THE QUEEN'S CLUB
STORY 1886–1986

The signed portrait of HM Queen Victoria presented by the Club's first Patron
in her Jubilee year

THE QUEEN'S CLUB

STORY 1886–1986

Roy McKelvie

FOREWORD BY LORD ABERDARE

Stanley Paul
London Melbourne Auckland Johannesburg

Stanley Paul & Co. Ltd

An imprint of Century Hutchinson Ltd

62–65 Chandos Place, London WC2N 4NW

Century Hutchinson (Australia) Pty Ltd
16–22 Church Street, Hawthorn, Melbourne, Victoria 3122

Century Hutchinson (NZ) Ltd
32–34 View Road, PO Box 40–086, Glenfield, Auckland 10

Century Hutchinson (SA) Pty Ltd
PO Box 337, Bergvlei 2021, South Africa

First published 1986
© Roy McKelvie 1986

Set in Linotron Erhardt by
Input Typesetting Ltd, London SW19 8DR

Printed in Great Britain by
Butler & Tanner Ltd, Frome and London

ISBN 0 09 166060 2

CONTENTS

ACKNOWLEDGEMENTS

In putting together this jigsaw story of The Queen's Club I have learned, among other things, that records of past events are almost universally badly kept. I have found that with few exceptions – the Wimbledon Library among them – individuals have been more abundant and enthusiastic sources of information than organizations. When, for instance, I set out to piece together the Club's fortunes in the Bath Club Cup, the first organized squash rackets team competition in this country, it caused some panic within the Squash Rackets Association. They had no record.

Brian Phillips, an old friend and rival on the court, came to the rescue, spending time going through past issues of *The Times* at his local library. It is with his help and that of Dugald Macpherson (a man of prodigious memory), Alan Chalmers, Robert Dolman, Jonathan Leslie and Rex Bellamy of *The Times* that the brief account of this game at the Club has been put together.

E. B. Noel, scholar, journalist, author and the highly popular Club secretary in some of its 'golden years', left some fascinating notes which Rosemary Jones unearthed and deciphered. These I have drawn upon liberally in several games, notably real tennis. Where Noel left off, the Railing family came to the rescue with their comprehensive scrapbooks of cuttings from *The Times, Telegraph, Morning Post* and *Manchester Guardian*. Then came William Stephens with his Tennis and Rackets Association records while Dugald Macpherson, Henry Johns (the doyen of professionals), and Reg Routledge (a man of many interests) have made their contributions.

John Thompson, a Marlborough schoolmaster, former rackets champion and first-class cricketer and squash player, has meticulously dealt with the rackets, of which more is and has been played at Queen's than anywhere else. Comments from two old champions, Tom Pugh and John Pawle, have added colour.

Lawn tennis is, as Noel has pointed out, the most popular game played at Queen's and though I am responsible for the various accounts I have had help from, among others, Alan Little, the Wimbledon librarian, Mary Hare, a Wightman Cup player, Geoff Paish, a former Davis Cup player, Bunny Austin, a Wimbledon runner-up, Dick Robinson of the LTA, Jean Borotra, King of the Covered Courts, Brian Hatton of the International Club of GB, and, of course, Dickie Ritchie, a considerable player and former Club secretary and president.

One of the pleasures of researching has been the renewal of old friends and acquaintances. Shortly after the last war when I joined the *Daily Mail* I handed over the task of athletics correspondent of *The Star* to Norris McWhirter, without whom the story of the Oxford and Cambridge athletics contest would not have been possible. In between the wars Sandy Duncan, former secretary of the British Olympic Association, and I were together at St Andrews Prep School, Eastbourne, and then at Malvern where we shared a study. He and R. T. S. Macpherson, whom I used to meet while watching the London Scottish play rugby, have filled in gaps, notably with reference to the Achilles Club. And on my file is a letter from that old high jumper, Arthur Selwyn, whom I have not seen for some fifty years.

The Oxford and Cambridge rugby match has been well documented but not so the soccer and I am indebted to two 'old blues', Tony Pawson of the *Observer* and David Miller of *The Times* for their help.

In general terms a great deal of the digging into the past and bringing the story up to the present has been done by Rosemary Jones, a pillar of The Queen's Club secretariat and member of the Fulham Archeological Society; and a professional researcher, Gordon Phillips, formerly of *The Times*. Thanks are also due to Gabrielle Allen, a professional picture researcher, who has unearthed a marvellous collection of photographs, to Dominique Shead, and to Roddy Bloomfield, the publisher, who has tirelessly supervised the planning and production of this ency-clopaedic book from start to finish. Without their help *The Queen's Club Story* would not have got off the baseline. That it got onto court at all is due largely to Dickie Ritchie, a great source of information and reminiscences, while from the side of the court encouragement and guidance have come from three club chairmen, Anthony Ward, Ivar Boden and Brian Palmer and the man who has guided the Club through its financial jungle, Errol MacSwiney.

Roy McKelvie

The author and publishers would also like to acknowledge the following sources:

Tennis – A Cut Above The Rest by Chris Ronaldson, Ronaldson Press
Sporting Pie by F. B. Wilson, Chapman & Hall Ltd, London, loaned by Neil Allen of the *London Standard*
The Willis Faber Book of Tennis by Lord Aberdare, Stanley Paul Ltd, London
The History of the Corinthians by F. N. S. Creek, loaned by David Miller of *The Times*
Corinthian Casuals and Cricketers by Edward Grayson, The Pallant Press
One Hundred Years of Wimbledon by Lance Tingay, Guinness Superlatives Ltd
Squash Rackets by Gerald Pawle, Ward, Lock & Co., London
The Story of Squash by Rex Bellamy
The Centenary History of the Rugby Football Union by U. A. Titley and Ross McWhirter, published by the RFU
Oxford v. Cambridge, The Story of the University Rugby Match, by Peter Howard, Clerke and Cockeran, London

The Barbarians FC by O. L. Owen, Playfair Books
Lawn Tennis & Badminton
Pastime
Squash Rackets and Fives, Tennis and Rackets
International Tennis Weekly published by the Association of Tennis Professionals
Inside Women's Tennis published by the Women's Tennis Association
Tennis & Rackets Association Records and Reports
The Times
International Club of GB
E. B. Noel's Notes
The Field
The Illustrated Sporting and Dramatic News
The Illustrated London News
The Cuttings Books kept by N. F. H. Railing and family
The Wimbledon Library and the Librarian, Alan Little
The British Olympic Association and K. S. Duncan
The Achilles Club and R. T. S. Macpherson
The Squash Rackets Association
The Queen's Club Files and Records

FOREWORD

This is a monumental work of fascination and those who have produced it deserve the gratitude of all lovers of the many games that have at one time or another been played at The Queen's Club. The variety of these games is incredible, ranging from the ephemeral Stické to the nucleus of the Club, lawn tennis and including real tennis, rackets, squash rackets, football and athletics.

In the years between the wars, I spent much of my holidays at the Club. In appearance it was not that different from today except for the small group of ball-boys squatting on the fence by what was then the office – amongst them some of the great players of later years. My proudest moment was in 1939 when, for the first time, at the age of twenty, I partnered my father, then aged fifty-four, in the Amateur Rackets Doubles. We reached the final but lost by 3 games to 4 to Cosmo Crawley and John Pawle.

This centenary book is above all a tribute to those many people who have kept the Club going over the past 100 years. They are accurately chronicled in its pages – the champions of various sports, outstanding administrators, the professionals, the ground staff, the office workers, the changing room attendants, the great characters of the Club. But fascinating as it is to recollect the past, I would like to end on a note of appreciation to those who have restored the Club to its ancient glories. Personally I have only had experience of half the 100 years of its existence but in my time I believe its reputation has never been higher, nor its services to its members better.

I warmly congratulate the many authors who have contributed to this splendid book and comend it to all lovers of sport.

Lord Aberdare

INTRODUCTION

As Lord's is to cricket, so surely The Queen's Club is to lawn tennis. But this book is much more than just a history of the centre of the British Lawn Tennis Association. The Club is also the head-quarters of the Tennis and Rackets Association, and has seen over its 100 years some twenty or more nascent English sports developed to their present popularity. Whether or not Queen's was the original venue, it may certainly be said to have fathered their development and rugby, soccer, cricket and athletics are just a few of the traditional English sports played here at the highest competitive level. World records have been broken, world champions have been created, and indeed today we still have some of the world's best in our midst.

Can there be another club whose buildings and grounds have housed such a diversity of sports throughout its first century, or whose walls have echoed with so many hallowed memories? Most exploits of the human frame have passed this way – sweat and toil, natural talent, inspiration, disillusionment.

Any sporting Club enthusiast will find much to fascinate him in this book, and many games chron-icled not normally associated with Queen's. Devotees of lawn tennis will gain fresh insight into their sport, seeing its growth from the days of the Dohertys and minor competitions to the modern phenomena of Boris Becker and the Stella Artois Championships.

The problems have been immense, not least the one of compiling a true and fair account which would do justice to the Club history. Roy McKelvie, the man who took on this massive task, has provided a record which is both interesting and exciting. The reader, I am sure, cannot fail to be caught up by his enthusiasm, his knowledge, and his love of the English sporting scene.

My own thirty years have seen the Club with its undeveloped potential and varying fortunes change dramatically for the better. With facilities much improved, Queen's is better equipped than ever before to fulfil its proper role in the future of British lawn tennis.

It has always been a source of tremendous enjoy-ment and enrichment of life, giving me, like so many others, an ever increasing circle of friends from all parts of the globe. One thing is certain: whatever the state of play at Queen's, there has always been and always will be, a sense of pride saying 'I belong to this great Club'.

Brian Palmer
Chairman

The first share certificate, issued in 1887

THE QUEEN'S CLUB STORY
1886–1914

ONE hundred years ago in late Victorian England, sport belonged largely to the privileged and leisured classes. Cricket, rugby, soccer, athletics and other games and pastimes, including that relative newcomer lawn tennis – Willie Renshaw won his sixth Wimbledon in 1886 – were dominated by men from the leading public schools, Oxford and Cambridge and officers from the services. Professionalism was in its infancy and was, as yet, irrelevant in terms of standards except in such restricted games as rackets and real tennis.

Socially the country was divided between those who had and those who had not; those in the gentlemen's professions – the services, the law, the church, medicine and land – and trade. There were ten percent unemployed, troubles with the Irish and occasional bomb-throwing. Lottie Collins, Marie Lloyd and Albert Chevalier played the music halls; women ('ladies' in those days) were beginning to take part in active sports including lawn tennis, and even appearing in high-class advertisements such as the ones for Elliman's Universal Embrocation at fivepence-halfpenny a bottle. Queen Victoria was approaching her Jubilee, the Royal Navy was the most powerful force in the world and child labour in factories was only just ending.

London's three leading sporting clubs were, and had been for some time, Lord's and Prince's, both named after their founders, and Hurlingham, the home of polo. The All-England LTC, Wimbledon, had yet to reach the pre-eminence it later achieved. Its Championships went into decline in the mid-nineties and, as we shall see later, there was some evidence suggesting the club was offered to Queen's for £30,000.

Prince's, 'that delightful playground' and the only multi-sports club in the country, was situated in the Cadogan Square, Lennox Gardens, Hans Place area; prime land for developers and far too expensive for the Club to renew its lease. So Prince's closed in 1887 to re-open the following year in Knightsbridge but with no facilities for outdoor sports. It was primarily a rackets and real tennis club. At the same time the Lillie Road sports ground, at which the Oxford and Cambridge athletic meeting had been held for some years, became unavailable, leaving London without a comprehensive sporting club.

Three men, the Hon. Evan Charteris, Colonel George Francis and the Hon. Algernon Grosvenor – all presumably members of Prince's – decided to establish such a club and set about finding a site. None appears to have shown any prowess at sport. Charteris, being in his early twenties, was by far the youngest, and though already commissioned into the Coldstream Guards, was at Balliol College, Oxford, at the time. Later he became the Hon. Sir Evan Charteris KC and by far the most distinguished of the trio – in the Army, at the Bar, in arts and letters.

THREE WISE MEN

With little transport outside Central London the three men could not cast their eyes, say, further than four miles from Hyde Park. In 1883 Messrs Gibbs and Flew, builders and developers in the Fulham area of West London, bought part of the Baron's Court Estate from the executors of the late Major-General Sir William Palliser. The parcel contained land and adjacent houses. The Pallisers had made their name and fortune from the development of armour-piercing projectiles to be used against the navies of Her Majesty's enemies.

The area covered Vereker, Palliser, Gledstanes and Comeragh Roads – on which Gibbs and Flew built more houses – and about eleven acres of land which had been a market garden – the Queen's Field. They maintained this as a cricket ground, though there is no evidence of much cricket being played on it. Known as 'The Queen's Cricket Club and Ground', it did attract the attention of Charteris, Francis and Grosvenor, who decided to buy and develop nine acres of it as an athletic club. This they did in 1886, one of their main aims being to provide a home for various Oxford and Cambridge sporting contests.

A company, The Queen's Club Limited, was formed with a capital of £60,000 divided into 6000 shares of £10 each. Algernon Grosvenor became chairman of the Board of Directors and remained so until his death in 1907. Charteris became a trustee for the company which was to carry on business for the purposes of lawn tennis, cricket, football, athletics sports, gymnastics *et al* and innumerable offshoots such as ice-manufacturing (this was soon scuppered by a local ice-merchant), hotel and restaurant keeping. All this was legally drawn up on 19 August 1886, which may be taken as the date of the birth of The Queen's Club.

Among the initial shareholders were Algernon and Richard Grosvenor, sons of Baron Ebury, and William Grenfell of Taplow, Bucks. Grenfell was not only heavily responsible for shaping Queen's but became a giant in the world of sport, commerce and public life – the famous Lord Desborough and a future president of the LTA.

Within a few years Queen's had collected a list of vice-presidents that included one marquis, fourteen earls, eleven lords and a committee containing three earls, a viscount and numerous other gentlemen, the sons of titled or prominent men in the world of sport, business and public life. In itself that gives a fair picture of the club in its early days.

THE FIRST MATCH

On 19 May 1887, nine months after the incorporation of The Queen's Club Limited – which cost £18 15s 0d – the grounds were opened for lawn tennis.

On 1–2 July Oxford met Cambridge in the first sporting contest to be held there. The result was a draw 9–9 and among the players was H. S. Scrivener (Oxford) who later became a noted referee and correspondent for the *Morning Post*. In my young days we knew him as 'Scriv' or 'Old Scriv'. He was the Wimbledon referee from 1906 to 1914, though never achieving quite the distinction of another Oxonian and his successor at Wimbledon, F. R. Burrow, the greatest crossword expert of his age. In November the Corinthians beat Oxford University at soccer and on 14 December Cambridge beat Oxford for the third year running at rugby – their previous two wins being at Blackheath.

It was Queen Victoria's Jubilee year and she not only consented to become the Club's Patron but also presented it with her portrait which still hangs there. In 1895 the Club produced a button with the Queen's head on it.

It took about eighteen months to complete the Club buildings, which were opened in January 1888 and consisted of a central pavilion facing east with a large club room running the whole length of the building and two floors of dressing rooms and bathrooms at the back. To the north side of the pavilion were the real tennis courts and an Eton Fives court. To the south were a couple of rackets courts and offices. William Marshall, runner-up to Spencer Gore at the first Wimbledon in 1877, was the architect and Bickley the builder.

At the back or west side of the pavilion were two covered courts, the East and West, reached by a covered way that today is probably just as draughty as it was then. The third covered court was not built until 1905. Basically this lay-out was the same as it is today, though the Eton Fives courts have disappeared and the second rackets court was converted into two squash courts shortly after the Great War. On the south side of the rackets courts was an asphalt area on which covered courts 7 and 8 now stand. When flooded this provided the Club with what was, at the time, described as 'the finest surface for skating ever seen in London'. It measured 3000 square yards (100 × 30), was floodlit – which was more than the covered courts were – and remained open until eight in the evening.

The snag was that when it thawed or the freezing plant broke down, which seems to have been fairly frequently, the water drained away into a nearby street (probably Greyhound Road) and flooded the local houses. Eventually the rink, the largest of its kind in the country, was abandoned. Some of its devotees tried roller skating on the covered courts but it was soon found that this damaged the surface.

In what used to be the old cricket ground there

was space for about thirty grass courts – out of the football season of course – though early photos suggest that no more than four were laid out until the Grass Court Championships were first held in 1890. Occasional cricket matches were played, but it was not an organized sport like football. There were nets and sometimes a professional in attendance. The last cricket match on record was played at the end of the Great War between London Boys' clubs.

The football pitch, rugby or soccer, was near the Palliser Road entrance. The running track around the perimeter was three laps to the mile until changed to four after the war. The track and field facilities were expressly laid out for the University Sports meeting which lasted longer at Queen's than any other 'extra-mural' sport: forty years from 1888 to 1928. Moreover, the early meetings between Oxford and Cambridge and Harvard and Yale were probably the first international athletic matches held anywhere in the world. Of light soil and well-drained, the track was said to be one of the fastest 'running paths' in England, a claim confirmed by the Achilles Club many years later.

On the formation of the Club in 1886 Henry Becks was appointed secretary, thus completing the officers, with Grosvenor as the first chairman of the Board and the Earl of Wharncliffe as the first president. The Earl was a Yorkshireman, a retired naval officer, a JP and DL and one of the Club's original forty-six shareholders.

A view of the Club in the 1890s

MONEY LOOMS

Becks, though he certainly helped lay the foundations of a successful club, remained a largely anonymous character. The first reference I found to him appears in the Club minutes dated 9 August 1887. He had convened an Extraordinary General Meeting for 21 July at 79 Perham Road, West Kensington, to discuss taking out an £18,000 mortgage with the Directors to borrow £10,000 on their personal guarantee. This resolution was passed and later confirmed at another EGM at the same address. Occasional references to Becks and the way he ran the University Sports meeting, the most successful financial venture undertaken by Queen's in those days, appeared in the illustrated periodicals. Becks retired in 1903, by which time the Club was well established.

Transport in those early days was mainly by horse. A chocolate-coloured four-in-hand horse bus made daily regular trips from Hyde Park Corner to the Club before the opening of Barons Court Underground station in 1906. There was stabling at the Club and horses were kept to draw the heavy rollers over the grounds. The last, Tom and Paddy, retired in the 1920s.

The Club took on its first two professionals on 1 January 1888. Charles Saunders was already a player of considerable prowess at real tennis and Peter Latham from Manchester was already World Rackets Champion though only twenty-two. Saunders left after a few months and Latham took over the real tennis as well. Such was his genius that within seven years he had won the world title at that

Anyone for tennis? The horse bus pick-up point at Hyde Park

game and became the first man to win both titles. In modern times two other Queen's Club men, Jim Dear and Howard Angus, have achieved the same mark.

The real tennis courts were officially opened on 28 January 1888 when J. M. Heathcote, an amateur and winner of the MCC Gold Racquet seventeen times between 1867 and 1886, played George Lambert, and the Hon. Alfred Lyttleton, a cricketer of great distinction, met Saunders. Later that year a competition limited to members was, needless to say, won by the assiduous Heathcote. The following year it became the Amateur Championship.

It took some time for 'the Amateur' to reach the exalted position it later achieved and still holds. The MCC Gold and Silver prizes, being longer established were more highly rated. Lyttleton, Gold Racquet winner until the mid-1890s, never played in the Amateur though he regarded himself as the champion.

The first amateur champion proper was Sir Edward Grey, an eminent politician who, as Foreign Secretary, announced the declaration of war against Germany in 1914. He became Viscount Grey of Falloden.

DOUBTFUL SERVICE

How good Grey was became a matter of some discussion. He won the amateur title five times in the ten years up to 1898. E. B. Noel claimed he might have been stronger had he 'taken more pains to learn service'. *The Field* made the same comment with: 'He persistently delivers but one service from one position.' But he did challenge Lyttleton for the Gold Racquet in 1896 – and won.

The courts, having been designed by the same architect (Marshall) and erected by the same builder (Bickley) were as uniform as could be and the Badminton Library listed them among the seven courts which 'most nearly approach perfection'. Noel, the most famous of all The Queen's Club secretaries and the 1907 Amateur Champion, had this to say: 'The east court has a character of its own not quite like any other. Nowhere else does a well-cut stroke feel more satisfying or the ball come onto the racket with more life. The west court is very different, the ball coming higher on the bounce.'

Early in the 1890s alterations and improvements were made to the east court *dedans*. The result was to turn it into a reading and smoking room where whist and chess were played. Today the *dedans* remains virtually the same, though it has lost its social purpose and 'no smoking' signs are up.

1888 was the year Queen's became established as *the* centre for sport. Noel claimed that twenty-five different games and pastimes were played there. Though some, like Pallone (an Italian game) and Stické had very brief lives and others like hockey and lacrosse were only very occasionally played, there cannot, anywhere in the world, have been a sporting club with such a record for versatility.

In February 1888 Oxford beat Cambridge 3–2 at soccer and, in March, the Oxford and Cambridge Sports, established in 1864 and the oldest track and field meeting in the world, first met at Queen's. That notable athlete and rugby player F. J. K. Cross won the third of his quartet of mile victories for Oxford in just under 4 minutes 30 secs.

On Saturday, April 13 the covered courts were opened with a singles exhibition between the reigning Wimbledon champion, H. F. Lawford, and his immediate successor, Ernest Renshaw. They were then joined for a men's double by E. W. Lewis, the Covered Courts champion – the competition was then held at the Hyde Park LTC – and C.H.L. Cazalet.

The players reserved their opinions of the floor which was made of rectangular blocks of wood laid herring-bone fashion on a bed of half-inch thick felt on a concrete base. It cannot have been satisfactory as the blocks were soon replaced with more American maple, one inch thick, three-and-a-half wide, laid on joists. These warped and the stain made them slippery. Finally they were replaced by American white wood and stained green. Expensive, but it produced a splendid playing surface.

LATHAM WINS

Rackets took off, Peter Latham resisting a challenge from Walter Gray of Charterhouse for the World title; C. D. Buxton of Cambridge winning the Amateur and Charterhouse the Public Schools. The University match was shared.

Within a year of the grounds being open for play the scene was set for a successful future. Oxford and Cambridge became thoroughly established at the Club, the Corinthians soon followed. Rackets and real tennis began their long history of events that made the Club what it is today, the headquarters of both games. It was another couple of years before lawn tennis expanded and the Grass Court and

Covered Court Championships took root.

Years later E. B. Noel wrote: 'The Varsity rugby match at Queen's was one where the spectators let themselves go. The whole spectacle of the match was peculiarly English, full of real keenness and genuine sportsmanship'. That first match at Queen's had drawn a 5000 crowd. The University soccer match attracted good crowds but not comparable with the rugby. But these and other football matches of both codes became a major source of income as the clubs involved paid the expenses and shared the gates.

In effect Queen's consisted of two clubs; for members and for visitors. The 1200 or so gentlemen members (five guineas ordinary, three guineas country, University and Services) could daily enjoy the Club for its facilities and amenities whether at real tennis or billiards, chess or the bar. The visitors were confined to their particular sports and organizations, especially later when the number of rugby and soccer clubs using Queen's proliferated. It provided a good source of income but in the end became counterproductive and turned against the interests of both the Club and the members.

The men who guided the Club through its early years came largely from the world of sport, big business and the aristocracy. On the Committee in the mid-1890s were, among others, two Wimbledon champions, William Renshaw and H. F. Lawford, that great authority on real tennis, Julian Marshall, an advocate and keen real tennis and rackets player, G. E. A. Ross whom *The Times* described as 'a slow and dreary speaker' and Sir Charles Tennant, a multi-millionaire whose Glaswegian father had invented bleaching powder. There seemed to be a lot of Harrovians on the committee including A. J. Webbe, a notable Cambridge and Middlesex cricketer and Silver Racquet winner, and the Earl of Clarendon who, at different times, was both president and chairman and sold his horse to the Club in 1896 for £12 10s 0d. I have been unable to discover the reason unless Queen's needed it to pull a roller or grass-cutting machine. There was also Sir Charles Pontifex, one of the few men to play cricket and lawn tennis for Cambridge. He became a judge of the Bengal High Court.

There was, however, one founding father and committee man whom *The Times* described as 'one of the greatest of all-round sportsmen' – W. H. Grenfell of Taplow, Bucks who, in 1905, became Lord Desborough of Taplow. He too was a Harrovian.

GREAT ALL-ROUNDER

At school Grenfell excelled at cricket and running. He took a first at Balliol College, Oxford, and was president of both the Boat Club and Athletic Club. In 1877 he ran for Oxford against Cambridge on a Friday and then rowed No. 4 in the following day's Boat Race that ended in a dead-heat. Later he stroked an eight across the Channel and then crossed it single-handed in a skiff.

Then Grenfell twice swam Niagara, the second time to satisfy a sceptical American. He caught giant tarpon off Florida, climbed half a dozen Alpine mountains, including the Matterhorn, in eight days, was once chased by a mad elephant and then by dervishes in the Sudan. He won punting and fencing titles, was heavily responsible for the organization of the 1908 London Olympic Games – Queen's held the Olympic Covered Courts meeting – was president of the MCC and the LTA and, among others, the Bath Club. At one time he sat on 115 committees. In 1930 *The Times* prematurely reported his death, mistaking 'Bessborough' for 'Desborough'. He lived another twenty-five years. He was in his early thirties when first he became involved with Queen's.

The gap left by the closure of the ice-skating rink was soon filled by the new craze for bicycling. It began in 1890 when the Club hired ladies' bicycles for twenty-five shillings a month and let them out at two shillings and sixpence an hour. The cinder track around the ground's perimeter was especially popular with the ladies who, if they were going to fall off, preferred the privacy of Queen's to the open parks of London.

So popular did this pastime become that in 1894 the Club bought fifty bicycles and engaged two instructors. The cost of hiring a cycle had, by then, been reduced to sixpence an hour or one-and-six with an instructor. For men it was a shilling or two shillings with an instructor. The Club even considered setting up a factory to manufacture bicycles but discovered that the Club's articles would not permit it.

In July 1896 a bicycling fete was held. *The Illustrated Sporting and Dramatic News* reported the event and carried a photograph of some of the women competitors. It wrote: 'There was a very good attendance at the first bicycling fete held at The Queen's

Club, the contest being similar to those held at Rane-lagh. Of the thirty competitors sixteen were ladies, fourteen were gentlemen and the prizes awarded were according to the aggregate number of points gained.'

The journal listed some of the events – 'The first, after a parade of lady riders, was a contest in plank riding. This was followed by an amusing race to see who could cover 100 yards in the shortest time carrying an egg in a spoon.' Then there was a needle-and-thread race, a tent-pegging contest for gentlemen, a ladies' competition in mounting and dismounting and an obstacle race for both sexes. 'The tortoise race over 100 yards, with the last to arrive being the winner, proved the most entertaining of the whole series which ended with a speed race for ladies.' Among the judges was the Club secretary, Henry Becks, but the report unfortunately failed to carry the names of any winners.

SYMPATHY BUT NOT TEA

Inevitably, though not necessarily in competition, there were accidents and when one lady fell and

The feathers fly – the first bicycling fete in July 1896

broke a leg she was comforted with a sympathetic letter from the committee. Coinciding with the bicycling craze, largely for the women, came billiards for the men. The lunch room was turned into a billiard room – men only – with a charge of ten shillings and sixpence which included half-a-crown for the marker and sixpence for the caretaker who was responsible for locking up at night. It was not until after the last war that the Club, or the members, could no longer afford a marker.

The position of women at the Club was ambivalent and membership was restricted. Members could introduce women by ticket. Even that privilege was restricted to just one lady on such occasions as the University football matches and Sports. At one time there was a rule barring nursemaids but not governesses; that is until someone realized it was impossible to distinguish one from the other.

It may have been the influence of these females but members began asking for afternoon tea to be served in all parts of the ground including the courts. The staff could not cope and thenceforward tea areas were restricted to the Club house and in front of the pavilion, as they are today.

The arrival of the 1890s saw a number of 'firsts' including the launching of the two major lawn tennis tournaments, both in 1890. The first few Covered Courts Championships were restricted to women's singles and men's doubles as the men's singles were held at the Hyde Park LTC, Porchester Square.

G. W. Hillyard, later to become secretary of the AELTC Wimbledon, and H. S. Scrivener were the first doubles winners. A Miss M. Jacks, for whom not even the Wimbledon Museum have been able to find a provenance, won both the covered courts and grass courts singles titles and H. S. Barlow took the grass court title. (These two events are fully covered in another section.)

Two more firsts were the Amateur Rackets Doubles Championship and the Oxford v Yale athletic match. Percy Ashworth, whom Freddie Wilson of *The Times* described as 'the perfect doubles player' and W. C. Hedley won the title. Yale's visit was a pioneering effort, possibly the first modern

international match, and led to further exchanges. In 1895 Oxford and Cambridge beat Harvard and Yale 5–4, watched by the Prince of Wales and the Duke and Duchess of York. The gate for that match was a massive £3549 – when next did Queen's take a gate as good as that? – and the Club took a third share.

Croquet was added to the growing list of games played at the Club when an arrangement was made with the All-England Croquet Association for restricted membership with the gentlemen having the right to introduce two lady members. Then along came the England Women's Hockey Association and played a match or two. No wonder, as the nineteenth century passed, the Club seemed prepared or resigned to accept lady members though the process was very slow.

WIMBLEDON FOR SALE

During this last decade, in which Queen's expanded its horizons and grew in stature and popularity, something happened that aroused little interest at the time but, ninety years later, has become an intriguing mystery. On 22 January 1895 and under the heading 'Wimbledon' the following appeared in the minutes of a committee meeting: 'I/Grosvenor made a statement with regard to the new scheme proposing that this company should take over an optional agreement for the purchase of the property at £30,000, the options being for six months.' In another of the minutes the Hon. A. H. Grosvenor pointed out that a sum of £40,000 would be needed to service such a mortgage and that while the income from the acquisition should be some £3660, expenditure including interest, rates, taxes and working management would be some £3000.

Did this mean that the Club was being offered the AELTC Wimbledon for £30,000? It has been assumed so for some time. The few historians, the late Tom Todd among them, who knew or know of the offer have accepted it as a fact largely because both the AELTC and the Wimbledon Championships were in decline at the time. But Wimbledon, claiming that there is no reference to the offer in their minute books, have persistently denied it.

Dick Robinson, a former LTA chairman and member of the Championships management committee, has done some research which leads to the theory that the club in question (Wimbledon) was not the All-England but the Wimbledon Covered

Courts Club, also in Worple Road. One of the clues is found in the breakdown of the income to be received from the venture. Subscriptions from 450 members was one source; from 600 to 700 skating members and fees was another. There is no mention of court fees and the AELTC is restricted to 350 paying members. And where did they skate in Worple Road?

Herbert Chipp, the LTA's first secretary, in an article 'Some noted Covered Courts of the past' in *Lawn Tennis* of 18 May 1898 mentions the Wimbledon Club as a survivor of the old rinking days. *Kelly's Directory* of 1890 and 1891 also mentions the Club. As the popularity of ice skating declined, so some members of the AELTC bought up the skating club and converted its asphalt floor to two courts, one singles, one doubles. Obviously Queen's in considering the offer had ideas of using the club for both skating and lawn tennis.

My only reservation is the cost. Would a converted ice rink with a corrugated roof be worth £30,000? Chipp says the place was eventually sold to the local Roman Catholic community as a children's playground. Could they have forked out £30,000? In 1895, whatever the truth of the matter, Queen's showed little interest in buying 'Wimbledon' and the affair died.

The year 1900 saw H. K. Foster, one of seven sons of a Malvern housemaster and a member of the greatest of all games-playing families (their one sister was a hockey international), win the Amateur rackets title for the seventh year running, Eustace Miles coming up to his peak at real tennis and H. L. Doherty dominating the Covered Court Championships. 1900 was also a year when ten sheep grazed on the grounds. They cost £1 18s 0d each and were sold for two guineas – not much profit. The same year, club member P. W. Le Gros refused to pay two shillings for a game of lawn tennis played on 20 May.

How good was H. K. Foster, after whom the Public Schools singles championship – the Foster Cup – is now called. Freddie Wilson, *The Times* sporting journalist who covered some twenty different games and sports, considered him one of the three champions (amateur) among champions, along with Sir William Hart-Dyke, the first amateur world champion, and E. M. Baerlein. 'Having retired Foster returned to the game in 1904 and beat Baerlein 3–0. He was the prettier, perhaps one should say more spectacular player. He did not play nearly as much as Baerlein did – perhaps only three weeks a year. To see Foster play Latham for a few strokes only you would have thought Foster the greater player of the two. In fact Latham could give him five and win when he wanted to. It was Latham's opinion that with both men at their best Baerlein would beat Foster four matches out of seven.'

GOOD FOOD GUIDE

E. H. Miles, who dominated real tennis for a number of years, was an ascetic character, vegetarian and teetotaller. Of the great champions of this period Wilson wrote: 'It is hardly possible to say how the Hon. Alfred Lyttleton, Eustace Miles and Baerlein would have stood in order of merit had they all been at their best at the same time.' In 1906 Miles opened a restaurant in Chandos Street that served no fresh meat or flesh foods. 'The premises are well ventilated' commented *The Times*.

The third member of this galaxy of great court game players straddling the end of the nineteenth and the beginning of the twentieth centuries was H. L. Doherty, five times Wimbledon champion from 1902 to 1906 inclusive. Laurie or 'Little Do', younger brother to R. F. (Reggie) Doherty, is, even today, regarded as one of the all-time greats. However two Queen's Club professionals, Cowdrey and Charles Heirons, claimed that Reggie was the more difficult to beat because of his brilliant service, well-placed rather than fast.

Laurie Doherty had already won the Covered Courts title four times, twice beating M. J. G. Ritchie in the final, when they met in the third round of the 1904 London Covered Court Championships, a lesser event played for some years in the autumn. Ritchie won 6–2 6–4 8–10 1–6 6–4 in what '*Lawn Tennis and Croquet*' described as 'one of the greatest surprises the tennis world has seen for some years'. Ritchie who, today, might be called 'a hard grafter', played the game of his life, while Doherty's return of service, it was said, was indifferent. Ritchie's name threads its way through the The Queen's Club story and is carried on by his son R.J. who became the Club secretary just before the Second World War and, in 1981, the president – a family span covering over ninety years.

1904 was a notable year for sport at the Club. The Prince of Wales watched the University sports that saw K. Cornwallis break the half-mile record for Oxford with a time of 1 min 54.8 secs; another

Lyttleton, the Hon G.W., arrived on the scene and won the shot putt for Cambridge and W. E. Lutyens won the third of his quarter-mile victories for Cambridge.

A revealing anomaly: the first lady shareholder was not permitted to be a member

GOOD GATES

The gate for that match was £1432; good enough but far exceeded by the £3530 taken for the meeting between Oxford and Cambridge and Harvard and Yale, the latter the winners by 6–3.

The outstanding event was the Corinthians' overwhelming victory over the FA Cup-holders, Bury, 10–3. The professionals had won the Cup the previous season with a record 6–0 win over Derby County. The Corinthians had had such a poor season that it was debated whether Cambridge University would be more suitable opponents for the Sheriff of London Shield match. After a hesitant start Corinthians clicked. G. O. Smith, then in partial retirement, later wrote: 'I should imagine it will stand as the greatest performance in Corinthian annals.'

The Corinthians (as may be seen in another section) were formed in 1882–3 as a club composed of the best amateurs in the kingdom to try to combat Scotland's supremacy on the football field. They had adopted The Queen's Club as their home ground in the early 1890s. Though soccer was a rough, robust game in those days they refused to wear shinguards – considered a sign of weakness – and if they gave away a penalty would stand aside and leave their goal open.

Henry Becks, the Club secretary from the start, retired in 1903 and was succeeded by C. J. B. Marriott, a Blackheath and England rugby international. Marriott did not stay long before becoming secretary to the Rugby Union, an office he held with distinction for many years. His brief reign was a busy one. Tenders were put out for the building of another covered court and two squash courts. The lowest, just under £4000 including additional galleries, came from Holliday and Greenwood and was accepted. They had built the Victoria and Albert Museum, the London Hippodrome and the Lambeth Infirmary and were said to be 'respectable and well-spoken'. Albert Slazenger's offer of a mortgage was turned down.

FEMALE RESTRICTIONS

The minutes of 1906 reported that women members were to be admitted at half the normal subscription of five guineas. However they were not allowed to propose men candidates or book the covered courts. They were also barred from playing on the east court on Saturdays and Sundays and the west after 12.30 p.m. This does nothing to clear up the mystery or confusion surrounding the admittance of lady members to the Club. Was it in 1900 or 1906?

Marriott left Queen's in September to take over the Rugby Football Union and, on 1 October, was succeeded by A. E. Stoddart at £300 a year. Stoddart was also a rugby international having, in 1886, played in the same England team as Marriott. But he was more famous as a cricketer and as one of the only two men who have captained England at both games.

Almost immediately Stoddart took up real tennis with all the enthusiasm he had shown for his other

sports. According to Freddie Wilson he emerged from his first lesson with André, Queen's famous professional and racket stringer, thoroughly mystified. 'I don't understand this game. The fellow kept on saying "Keep your head up, Sir, keep your head up" till I was looking at the skylight and couldn't see the blessed ball at all. All I've got out of my first lesson is a crick in the neck.'

'Stoddie', as he was christened by W. G. Grace and others, got a touch of tennis elbow but continued to play until it was so bad that it affected the whole of his games-playing life and he could not play lawn tennis, golf or cricket. Earlier in his career he had scored 485 in one day for Hampstead against the Stoics without having gone to bed the previous night. Immediately after that mammoth innings he had played a lawn tennis match, gone to the theatre, then to a supper party and bed at 3 a.m! A tireless man.

The 1908 Olympic real tennis, rackets and covered courts lawn tennis events were held at Queen's and were a flop. Jay Gould, the American, well known at Queen's and possibly the best amateur the game had seen up to the Great War, won the real tennis; E. B. Noel won the rackets, most players having scratched; and Vane Pennell and J. J. Astor won the rackets doubles. A. W. Gore and Gladys Eastlake-Smith won the lawn tennis singles; Gore and H. Roper Barrett the doubles. Total gate receipts were under £90, only fifty-eight seats were reserved and 102 programmes sold. Real tennis and rackets were dropped from future games.

STICKY GAME

During this first decade of the twentieth century, more games and pastimes were added to The Queen's Club bag, among them lacrosse, miniature rifle shooting and Stické. Oxford and Cambridge met at lacrosse in 1906 and the following year London entertained the Capital Club of Ottawa. A Stické court was built adjoining the new No. 3 covered court and the fee was a shilling an hour per player. It was opened by Eustace Miles and R. E. 'Tip' Foster, another of the Foster tribe who scored a record 287 for England against Australia in 1903 and captained England at both cricket and soccer.

The game of Stické which never caught on resembled lawn tennis played in an enclosed court – hard floor, wooden walls – with a tennis racket and coverless tennis ball with a net across the middle.

Noel described it as 'by no means a bad game: in fact if one had nothing better to do it would be a godsend'.

W. D. Macpherson, that distinguished Queen's Club squash and real tennis player, played a few games on a court in Buckinghamshire just after the Great War. He said: 'It was good fun for people getting too old for squash. I used to play Gerald Robarts, a squash player. We had long rallies but as he never cut the ball he never made a winning stroke. If I could get the ball past him with cut he never returned it.' In its brief existence the Stické court was once used for a duel with pistols and wax bullets. Who the contestants were is unrevealed but Sir Cosmos Duff Cooper provided the weapons.

Peter Latham had left Queen's in 1901 to go to Sir Charles Rose's court at Newmarket. André, Alfred Dooley and Toby Chambers, the rackets professionals at Queen's, were joined a year later by Jamsetji from Bombay who actually succeeded Latham as world champion when the latter resigned the title in 1902.

In 1911 Charles Williams, aged twenty-two and a protégé of Latham, took the world title off Jamsetji in matches at Queen's and Prince's. Williams, supremely fast about the court and a formidable striker, also played a home-and-away (Queen's and Manchester) match against Baerlein. The amateur led 2–1 at Queen's when he was hit on the 'funny bone' of his left elbow by a full-blooded stroke. It nearly crippled him. Williams took that leg 4–2 and won again at Manchester.

The following year Williams who had, as a young man, the choice of becoming a welterweight boxer

The Stické court, 1910. One of the many early experiments

or a rackets professional, went down with the *Titanic* while crossing the Atlantic to play George Standing in New York. After spending nine hours adrift in a small boat he survived and joined Queen's after the war. Latham, by the way, returned to Queen's in 1913.

TRUE AMATEURS

There were men at Queen's in those days and later – Vane Pennell, J. C. F. Simpson, Nigel Haig, Kenneth Gandar Dower among them – who would challenge anyone to play every game at the club in one day. Pennell and Haig, a prominent Middlesex cricketer, liked to play for money. Two who played more for honour and glory were F. A. Sampson, who was in the 1909 rugby rackets pair, and H. W. Leatham, a Carthusian who won the Amateur rackets doubles championship seven times, once with his school partner, H. A. Denison, and six times with the Hon. C. N. Bruce (Lord Aberdare).

Their Olympian contest in 1911 began in the Stické court and was followed by lawn tennis on the covered, squash, and then ping-pong, a game that went up-market, called itself 'table tennis' and became vastly popular at the Club in the thirties. They got in their game of rackets before lunch after which they met at billiards, real tennis, the quarter-mile which, someone reported, Leatham surprisingly won by a yard, and then played single wicket cricket. On they went to throwing the cricket ball, hitting a rackets ball, and ending with bowls which enjoyed a brief period of popularity at the Club. Leatham was the overall winner. The sole stake of this mammoth exercise was a drink. (In between the wars I recall a similar contest that attracted the attention of some national newspapers between two undergraduates, J. M. F. Lightly of Cambridge and Wake Thring of Oxford.)

King George V attended the 1912 Army v Navy rugby match which provided further evidence of the inadequacy of the Club's accommodation for such games. In 1910, for instance, over 2750 paid to watch the game, producing well over £100 for the Club. The crowds for the University rugby match were considerably larger and Oxford and Cambridge were already putting pressure on the Club to improve the facilities. The Club countered by asking for a five-year guarantee.

A billiards handicap at the Club in 1907

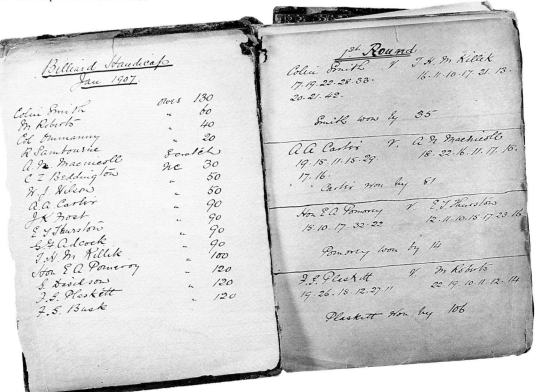

An early assembly of the Queen's Club staff, complete with ball-boys

The suffragette movement was disturbing London and the Club, being male-orientated and, some might consider, chauvinistic was regarded as a possible target. Three nightwatchmen were hired. So was a dog – until it bit the secretary!

That was not the reason for Stoddart, secretary since 1906, retiring in the autumn of 1914. He had suffered ill-health for some time and then had a nervous breakdown. An attack of 'flu left him moody and depressed and in April 1915 he shot himself. This was a tragic end for a great games player and, judging by the Club's popularity and success during his years of office, a first-rate secretary. In his heyday as an England cricketer and rugby player – captain of both – he was immensely popular. In Australia, where he toured four times, his name was a household word.

Among Stoddart's many achievements were 215 for Middlesex against Lancashire in 1891 and an average of 52 for the season. Also in that year he dropped a goal for Middlesex against Yorkshire in the County Rugby Championship that caused the rules of scoring to be altered. In those days a goal overtook any number of tries and Yorkshire had scored four!

Shortly after the outbreak of war in the summer of 1914 the army cast its eyes on Queen's with a view to a possible takeover. The Club reported that it then consisted of two real tennis courts, two rackets courts, two squash courts, three covered lawn tennis courts, five hard courts, (laid down in 1913 by the Perfect Hard Court Company for £360), over twenty grass courts, a running track and a football ground. The threat never materialized though later the Club became a balloon site. Life at the Club under a new secretary, E. B. Noel, went on with as little unseemly alteration as possible, and Queen's with a reduced staff made its contribution to the war in helping to entertain troops from home and overseas.

TENNIS AT QUEEN'S CLUB

*E. B. Noel**

THERE are not many athletic and games clubs either in this country or anywhere else with such varied activities as The Queen's Club. In its history of only thirty-two years the ground and buildings have been the scene of twenty-five different sports and games of which twelve – cricket, rugby, Association football, athletic sports, baseball, lawn tennis, real tennis, rackets, squash rackets, Eton fives, bowls and billiards – now take place daily, periodically or at rare intervals.

But there is no question that the great majority of members and visitors are primarily interested in 'lawn tennis' which, at The Queen's Club, includes the game on wooden courts, hard courts and grass courts. Lawn tennis is infinitely more played than any other game at the Club and, of the daily activities, is the best known and most popular.

Lawn tennis is recognized as, perhaps, the most cosmopolitan of pastimes. At Queen's it has been played by competitors from well over twenty countries as well as our dependencies and colonies and members of the *Corps Diplomatique*. There is a slight fallacy in some quarters that if people play at The Queen's Club they must necessarily be good. This is very far from being so. There is play of all kinds and descriptions. I have seen at the Club some of the greatest skills ever exhibited at lawn tennis. I have seen some aspirants whose inefficiency was almost incredible; whom the most patient and painstaking professional would have to give up as a hopeless case. Yet they enjoyed their so-called game which consisted largely of double-faults and a return of any description was an exception.

The Queen's Club does not go back to the earliest days of lawn tennis but to a time when the game was very different from now. For some years there existed near the Gledstanes Road end of the ground one of the old-fashioned long courts, about 90 ft. I believe, which was very popular. When the Club was opened the Renshaw brothers were still in their prime. These famous players, the real inventors of the modern game, to whom their successors owe so much, were constant frequenters and keen supporters of the Club, as later, were the Doherty brothers.

Since Queen's was founded the game has had its ups and downs. There was a time of lost popularity followed by a partial recovery. But it has not been until recent years that the game has established for itself a position which its original inventors would hardly have believed possible. At the moment it seems to be at the height of its popularity and yet I fully believe the crest of the wave is not yet reached. The game has emancipated itself from being scoffed at as a garden party game and, as was said of its kingly forebear, tennis, in Tudor times: 'There were the great days of the game when everybody played.'

The grass courts and covered courts go back to the early days of the Club. The hard courts are a more recent development. Queen's is, perhaps, proudest of the covered courts which have a character all of their own. Nowadays there are three. The east and west are in the same building and stand behind the pavilion. Except for the floor, which has been altered and renewed more than once, no great change has been made since they were built thirty years ago. The light is provided by roof lights; the walls, nowadays, are painted black halfway up and then terracotta. Green baize is hung on the end walls of each court.

*A precis of an article by E. B. Noel that appeared in *The Illustrated Sporting and Dramatic News*, 16 November 1918.

There is a gallery attached to the east court, a narrow strip with room for about two rows of spectators, and a larger one at the back. On occasions a stand and seats have been put on the west court. The present floor was laid in 1914. It is painted black, a colour proved to be the most satisfactory. The new court, perhaps the most popular nowadays, was built early this century at the southerly end of the pavilion. It has a spacious gallery at the back but none at the side.

FAST COURTS

These courts provide a fast game, faster perhaps than on any other surface. The floor does not grip the ball. Rather, it skids off it and it takes some time to become accustomed to the game. Tournaments have been held on the covered courts since the early days and such important events as the 1908 Olympic Games. The two annual tournaments were the London Covered Court Championships in the autumn and the Covered Court Championships in springtime, the latter being the more important of the two.

Almost every great player, male and female, past and present, has played on the covered courts; the Renshaw brothers, E. W. Lewis – one of the greatest covered courts players – H. S. Barlow, who played any ball-game well and poor Harold Mahony, a most popular player, who was killed in an accident in his native Ireland. When only thirty-eight he was found dead at the foot of a mountain, having fallen off his bicycle. Mahony was the life and soul of many a game and many a frolic. How often we heard him give his views on the game in his own delightful way, in all parts of the Club and in all sorts of costumes.

A pair of the 1890s was G. M. Simond and G. A. Caridia. The latter had an attractive style that was a delight to watch. His characteristic stroke was one that, perhaps, should be called a half half-volley. It excelled on these wood courts. Round about 1900 came the summit of the Dohertys' career and they were constantly at Queen's. There was no keener supporter than M. J. G. Ritchie, who has played as many games on these courts as anyone. One of the great triumphs of his life was a victory over H. L. Doherty in the spring tournament. The late A. F. Wilding played a good deal at the Club; so did that great athlete and fine man, Kenneth Powell.

Many ladies have made their name at Queen's and among those who have been closely associated with the Club one would mention Miss T. Lowther, a splendid player at her best, Mrs G. Greville, Mrs G. Lamplough, a pupil of Mahony and the Dohertys and a delightful stylist, Mrs Satterthwaite, Mrs Beamish and Mrs Lambert Chambers, the lady champion.

The President of the Club, Mr A. J. Balfour [later Lord Balfour] is very fond of a game on the covered courts as are Mr Bonar Law, Sir F. E. Smith [later Lord Birkenhead] and Sir H. O. Steel-Maitland.

The increase in number and popularity of the hard courts has been one of the features of modern lawn tennis. Some people go so far as to prophesy the decline, if not the ultimate disappearance, of grass as a surface for the game. It has its drawbacks especially in this climate when in summer months like last July play was stopped day after day. Grass also has its compensations; the feel of it to the feet and the freshness and smell on a real summer day do contribute to the pleasure of the game. There is no better surface than a good grass court.

At one time Queen's was able to have nearly thirty grass courts. They were reduced to about twenty-five when the hard courts were laid on a raised strip of ground at the Greyhound Road end. In the days just before the war the three most fashionable courts were in front of the pavilion. In the south-east corner of the ground, protected by a privet hedge and more sheltered than any other part, is a small but delightful piece of turf. In the Dohertys' time there were two courts there and very popular they were. Later they were turned into a bowling green but since the war have been used for lawn tennis again.

Many great events have been held on the grass courts at Queen's. There was the annual tournament which, of late years, has preceded Wimbledon by a week. The chief event, the Championships of London, is no less distinguished than the Covered Courts Championships and several notable names figure in the list of winners; Joshua Pim, H. S. Barlow, C. P. Dixon, Holcombe Ward, G. Greville and Kenneth Powell.

In 1905 Davis Cup matches involving Australasia, Austria, France and the United States were played there with the Americans, Beals Wright, William Larned and Holcombe Ward proving too good for Australasia's Tony Wilding, Norman Brookes and A. W. Dunlop. In 1913 Canada beat South Africa in the first round.

For many years the Oxford and Cambridge match was played at Queen's – I believe the first-ever one was played there. Of the eighteen so far played Cambridge have won eight, Oxford two, seven were drawn and one abandoned.

In 1910 the Army Championships, particularly the Inter-Regimental Doubles Cup, was inaugurated largely through the work of Captain A. S. Berger (now Colonel) and Capt. A. H. Jones (now Brigadier-General). The tournament was usually played in early July, often corresponding with the Eton and Harrow match at Lord's. In 1914 there was a Parliamentary handicap tournament which, I hope, will become an annual event now that the war has ended.

Since the war the grass courts have been the scene of exhibition matches for charity. In the summer of this year (1918) Colonel H. G. Mayes of the Canadian Forces organized a series of matches between sides chosen from the Services of the British Isles, the Empire and America. There were five teams, the British Isles, American, Canadian, Australian and South African Services, each team playing each other, the matches being played on Wednesdays throughout July and August. Then there were matches between the British and American navies and the British Empire and American armies. Players such as Major A. H. Lowe (England), Colonel Mayes (Canada), Colonel A. R. F. Kingscote (England), Major W. A. Larned (America), Lt Pat O'Hara Wood (Australia) and Captain Le Sueur (South Africa) took part.

Even the ball-boys wore long trousers: Davis Cup competition in 1913

In 1915 the hard courts were entirely re-topped. There were originally five courts, four running north and south and the fifth (a morning court) east and west. The last is temporarily out of commission, but an extra singles court has been added so that there will be six in all.

The part played by the professionals in the development of the game is very considerable. Some years back, when the number of professionals was very much smaller than it was in 1914, practically all of them came from Queen's. In a year or so before the war they multiplied rapidly, but even so in 1914 it would not have been long odds against any professional having emanated from Queen's.

THE PROFESSIONALS SPREAD

The first lawn tennis professionals at West Kensington came from the old Prince's Club. One was Thomas André whose nephew is still engaged at Queen's. But the first to hold the post as now constituted [probably head professional] was Tom Fleming, son of Tom Fleming of the old Maida Vale Club. He is a fine player and good teacher, now at the Roehampton Club.

Tom Fleming was succeeded by Charles Heirons who still holds the position. He manages the lawn tennis department with tact and skill as well as being a good player, delightful stylist and the best and most patient of teachers. Never does he seem tired or bored with the game and he can pass from the worst of pat-ball to the hardest of first class 'fours' with

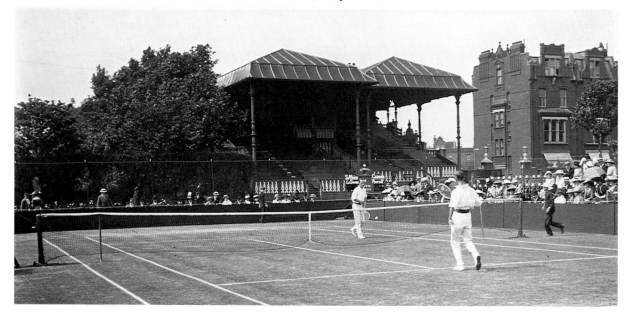

wonderful adaptability. With Heirons before the war, when he joined up, was Henry Cowdrey, a player of different style but of very great natural ability. He had command of any number of strokes and at his best his half-volleying was quite wonderful.

Many other budding professionals have passed as ball-boys through Heirons' capable hands and have gone out to various places. One may mention William Seymour and Lockyer who both remained at Queen's for some time and Haggett, son of a former head groundsman, who became a very fine player. Other members of the staff whose duties were not primarily connected with lawn tennis but who played a good deal were John Laker, now the popular rackets professional at Malvern; Walter Hawes who holds a similar post at Wellington and, before the war, Charles Read. Robert Nash, discharged from the Army after serving in France, has been in the last eighteen months an able second to Heirons and André, formerly a tennis professional, has given much help. As a stringer of rackets he has no superior.

E. B. Noel

Above: Canadian Davis Cup player B. P. Schwengers
The South African Davis Cup squad (left to right): V. R. Gauntlett (Capt.), R. F. le Sueur, L. E. N. Girdlestone and C. R. Leach

THE LONDON GRASS COURT CHAMPIONSHIPS 1890–1914

THE London Grass Court Championships moved to Queen's from the London Athletic Club, Stamford Bridge, Fulham, in 1890 and, apart from the interruptions caused by two world wars, have been held there ever since. 'To judge from the satisfactory manner in which the first open tournament held at Queen's on grass was conducted, the London Championships are likely to flourish exceedingly in their new abode. The courts were in splendid order and the ground man, André, deserves credit' was the comment from *Pastime*, the sporting journal of that era. The comment was not always so kind but one hundred years later *Pastime*'s prophecy remains true. The Championships have flourished, the courts are in splendid order and the groundsman (the modern term), David Kimpton, also deserves credit.

The champions that first year were H. S. Barlow and Miss M. Jacks. Barlow, warding off the challenge from Wilfred Baddeley, aged eighteen, 3–6 6–8 6–1 6–2 6–2, was an inconsistent player with a long reach who had achieved fame, indeed immortality, at Wimbledon the previous year when playing William Renshaw for the title. Barlow stood at match point when Renshaw slipped, fell and lost his racket. Barlow had only to place a shot but chose to 'dolly' the ball and give Renshaw time to recover. That cost him the title. Quixotic or sporting? Who knows? Miss Jacks, about whom very little is known, resisted the challenge from Maud Shackle, the first known ambidextrous woman player, 6–2 6–1. Their rivalry extended to the Covered Court Championships.

In those days the champions did not have to play through and thus had only to appear for the final day. It did not always work to their advantage. Barlow, for instance, appears to have been playing in Bath all week before coming up to London to meet young Baddeley – 'For two sets Barlow's play was slow and lifeless' was *Pastime*'s comment.

It was also the age when everyone entered the handicap events and Herbert Baddeley, an identical twin, won the event off owe-40. The twins won the Wimbledon doubles title in 1891.

That year there were three singles events in the London Championships – the Open, the Queen's Cup and the Handicap. This gave the players a lot of matches and the referee, the renowned Herbert Chipp, another pioneer ambidextrous player and, later, the first LTA secretary, a lot of headaches. It also produced some strange twists. Barlow, for instance, won the London title for the third year running, beating the Irishman, Joshua Pim, 6–4 2–6 6–0 7–5. But Pim beat him when they met on level terms in the handicap singles while another Irishman, H. S. Mahony, an ebullient fellow whose name is written all over the early history of lawn tennis at Queen's, beat him in the Queen's Cup. Pim, the winner of that event, was judged the player of the week – 'He has certainly never played a better game than in some of his matches at Queen's. He appeared able to return anything and the grace and ease with which he accomplished the most difficult strokes earned the admiration of all beholders' wrote a commentator of the time. And just to show that doubtful line decisions are no modern phenomenon it was claimed that Chipp was done out of the second set against Mahony by several!

Miss Shackle prevented Miss Jacks from winning the women's title for the third year running, winning 6–2 4–6 6–3 and then rubbing it in with a 6–0 6–1 victory in the Queen's Cup final. The winner with 'unerring precision' retained the London title the following year, beating Miss Ethel Austin, the future Mrs G. Greville, 6–2 6–3.

In that year, 1892, the spotlight focused on another young lady, Miss Charlotte 'Chattie' Cooper, beaten 6–4 8–6 by Miss Austin. 'The loser did not succeed in winning a set but she offered most determined resistance. Miss Cooper ought to make a name for herself for her all-round play. She is not afraid to follow a sound return to the net' ran a contemporary report. Fulfilling the writer's predictions, three years later Miss Cooper won the first of her five Wimbledon titles.

DOUBLE-FAULTER

The first of the overseas invaders appeared in the men's singles. He was Oliver Campbell, who had won the US title in Philadelphia at the age of nineteen. This was written of Campbell: 'He probably serves more double-faults than any known player, often presenting his opponent with 30, odds he can scarcely afford to concede.' Not surprisingly he went out to Pim who was then beaten to the title by E. W. Lewis.

The drought of 1893 affected Queen's more than most clubs and 'when the rain that was to obliterate the traces of winter football and the antics of the (so-called) golfers never came, there were doubts whether the courts would be ready in time.' Through the efforts of Banks, the head groundsman, however, and helped by a few showers, they were what was described as 'presentable'. Ironically thunderstorms came near to wrecking the finals.

The men's Challenge round was an all-Irish affair, Pim beating Mahony in five sets and most of the match being played on covered courts owing to a thunderstorm. Maud Shackle retained her women's title, again beating Edith Austin on the way. This time, however, she really rubbed it in by beating Miss Austin in the Queen's Cup after the loser had had a match point and, for a third time in the week, in the handicap singles; Miss Shackle off owe-40, Miss Austin off owe-30. Charlotte Cooper and Miss E. Lane also met in all three events, the latter player winning two of them.

The first rumbles of discontent over the effect of winter football on the grass courts were heard in 1894. In hot weather the courts became 'fiery and bumpy' and *Pastime* suggested that 'The powers to be at this influential club should consider improving the playing portion of their attractive ground'. It was

nearly thirty years before football, rugby and soccer finally departed from Queen's.

In the early nineties the growth of lawn tennis had slowed down, and its popularity waned. Even Wimbledon showed a decline and Queen's did well to get an entry of twenty-nine men including half a dozen past, present or future Wimbledon champions and ten women in 1894. Mahony (*Hic & ubique* they called him) was the winner but in the first round of the handicap singles he failed to give Arthur Gore 4/6. Edith Austin won the women's title for the first time.

The turf was relaid the following year but dry weather did not hold and, it was recorded, false bounces were as plentiful as ever. In 1896, though, Haggett, the head groundsman – they seemed to come and go in those days – was praised for the splendid condition of the thirteen courts – the first reference to the number of grass courts at Queen's or the number used for the meeting.

The meeting that year was notable for the entry of Laurie Doherty, later to become one of the all-time greats, and William A. Larned who, a year or two later, won the US Championship and played in the early Davis Cup matches. Laurie Doherty beat Larned but lost to Mahoney 10–9 in the fifth set and it was written of him: 'With a little more severity he should not be far removed from the very topmost rank.' Mahony went on to beat the elder Doherty, Reggie, for the title and then win Wimbledon. 'Chattie' Cooper won her first London title and the first of her five Wimbledons.

MARATHON MATCH

Laurie Doherty dominated Queen's for the next two years, even winning the handicap singles from owe-15, while M. J. G. Ritchie, well beaten in the final by the younger Doherty, made the first of his many impacts on Queen's and the game as a whole. The match of the 1897 meeting was between Ritchie and A. W. Hallward. They went on court at 3.30 p.m. precisely and came off at five minutes to seven – three hours and twenty-five minutes, which must have been a near-record in those days. Ritchie won 4–6 6–1 7–5 5–7 8–6.

'Chattie' Cooper retained her title but only after a tremendous semi-final tussle with the left-handed Miss Beryl Tulloch, the severest hitter the women's game had yet seen, 8–10 6–3 8–6. She won it for the third successive year in 1898 after a mighty close struggle with Miss Austin, who led 5–4 in the final set before going down 6–4 3–6 8–6. The players, by the way, complained about the spectators continually passing from court to court close to the baselines!

The last year of the nineteenth century was a bad one for Miss Cooper. Her old rival Miss Austin beat her four times, in the Covered Courts Championships, Chiswick, Beckenham and at Queen's where, it was claimed, a bad line decision cost Miss Cooper the match. Miss Austin won 12–10 2–6 9–7 – 'Probably the most severely contested match which these rivals in many a stubborn match have ever struggled through'. Miss Cooper then lost her Wimbledon title to Mrs. G. W. Hillyard.

The first few years of the twentieth century saw a changing scene among the men but not the women. There was some hot weather too, up to 90° in the shade in both 1901 and 1902. A. W. Gore, who was to win his first Wimbledon the following year, was the 1900 winner. Laurie Doherty played only in the handicap singles, losing in the first round off owe 3/6. Chattie Cooper regained her title and Miss Dorothea K. Douglass, later the formidable Mrs Lambert Chambers, made her first appearance.

When the 1901 meeting came around, Miss Cooper had become Mrs A. Sterry and her defeat by Mrs G. Greville, formerly Miss Austin, was a major upset. 'Mrs Sterry occasionally got the ball as far as the net. If it went over Mrs Greville did as she wished with it'. She went on to beat Miss E. W. Thomson in the final.

One report claimed that the men's play that year was, in some instances, better than Wimbledon which, of course, it followed, not preceded, in those days. A description of C. P. Dixon's play in the final against G. Greville, whom he beat 6–1 6–0 4–6 6–4, is illuminating: 'Some of his forehand drives even when taken from outside the baseline were hit with such cleanness and power that Greville could not match them – and, if he did, returned only weakly. On the forehand Dixon now plays the ball before it gets to the top of its bounce and his opponent is continually on the strain to return it. Not so the backhand. The ball is taken anywhere after it begins to fall, sometimes just before it would reach the ground. The result is that it is returned without reason, direction or purpose.'

The writer did not think much of Greville – 'His racket met the ball at all sorts of funny angles. He hasn't a single shot that is true.' The following year the commentator was in equally clinical form when claiming that Mrs Sterry 'was in the right mood' and Mrs N. Durlacher, whom she beat 6–0 6–0 in the women's final, 'was in the wrong mood and was puzzled by the screw Mrs Sterry put on the ball'.

Two new names appeared on the winners' board in 1903 – G. M. Simond, a regular Wimbledon last-eighter and later a referee, and Miss Agnes Morton, an Essex girl who won the Wimbledon doubles in 1914 (with Elizabeth Ryan) and who married late in life to become Lady Hugh Stewart.

The men's and mixed doubles were added to the Championship programme for the first time the following year. That brought Reggie Doherty back to Queen's to win the men's with W. V. Eaves, one of the founding fathers of Australian tennis before he settled in Britain as a doctor. Eaves was merely the harbinger of the flock of players from Australasia and the United States that invaded Queen's and Wimbledon in succeeding years.

1905 was a big year for Queen's. The London meeting was moved to a pre-Wimbledon date and after Wimbledon the Club staged a series of Davis Cup matches involving the US, France, Austria and Australasia to decide which nation should challenge Britain, the holders. Thus the London meeting was dominated by men from the US and Australasia. There was a massive entry for all events from home players.

AMERICANS SET THE PACE

The Australian, Norman Brookes, in his first match beat J. M. Flavelle, a respectable Wimbledon player, 6–0 6–0 6–0. This was described as 'sensational'. Brookes eventually fell to the American, Beals Wright, after leading two sets to one and 4–2. The pace began to tell on Brookes and Wright proved a better general and overhead volleyer. It was, according to one observer, 'one of the best matches it has been our privilege to have seen'.

Another American, Holcombe Ward, produced a twist service that puzzled all his opponents including Arthur Gore, whom he beat in the semi-finals. That serve became known as 'the American twist'. Wright retired to Ward in the singles final and together they lost the doubles final to two more Americans, W. A. Larned and W. J. Clothier.

Larned and Clothier, members of the first US Davis Cup team to visit this country, had only just landed when the meeting began. They still had their sea-legs and were a trifle shaky when they went on

The London Grass Court Championships 1904, won by M. J. G. Ritchie

to court for their opening match which they lost in two sets. Back in the changing room the referee asked them the score and when they mentioned two sets he pointed out the match should have been the best-of-five and they had better all go out again and finish it. They did and the Americans won the next three sets and later the tournament!

Australia was represented in the mixed final with A. W. Dunlop and Norman Brookes on opposite sides of the net. Dunlop's partner was the singles winner, Miss E. W. Thomson who, seven years later, won Wimbledon as Mrs Dudley Larcombe.

The courts came in for some ripe criticism in 1906. It was claimed that 'Haggett did all in his power to make the courts as good as possible. Nos. 1, 2 and 3 were very good comparatively (whatever that means – Ed.). The less said about the others the better'.

The first appearance of Tony Wilding, a New Zealander at Cambridge, and the defeat of Wimbledon champion, Mrs Lambert Chambers, were the next year's highlights. Wilding had the easiest final over M. J. G. Ritchie 6–2 6–1 6–0 and it was said of the loser: 'Ritchie appeared to take little interest in the game after the first set.'

Mrs Lambert Chambers, already a three-time Wimbledon winner, fell to Miss V. Pinckney 2–6 6–3 6–4. A report said, 'The winner played the game of her life keeping her opponent on the run and at an admirable length. Mrs Chambers was not at her best and the Wimbledon title will change hands if there is no improvement.' It did. May Sutton from the US beat her.

The Championship of Europe (men) was held in conjunction with the normal meeting in 1908 and two five-set singles championshis in one week proved too much for some players. W. C. Crawley retired with cramp in the European final to Ritchie midway through the third set (one set-all). Then Ritchie, a set down and 3–3, retired to K. Powell in the London final. Miss Pinckney again beat Mrs Lambert Chambers in the women's final.

Wilding, having helped Australasia win the Davis Cup in 1909, became the dominant player not just at Queen's but at Wimbledon during the years 1910–1912 inclusive. He went through those three years at Queen's without losing a set. Indeed, in 1910, he dropped only 15 games in 12 sets in reaching the final where Ritchie, completely off form, retired when down two sets. He beat A. E. Beamish in 1911 and the following year the German, Otto Froitzheim, who having suffered two five-setters against Ritchie and J. C. Parke, retired with a swollen hand.

The American, Beals Wright, had withdrawn in 1910 when prohibited from playing in spikes. He did borrow some 'rubbers' but found them uncomfortable and retired at set-all to A. Hendricks. Neither Queen's nor Wimbledon permitted spikes unless the referee considered that the ground condition warranted them. There was more grumbling the next year, too, and the comment appeared in print that 'The courts are such that if we played with toboggan rakes on our toes I don't think we could hurt them.'

DAMP GERMANS

There was some interest in the appearance of the Germans, Froitzheim, F. W. Rahe and H. Kleinschroth in 1911. It was a damp year and they were disconcerted by the low bounce and soft courts. But, it was said, 'When the ball occasionally bounced up they swooped it back in their beautiful free style.'

During those three years there were three different women champions. The first was Mrs G. Lamplough, formerly Gladys Eastlake-Smith. She beat Miss E. G. Johnson in the final and then lost to her in the semis at Wimbledon. The winner's game was a strong and fast one and after her easy win over Miss Johnson a rival was heard to say, 'If you don't start at once against Gladys you find yourself back in the changing room still thinking about the first service.' Miss Johnson obviously learned her lesson.

Miss M. Coles, a Wimbledon quarter-finalist, succeeded Mrs Lamplough, beating Miss Agnes Morton, later Lady Hugh Stewart, in less than half-an-hour. The third champion was Mrs Dudley Larcombe, who won her one-and-only Wimbledon that year, 1912, and the London title at Queen's for the next two years as well.

Also in 1912, the year that H. S. Scrivener took over as referee from G. M. Simond, an interesting men's doubles team appeared on court – R. B. Powell and the Frenchman A. H. Gobert. If Powell shouted 'out' Gobert invariably took a swipe at the ball. In retaliation Powell repeatedly tried to poach Gobert's shots with the inevitable clash of rackets. They did well to get to the third round.

The Germans were back in 1913, and among the spectators was one of the Kaiser's nephews, Prince Frederick Karl. He saw Rahe and Kleinscroth win the doubles. In political contrast Mrs Winston Churchill, whose husband was First Lord of the Admiralty, played in the handicap singles, losing to Miss L. Davenport.

Wallace Johnson, ranked third in the US and a specialist in fast spin, reached the men's final but despite his chopped drive and adroit lobbing lost to F. Gordon Lowe in five sets. Johnson led 4–2 in the final set and then went for the lines – and missed. Lowe won again in 1914, beating P. M. Davson, designer of No. 3 Covered Court.

Brookes and Wilding made their last appearance at Queen's and, standing well inside the baseline to receive serve, beat W. C. Crawley and Davson.

A. E. Stoddart (left) former Middlesex and England
cricketer, with his tennis partner

THE COVERED COURT CHAMPIONSHIPS
1890–1914

THE Covered Court Championships, the first event of their type in the world, were first held at the Hyde Park LTC, Porchester Square, in 1885, eight years after the birth of Wimbledon. They consisted only of men's singles and did not flourish. When it was decided to hold a championship for women's singles and men's doubles, The Queen's Club, already a name in sport through its football, athletics and University sport in general, was the obvious choice. Those two events were first played there in 1890 but the men's singles remained at the Hyde Park LTC until 1895.

The first champion at Queen's to win Wimbledon was Miss Charlotte 'Chattie' Cooper in 1896. Curiously she never again won the Covered Court title though, like Miss Cooper or Mrs A. Sterry, she won five Wimbledons before the war. Thereafter Queen's champions thrived at Wimbledon, Mrs G. W. Hillyard winning that title six times, Miss D. K. Douglass, later Mrs Lambert Chambers, seven times and Miss Dora Boothby once.

Among the men the Doherty brothers, Reggie and Laurie, who, it has been said, were given £2000 a year each by their parents to play lawn tennis, dominated Queen's just as they did Wimbledon and wherever else they played. Between 1898 and 1906 inclusive there was not a year when they did not win the singles or doubles, or both, at Queen's. Their achievements overshadow those of Arthur W. Gore, who between 1888 and 1927 inclusive played 182 matches at Wimbledon, winning the title three times. Goodness knows how many he played at Queen's as his name, like that of M. J. G. Ritchie, seems to crop up year after year.

The first singles winner at Queen's, in 1890, was Miss M. Jacks, about whom nothing is known other than that she was one of the only four entrants for the Wimbledon women's singles. Her final opponent was Miss M. Pick, whom she beat 6–0 6–1. The predominant player in the first few years was Maude Shackle, the winner three years running and the first known ambidextrous player. Her mixed partner, Herbert Chipp, the first LTA secretary, was also ambidextrous. Miss Shackle's daughter, Joan Reid-Thomas (later Mrs F. M. Strawson), won the title in 1925.

When Miss Shackle won the first final of her hat-trick in 1891, beating Miss Jacks 7–5 6–3, both women played from the baseline, 'as they usually do', said one report. It was not much different the following year when Miss Shackle beat May Arbuthnot, one of three competing sisters. But at least she volleyed once – in the last game. The loser's serve was said to be 'short and easy'.

Miss Arbuthnot improved her serve the following year. With the help of a netcord she led 5–4 in the final set, only to lose it 7–5 due to Miss Shackle's steadiness. Whether or not the winner played another volley is not recorded. Miss Shackle was succeeded by Miss Edith Lucy Austin, who survived a match point to beat Miss Arbuthnot and win the first of five titles before becoming Mrs G. Greville, a regular Queen's Club competitor with her husband.

So far, that is up to 1894, the men's activities were confined to the doubles, with G. W. Hillyard and H. S. Scrivener winning the first two years. Hillyard became Secretary of the All England Club in 1907, an office he held until 1924. Scrivener took to refereeing and became a distinguished correspondent for the *Morning Post*. He had earlier played in the first Oxford and Cambridge match played at Queen's.

FULL GALLERY

That first year, 1890, Hillyard and Scrivener beat Ernest Renshaw, already a Wimbledon singles and doubles winner (with his brother William), and H. S. Barlow, also a Middlesex County cricketer, 6–4 6–3 8–6. A report said that the gallery was so full that the overflow spectators had to stand on the floor of the adjoining court, something not appreciated by the players. Hillyard seems to have been the star, the most severe hitter on court; while Scrivener excelled in the use of the short cross, clever placing and the lob.

Two years later they lost the title to E. G. Meers and H. S. Mahony, one of the three Irishmen to win Wimbledon, who was said to be 'the life and soul of Queen's Club'. He played for years in Championships held at the Club under his own or assumed names, had poor groundstrokes but was an adept volleyer, which no doubt helped him on the fast courts and contributed to his success in both Championships. Mahony was a distinctive character.

By 1895 the growing popularity of The Queen's Club and the decline in interest of Hyde Park was such that it was decided to transfer the men's singles from Porchester Square to Barons Court. Mahony, the last singles winner at Hyde Park, caught 'flu and though a postponement was offered was unable to play what was then the Challenge round. E. W. Lewis, five times the champion from 1887–91, thus regained the title.

Miss Charlotte 'Chattie' Cooper made her first appearance in these Championships that year and deprived Miss Austin of her title by 6–4 3–6 6–1. Miss Austin is said to have played timidly but the fact was that Miss Cooper was a fine volleyer 'with a constitution of the proverbial ostrich who scarcely knew what it was to be tired'. She won the first of her five Wimbledons that year, the last as Mrs A. Sterry in 1908 and became one of the game's legendary figures, dying in her nineties.

Lewis won the men's title for the seventh time in 1896 after an extraordinary match against W. V. Eaves, an Australian doctor resident in England and an old rival, 6–4 6–1 6–8 4–6 7–5. Lewis lost three match points in the third set and later, when leading 5–1 in the fifth, temporarily collapsed only to recover at the last moment. Both men were notable volleyers and Eaves, the previous year, had come within a point of winning Wimbledon when playing Wilfred Baddeley in the All-Comers final.

REAL TENNIS BLAMED

W. V. Eaves turned the tables on E. W. Lewis in 1897 and had a distinguished tournament. First he beat the well-known real tennis player, Eustace Miles, 6–4 6–3 8–6. Miles, it was said, 'Imparts too much cut to his returns and the royal game is to blame for this. He also stands too near the ball for the backhand which, in consequence, he chops.'

Having dealt with Miles, Eaves put out the brothers, R. F. and H. L. Doherty, the latter competing for the first time. Both matches probably hung on their long first sets. H. L. Doherty, for instance, lost the 21st game on a very doubtful decision and was beaten 12–10 6–2 6–4. Eaves then beat the Irishman, H. S. Mahoney and, in the Championship round, E. W. Lewis, 6–3 6–3 7–5; the loser being short of practice, nursing an arm injury and doing much of his volleying from behind the service line.

Miss Edith Austin retained her singles title but only after the longest ladies' final yet recorded. She beat Miss R. Dyas 9–11 6–4 12–10 in just over two hours. The loser had a match point at 9–8 and 40–30 in the final set.

With the growth in popularity of both The Queen's Club and these Championships, mixed doubles was added to the list of events in 1898. It was won by R. F. Doherty and Charlotte Cooper over G. Greville and Miss L. Austin, 6–3 5–7 6–4. R. F. Doherty, 'Big Do', was already the king of Wimbledon, though he was soon to surrender the crown to his younger brother 'Little Do'. They won the men's doubles title, R. F. and Miss Cooper retained the mixed but H. L. Doherty lost 6–4 7–5 6–3 in the Championship round to Dr W. V. Eaves, the holder. Eaves's service bothered his opponent and he excelled in the use of the half-volley, a popular stroke in those days.

Miss Austin retained her title, beating Miss P. Legh. The surprise result was Miss Legh's defeat of Charlotte Cooper who, it was said, had sprained a wrist and was short of practice. A few months later Miss Cooper won Wimbledon for the third time.

The last year of the century saw the first appearance of M. J. G. Ritchie and he was surprisingly beaten by R. B. Hough who, it was said, 'rushed the persistent Ritchie off his game'. Ritchie's name, however, appears in these annals for many years to come.

W. V. Eaves retained his men's title, beating H.

Covered Court cartoons of the 1890s

S. Mahony in five sets despite being in poor health. The match was played in bad light, a yellow fog pervading the court. Miss Austin won her fourth successive title, again beating Charlotte Cooper though both players were well below their best.

With W. V. Eaves away in the Boer War in South Africa, A. W. Gore, who had already been competing at Wimbledon since 1888, won the first of his two titles, beating M. J. G. Ritchie 6–1 7–5 6–3 in the 1900 Championship final. Gore had a most remarkable career as he won Wimbledon three times and last competed there in 1926 when, at the age of fifty-eight, he and H. Roper Barrett beat the Duke of York (later King George VI) and Louis Greig.

There was general public regret that the Doherty brothers did not compete in the singles and some disappointment when they won the doubles with the utmost ease. Miss L. Austin, who had become Mrs G. Greville, did not defend her singles title and that fell to Miss T. Lowther who beat Charlotte Cooper and Miss Beryl Tulloch in the last two rounds.

Their father subsidized the remarkable Doherty brothers

DOHERTY DOMINATION

For the next few years, six in the case of the singles, the men's events were dominated by the Doherty brothers, Reginald and Laurie, and by the latter in particular. Wimbledon, if not Queen's, had suffered some decline in the 1890s which, it has always been claimed, the Dohertys arrested. The brothers' overall record at Queen's was remarkable – H. L. singles champion six times, with R.F. doubles champion seven times, with G. W. Hillyard doubles champion twice and with Miss T. Lowther mixed doubles champion twice – seventeen titles in all. Reginald never won the singles but shared his brother's seven doubles titles and won the mixed four times, thrice with Charlotte Cooper and once with Gladys Eastlake Smith.

During his six years as singles champion Laurie Doherty did not always have it all his own way. His first title, however, was clearcut and he lost only one set, to that half-volley expert G. A. Caridia in the first round, before taking the title off A. W. Gore 6–3 6–1 6–1. The following year, 1902, he had a Championship round battle with M. J. G. Ritchie,

who had not dropped a set in reaching that stage, before winning 6–4 6–3 5–7 6–3.

G. W. Hillyard was Laurie Doherty's opponent in 1903 and he was beaten in four sets. For the next two years the persistent M. J. G. Ritchie was his challenger and, in 1904, they had a rare battle before the champion won 6–2 8–10 5–7 6–4 6–3. Ritchie won the second set with two crosscourt drives and an overhead error from Doherty. He was up 3–1 in the third set, but lost the next four games before taking Doherty's service to love to go two sets to one up. Ritchie led 3–0 in the fourth set and his volleying and smashing took him to 3–1 in the final, but that was his limit. The champion, not feeling his best so it was said, crawled home. In his six years' reign that was by far the hardest singles match Laurie Doherty played.

Doherty beat Ritchie again in 1905 in three sets and in his last year defeated A. W. Gore 6–2 6–4 8–6. That year was notable not so much for Laurie Doherty's sixth win as for the arrival of A.F. (Anthony) Wilding, a New Zealander at Cambridge University and future Wimbledon champion. Wilding beat Ritchie in the second round. Against Gore in the semi-final, Wilding began by playing mostly from the back of the court. To go two sets up Wilding brought the volley into play. He let the third set slip as Gore showed more dash but was ahead 3–1 and 6–5 in the fourth. Gore saved that set and from 3–3 in the fifth volleyed with great judgment to win 4–6 2–6 6–0 8–6 6–3. Needless to say, he had little left against Doherty.

These Doherty years saw the rise of another great champion: Dorothea Douglass, later Mrs Lambert Chambers, who won both the Covered Courts and the Wimbledon title seven times. In 1901, however, she fell to another multiple Wimbledon champion, Mrs G. W. Hillyard (formerly Blanche Bingley) who went on to win the title for the only time beating Mrs A. Sterry (Charlotte Cooper) and the holder, Miss T. Lowther. Mrs Hillyard did not defend in 1902 and Miss Lowther had it very much her own way that year and the following.

Miss Douglass won her first singles title in 1904, her final opponent being a former champion, Mrs G. Greville (Miss L. Austin). She did not defend in 1905 when Miss H. Lane, who had not previously played at Queen's, came up from Brighton and beat Gladys Eastlake-Smith for the title. Miss Lane, in defending her title against Miss Douglass the following year, won only two games.

With the end of the Doherty era, Anthony Wilding swept the board at Queen's winning all three events in 1907, partnered by M. J. G. Ritchie in the men's doubles and by Gladys Eastlake-Smith, the women's champion, in the mixed. The hardest match Wilding had was his first against Ritchie, whom he beat 6–0 3–6 7–5 6–3. Ritchie had beaten Wilding in Cannes not long beforehand and when, with some telling volleying and lobbing, he took the second set and led 4–1 in the third, it looked as if he might repeat that win. Wilding's fitness got him home.

A. W. Gore, who had beaten Wilding the previous year, was beaten by an American, D. P. Rhodes, in five sets after leading 4–1 and 40–30 in the final set. The American's volleying and service worried Gore but not Wilding when they met in the fourth round. To win the title Wilding beat G. A. Caridia easily.

STRANGE NAMES

In 1908 a printed programme was issued for the first time and in it the use of pseudonyms was deplored. In this history I have translated as many pseudonyms as possible. The worst offenders were H. S. Mahony and H. Roper Barrett. Among the variety of pseudonyms were the obvious 'N. O. Good' and 'T. Ennis' but strange ones such as 'Cregan' and 'Hardress Cregan', 'A. Mough' and 'R. H. Roberto'. They were used mainly by players who, for one reason or another, wanted to disguise or hide the fact that they were playing at Queen's.

A. W. Gore beat both his chief rivals: M. J. G. Ritchie 6–4 6–2 6–3 in the final and Tony Wilding (holder) 4–6 8–6 6–0 8–6 in the Challenge round. Gore's driving against Ritchie was in splendid order; he ran his man from corner to corner and did more or less the same to Wilding in a largely baseline duel. 'Neither man could afford to go to the net,' said a report. Mrs Lambert Chambers, her service improved – 'It now has more sting in it' – returned to regain the singles title from Gladys Eastlake-Smith. The weather that year was volatile. The light on the second day was, it was said, 'atrocious' and rain came through the roof. Much sawdust was needed. And the fifth day was far too hot for indoor play.

After ten unsuccessful years of trying, M. J. G. Ritchie at last won the title and without dropping a set! He outplayed A. W. Gore (holder) 7–5 8–6 6–3 in the 1909 Challenge round. At 5–4 in the first set

MISS G. EASTLAKE SMITH — THE NEW LADY
COVERED-COURTS CHAMPION.

AN IMPRESSION OF MR M. J. G. RITCHIE

MR G. A. CARIDIA.

MR A. F. WILDING
WINNER OF THE MEN'S
SINGLES CHAMPIONSHIP

MR A. W. GORE. IN ACTION.

THE OFFICE OF UMPIRE IS NOT A MATTER
OF MUCH COMPETITION AMONG CLUB
MEMBERS

DUDLEY CLEAVER 07

MR D. F. RHODES WHO GAINED AN UNEXPECTED VICTORY
OVER MR GORE

MISS M. COLES.

The Gentlemen's Double Final in 1910: Doust and Poidevin v. Gore and Barrett

Gore made two unexpected errors and at the same score in the second suddenly put three into the net. (In those days, by the way, the rallies were still called 'rests' as in real tennis.) Ritchie beat two other interesting opponents: Kenneth Powell, who had beaten him in their three previous meetings, and the dogged C. P. Dixon.

Dora Boothby, who won her only Wimbledon singles title later that year, became the women's champion, beating Mrs O'Neill, an underhand server, 6–1 6–3. Gore and Roper Barrett beat the Lowe brothers, A.H. and F.G., to take the men's doubles.

Two most interesting challengers appeared in 1910: André Gobert from France, six foot, aged nineteen, a powerful hitter and soon to dominate the men's singles, and Miss Molla Bjurstedt, a Norwegian-born American who later won the US Championship seven times. In 1921 as Mrs Mallory she inflicted on Suzanne Lenglen the worst defeat the French lady ever suffered in competition. But here

left Covered Court contenders in 1907

at Queen's the young Miss Bjurstedt lost in the first round to Miss B. Tulloch.

The Lowe brothers dominated the men's singles, F.G. beating A.H. 6–4 6–0 6–1 in the title match. But earlier F.G. had a narrow escape from defeat by Gobert, who had a match point at 5–3 in the fifth set. Lowe passed him down the sideline and the Frenchman, exhausted after some long rallies, 'went to the sliding door at the side of the court to inhale outside air'. F.G. won 4–6 6–1 6–2 3–6 8–6. Mrs Lambert Chambers beat Mrs O'Neill 6–4 6–3 for the women's title.

Gobert, now twenty years old, beat A. H. Lowe, P. M. Davson, M. J. G. Ritchie and finally F. G. Lowe (holder), all in three sets, to win the title in 1911. Gobert's service proved to be almost untakeable. Ritchie, having beaten Tony Wilding in five sets, had to stand almost touching the backstop netting to receive it; F. G. Lowe actually hit the netting in his attempts to return serve. The run-back was considered on the short side. Gobert and Ritchie won the doubles and Mrs Lambert Chambers retained the women's title, beating Miss H. Aitchison 6–3 6–1.

The 'new' court (No. 3) was used for the first time in the 1912 Championships as the floor of the west court had been uneven for some time. Players claimed the 'new' court was the best of the three.

Gobert retained his men's title after a mighty battle against Tony Wilding, whom he beat 3–6 7–5 4–6 6–4 6–4. The loser had led 3–0 in the fourth set. Audacious play saved the Frenchman that set but then he lost a 4–0 lead in the final. He served fourteen double-faults in the first two sets, eight in the next three!

Stanley Doust, an Australian and later lawn tennis correspondent for the *Daily Mail*, first appeared at this meeting in 1910 and won the men's doubles – he won again with Wilding – beating the holders, Gobert and M. J. G. Ritchie. Miss E. D. Holman won the first of her four singles titles, beating Mrs H. Edgington 6–2 6–0.

1913 was A. E. Stoddart's last year as the Club secretary. D. R. Larcombe, later to become secretary to the All England Club, was the referee, having taken over in 1911 from G. F. Simond. Few anticipated that the men's winner would be P. M. Davson and that his final opponent would be E. Larsen, the Danish champion, whom he beat 5–7 6–2 6–3 6–2. Davson was a patient, thoughtful player with a good variety of strokes and a sense of placement.

The more favoured players were beaten; the Lowes, and M. J. G. Ritchie by Stanley Doust, who in turn fell to Larsen. But Doust did win the two doubles titles, with Tony Wilding and Mrs Lambert Chambers. That good lady, needless to say, regained the singles title, losing seventeen games in four matches and ending by beating the holder, Miss E. D. Holman.

Davson's reign was brief and as war began to threaten in 1914 M. J. G. Ritchie, who by then knew every crack in The Queen's Club floor and every sparrow in the rafters, won for the second time. He beat Davson 8–6 6–3 6–1. Mrs Lambert Chambers had an injured foot and Miss E. D. Holman recovered the women's title. Because of the war it was to be five years before any of these players met again in competition.

REAL TENNIS
1888–1914
E. B. Noel

ON 1 January 1888 two famous professionals entered the services of The Queen's Club. The first, Charles Saunders, then at the height of his form as a tennis player, only remained a few months and then left to take a position at Prince's Club, Knightsbridge. He had formerly been at 'Old' Prince's in Hans Place. The other, Peter W. Latham, then a young man of twenty-two, became the most noted of racket and tennis players of the time. He was born on 10 May 1865 and went as a boy into service of the Manchester Club who may be said to have discovered him. He showed the most astonishing prowess at rackets and as early as 1887 he wrested the Championship from Joseph Gray of Rugby. The first ten years of Latham's engagement at Queen's took him to the zenith of his fame. He came to the Club as rackets professional, but when Saunders left he took over tennis as well.

In 1895 his admirers made him a presentation, in the big room at Queen's, on an occasion when he played a match with the Hon. Alfred Lyttleton, giving him 15. Only a few years earlier the odds would have been the other way.

In all the early years of the nineties tennis was very popular at Queen's and it was, I think, very largely due to Peter. The years 1895–98 were the crown and summit of his career. In this time he played his two greatest matches against George Standing at rackets and against Tom Petitt at tennis and won them both.

Soon after that he left Queen's to go to his old patron, Sir C. D. Rose, with whom he stayed first at Newmarket and then at Hardwick near Whitchurch until Sir Charles's death in 1913.

Peter resigned the Championship of rackets in 1903 having held it for sixteen years and having won

five matches and lost none. In 1904 he beat C. 'Punch' Fairs for the Championship of Tennis but in 1905 in a home v home match Fairs beat him at The Queen's Club and at Prince's. It was rather curious that Peter's one-and-only defeat in a Championship match should come in the court he knew most intimately. In 1907 he recovered the Championship from 'Punch' at Brighton and thus ended his career in a blaze of glory. In all he won nine out of ten of the contests.

In 1916 he returned on 1 May as head professional at Queen's with his powers and skill very little abated at rackets in spite of his fifty years, and he still clearly loves to get into the racket court. He is pre-eminent as a teacher as well as a player, and in the profession of both tennis and rackets he has been an outstanding figure for many years.

Other professionals at the Queen's Club in the early days were Bill Holden, who also came from old Prince's, and George Cott, half French and grandson of the celebrated Edmond Barre, World Champion in 1829. He afterwards returned to the Paris courts and died in 1917 as the result of an accident. Frederick André was another of the firstcomers and is still in the Club's employ. When Peter left to go to Newmarket he took over the management of the courts. There were also Alfred Dooley and Toby Chambers.

BIRTH OF THE AMATEUR

In the spring of 1888 an event known as The Queen's Club Cup was contested, which was won by H. J. M. Heathcote. During the next spring the competition was thrown open to all amateurs and has become known as 'The Amateur Championship',

J. M. Heathcote (centre) with Lyttleton, Marshall, Pepys and Langham. Five of Heathcote's rackets, all dated 1888, were found recently at the Club. One was inscribed 'the best I ever played with'

the most famous of all competitions of the kind. It was not always held in the precise and mathematical manner that characterized it in the few years before the war. Indeed, up to the beginning of the century, the matches in the preliminary rounds were played by mutual arrangement at any time before a given date. The time of year, however, was always late April or early May.

At first the competition did not occupy the same exalted position as the MCC Gold and Silver Prizes and the Hon. Alfred Lyttleton, who was holder of the Gold Prize until 1896 and, as such, amateur champion of the game, never played in the event at The Queen's Club. But after the disappearance of the famous old Lord's court and when competitors from France and America started to come to Queen's, the competition began to be regarded as the more important of the two, and its winner as the veritable amateur champion of the year.

The actual date of the change of headquarters cannot be precisely determined, but it may be said that in 1903 the MCC prizes were still the more important and the transition years were from 1904–6. After Mr Gould's visits in 1906, 1907 and 1908, there is no question that the Queen's event was, in fact as well as name, the blue riband of amateur tennis.

At tennis there is generally a distinct dividing line between the really first-class player and the merely good player, and the list of the winners of the Championship and of the runners-up does not present a great number of names – only eleven in the twenty-nine years. Sir Edward Grey won the first competition in 1889 with E. B. C. Curtis, his confrère in the University tennis matches of the early 1880s, as second. The latter won in 1890 when Sir Edward gained the second prize. Then from that year until 1896 Sir Edward and H. E. Crawley – constant antagonists and very equally matched – divided the Championship between them. Sir Edward won first prize in 1891, 1895 and 1896 and Mr Crawley in the three years from 1892–4.

As already mentioned, the matches in the 1890s were rather casually arranged, and more than once Mr Crawley and Sir Edward settled on playing early in the morning, when no one knew anything about it, and consequently there were very few spectators. Of the many close struggles between the pair, that of 1892 is most memorable, for the whole five sets were played and each set was five games-all.

GRILLE BASHING

In 1897 that beautiful player, James Byng Gribble, whose early death robbed tennis of one of the most stylish of its exponents, was the winner. In 1898 Sir Edward won again and in 1899 began E. H. Miles's series of successes which were unchecked until 1904. Of all the amateur players most closely connected with Queen's, Miles is the most distinguished. In all his greatest years, from about 1898 until 1910, when he began to lose some of his activity, he played at Queen's pretty regularly and here he perfected his characteristic and peculiar game. Nowhere did he 'pound' the grille more constantly, straight or boasted, with greater accuracy than at Queen's.

From 1899–1902 Gribble won second prize and Vane Pennell – a player of the greatest brilliance though of mercurial temperament – followed him in 1903. At his best Pennell might beat anyone; at his worst he might be beaten by anyone. He did succeed in beating Miles in 1904, in a game which was one of the closest of the whole series, by 3 sets to 2. No one who saw that match would be likely to forget it.

Below Eustace Miles and Vane Pennell in their needle match in 1904

Right E. H. Miles (right), 'easily upset by trifles', seen here with James Byng Gribble and Peter Latham (leaning on the net)

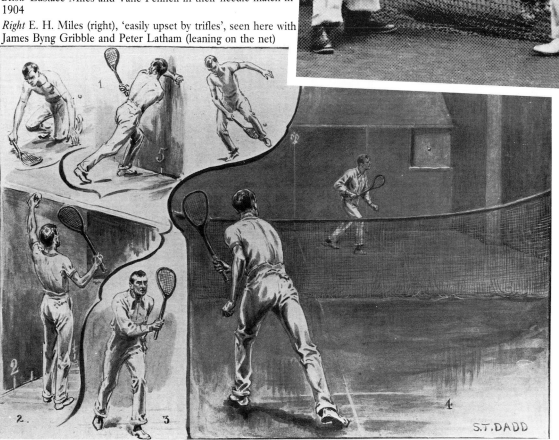

S.T.DADD

Transatlantic onslaught – the great Jay Gould

Miles in those days was rather easily upset by trifles and Pennell upset him that day. Pennell would kneel on the floor after a protracted rest (as the rally at tennis is called) puffing and panting and would wait like this while Miles delivered the service, whereupon he would spring up quicker than a cat and produce some wonderful boast or volley. His antics, if one may so call them, on one occasion drew from Miles the comment: 'This isn't a Harlequinade, Pennell.' 'Don't talk on the stroke, Miles,' came the immediate reply.

Miles in those days used to drink a temperance mixture of which I forget the ingredients; Pennell was a firm believer in champagne. In the last game of the last set he remarked to the *dedans*: 'This match is Fiz *v* Tea and I back Fiz' – whereupon he produced two dead nicks with his powerful American service. It was an exciting and in many ways amusing match for the spectators.

The years 1905–8 were the most famous in the history of the Championship. There were several competitors from other countries and English amateur tennis was at high tide. In 1905 America was represented by Joshua Crane, who had been holder of the National Championship of the States in the three preceding seasons, and France by Albert de Luze, holder of the *Coupe de Paris* and *Coupe de Bordeaux* and the best French amateur of the year. *M.* de Luze in the end did not actually compete in the Championship, but he played several other matches, his best performance being to get a set from Miles in an exhibition match. He was a fine, hard-hitting left-handed player with a particularly fast railroad service.

H. J. Hill, a former holder of the Gold racket of the Melbourne Club (the amateur championship of Australia) and a member of Queen's, accomplished the best performance of his career in beating Crane. He was a very effective and determined if ungraceful player with an overhead service of considerable merit. Miles in the end won back the Championship that Pennell had taken from him the year before.

THE GREAT GOULD

Already there was much talk of the prowess of a young American boy, Jay Gould, and during the next three years Queen's was to witness the rise of the greatest star in the history of amateur tennis and enjoy the excitement of the most tremendous and interesting contests of all the Championship years.

In 1906 Joshua Crane came over again, as did *M.* de Luze, who this time competed. Crane was unfortunate enough to draw Gould in the first round and the latter at a bound established his fame here by administering a severe defeat on his fellow-countryman. Major A. Cooper Key disposed of *M.* de Luze and Gould walked through to the Championship round where he was to meet Miles. That year Miles beat him, though not easily, by 3 sets to 1. Gould was then under twenty, but even so it was obvious that there was very little to choose between them, and their meeting in 1907 was anticipated with the utmost interest.

Gould again went through the preliminary rounds easily, the present writer having the honour of getting more games against him than anyone else.

The Championship match before a record *dedans* proved to be a terrific struggle. At a critical moment Gould got cramp in his arm. Miles most gallantly allowed him a considerable rest to get rubbed and rather foolishly waited in the court and so got cold. It came to 2 sets-all and then Gould edged home. At this time there was not a pin to choose between them, but in the next year Gould definitely passed his rival.

Miles went to America in the spring and was beaten by Gould 3 sets to 1; in the home championship the score was the same and in the Olympic Games event Miles did not get a set. So ended the battles between these two famous players – so utterly different in style. Gould from that time went from strength to strength until he became World Champion in 1914. His overhead service was brought to a pitch of accuracy perhaps never equalled and he combined this with an absolute mastery of many strokes and great attack on the openings if he needed it – his volleying being especially brilliant.

In 1909 and 1910, in Gould's absence, Miles won back the Championship, the runner-up in both years being the Hon. N. S. Lytton, who was improving by leaps and bounds. In 1911 Lytton beat Miles decisively and won his first victory. The year 1910 proved to be Miles's last success after a wonderful career. He won in all nine Championships and was beaten in the Championship round three times.

In 1912 came a new star, E. M. Baerlein. He had had an unrivalled career at tennis and rackets at Cambridge from 1899–1902, but he had partially given up the game since going down, though he played on occasion in his home court at Manchester. Baerlein took to tennis seriously again in about 1911 and soon regained his old form and skills. His defeat of Lytton in 1912 was a triumph of head work, leg work and return over greater attack and less accuracy. Lytton had his revenge the next year when he gave an especially fine performance and beat Baerlein by 3 sets to 2.

Joshua Crane came over to England again in 1914 and there was by far the largest entry on record. Great keenness was shown in tennis at the time. Lytton was in America and so there was no challenge round. Crane, who appeared even stronger than he had done in 1905 and 1906, easily reached the final. Baerlein was, however, at the top of his form and defeated him handsomely by 3 to 0. So ended the latest championship that has been held.

RACKETS BEFORE
THE FIRST WORLD WAR

J. R. Thompson

To all players of rackets, Queen's has become the Mecca of the game. As Lord's is to cricket and Wimbledon is to lawn tennis, so is Queen's to rackets. The game has an unusual history. It was born in the debtors' prisons of eighteenth century London, when 'gentlemen' debtors improvised a variant of tennis to play against the high prison walls. Despite these inauspicious beginnings, by the early nineteenth century it had been taken up in a number of clubs and public schools. Competitions were started and, until Queen's came into existence, the venue for rackets championships was Prince's Club in Hans Place. Prince's old site was demolished in 1886. It was in this year that Queen's ordered the building of two rackets courts; from that period it became the national home of rackets.

Originally there were two courts, the north and the south, which were first opened for play in 1888. They were built by Joseph Bickley, who constructed most of the rackets courts in the last half of the nineteenth century. That many of them should have lasted so well is a tribute to his constructional expertise and to the skill of his plasterers. Sadly for rackets, the demand for squash courts after the First World War led to the conversion of the south court into squash courts in 1926. Fortunately the north court was spared and lighting was added after the war. It continues to stage most of the important matches to the present day.

Every major national rackets championship now takes place at Queen's. These include the British Open Rackets Championship, the Amateur Singles, the Amateur Doubles, the Public Schools Rackets Championship, the Public Schools Old Boys' Rackets Championship (the Noel-Bruce Cup) and the Services Championships. There is also the University Rackets match; apart from the Boat Race, this is the oldest annual contest between Oxford and Cambridge.

On the international level, the predominant event is, of course, the World Championship, in which Queen's has been the setting for many historic matches. We start the history of rackets at Queen's with an account of the early years of this major competition.

The World Championship

The first official World Championship Challenge Match took place at Belvedere Gardens, Pentonville Road in 1838 when John Lamb defeated John Pittman by 8 games to 4. In the next fifty years there were five further matches for the World title. In the last of these, Peter Latham, then twenty-two and professional at the Manchester Racket Club, won the title for the first time, defeating Joseph Gray, the holder and professional at Rugby School, by 7 games to 4 at Rugby and Manchester.

Since 1887 there have been twenty-five challenge matches for the World Championship, each played over two legs on a home-and-home basis, the winner being the one to win the most games on aggregate in the two legs. The Queen's Club has staged twenty-two of the matches, where at least one leg has been played. Queen's has been the most popular venue for these matches.

In 1888 Peter Latham was appointed professional for Rackets and Real Tennis at Queen's. Following his arrival he was immediately challenged by Joseph Gray's brother, Walter Gray, the professional at Charterhouse. Latham won the 1st leg played on his home court at Queen's with some ease by 2–15,

15–12, 15–7, 16–14, 15–6, largely owing to his dominating service. In the 2nd leg a week later at Charterhouse, Latham faced a very partisan gallery who cheered Gray's every stroke. The match was close, but Latham managed to win the two games necessary for victory by 8–15, 15–4, 12–15, 15–9.

US CHALLENGE REBUFFED

Three years later in 1891 came the first American challenge for the World Title from George Standing, professional at the New York Racquet Club. He had learnt his rackets at the old Prince's Club, Hans Place. The match was for a stake of $5000. Latham won the 1st leg easily at the Prince's Club by 15–6, 15–12, 15–9, 15–5 and had no difficulty in winning the first game of the 2nd leg at Queen's, by 15–6. In 1897 Latham again withheld a further challenge from Standing for a stake of £2000, Latham winning by 15–11, 15–13, 15–10, 15–18, 15–4 at Queen's. The 2nd leg, played in New York was a close match

which Latham eventually won by 15–2, 16–18, 3–15, 15–9, 17–16, 15–1.

Latham defended his World Title once more in 1902 against Gilbert Browne, professional at the Prince's Club. Latham won comfortably by 16–13, 15–10, 15–0, 15–2, at Queen's and, taking the first game by 15–11 in the 2nd leg at Prince's, retained the title. After this match Latham resigned his World Title in order to concentrate on real tennis. He was then thirty-seven and he had dominated the rackets scene for fifteen years and is arguably the greatest rackets player of all time. For a full account of his career see p. 198.

In 1903, with the World Title vacant, a match was arranged between Gilbert Browne, Latham's last challenger and J. Jamsetji, the Indian professional at the Bombay Club. In a somewhat disappointing match at Queen's in the 1st leg, Jamsetji won by 15–11, 18–16, 13–16, 15–18, 15–4 and by 15–5, 11–15, 15–5, in the 2nd leg at Prince's, to become the first overseas player to hold the World Title. Jamsetji held the title for eight years without a challenge until Charles Williams, a brilliant young

World title – Charles Williams v. Jamsetji of India

professional at Harrow School, appeared on the scene. In the 1st leg at Queen's Williams won very easily by 18–15, 15–2, 15–9, 15–8 and won the first game by 15–7 in the 2nd leg at Prince's. Williams's hard hitting overwhelmed the Indian.

The next twenty-five years were dominated by Williams and Jock Soutar, a Scotsman who had learnt his rackets at Prince's and had emigrated to become professional at the Philadelphia Racquet Club in 1907. In the meantime, Williams had become the rackets professional at Queen's. In their first match at Queen's, Williams won by 6–15, 15–12, 15–11, 15–10, 9–15, 15–6, but in the 2nd leg at Philadelphia, Soutar won easily by 15–2, 15–8, 15–4, 15–3. Williams failed to do himself justice on a hot day in 1914 and so the title went to the USA shortly before the outbreak of the First World War.

The Amateur Singles Championship

The Amateur Rackets Singles Championship, instituted in 1888 at Queen's has been played there ever since, except for the war years, 1915–1919 and 1940–1945. Up to 1971, when the British Open Singles Championship was made an annual event, the Amateur Championship had carried the greatest prestige in the rackets calendar.

In the early days the Championship was played by a challenge system, whereby the holder awaited the result of a knock-out competition before being challenged by the winner. This system appears to have continued until the First World War, after which the Championship became a straightforward knock-out competition as it remains today.

The first three winners of the Amateur Championship, C. D. Buxton (1888), E. M. Butler (1889) and P. Ashworth (1890), were all undergraduates at Cambridge University at the time. Since then, many of the great rackets players' names have appeared on the Championship silver rose bowl. F. Dames-Longworth, who did so much for Carthusian rackets, won in 1892–93 and 1901. He was followed by the legendary H. K. Foster, who won seven years in succession (1894–1900). He then retired, only to return in 1904 to defeat the young pretender, E. M. Baerlein, in a historic match. Baerlein went on to win the Championship on nine occasions, (1903, 1905, 1908–1911, 1920–1921 and 1923) and this remains a record to this day.

Edgar Baerlein. Unbeatable for many years

The Amateur Doubles Championship

The Amateur Doubles Championship at Queen's was first played in 1890, two years after the Singles Championship began. It has been played at Queen's every year since, except during the World Wars, 1915–1919 and 1940–1945.

The Doubles has always attracted an entry from the leading amateur players of the day and has been a popular event. As the public schools have always given more importance to their Doubles Championship and amateur players have learnt the game at school, their liking of the doubles game is understandable. Doubles encourages improvisation, variety of stroke and the use of the angles. It is also a fine spectator sport and those in the gallery have enjoyed many exciting and tense finals over the years.

In the early days there does not appear to have been any permanent partnership who won consistently. H. K. Foster, in his eight doubles victories won with five different partners, P. Ashworth (1896, 1897, 1899 and 1900), F. H. Browning (1893), C. F. Ridgeway (1894), W. L. Foster (1898) and B. S. Foster (1903). The Foster brothers won together on three occasions, H.K and W.L. in 1898, H.K. and B.S. in 1903 and W.L. and B.S. in 1907 and brothers have never won as a pair since.

E.M. Baerlein won on six occasions, with P. Ashworth (1902, 1904, 1905 and 1909) and with G. G. Kershaw (1914, 1920). In 1910 the winning public school pair from Charterhouse, H. W. Leatham and H. A. Denison reached the final (before the challenge round) when they were beaten by B. S. Foster and the Hon. C. N. Bruce, who went on to win the Championship. Leatham and Denison won two years later in 1912.

The Hon. C. N. Bruce (later Lord Aberdare) and Dr H. W. Leatham

The Public Schools Championship

The public schools with an interest in rackets have, of course, always exerted an enormous influence on the game, producing almost all the champions and ensuring that a steady supply of good club players is maintained. For the past 100 years the crowning ambition of promising rackets players at the schools has been to play at Queen's in the Public Schools

Two of the seven brothers of the great Foster family

Championship. The first schools doubles championship was held at the old Prince's Club, Hans Place in 1868. Credit for this must be given to the Rt Hon. Sir William Hart Dyke, Bt, P.C., an old Harrovian, who was the first amateur to win the World Championship in 1862. He had a great deal to do with bringing together Eton, Harrow, Cheltenham and Charterhouse to take part. It was won by Eton (C. J. Ottaway and W. F. Tritton), who beat Cheltenham (J. J. Read and A. T. Myers) by 4 games to 3 in the final.

For the first nineteen years, when the doubles championship continued to be played at Prince's Club, Harrow were the winners on twelve occasions and Eton on six, with Rugby the single intruder in this series. The dominance of Eton and Harrow ceased after the championship moved to Queen's in 1888 and more schools entered. Between 1890–1910, the names of the greatest of all racket-playing families appear, the seven Foster brothers of Malvern, who all represented their school at Queen's and who, as we have seen, went on to success in the Amateur Doubles. Five of the seven brothers were in pairs which won and on two occasions, two brothers were partners. In 1909 and 1910 appeared the famous Charterhouse pair, H. W. Leatham and H. A. Denison. Having won the Championship in

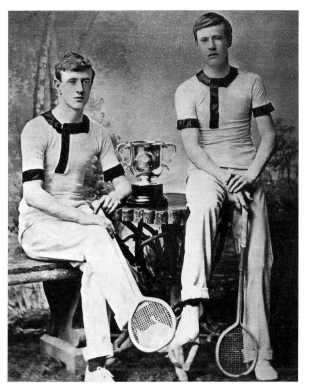

Enthusiasm. Serving. Just saved. Volleying. On the wood. Eton v. Harrow. A couple of Veterans. S.T. DADD.

The Public Schools Championship moved to Queen's in 1888

1909, they coasted through the 1910 championship without losing a game and, while still at school, reached the final round (before the challenge round) of the Amateur Championship. The following year also marked a record when C. F. B. Simpson was first string for Rugby for the fifth year and in 1911 he finally won the cup with his partner, W. H. Clarke. Two years earlier Simpson and F. A. Sampson had won the first three games against the redoubtable Leatham and Denison in the second round, only to lose the next four, the final game by 17–16.

The University Match

The first Oxford *v* Cambridge rackets match was played at Oxford in 1855, consisting of a doubles match only. From 1859–86 annual contests took place, consisting of a doubles and one singles match at the Old Prince's Club, Hans Place. The series was continued at Queen's in 1888 and has been played there ever since, except for the war years,

1915–19 and 1940–46. A second string singles match was added in 1921, but this did not count towards the result until 1937.

The Tennis and Rackets Association

A history of rackets at Queen's would not be complete without some mention of the Tennis and Rackets Association. It was formed in 1907, under the chairmanship of G. E. A. Ross. A year later the T. and R. A. adopted its own rules for tennis and rackets and from that time the Association has been the controlling body in Britain for both games. E. A. Biedermann (later Best) was appointed as the first Hon. Secretary and he served in this capacity until 1920.

To advance the story of the T. and R.A. beyond this particular period, after the 1914–18 War, Sir William Hart-Dyke became President. In 1921, The Queen's Club generously agreed that the T. and R.A. Committee should decide the venue and make arrangements for Tennis and Rackets Championships. Major H.M. Leaf became Hon. Treasurer in

1919 until he was succeeded by his brother, E. H. (Ted) Leaf in 1930, who did noble service until 1955. He also acted as Hon. Secretary during the Second World War, 1939–45.

After the War, M.B. (Maurice) Baring became the Hon. Secretary for a year, to be succeeded by Col. N.S. (Nigel) Renny. He was an outstanding administrator and he rendered wonderful service for twenty-five years in organizing Tennis and Rackets Championships until he died in 1971. He was succeeded by Guy Bassett-Smith (1971–75), Col. Nigel Bruce (1975–82) and by William Stephens in 1982. Nigel Bruce established a T. and R.A. office at Queen's from where William Stephens has continued to run the T. and R.A. affairs with great enthusiasm.

Sir Kenneth Hunter was Chairman (1945–60), Lord Aberdare (1960–71), Peter Kershaw (1971–79), Dick Bridgeman (1979–82) and David Norman (1982–). G. N. (Geoffrey) Foster and Capt H. F. H. (Herbert) Layman acted as Hon. Treasurers (1955–66), to be succeeded by J. R. (Richard) Greenwood, who has also acted as Hon. Membership Secretary for the past twenty years. His enthusiasm has done much to increase the membership and thereby the funds of the T. and R.A.

The Professionals

Many distinguished players at one time or another have held appointments as rackets professionals at Queen's. Some started there on leaving school at the age of fourteen acting as ball-boys at the beck and call of the senior professional of lawn tennis, rackets or tennis. Begging or borrowing racquets and equipment as best they could from the generosity of their elders, they learnt to play these games in any spare time available. In the old days, not even the senior professionals were permitted to enter the clubhouse or bar, as they were the sole preserve of the members.

The first rackets professional appointed in 1888 was Charles Saunders, who was succeeded in the same year by the legendary Peter Latham whose achievements in the World Championship have already been mentioned. Peter came to Queen's at the age of twenty-three as senior rackets professional, having defeated Joseph Gray for the World Rackets Championship the previous year. He held the World Rackets Championship from 1887–1902 and the World Tennis Championship from 1895–1905 and again from 1907–1908. He held both titles simultaneously from 1895–1902, a unique achievement.

In 1902 Charles Read joined Queen's as a ball-boy and then spent three years at Harrow learning rackets and squash rackets under the professional Judy Stevens. He returned to Queen's in 1906 at the age of seventeen to be senior rackets professional and remained there until the Second World War. A short stocky figure with a prominent beaky nose, he became Professional Rackets Champion from 1925–1932, Professional Squash Champion from 1920–1929 and Professional Lawn Tennis Champion from 1921–1928. For over thirty years he served the club with distinction. J. Jamsetji, the Parsee rackets professional at Bombay and the World Rackets Champion from 1903–1911 spent a brief period at Queen's during this time. In 1923 Charles Williams, World Rackets Champion from 1911–1913 and from 1929–1935 was also at Queen's for a brief period before taking up an appointment at the Chicago Racquet Club, USA.

THE CORINTHIANS AT THE QUEEN'S CLUB

'It is no wonder that footballers who have met in rivalry on the field at The Queen's Club in the Varsity match join together after and strain every nerve to keep the Corinthians in the position they have always held' – Stanley S. Harris, Westminster, Cambridge, Corinthians, England, 1905.

THE Corinthians, to most people today, are no more than a sporting legend; a romantic episode in the evolution of soccer extending from its early days, when the best amateurs were better than the professionals, to the time when they could no longer compete on equal terms. To some of us who saw them play or even played with or against them, the Corinthians in their fifty-one-year history, from 1881 to 1932, are more than that. They evoke a sense of reverent nostalgia, recalling a glorious epoch in the history of sport and sportsmanship. If a penalty were given against them they would leave their goal open!

The Queen's Club is part of the Corinthians history. They opened the new ground with a match against Oxford University on 9 November 1887. According to *Pastime* it 'was not favoured by fine weather. The fixture for the occasion was an attractive one and had the elements been less unpleasant, a fairly good attendance of spectators would, in all probability, have been secured.' *Pastime* further commented that though the ground was slippery – much rain had fallen – it played well and that the accommodation for spectators and players was excellent.

The Corinthians beat the University 4–2 and among their team was Arthur Dunn, an Etonian who played for England and, in 1892, founded Ludgrove which became a famous prep school. It had one pupil when it opened. Ten years later when Dunn died at the early age of forty-one, it had a waiting list for the following ten years. Dunn undoubtedly enjoyed that first game at Queen's – in the rain. The great *Times* sporting correspondent, Freddie Wilson, wrote of him: 'He was desperately quick, wonderfully strong and certain on his feet. He was at his very best on treacherous ground and the worse the soup, the more easily he slipped over the top of it.'

Thirty-four years later the Corinthians played their last match at Queen's, losing to Cambridge University on 29 October 1921. During that thirty-four-year span they had, in 1895, adopted Queen's as their home ground and, in all, played 134 matches at the Club, winning 75, drawing 27 and losing 32. At one time or another they played most of the leading professional clubs, carried on their brotherly rivalry with Queen's Park, Scotland's great amateur club, encouraged the game at the ancient universities and the public schools and took soccer to many parts of the world.

The Corinthians' time at Queen's was highlighted by two events, their sporting trial of strength with the Barbarians Rugby Football Club in April 1892 and their defeat of Bury, the FA Cup-holders, 10–3 in the Sheriff of London Shield (now the FA Charity Shield) on 5 March 1904. In the first the Corinthians showed their versatility as athletes and games players and in the second they reached a peak probably unequalled even by their famous draw with Manchester City in 1926. These two achievements are worth describing at some length.

GAUNTLET ACCEPTED

The Corinthians in 1892 threw down a challenge: 'to meet any other Association Club at football, cricket and athletic sports, the proceeds to be given to charity'. It was, however, taken up by the élite Barbarians Rugby Club which, like the Corinthians, drew its members from the universities and public schools and carried the rugby code far and wide. Rugby, of course, was added to the list of events and in the end the Corinthians proved triumphant 3–1, winning the soccer, rugby and athletics but losing the cricket match.

The soccer match and half the athletic events took place on Saturday, 9 April 1892. It was also Boat Race day and a lot of potential spectators, thinking the soccer match would be a farce, chose the towpath at Putney rather than the sporting arena at Queen's. About 2000 turned up on Saturday and about half that number on Monday when the athletic contest was finished and the rugby match played. The Corinthians won the soccer match 6–0. Among the six full internationals in their exceptionally strong side were the famous Walters brothers, A. M. and P. M., a pair of full-backs who played over twenty times for England and a hundred matches for the Corinthians. They had been in virtual retirement for a year.

The game was played thirty-five minutes each way instead of forty-five. The Barbarians appeared well-versed in the rules, though they occasionally warded off opponents by pushing and using their arms. Understandably they were incapable of coping with the pace, passing and teamwork of their rivals. The Corinthian goalkeeper, W. J. Seton, had only one shot to save but the Barbarians showed enough vigour in defence to restrict the scoring. G. L. Wilson, who dislocated a thumb, Winckworth, Lindley (3) and Sandilands scored for Corinthians. The teams:

Corinthians – W. J. Seton, P. M. Walters, A. M. Walters, A. K. Brook, C. B. Fry, W. N. Winckworth, G. L. Wilson, G. H. Cotterill, T. Lindley, R. R. Sandilands, J. G. Veitch.

Barbarians – W. H. Manfield, W. W. Rashleigh, A. S. Johnson, H. M. Taberer, W. P. Carpmael, F. Evershed, J. le Fleming, R. D. Budworth, C. M. Wells, R. F. C. de Winton, E. H. G. North.

Surprisingly, the Corinthians won the rugby match 16–13 (two goals, two tries to two goals and a try) and this was not entirely due to any indulgence on the part of the Barbarians. *Pastime* summed up the match this way: 'This surprising result may be accounted for partly by the extraordinary speed and energy shown by the winners towards the end of the game and partly by the carelessness of the Barbarians who, after neglecting their opportunities and allowing the game to become a loose scramble, were unable from exhaustion to retrieve the day.' *Pastime* did suggest the Barbarians lost much by not claiming penalties, especially for offside and picking up the ball in the scrum. Nor, until late in the game, do they appear to have used their scrummaging power, preferring to heel quickly and start passing moves.

BARBARIAN BLUES

The Corinthians caused some amusement by their pre-match attempts at drop-kicks and later by their ignorance of where to position themselves at the kick-off and A. M. Walters' use of the soccer throw-in at the lines-out. C. B. Fry, however, soon showed himself to be an accomplished wing three-quarter. The Barbarians squandered an early chance when Johnston missed a penalty shot from in front of goal. Their sprinter winger, Monypenny, was caught near the line by P. M. Walters but managed to get the ball to de Winton, who crossed the line but was tackled and wrestled into dispossession by the wiry Winckworth.

When Hooper scored the first Barbarian try at the posts, Johnston's kick hit a post, a failure that eventually cost his side the match. Lindley matched that try with one for the Corinthians. Then Taberer and Hooper, with Johnston's conversions, gave the Barbarians a strong lead of two goals and a try to one try shortly after half-time. The Corinthians, showing an increasing taste for scrummaging, scored their second try through A. M. Walters, who charged through his opponents soccer-style and, having planted the ball behind the posts, sat on it! Fry scored a brilliant try and with Ingram's conversions the scores were level. Finally another run by Fry, backed up by Cross, who kicked over the line, led to Lindley following up at tremendous pace, scoring the winning try for the Corinthians. Teams:

Corinthians – P. M. Walters, C. B. Fry, W. J. Seton, R. C. Gosling, F. J. K. Cross, T. Lindley, A. M. Walters, G. H. Cotterhill, W. N. Winckworth, W. S. Gosling, A. K. Brook, C. Wreford-Brown, J. G. Veitch, R. R. Sandiland, F. M. Ingram.

Barbarians – A. S. Johnston, J. le Fleming, C. A. Hooper, C. M. Wells, C. J. B. Monypenny, R. F. C. de Winton, H. M. Taberer, F. Evershed, C. Ekin, W. P. Carpmael, C. B. Nicholl, W. H. Manfield, W. W. Rashleigh, R. D. Budworth, A. Allport.

The Corinthians won the athletic (track and field) contest by five events to four, winning the half-mile, mile, long jump, high jump and putting the shot but losing the 100 yards, the two miles, the quarter and the 120-yard hurdles. C. J. B. Monypenny, the Barbarians' wing three-quarter and university sprinter, won the opening event, the 100 yards, in 10.2 secs (measured 10 $1/_5$ secs in those days) beating the Corinthian, C.B. Fry, by a foot. Next came the two miles. A.M. Walters and W. N. Winckworth ran for the Corinthians; C. E. Ekin, W. W. Rashleigh and R. D. Budworth for the Barbarians. Soon only Winckworth challenged Ekin but even he dropped out after a mile-and-quarter. Ekin came home in 10 mins 33 secs.

The quarter-mile also went to the Barbarians. Monypenny had done 49.8 secs the previous day in the University Sports. Cross was considered capable of holding him but had suffered a severe cold while training. C. E. Hooper and R. C. Gosling started but were left behind after the first corner. Cross held his rival until the straight but faded and was beaten by a dozen yards in 50.2 secs.

The first Corinthian success came in the long jump, regarded as a certainty for C. B. Fry, the current record-holder. He won with 21 ft 9½ in but was heavily challenged by his colleague F. J. K. Cross, who jumped 21 ft 6 in, and by the Barbarian, H. M. Taberer, who landed with a jump of 21 ft 5 in. Thus at the end of the first day the Barbarians led by 3–1.

CORINTHIAN FALLS

Monday opened with the half-mile, which resolved itself into a battle between the Barbarian, Monypenny, and the Corinthian, Cross, after Taberer had made the early pace. Three hundred yards from the tape Monypenny faded and Cross finished in 2 mins 1.8 secs. J. le Fleming won the 120-yard hurdles easily for the Barbarians from his colleague, C. A. Hooper. G. H. Cotterill and C. B. Fry ran for Corinthians, the former holding second place until the last hurdle, when he slipped and fell.

C. B. Nicholl was expected to win the shot putt for the Barbarians and that would have meant overall victory. But he strained his arm and was beaten by the Corinthian, Cotterill, with a throw of 34 ft 1 in. With Fry winning the high jump for the Corinthians with 5 ft 3 ¾ in, the two teams were level with one event, the mile, remaining.

Cross and F. M. Ingram ran the race for the Corinthians, W. W. Rashleigh and C. E. Ekin for Barbarians. Rashleigh gave up after one lap and Cross after half a mile. Ingram, instead of succumbing, stayed with Ekin, the favourite, and wore him down to take the lead as they entered the last straight. Ingram's winning time was 4 mins 34 secs.

The Corinthians thus established a winning lead of three sports contests to nil and in reviewing this unexpected turn of events, especially at rugby, O. L. Owen in his history of the Barbarians had this to say: 'No doubt the Corinthians who, at that time, included some magnificent athletes like C. B. Fry, P. M. Walters, T. Lindley, R. C. Gosling and F. J. K. Cross, were given a lot of latitude whenever they offended against the complicated rugby rules, but for all that the Corinthians were entitled to the glory that follows a fully substantiated challenge. The totally unexpected victory of the dribblers and chargers – and the Corinthians of 1892 knew how to do both – over the handlers, scrummagers and tacklers was, however, not merely good fun but interesting sport. It may well be that the success of the fast and powerful Corinthians, forwards as well as backs, led to the speeding up of rugby forward play.'

'Nettled by this reverse', as the old-time reports used to say, the Barbarians roused themselves to a supreme effort in the cricket match, also played at Queen's, on 30 April of the same year. The Corinthians were dismissed for 170 runs. The Barbarians made 173 for 6 and no longer felt quite so sheepish. The Corinthian score was notable if only for the dismissal of one of its batsmen, a mysterious 'A. Fryer' for 25 runs. C. B. Fry was cheap at the price, even in 1892!

So ended one of the most romantic episodes in the history of British sport and it all took place at The Queen's Club.

CUP-HOLDERS SUNK

Twelve years later, in 1904, the Corinthians registered their famous victory over Bury in the Sheriff of London Shield, a victory described by the immortal G. O. Smith, Charterhouse, Oxford, Corinthians and England, as possibly 'the greatest performance in Corinthian FC annals'. Smith was unable to play in that match and, indeed, thought little enough of the team beforehand to comment that, 'I should put few, if any, in the best Corinthian side of all time.' The Club's form that season had been so modest that it was at one time doubtful whether they would be chosen to represent the amateurs.

The idea of the Shield was conceived by, among others, N.L. 'Pa' Jackson, one of the Corinthians' founders, and Thomas Dewar (later Lord Dewar). The idea was that the best amateur and professional sides of the year should meet and the proceeds be given to charity. Only once, in the 1888–9 season, were the Corinthians not chosen, being replaced by Queen's Park, the famous Scottish Club.

In the weeks immediately preceding the match, the Corinthians found some form, beating Southampton and Stoke, both at The Queen's Club. Bury's record was well established. They had gone through the FA Cup the previous season without conceding a goal and their final 6–0 win over Derby County set a record unbroken for over half a century.

Playing against a stiff breeze the Corinthians were down two goals in the first quarter-of-an-hour. Edward Grayson in his *Corinthians and Cricketers* describes their comeback: 'The [Corinthian] forwards swung into action, finding their men with dashing rushes in the true Corinthian passing and dribbling style which the professionals' defence could not counter. In less than ten minutes G. S. Harris reduced the lead and S. H. Day snatched it with two fine shots. S. S. Harris notched another before half-time and the Corinthians then led 4–2. In the second half Bury held out for a quarter-of-an-hour. Thereafter the Corinthian bombardment prevailed; with their forwards in full cry the halves and backs could devote themselves solely to breaking up the not infrequent Bury attacks. S. S. Harris scored a hat-trick and G. S. Harris his second goal. Bury never gave up the hunt and came once more through Swann, who had a fine match. The Harrises each scored once more to set up double figures. The Corinthians had beaten the Cup-holders 10–3 and the famous old name was redeemed.'

Grayson describes the Corinthian technique of the wings taking the ball to the corner flag before making the centre. The ball was then passed backwards along the ground for the insides to run on to. That such tactics were so successful is proved by the fact that the three inside forwards, S. S. Harris (5), G. S. Harris (3) and S. H. Day (2) scored all the goals.

The teams:

Corinthians – T. S. Rowlandson, Rev. W. Blackburn, W. U. Timms, H. Vickers, M. Morgan-Owen, H. A. Lowe, G. C. Vassall, S. H. Day, G. S. Harris, S. S. Harris, B. O. Corbett.

Bury – Monteith, McEwan, Lindsay, Ross, Thorpe, Johnston, Plant, Wood, Sagar, Swann, Richards.

When the Corinthians were originally formed on 18 October 1882 as a club composed of the best amateurs in the kingdom there appeared no need for a ground or a subscription. Membership was limited to fifty. The reason for the formation was simply that England were regularly being beaten by Scotland and one of the causes was thought to be that the best players in England had few chances of playing together other than in international matches. One could almost say that holds true today!

In their first few years the Corinthians used Upton Park, the Oval, Leyton, Richmond and, very occasionally, The Queen's Club for their home matches, mostly against Oxford and Cambridge. In 1891–2 they played five matches at Queen's beating, among others, Preston North End who, with Blackburn Rovers, were among the best professional sides in England and, for 'Corinth', had become annual fixtures. In the next three seasons the Club played only four matches at Queen's but in 1895 decided to make it their HQ.

Corinthians celebrated their first season at The Queen's Club with wins over the Army, Edinburgh St Bernard, Sunderland, West Bromwich Albion, Exeter and Dundee. They lost to Notts Forest, Queen's Park and Sheffield United but drew with Middlesborough and Derby. It was about this time that the Corinthians were occasionally selected *en masse* for England. On one such occasion England drew 1–1 with Wales at The Queen's Club. The England goalkeeper was G. B. Raikes, who took Holy Orders after leaving Oxford and played little thereafter. W. J. Oakley, G. O. Smith – still regarded as one of the greatest-ever centre forwards – and C. Wreford-Brown were among the Corinthian giants in that team.

TWIN WINS

In November 1897 the Corinthians brought off a remarkable feat in playing two matches against leading professional sides on the same day without being beaten. They beat Blackburn Rovers 3–1 at Queen's and drew with Sheffield United at Bramall Lane.

1897–8 was a peak season, during which they played eleven matches at Queen's beating Blackburn Rovers, Sheffield Wednesday, Sheffield United, Liverpool, Queen's Park, Notts County and Preston North End, and losing only to Edinburgh St Bernard. By then C. B. Fry had added his considerable talents to those of G. O. Smith, Oakley and others. The average gate at Queen's in this period was in the region of 5000, satisfactory enough considering the facilities, but modest compared with the 15,000–20,000 or more the Club drew elsewhere. Indeed 30,000 attended the 1905 contest against Queen's Park at Hampden.

1900–1 was another successful season. By then the Club, still led by G. O. Smith and with C. B. Fry at full-back, were supplemented by two more England cricketers, R. E. Foster and C. J. 'Pinkie'

Burnup, both Malvernians. A decline followed, which was eventually reversed by that remarkable win over Bury in 1904. That revived the Club's fortunes. They were unbeaten at Queen's in 1905–6 and, curiously, lost only to Oxford and Cambridge the following year while beating such teams as Spurs, Birmingham and Notts County. That was the last season before what became known in soccer as 'the Split' took place; something that had already happened in rugby, though in a different way.

At the time soccer, irrespective of whether amateur or professional, was run by the Football Association. Some amateur organizations objected to this and as a result the Amateur FA was formed. This meant that the Corinthians were excluded from playing clubs affiliated to the FA and that just about ruined their fixture list. From 1907 to the outbreak of the 1914–18 War, Corinthians' opponents at The Queen's Club were confined to Oxford and Cambridge. Even the annual contest, tantamount to an amateur international, between Corinthians and Queen's Park, ceased until it was revived in 1920.

Their first meeting at Queen's was in 1892 and with few exceptions their matches alternated between

The Corinthians of 1901, with (back row, fourth from left) C. B. Fry at fullback and (on his left) A. T. B. Dunn, after whom the Arthur Dunn cup is named

A Members v. Staff football match

Queen's and Glasgow until 1907. Their last match at Queen's was in 1921, a 0–0 draw. As a matter of interest, when their contest ended in 1931, they had met 63 times, Corinthians winning 31, and losing 21 with 11 drawn. Of the 13 matches played at Queen's Corinthians won 7 and drew 2.

When the Corinthians re-formed after the First World War, one of their problems was finding a suitable home ground. Queen's, seeking to expand their lawn tennis facilities, were not too happy to see their turf cut up by Corinthian or any other boots. In the 1920–21 season Corinthians played only four matches at Queen's – against the Army, Oxford and Cambridge, the Public Schools and Queen's Park. Their last at the Club was against Cambridge on 29 October 1921. In the meantime Corinthians had secured Crystal Palace, a former Cup Final ground, as their home; at least, for the next ten years. And The Queen's Club began to take shape as, fundamentally, a tennis club.

THE OXFORD AND CAMBRIDGE RUGBY MATCH
1887–1920

IT is hardly surprising that rugby football, having taken root at The Queen's Club in 1887 with the Oxford and Cambridge match, received considerable encouragement, despite some lurking doubts among the Committee, in the early years of this century up to the Great War. The Club's two secretaries most involved in that period were both England internationals.

Charles J. B. Marriott, 'a formidable man', so it was said, took over the secretaryship of the Club from Henry Becks in 1903 and remained there for two years before becoming secretary of the Rugby Union in 1907, a post he held until 1924. He was succeeded at Queen's by Andrew E. Stoddart in 1906, whose office lasted until 1914.

Marriott, a forward, played rugby for Cambridge in the early 1880s, one of four Tonbridgians in the side one year, followed by winning seven caps for England and captaining Blackheath. By profession he was a schoolmaster, though he appears to have spent little time at it. He was also a Sussex land-owner, Lord of the Manor of Fleed Hall and a founder of the Public Schools Club, London.

Stoddart, though he won eleven caps for England between 1885 and 1893, was better known as a cricketer – 'a dashing batsman' according to Sir Neville Cardus. He was playing cricket for England in Australia when the England rugby team toured that country in 1888. He joined the party, was an object of wonder to the Australians because of his skill not just at rugby but also Australian Rules football (both codes were played on that tour) and took over the England captaincy when R. L. Seddon was drowned in a sculling accident. He was also one of the 'two great batsmen' mentioned by C. B. Fry while recounting the story of his two hat-tricks for Oxford against the MCC. At one time Stoddart was articled to an architect and was later a member of the Stock Exchange. He died tragically in 1915, a year after he left Queen's.

The University rugby match, still one of the sporting events of the year in this country, was played at The Queen's Club twenty-nine times, from 1887 to 1920 inclusive, during which period Oxford won on thirteen occasions, Cambridge eleven with five matches drawn. The earlier matches – the series began in 1871 – were played at Oxford and Cambridge respectively, then at the Oval and, before the move to Queen's, at Blackheath. From Queen's in 1920 the match moved to Twickenham where it remains.

The public clearly appreciated the move from Blackheath to nearer the centre of London as 5000 spectators turned up for the match in 1887. That crowd increased to 8000 the following year when Cambridge completed a run of four wins. Ten years later a crowd of 10,000 was recorded. In 1908 came the stampede. The experiment of playing the match on a Saturday, instead of the traditional Tuesday, was tried for the first time. It proved far too popular as 16,000 tried to get into Queen's. Not only was the accommodation for such a crowd totally inadequate but there were only two entrances into the grounds, Palliser Road and Greyhound Road. One of these was rushed, though luckily without serious consequences.

This was a significant indication of the growing popularity of the match increased, perhaps, by the fact that Oxford had an all-international back division. Among the caps were H. H. Vassall and F.

N. Tarr in the centre, G. Cunningham and R. H. Williamson at half-back. G. V. Portus, twice capped at half-back by England the previous season, could not get into the side. The Oxford pack included two internationals, H. A. Hodges and G. D. 'Khaki' Roberts, well known at Queen's for many years as a real tennis player. He also became Recorder of Gloucester.

The Club never again saw a crowd like the year of the stampede, not even when King George V attended the first post-war match in 1919. And it was not until after the Second World War that the universities again played the match on a Saturday, at Twickenham of course. It was a flop.

LEADERS OF CHANGE

The rugby game, during its thirty-four years at Queen's – that period includes the five war years – underwent many radical changes and the universities were responsible for a good many of them. Oxford, for instance, led the game out of the maul and wrestling era largely through H. Vassall, a forward and uncle of the great H. H. Vassall who played in the 'stampede' match. By the time the first match was played at Queen's the game had achieved some semblance of order. It was also helped by the law ruling that players must release the ball on being tackled. Despite this the 1892 match 'degenerated into a scramble in the mud' following torrential rain after the removal of the straw laid on the pitch to protect it from frost.

In 1893 the two universities adopted the four three-quarter line-up, reducing the packs from nine to eight men. It not only aimed at speeding up play but also heralded the age of specialization, e.g., the development of half-back play. This, in turn, helped to produce great and imaginative halves such as E. J. Walton, F. Munro, G. Cunningham and Adrian Stoop – all of Oxford.

Ironically, these changes in style did not immediately help Oxford, who tended to be the leaders of change. When Cambridge won in 1895 The Times commented somewhat ruefully that, 'The score ill-represents the Light Blues' superiority [at Queen's Club yesterday]. There was nothing in the Oxford three-quarter game to justify the common regard in which the short passing of the four three-quarters is now held. Essentially it was a forward game . . . and the result a triumph for the art of forward play.'

When, two years later, Cambridge repeated that victory The Times chortled that it was: 'A triumph for honest scrummaging over futuristic three-quarter play'. This seemed hardly fair, as fog – a fairly frequent hazard at Queen's at that time of year – obscured much of the play. Apparently, the two sides could only be distinguished by the colour of their shorts – knickerbockers in those days – with Cambridge white and Oxford dark blue.

The Times remained scathing of new ideas and hopes and after the 1898 match, watched by 10,000, commented, 'The contest degenerated into an entirely forward battle in which it was simply a question of which side would shove the harder. The modern Rugby Unionists pretend to talk about the efficiency of three-quarter play . . . The forward has been and will remain the dominant element in rugby football.' It certainly was in 1899, when Cambridge had what some considered their greatest-ever pack and won 22–0 (two goals, four tries to nothing), the heaviest defeat so far inflicted on Oxford. Sooner or later every member of that Light Blues pack played for England or Scotland.

Snow had fallen before the match but when it was swept away the pitch was in excellent condition. At times the Cambridge forwards shoved right through Oxford, picked up the ball and began passing moves. In the end Oxford were submerged by the remorseless tide of Cambridge foot rushes and their line crossed six times. Among the Cambridge giants that day were Darkie Bedell-Sivright who captained the 1904 British Isles team to Australia, J. R. C. Greenless and John Daniell.

Those three men were in the 1900 Cambridge pack which included the younger, Bedell-Sivright, J.V. and B.C. 'Jock' Hartley, a future Rugby Union President. Oxford beat them 10–8, as unexpected as any victory in the annals. The game was stopped shortly after the start as the Oxford touch-judge had failed to arrive. Then, with the pace already hot, Oxford lost their right wing, J. W. F. Crawford, injured. Against such a powerful Cambridge pack Oxford decided not to replace him for the moment with a man out of their own pack.

With no score at half-time Oxford changed their minds. Soon they were eight points down and their abbreviated pack were being hammered by Daniell's forwards. Instead of capsizing Oxford decided to counter-attack and began a move on their own line. It ended with a try by fly-half, E. J. Walton – one of the great tries, it has been said.

SHORTS TORN

Briefly Daniell was off the field changing his shorts – they don't bother to leave the field nowadays – and on his return Oxford scored again, through winger J. E. Crabbie. With both tries converted, Oxford secured and held on to a two-point lead.

Daniell, seven times captain of England, who became known as 'the Prophet', scored a hundred one year and 99 the next in the University cricket match, played for Somerset, became an England selector at both games and was, just after the Second World War, President of the Rugby Union.

Adrian Stoop, later to become one of the game's legendary figures, first appeared in the Oxford side in 1902. He had come up from the birthplace of the game, Rugby School, and brought with him a natural instinct for the game plus imagination and a sense of innovation. Stoop and his outside-half partner, A. M. P. Lyle, saved Oxford from defeat that year when the Cambridge pack, with the two Bedell-Sivrights and another Scot in J. B. Waters, were as formidable as ever. It was a draw.

Stoop lived rugby and the game gained much from him, not least in his ideas of attacking from anywhere in the field and especially out of defence. 'There is no mechanism about Stoop. He masks his game until the opening for his three-quarters is made,' wrote one newspaper. Of himself and his ideas he said, 'As I lay in bed at night before going to sleep, the best time of all to make plans, I mapped out my ideas, and then tried them out on the field.'

After Oxford Stoop, a barrister, went on to captain the Harlequins and England, among other teams, before becoming President of the Rugby Union. He restored England's international pride and created a remarkable breed of Harlequins; so much so that at one time he conceived the bizarre idea of mating them with the most attractive and most suitable young ladies in London to produce a perfect breed of Harlequins. He played his last game for that club at the age of fifty-six!

Oxford's inventiveness and enterprise paid off when, in 1906, they began a run of five wins and one drawn game in the next five matches. The arrival of Rhodes Scholars – W. W. Hosken from St Andrews, Grahamstown being the first in 1904 – was one factor. A stream of great backs including H. H. Vassall and Ronnie Poulton was another.

A commentator in the *Bystander* had this to say about the 1906 match: 'It was so well worth seeing that it was a great pity that during the second half it could only be seen properly while the game was going on under one's nose. It was the old story – an unpunctual start ten minutes after the advertised time (2.30) which was, in itself, too late; the delay on this occasion being due to the fact that the referee was behind time and somebody had to be fished out to take on the job until he turned up. There was a little of the usual Queen's Club mist about, though not much, but to make matters worse one of the Club chimneys got on fire and there was just enough wind to distribute a thin cloud of smoke all over the ground.

'I believe Cambridge made a great mistake in putting McLeod [the great K.G.] on the wing when it was found that Koop was not fit. I don't say they would have won if they had not done so but I do think

The 1910 Varsity Rugger match. Oxford beat Cambridge 23–18

they would have had a better chance of winning. The great man of the side, who is equally formidable in attack and defence, ought to be in the middle where he is pretty sure of getting most of the work of both kinds. As it was, Vassall, the Oxford right centre, who proved himself the great man of the Oxford side, was the most conspicuous three-quarter on the field because he was the right man in the right place.'

DECEPTIVE LOOK

Isis, the Oxford University magazine wrote of Vassall who, because he did not always do the expected, was sometimes accused of selfishness: 'One can well imagine him strolling onto the field with his hands stuck deep into his pockets and an extreme look of boredom on his face. We know that look so well now but we also know what it means.'

In 1909 Oxford, down to fourteen men for most

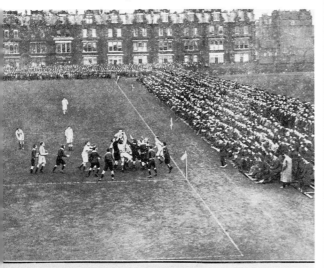

of the match and thirteen for part of it, won 35–3; a remarkable score as there had been torrential rain for the two days preceding the match. It became known as 'Poulton's Match'. He scored five tries. Poulton was tall, fair-haired and thin-legged, giving the illusion of frailty. In fact he was a well-muscled athlete of whom an opponent once said, 'How can you stop him when his head goes one way, his arms another and his legs straight on?'

After Oxford won the 1911 match *The Times* wrote of Poulton-Palmer, as he had then become (his uncle the Rt. Hon. G. W. Palmer of Huntley and Palmers left him a fortune) describing his style as 'swinging the ball from side to side as if rhapsodizing on a concertina, compelling the defence to follow him spell-bound'. While Ireland's captain, Dickie Lloyd, said, 'It is not what he was doing but what he was going to do that made him a great player'. He was not notably fast but mesmerizingly deceptive. Also a hockey 'blue', Poulton-Palmer was killed by a sniper's bullet in France in 1915 and, it is said, a visiting officer found all his men in tears.

There was a heavy drizzle, almost as bad as fog, in 1912 when Cambridge gained their first win since 1905. With five internationals, including those great outsides, C. N. Lowe and B. S. Cumberlege, they did so again the following year, the last match before the Great War. When the two university teams were mustered in 1919 after the war they were fortunate in having two pre-war senior players, E. G. Loudon-Shand (Oxford) and J. E. Greenwood (Cambridge) to lead them. They had been at Dulwich College together before going up to university.

Greenwood's five appearances for Cambridge spanned nine years. Until 1919 the rules of the University match ordained that no one could play in more than four. But Oxford agreed that Greenwood, nicknamed 'Jenny', who had begun the war as a private in the Artists Rifles and ended as a captain in the Grenadier Guards, should return to Cambridge to lead them a second time. Already an international, he gained thirteen caps for England as a forward, became President of the Rugby Union and is, of course, father of Richard Greenwood, the Hon. Treasurer of the Tennis and Rackets Association which has its HQ at Queen's.

Cambridge won that first post-war match by two points, a dropped goal by A. M. Smallwood – he landed a famous one for England against Wales later – who achieved further distinction as a gardener and as a bassoonist with the Stamford Symphony

OXFORD v CAMBRIDGE.
1919.

J. E. Greenwood being presented to H. M. King George V before the 1919 Varsity rugger match. H.R.H. Prince Henry and Oxford captain E. G. Loudoun-Shand look on

A good luck telegram for Greenwood from Prince Albert and Commander Grieg

Orchestra. By now it was clear that the annual match was outgrowing Queen's while lawn tennis, spurred on by *Mlle* Suzanne Lenglen's successes at Wimbledon, was assuming increasing popularity. The football games restricted the use of the Club's turf.

Oxford won the last match played at Queen's in 1920 with a side that contained, among others, H. L. Price, who played rugby for England one Saturday and hockey for England the next, and B. L. Jacot, a winger. Jacot was one of the few men to have climbed the Martyr's Memorial at Oxford. Of formidable strength, he once picked up an England forward in a match at Northampton and dumped him in the pond at the end of the ground. The University match then moved to Twickenham where it remains today.

Throughout the story of this match there were

men who distinguished themselves in life and sport other than rugby. Sammy Woods, a Cambridge forward of the late 1880s, took thirty-six wickets for Cambridge against Oxford in his four appearances; took all ten in another match for his university; played in representative English teams abroad and turned out three times for Australia *v* England. In the Great War and at the age of forty-seven, he acted as a stoker on an overheated transport ship in the Dardanelles.

G. McGregor – the McGregor of McGregors – of Cambridge kept wicket for England and played full-back for Scotland. W. Neilson, who played for Cambridge in the 1890s, was capped for Scotland at the age of seventeen-and-a-half. Frank Mitchell, the 1893 Cambridge captain, played rugby for England and cricket for Yorkshire and South Africa, though he toured that country with Lord Hawke's team in the late 1890s. He was also a shot put blue. Another who played cricket for South Africa was R. O. Schwarz, a goodly bowler who was the Cambridge scrum-half in 1893. E. R. Balfour, after three years in the Oxford team, became a rowing blue and later won the Silver Goblets at Henley with 'Gully' Nicholls.

The famous K. G. McLeod first appeared in the

A cartoon celebration of the 1919 Oxford v. Cambridge Rugby
Match. Cambridge won 7–5

1905 Cambridge side partnering his brother in the
centre. McLeod won ten caps for Scotland before
he was twenty-one, won the 100 yards twice and
dead-heated once against Oxford, also at Queen's.
In 1910 F. T. Mann became the first product of
Malvern, a soccer bastion, to win a rugby blue at
Cambridge and went on to captain England at
cricket. The Cambridge full-back that year was C.

Pinkham who also won blues for soccer and lacrosse.
The first of the Bruce-Lockhart clan, J.H., was also
in that side.

There is, however, one Cambridge player who
fascinates me more than these: R. L. Alston of 1889.
Somehow he managed to be educated at Cheltenham, Westminster, Berkhamsted and Tonbridge.
That was some achievement – or was it?

THE OXFORD AND CAMBRIDGE SOCCER MATCH
1888–1921

THE university soccer men followed their rugby colleagues to The Queen's Club during the 1887–88 season. The switch from the Oval to West Kensington brought a change in Oxford's fortunes. Having lost the five previous contests, one by 5–0, the largest margin in the first fifty years of the series, Oxford won 3–2 on 22 February 1888 – an inspired performance. Down 3–1 at half-time Cambridge pulled back with a goal by their captain, Tinsley Lindley, regarded as the best of all centre forwards until the arrival of G. O. Smith. But Oxford survived a final bombardment. Five of their side later became internationals.

Oxford attributed their unexpected win first to a macabre superstition that passing a funeral was worth a goal – they passed three on their way to Queen's – and second to the outstanding play of their goalkeeper, L. Cooper, a man so tall that he was reputed to be able to put his hand over the cross-bar and scratch his head!

The normal formation in those days was a goalkeeper, a back, two halves and seven forwards.

It was only a few years prior to the move to Queen's that the universities had awarded full blues for the two football games. Oxford were first in the early 1880s but when H. G. Fuller and F. W. Pawson, respective captains of rugby and soccer at Cambridge, applied they were turned down by the cricket, boating and athletics authorities who tried to maintain their exclusivity.

Eventually the two teams awarded themselves blues and appeared for their respective matches in light blue coats. The boating authorities brought the matter to a head with a debate in the Cambridge Union condemning the football clubs' action. They

were sunk without trace, an overwhelming majority favouring the footballers.

The second match at Queen's, in 1889, ended in a draw 1–1. The Cambridge side contained W. E. Pryce-Jones who later won five full Welsh caps. While at Shrewsbury, it was often claimed, Pryce-Jones and H. A. Rhodes, a member of the 1890 Oxford team, took the ball the whole length of the field using only their heads, until finally Rhodes scored with his foot.

In the Oxford side that year was H. M. Walters, younger brother of the famous twins, A. M. and P. M. Walters, full-backs for England nine times. He had been brought up to play rugby but had developed into a strong 'rushing inside forward'. Playing under instructions to take the man and let his wing take the ball Walters met an opponent's knee in one of his rushes and later died of the injury.

There were no goal nets in those days and Oxford felt themselves cheated claiming to have scored the winning goal, whereas the referee believed the ball passed outside the posts. It was fast approaching dusk at the time.

Cambridge, with an all-international forward line, won for the first time at Queen's in 1890 beating Oxford 3–1. Those goals may not have been painlessly achieved for one Oxford back (the team formation had changed to 1–2–3–5) was the redoubtable E. Jackson. A fellow player claimed that he had been knocked down more often by Jackson than any other back he had met, though C. B. Fry had knocked him further at one go.

The great C. B. Fry came on the Oxford scene in 1892, and that year's team also contained an outstanding dribbler, W. E. Gilliat, a Carthusian who won a full cap for England the following year. But Oxford were trounced 5–1. Gilliat's suspect knee went in the first few minutes and the rest of the Oxford forwards were accused of 'probably the worst shooting ever seen in a Varsity match'. Fry was no help, giving away two goals by his 'fancy kicking'. Though a freshman, Fry was cocky enough to comment: 'I never want to play again with such a lot of ***** crocks.' He did, however, play for Oxford for the next three years.

There arrived at Oxford in that disastrous season G. O. Smith, another in the line of great Carthusians and, perhaps, the greatest of them all – a nonpareil who won over twenty full caps for England and later became headmaster of that famous prep school, Ludgrove, founded by Arthur Dunn who gave his name to the Arthur Dunn Cup.

VERSATILE FORWARD

At Charterhouse Smith had played outside-right for his first two years and centre-forward for the last two. He appeared in the 1893 Oxford side at centre-forward and scored the first of the three goals by which they rubbed off a Cambridge half-time lead of 2–0 to win 3–2. He was immediately chosen for England against Ireland but at inside-right. After that he never played anywhere else other than centre-forward and was rated as the greatest player of his generation (some say any generation) in that position.

The 1894 Oxford side, with Fry as captain backed up by such players as G. B. Raikes (later the Rev.) in goal, W. J. Oakley at full-back, and G. O. Smith – they won a multitude of England caps – were strong favourites. Before the University match they had recorded 14 wins, 2 draws and 1 defeat.

The Queen's Club pitch was bone hard and uneven through frost. Fry rejected a postponement and brought his team to Queen's with long studs in their boots as it had already thawed at Oxford. Not so at Cambridge, where the ground was still frozen and their players equipped themselves with boots with shallow bars. The result was a 3–1 win for Cambridge over what some claimed was the best-ever Oxford team.

In the next two years Oxford, in their build-up to the University match, were often deprived of their best players for, as one player wrote, 'Oxford football was to all intents G. O. Smith, W. J. Oakley and G. B. Raikes. True, we did not see much of them in

the October term as England needed them and they also had to play regularly for the Corinthians. But in the next term they appeared in all the Oxford matches and what a difference that made!'

Indeed, it did. Oxford won both years and G. O. Smith completed his four years in the side with three wins and one defeat. There were nearly 8000 spectators to see him score the only goal, the winning goal, in 1896 in a match described by *The Times* as: 'A game that exceeded anything seen in the University match for many years.' Smith, near the corner flag, noticed that the goalkeeper had stepped forward to intercept a centre (cross is the modern word). He hit the ball with a left foot slice to screw it just over the goalie's head and under the bar.

One of the more notable Cambridge players during this period was L. H. Gay from Brighton College. Later he became a double international, keeping goal and wicket for England and never being on the losing side at football. G. O. Smith described him as one of the three best Corinthian goalkeepers along with W. R. Moon and G. B. Raikes – 'Howard Baker was the best of the rest'. A. E. Stoddart, later to become The Queen's Club secretary, chose Gay to keep wicket for England in Australia 1894–5 without ever having seen him play.

Another Cambridge man of the time was T. T. N. Perkins, a busy centre-forward ever eager to have the ball. So eager, in fact, that aspirants for blues in the year he was captain spent all their time passing to him. He was largely responsible for that 5–1 Cambridge win on a near-frozen pitch. Before the game began some old hand was heard telling the new blues: 'Now you have your blues stop all that damn silly passing to Perks.'

The Oxford captain in 1899 was G. C. Vassall, whose brother was a distinguished and innovative Oxford rugby captain. G. C. Vassall was picked to play for England against Ireland on the same day as the University match. Naturally he chose to lead Oxford onto the field at Queen's – they were beaten 3–0 – and was never again invited to play for his country.

That year's Oxford side later toured Europe. In Vienna they won 12–0 and 15–0, the Oxford goalkeeper, Russell, spending most of his time signing postcards for the spectators or sitting on a chair eating sweets.

After four successive defeats Cambridge won the 1904 match by the same record margin they had achieved in 1886 – 5–0. The following year the

An Association Football match between Oxford and Cambridge Universities in 1905

Bystander of 22 February commented: 'The excellence of their forwards made Cambridge the favourites but it was the fine play of the Oxford halves and backs that won the contest.' The Cambridge goalkeeper, R. P. Keigwin, a Cliftonian who was four years in the cricket XI, was held responsible for letting through the winning goal but, according to the *Bystander*, 'made two exceptional saves and stopped other shots that would have scored nine times out of ten'. Years later Keigwin appeared in The Queen's Club rackets court with a Pelota basket!

PULPIT AND PITCH

By 1908 and with three wins in the past four years Oxford drew level with Cambridge, each team winning seventeen times. One of Oxford's key men was K. R. G. Hunt (later the Rev.) who, a week after helping his side beat Cambridge 4–1 in 1908, scored the first goal for Wolverhampton Wanderers in their victorious Cup final against Newcastle United. He formed a formidable half-back line with G. N. Foster, one of the seven Foster brothers at Malvern, and E. L. Wright.

The Cambridge captain that day was F. H. Mugliston, a Rossallian who joined the Sudan Civil Service with Guy Pawson. Pawson was the Oxford cricket captain, and father of Tony Pawson, a Wykehamist

like his father, a double blue and co-author of these notes. Mugliston's stay in the Sudan was brief. The British Army ran the country and the Governor of Kordofan, a general, took exception to a chatty note from 'Mugs' which did not address him properly or list his decorations. Mugliston's response to a frosty reply ended with 'and in future, General, you will address me not as Mr Mugliston but as F. H. Mugliston Esq., BA (Cantab)'. He was put on the next boat home.

The Cambridge forward line in 1911 was reckoned to be as good as their 5–0 winning predecessors in 1886 led by W. N. Cobbold, the 'Prince of Dribblers' and nicknamed 'Nuts' ('all kernel but very hard to crack,' said C. B. Fry) and that of 1904 led by Stanley S. Harris, one of a generation of fine players from Westminster. The Cambridge captain, H. G. Bache, who scored some fifty goals that season, must have hoped to emulate them. And among the Cambridge wins was one of 7–2 over the Corinthians.

Bache did put Cambridge ahead after a goal by the Oxford captain, J. B. Bickersteth, and had some ill-luck when Short hit a post and an Oxford back trying to clear with a fancy overhead kick slammed the ball back onto the same post. Oxford, who had suffered half a dozen defeats that season, took charge and won 3–2 with goals by Cardew and Maples.

Cambridge made up for that by winning the following season, scoring twice in the last three minutes.

Bache went on to distinguish himself for West Bromwich Albion before being killed in the Great War. He was one of the last of a notable era of Cambridge men to play at Queen's, the final name being Max Woosnam, a Wykehamist and son of a canon who played in the last three years before the war and after it for full England. He played four different games for Cambridge, was twelfth man at cricket and won the Wimbledon men's doubles title with Randolph Lycett in 1921. Like C. B. Fry before him and Howard Baker later he was one of the great all-rounders. Oxford covered that pre- and brief post-war period at Queen's with such men as F. W. H. Nicholas from Forest School and Miles Howell from Repton, who gained their full caps just after the war. And Oxford won the last University match played at Queen's in 1921, 2–1.

ATHLETICS AND THE OXFORD AND CAMBRIDGE SPORTS

ONE day Howard Baker, a great all-rounder and wearing his LTA bow-tie – he is a Life-Councillor – was walking across The Queen's Club grounds. As he passed one of the hard courts close to the Fencing Association HQ he remarked to his companion, 'That's where we used to high jump.'

That chance remark brought to light a one-off event that took place at Queen's in 1920 which was probably the most successful promotion, financially and in prestige, held at the Club up to that time and, for that matter, thereafter until John McEnroe and Jimmy Connors filled the arena during the Grass Court Championships. I refer to the athletics match between the British Empire and the USA held shortly after the 1920 Olympics in Antwerp. It was inspired by the Achilles Club, largely composed of men from Oxford and Cambridge.

The Achilles Club, an élite organization of athletes, was in the process of being formed that Olympic year. Some of the leading .founder members, among them Bevil Rudd, who won the 400 metres gold medal, Philip Baker (later Lord Noel-Baker) second in the 1500 metres, and A. N. S. Jackson, the 1912 Olympic 1500 metre champion, were asked to try and get the Americans to come to London for a match against the British Empire. 'We had agreed with The Queen's Club that the meeting should take place on its excellent track, then the best in Britain. We also approached the Canadians, Australians and others before we said anything to the Americans. They were all keen to come to London,' wrote Lord Noel-Baker later.

The Americans were also enthusiastic but wanted a £1200 guarantee to cover expenses. 'None of us could have raised that sum but unblushingly we gave the guarantee, confident that the gate-money would

cover it,' added Lord Noel-Baker. Despite the number of Olympic champions taking part and an excellent Press the tickets did not sell. On the Wednesday before the match – a Saturday – only a handful of people had booked seats. Lord Northcliffe, obsessed with the need for Anglo-American friendship and co-operation, came to the rescue with his stable, which included *The Times, Daily Mail* and *Evening News*, doing a blanket operation.

By Saturday morning every seat was sold and those without tickets were clamouring at the Club entrances; so much so that the promoters had to pay Queen's £200 to repair the damage. After paying the Americans' expenses the net profit, shared between the Achilles Club and Queen's, was £3000; a hefty sum for which E. B. Noel, the Club secretary, expressed his gratitude.

The match? With each side winning four events, it came down to the decider – the High Jump – which resolved itself into a contest between the new Olympic champion, Dick Landon, a New Yorker who wore glasses, and Howard Baker, unplaced in Antwerp. Howard Baker won and, the following year, jumped 6 ft 5 in, in Huddersfield, to establish a British record that stood for twenty-six years – until 1947!

Footballer, athlete, swimmer and Wimbledon lawn tennis player, Howard Baker's achievements in sport are legendary. He played a record number of 176 matches for the Corinthians and 120 for Chelsea and Everton, as well as playing for full England. According to David Miller of *The Times* he only became a goalkeeper because of damage to an ankle while serving on a minesweeper during the Great War. He was such a formidable kicker that he would often take the penalties and, it is claimed, an opposing goalie once asked him not to shoot straight at him as he did not want to get hurt!

Tall and good-looking, Howard was, according to Miller, 'the dandy socialite of the twenties, as well-known to wine waiters and hall porters as was Douglas Fairbanks'. His background, therefore, was very different from that of C. B. Fry, Repton and Oxford, or Max Woosnam, Winchester and Cambridge, two other great all-rounders who expressed themselves on the field and courts of Queen's.

OLDEST MEETING

The Oxford and Cambridge athletics meeting is the oldest in the world. First held in 1864 it moved from Lillie Road to The Queen's Club in 1888 and remained there, apart from a seven-year gap caused by the First World War, until 1928. It was the last major event, other than lawn tennis, real tennis and rackets championships, to be held at the Club.

Next to the University rugby match the Sports Day, according to E. B. Noel, was the greatest of the year at the Club and always drew a large crowd despite the uncertainty of the weather in March. Its popularity went back a long way to the days of Henry Becks, the first Club secretary. In 1899, for instance, *The Illustrated Sporting and Dramatic News* made this comment while reporting the Sports: 'With each succeeding year Mr Henry Becks, The Queen's Club secretary, has brought his tact and experience so serviceably into play with reference to the general arrangements that perfection has now been so nearly reached and further improvement seems to be quite impossible.'

The weather that year was cold and cheerless but that did not deter the public or a whole host of celebrities from attending the meeting. Among the more distinguished were the Earl of Jersey, W. N. Cobbold, known as the Prince of Dribblers on the soccer field and a Cambridge blue for lawn tennis, E. Temple Gurdon of Cambridge and England rugby fame, and H. D. Leveson-Gower, the cricketer.

In 1909 the gate takings were £797 and went up to £946 the following year. That seems a considerable sum for those days. The popularity of the meeting continued after the First World War and in 1920 and 1921 the gate takings were £1259 and £1117 respectively. Understandably the Club found Sports Day a useful source of revenue as they took about a third of the profit after expenses.

The original track was three laps to the mile and was run anti-clockwise. The main straight lay at the south end of the Club grounds, between the grass courts and the hard, and was overlooked by a covered stand holding over 300 people. The course of the track was similar to that nowadays taken by joggers at the Club.

For the long jump there were two pits, one at each end of a narrow cinder track, so that advantage could be taken of any wind. Similarly the hurdles were run north to south or *vice-versa*. In 1920, the first post-war meeting, the track was reconstructed to four laps a mile.

Three times before the Great War, Oxford and Cambridge met Harvard and Yale at Queen's, winning twice. The impact these four great universities made on the modern Olympics, especially in the earlier years, was considerable.

An Oxford man, George Robertson, later Sir George Robertson QC, winner of the hammer throw in 1893–4–5, happened to be in Greece for the first of the modern Olympics – 'anyone could enter' – and took part in the discus, weight putt and lawn tennis, there being no hammer in those days. But it was not at any of those events that he achieved international acclaim. It came from the fact that he was the first Olympic athlete since 770 BC to win a prize for a Greek ode! A scholar *par excellence* he was, when I met him in 1962, the sole survivor of those Olympics.

Many famous men, games players and athletes passed through The Queen's Club gates and took part in the Sports. R. Goddard, an Oxford sprinter, became the Lord Chief Justice of England, Lord Goddard. Arthur Porritt, another Oxford sprinter, became a famous surgeon and member of the House of Lords. And yet a third Oxford sprinter, Noel Chavasse, became one of the only three men to win two VCs.

THE MAGIC MILE

Milers were among the heroes of the late Victorian era – have they ever ceased to be heroes in this country? – with Oxford's F. J. K. Cross lowering the record in 1889 to 4 mins 23.6 secs at his fourth attempt and W. Pollock-Hill, also of Oxford, lopping two seconds off that the following year. The Light Blue, W. E. Lutyens beat that with 4 mins 19.8 secs in 1894.

C. B. Fry, often regarded as the greatest all-rounder this country has produced – England cricket

The Hundred Yards in 1893: C. B. Fry and A. Ramsbottom
dead-heat at the tape

and soccer player; England reserve at rugby; athlete, scholar and writer – broke the long jump record for the meeting with 23 ft 5 in, less than a week after beating the world record in 1892.

The following year *The Illustrated Sporting and Dramatic News* reported that 'The gathering at Queen's Club on Thursday the 23rd of March was in every way a most successful one. With glorious weather, as warm as June, the attendance was far larger than ever before and the performances were in many cases exceptionally good, especially in the High Jump and Three Miles. The latter resulted in a fresh record being made (F. S. Horan of Cambridge) and was a splendid exhibition of running. 'Some disappointment was felt at C. B. Fry failing to improve on his wonderful long jump of 23 ft 5 in last year. He has since then tied the American record of 23 ft 6½ in and it was hoped that on this occasion he would be able to beat it. The Oxonians were even more successful than was anticipated and won seven of the nine events. However, Cambridge had five seconds to four of Oxford.' Fry, by the way, dead-heated the 100 yards with the Oxford President, A. Ramsbotham.

Into the Edwardian era, R. W. Barclay (Cambridge) became the first athlete to record six track wins with the 100-yard dash and 440 doubles in 1902–3–4. In 1895, C. C. Henderson, later killed in the Great War, set a mile record of 4 mins 17.8 secs that withstood all assaults including those of Jack Lovelock until Roger Bannister's third win for Oxford in 1949.

Cambridge predominated from 1908 until the Great War with men such as K. G. McLeod, a great Scotland rugby centre, in the 100 yards, Kenneth Powell, a hurdler and frequent lawn tennis competitor at Queen's, P. J. Baker, later Lord Philip Noel-Baker, in the mile-and-a-half, the sprinters, D. Macmillan and H. M. Macintosh, and the most versatile man in the history of the Sports, H. S. O. Ashington. He won the half-mile, the high hurdles (twice), the high jump, the long jump (thrice) and even ran in the 1911 mile. Oxford's A. N. S. Jackson won the mile in 1912–13–14 and, of course, the Olympic 1500 metres in Stockholm in 1912. G. M. Sproule set a three-mile record in 1913 that stood for thirty-six years.

MULTIPLE WINNER

After the war along came Harold Abrahams, with a total of eight individual wins for Cambridge including the long jump record. Between 1920 and 1923 he won the 100 yards four times, the quarter-mile once and the long jump three times. Other Cambridge men with three or more track wins were the miler, H. B. Stallard, quarter-milers Guy Butler and J. W. J. Rinkel, the double Olympic 800 metres champion Douglas Lowe, and Lord Burghley (later the Marquess of Exeter) who scored a hurdles double three years running. Arthur Porritt won the 100 yards twice for Oxford during that period.

By the time the Sports left Queen's for Stamford Bridge after the 1928 meeting, Oxford had won 25 times, Cambridge 29 with 6 ties. The most famous of all scions of the University Sports must be Harold Abrahams' whose Olympic victory in the 1924 Paris Games was immortalized in *Chariots of Fire*.

Rex Alston, BBC cricket commentator and sporting journalist, ran with Abrahams at Queen's and recalls a memorable occasion in 1923 when Cambridge were short of a quarter-miler of any class. 'There being no prominent quarter-miler, Harold plotted with our enthusiastic little coach, Alec Nelson, to try and undo Oxford's crack runner, the reigning American champion, W. E. Stevenson. The Queen's Club track was a quarter-mile round and the start was very near the finish. It was vital for Abrahams to use his speed to reach the first corner and so lead the other three runners down the back straight.

'The plan was for him to slow down the race so that with his finishing sprint he would have a chance against a far better quarter-miler. It worked like a dream and Stevenson fell into the trap. Instead of taking the lead down the back straight, Stevenson allowed Harold to set such a slow pace that when it came to the last two hundred yards or so Abrahams was still in the lead and Stevenson had no hope of catching such a brilliant sprinter in the run-in. It was a marvellous tactical victory for a man who dominated that day's sport.'

Alston, in fact, was Harold's second string in the 100 yards against J. Bird. 'I had a close race with Bird and I remember being sickeningly nervous because we had two false starts, both his fault, not mine. When we did get started, Harold streaked away and I just pipped Bird for second place.'

In winning the long jump that year, Abrahams beat the record with a leap of 23 ft 7¼ in. His first leap

Above The Mile 1898, with H. E. Graham (Cambridge) leading

Right The 1898 Hundred Yards, showing R. Goddard (extreme left) and C. R. Thomas (extreme right). Goddard failed in the race but succeeded in life

was a 'no jump'; his second beat the record, after which he put on his sweater and left the arena, so certain was he that no third jump would be required to keep Oxford at bay.

Norris McWhirter, himself an Oxford blue sprinter and statistician, has set down the highlights of University Sports which took place at Queen's for forty years, from 1888 to 1928.

Athletics Diary by Norris McWhirter

Having moved from Lillie Bridge, the Sports were first held at Queen's on Friday, 23 March 1888, Cambridge winning by five events to four. The world's fastest half-miler of the day, Francis J. K. Cross (later the Reverend) won the mile by 25 yards in 4 mins 29.4 secs. He won again, and so did Cambridge, the following year. Four years later Cross took part in that gladiatorial contest between the Corinthians and the Barbarians, won by the former three events to one.

W. Pollock-Hill lowered the mile record to 4 mins 21.6 secs and W. B. Thomas set a new quarter-mile record of 50.2 secs, both for Oxford in 1890. Two years later, Charles Burgess Fry, Repton and Wadham College, Oxford, appeared on the scene winning the long jump with 23 ft 5 in and establishing himself as the world's best performer. C. J. B. Monypenny broke the 50-second barrier in the 440 yards and shortly afterwards turned out for the Barbarians in both the rugby match and athletics contest against the Corinthians. In 1893 the two Oxonians, Fry and A. Ramsbottom dead-heated in

J. K. Macmeikan in the 1904 High Jump. The Eastern cut-off?

the 100 yards in 10.2 secs and Ramsbottom also took the 440 yards by a margin of 4 yards while Fry retained his long jump title with 23 ft 0½ in. In 1894 Fry was beaten into last place in the 100 yards but took the long jump for the third time with 22 ft 4 in.

In 1895 the track was in such a bad state owing to frost that the Sports had to be postponed to the more sensible date of 3 July. On this occasion Fry was beaten into second place in the long jump by W. Mendelson by 8½ inches with the Cambridge man doing 22 ft 5½ in.

In 1898 the Sports again had to be postponed from 25 March to 29 June because of bad weather. A postponement cost the Oxford sprinter R. Goddard dear because he was unable to train for a second peak. The winner was C. R. Thomas, also of Oxford, in 10.4 secs. Goddard was last. Later he became Lord Chief Justice of England. When asked what became of Thomas he replied, 'I never heard of him again. I believe he may have been a parson in South Wales.' Thomas went on to win again in 1899 and 1900.

In 1902 the Oxford shot-putter W. W. Coe, from America, won with 43 ft 10 in and later became the world's best performer at this event. In 1904 K. Cornwallis of Oxford set a new 880-yard record, winning by 15 yards in 1 min 54.8 secs. The following year there was a new mile record by C. C. Henderson-Hamilton with 4 mins 17.8 secs. He was killed at Gallipoli in the First World War.

In 1906 the famous Scottish rugby international, Kenneth McLeod, took the 100 yards title by inches. In 1906 came the first appearance of the famous Chavasse twins, Christopher (C.M.) and Noel (N.G.) from Trinity College, Oxford. Christopher was third in the 440 yards. In 1907 Noel won the 100 yards in 10.5 secs in a dead-heat with McLeod, with Christopher third. In the 440 yards the twins finished first and second with Christopher getting the verdict by half-a-yard in 50.6 secs. The 3 miles was won by N. F. Hallows, who later became the school doctor at Marlborough College, and competed in the 1908

PROGRAMME

SATURDAY, MARCH 27th, 1920

OXFORD.	CAMBRIDGE.
President—B. G. D. RUDD, Trinity	President—A. C. TELFER, Selwyn.
Hon. Treas.—G. C. VASSALL, M.A., Oriel.	Hon. Treas.—Canon J. H. GRAY, M.A., Queens'.
Hon. Sec.—E. A. MONTAGUE, Magdalen.	Hon. Sec.—G. M. BUTLER, Trinity.

2.15 Hundred Yards.

1. R. STAPLEDON, Queen's (dark blue).
2. B. G. D. RUDD. Trinity (red),
    or G. F. WOOD, Trinity (red).
3. H. M. ABRAHAMS, Caius
               (light blue).
4. G. M. BUTLER, Trinity (red).

2.25 High Jump.*

1. H. S. WHITE, B.N.C., (dark blue).
2. W. DOWLING, St. John's (red).
3. E. S. BURNS, St. Catherine's
               (light blue)
4. A. K. BIRD, Emmanuel (red).

2.25 Putting the Weight.*

1. S. YOVANOVITCH, New College
               (dark blue)
2. G. F. WOOD, Trinity (red).
3. R. S. WOODS, Downing (light blue).
4. H. WATERHOUSE, St. John's
               (red).

2.50 440 Yards.

1. B. G. D. RUDD, Trinity (dark blue).
2. H. B. ANDERSON, Magdalen (red).
3. G. M. BUTLER, Trinity (light blue).
4. J. C. A. DAVIS, Christ's (red)

3.0 One Mile.

1. W. R. MILLIGAN, University
               (dark blue).
2. E. BEDDINGTON-BEHRENS,
    Christ Church (red).
3. W. A. GRACE, Queen's (yellow).
4. H. B. STALLARD, Caius
               (light blue).
5. W. G. TATHAM, King's (red).
6. W. MABANE, Caius (gold).

3.10 Hurdle Race.

1. H. P. JEPPE, Trinity (dark blue).
2. J. N. C. FORD, Hertford (red).
3. A. N. CAMERON. Pembroke
               (light blue).
4. B. D. NICHOLSON, Trinity (red).

3.20 Long Jump.*

1. L. St. C. INGRAMS, Pembroke
               (dark blue).
2. B. G. D. RUDD, Trinity (red),
    or G. F. WOOD, Trinity (red).
3. H. M. ABRAHAMS, Caius
               (light blue).
4. K. R. J. SAXON, Emmanuel (red).

3.20 Throwing the Hammer.*

1. M. C. NOKES, Magdalen (dark blue).
2. G. A. FEATHER, Wadham (red).
3. H. R. FERGUSON. Caius
               (light blue).
4. J. M. LIPSCHITZ, Clare (red).

3.40 Three Miles.

1. E. A. MONTAGUE, Magdalen
               (dark blue).
2. S. L. O'NEILL, Balliol (red).
3. J. G. BROADBENT, Magdalen
               (yellow).
4. W. R. SEAGROVE, Clare
               (light blue).
5. L. R. ANDREWS, Pembroke (red).
6. W. T. MARSH. Queens' (gold).

4.0 Half Mile.

1. B. G. D. RUDD. Trinity
               (dark blue).
2. B. E. HENTY, New College (red).
3. E. D. MOUNTAIN, Corpus
               (light blue).
4. R. C. GREGORY. Trinity (red).

N.B.—Every Competitor will wear upon his **Left Arm** the Colour stated in this Programme opposite his name.
  * The progress of each round of these events will be marked by dark and light blue flags, and at the conclusion of the Competition the Winner's Throw or Jump will be indicated on the Telegraph Boards.
  In addition to this, the respective Colours of the Competitors who have been placed first and second will be hoisted at the Telegraph Board to indicate the result of each event.

— A 1920 programme showing Harold Abrahams' events —

RESERVED SEATS in Covered Stands A, B and C are 12s. 6d. each, including admission.

OXFORD & CAMBRIDGE SPORTS, SATURDAY, MARCH 27th, 1920,
AT 2.15 O'CLOCK.

PLAN OF QUEEN'S CLUB, SHOWING THE TRACK AND WINNING POSTS.

Also Position of Reserved Seats and Entrances.

Perham Rᵈ Entrance 2/6 and for holders of Stand "C" Tickets

Track 4 laps to the Mile.

Transfer to 5/- Part.

Comeragh Road
To West Kensington Station →

Transfer to 5/- part.

● Throwing Hammer.

Start Hurdles

Start 100 yards.

5/- PART

Covered Stand "C" 1st 2nd & 3rd Rows

185 to 240

137 to 184

73 to 136

1 to 72

ENTRANCES

Grass Lawn Tennis Courts.

5 Hard Courts (Lawn Tennis)

● Putting Weight.

Palliser Road
← To Barons Court Station

5/- Entrance and for Members & their Friends

Telegraph Office

● Start 3 Miles

Covered Stand "B"

Stand "B" consists of 20 Rows lettered from A to V – The front row is "A". The numbering of each row begins with 1 at the left-hand end of the row as you enter the stand.

● Long Jump.

● High Jump

Winning Post

Winning Post. 100 yards, ¼ Mile ½ Mile, 1 Mile, and 3 Miles.

To other side of Ground

Start ½ Mile

Start ⅓ Mile

Start ¼ Mile

Tickets for Reserved Stand "C" Seats sold here (if any left on day).

Tickets for Reserved Seats A & B sold here (if any left on day).

Enclosure for Members, Blues & their Friends

"A" Stand for Friends of Members

Enquiry Office

Eton Fives Court

| 324 to 382 | 207 to 323 | 89 to 206 | 1 to 88 |

Royal Tennis Courts

Members Pavilion

Offices

Racket Courts

Miniature Rifle Range

Squash | Courts

New Covered Lawn Tennis Court

Tea Room & Covered Lawn Tennis Courts

Remittances must accompany every application for tickets or they cannot be sent.

A plan of the grounds in 1920

Olympics 1500 metres in which he won the bronze medal. In fourth place in the 3 miles was S. P. B. Mais of Oxford, later to win fame as a prolific novelist. The 120-yard hurdles was won by Kenneth Powell of Cambridge, who was regarded by many as the finest high-hurdler in the world.

In 1909 McLeod again won the 100 yards with Noel Chavasse third, while Christopher was second in the 440 yards. Christopher later became the Bishop of Rochester, while Noel Chavasse was one of only three people in history to win a bar to the Victoria Cross. He was serving as a captain in the RAMC on the Western Front and his second award was posthumous. Both the twins ran in the 1908 Olympic Games at the White City Stadium in London.

GLITTERING PRIZES

In 1910 the half mile was won by P. J. Baker (later the Rt Hon. Lord Noel Baker) winner of the Nobel Peace Prize and winner of a silver medal in the Olympic 1500 metres of 1920. The following year, Baker won both the half mile and the mile and in 1912 again took the half mile.

In 1912 the mile winner was Arnold Nugent Strode Jackson of Brasenose, Oxford, who won handily by 8 yards in 4 mins 21.4 secs. The high jump winner was the famous intelligence expert J. C. Masterman. Jackson represented Great Britain at the 1912 Olympic Games in Stockholm and defeated a trio of American champions to set a new 1500 metres world record of 3 mins 56.8 secs. He carried on to win again in 1913 by the extraordinary margin of 100 yards in 4 mins 24.2 secs. That meeting was notable also for the long jump record of H.S.O. Ashington of Cambridge (23 ft 5¾ in) so bettering C. B. Fry's jump of nineteen years before. Ashington in 1914 took both the high jump and long jump, the latter being yet another record, 23 ft 6¼ in.

After a lapse in the war years the Sports returned to The Queen's Club on 27 March 1920. Harold Abrahams opened his count by equalling the 100-yard record of 10.0 secs beating Bevil Rudd by a foot with Guy Butler third. Rudd, who later went on to win the gold medal in the Olympic 400 metres at Antwerp, won the 440 yards in 49.6 secs. The mile was won by Henry Stallard, who later became a famous opthalmic surgeon. The track for the first time had been reconstructed to make four laps instead of three laps for the mile. The 3 miles was won by Evelyn Montague, who was a member of the family which owned the *Manchester Guardian*. Abrahams also won the long jump and in second place was L. S. Ingrams, father of the editor of the notorious *Private Eye*, Richard Ingrams. The shot putt was retained from 1914 by the remarkable Rex Salisbury Woods, who is still living as a nonagenarian doctor in Cambridge.

In 1921 Abrahams retained the 100 yards by 2ft over Guy Butler but was shunted to third in the long jump which was won by Ingrams with 22 ft 0½ in. Butler defeated the Olympic champion in the 440 yards. He was the cousin of R. A. Butler and was the only male British athlete ever to win gold, silver and bronze medals on the track in the Olympics.

SPIDER MAN

In 1922 Abrahams beat Butler by a yard in the 100 yards and again took the long jump, this time with Ingrams fourth. The hammer was omitted from the programme for lack of competitors and a 220-yard low hurdles was introduced and was won by W. S. Bristowe, who later became the world's greatest authority on spiders.

In 1923 Harold Abrahams won the 100 yards for the fourth time, beating cricket journalist Rex Alston by 3 yards in 10.0 secs. Harold also won the 440 yards and, again, the long jump, this time with a new record of 23 ft 7¼ in over the bounding Baronet Sir Thomas Devitt. The 1923 match also saw the appearance of Douglas Lowe, who won the half mile and who was later to win Olympic gold medals both in 1924 in Paris and in 1928 in Amsterdam. The mile winner was W. R. Milligan, who later became the Lord Advocate or Senior Judge in Scotland.

In 1924 Douglas Lowe achieved a double in the half mile by 4 yards and the mile by 20 yards. In 1925 Arthur Porritt, the New Zealander, broke the 100 yard-record with 9.9 seconds. He had won the bronze medal behind Harold Abrahams in Paris the year before. The 440 yards was won by W. E. Stephenson, who won a gold medal in the 4 × 400-metre relay in Paris, while Douglas Lowe took his third half-mile title. Lord Burghley won both the high and low hurdles medals by 3 yards and 4 yards respectively from Porritt. In 1926 Porritt retained his 100-yard title, as did Lord Burghley in the two hurdle events.

The pole-vault had been introduced in 1923 and in the 1926 match R. L. Hyett of Oxford set a record of 11 ft 10 in. Lord Burghley won his third hurdle double in 1927 with an inches victory over the South African Olympic champion G. C. Weightmann-Smith.

The Sports were held for the last time in 1928 at The Queen's Club before moving to Stamford Bridge, and the 100 yards and 440 yards were won by J. W. J. Rinkel, who retained his 100-yard title and achieved a hat-trick of 440-yard titles. His 100-yard victory was over E. R. Smouha of Cambridge. Smouha's address in Egypt was Smouha City and he was one of the very few athletes to run successfully wearing a monocle. Weightmann-Smith won a hurdles double by substantial margins with a new record of 15.4 secs in the high hurdles and equalling Lord Burghley's low hurdle record of 1925 with 24.8 secs.

THE QUEEN'S CLUB–THE WAR YEARS
1914–1918

THE country was at war when E. B. Noel, tall and spare, succeeded A. E. Stoddart as secretary in December 1914. Affectionately known as 'Nolly', Noel was already a well-known figure in the rackets and real tennis fraternity as well as in the world of sporting journalism at Printing House Square – *The Times*. A left-hander educated at Winchester and Cambridge, 'Nolly' won the Amateur rackets singles title in 1907 and the Olympic singles the following year as well as the MCC Silver racket at real tennis. He was a prolific writer on both games.

Once settled into Queen's, Noel and his family moved into a house on the corner of Palliser Road and Comeragh Road that overlooked the Club. His daughter, Susan, recalls a bridge being built from the Comeragh Road garden into the Club grounds so that the family could by-pass the main entrance.

When and how he found time to write all that he did is something of a mystery as, according to his daughter, he did not get up until 10.30 in the morning, never ate very much, driving his wife to despair on that subject, and sometimes repaired at mid-day to the 'Three Kings' or 'The Baron's Keep' usually in the company of Peter Latham, the head real tennis and rackets professional. Among his wide circle of friends were many from the world of variety and the theatre who, during the war, spent time at the Club. It does appear that the job of Club secretary at that time was as much social as administrative. Meanwhile, there were people like Mr Dodds to run the everyday life of the Club.

The war, certainly in the early stages, did not greatly affect the life of the Club. Late in 1913 the Army and Navy Store had taken over the catering which, in the first nine months, made a profit of over £50, much to everyone's delight. Their contract was immediately renewed and carried on at least until the end of the war, though the A & N did try to break it in 1917 but relented.

These facts suggest that rationing, certainly in the early part of the First World War, was not as severe as in the second conflagration. In fact, down the road, adjoining Barons Court station, there was a Fuller's Tea Shop advertising best-quality chocolate and, of all things, chewing gum. Anyone who recalls Fuller's will know how delicious were their iced cakes, scones and tea. You might, today, find their equal at Fortnums!

Some major decisions relating to the Club and the war were made while Stoddart was still secretary and Lord Clarendon, who died later that year, was in the chair. One was that no action should be taken against German and Austrian members – Turkish were added later – and that all the usual annual competitions be cancelled. There was to be no gate money charged for any events taking place at the Club except for charity.

One of the first 'charity' soccer matches was between the Public Schools and the Northern Command. It raised just over £13 for the Prince of Wales Fund. It was followed by a match between the Corinthians-under-Arms and the Aldershot Command. That raised £31. The big money-makers, the rugby matches between the New Zealanders (the All-Blacks) and the South Africans (the Springboks) came later. The Public Schools Headmasters decided against holding the annual schools rackets competitions at Queen's but the Club did organize handicaps for boys during the holidays.

The Club, of course, suffered considerable loss of revenue from the cancellation of events and matches normally taking place there; the Oxford and Cambridge rugby and soccer matches and the athletic sports, for instance, as well as all the matches the Corinthians and other clubs usually played there. Normally the Club not only charged those clubs and organizations rental but also took a share of the gate. In 1916 the Club did impose a ten percent charge on the use of the grounds to cover wear and tear.

WHITHER WOMEN?

The war did not appear to affect the membership which, from its early beginnings, had been restricted to 1200 ordinary members. In 1901 there were 1188 members. In 1915 there were 1198 – none of them women, though there were clearly plenty involved in the social life of the Club. This fact merely confuses the issue of lady membership because according to some sources women were admitted as members in 1900 and eighteen were listed in 1901!

The first big wartime party held at Queen's was at Christmas 1915, for wounded soldiers. This was organized by A. W. Dunlop, an Australian lawn tennis player of pre-and-post war distinction, and a Mrs Hall Walker. It included a soccer match between the Scots Guards and the RAMC and exhibition games of lawn tennis, real tennis, rackets and billiards. After tea there was a challenge match at billiards between Miss Ruby Roberts, the reigning women's champion, and Colin Smith, the Club's best player. The lady won.

There followed entertainment organized by Mrs R. A. Waller who later became Lady Wavertree. Among the renowned artists were Miss Phyllis Dare, Paul Rubens, Nelson Keys and Henry Ainley, all well-known figures in the theatre or music-hall. Gerald du Maurier (later Sir Gerald), a regular member of the Club, managed the affair. About 240 wounded soldiers were present from the Fulham, Hammersmith, Roehampton and other London Hospitals and were taken to and from the Club in motor buses! Sundays seem to have been a fairly regular day for entertainment and Ivor Novello is said to have played his own 'Keep the Home Fires Burning' at the Club.

There did not appear to be too many restrictions at that stage of the war. For instance, the hard courts, laid down by the Perfect Hard Court Company in 1913, needed a new top dressing two years later. The work was carried out by En-Tout-Cas.

Economy called for a reduction in staff wages in 1915 but not in personnel. A Mr Platt from the Army and Navy presided over the catering with Richardson the waiter and Caves the barman. The kitchens could cater for forty. Mr Cowdrey, one of the senior professionals, was called up and Charles Read, who was to make his mark on lawn tennis and squash after the war, was given a temporary exemption which appeared to extend throughout the war. Robert Nash was discharged from the Army after serving in France. Latham remained as head professional at real tennis and rackets as did Charles Heirons at lawn tennis for many years to come. Also around at this time, among others, were Tom Jeffrey, who later moved to Roehampton, and André, the expert racket stringer.

During the first two years of the war the activities of the Club were largely connected, as already

The Wounded Soldiers Christmas party organized in 1915

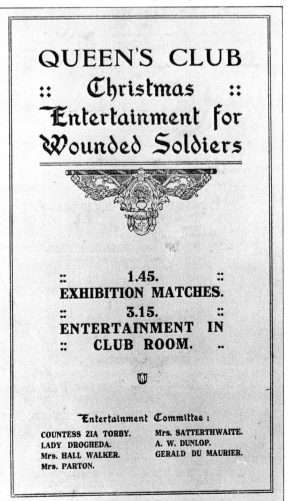

Above Tennis as usual in 1918, barrage balloon notwithstanding
Left The three kite balloon hangers loom behind Miss May Turner's backhand

mentioned, with raising money for charities, through the loan of the grounds to military and other organizations. Football of both codes, hockey, cricket and all the racket games were exploited. Walter Hawes, who had left Queen's for Wellington, and Ernest Jones, the Eton professional, beat Latham and Read 4–3 in a rackets match and raised a few pounds.

Australian Rules Football in aid of the Red Cross

In 1916 the War Office took over part of the grounds, though none of the buildings, and erected three kite balloon hangers. The Club became a balloon testing station under a Colonel Pryce and Major Brown, both of whom were keen sportsmen and used the facilities, especially the squash courts. The Club lost a fair amount of ground including the three grass courts in front of the pavilion. The football pitch had to be re-arranged to run north-south from the main entrance.

YANKS AND AUSSIES

By this time the country had become a reservoir for American and Commonwealth (Empire in those days) forces and two new games were introduced to Queen's – baseball and Australian Rules football.

In the autumn of 1916 three exhibition games of Australian Rules, a combination of rugby and soccer between sides of eighteen players, were given, followed by a match between the Third Australian Division and the Australian Training Units. Then the USA and Canada met at baseball to play a 'Championship of the British Isles' match in aid of the Russian Women's Battalion of Death which had fought with the utmost bravery on the Austrian front. The patron of that particular charity was Earl Grey who, nearly thirty years earlier, had become the first amateur real tennis champion.

The Scots Guards under Colonel R. S. Tempest DSO held a sports meeting, the four events being the 100 yards, the long jump, putting the shot and tossing the caber. There was nothing remarkable about that except that the prizes for the first three places in each event were one pound, ten shillings and five shillings – an awful lot of money in those days when a soldier was lucky to get a shilling a day.

Lawn tennis made its contribution. A Queen's Club team that included G. Greville, M. J. G. Ritchie, G. Caridia, P. M. Davson – all well-known pre-war Covered Courts performers – and the Hon. F. M. B. Fisher and A. Wallis Myers played C. P. Dixon's team that included A. D. Prebble and Stanley Doust. Near the end of the war Colonel H. G. Mayes of the Canadian Forces organized a Services competion which was won by the British Isles with Canada, Australia and South Africa following and the USA last!

The social life did not appear to decline. After one mixed doubles handicap won by E. A. C. Druce, a real tennis player of some distinction, and his daughter, there was a dinner and dancing on the grass. Such frolics were not uncommon and after one sports meeting there was dancing in a rackets court. The other court, by the way, had been used to store ammunition since the outbreak of war.

QUEEN'S CLUB, WEST KENSINGTON.

Programme

Lawn Tennis

SATURDAY, APRIL 15th, 1916,

— At 2 o'clock, on the Hard Courts. —

QUEEN'S CLUB

v.

Mr. C. P. Dixon's Team

GENTLEMEN'S DOUBLES.

Admission - - - 2s. 6d.

The proceeds will be given to the Ambulance Column attached to the London District.

THE SIDES ARE:

QUEEN'S CLUB.		MR. C. P. DIXON'S TEAM.
G. GREVILLE and M. J. G. RITCHIE	v.	C. P. DIXON and M. R. L. WHITE.
G. A. CARIDIA and P. M. DAVSON	v.	A. D. PREBBLE and S. N. DOUST.
Hon. F. M. B. FISHER and WALLIS MYERS	v.	W. A. INGRAM and A. N. OTHER.

If wet, as much of the programme as possible will be carried out in the Covered Courts.

SCORE CARD.

BASEBALL CHAMPIONSHIP OF THE BRITISH ISLES.

AMERICANS v. CANADIANS.

QUEEN'S CLUB GROUNDS, SEPTEMBER 28TH, 1918, 2.30 P.M.

PROCEEDS IN AID OF MAIMED & WOUNDED OF "THE RUSSIAN WOMEN'S BATTALION OF DEATH." (SEE BACK PAGE.)

PRICE THREE PENCE.

F. J. Parsons, Ltd., "Herald" Works, The Bayle, Folkestone.

Lawn Tennis for the ambulance service and baseball for the Russian Women's Battalion casualties

Top The Americans beaten at their own game by Canada in 1918
Above American football minus padding, 1918
Left M. J. G. Ritchie and Stanley Doust carrying an injured
member, King Manuel, into the clubhouse

Top War or no war, polite society continued at the Club: A rather flash Mr Scott Robson, with Capt. Anson, Capt. Compton, Miss S. Robson, Miss Farquharson and Mr Gordon Lennox

Above Lady Medina and Lady Mainwaring in the motor; Mrs Mathieson and Lady Headfont

The Club did suffer some air raid (zeppelin and aircraft) damage but nothing like it did in the Second World War. When finally it rendered its claim it included in the £5780 some loss of revenue from sporting events normally held. There was, as one might expect, much to-ing and fro-ing of letters between the Club and the War Office. At the same time the Club raised its fire insurance from £24,000 to £34,000.

That horses were stabled at Queen's during the war is clear from the forage bills. There was nothing unusual about that but it would be fascinating to know where Lady Derby had stabled her Shetland pony before parking it on Queen's in 1916. And anyway what was a Shetland doing in London at that time?

Top Lord d'Abernon, Lady M. Cavendish, Lady d'Abernon and Col. Greene
Above right Mme de Tessier
Right The Hon. Mrs E. Lascelles – how would E. B. Noel have described her game?

THE QUEEN'S CLUB STORY
1919–1939

THE Club, having come out of the war relatively unscathed – a few thousand pounds worth of war damage was claimed and received – soon faced a crucial decision. Was it to remain a multi-sports complex open to a host of visiting organizations or was it to become a members club predominantly given over to court games? Boiled down this meant a tussle between the field sports such as rugby, soccer and athletics and the court games, the most popular of which was lawn tennis.

E. B. Noel, thoroughly established as a most popular and successful secretary, wrote that 'with 1500 members the interests of the Club are very diversified. Some members are chiefly interested in the great football and athletic events which take place at the Club; some in billiards; some in tennis (real) and so on. But there is no question that by far the majority are interested in lawn tennis.'

This had not always been the case. Freddie Wilson of *The Times* wrote in his 'Sporting Pie' that early on in the Club's history there was a certain amount of bickering between the lawn tennis players and the rackets and real tennis fraternity: 'The tennis and rackets players pretend that they play lawn tennis because it is a nice slack way of getting out in the sun and having a rag. This annoys the lawn tennis players immensely.'

With the arrival of Suzanne Lenglen at Wimbledon and later Bill Tilden, who made his first appearance at Queen's in 1920, the popularity of 'lawners' soared. It became very much the in-game. With the members it has remained the No. 1 sport ever since and today, one hundred years after the foundation of the Club, it is thriving as never before. So too, for that matter, are rackets and real tennis.

In order to put the case for court games against field sports into perspective it is necessary to go back to the Club's beginnings and its *raison d'etre*.

Lawn Tennis or Football – The Crisis?

In the beginning Queen's enhanced its reputation and derived a considerable part of its income from football of both codes and the Oxford and Cambridge athletic meeting. These University contests, rugby, soccer and athletics, each made more money than the Covered Court Championships. Financially real tennis and rackets meant very little, a few guineas profit here and there.

In the early part of this century the Club, ever watchful of its finances which were rarely better than precarious, became conscious of the amount of football of both codes being played on its grounds and the financial returns. The Earl of Clarendon, then chairman of the Club, reported that of the matches played in January 1904 only the Corinthians *v* Southampton showed a reasonable profit while two rugby matches played by the London Welsh, who used the ground a good deal in those years, produced only two shillings profit. It was a shade better in February and March when the Oxford and Cambridge soccer match made £103 (£149 in 1905 and £386 in 1909), the Corinthians *v* Notts County £36 and the Old Carthusians *v* Old Rossallians £33.

Too Much Football

The number and diversity of football clubs of both codes that used the grounds was considerable. The Army and Navy rugby match was played there; so were Hospital Cup ties and the Arthur Dunn Cup matches at soccer. Great rugby clubs like Newport,

Bristol and Gloucester visited Queen's. Oxford and Cambridge played matches under both codes in addition to their own annual battles. Some were profitable, most were not.

In 1909 and 1910 the Army and Navy rugby match receipts were £195 and £305 respectively. Not quite as fruitful as the University rugby match or athletics meeting. The Sports took £800 in 1909 and £946 the following year. But an England v Ireland hockey international (yet another game played at Queen's) made a divisable balance of £58 of which the Club benefited by £19.10s.6d! And six soccer matches played by Oxford and Cambridge against such sides as the Old Carthusians and Old Malvernians realized

only £12.10s.0d.

The growing popularity, or rather explosion, of lawn tennis just after the Great War forced the Club to examine its purpose and ethos. The conclusion it came to was that its green acres could be better (and more profitably?) used by the growing band of lawn tennis players and that its members would be best served by having more and improved grass courts, even if this were to mean the sacrifice of football pitches.

An analysis of the gross income derived from the Grass Court Championships, The University Sports and the multitude of football matches from 1919 to 1921 revealed the following:

'A most popular and successful secretary' – E. B. Noel

1919 – Grass Court Championships £345; University rugby match £400; University Soccer match £173; University Sports £451.

1920 – Grass Court Championships £455; University Rugby match £423; University Soccer match £129; University Sports £412.

Against these figures twenty-six other assorted football matches played in the 1919–20 season grossed £216 and the same number in the following season produced only £178. In 1921–22 only seven other matches were played grossing £20. Queen's had almost become a benevolent society for wandering football Clubs since the cost of labour and ground upkeep was at least £300 p.a.

At the same time it was realized on both sides that the University rugby match was becoming increasingly popular and had already largely outstripped the Club's capacity. The universities wanted more and better facilities and the Club was unwilling to provide them. On 5 October 1921 the Directors of The Queen's Club and the Committees of the Oxford and Cambridge Rugby Football Clubs met to discuss the arrangements for the forthcoming University match. After the meeting they issued the following statement: 'The Directors, having in mind the many athletic activities of the Club, other than Rugby football, for which they have to provide equally, explained that they were unable to offer the very largely increased covered stand accommodation for spectators which the University representatives considered essential. In these circumstances it was mutually and reluctantly decided that the match must be played elsewhere.' It was signed by, among others, Major A. Cooper Key, chairman of The Queen's Club, R. Cove-Smith, Cambridge University captain, and E. Campbell, Oxford University captain. Cooper-Key (later Sir Aston) had taken over the chairmanship from G. E. A. Ross in 1919.

The University soccer match followed the rugby men's lead; they departed to Chelsea, the rugby to Twickenham, the latter in a hurry as they had less than two months to make the switch. That left the Corinthians, for whom few of the pre-war giants were available; some like F. N. S. Creek were still at university and others like Max Woosnam and A. E. Knight were playing for professional clubs. Moreover with the extension of the leagues and the number of clubs involved Corinthian showpieces against leading professional clubs on Saturdays were

impossible and that, of course, meant loss of gates and, in the case of The Queen's Club, revenue.

The Corinthians wanted to stay at Queen's but under their own terms, which meant that the Club would virtually lose control of its own grounds. The Corinthians wanted sole use of the grounds with the right to sub-let for any match or event they chose including the University Sports, a regular money-maker. For this the Corinthians were prepared to pay £1000 a year plus a percentage of their profits. A memorandum was prepared, whether by E. B. Noel, the Club secretary, or the business manager is not clear, and sent to Major Cooper Key to be considered by the full board. It made some valid points:

1 We must realize that if we allow the Corinthians to take over the ground we are jeopardizing the Sports because the Corinthians *might* insist upon too onerous terms and lose the event.

2 The Corinthians may be a very fine team but there are no amateur teams who will be able to give them a good enough game to justify a substantial 'gate'.

3. With the heavy programme now undertaken by professional clubs I do not think they are likely to get many matches against professional teams apart from the possibility of a lucky draw in the English Cup. I therefore do not think we can count on the percentage of profits as being anything tangible.

4 A far bigger question is posed by the fact that 1000 out of the 1200 members of the Club belong to it mainly for the lawn tennis. The subscription income from these members is probably £8000 a year. The subscription rate has recently been increased and I know that the great majority of members are looking for substantially increased facilities.

5 If football is played, as it would be by the Corinthians from October to April, lawn tennis on the same ground is an utter impossibility. That leaves the Club with just ten grass courts. And who will want to pay 10 guineas a year for the privilege of using a court (for an hour-and-a-half) once a week or even less?

6 I believe, if we added twelve first class courts, Queen's would become the Mecca of lawn tennis in London (Wimbledon is too far out for ordinary purposes) and that we would get a further 200 members at the ten guineas subscription.

I feel that the decision that now has to be made is of such far-reaching importance that it should not be made without a reference to the Members of the Club at a General Meeting. Personally, I have little doubt that their verdict would be almost unanimously in favour of lawn tennis.

A landscape painting of the entrance to the Club. The grandstand gave way to the Lawn Tennis Association's head office

ADIEU CORINTH

The case for lawn tennis vis-à-vis field sports was won. The Corinthians found a new home at the Crystal Palace and, for a few years, new glories. The University Sports meeting and the activities of the Achilles Club which did not interfere with lawn tennis remained with the Club until 1928. The only recorded complaint came eight years later from A. K. H. Neale, who beefed that in days past one could see first-class football and athletics at the Club and 'now what does one get for one's sub other than the right to enter the Club?'

Shortly after the agreement with the Corinthians, in the autumn of 1921, Noel fell ill and was unable to work. He was not a robust man and his weak health may have persuaded the Club, a couple of years later, to appoint Vice-Admiral Sykes CMG as manager. That meant looking after the business side of the Club. Sykes had served in German East Africa during the war and commanded HMS *Challenger* at Dar-es-Salaam. His stay at the Club was brief and within a year he had resigned. The reason could well have been an incident concerning the Prince of Wales (Duke of Windsor).

The Prince used to come regularly to the Club for a game of squash with Charles Read, one of the professionals and a champion player at court games other than real tennis. There had been a spate of pilfering at the Club and the Admiral had posted a notice telling members not to leave their coats outside the courts. The Prince either did not see or disregarded the notice and was playing with Read when the manager Sykes, passing by the court, observed a coat hanging outside it. He burst in prepared to deliver a rocket and may well have done so for the Prince never again came to Queen's. If I recall correctly he repaired to the Bath Club and played with Charles Arnold.

That, however, certainly did not break the Club's connection with Royalty, which from the outset had always been strong. The Duke of York (King George VI) continued to play lawn tennis there and in 1936 King George V, a frequent visitor when Prince of Wales, became the Club's Patron following the tradition set by Queen Victoria.

Vice-Admiral Sykes was succeeded as business manager by W. J. Wood and eventually this post appears to have lapsed. A Mr Pott seems meanwhile to have been the most important link in the clerical chain, joining the Club as bookkeeper and minute writer in 1900 and remaining in office for fifty years.

WAR SERVICE

En-Tout-Cas, who had serviced the hard courts even during the war, laid down three more at a cost of about £700 early in the twenties. During the winter of 1922–3 twelve grass courts replaced what had previously been the football pitch to bring the total number of outside courts to thirty grass and eleven hard.

The Club gave a lunch in May 1923 to celebrate the opening of these new courts, each one of which was self-contained with a good background. Walter C. Bersey, a member of the Club committee, keen player and wealthy businessman, presided. Among those at the lunch were Mrs Lambert Chambers, seven times Wimbledon champion, Mrs A. E. Beamish, M. J. G. Ritchie, still merrily competing, F. R. Burrow, the referee, and an assortment of players and/or writers such as Stanley Doust (*Daily Mail*), A. Wallis Myers (*Daily Telegraph*), H. R. McDonald (*Evening News*), F. B. Wilson (*The Times*), S. Powell Blackmore and H. V. Dorey (*Lawn Tennis & Badminton*).

Walter Bersey announced that at the forthcoming Grass Court Championships the doubles would be played on the American system, in groups of six pairs. The idea was not universally popular, nor did it last long. But the Club was shrewd enough to offer some inducement to competitors as the following letter, signed by 'Glutton' and appearing in *Lawn Tennis & Badminton*, shows:

It is a pleasure after hearing continually from so many people what little value they consider they derive from their entry fees at various meetings to put on record the splendid value accorded to entrants at the last Queen's tournament. The 'free teas' gave many competitors that glorious 'something for nothing feeling'. There were certainly enough cakes and some to spare to admit of a cake-eating event on the knock-out principle. The American doubles event was in every way delightful. The courts were in excellent condition and no less a personage than Vincent Richards acclaimed them as much better than those in the States.

To anyone familiar with grass courts in the US that would not be difficult to believe but it spoke well of Jim O'Leary who had succeeded Wilson as head groundsman. O'Leary, a man of character and considerable beer-drinking capacity, had joined the Club just before the war and remained with it full-time until 1960; almost as long-serving a member of the staff as Mr Pott the bookkeeper.

The American invasion at the Grass Courts meeting and the French at the Covered Courts had already begun. Tilden and 'Little Bill' Johnston competed in the Grass Courts in 1920, Vincent Richards, Frank Hunter and Elizabeth Ryan appeared in 1923. The Frenchman André Gobert stormed through the Covered Courts for three years, 1920–2, depriving the Englishman P. M. Davson of his title in 1920. Davson and his brother A.M. were the architects of the two new covered courts built in 1925 for just over £9000.

Despite the new names, the fresh kings and queens of the courts, many of the old favourites, M. J. G. Ritchie among them, who had supported the Club's major tournament for years, continued to play. They were immortalized by an unknown writer who produced this piece of doggerel that appeared in *Lawn Tennis & Badminton*:

I met a young fellow named Doust,
Whom I tried in a single to oust.
   I would have played better
   Relieved of my sweater
And freed from superfluous frowst.

I played a young sportsman named Wheatley,
Whose service deceived me completely;
   My game was too staid
   And I felt that I played
Anciently and obsoletely.

I met that young veteran Ritchie
On a day that was dull, dark and pitchy;
   But I'm far too stout
   For running about,
And my tummy was painful and 'stitchy.'

I played a young fellow named Higgs,
But my game wasn't fit for the pigs;
   I was thoroughly beat,
   He was good with his feet,
While *I* was all for trots and jigs.

At Hendon I met Gordon Lowe
And said, 'My boy! Gadzooks! What!'
   He gave me the shove,
   Six-love, six-love,
I was 'napoo' that's Scotch for 'no go'.

Next I met C. Ramaswami,
Who was so collected and calm, he
   Killed me quite nicely,
   Clean and precisely . . .
In Heaven it's beautifully balmy.

I ran into Mavrogordato,
Who crushed me just like a tomato;
   It really was thick,
   His game was too quick,
While mine was all 'tempo rubato.'

I met a young Frenchman named Cochet,
But my game was too feeble and washy,
   And when it was over
   He sailed back from Dover . . .
Now I'm taking up knitting and crochet.

I played against A. Wallis Myers
And tried to manipulate skiers;
   They led me off sobbing,
   Killed by his lobbing,
And said I was one of the triers.

I met Crawford, whose prefix is Leighton,
And found him as cunning as Satan;
   I entirely forgot
   He is stuff that is hot,
And a single's the game he is great on.

I played v. that demon Asthalter,
But never for once did I falter;
   I was cut up and hashed,
   Like sausage and mashed,
And now I sing psalms from a psalter.

Downstairs

The war had little effect on the Club membership, which stood at 1500. The number of titled gentry may have declined but members still came from the leisured classes. Trade was not encouraged. Nor, it seems, were women as, in 1920, the female membership, limited to seventy-five, was increased by a meagre ten with subscriptions at five guineas, whereas the men paid ten. Nevertheless this was better than the All England Club who had yet to admit women and then restricted the number to seventy-five. Not until 1928, some forty years after the Club's foundation, did women really come into their own when three hundred were admitted as full members exclusive of honorary, courtesy and diplomatic.

MORE PROS NEEDED

Lawn tennis was a class game and remained so for many years. With the Club now largely devoted to it, and with the extra number of courts, came the need for an enlarged professional staff. The original lawn tennis professionals, like those at rackets and real tennis, came from the old Prince's Club. André, whose nephew followed him to Queen's, was one. Tom Fleming, who became the equivalent of head professional, was another. His father had been head professional at the old Hyde Park Club where the Covered Court Championships began. When Fleming left he was succeeded by Charles Heirons, the best-known and longest-serving head pro of any. He celebrated his fortieth year at the Club in 1932.

Noel thought highly of Heirons – 'a fine player and most delightful stylist, the best and most patient of teachers. He looks after the management of the lawn tennis department with much skill and tact.' His wage in 1916 was five shillings a week!

Charles Read came to Queen's from Harrow in 1906 as head rackets professional, replacing Walter Hawes who went to Wellington. Read was still at the Club thirty years later having been professional champion at lawn tennis, rackets and squash. Read's early contemporaries included Henry Cowdrey, an expert half-volleyer, Lockyer, William Seymour and Haggett, son of an early head groundsman. In between the wars there was a whole host of lawn tennis pros: Tom Jeffrey, who went to the Melbury Club, Tom Jones, formerly one of the Club's waiters, Fred Poulson, Joe Pearce, Bill Young, Bill-Holmes, Ernie Lowe and Bill Dear, brother of Jim, among them.

Peter Latham had returned to the Club just before the war and was made an honorary member just after it. He continued to teach real tennis and was joined in 1923 by Charles Williams, former World rackets champion from Harrow, and Ernest Ratcliff from Manchester. Arthur Ashford, father of Peter who was at the Club after the Second World War before moving to Winchester, was another member of the rackets-real tennis staff; Albert Cooper, the 1934 open rackets champion, joined in the mid-twenties and Jim Dear, later world champion at rackets and real tennis, some years later.

There were so many professionals at Queen's shortly after the Great War that new changing rooms had to be built in what is now the Cottage occupied by Reg and Barbara Routledge. The great majority of the professionals began their careers as ball-boys and, among that post-First World War generation were Henry Johns, briefly at Queen's before going to Prince's and later becoming the master-teacher at Lord's, and Dan Maskell. When Maskell was fourteen-and-a-half the question arose as to whether he should leave school or go on to Latymer Upper. During the holidays he had ball-boyed at Queen's and shown interest in learning about the games, especially lawn tennis.

LOTS OF BALL-BOYS

There were some thirty full-time ball-boys at the Club during the summer, twenty in the winter. Maskell and Johns differ as to what they got paid; the former saying ten shillings a week and just over fivepence a court, the latter halving that amount. At the end of each summer Charles Heirons would pick out the boys most likely to make teaching professionals.

In the summer the days were long, play starting on the hard courts at eight in the morning and finishing on the grass, which opened at two o'clock, after eight in the evening. In the winter the ball-boys were on duty just after seven to sweep out the covered courts, which were increased from three to five in 1925 when lighting was first installed.

There was a room adjoining the courts in which were kept the brooms, brushes, buckets and sawdust used for sweeping them. It was a ritual that when anyone became a full-time ball-boy he was thrown in the sawdust like the stable boys at Newmarket are thrown into the manure. The head ball-boy was called the book-boy because he had to record details of the work the boys did; time, court number, member's name and so on.

The staff assembled, late 1920s

THE QUEEN'S CLUB

DETAIL OF DUTIES OF GROUND STAFF.

Head Groundsman- J. O'LEARY.
Second Groundsman- F. S. KEEN.
Groundsmen- A. JEFFEREYS, J. STIMSOM,
A DOWDEN

(1)   The Head Groundsman will be in charge of all groundsmen under him, including extra hands taken on from time to time for work on the ground. His duties under the Secretary will be -

(2)   To keep a book at the Gate in which each man of the Ground Staff will enter his name and the time on arrival each morning.

(3)   To draw up Daily and Weekly scheme of work for his staff and submit it to the Secretary daily.

(4)   To bring to the notice of the Secretary, all matters connected with the ground, or any slackness on the part of his groundsmen.

(5)   To report to the Secretary his requirements in mould, fertilizer, seed, manure, worm killer, tools, petrol, oil, etc., or any extra labour required for indent through the Manager.

(6)   To keep the grass and hard courts in first class condition for play during their seasons, and be responsible during the grass court season for the erection of the screens and netting.

(7)   To perform all minor repairs to netting, screens, posts, gates, tools, machines, etc., to keep them in good condition and see that all gear not actually in use, is properly stored and kept in serviceable condition.

(8)   To put courts out of play in regular rotation for watering, rolling, etc., informing the Bureau staff each morning. He will report via the Secretary to the Bureau, when he considers courts are not playable.

(9)   To keep in order the hedges, borders, paths, flower beds and allotments.

(10)   To erect spectators' stands as required before Tournaments, and put out seats, umpires' chairs, name boards, etc.

(11)   To keep the Hard Lawn Tennis Courts in good condition for play, and put up nets and keep netting in good repair.

May, 1931.

'Queen's Staff Race', 1930

Lunch and tea provided by the Club were regarded as part of the wages and Maskell recalled how they supplemented their rations. 'Near the Club there was a high-class baker's shop and confectioners, Gerrards. The area was a middle-class dormitory. When I had become book-boy I heard that they sold off stale cakes. Most of us came from poor families without too much to eat. I went to Gerrards, told them who we were – most people in the area recognized Queen's ball-boys because of our red jerseys – and made an arrangement to pay so much a day to buy up the cakes. Six days a week one of us would go up to Gerrards and collect the cakes left over from the day before. It cost us very little. When Charles Heirons heard about it he said "Well done, young fellow".'

It was part of the boys' apprenticeship to learn line-judging and umpiring and the best of them were used in the early rounds of the various tournaments. They had also to help mark out the courts but were

Left Ground staff duties, 1931

not allowed to play on them. Most began playing by knocking-up on the old skating rink (on which covered courts 4 and 5 were built) with wooden bats. Maskell managed to acquire an old real tennis racket which he strung with rackets gut. That became the fashion among the ball-boys. Maskell bought his first proper racket for a shilling from Jack Jenkins, the head dressing room attendant. It was a second-hand SND – the initials of Stanley Doust. Jenkins had an eye for young talent, and saw it in Maskell. Some years later he also encouraged Fred Perry when both were living in Ealing.

The Maharanee of Baroda presented the Club with a Cup to be played for by the ball-boys. Maskell won it from owe-30, was promoted to assistant professional and was asked to play with the Maharanee. 'She arrived in a Rolls-Royce with a couple of bodyguards or attendants. She would only play on Court 3 because it was on its own and could be closed. The attendants were posted in opposite corners of the court. She played in a sari and must have been about seventy. But as long as I hit the ball within two or three yards of her she was all right. She must have been a useful player when younger.'

The Inter-Services Lawn Tennis Championships 1920: Front Row (seated) left to right: Instructor-Captain Card, Group-Captain Ludlow-Hewitt, Paymaster-Lieut-Commander Bell, Major A. R. F. Kingscote, H.R.H. The Duke of York, Commander H. G. D. Stoker, Instructor-Commander Holt. Back Row (standing) left to right: Mr S. A. E. Hickson, Captain J. L. Ritchie, Lieut. T. Bevan, Squadron-Leader Hunter, Squadron-Leader Young, Major Dudley, Wing-Commander Louis Greig, Squadron-Leader Saul, Flying-Officer Gilbert, Paymaster-Lieut. Worthington, Mr Fraser

DUKE'S COURT

No. 3 court, because it was on its own, was popular. The Duke of York and Louis (later Sir Louis) Greig, an RAF surgeon and future chairman of the All England Club, used to practise on it against Heirons and Read. The Duke and Greig competed in the RAF Championships and, in 1926, played at Wimbledon where they were comprehensively beaten by A. W. Gore and H. Roper Barrett, a pair of real veterans.

Maskell ball-boyed for them at Queen's and said of the Duke's game: 'He was a left-hander who had a useful top-spin forehand but no backhand. His first serve was quite useful but his second poor. His best shot was a shoulder-high volley.' As an assistant professional Maskell moved into the professionals' room which, as distinct from their changing rooms in the Cottage, was where the Press room and Miss Rosemary Jones' office now are. As the junior to Heirons, Read, Jack Jeffrey, Charles Williams and others he had to collect their meals – 'Members were upstairs, we were downstairs. There was definitely class distinction, though the members were friendly.'

However illustrious the professionals were, none was allowed into the lounge, bar or dressing rooms. That is, except Peter Latham, whom Noel had made an honorary member shortly after the war. 'You played with someone, maybe a Lord as we had quite a few in those days, and he said "Have a drink" and we all had to stand outside the bar. We accepted it as normal in those days,' said Maskell, who added, 'I must say I found things very different when I went to Wimbledon.' Those days may appear feudal but there are undoubtedly some members today who think the pendulum has swung too far the other way.

Having established himself as a teaching professional, Maskell then took the professional title off Charles Read. In the semi-final Maskell played F. W. Donisthorpe, a former Wimbledon player who had invented the large-headed racket – the prototype of the modern Prince. The patents for 'the Donisthorpe' racket are today in the Wimbledon Museum.

As it was raining Maskell and Read played on the east covered court. 'There was a huge crowd. I'd never seen anything like it – people with their legs dangling over the side of the gallery. I won three sets to love and Jack Jeffrey, one of the other pros who later became head dressing-room attendant, told me I'd killed twenty-nine of Read's thirty-one lobs.' As champion, a fact noted by the LTA and AELTC, Maskell was much in demand. 'I found it embarrassing as a lot of people would only play with me and I was doing six and seven hours a day whereas some of the other pros were only doing three or four.'

EARLY BIRD

One of Maskell's regulars was Sir Samuel Hoare, a distinguished Foreign Secretary who later became Lord Templewood and president of the LTA. 'He liked to play early in the day before going to the House of Commons. Sometimes he would arrive in a small car, like an Austin Seven; sometimes in a Rolls-Royce – either one chauffeur-driven. His first remark was always, "Is the court ready, Maskell?" Invariably it was. He always had two ball-boys and insisted on new balls. We would begin on the dot of eight o'clock and never knocked-up. At the end of forty-five minutes and whatever the score, we stopped. Occasionally when he was especially busy at the House he would ask me to give his secretary a ring the day before. Nevertheless I always had a court booked for him on Wednesdays and Fridays – his regular days. He was a nice stylist with neat strokes. He was also, by the way, an expert skater.'

Ben Levy, the playwright, was another of Maskell's regulars and he used to complain, 'You're damned expensive to play with, young Maskell. I never feel I can play with you with a box of balls that have already been used. So I always have to buy new ones.' Another regular was Lord Charles Hope, who was a line-judge at the famous match between Suzanne Lenglen and Helen Wills in Cannes in 1926. He was a more than useful player until he developed tennis elbow so badly that he learned to play left-handed, like another Queen's Club stalwart and squash player, Frank Strawson, who damaged his right arm. In Lord Charles' côterie of players was the young Lord Rothermere (Esmond), proprietor of the *Daily Mail*.

Maskell was still learning his trade when the Americans, Vincent Richards and Frank Hunter, competed in the 1923 Grass Court Championships. Noel deputed him to 'look out for a chubby-faced young man wearing a corrugated straw hat [the fashion of the time] and carry his bag. That will be Richards.' Richards, a Tilden protégé, was hailed as the coming player, an accomplished volleyer. He duly came through to the final. The experienced Hunter, expected to win the title, was beaten by the Anglo-Indian, S. M. Jacob, a slow court specialist.

The Richards-Jacob final caught the public imagination and the Club had some difficulty in controlling the crowd, who tried to make an extra stand out of the garden seats around the hard courts. Richards won easily enough but Maskell, having already become interested in technique, recalled noticing how long his racket work was. 'He used to swing his racket round in a circle and volley from well back in the court. That would not do today.' The following day, Richards played an exhibition against another American, 'Little Bill' Johnston. 'Here was a man, Johnston, with a western grip like Borg which everyone said could never win matches on grass because the ball didn't bounce high enough. But he won Wimbledon.'

Lawn tennis was not the only game at which Maskell excelled and while the LTA and Wimbledon had their eyes on him for that game, others saw him as a rackets player.

In 1920 the Club had agreed to surrender the control of the real Tennis and Rackets Championships to the Tennis and Rackets Association. This, as Noel pointed out in his letter (of 25 November, 1920) to Henry Leaf, was 'purely as an act of grace and without prejudice to the rights of Queen's Club in the matter'. Those rights were exercised in 1925 when the Club, sensing the rise of squash, converted the No. 2 Rackets court into two squash courts.

SHORT SUPPLY

However, in those early days after the war it was soon realized that there was a dearth of young rackets professionals capable of becoming the successors to such men as Ernest Jones at Eton, the Crosby family at Harrow and Winchester, 'Stu' Green, a former Queen's Club ball-boy now at Malvern and, of course, Charles Williams, the champion. The Tennis and Rackets Association organized a junior professional championship and Maskell won it, beating Bill Dear, Jim Dear's elder brother, in the semi-final, and Albert Cooper, then at Wellington, 3–0 in the final.

Freddie Wilson wrote that Maskell had a great future as a rackets player. Maskell, however, was adamant – 'I enjoyed rackets whether playing or marking but was fonder of lawn tennis. One of my most vivid memories is marking a match in which J. C. F. Simpson played R. C. O. Williams. Simpson was a tremendous hitter, nearly as fierce as Charlie Williams. They used 273 balls. At threepence a time, too!' In June 1929 Maskell joined the All England LTC, Wimbledon, as their professional.

On Court

This inter-war period saw the Club not only transformed from a multi-sports complex to the country's leading court games centre but also actively participate in the growing popularity of a relatively new game, squash rackets. Now it is universal. The Club's first two squash courts were built in 1905, alongside the No. 3 covered court, before a standard size had been established. They were longer and narrower, more like the American version, than are today's courts.

The first major event to be played at the Club was the Ladies' Championship inaugurated in 1922 and remaining there until the last war. In the early years it was dominated by the Cave sisters, Joyce and Nancy, and Cicely Fenwick, all of whom came from families possessing private courts. Then along came two champions who were Club members, Susan Noel, daughter of the Club secretary E. B. Noel and thus brought up on the premises, and Margot Lumb. Both were also lawn tennis internationals. They won eight championships and turned women's squash into a skilful and athletic game. Miss Noel, by the way, played her first match for the club at the age of thirteen – against the men!

The Club also produced two mens champions during these years: Dugald Macpherson and Kenneth Gandar Dower, both Harrovians like so many involved in The Queen's Club story, and versa-tile games players. At the same time the Club professional was Charles Read, for many years undisputedly the best player in the land. Macpherson, who also won the Amateur Real Tennis title in 1938, the same year that Gandar Dower took the squash championship, was a talented, artistic player of no great physical strength. He played games for fun and deplores the modern trend of more and more competition backed up by commerce and sponsorship. He had a wonderful squash record for Queen's, leading the team to four Bath Club Cup victories, playing between eighty and ninety matches with only four defeats and beating, among others, Amr Bey, the 'king' of the game in the thirties.

STRANGE COMPANIONS

Gandar Dower was one of those versatile and somewhat eccentric characters whose talents were spread in all directions. He travelled, wrote at least two books – *The Spotted Lion* (1937) and *Outside Britain* (1938) – and at one time kept a pair of cheetahs which he raced at the White City and once brought into the bar at Queen's. 'The Gandar' and George McConnell, a Harrow housemaster, won the Kinnaird Trophy at Eton Fives but Gandar Dower was almost impossible to follow in the doubles game at that or Rugby Fives, at which he also excelled. In 1938 he played Don Budge at Wimbledon on the Centre Court and the story goes that while at Cambridge he played in a cricket trial and lawn tennis trial at the same time, skipping over the fence at Fenners from one game to the other.

Peter Latham, the first man to win the world title at rackets and real tennis and in partial retirement though still at the Club at this time, and Edgar Baerlein, amateur champion at real tennis and rackets many, many times, must take pride of place as the two greatest players of these specialized games the Club had so far seen. Latham still gave lessons to those whom he thought worth it – Jim Dear was one – and 'The Stroke' had become so ingrained on his mind that Freddie Wilson recalled seeing him walk down the street, stop, hold his stick as a racket, stoop and play two or three theoretical strokes. He was still watching both games after the Second World War.

Wilson described Baerlein as 'the supreme amateur'. James Agate, the theatre critic, asserted that he had 'the grace of a Driscoll, the strength of a Ledoux'. Others knew him as 'the Little Man' and

Hubert Winterbotham, the *Daily Telegraph* correspondent, used to tell the story of a car ride through the deserted streets of Manchester one Sunday morning. 'He was driving at break-neck speed when a small boy suddenly appeared on the curb ready to cross the road. Baerlein did not slow down and when I suggested he might have run the boy down he replied, "Impossible. He was on the wrong foot".'

Baerlein, fifty-one when he won the Open Real Tennis title for the last time, had few rivals. The Hon. C. N. Bruce (later Lord Aberdare) whom I first saw on the cricket field – a most attractive batsman and immaculate cover point – was one at both games. His greatest rackets successes came in doubles and he won the Amateur Championship ten times with four different partners. Charles Williams, taught by Latham, was another such rival. He used to give Cyril Simpson and R. C. O. Williams five and beat them but did not bother much with doubles. Walter Hawes once said, 'He would stand in the middle of the court and shout "Yours".' He became professional at the Chicago Racquets Club in 1923.

Freddie Wilson wrote of Simpson, 'Though slight and apparently fragile, Cyril Simpson owing to a wonderful wrist and perfect timing hit harder than any player except Charles Williams.' He was also eccentric, once arriving for a match at Queen's wearing his pyjamas.

In the thirties Lowther Lees from Manchester, a notable game shot, dominated the real tennis and David Milford, a Rugbeian and a master at Marlborough, the rackets, culminating in his win over Albert Cooper, the senior rackets professional at Queen's, for the Open rackets title in 1936 and the world title the following year over Norbert Setzler of New York. Milford, like Gandar Dower, was one of those gifted games players to whom sports came naturally – an international hockey player, minor counties cricketer, county lawn tennis player. I played cricket against him once and when C. D. Williams, an Oxford rugby player, hit him out of the ground three times running he walked off the field in disgust – at his own bowling!

Lawn tennis also produced great players, personalities and events. In 1920 the London Covered Court Championships, junior in age and prestige to *the* Covered Court Championships, was elevated for one year to the grandiose title of the World Championships by the International Federation. The entry was largely a domestic one, F. G. Lowe and Mrs A. E. Beamish winning the singles, the latter beating Miss Kitty McKane, who later won Wimbledon in 1924 and 1926.

AUSTIN TO THE RESCUE

Then, in 1930, there was that exciting Davis Cup match, accompanied by a zeppelin, in which Britain beat Germany after being down two-love on the first day. On the last Bunny Austin beat Dan Prenn, who later came to live and work in this country and in the 1980s saw one of his sons, John, win the world rackets title. Three years later Australia and South Africa met in the Davis Cup for the first time and the former, up two-love after the first day, won in the deciding rubber when Jack Crawford beat C. J. Robbins in three sets. Three weeks later Crawford, unable to defend his London Grass Court title because of that tie, won Wimbledon.

Crawford was only one of a line of Wimbledon champions who played at the Club between the wars. Others were 'Little Bill' Johnston, Bill Tilden, Ellsworth Vines, Don Budge, Bobby Riggs, Helen Wills-Moody and the man who made a greater impact than anyone else on the game at Queen's – Jean Borotra. Between 1926 and 1938 Borotra won the Covered Courts title nine times. He was beaten only three times. Moreover, playing for the IC of France against the IC of GB from 1929 to 1938, at Queen's, Borotra lost only three matches, all to Bunny Austin. He carried on after the war and was fifty-one when last he won the Covered Courts title in 1949. And he was over eighty when he played in the last match between the Clubs contested at Queen's in 1980. His deeds are recalled elsewhere in this story.

Off Court

The death of E. B. Noel in December 1928 was a sad blow. He was a much-loved man, a splendid games player and sportsman, a scholarly sort who never enjoyed robust health. He was forty-nine and suffering from tuberculosis. In his early days, after Winchester and Cambridge (for which he played rackets and real tennis), being director of the sporting department of *The Times* he was told by his doctor that night work was bad for his health. Thus he became secretary to The Queen's Club and the prosperity and popularity of the Club owed much to him.

The Times paid him this tribute – 'Noel was a man of great personal charm loved by all who knew him and, at the same time, he was a dour fighter. He fought for many years against ill-health and seemed again and again to have overcome that enemy. He was also a great fighter at the many games at which he excelled especially tennis (real) and rackets. There was nothing personal about his duels. Another of his individualities was that he was completely ambidextrous. He batted, bowled and threw at cricket with his right arm but played rackets and tennis with his left.

'In appearance he was a definite character. Tall, round-shouldered and thin he looked as little like a fighter at physically testing games as could be imagined. His face was finely drawn and his eyes set back in his head so that he looked at one rather like a wise old owl. He always appeared negligent of his clothes and was devoted to an old overcoat which he had outgrown many years ago and the sleeves of which finished half way up his forearms. He looked, and indeed was, different from other people.

'He was kind and amusing and very good company but behind it all he had a very definite idea of what he wanted as he showed by the way he controlled Queen's and the various great tournaments that were held there. He had a fine understanding of the weaknesses and failings of others and was an exceptionally good handler of men – and women – as the manager of any great club has to be.'

GREAT AUTHORITY

There were many other tributes in the Press and Lord Aberdare wrote, 'Noel's Gold Medal (won at the 1908 Olympic Games for rackets) should more deservedly have been awarded to him for his services to tennis and rackets as an historian – and Queen's Club secretary.' 'Nolly's' great friend, Freddie Wilson who, I imagine, was responsible for *The Times* obituary, considered him the greatest authority on real tennis in the world. And that was before Noel and L. O. M. Clark produced their classic two-volume work *The History of Tennis*.

Nolly's two children, Susan and Gerrard, were made life members of the Club. Susan had already shown her talent for courts games by reaching the final of the schoolgirls' championships, held at Queen's, the year he died. She later won the title, played for many years at Wimbledon, and was an outstanding ladies' squash champion. Gerrard, killed in the Second World War, played in the Amateur Squash Championships.

Noel was succeeded as Club secretary by Lt Col. G. E. Bruce MC, a retired Indian Army officer who, unlike his predecessor, was not a games player of note or quite as sociable a character. He played the occasional game of real tennis but took no special interest in lawn tennis, by then the Club's predominate game. I recall Eyre Bruce as a quiet gentlemanly figure, greying and with a military moustache – I saw many similar types in India during the war – but no great personality. I should add that my first wife, the late Alex McOstrich, a contemporary of Susan Noel, liked and respected him.

Bruce's arrival coincided with Lord Aberdare's long reign as chairman (1930–1954), the world depression and the Club's financial problems, which haunted him throughout his ten years in office. The Colonel instituted a complaints book which mentions some of the Club's characters and provides some amusing reading. The women, though outnumbered heavily, were more vociferous than the men. Miss G. E. Tomblin, Mrs Violet Cobb and Mrs Bengough were the leading complainees and the subjects were diverse. Miss Tomblin, a modest tournament player, wanted ladies' doubles included in the Covered Court Championships. They were in 1935. Then she and Mrs Cobb wanted a practice wall. That was not forthcoming for a good many years as some time later Mrs Bengough added her voice to the request. She claimed that she was unable to use the rackets court after lunch at weekends as it was occupied by young members. It is surprising that anybody was ever allowed to use the rackets court for lawn tennis practice.

The women's changing room, presided over by the motherly Mrs Tutt and Mrs Tarrant, was a frequent topic. Joan Ridley, the 1930 Covered Court Champion, and Mrs Cobb wanted an iron and ironing board in there. They were supported by a man, John Olliff! Others claimed the dressing room was overcrowded, lacking mirrors over the basins and even that it smelt. Miss Tomblin eventually left the Club. The imposition of a sixpenny charge for a bath – men and women – provoked much comment and criticism and, it was suggested, some members even avoided taking baths. That may have been responsible for the smell complained of, and Ted Avory commented that such a charge 'should not encourage members to go unwashed'.

MISSING PAPERS

The frequent disappearance of the Club's newspapers was a constant source of irritation – 'unheard-of behaviour' claimed Eric Peters – and Mrs Bengough became a self-appointed custodian. Once she said she saw a lady member borrow *The Times* from another, stuff it into her fur coat pocket and leave the Club. Mrs Bengough, blonde and liberally made-up, was one of the Club's characters. She positioned herself in the lounge so that she had the maximum view of what went on there and outside the windows. It was impossible to pass into the cafeteria without being detained for some considerable time. Consequently some members sought a long way round, through the Bridge room in which occasional committee meetings were held. It was thought better to incur the wrath of a committee of eighteen rather than be trapped by the lady. She never ceased to complain about this and that, no doubt in good faith, and when finally she departed this world in the sixties there seemed a void in the life of the Club.

Curiously, when it came to food, it was the men who did most of the complaining. H. T. Mills wanted cakes *not* containing almonds which he found 'disagreeable to some tastes'. H. A. Milne and others wanted hot toasted scones served with tea – 'served really hot and well-buttered. In a covered dish'. Eric Peters thought that the quality of the fish and meat had deteriorated though there was a greater variety of food available. E. Crawshay Williams, author of *Night in a Hotel*, wanted the fruit tarts to be served hot rather than cold and claimed 'Some members prefer their pastry crisp'. In the late twenties when the peripatetic bar happened to be situated over the Club boiler room, members complained that the temperature of 75 degrees was too high for minerals and alcohol. Justifiably.

It may have been too hot in the bar but in the world outside the financial temperature was sinking as the effects of the North American depression began to be felt in Britain. The warning shots of economies to come at the Club were fired in 1929 when it was proposed to dismiss three professionals including Joe Pearce. Eric Peters complained that Fred Poulson would be the only professional left capable of giving anyone (Peters meant players of his own class) a decent game. The fact was that neither Peters nor others among the Club's best players spent much money playing with the professionals.

The records show that Pearce was in fact re-appointed to the Club staff in June 1933 at thirty shillings a week plus fees of about twelve pence an hour. Since Ernest Ratcliff and Tom Jones had been on the professional staff in the late twenties at around £3 a week, Pearce's wage seems mean. Yet it reflected the economic stress of the period and that year there was a general cut in wages. Albert Cooper, the head rackets professional, was only getting twenty-six shillings a week plus fees.

At a directors' meeting in October 1931 it was reported that there had been a large number of resignations owing to the depression. It was suggested that it might be advantageous to members to pay their subscriptions (now ten guineas for men, seven for women) half-yearly or that members might like to take out a two-guinea reduced annual subscription providing they did not use the Club during the period covered. All salaries and wages were cut by ten percent and five members of the staff were dispensed with.

Briefly, in mid-1934, the Club's finances appeared to be improving. Half the wage cuts were restored (they were re-imposed in 1938) and so were entrance fees, eight guineas for men, five for women. But early in 1936 two of the Club's great old retainers, Peter Latham and Charles Read, champions at every game they played, were given notice. Read became so depressed at this that he had a stroke. Numerous measures were discussed for raising funds and increasing the Club's waning popularity, including advertising and posting notices in the Oxford and Cambridge colleges. Though the Club did not recognize it, the social revolution was beginning and those two universities no longer formed the bulk or even basis of the membership. This mid-thirties period in the Club's history shows a general decline in fortunes.

GOOD OLD DAYS

Back in the halcyon mid-twenties in contrast, the lighting of the covered courts was celebrated with an evening social tournament known as 'Nolly's Follies' and later as the 'Midnight Follies'. Reflecting the gaiety of the period they were fun; dinners and dancing to a band, champagne at six or seven shillings a bottle. The men's card room was used as a ladies' bar after John Olliff had complained of them being unable to get a drink after eight o'clock. Dickie Ritchie, who later became the Club secretary, recalls partnering Joan Ridley, a strict teetotaller, in the mixed and having to be careful what he drank before playing. Olliff was not so frugal and he once went on court wearing a dinner jacket and lined up glasses of Pimms No. 1 along the tramlines. Eventually he said to his partner 'Which ball do I hit? There are three of them.' 'The middle one,' replied Daphne Clarke, who later became Ritchie's wife.

Like the age such frolics couldn't, and didn't, last. In 1936 and 1937 the 'Follies', played in the late autumn, and the Spring Covered Courts tournament, were abolished. Both were losing money and had done so for some years. In 1936 a spring hard court tournament was held for the first time. It lost about £30. The schoolboys' and schoolgirls' competitions, run for many years by Mr & Mrs G. T. C. Watt, lost money too.

The two profitable events were the Covered Court and Grass Court Championships, though there were years in the twenties when even they lost money. In 1925, for instance, the grass court meeting lost £176. Gordon Lowe won the men's singles and he was certainly not an exciting player to watch. Ironically in the following year the Covered Courts lost £65. I say ironically because it was Jean Borotra's first year and people had yet to realize what a covered courts genius he was; a colossus who dominated the meeting and packed the galleries for more than twenty years. Indeed, he was still playing at Queen's over fifty years later, for the I.C. of France against Great Britain.

At the end of the 1920s and despite the signs of coming depression the Club did spend some £15,000 on reconstruction by Higgs and Hill. This included cork-tiling the men's dressing-room floor – and what a blessing that was. Among other improvements were the conversion of the old billiard room into a lobby, and of the balcony over the pavilion and in front of the men's dressing room into a stand and the secretary's office into a card room. The money came from the H. L. Beckett Trust which had taken over the Albert Slazenger mortgage and from an arrangement with Lloyd's Bank for a £10,000 overdraft. It was about the last major expense the Club was able to afford until well after the next war.

There were no great celebrations even in the Club's Jubilee Year, 1937, recorded in the *Sunday Times* and *Observer*, *The Illustrated Sporting and Dramatic News* and *Lawn Tennis & Badminton*, though King George VI did consent to become the Club's Patron. The cloth and cushions on one of the billiard tables was renewed and the covered courts painted,

much to Borotra's disgust as it slowed them down. The old Eton Fives court behind the garage was re-conditioned, given a glass roof and electric light. But, as it was also Coronation Year, the Club generously allotted fifty complimentary tickets a day and twenty reserved seats on Friday, and Saturday to visitors 'from the Dominions, India and the Colonies' for the Grass Court Championships, won by Don Budge and Jadwiga Jedrzejowska.

FIRST BROADCASTS

Historically it was the first time the BBC, ambitiously spreading its wings into live broadcasting of outside sporting events, gave running commentaries on the Noel Bruce Cup for rackets, the Covered Courts finals in which Bunny Austin beat Karl Schroder of Sweden and Peggy Scriven defeated Phyllis King and, thirdly, the World Rackets Championship won by David Milford, a Marlborough schoolmaster, over the American, Norbert Setzler. Milford was the first amateur to win that title since Sir William Hart-Dyke in 1862.

Outside tournaments such as the *Evening News*, the *Star*, the London Postal LTA, the National Association of Local Governments Officers and the Insurance Brokers LTA continued to play their last rounds at the Club, though they do not do so today even if they exist. Some years earlier the *Evening News* tournament, by far the largest of these extraneous events, had been won by a young and relatively unknown player – Fred Perry! His appearances at Queen's were extremely rare.

Arthur Whetton from Haileybury took over as head rackets professional as Albert Cooper, the professional champion, moved to Eton. John Ridgers led the Club squash team to win the Bath Club Cup. Two Eton Fives courts were going strong and the Club appointed a new head waiter, G. Nancollas. That was the Jubilee Year that was.

It was about this time that E. W. Sutton, a landmark at the Club like Mrs Bengough, got himself arrested. Sutton was a quiet old gentleman who had lunch and tea every day, seven days a week at the Club and indulged in a glass of vintage port. Occasionally he entertained the ladies such as Miss E. D. Holman, a very useful tournament player in her time. Some members thought Sutton's membership was in defiance of the Club rules which said that no member may use the Club for professional purposes and carry out his business there. As he was always at the Club it was obvious he did no other business and as he was always working at a desk, one of those facing the windows in the lounge, it seemed clear he was up to something.

It turned out that he was a law examiner and spent his time at the Club correcting papers, which seemed a harmless enough occupation. Sutton wore a long and rather tattered coat and always walked to and from the Club to catch the tube at Barons Court carrying his rackets. One day a policeman noticing this rather shabby figure shuffling towards the underground accosted him on suspicion of stealing rackets from the Club. It required the Club secretary to convince the constable that Old Man Sutton was a respectable character – and a member.

MEMBERSHIP MYSTERY

By 1938 the membership was falling and no one could fathom why. In its very early years the membership was about 450. By 1900 it had risen to nearly 1200, a figure it reached, oddly enough, by 1918. By the mid-1930s it was well over 1500. Then it began to slip: by 75 one year, 21 another. The immediate reaction was to reduce the Country membership specification from fifty miles to twenty-five. Colonel Bruce was instructed to prepare plans to reduce the Club's expenditure by £1000 a year. That may seem a paltry sum these days but it gave the Colonel a hard time.

He pointed out that the office staff was already one short and fully stretched. The women's dressing room could hardly do without Mrs Tarrant, or indeed Mrs Tutt – who was so popular because she would do anything, including laundry, for those members she liked. Nor could the men's room dispose of Jack Jenkins, Charlie Shepherd, Mr Bush and Mr Simes. That was the minimum number needed to keep the rooms clean and, among other things, guard against pilfering that was becoming prevalent – some members had the horrible habit of pinching the soap. The cleaning staff, led by Mrs Fagan, was at its barest. So was the catering staff who had to feed not only the members but eighteen staff as well.

Savings could be made if the seven-strong groundstaff under O'Leary were reduced to five. But half the hard courts would have to be put out of play and expenses on grass seed and fertiliser reduced. That might save £300. Another £350 could be saved by dispensing with two professionals – their wages

were £2 10s 0d a week each – and reducing the ball-boy staff from seventeen to eight. The most interesting part of Bruce's observations and suggestions concerned members' payment for the courts, balls, ball-boys, professionals and lights. In the past Admiral Sykes, when manager, and Walter Bersey, that wealthy businessman, keen player and committee member had tried without success to enforce cash payments. Over £150 in bookwork could be saved if everything were paid for in cash. The situation of the bureau, as the office was called in those days, adjoining the women's dressing room and facing the centre court, did not help. It was not necessary to pass it when leaving the Club and a lot of time was spent catching up with members who did so without paying their bills. This geographical fact had been pointed out many years before, in Henry Beck's time, yet nothing was done about it until the relatively recent arrival of the Portacabins.

To save money the directors waived their fees though Rory McNair, a staunch club man and senior LTA official, objected on the grounds that he needed the money – £250 a year – to live on. The Club offered a portion of land to the Fulham Borough Council and, ironically in view of what happened just after the Great War and later after the second, was turned down. In desperation even an offer from the Rover Car Company to buy a whole bank of hard courts on which to build offices was entertained.

To compound the Club's problems the directors, of whom Olliff was one, decided that the Club needed a new secretary. Colonel Bruce lacked the love of games and the social flair of his predecessor E. B. Noel, and, perhaps, a younger man was needed. Olliff was deputed to sound out R. J. Ritchie, son of M.J.G. and a Cambridge 'blue'. Dickie Ritchie, who later became the Club president, was working for W. H. James, a subsidiary of Prossers, rackets manufacturers, and was unaware that he was being considered for the job. 'I didn't apply for the job. I didn't even know Colonel Bruce was leaving until John Olliff, a close friend of mine, asked me whether I would take it.'

Ritchie took over as secretary in 1939, in time to run the last Grass Court Championships before the war – a meeting memorable for the confrontation between Baron Gottfried von Cramm and the American Bobby Riggs, the two favourites for Wimbledon. Von Cramm won easily because, it has always been claimed, Riggs threw the match to lengthen his Wimbledon odds with the bookmakers. He succeeded and won a lot of money. Ritchie recalled the US Ambassador arriving at the Club to see von Cramm, a known homosexual, and find out whether he was contemplating going to the US later that season. He need not have worried as Hitler ordered von Cramm back to Germany.

In July secretary Ritchie, a Territorial with the Bedfordshire Yeomanry, was called up and eventually went to the Far East, where he was captured and spent the war as a Japanese POW. As directors of the Club Olliff and T. D. Wynn Weston, a very keen but modest player and a director of the Rover Car company, sent a letter to all members stating, among other things:

1   The Club will be open during the war, play taking place on all courts.
2   The bar will remain open.
3   Owing to lighting restrictions there will be no play under artificial light.
4   There will be no charge for play on hard or grass courts.
5   There will be a restricted professional staff.
6   All payments are to be in cash.
7   Mr G. Greville is to be honorary secretary of the Club in the absence of Mr R. J. Ritchie.

The Club went to war with a few of the old retainers. Stanley Suffling, the last of the billiards markers, whose brother was known under his *nom-de-guerre* as Phil Scott the heavyweight boxer, was one. O'Leary, the groundsman, and Joe Richardson, a waiter, were others. Jack Jenkins from the men's changing room moved through the Club acting, at one time, as manager. Mrs Fagan stayed on as the cleaner but most of the professional staff, including Joe Pearce, Bill Holmes and Bill Young, were eventually called up. Dear Mrs Tutt stayed, of course.

THE LONDON GRASS COURT CHAMPIONSHIPS 1919–1939

THERE was a massive entry the first year after the war, 1919. There was rain, too, on the Friday and Saturday and the meeting was finished on Sunday. Was this the first time an English tournament was played on a Sunday? It was certainly fifty-three years ahead of Wimbledon where, owing to a wet Saturday, Stan Smith and Ilie Nastase played their memorable final on a Sunday in 1972. It was not until the 1980s that Sunday Championship play was introduced at both Queen's and Wimbledon.

Apart from such notable overseas men as Pat O'Hara-Wood (Australia), returning from the war, and the South Africans, B. I. C. Norton and Louis Raymond, there were some interesting competitors. Among them was F. W. Donisthorpe, the inventor of a large-headed racket similar to the present-day Prince. Donisthorpe took out a patent, copies of which are held in the Wimbledon Museum and, from time to time, would-be manufacturers of such rackets visit the place to examine them.

Among other competitors were the eccentric H. M. 'Buns' Cartwright who, as a small boy from Australia, talked his way into Eton and later was a pillar of the Eton Ramblers cricket club, A. Wallis Myers, the distinguished lawn tennis correspondent of the *Daily Telegraph*, Hamilton Price, a future Wimbledon referee, Sir George Thomas, a great badminton player, and Leo Lyle, later Sir Leo MP and then Lord Lyle of Westbourne. And there was also Max Woosnam, a Canon's son and a Wykehamist, who won four blues at Cambridge and was its twelfth man at cricket. He was also a Corinthian and a full international at soccer. In 1921, he won the Wimbledon men's doubles with R. Lycett and reached the final of the mixed. Someone wrote: 'His wrist work when volleying is beautiful to behold.'

The first round surprise was the defeat of 'Boy' Norton – not yet quite the force he was to prove the following year when he reached the Wimbledon Challenge round – by the American, A. M. Lovibond, 2–6 1–6 6–1 6–1 8–6.

O'Hara-Wood, concentrating on his opponent's backhand, beat the left-handed Raymond 6–4 6–0 2–6 7–5 to win the men's title, having had a desperately close semi-final with the Romanian, N. Mishu, whom he beat 8–6 in the final set. Wood had trouble volleying Mishu's top-spin, while some critic of the time somewhat unkindly wrote: 'Mishu, unlike most continentals, never gave up trying.' The British disdain for anyone from across the channel was strong.

Mrs D. R. Larcombe, the 1912 Wimbledon champion, won the women's title beating Miss E. D. Holman 6–4 8–6, having dismissed Elizabeth Ryan 'with pathetic ease' in the semi-final.

1920 saw the start of the American invasion and dominance that was to carry on intermittently throughout the twenties and thirties up to the start of the Second World War. It also brought renewed criticism of the courts that, a couple of years later, virtually brought about the end of rugby and soccer on the grounds. 'It is a great pity the courts compare so unfavourably with those of other clubs in the Metropolis', commented *Lawn Tennis & Badminton*.

During the previous year's meeting the playing of five sets by the men had been questioned largely because of the huge entry. In earlier days the best of five was considered good practice for Wimbledon but with such enlarged entries it became a burden not just for the players but for the organizers, notably the referee, Major Dudley Larcombe. This year it was reduced to the best of three.

America's one, two and three that year, Bill Tilden, Bill Johnston and Richard Williams, led the men's charge. Williams was 'sensationally' beaten by the veteran M. J. G. Ritchie but inevitably Tilden and Johnston reached the men's final. It was the first time this country had seen these two giants, who had come here to chase the Davis Cup apart from competing at Wimbledon. A contemporary scribe wrote of the two Americans – Big Bill and Little Bill – 'It would be difficult to find such a well-balanced player as Johnston, who has mastered practically every stroke in the game. His forehand drive is fast and destructive and when he has made it he is "unstretched" for the next shot. He can read the other man's intentions and his anticipation is super-excellent. Tilden is a much quieter exponent of the game but looks a player of considerable brain-power and understands the art of lobbing, which once helped him beat Norman Brookes. He calls "peach" to his opponent's best shots.'

TANKERS?

When Johnston won the final 4–6 6–2 6–4 there were suggestions that neither player tried his hardest or best. Tilden shrugged it off with: 'Bill wins one time and I win another.' Tilden, already twenty-seven, went on to win his first Wimbledon, and the pair of them thrashed Britain 5–0 in the Davis Cup.

Molla Mallory had lost her US title – she regained it later that year – when she made her first appearance here. Even so she failed to justify her reputation and was well beaten by Mrs Larcombe, who had to retire to Miss E. D. Holman in the final.

The 1921 Championships were undistinguished except for the remarkable performance of the Japanese, Zenzo Shimidzu, who went through six rounds for the loss of only thirteen games. His last three opponents, Alain Gerbault of France, P. M. Davson and Mahommed Sleem, all class players, mustered eight games between them. Shimidzu was quick about the court, a useful volleyer and a resourceful player with a 'beatific' expression when beaten by a shot. The match of the meeting was Sleem's win over BIC 'Boy' Norton 1–6 6–2 7–5. Having won the first set easily, Norton played the fool and found himself down 0–5 in the final set. The gap was just too wide.

Mrs R. C. Clayton won the women's title, hitting too hard for Miss Holman who persisted in taking the ball as it dropped. This persuaded a critic to write: 'If only more ladies would take the ball at the top of its bounce as does Mrs Mallory or, better still, earlier, then there would be less pat-ball in our English tennis.'

The 1920 all-American final: Bill Johnson on his way to victory over Bill Tilden—a carve-up?

Despite some competition from Roehampton, there was over the next few years no decrease in the number of entries especially among the men. One hundred and four entered in 1922 when Colonel H. G. Mayes, who had come here during the war with the Canadian Forces, beat Donald Greig, a player with a fast serve. Even more played the following year when the scholarly F. R. Burrow, one of the greatest crossword experts, took over as referee. He was, by the way, Wimbledon's referee from 1919 to 1936.

Vincent Richards who, at sixteen, had beaten Tilden to win the US Covered Courts title and was hailed as a 'wonder player', appeared on the English scene in 1923. He lost a set to Donald Greig – he won the second in ten minutes going up on every shot – but thrashed the Indian Davis Cup player S. M. Jacob 6–2 6–2 in the final. Richards was a great volleyer with a strong top-spin forehand and a slice which he used to his opponent's backhand.

Elizabeth Ryan, an American already living in this country and destined to win nineteen Wimbledon doubles titles, took the singles for the first time, showing greater stamina than Mrs A. E. Beamish in a temperature approaching 100°.

The men's and women's doubles were altered from the normal format to an American tournament; the Americans Richards and F. T. Hunter winning the men's, Miss Ryan and Mrs Lambert Chambers the women's. Among the competitors was Lady Beaverbrook, wife of the then owner of Express Newspapers – the famous 'Beaver'.

1923 was also the first year that The Queen's Club turf had not suffered during the winter from the studded boots of football, rugby and soccer. The University rugby match had gone to Twickenham and the Club had taken the chance to lay down some new grass courts during the winter. An additional twelve courts were created, bringing the Club total to thirty grass and eleven hard. That number of grass courts allowed the head groundsman to take out four at any one time to rest. Each court was self-contained.

Fifteen courts were used for the Championships the following year and were described as being in excellent condition, even better than in 1923. The effect of Roehampton's rival tournament may have diluted the quality of the entry but not the numbers and, as was the case in other tournaments at this time, the men's singles was divided into two classes.

Norman Brookes should have won the men's singles but when leading Algy Kingscote 5–1 in the first set of the semi-final he was hit in the eye by a ball that glanced off both the net and his racket. That put Kingscote through to the final, where he beat Gordon Lowe, the winner in 1925. Miss Ryan easily won the women's title but a Miss K. J. Keymer attracted some attention by hitting her backhand with the same face of the racket as her forehand!

The assiduous Colonel Mayes then had his successes, engaging Gordon Lowe in a stonewalling contest in 1926 and beating the two Japanese T. Harada and Y. Ohta in 1927. The lovely Eileen Bennett appeared on the scene and so did two fine South African players, Bobby Heine (later Mrs Heine-Miller) and Mrs G. Peacock, who later became the first lady to appear on the Centre Court without stockings. The Hon. Esmond Harmsworth, later Lord Rothermere, the *Daily Mail*'s proprietor, was among the competitors.

BIG BILL BACK

The meeting was back to its best in 1928, when it drew by far the strongest entry since Tilden had last played at Queen's in 1920. Tilden headed the US squad which included his sixteen-year-old protégé, W. F. 'Junior' Coen and F. T. Hunter. J. H. Crawford and Harry Hopman from Australia, R. Boyd and E. Morea from the Argentine and, in doubles only, Henri Cochet and René Lacoste from France and the evergreen Norman Brookes, who reached the final of the mixed, were notable competitors.

Tilden won the singles and doubles, dropping only 17 games in 10 sets in the former, including his final win over Hunter 6–3 6–2 6–1. He gave his most impressive display against Coen, whom he beat 6–2 6–2 in the semis. 'Tilden hit with terrific speed and served his famous cannonball which he had not done against previous opponents,' wrote a critic. Against Hunter he showed an infinite variety of attack, varied in conception and technique and such a wealth of return that Hunter, the US No 2, was made to look second class. Hunter had earlier been given a rough ride by the Australian, Hopman, a brilliant volleyer.

The men's doubles was interesting. The Frenchmen, Cochet and Lacoste, did not make an effort against Tilden and Hunter. This was most probably for strategic reasons since France was defending the Davis Cup against the US in Paris the following month. But there was no question of the Australians, Crawford and Hopman, not trying against Tilden

Big Bill Tilden – called 'peach' to his opponent's best shots

slipped about despite being shod in spikes. Tilden and Hunter eventually won 9–11 6–2 7–5 6–3.

The winners dropped service four times, Hunter thrice in the first set, Tilden once in the third. Allison's serve was the more vulnerable of the losers. The winners' return of service and astute lobbing was mainly responsible for their success. Van Ryn was the better of the losers, 'slapping the ball good and hard without any fancy work,' wrote H. S. Scrivener, adding that the quality of the play was so high it put everything else that happened during the week in the shade.

Allison and van Ryn took their revenge at Wimbledon, beating Tilden and Hunter in the semifinal and Colin Gregory and Ian Collins in the final. They then played the doubles for the US against France in the Davis Cup Challenge Round, unavailingly as it turned out.

Tilden and Hunter divided the singles in view of the weather, though they were some distance ahead of anyone else. Such British players as H. F. David, J. S. Olliff and H. G. N. Lee made some impression, as did *Fräulein* Cilly Aussem and Dorothy Round, both future Wimbledon champions, among the women. As notable a performance as any came from Mrs Bundy who, as May Sutton, had won her first Wimbledon twenty-four years previously, in 1905. She reached the fifth round of the singles, beating Joan Ridley the holder 6–1 6–0 before losing to Miss Ryan, and also the final of the women's doubles.

Poor weather caused numerous players, including Tilden, to withdraw from the meeting in 1930 even after some had played a match or two. Yet two Americans met in the final: Allison who, a couple of weeks later, became the first unseeded player to reach the Wimbledon final – he was beaten by Tilden – and G. S. Mangin. Allison won 6–4 8–6, 'being less liable to belt the ball as hard as he could when there was no need to do so'. Mangin, having earlier beaten the US No. 3, John Doeg, was impetuous.

George Lott and Doeg, the US champions, beat Allison and van Ryn, the Wimbledon champions, in a four-set doubles final. There were only four service breaks in this 12–14 6–3 6–4 6–4 match and the losers reversed the result in the Wimbledon final.

After three years of American domination, the men's singles now returned to this country and produced a strange final in which John Olliff beat Ted Avory 3–6 6–4 6–2 – strange because Avory led by a set and 4–0 and was twice within a point of 5–0.

and Hunter in the final. The Americans led two sets to one and 5–2 but only got away with it 4–6 6–1 8–6 6–8 6–4.

Tilden and Hunter were back in 1929, joined by their compatriots, W. L. Allison and J. van Ryn. The doubles rivalry between these two pairs was such that with the weather doubtful on finals day they asked for it to be played before the singles final. The match was played in a light rain, causing Tilden and Hunter to play in their socks while Allison and van Ryn

Lawn Tennis & Badminton wrote: 'Olliff by downright bad play let Avory gain the lead. He recovered in the nick of time and made Avory look second rate.' Avory, by the way, strongly denies a suggestion that Olliff 'fooled about' with lobs and drops in breezy conditions. Both men beat some useful players *en route* to the final. Avory's scalps included I. G. Collins and George Lyttleton-Rogers, the giant Irishman.

Mrs J. B. Pittman (formerly Elsie Goldsack) beat *Fräulein* Krahwinkel who later reached the Wimbledon final – she lost to Cilly Aussem – in three sets and then defeated Mrs Kitty Godfree, the 1924 and 1926 Wimbledon champion, 9–7 6–4. 'Mrs Godfree volleyed beautifully on occasions, those backhand push volleys bringing back memories. But the loss of the first set was a little too much for her,' said one report.

It was almost a clean sweep for overseas players in 1932. Dorothy Round and Mrs Peggy Michell were the only home players to reach any final – the doubles, which they won.

THE TORNADO ARRIVES

The first appearance here of Ellsworth Vines, regarded as the natural successor to Tilden and Allison, provided considerable interest. Though Vines spent his first weekend practising on grass at Wimbledon he immediately ran into difficulties at Queen's, where his first opponent was R. J. (Dickie) Ritchie, son of M. J. G., a Cambridge 'blue' and future secretary of this Club. 'When I saw who I had to play I was prepared for the worst, hoping to salvage a few games before he became used to our grass courts and a different make of balls. To my surprise I survived until six-all in the final set,' recalls Ritchie.

After an hour-and-a-half Vines won 5–7 6–4 8–6 after Ritchie had saved a match point at 4–5 in the final set. Vines was noted for his blasting serve and forehand and it was some feat on Ritchie's part to break his serve twice in the final set – something Bunny Austin failed to do in the Wimbledon final where he was thrashed 6–4 6–2 6–0.

Vines, clearly practising his low volley (never a strong point) and suffering a blistered hand, fell to the Australian Harry Hopman 0–6 6–2 6–3. Hopman then went out to that remarkable Cambridge all-rounder, Kenneth Gandar Dower and that left the field pretty clear for Hopman's countryman, Jack Crawford, who beat the Japanese,

Jiro Satoh, and the Dutchman, Hans Timmer, in the last two rounds. The Australians then combined to win the doubles, unseating the holders, Gottfried von Cramm and Jacques Brugnon. Mrs Elsie Pittman lost her title to the American, Mrs Dot Andrus Burke.

All the finals were washed out in 1933 but not before there had been some stirring play. A formidable quartet of Americans including Wimbledon champion, Ellsworth Vines, filled the last four places in the men's singles. Three American women including Wimbledon champion, Helen Wills-Moody, reached the same stage in their event.

The odd player out was Mrs Elsie Pittman, the 1931 winner, whose major achievement was to beat the Polish lady, Jadwiga Jedrzejowska, 7–5 5–7 6–3 in the semis. 'Mrs Pittman must have covered miles in retrieving the Polish lady's shots,' was one spectator's comment. Mrs Moody, the other finalist, beat, among others, Susan Noel, daughter of the former Club secretary and a talented court games player – she became the squash champion. Mrs Powell (as Miss Noel became) recalls playing the great lady: 'It was pure joy. Her classic game made me feel as if I were playing immaculately even if I didn't get many games.'

The big match saw Vines beat Keith Gledhill, his countryman and partner – they held the Australian and US titles – 6–8 7–5 6–3 in one semi-final. Vines took the affair casually until he was down 2–4 and love–40 in the second set. 'We then saw the 1932 champion. He won 13 consecutive points bringing out his cannonball serve for the first time,' wrote a critic.

Lester Stoeffen and Cliff Sutter provided a sharp contrast in styles in the other semi-final, which ended when the latter retired with the score 12–10 12–12 against him. Stoeffen looked like another Vines in height and hitting power – he was too erratic to become a champion – and Sutter was dubbed the American Lacoste.

Ted Avory, who scored a notable win over South Africa's C. J. C. Robbins, and Dickie Ritchie both fell to Gledhill. Ritchie had three points for 5–5 in the second set against Gledhill but recalls 'being unable to disturb his composure'.

The US Davis Cup team, Sidney Wood, Frank Shields, George Lott and Lester Stoeffen, entered *en bloc* in 1934 preparing not just for Wimbledon but their eventual challenge to Britain, the Cup-holders. Inevitably they lined up in the singles semis, though

Wood was at one time down a set and 2–4 to Stoeffen before taming the big server. Wood then beat Shields 11–9 6–0 for the title.

More encouraging from Britain's viewpoint was the doubles success for Ian Collins and Frank Wilde. On Friday and without leaving the court they defeated first Shields and David Jones 6–4 6–2 and then Lott and Stoeffen, the US Davis Cup pair, 6–0 11–9. Against four of the heaviest servers in the game this was an achievement constructed largely on Wilde's excellent serving and deadly overheads plus the clever play of Collins, whose forecourt game with his cut-ins and cross-volleys was often brilliant. They had little trouble with Gandar Dower and Cam Malfroy in the final.

COMPÔT DE FRANCE

The women's events and the mixed were dominated by the French. *Mlle* Goldschmidt became the first Frenchwoman to win the singles; *Mlle* Collette Rosambert, *Mme* Sylvia Henrotin and *Mme* Simone Mathieu were involved in the two doubles finals.

In 1935 the Americans, with David Jones, Wilmer Allison and Don Budge reaching the semis, again dominated the singles but, for the third time since the war, both singles finals – *Sta* Anita Lizana and *Mme* Sylvia Henrotin were the two ladies – were washed out by rain.

As in the previous year it was a British doubles pair that made the news. This time it was Pat Hughes and Raymond Tuckey who, in winning the event, beat Wilmer Allison and John van Ryn, former Wimbledon and US champions, Sidney Wood and the Spaniard E. 'Booby' Maier, and then Budge and Gene Mako, the current US Davis Cup pair. This seemed to answer Britain's problem of finding a Davis Cup partnership as they prepared to play the US or Australia in the Challenge Round.

Hughes and Tuckey, a new combination, displayed both an understanding and a vigorous blend of attacking tennis. Hughes was generating more pace on his drives and hitting a flatter and faster service than before. Tuckey's game showed the same dash as had Colin Gregory's and he had a scoring serve and deadly smash. Moreover Tuckey played in the backhand court, leaving Hughes to his favourite right. Against Budge and Mako, whom they beat 4–6 6–3 6–4, their dipping service returns were most effective. The following year they won Wimbledon.

This was Anita Lizana's first experience of grass and to beat Miss Ermyntrude Harvey, Joan Hartigan, an Australian, and Susan Noel, who led by a set and 2-love, was no mean feat. Her trademark was the dropshot which she could play from anywhere in the court.

The American line of giants continued; Johnston in 1920 followed by Tilden, Richards, Allison, Vines, Wood and now, in 1936, Don Budge. The final in which he beat his countryman, David N. Jones, 6–4 6–3 was notable principally for its service statistics. Jones served 9 times, scoring 22 aces out of the 49 points he won all-told. He also served 8 double-faults. Budge tried standing in to take serve but the pace still beat him. Nevertheless 15 of his 65 points were aces – and only one double. Someone wrote: 'His flat-hit backhand down the line has few, if any, equals in men's tennis and he can swing the ball to any part of the court.'

Budge and Mako's win over the US Champions, Allison and van Ryn, 6–3 6–3 was their sixth that year and they were chosen for the Davis Cup match against Australia. Budge scored a triple by winning the mixed with Sarah Fabyan.

The Polish player, Jadwiga Jedrzejowska, had been moving up the ladder for some years and was nearing her peak when she beat Susan Noel 6–2 6–4 in the women's final. As doubles partners they knew each other's play pretty well and Mrs Powell, as Miss Noel became, has this comment to offer: 'I knew her game well yet could never make much impression on her. Her backhand was wholly defensive but was safe and sure. The main hope of getting into the game came when she cracked that devastating fore-hand of hers out of court. That didn't happen too often. But it did offer some hope.'

Budge had no difficulty retaining his title in 1937. He lost an average of fewer than three games in the five matches he played and ended by crushing Bunny Austin 6–1 6–2 in half-an-hour, a preview of their Wimbledon final the following year.

Miss Jedrzejowska retained her title, too, beating three leading British players, Valerie Scott, Peggy Scriven and Kay Stammers, all without the loss of a set, in the last three rounds. Shortly afterwards she took Dorothy Round to 7–5 in the final set in the Wimbledon final.

The great Helen Wills Moody played her first Wimbledon in 1924 and her last in 1938, winning the title eight times. But only twice did Helen play Queen's – 1933 and 1938 – and this time she lost in the semi-final 8–6 6–2 to *Frau* Hilda Sperling. Moreover, at St George's Hill, Weybridge shortly before Queen's, Helen had been beaten by Mary Hardwick. But when Wimbledon came along Helen was once more invincible. She beat *Frau* Sperling in the semi-final 12–10 6–4 and her old rival Helen Jacobs in the final and, as far as I know, has never been back to England since. *Frau* Sperling beat the great Helen at Queen's because of her stubborn defence – she had long legs and a long reach – and the fact that the American never moved off the baseline. After losing leads of 5–3 and 6–5 in the first set, Helen appeared to lose some interest. The winner was then 'blown off court' by Miss Jedrzejowska, who won the title for the third successive year.

Bunny Austin added his name to the list of winners with an easy final win over Kho Sin Kie, 6–2 6–0. His hardest match came in the semi-final against the Yugoslav, F. Kukuljevic. He not only tamed the European's two-way kicking service but also undertook a volley campaign, most unusual for him, to win an exciting match 6–2 6–4.

In the last meeting before the Second World War the crushing defeat of the US No. 1. Bobby Riggs by Gottfried von Cramm, 6–0 6–1 was a major talking point. Did Riggs 'throw' the match so that he could get a better price on himself for Wimbledon? It was discovered later that Riggs had backed himself fairly heavily to win all three events in the Championships. He succeeded in all of them and made a hefty sum of money.

The only alternative answer was that he had come straight off clay courts in Paris on to rain-soaked dead grass at Queen's. But he had had three matches before meeting von Cramm, who would probably have been seeded one at Wimbledon had not Hitler ordered him back to Germany. Earlier von Cramm had beaten Riggs's compatriot, Elwood Cooke while Bunny Austin, who was top seed at Wimbledon, fell to Kukuljevic. Von Cramm won 61 points to Rigg's 26 and made only seven errors in the whole match. Miss Jedrzejowska won her fourth successive title, beating Hilda Sperling again.

THE COVERED COURT CHAMPIONSHIPS
1919–1939

'When you go to the net on the east court at Queen's, always do so very gently on your toes. When you stay back on the baseline, bang your feet on the court and your opponent will think you are going to the net. The accoustics on that court are different from any others.'

Advice from Leighton Crawford to Mary Hardwick (Mrs Charles Hare) before she beat Peggy Scriven in 1936.

THERE was a lawn tennis boom just after the First World War, sparked off by the relief felt at the war's end and also by the arrival at Wimbledon of that remarkable French player, *Mlle* Suzanne Lenglen, and shortly afterwards by the American, Bill Tilden.

Suzanne never played at Queen's and Tilden did not play there until the mid-twenties, and then only in the Grass Court Championships, but the new-found enthusiasm for the game rubbed off on the Club and its various tournaments, not least the Covered Courts. E. B. Noel, that distinguished Club secretary and historian, wrote: 'Lawn tennis at Queen's means three things – the covered courts, the grass courts which date back to the earliest days of the Club and the hard courts which are of more recent construction. And, perhaps, Queen's is proudest of the covered courts in which so many great games have been played and which have a character of their own.'

Noel might well have added 'and so many great players have competed' for, as we have seen in the earlier section of this story of the Covered Courts Championships, Wimbledon champions abounded: H. F. Lawford, Laurie Doherty and his brother Reggie, A. W. Gore, Blanche Bingley (Mrs G. W. Hillyard), Chattie Cooper (Mrs A. Sterry), Dora Boothby (Mrs A. C. Geen) and Dorothea K. Douglass (Mrs Lambert Chambers).

This new era between the wars became part of what is known as 'the Golden Age of Lawn Tennis' and one of the characters who helped create that image was Jean Borotra of France, whose deeds at The Queen's Club were momentous. And, linking the past to the present, one name recurs year after year – M. J. G. Ritchie, twice the champion. He first competed in 1894. He was still going strong at sixty-three in 1933 and by then his son, R. J. 'Dickie' Ritchie, a future Club secretary, had joined him as a competitor in the Championships.

The first tournament held in England after the 1914–18 War was the Covered Court Championships at The Queen's Club. Played at the beginning of April 1919, it not only drew a distinguished entry including the last Wimbledon women's champion Mrs Lambert Chambers but also record crowds. 'Not even the much-increased admission charges and the prospect of suffocation kept the spectators away,' was how a contemporary writer put it. Such was the relief from war.

Among the men to make their first appearance were Gerald Patterson, an Australian hailed as a second Norman Brookes; the rising American, Watson Washburn; two South Africans, B.I.C. 'Boy' Norton and Louis Raymond, and the Romanian, N. Mishu. A few months later Patterson won the first post-war Wimbledon. The key men's match was P. M. Davson's win over Washburn 6–0 6–3 3–6 7–5. They were players of similar style and method, outplaying rather than out-hitting their opponents.

In this case Davson was more used to the courts than the American. Davson went on to beat Patterson in the final and the holder, the evergreen M. J. G. Ritchie, 6–2 6–3 8–6 in the Challenge Round.

Mrs Lambert Chambers was in a class of her own. It was said that her opponents were proud of every game they took from her. She beat the American, Elizabeth Ryan, 6–2 6–1 and finally the holder, Miss E. D. Holman, 6–3 6–3. The Australian, Randolph Lycett, won both doubles, the men's with R. W. Health and the mixed with Miss Ryan.

Davson's reign was brief and in 1920 he was deprived of his title by a newcomer from France, A. H. Gobert, a strong hitter of the ball. Gobert beat M. J. G. Ritchie in the final and Davson 6–4 7–5 6–2 in the Challenge round. Davson tried unsuccessfully to slow down the Frenchman, who was severe on service and overhead and was, among other things, an adroit volleyer.

Mrs Lambert Chambers did not defend her title. Indeed, a year later she retired from singles on doctor's orders. In her absence Miss Ryan won the title, beating Miss E. D. Holman 6–3 6–0 in the second round and Mrs D. K. Craddock 6–4 6–2 in the final. Miss Ryan, curiously not recognized as a great doubles player, retained her mixed title with Randolph Lycett.

LYCETT SLIPS

The match of the 1921 Championships was W. C. Crawley's win over Randolph Lycett 4–6 14–16 7–5 9–7 6–3 – seventy-seven games in three-and-a-half-hours' play. (How long would such a match take today?) Lycett led 4–2 in the third set and had match points at 5–3, 5–4 and 7–6 in the fourth. It appears he did not volley enough at crucial moments. Crawley's placing was the better and he made Lycett do most of the running. This win was the more remarkable since, early in the week, Crawley had suffered neuritis in his shoulder which nearly cost him his match with Stanley Doust. And in the challenge round he only narrowly went down to André Gobert, 6–2 6–4 4–6 0–6 7–5. No one quite knew whether Gobert would arrive from Paris for the match.

Miss Elizabeth Ryan did not defend her women's title and Miss E. D. Holman won it for the third time, beating the South African, Mrs G. Peacock, 6–1 3–6 6–4. Remarkably, Gobert and Lycett were upturned in the men's doubles by P. M. Davson and T. M. Mavrogordato.

André Gobert scored his hat-trick in 1922 when, arriving at Queen's after a night journey from Paris and in time for only a brief knock-up, he warded off BIC 'Boy' Norton, the 1921 Wimbledon All-Comers winner, 4–6 6–1 6–8 6–4 6–2. Norton, a South African, may have been stout-hearted but he was up against a man in crushing form. In the final Norton had beaten Randolph Lycett 8–6 8–6 6–3, the loser becoming exhausted.

Lycett regained both doubles titles, the men's with Stanley Doust and the mixed with Miss Kitty McKane, a new partnership. Miss E. D. Holman won the women's title for the fourth time, beating Mrs D. K. Craddock 6–2 6–1.

The 1923 entry was about the weakest since the war and it was decided that holding the meeting in April instead of the more traditional October was the cause. André Gobert did not defend and he was succeeded as champion by South African-born J. P. D. Wheatley, a competent player without any punishing strokes who had made his first appearance in this event in 1921.

There being no Challenge round – Wimbledon had abolished the system the previous year – Wheatley took the title when he beat the Indian Davis Cup player, Dr A. H. Fyzee, 1–6 6–2 6–4 6–4 in the final. He was less successful in the doubles events, losing the final of the men's with Hamilton Price, later a notable Wimbledon referee, to Stanley Doust and A. W. Asthalter and the mixed with Miss Evelyn Colyer to Asthalter and Mrs Edgington, also in the final. Mrs R. C. Clayton emerged as the best of a poor women's entry, beating Mrs Edgington 6–3 6–2 in the final.

The 1924 Championships reverted to their traditional October date. Pat Wheatley lost his title to another South African expatriate, P. B. Spence, a London medical student, who beat him 6–2 6–2 4–6 6–1 in the final. Pat Spence was an attacking player and a good volleyer, as he showed in his earlier defeat of the persistent S. M. Jacob, who thrived on long rallies. Jacob, by the way, had previously outrallied M. J. G. Ritchie, described at the time as 'England's priceless old man'. Spence scored a double winning the men's doubles with Charles Kingsley.

Nigel Sharpe began to make his presence felt, beating Col. H. G. Mayes and losing to Wheatley in four close sets. Phillip Le Gros, later to become a respected Queen's Club chairman, was among the competitors. Mrs A. E. Beamish won the women's title, beating Mrs Craddock 6–4 6–4 in the final and a new group of ladies began to emerge. Among them were Lumley Ellis, Joan Ridley, Christobel Hardie, Effie Hemmant and Joan Reid-Thomas.

The first of that group to distinguish herself was Miss Reid-Thomas whose mother, Maud Shackle, had won the title three times in 1891–2–3. Joan Reid-Thomas followed her mother and won the title in 1925, beating the Hon. Mrs Colston 6–2 7–5 in the final. Her closest encounter was with the redoubtable Mrs Edgington, whom she beat 9–7 in the final set after being down 2–4. The winner, it was said, showed a much-improved backhand.

Pat Spence lost his men's title to S. M. Jacob, who won 3–6 7–5 6–0 3–6 6–3; a tactical triumph for the winner who spent much of the first two sets making Spence work hard for every point and then frustrating him with drives of varying length and pace as well as lobs. Jacob looked tired at the end. Spence was exhausted but later won both doubles events, the men's with Charles Kingsley and the mixed with Evelyn Colyer. Jacob had only beaten E. E. 'Teddy' Higgs in five sets, the loser winning two more games than the winner.

THE BOUNDING BASQUE

That 1925 meeting was merged with the London Covered Court Championships and held in March. The following year saw the beginning of an era when the meeting became established in October, with artificial light installed, to be used only if the players agreed and, more dramatically and significantly, it saw the start of Jean Borotra's historic reign.

Borotra's entrance to The Queen's Club and the Championships in 1926 was characteristic. He arrived late, playing his first opponent, an Italian Count, under artificial light. Full of apologies he was late for his next match against George Stoddart, who had been changed and waiting for some time. They eventually played at 9.15 a.m. the following day. That same afternoon Borotra met G. R. Crole-Rees, a notable doubles player. It was touch-and-go whether the light would last when Crole-Rees led 5–3 in the second set and won the third. Borotra in fact won sixteen successive points to take the second set and later won the match 6–3 7–5 3–6 6–3. Crole-Rees won the doubles with C. G. Eames, the first of their three victories.

Mahommed Sleem, an Indian barrister, returned to the scene after a couple of years absence, only to be beaten in the semi-final by Donald Greig. For an attacking player Greig showed remarkable restraint meeting Sleem's 'slow-balling' with rallies of a dozen-or-so strokes before 'going for broke' – usually down the middle followed by a volley. Greig won in four sets but, according to accounts, was 'cooked' at the end. Borotra beat him in the final 6–3 6–2 6–4.

The women's singles was overshadowed by Borotra's appearance but was won by Peggy Saunders, later Mrs L. R. C. Michell, who beat Betty Dix in the final. Earlier Miss Dix had put out Joan Ridley and Eileen Bennett.

Borotra did not defend in 1927. Teddy Higgs, who had been in the forefront of the British game for the past few years, and the glamorous Eileen Bennett became the champions. Someone wrote that Miss Bennett played the game 'as beautifully as it can be played'. In beating Mrs John Hill and Christobel Hardie in the last two rounds she was never in much trouble.

Higgs did not have an easy journey. He was within a point of losing to Nigel Sharpe at 4–5 in the fifth set and then came up against Donald Greig. When Higgs, a driver of the ball, and Greig, a volleyer, had shared four sets – 3–6 6–1 8–6 3–6 – the light failed. It was decided to re-play the match on the following Monday. But both men were so 'fed-up', to use the description of the time, that they agreed that as soon as one man had won two sets the other would retire. Higgs took the first two sets 6–2 10–8 and went on to beat C. R. Crole-Rees 6–4 6–3 6–4 in the final. Crole-Rees and C. G. Eames retained their doubles title at the expense of Higgs and Greig.

1928 saw the start of Borotra's astonishing run of six successive Championships, equalling that of H. L. Doherty from 1901 to 1906. It also saw Mrs Kitty Godfree, twice Wimbledon champion, win the title for the first and only time in her distinguished career. Borotra's play throughout the week was patchy, though he managed to raise his game when needed. He demolished Pat Wheatley, a former holder, and then played a slack five-setter against Eric Peters, who had a point for a two-set lead before losing 4–6 8–6 3–6 6–2 6–0.

Nigel Sharpe, having scored his first win over Pat Spence, gave Borotra a good run for four sets, as did C. R. Crole-Rees, serving splendidly, in the final. Crole-Rees, by the way, won his semi-final match against Charles Kingsley by the curious score of 6–4 0–6 6–0 6–0.

Joan Fry and Mrs Fearnley
Whittingstall in 1930

Mrs Godfree narrowly beat Betty Dix 1–6 6–2 8–6 in the quarter-final but was otherwise free from trouble. She defeated Mrs B. C. Covell, who had put out Joan Ridley, in the semi-final and trounced Eileen Bennett, conqueror of Mrs L. R. C. Michell (née Peggy Saunders), 6–1 6–2 in the final. In a 58-game mixed doubles semi-final Wheatley and Miss Bennett beat Spence and Betty Nuthall 7–9 7–5 16–14!

Borotra dropped only one set in 1929 – to Eric Peters in the semi-final. H. S. Scrivener, one of that era's leading scribes, wrote, 'Peters deals in the stroke that makes things awkward for the other player without being positively deadly'. He once wore down Bill Tilden in the south of France. In the final,

Borotra beat Nigel Sharpe 7–5 6–2 6–2 after the loser had led 5–1 in the first set, a situation that stirred the Frenchman into action.

Mrs Peggy Michell won the women's title for the second time. She lost only one set, to Effie Hemmant in the second round, and then successively beat Susan Noel, Mrs F. M. Strawson (née Joan Reid-Thomas) and Joan Ridley for the loss of only eleven games. Mrs Michell also won the mixed with C. R. Crole-Rees and an invitation women's doubles event with Betty Dix. The meeting also saw the rise of Phyllis Mudford, Vera Montgomery and Elsie Goldsack.

NO HAT-TRICK FOR AUSTIN

Despite a cold, Borotra completed his hat-trick (and his fourth title in all) in 1930. It was also the start of his rivalry in this event with Bunny Austin whom he beat 6–1 0–6 2–6 6–2 6–1 in the final. Though the more tired of the two towards the end, Borotra's remarkable will to win pulled him through. They had already met twice that season on the same court, in the Spring meeting and International Club match, Austin winning on both occasions.

'Toto' Brugnon, another member of France's champion Davis Cup team, made his first appearance, won the first two sets off Charles Kingsley, got cramp and lost the next three and the match 1–6 3–6 6–1 6–0 6–0. In the semi-finals Borotra put out John Olliff and Austin beat Kingsley.

Joan Ridley won the women's title, beating Freda James 9–7 6–4 in the semi-final and Joan Fry 6–2 6–2 in the final. Jeanette Morfey, Betty Soames, Nancy Lyle and Billie Yorke were other names that would attract notice in the following years. A young Frank Wilde, partnered by W. A. Ingram (father of Joan), reached the men's doubles final, losing to Austin and Olliff.

Borotra, despite trying to convince people that his game was deteriorating, was in better trim while recording his fifth win in 1931. Bunny Austin did not compete but the Frenchman had a worthy final opponent in the Japanese, Jiro Satoh, whom he beat 10–8 6–3 0–6 6–3. They had met twice previously, at Wimbledon and in Paris, Borotra winning each time.

Satoh with a stop volley gained a point for the first set at 6–5 but netted a volley off a shot that might well have gone out. Satoh led 7–6 and 8–7 but then Borotra's service became 'deadly'. Borotra played the

A young Dan Maskell and Kay Stammers on their way to practise

second set from the baseline and chucked the third before making his major effort in the fourth.

In the semi-finals Borotra was taken to five sets by E. R. Avory, a Cambridge 'blue', while Satoh, having put out Oxford's Bob Tinkler, beat John Olliff. Father and son, M. J. G. and R. J. 'Dickie' Ritchie, competed for the first time; the young Ritchie taking Olliff to five sets.

Three former champions, Mrs A. E. Beamish, Mrs L. R. C. Michell and Mrs F. M. Strawson challenged for the women's title but only the last named reached the semi-final. The title went to Mary Heeley, who beat Kay Stammers in the semi-final and Jeanette Morfey in the final.

The entry for the 1932 Championships was so large that it had to be restricted to thirty-two for the singles events. Borotra recorded his sixth win with one of his most sustained performances. There were six Wightman Cup players among the women.

Borotra dropped the first set to Bob Tinkler in the quarters, beat Cam Malfroy, a Cambridge 'blue' and New Zealander, in three sets, two advantage, in the semis and then beat Harry Lee, sometimes outplaying him from the back of the court, 6–2 6–3 6–3 in the final. That match took only forty-five minutes – about the time, fifty years later, that John McEnroe took to play one short set.

En route to the final Lee beat the famed Kenneth Gandar Dower, a multiple Cambridge 'blue', and the Japanese, Jiro Yamagishi, 6–4 6–3 6–2, the loser fading badly midway through the second set. The Grand Old Man of the meeting, M. J. G. Ritchie, took P. F. Glover to five sets and The Queen's Club chairman, Judge Hargreaves, did the same with Teddy Buzzard, an Oxford 'blue' and St Thomas's Hospital medical student.

A new generation of women players led by Peggy Scriven, the winner aged twenty, made their presence felt. On her way to the final Miss Scriven outplayed the experienced Ermyntrude Harvey and then survived a 5–7 6–4 7–5 contest with Mrs M. R. King (née Phyllis Mudford). The tenacious Mrs King led 5–3 in the final set but was beaten by a burst of fierce but well-controlled driving. In the final Miss Scriven beat Kay Stammers 6–2 6–4, the loser having put out two former champions, Mrs Peggy Michell and Mrs B. C. Covell and, penultimately, Jeannette Morfey.

The biggest surprise of the meeting was the defeat of Miss Dorothy Round by the left-handed Alex McOstrich, whose sense of match play and forehand driving were excellent but not quite good enough to beat Miss Morfey later.

THE OLD FOX AGAIN

In 1933, the forty-fifth meeting, there occurred one of those dramatic incidents that became part of the history of the game. Needless to say it concerned Borotra. The other participant was Bunny Austin who clearly remembers what happened: 'I led 4–love and deuce in the final set. Borotra seemed to be quite exhausted and hardly able to continue. At deuce he served, came into the net and I hit the ball to his backhand. He tried to volley, fell, knocked out the net post and lay on the court, prone.

'I dashed round, helped him to his feet and to a chair, where he sat for a few minutes. He seemed so exhausted I thought he would retire. But up he got and went back to the court. The umpire called "advantage Austin". Borotra said, "No, it is my advantage. The ball was dead when it hit the net". I didn't think it worth arguing as I felt I was bound to win. How wrong I was. I never won another game.' The Frenchman won 6–3 5–7 6–4 1–6 6–4, taking twelve of the last fourteen points and ending the match in a state of semi-collapse.

In earlier matches Austin had recorded his fourth win in six meetings over Dan Prenn and Borotra had fended off the American D. N. Jones, whose service was described as one of the best in the game – 'He aims his first for the lines, the second down the middle.'

Austin was not fooled by Borotra the following year and when he led 4–2 in the final set he made quite sure he finished it off – 6–2 4–6 6–0 6–8 6–2. There were some interesting results that year.

The England rugby player, S. W. Harris, beat a young Bob Mulliken in five sets. Years later Mulliken became the rackets professional at Wellington. C. M. 'Jimmy' Jones made his first appearance and beat J. G. Smyth (later Brigadier), a First World War VC, in five sets before being forced to retire to Nigel Sharpe at 2–2 in the final set with an ankle injury. Austin put out the 'sob' writer of the period, Godfrey Winn, and John Olliff beat the budding actor, Peter Graves. And the perennial M. J. G. Ritchie celebrated his sixty-third birthday by holding V. G. Kirby to 6–4 10–8 6–4. It was forty years since Ritchie had first competed at Queen's.

Mrs Phyllis King retained her title in 1934 – she had beaten Kay Stammers the previous year – at the expense of the up-and-coming Mary Hardwick, who still has vivid memories of the meeting. 'It was a kind of breakthrough for me. I beat Joan Ridley on the east court, Alex McOstrich on No. 3. Meeting Phyllis King was my first big final and I shall never forget the creaking floorboards as the spectators walked along that long passage to the members' stand. That was the last time I lost to Phyllis.'

Miss Hardwick was out of luck the following year when she lost to Ermyntrude Harvey on a line decision – 'a very bad one too' according to the loser – after considerable fuss. Peggy Scriven regained the title at a meeting now dubbed 'The National Covered Courts Championships'. The women's doubles were held for the first time and won by Billie Yorke and Mrs J. B. Pittman (née Elsie Goldsack). Borotra not only regained the singles title but won the mixed for the fourth year running, 1932–33 with Betty Nuthall and 1934–35 with Peggy Scriven.

Jean Borotra, Bunny Austin and the home-grown leading ladies were brushed aside in 1936 by two newcomers from overseas, Karl Schroder, the Swedish champion, and *Senorita* Anita Lizana from Chile, who later married a Scot and settled in that country until he died. She now lives in Ferndown, Dorset.

When the massive Schroder appeared at Queen's he had been absent from the game for four months. It had little effect on his play. Aged twenty-two and weighing 14 stone he had already beaten players such as Borotra and Gottfried von Cramm in Europe. He moved with remarkable speed and was difficult to beat at the net. He masked his strokes, especially his forehand, which was reproduced some forty years later by another and more famous Swede, Björn Borg.

'Bunny' Austin, whose dispute with Borotra over an advantage point
caused him to lose the match

Don Butler and Frank Wilde gave Schroder the practice he needed to meet Austin in the semi-final. The result was a massacre, 6–2 6–1 6–1 to the Swede. In twenty-two games Schroder hit twenty-two winners off the floor.

In the final Schroder beat Borotra 8–6 6–1 9–7 in ninety minutes, the first set proving the decisive one. Borotra was three times within a point of winning it at 5–4 and once at 6–5. Schroder saved these set points with passing shots, held his serve after four deuces for 7–6 and then brought off three more passing shots to capture Borotra's serve for the set.

Miss Lizana was a drop-shot expert as well as being exceptionally quick about the court. To win the title she beat Joan Ingram, Nancy Dickin and Ermyntrude Harvey without losing a set and, in the final, Mary Hardwick 6–3 6–0. That was pretty conclusive, seeing that Miss Hardwick had put out Peggy Scriven, the holder, and Freda James. Charles Hare and Frank Wilde won the men's doubles; Mary Whitmarsh and Billie York the women's.

BIG SWEDE SQUASHED

Bunny Austin got his revenge in 1937, taking the title off the big Swede, Karl Schroder, 6–2 3–6 7–5 6–2. In that final he failed to return serve only twenty-five of the 200 or more times he received. It was probably the best tournament win of Austin's career. Austin may well have been helped by the fact that the east court had been repainted and was therefore slower than normal. His cold-blooded win, 6–1 6–1 6–1, over Borotra in the semi-final seemed to confirm this, though Austin did appear to be taking an earlier ball than usual and making more frequent use of the half-volley.

Peggy Scriven won the women's title for the third

time, beating a former holder, Mrs Phyllis King 6–1 6–2, in the final, *Mlle* Goldschmidt in the semi-final and the fast-improving Valerie Scott, to whom she dropped a set, in the quarters. Two young players distinguished themselves; Rosemary Thomas, the junior champion, beating Nina Brown, and Betty Smith defeating Betty Nuthall. Miss Scott and Jean Saunders won the ladies' doubles.

The last Championships before the war were held in October 1938, providing Jean Borotra with his ninth title and Peggy Scriven with her fourth. Overall these two were the outstanding players seen at this meeting in the twenty years between the wars. Borotra became the third man over forty to win the title following the example of A. W. Gore and M. J. G. Ritchie. He also managed to shrug off the effects of a ski-ing accident earlier in the year.

As usual, Borotra dropped sets on his journey. C. M. 'Jimmy' Jones took him to four in the quarters, as did Murray Deloford in the semis. In the final Don Butler was level-pegging at set-all and 3–3 when Borotra suddenly put on a spurt to win 6–0 4–6 6–4 6–2.

In a final battle between two left-handers Peggy Scriven beat Mrs R. D. McKelvie (Alex McOstrich) 6–3 4–6 6–1. Miss Scriven, whose fourth title this was, had the greater range of winning shots but Mrs McKelvie showed a good sense of match play until she tired in the final set. In the semis Miss Scriven beat Gem Hoahing and Mrs McKelvie put out the evergreen Ermyntrude Harvey – both in two sets.

Borotra and Miss Scriven, twice mixed doubles champions, were beaten by C. M. Jones and Miss Harvey who went on to win the title. Joan Ingram and Evelyn Dearman deprived Valerie Scott and Jean Saunders of the women's doubles title and Henry Billington and John Olliff won the men's.

So, down with the curtain!

REAL TENNIS
1919–1939

PETER Latham, having left Queen's in 1898 to serve his great patron, Sir Charles Rose, returned to the Club in 1916. He was then over fifty but still capable of giving a first-class amateur, Nigel Haig for instance, thirty and a beating. E. B. Noel, the Club secretary and a great admirer of Latham, was delighted to have him back and when the war ended the game was flourishing at the Club as if there had been no interruption.

When Henry 'Toby' Chambers, who had already made a name as a marker, returned in 1919 from war work – he died in 1926 – the Club boasted four professionals. Frederick André, famed as a stringer of rackets, had been with the Club a number of years. He retired in 1922. Emil Latham, Peter's son, made the fourth. Then there were the ball-boys, some of whom were budding professionals.

Dan Maskell was one who began as a ball-boy but, despite his prowess at rackets, stuck to lawn tennis. Henry Johns, today the doyen of the game's professionals, began his career at the Club in 1924, and two years later Ernest (Willy) Ratcliff joined from Manchester. Ratcliff later won the British Open Championship. Another of the Johnson clan, Albert, was briefly on the staff in the thirties and beat Jim Dear in the Young Professionals competition.

The outstanding amateur in this country was Edgar Baerlein: 'The Little Man' as Freddie Wilson and others called him. He and another Mancunian, Lowther Lees, dominated the twenty or so years between the wars.

Baerlein, a rackets player at Eton, learned real tennis at Cambridge where he was a contemporary of Noel and Freddie Wilson, both of whom he partnered in the doubles against Oxford. In his four years in the Cambridge team Baerlein lost only one set and his progress at the game was so rapid that he even tired out the reigning amateur champion, Eustace Miles, after three hours' play. He also smoked a meerschaum pipe, puffing clouds of smoke into his and other people's rooms, and once played Lord Howick on bicycles.

Baerlein, by then in business in Manchester, won the amateur title twice before the war, in 1912 and 1914, and for the first nine years after it. That run was eventually broken in 1928 by Lowther Lees though the 'Little Man' recovered the title the following year. There were twenty-one Championships between the wars and these two men won eighteen of them!

In his first post-war win Baerlein beat a former champion, Vane Pennell, after a close match in which, it was said, the loser, despite losing a 3–1 final set lead, played brilliantly. Pennell not only refreshed himself during matches with champagne but was described by Noel as being 'Of the modern school, relying chiefly on his railroad service, hard and quick hitting, plenty of boasting and attack on the openings' – shades of some of the present-day champions. He was not, however, a dependable player and could play as slackly as he could play well.

Baerlein's championship match opponent in 1920 was E. A. C. Druce, a Cambridge hockey blue who gave his name to the Club handicap competition. The match of that season at Queen's, however, appears to have been a club affair in which J. J. Freeman of Hampton Court at the age of seventy beat G. M. Chessey. The winner's last two strokes were to beat worse than a yard and worse than two on the floor, 'quietly and deliberately. Perfection,' said *The Times*.

Three times between the wars, in 1922, 1926 and

1931, the Amateur was played in Manchester out of deference to Baerlein and later his successor, Lees.

The first American after the war to challenge for the title was C. Suyden Cutting, runner-up to the great Jay Gould in the US Championship. Baerlein dismissed him without difficulty in the 1921 Challenge Round. The 'Little Man' was fifty when, in 1930, he won his thirteenth and last Amateur, beating another American, Bill Coxe Wright, 3–0. But in 1931 he beat W. A. Groom (Lord's) for the Open Championship.

THE RABBIT

According to Freddie Wilson, Baerlein wore 'a frozen expression' while playing games. Off court his bark was worse than his bite and he described lesser players, even those who won the Silver Racquet at Lord's, as rabbits, though admitting that he too was a 'rabbit' to Peter Latham. Up to that time he was probably second only to Jay Gould among the best amateurs the game had yet seen.

James Agate, the distinguished theatre critic, was one of his great admirers, claiming that Baerlein's passion was an ice-cold demonstration of superiority and that his brain was the quickest and his mind the most exact he had ever known. He had, moreover, calculated the odds against an after life at a shade worse than five to two.

Peter Kershaw, another Mancunian and later Amateur Champion, described Baerlein as stocky of stature, nimble of foot and a great match player. He has recalled watching him practise his underhand twist serve 'Just so I can start the game and get my opponent to put the ball where I want it.'

The Hon. Clarence Bruce (later Lord Aberdare) suffered more at the hands of Baerlein than any other single player, losing to him in four successive finals from 1924 to 1927. In that last year Bruce had won a two-and-a-half-hour marathon against the American, Bill Coxe Wright, 5–6 6–2 6–1 2–6 6–5. At 5–5 and 30-all in the final set Wright had only to beat the door to reach match point. Bruce put the ball on the penthouse just above the grille and it trickled down into the corner. Wright was unable to scoop it out. After all that Aberdare had to face his nemesis, Baerlein.

Noel had a high regard for Bruce who, among his other achievements, played cricket for the Gentlemen, but did not live to see him win the Amateur Championship. He wrote 'Bruce has an attractive style, splendid return and is really a fine match player in lasting power, judgment and determination. His stroke is improving and gaining in power though he does not get down to the ball quite enough.'

The influence of Latham had made everyone very conscious of getting down to the stroke, as *The Times* reflected when reporting a match Richard Hill won in the Amateur during the mid-twenties, 'Above all he stooped. Once he so stooped as to tap the hoop of the racket on the floor when making a chase better than two.'

Three new competitions appeared in the early nineteen twenties; the Bathurst Cup, an international team event, the Bailey Cup, an inter-club four-handed competition and the Henry Leaf Cup for Old Boys teams. All were first held at Queen's and the Henry Leaf has never been played elsewhere. The Bailey Cup followed the Amateur Singles and is now the Amateur Doubles Championship.

The Illustrated Sporting & Dramatic of 22 May 1922 recorded the first Bathurst Cup with 'It was a happy idea to inaugurate an international team competition for tennis and the first contest for the beautiful Cup presented by Lady Bathurst was held at Queen's last week . . . The British Isles represented by the Hon. C. N. Bruce, V. H. Pennell, E. M. Baerlein and W. Renshaw won all five matches (against France) easily and secured the Cup for the first year.'

France, the USA and, more recently, Australia are the other countries involved in this peripatetic competition and except for 1926 when it was held at Prince's, Queen's has always been the home pitch.

Possibly Baerlein's finest accomplishment was to beat the American, Jay Gould, the 1914 World Champion, in the 1923 Bathurst Cup, albeit in Paris. Baerlein was delighted and explained 'There was just one way to beat him and I discovered it.' What he discovered he did not say but it did not work a second time and Gould took full revenge at Queen's the following year.

BAERLEIN'S SWANSONG

Baerlein's last appearance in the Cup was in 1931 when he and Lowther Lees beat the Americans, Wright and Gould. That was the 'Little Man's' last year of Championship tennis though he continued to play for Manchester in the Bailey Cup until 1937 when he and Lees won it for the fourth year running and seventh time in all. He took to shooting and fishing and lived to ninety-one. It was also Gould's last appearance in this or any other competition this side of the Atlantic. He died in 1935 aged forty-six.

Needless to say Manchester with Baerlein, Renshaw, Max Woosnam and Lees were the dominant Bailey Cup team between the wars, winning it thirteen times. American teams won it twice when, in 1924, Gould and Suyden Cutting represented Paris and, in 1927, Gould played with Bill Coxe Wright for Philadelphia, very narrowly beating Manchester in the final. The score against Lees and Woosnam was 6–3 3–6 6–4 3–6 6–5 owing, *The Times* said, to Gould's wonderful shots for the grille in the final set crisis. It also commented that the feature of the match was 'the wonderful volleying duels between Gould and Woosnam'. That is understandible as Woosnam, with Randolph Lycett, won the Wimbledon men's doubles title in 1921. An England, Corinthian and Manchester City footballer and useful cricketer, Woosnam was one of the great all-round games player of that or any other age, like C. B. Fry, Howard Baker and R. E. Foster.

Queen's, between the wars, won the Bailey Cup five times. Those successes were due to the fact that, apart from Baerlein and later Less, the Club had the best amateurs in the country; Bruce (later Lord Aberdare), Richard Hill, E. A. C. Druce and later Dugald Macpherson. By the year 1938 the Club was so strong that two teams were entered and in the final Queen's I (Aberdare and Macpherson) beat Queen's II (Billy Ross-Skinner and Michael Pugh).

A triangular competition between Queen's, Prince's and MCC and intended for Club players was begun in 1931 and it was in this that Pugh first made his mark along with Norman Freudenthal, Rory McNair, D. J. Wardley, E. C. Holt, G. E. Bean, C. M. N. Baker and others. The rivalry did lead to some team packing and Lord Aberdare was constrained to write to Freudenthal suggesting that he, Ronnie Aird of MCC and Ross-Skinner, then playing for Prince's, should stand down from the competition.

The third of these innovative competitions was the Henry Leaf Cup for Old Boys' teams and this was the one event neither Baerlein of Eton nor Lees of Wellington could dominate. First held in 1922, it was not until 1948 that Eton with Lord Cullen, Aird and R. St. L. Granville first won the Cup and Wellington have yet to do so.

The outstanding team throughout the history of this event has been Winchester followed by Rugby and, to a lesser degree, Harrow. Winchester with Bruce, Hill and G. D. Huband won the initial competition and every other year between the wars apart from 1923 (Rugby) and 1939 (Harrow).

WINCHESTER SUPREME

So strong were Winchester that in 1923 they entered two teams and in 1925 Ross-Skinner, having come down from Cambridge where he won a Rugby blue, had to play Douglas Jardine, a member of the 1924 winning side and later England's controversial body-line cricket captain, and Freudenthal for the third place in the first team. He succeeded.

Aberdare, sandwiched between Baerlein and Lees in the Amateur Championship heirarchy, played in the majority of these inter-war finals, backed up by Hill, Ross-Skinner, Freudenthal, N. F. H. Railing, A. L. Grant, Woosnam and Archie Hamilton, later *The Times* real tennis, rackets and squash rackets correspondent, despite being half-crippled by arthritis.

In 1927 Bruce scored his first win over Baerlein. That was also the first time Baerlein, nearly forty-eight, had been beaten by an amateur from this country since N. S. Lytton deprived him of the Amateur singles title in 1913.

In 1931 Henry Leaf, the donor of the Cup, was knocked down by a bus and killed. A useful cricketer, he was an expert at the draw stroke between the legs, known as the dog shot, something that even Ian Botham has not yet exploited.

Lowther Lees won his first Amateur Championship at the age of twenty-five, in 1928, the first season the Challenge round was abolished and the champion had to play through. He was taken to five sets successively by Macpherson, Bruce and Richard Hill, in the final. Among the spectators was R. C. Glanville who, seventy-one years earlier (1857), had won the Silver Racquet at Oxford! Introduced to the game in Manchester, Lees had just come down from Cambridge where he and Ross-Skinner had followed Macpherson and Hill as the University's top players. That win was only a summary foretaste of his later successes, as Baerlein was back for the next two years and it was not until 1931 that Lees beat the 'Little Man' in the final. That was the last time Baerlein played in the Amateur.

That left Lees and Aberdare to fight it out. Aber-

Queen's Club v. United Universities: Top row, left to right: Mr M. Roberts (Queen's), Mr G. Ashton
(Cambridge), Mr S. H. Geldard (Queen's), Mr R. H. Hill (Cambridge), Mr E. B. Noel (Queen's), Mr V. A. Cazalet
(Oxford), Mr Justice Page (Queen's), Peter Latham (head professional, Queen's Club).
Sitting, left to right: Mr W. D. Macpherson (Cambridge), H. Chambers (professional at Queen's Club),
E. Latham (professional at Queen's Club), Mr D. R. Jardine (Oxford), Captain R. K. Price (Queen's),
Mr C. E. Tatham (Queen's)

dare by then was nearer fifty than forty and had yet to win the title. He finally succeeded in 1932, beating Lees 3–2 in the final after holding a match point in the third set. Aberdare used the underarm twist or giraffe service; Lees persisted with the American.

SHORT OF STROKES

That year also saw the first appearance of Kenneth Gandar Dower in the Amateur. A man of many Cambridge blues, he met Jimmy van Alen, an American, and was beaten 3–1. *The Times* commented 'Gandar Dower extended a really good player for two and a half hours without making a single properly cut tennis stroke.'

For the next five years Lees sat comfortably on the throne, beating Aberdare in three successive finals, C. M. N. Baker, a Cambridge blue, and Richard Hill in the other two. *En route* to his 1934 title Lees beat Gandar Dower in the semi-final.

The Gandar's appearances in the Championships fascinated people. That year he beat Freudenthal to reach the last four and Hubert Winterbotham in the *Daily Telegraph* described him as 'This tennis philistine' and 'This iconoclast who walks into the court with his tongue in his cheek.' John Armitage wrote that Gandar Dower's serve was 'a mere pat on the penthouse' and that 'he cannot, except for good fortune, lay a short chase'.

The following year Freudenthal did reach the semi-final where he met Aberdare. Before the match he received a letter from Billy Ross-Skinner that read 'Dear Norman, I think you might do it today if you feel fit. Wouldn't it be grand if you were in the final. Good Luck, Billy'. He did not make it but took a love set off Aberdare.

Lees's last title before the war was in 1937, the year that Latham, then seventy-two, retired after fifty years, on and off, at Queen's. It was also the forty-fifth Amateur Championship and Peter Kershaw, still at Oxford, was among the competitors. He lost to Hill, who then beat Aberdare in five sets before being demolished 6–0 6–2 6–0 by Lees in the final. The quality of Lees's play, it was said, had not been equalled since Etchebaster beat Walter Kinsella for the World title at Prince's in 1930.

Lees was a handsome player, a natural and he needed little practice before competing. According to Kershaw he used a well-controlled American service often followed by a volley which was well cut and died away in the area of the grille. He was quick about the court which, combined with a crushing weight of stroke, made him a formidable player. His weakness was that sometimes while playing a lesser man he would become uninterested and lose matches he should have won.

Aberdare was fifty-three when he won his second title in 1938, the oldest man ever to have won it. It was also fourteen years since he first appeared in the final. It took him three hours to subdue Lees, the holder, 5–6 1–6 6–5 6–3 6–5 in the semis – a wonderful feat of determination and endurance, especially as Lees had led by two sets and 3–1. Richard Hill was seeded to come through the other half but, suffering from an injured wrist, lost to Ross-Skinner in the first round. The latter, who revelled in a hard-hitting game, made little impression on Aberdare in the final.

Dugald Macpherson's win in the last Championship before the war was a great surprise. Aged thirty-eight and only the fourth man to win the title between the wars, he beat Lees 6–5 5–6 6–5 6–1 in the final. That kept the pecking order correct as Lees had been his second string when at Cambridge. The *Manchester Guardian* commented that Lees's play was in and out, 'He would relapse from his high estate'. *The Times* said 'As a returner of the ball Macpherson is unequalled.'

Macpherson put it this way: 'Lees was a far better player than ever I was and it was rather sad that owing to his drinking too much beer in Manchester I succeeded in beating him. I was never a good tennis player and I only won matches because I played reasonably good squash in the tennis court, by which I mean I kept the ball going longer than people liked or expected!' Modesty!

It was another seven years before Lees got his chance to relieve Macpherson of the title.

Real Tennis: Dugald Macpherson Looks at the Leading Players

The two outstanding players, I would say, have been Pierre Etchebaster and Jay Gould. They are followed by Peter Latham, Fred Covey, Jim Dear, Edward Johnson, Jock Soutar, Norty Knox, Howard Angus and Chris Ronaldson. Just behind that group come Edgar Baerlein, Clarence and Morys Aberdare, Geoffrey Atkins, Alan Lovell, Ogden Phipps, Alistair Martin, Pete and Jimmy Bostwick, Frank Willis, Jack Groom, Henry Johns, Charles Cullen and Richard Hill.

Jay Gould's record of winning the US Championship from 1906 to 1925 speaks for itself. I saw him win the 1924 title when he beat Hewitt Morgan, who had beaten me in the semis. Gould, by then, had become too fat to run about the court but his ball control was so remarkable that he was in charge of the game throughout. His volleying and railroad service were so accurate that Morgan was always on the defensive. When volleying he nearly always cut the ball so that it would have laid chase better than 2. He had the perfect tennis stroke (better than Pierre Etchebaster's).

Both he and Pierre were masters of the railroad. They stood about a yard from the gallery wall and, unlike a lot of present-day experts, did not serve fast. They could decide whether the ball would touch the penthouse once or twice. If it touched twice and the receiver managed to volley it, then they would serve only one bounce off the penthouse. That prevented the receiver volleying and the ball would shoot off the back wall into the side wall.

It is sometimes suggested that Baerlein was in the same class as Gould because he beat him two sets to one in a Bathurst Cup match in Paris in 1923. I understand that Jay had travelled to Paris from the Riviera overnight expecting to practise the next day

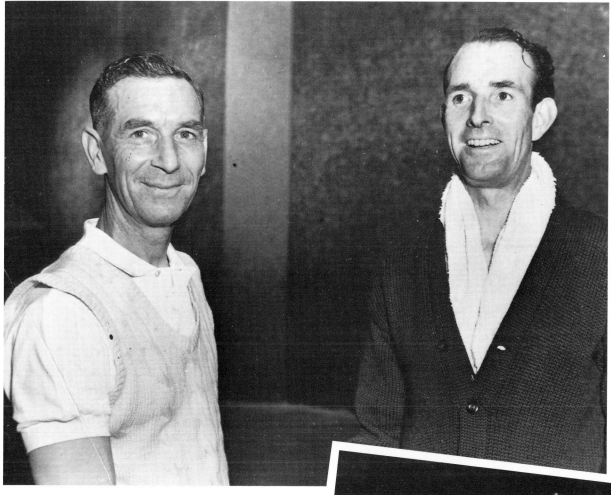

Jim Dear in action and (above) with Albert Johnson of the New York Tennis and Racquets Club

but found he had to play Baerlein immediately. The following year Gould beat Baerlein 3–0 in a Bathurst Cup match at Queen's, though he could not run.

In his prime Gould beat Fred Covey for the World title (1914) and when I was at Cambridge in 1921 or 1922 I saw Covey beat Baerlein very easily in an exhibition, giving him 15 as well. Covey was altogether too fast and strong for Edgar. Gould cut the ball in a more correct or classical style than Pierre Etchebaster, who admitted that he 'carved' the ball rather than cut it. I think that if they had met when both were at their peaks Pierre would probably have won because there was never a player (Baerlein and Angus not excepted) who devoted so much time and thought to the game and tactics.

When Pierre Etchebaster lost to Covey in their World Championship match at Prince's in 1926 he is alleged to have said, 'I shall be back next year when

I will win'. He had lost to Covey mainly because he had never previously met a player who cut the ball so heavily (much as Gould cut it) or hit harder and faster, making it extremely difficult to return the ball off the back wall. When they met again Pierre had trained himself to take such shots before they reached the back wall. This suggests that Pierre could or would have done the same with Gould's heavily cut strokes. He was also a more accurate and attacking volleyer than Jay and would spend unlimited time practising or perfecting special strokes.

I never saw Peter Latham in his prime but his record shows that he could cope with all types of players and E. B. Noel considered him the equal of any player he had seen. If Covey had been able to devote all his time and interest to tennis he might well have delayed his defeat by Pierre for a few years. Unfortunately tennis became more or less a sideline owing to the attitude of his employer, Baroness Wentworth.

Jim Dear was probably the most natural ball-games player and mover I have ever seen, excelling at squash, rackets and tennis. Unfortunately he did not possess the character requirements – mainly determination to win – that are necessary in world class competition. I refereed the three squash rackets challenge matches between him and Amr Bey in the 1930s and it was disappointing to see him try foolish drop-shots from the back of the court when hand-in and game-ball.

On the second day, or leg, of his World Challenge match with Pierre in New York in 1948, Jim played so well that he got on top of the champion; something previously unseen. At the end of that day's play Jock Soutar was heard to say, 'The "Little Man" is going to be beaten – at last.' But Pierre had made Dear run so much that the Englishman's legs gave out in the third and decisive leg. Jim eventually won the title when Pierre retired but he should never have lost it in 1957 to A. B. Johnson. I put that down to inadequate preparation; he spent most of the time coaching young people at lawn tennis and squash.

Soutar was an Englishman, trained at Prince's, who emigrated to the US and spent most of his life at the Philadelphia Club. He, like Dear, was an all-rounder; world champion at rackets and world standard at tennis and he once beat Pierre in an exhibition match receiving only half 15.

Lowther Lees was my second string at Cambridge. In the 1930s he became open champion before losing the title to Jim Dear. A fine volleyer and playing a fast game his career was shortened by his lack of attention to his health.

There has never been a fitter or more sporting amateur than Howard Angus. He re-introduced the speeding up of the game, just as Tom Pettitt had done in the late 1800s. His main new stroke, which won him many points, was hitting the ball on the half-volley very hard into the main wall so that it skimmed over the low part of the net before dying under the winning gallery. It is an extremely difficult ball to return in a satisfactory way. My view is that Pierre would have dealt with Howard's game by playing short and slow.

Chris Ronaldson is clearly a very good match player, able to cope with the faster game that most professionals play nowadays. He makes use of numerous services, which is one of the attractions of tennis, but I doubt whether either he or Angus have as accurate a railroad as did Gould and Etchebaster.

Although Edgar Baerlein had a long innings (1914–31) as Amateur Champion or Gold Racquet winner, I do not consider him a player of the very top flight and I did see a large number of his matches. He was fortunate in not facing really high-class opposition until he met Lowther Lees. He was successful because he treated his games very seriously and, no matter whom he was playing, always tried to win every game to love.

Edgar had no great serve and did not cut the ball in the classic way. But he did play to a length and his powers of return were remarkable. His volleying was defensive like most English players compared with American. He established a psychological ascendency over Clarence Bruce (Lord Aberdare), his main opponent, who was almost but not quite his equal in accuracy of return and placement. His knowledge of the game was profound but I doubt whether he would have achieved the same results in the faster game played today.

And what of the Aberdares, father and son, Clarence and Morys? Clarence was a wonderful ball-game player with an excellent eye (he scored several hundreds for Middlesex at cricket). His return and volleying were as good as Edgar's but he was not quite so accurate in his direction and length. It was his safe volleying that helped him win the amateur doubles title with various different partners. I do not consider him as good a stylist as his son, Morys, who also cut the ball more than his father did.

Geoffrey Atkins was more involved in the world

rackets but on the tennis court he showed the same qualities that made him the rackets champion: perfect footwork, timing, anticipation and stroke play. He would have been top class had he been able to devote more time to the game. Alan Lovell, too, has all the makings of a first-class player providing he can give the time to the game.

The most attacking volleyer and most aggressive and powerful player I have seen, or played against, was the American, Ogden Phipps. In his challenge matches against Pierre Etchebaster I understand he was able to compete on equal terms for a set. But he was a big man, not too active on his feet, and Pierre would then run him about too much.

I met Phipps in the 1949 Amateur Championship final. I knew I had to return his strokes before the back wall. For three games I succeeded but then pulled a leg muscle and could only limp thereafter.

The following year I lost to another American in the final, Alastair Martin. A delightful fellow, he cut the ball beautifully and was an excellent volleyer. Strangely I never saw the Bostwick brothers, Jimmy and Pete, play.

Finally, I should mention two players who, for different reasons, never really fulfilled themselves. Both were beautiful players. Charles Cullen's best stroke was his forehand. Though he won the Amateur twice and the doubles title three years running with me defending the side galleries and later twice more with Morys Bruce, Charles did not have the time, interest or physique to maintain top-class form. I certainly believe that Richard Hill could have been a world champion if his health and character had allowed. He had the best backhand stroke I have ever seen. And I have seen quite a few in my time.

RACKETS
1919–1939

J. R. Thompson

AS Club secretary at Queen's from 1914 to 1928, E. B. Noel did much to increase the membership of rackets players. He was in the Winchester pair in 1897 and 1898 and reached the final of the Public Schools Championships with his partner, R. A. Williams. He won the Amateur Rackets Singles in 1907 and is the only person ever to win an Olympic medal for rackets singles, which he did in 1908. Only a few British players entered and there were many retirements: maybe his Gold Medal would have been more fitting for his services to rackets as a historian and as Secretary of The Queen's Club!

The World Championship

For some years after the First World War the World Championship was contested in the USA. The two leading players were Jock Soutar and Charles Williams, the latter having left Queen's in 1923 to join the Chicago Racquet Club. Soutar had been champion at the outbreak of war, but eventually Williams regained the World title in 1928 by at last defeating Soutar by 7 games to 3, an interval of eighteen years since he had first won the title. Williams died in 1935 so that the title again became vacant. It was agreed to arrange an Anglo-American, home-and-home match. The British challenger became David Milford a master at Marlborough College. As Amateur Champion, he then defeated Albert Cooper, the Professional Champion, in two great matches at Queen's in 1936, by 8 games to 3. Milford's speed about the court and ability to conjure up remarkable winners had enabled him to nullify Cooper's glorious hitting. Quite unexpectedly, Norbert Setzler, the New York Professional, had

defeated the much-fancied Bobby Grant in the North American Open Championship, so that he became the American challenger.

In 1937 they met for the first leg in New York, in what was a very close match which Setzler won by 4 games to 3, 9–15 15–9 10–15 15–10 15–8 12–15 15–12, after Milford had led by 11–9 in the last game. However, in the second leg at Queen's, Milford was an easy winner by 15–4 15–4 15–9 15–12 to take the World title by 7 games to 4. In so doing he became the first amateur since Sir William Hart Dyke in 1862 to do so. Milford's amazing fleetness of foot and wonderful eye and wrist enabled him to play strokes of sheer genius and he was a worthy champion. Milford held the title for the next ten years unchallenged, until he resigned after the Second World War in 1947.

The Amateur Singles Championship

In the Amateur Singles Championship between the wars, the name of the Hon. C. N. Bruce appears regularly in the final. He became champion in 1922 and again in 1931 as Lord Aberdare. The year 1925 records the only American winner in C. C. Pell, to be followed by a three-year reign by the talented left-hander, J. C. F. Simpson (1926–28). D. S. Milford won for the first time in 1930 and if his hockey and schoolmastering duties had allowed him to play more often, he would undoubtedly have won more frequently. I. Akers-Douglas won for three successive years (1932–34), to be followed by the equally consistent Milford for the next four years (1935–38). P. Kershaw from Manchester was the winner in 1939, the last championship before the Second World War.

Ten times triumphant in the Amateur Doubles, Lord Aberdare – seen here with his son, Morys Bruce, the present Lord Aberdare

The Amateur Doubles Championship

When the Amateur Doubles Championship was resumed after the war Lord Aberdare added eight wins to his two previous victories with B. S. Foster (1910 and 1911). His most successful partnership was with Dr H. W. (Bill) Leatham, the Charterhouse doctor, but he also won with A. C. Raphael and P. W. Kemp-Welch. Next to Aberdare J. C. F. Simpson (later Sir Cyril Simpson Bart) was the most successful doubles player of the period, winning three times with R. C. O. Williams and the same with C. S. Crawley. Kenneth Wagg and Ian Akers-Douglas won the title three times.

The British Open Championship

In 1929, Major-General S. H. Sheppard presented a cup for the British Open Championship. The first winner, J. C. F. Simpson, defeated the Queen's

Finalists in the Public Schools Championship of 1926, Harrow v. Wellington.
The Prime Minister, Old Harrovian Stanley Baldwin, stands in the gallery
front row (fourth from left). Wellington (R. C. Dobson and J. Powell) beat Harrow
(N. M. Ford and A. M. Crawley) 4–3.

professional, Charles R. Read, by 5 games to 1 in a two-leg, best of 7 games match. In 1931, Lord Aberdare, having defeated Simpson in the Amateur Championship, challenged him for the Open Title and won handsomely by 6 games to 2 at the age of forty-six.

The Public Schools Championship

During the war years 1914–1919 a handicap singles event was started for the schools, and continued until 1954, when a cup was presented by the Foster family in memory of H. K. Foster. The event then became a level singles championship for the best sixteen selected school players. The first Public Schools Championship after the war took place in 1919 at Queen's.

BETWEEN THE WARS

In 1919, the first championship at Queen's after the war, Marlborough (G. S. Butler and G. W. F. Haslehurst) defeated Malvern (C. G. W. Robson and N. E. Partridge) in the final by 4 games to 1. The name of D. S. Milford soon catches the eye, as from 1921–1924 he was first string for Rugby for four years, winning the cup for the last two, first with G. M. Goodbody and then with E. F. Longrigg. Mr Stanley Baldwin, an old Harrovian, watched the great final of 1926 when Wellington (R. C. Dobson and J. Powell) defeated Harrow (N. M. Ford and A. M. Crawley) by 4 games to 3.

In 1929, the Hon. C. N. Bruce and E. B. Noel instituted the Old Boys' Championship for the Noel-Bruce Cup. This competition has continued ever since, gathering momentum and increasing in popularity as the years have gone by. In 1932, Harrow (R. Pulbrook and J. H. Pawle) defeated Rugby (R. A. Gray and R. F. Lumb) in the final by 4 games to 2, but the following year Gray and Lumb had their revenge defeating Pulbrook and Pawle by 4 games to 2.

In 1934–1938, Malvern came into the news again with P. D. Manners who was in the pair for five years, winning the championship with N. W. Beeson in 1936 and 1937. Having won the final against Clifton (W. E. Brassington and S. G. Greenbury) by 4 games to 0 in 1936, they were given a splendid fight by Tonbridge (J. R. Thompson and P. Pettman) before winning by 4 games to 3, in the 1937 final.

The Noel-Bruce Cup

Public schools rackets was given a fillip in 1929 with the introduction of a competition for the Noel-Bruce Cup, otherwise known as the Public Schools Old Boys' Rackets Championship. This ever-popular doubles competition for Old Boys' pairs was the brainchild of the Hon. C. N. Bruce, who was

The Prime Minister presents the trophy to the victorious Wellington pair, J. Powell (left) and R. C. Dobson

Amateur Doubles Champion at the time, and E. B. Noel, then secretary of Queen's. Both had previously represented Winchester at Queen's in the Public Schools Championship. Ever since its institution in 1929, it has been played with ever-increasing enthusiasm, except between 1939–1945, during the Second World War. This competition, more than any other, has helped to encourage those who have learnt their rackets at school to continue to play after leaving. There have been occasions when as many as ten pairs have entered from one school; the entries depending very much on the enthusiasm and efficiency of the Old Boys' rackets secretary of a particular school. The competition has always been well supported by the prominent amateur players of the day and the finals have often attracted a packed gallery, vociferous with partisan support for their old school.

Eton (R. C. O. Williams and Ian Akers-Douglas) won the first competition but thereafter in the next nine competitions before the War, Rugby won seven times with David Milford and Cyril Simpson for four years and with Raymond Lumb and Peter Kershaw for three. Their sequence was only broken in 1932 by Eton (Kenneth Wagg and Ian Akers-Douglas) and in 1935 by Winchester, for the only time, with Norman McCaskie and Julian Faber.

The Professionals

Between the wars, the Club's rackets professionals continued to make their mark. Albert Cooper, a tall brilliant hard-hitting left-hander who learnt to play at Wellington under Walter Hawes, was employed by Queen's in the 1930s before moving to Eton. He was British Open Rackets Champion from 1934–1936. Shortly before the Second World War, Arthur Whetton, a most promising young red-haired player was at Queen's before he moved to Haileybury but sadly he lost his life in the War. Mention should also be made of Dan Maskell, the distinguished former Professional Lawn Tennis Champion for many years and now so well known as the BBC TV commentator on lawn tennis. He too joined Queen's as a ball-boy and in 1926 he won a Junior Professional Rackets Championships. He would have made a fine rackets player, but in 1927 he was lost to the game when he went to the All England Club as lawn-tennis professional.

In 1924, Jim Dear joined his elder brother as a ball-boy at Queen's at the age of fourteen. At first he hated games and was nearly sacked at seventeen for showing no promise. He was transferred to Prince's to learn rackets and squash. There he met Amr Bey, then the Open Squash Rackets Champion, who encouraged him and realized his talent. Thereafter Jim's record at court games is unique. He was Open Squash Rackets Champion from 1938–46 World Rackets Champion from 1947–54 and World Tennis Champion from 1955–57. He returned to Queen's from 1946–51 and from 1953–56 and also held professional appointments at the New York Racquet Club, Wellington and Eton. Compactly built and a beautiful mover with an individual style, he possessed superb ball control and tactical skill at all court games.

His wry comments were much appreciated by his many admirers: 'It's not the racket that hits the ball – you hit the ball with the racket!' Or, 'There's one thing about refereeing; you can make mistakes but you are always right!' Or, 'The trouble with these games is that they are so easy no one can play them.'

John Pawle on Rackets

John Pawle, amateur champion from 1946 to 1949 inclusive and twice challenger for the World title, learned the game in between the wars and offers some comments on the players of that generation.

It is impossible, in my view, to compare the champions of different ages in any sport. Rackets is no exception especially when played, as it was up to the 1950s, with a stitched kid-covered ball that made it a totally different game. 'Cut' applied with the classic stroke could make the ball die on the floor and to dig it out from the back was well nigh impossible.

One talked about cutting the cover off the ball and this was literally true. Sufficient cut could sever the stitches on the seams. Any player who failed to kill the ball nine times out of ten was considered inept. The modern game played with something like a golf ball has to be faster but, and I admit I am prejudiced, is less skilful. For instance, the drop shot – not the poopy variety as played in the squash court but the heavily cut masked shot that died on the floor – is now an impossibility. The speed of the hammer service as delivered by Willie Boone is quite breathtaking but the classic up-and-down game is now too often a round-the-houses bash, especially with lesser players. That is the fault of the modern ball.

Without trying to compare across the generations I think Charlie Williams was probably the greatest all-time striker of the ball [others tend to confirm this – Ed.] and, like a lot of geniuses, one of the worst coaches. Cosmo Crawley has said that his only advice was "it it like me, sir'. Of course no one in the world could "it it like "'im" and the result in Crawley's case was that he and his partner, Leonard Crawley, broke a record number of rackets while at Harrow.

Cosmo Crawley and others considered Cyril Simpson to be the best amateur between the wars, a period that included David Milford and Ian Akers-Douglas. I would qualify that by saying 'on his day' because Simpson, an amusing and light-hearted fellow, did not always give himself the best of chances. He trained at the '400' Club and was known to have turned up for a match at Queen's still in his dinner jacket. [There is another version that says he arrived for a match wearing his pyjamas – Ed.]

In my view the best player in the game by 1939 was Arthur Whetton, the Haileybury professional. He was taught by Fred Crosby at Harrow. Tragically he was killed in the war, otherwise he and Jim Dear might have been battling it out for a decade or so afterwards.

In my days Walter Hawes at Wellington was considered the finest coach. He was a lovely man, though I thought Fred Crosby was just the better teacher. As to courts I have no hesitation in saying that Queen's, despite being a draughty place, had the finest in the world bar none. Because it was so fast and took cut I thought it impossible to play on when first I competed there. But, that was the beginning of a love affair.

In my days we had some great doubles teams; Cosmo Crawley and Cyril Simpson, Ian Akers-Douglas and Kenneth Wagg, 'Bimby' Holt and Ronnie Taylor and that schoolboy pair, Raymond Lumb and Peter Kershaw of Rugby. There were characters too; Edgar Baerlein, Nigel Haig, Richard Hill and Peter Latham among them. Then there were Freddie Wilson of *The Times* and R. C. Robertson-Glasgow (*Crusoe*). I remember some young man playing a match wearing a wristwatch (commonplace nowadays but not then) and Wilson commenting in *The Times*, 'It did not appear to help him time the ball'. Then, in 1936, Robertson-Glasgow covering the Amateur Doubles semi-final in which Clarence Aberdare and Peter Kemp-Welch beat Richard Hill and myself 4–3, wrote, 'In the final game Hill distinguished himself by returning two strokes with a broken racket that wailed like a minstrel whose audience had fled!' They were colourful days.

THE QUEEN'S CLUB SQUASH
1919–1939

THERE was no standard size when the first two squash courts were built, along with the No. 3 covered court, in 1905. When the standard measurements were drawn up by the Tennis and Rackets Association – the SRA had yet to be formed – it was found that the Queen's courts were 2–3 feet longer and 2–3 feet narrower than the regulation.

E. B. Noel who did a great deal to encourage squash when, in 1914, he became secretary, wrote, 'Nevertheless they are excellent courts. Some think them better than the standard though they suffer from a fault common to the great majority of squash courts. Whatever ball is used it is very difficult to finish a rally with anything like good players. But it must be remembered that a club court is played on not only by expert players but by those of all grades of skill, or lack of it. Hence it is better not to have a club court too difficult. In the courts in the chief London clubs, Lord's, Prince's, the Bath Club, RAC and Cavendish as well as Queen's, it is not easy to kill the ball. With the greatest players I have seen rallies which lasted for over fifty strokes.' What would Noel think if he could see the present-day game?

The first match of any note The Queen's Club played was, according to Noel, against the Bath Club in 1908. The Club was represented by Noel, Cecil Browning (a jovial character whose son, Oscar, became a useful player) and P. Bramwell Davis. The Bath Club had J. E. Tomkinson (later Palmer-Tomkinson), the best amateur of the period, H. B. Chinery and R. E. 'Tip' Foster, who captained England at cricket and soccer and was one of the great brotherhood of seven. 'We were, as we expected to be, wonderfully beaten,' wrote Noel.

The finest player of the age, and for a good many years to come, was Charles Read, who had joined Queen's professional staff (lawn tennis, rackets and squash) in the early 1900s. Noel considered him 'the most proficient player ever seen'. W. D. Macpherson, one of the two best amateurs ever to play for Queen's, claimed that the reason for Read's dominance was that he realized that the man who held the front of the court always won the rally. 'That explained why Read beat Oke Johnson of the RAC so easily in 1920 and 1928,' wrote Macpherson, who had personally learnt that lesson playing in the US while at the Harvard Law School.

Like many others Macpherson did not think much of the Queen's courts except for No. 4, which was one of the two built in the No. 2 rackets court in 1924. He wrote: 'It was standard size and, in my opinion, as perfect as any court – and the gallery held few people, which suited me. No. 3 court with the old rackets court gallery played slow and the bounce was curious.' Indeed, the courts did not satisfy everyone. Some years later Frank Strawson repeatedly complained about them – 'appallingly unsatisfactory and unattractive conditions', 'condition of squash courts quite unworthy of the Club', 'poor lighting in No. 3 court, a hole in No. 4 court roof', etc. etc.

Macpherson's introduction to the Club came as a schoolboy, when he and W. H. Isaac were the Harrow pair in the Schools Rackets Championship in 1918. The following year he played with W. A. R. (Billy) Collins and unbeknown to him E. B. Noel, as was his habit with the more promising schoolboys, made him a member of the Club; a fact that remained undiscovered until his father received a bill for his subscription the following year! He played little at Cambridge, mostly it seems against Richard

W. D. Macpherson (right) with Victor Cazalet. Macpherson was
twice Amateur Champion

Hill, a notable real tennis player and colourful writer on court games for *The Times*. His squash development began seriously while in the US.

Macpherson won the Amateur Championship twice, a feat no other regular Club player has achieved. The first time, in 1924, he beat Jimmy Tomkinson in the final. Ironically, Tomkinson that season had chosen Macpherson as his training partner! Two years later he won the title again, beating a stern rival, Victor Cazalet, a man very difficult to dislodge from the front of the court.

It was as a Bath Club Cup player that Macpherson rendered his greatest service to the Club, leading the winning team four times in 1925–26, 1929–30, 1930–31, and 1931–32; a record only equalled by R. A. Dolman in the seventies. In 1948 'Mac' made a major comeback and led another victorious team, a fact of which he has no recollection though his memory is remarkably acute for his age. The 1925–26 team was Macpherson, R. G. de Quetteville and P. W. Le Gros, an all-round sportsman who played rugby for Richmond, and cricket for Bucks and, after the last war, became the Club chairman. When Queen's gained their hat-trick, Macpherson was joined by K. C. Gandar Dower, Frank Strawson, J. D. P. Wheatley and Le Gros. De

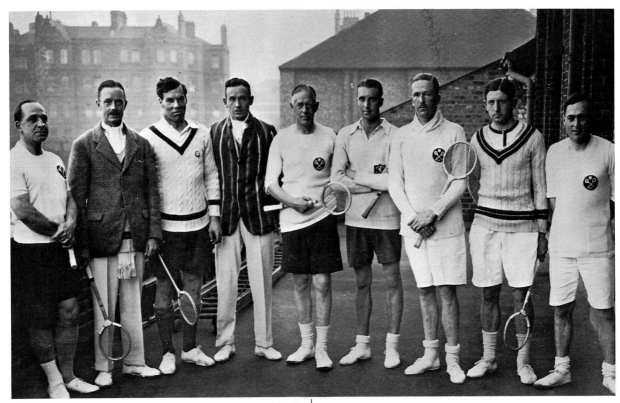

Inter-County Championship finalists 1930–31 (left to right): C. H. Medhurst (Yorks), J. C. Gregory (Yorks), S. M. Toyne (Yorks), Hon. B. M. O. S. Foljambe (Yorks), J. R. B. Knox (Yorks), J. B. Hyde-Smith (Kent) F. M. Strawson (Kent), G. O. M. Jameson (Kent), C. P. Hamilton (Kent)

Quetteville had moved to the Conservative Club. In 1932 Macpherson scaled the pinnacle of his squash career, beating Amr Bey (RAC) in the Bath Club Cup having lost to the new master in the final of the Amateur Championship. He then retired from serious squash but in 1938 made a surprise reappearance and, as second string, beat R. F. Lumb in a Cup match against Prince's!

Gerald Pawle in his book *Squash Rackets* claims that Macpherson was never beaten on the Club No. 4 court – the one he disliked – and lost only four Cup matches in his career; twice to P. Q. Reiss, once to Victor Cazalet and once, when the court was sweating, to Weston Backhouse. Both Reiss and Cazalet were players who took the middle of the court and made it very difficult for their opponents to get a clear view of, or swing at, the ball. Having played Cazalet once in the Amateur Championship I can vouch for that. I beat him but must have done twice the amount of running.

Gandar Dower, another Harrovian and Cantabridgian and wonderfully versatile sportsman,

succeeded Macpherson as the Club's leading player. They first met in the 1928 Amateur Championship when 'The Gander' was only twenty and still at Cambridge. Macpherson won. Cazalet proved his stumbling block in the next few years and for some time Gandar Dower gave the Amateur Championship a miss. But, in 1935–6, he did help Queen's win the Bath Club Cup with John Ridgers, Bob Tinkler and Sir William Lewthwaite.

In that season 'The Gander', less of an artist and more of an entrepreneur than Macpherson, met the champion, Amr Bey, then at the height of his powers, in a Cup match at the Club. On 14 November 1935, *The Times* carried this report:

The most important match in this year's Bath Club Cup competition was played at Queen's yesterday, when the home club met the holders, the Royal Automobile Club. Before the match the two clubs were level at the head of the competition with eight points each out of a possible nine. At the end of it Queen's headed the table with ten points to the RAC's nine and though both the teams will be without the services of their first strings in the second half of the competition, last night's match has probably determined the destination of the cup.

In the first-string match F. D. Amr Bey (RAC) beat K. C. Gandar Dower (Queen's) by three games to none (9–7

9–5 9–5). This was the best game seen, or likely to be seen, between amateurs this season, for the pair will not meet again in the Amateur Championship. Gandar Dower kept the Open champion on court for 52 minutes and thoroughly extended him in the first game, a feat of which no other British amateur is capable. The standard of play in this game was extremely high, both players producing wonderful shots of every description, and it had to be an exceptionally fine one to terminate a rally, when the return of both was so accurate and their pace about the court so great.

Amr's length for his hard-hit shot to the back of the court was not so consistently good as it became later and Gandar Dower, profiting by this, led 5–3, making a very useful run of four aces. Amr drew level at five-all with an unexpected backhand reverse angle shot, but five hands later his opponent led 7–5, scoring his seventh ace with a beautiful drop shot at the end of a rally of some forty strokes. Gandar Dower then made two mistakes, hitting a service out of court and putting an easy ball on the tin, and the score was seven-all. He was in hand once more but failed to score, and Amr, with an angle and drop shot – both made with perfect touch on the backhand won the game.

Afterwards the superior play of the champion gradually overcame the wonderful activity of The Queen's Club player. Amr also found the length of the court better, and though twenty-five hands were played in the second game Gandar Dower was always fighting a losing battle. In the third he could do little against Amr's relentless accuracy and scored only a single ace before the latter won the match with a run of four aces, the winning shot being a perfect straight drop in the forehand corner.

The two remaining ties, though good in their class, were insignificant in comparison. J. N. S. Ridgers, by superior stroke play and greater pace in the court, proved far too good for the steady return of O. Lerwill, winning by three games to none (9–7 9–3 9–4) and R. K. Tinkler so outlasted J. H. Stothert that after a finely fought third game he won the fourth without the loss of an ace, the score being 9–3 9–7 8–10 9–0.

The writer, 'Our Squash Rackets Correspondent' as *The Times* put it in those days, was Archie Hamilton, who suffered arthritis in his hands and wrote ponderously but meticulously and delivered all his copy by hand to the Old Printing House Square, down by Blackfriars Bridge, where *The Times* was then published.

THE CHAMPION BUMPED

Gandar Dower and Amr Bey did not meet again for another three years (9 November 1938) and then it

was also in the Bath Club Cup, this time played at the RAC. By then the matches had been reduced to the best of three games. Amr, still Amateur Champion, set off at a terrific pace and was dead accurate in all he attempted. His backhand volleys off Gandar's lobs, aimed at slowing down the game, were deadly and he took the game 9–1. At the start of the second game, Amr leading by a point or two, there was a fierce rally in the course of which Gandar, in seeking to move up court, shoved Amr in the back and sent him sprawling. The normally immaculate Amr did not approve and showed it in his glance at his opponent. But he was shaken and Gandar Dower squared the game 6–6 before Amr Bey recovered his poise and delivered the *coup de grâce*. The RAC beat Queen's 3–0 on that occasion but lost the return later that season.

That vignette was provided by Brian Phillips, a notable player of that period and after the war. He was Gandar Dower's opponent in the return match that season and was beaten 9–8 9–5. 'The Gander' led Queen's to their sixth Bath Club Cup in the last season before the Second World War, (1938–9) when a host of players including his brother, R. W., Bob Riseley, Michael Pugh, father of the post-war rackets brotherhood, John Olliff and G. J. Wardley turned out. J. de P. Whitaker and Bob Tinkler were the main props and Macpherson made that one unexpected appearance. That was also the year when 'The Gander' won his only Amateur Championship. He had not competed since losing to Cazalet in 1930 and Amr Bey had retired after his 1937 win. It was his chance and he took it, beating Edward Snell and Douglas Burnett in the last two rounds. I took a game off him in the second round but was then run off my feet.

THE WOMEN PIONEERS

The ladies, and only 'ladies' played squash in the early days, were just ahead of the men in establishing an Amateur Championship and from its start in 1922 to the outbreak of war in 1939 it was played at The Queen's Club. The first six meetings were played on the group system – group winners meeting in the semis or final – but in 1928 it became a knock-out event. Four players, three of them from families that had their own courts, dominated the first ten Championships. Joyce Cave was nineteen, six years younger than Nancy – there was also a third sister – when she won the first of her three titles. Nancy won three too and appeared in nine finals. Cicely Fenwick, whose family court was in Gloucestershire, also won three titles and the odd one out was Sylvia Huntsman.

The squash was pretty basic up-and-down in those early days but it was Miss Fenwick, with more strokes than the others, who took the game a step forward, a process developed further still by her successor as champion in 1932 – Susan Noel. Miss Noel, daughter of the late Club secretary, lived on the premises, you might say. Encouraged by their father she and her brother, Gerard, had the run of the Club and its courts and would play with professionals and ball-boys alike. She showed the same aptitude and skill for court games that had been inherent in her father. She did not win by pace and hustle but by brain and placement and made the game all the more pleasing to watch. She was only twelve when she first competed in 1924 and twenty when, in 1932, she won the first of her hat-trick of titles, beating Joyce Cave in the final. She was a female edition of the Charles Read-Dugald Macpherson school. To show that she could adapt her game she became the first overseas player to win the US title in 1933; a remarkable feat, seeing the considerable difference in the two games.

To win the third of her three titles in 1934 she beat the next of the 'modern' school of players, Margot Lumb, 9–7 9–0 9–6 in the final and the magazine *Squash Rackets and Fives* had this to say – 'Miss Noel set a very fast pace but she was not very much better than Miss Lumb in the first game, the points being won by really good shots. Nothing could stop Miss Noel in the second game. She played every shot she knew, and she knows many more than her opponent, with devastating accuracy. She led 8–0 in the third game before being suddenly checked. Miss Lumb drew up to 6–8 but was beaten by a side-wall shot that clung lovingly to the wall and Miss Noel won the match with a kill.'

For the next five years Miss Lumb, a left-hander and a Wightman Cup lawn tennis player, was as dominant among the women as was Amr Bey among the men and she too won the US title, in 1935. In those five years she dropped only one game, to Betty Cooke in 1938. Her forte was strength and great speed – both of shot and about the court. She ran her opponents into the floor not with exhausting rallies but by sheer pace.

Miss Noel missed the first four years of Miss Lumb's reign but returned in 1939 and reached the final. The clash with Miss Lumb evoked considerable interest and the gallery at Queen's was so packed that Gandar Dower, the men's champion, had to perch himself precariously on a ladder to watch it. Miss Lumb won 9–6 9–1 9–7 and that settled any arguments, but these two players had taken women's squash nearer the twenty-first century than many of their successors.

Early in the thirties Miss Noel and Mrs G. B. Wolfe presented a cup – the Wolfe-Noel Cup – for competition between Britain and the United States. The first match was played in the US in 1933 and the British team, winners 4–1, included Miss Lumb, Miss Noel and a third Queen's Club member, Mrs J. B. Pittman, also a leading lawn tennis player, with Mrs Wolfe as captain. The following year the match was played at Queen's. The British won 5–0 and the same three Club members were in the side. The last time the Club hosted the match was 1939, by which time Mrs Pittman had dropped out of the team.

Needless to say, with players of this calibre and others such as Rachel Sykes, Betty Hobson, Joy Cunningham, Alex McOstrich, Mrs W. H. Backhouse, Mrs F. M. Strawson, Mrs W. D. Porter and Miss M. Fraser, the Club were about the strongest in London. They won the Inter-Club Cup from 1935 to 1939 except for 1938.

ETON FIVES

A Kangaroo at Queen's!

Kenneth Gandar Dower, whose astonishing versatility ranged through most moving ball games to racing Cheetahs and big game hunting, was captain of Eton Fives at Cambridge, where he was a scholar, and in the Rugby Fives team for three years. According to a contemporary writer he had, when at his best, no superior at Eton Fives and, at Rugby Fives, was original and 'really good'. In one Varsity match an opponent was heard to remark 'I give up; it's no good playing against a Kangaroo!' The writer added 'As a doubles player he was less effective, as his partner could never quite know where he would be.' Gandar won the Kinnaird Cup twice with George McConnell and the amateur singles championship at Rugby Fives once.

The story of Eton Fives at Queen's is brief and sketchy. The game flourished there in the thirties and for a couple or so years the Club became the HQ of the Eton Fives Association. The first recorded committee meeting was held there in November 1934 and the last two years later. There were two courts, one built before the First World War, the other between the wars. The first, an open one, was at the end of No. 2 real tennis court adjoining the Cottage. The second was close to No. 3 Covered Court beyond the second squash court. It had a glass roof and electric light. Neither survived the last war.

In December 1936 A. J. Conyers, a leading player and member of the EFA committee, wrote to the Club suggesting that the old court, in poor condition and out of action, should be brought back into commission and provided with a glass roof and lighting and that the Association should reimburse the Club to the tune of £25 a year. In return the Association's members should have the right to use both courts at all times. The cost of the work was not expected to exceed £175 but it was agreed that estimates should be obtained. In return the Club asked for a guarantee of £25 a year for ten years apart, of course, from the court fees. This seemed to have caused relations between the two sides to become strained.

In 1938 the EFA complained to Colonel Eyre Bruce, the Club secretary, about the dirty condition of the courts and received an apology. Obviously something was done, as the courts were booked for the Kinnaird Cup, the game's leading competition, in February and March 1939. The event took place, Howard Fabian and J. K. G. Webb of the Old Cholmeleians beating George McConnell and Willie Welch of the Old Harrovians in the final. That was the end of Eton Fives at Queen's.

When the war ended Lord Aberdare, chairman of the Club's Board of Directors and holder of the purse strings, refused to consider rebuilding the courts until the War damage claim was settled, despite a proposal by the EFA and Jesters Club to pay half the refurbishing costs. With the Club in its usual parlous state nothing was done and interest lapsed.

Some distinguished games players appear among the winners of the Kinnaird Cup in the years it was played at Queen's. Howard Fabian, for instance, played soccer and cricket for Cambridge, soccer for England and Derby County. He won the Cup twice with Webb and once with J. Aguirre. He won it a fourth time after the war, with Webb.

Alan Barber, another double blue, one of the last great Corinthians and Yorkshire cricket captain, won it twice with his fellow Salopian, Desmond Backhouse, a leading squash player. Barber was also headmaster of that famous prep school, Ludgrove, one of the few in this country to possess an Eton Fives court. In those days Harrow, Shrewsbury, Highgate and Eton were top dogs.

THE QUEEN'S CLUB – THE WAR YEARS
1939–1945

LIFE at the Club during the war slowed down, though it never came to a halt. During the First World War, when the threat of enemy aircraft was negligible, there had been a social atmosphere. Now it was not quite the same. Life was sterner and more austere. The Allied Services still used the Club but not as much as before. The facilities – football, rugby, baseball, American football, cricket and even Australian Rules football – were not available as they had been in 1914–18. There were not so many charity exhibitions and, though Frances Day the actress became a member in 1942 and Bebe Daniels and Ben Lyon were also members, show people were not so much in evidence as they had been in the earlier war.

Erroll MacSwiney, the Club's financial director then and now, put it this way: 'During the week we were all working, some of us had two jobs, and mostly we came to the Club at weekends to play tennis, bridge and have a drink.' The Club revolved round these facilities – the courts, the bridge table and the bar.

Mrs Ellen Fagan, who still lives in Greyhound Road, came to the Club as a cleaner in 1942, a position she held for forty years. She had begun in service at the age of fourteen at ten shillings a week. She was bombed out of her home in Shepherds Bush and went to stay over a vegetable shop run by Jack Jenkins, a man of all trades at the Club. He got her the job as cleaner at one pound a week including Sundays and later persuaded Lord Aberdare to raise that by half a crown. Apart from cleaning, Mrs Fagan helped in the bar and kitchen and served tea through a cubbyhole, assisted by her 11-year-old daughter who buttered the bread. She relieved Stan Suffling in the bar at weekends and washed up the trays.

Her responsibilities included cleaning both the men's and women's changing rooms and tending the coal fires. She recalls the friendly atmosphere with the wives of members around the fire in the lounge and everyone looking forward to 'the boys' coming in to play. The staff, such as they were, would bring their own rations and sometimes donated their precious tea and sugar when the Club ran short. She remembers a 'Doodlebug' whining overhead in 1944 and two venerable members, Dr Shirley and Dr Lillis, hurling themselves flat on the court. They were not the only ones; Vera Woods, Patsy O'Connell, Joan Ingram and Vicky Valentine-Brown were playing a doubles and reacted similarly while Bruce Harrison, a Canadian serviceman, and Jack Jeffrey, then in charge of the changing room, climbed onto the Club roof to watch the bomb fall about a quarter of a mile away. Harrison claims that there was more whisky drunk in the Club that evening than during the whole war. Where it came from remains a mystery as by then only half-bottles of gin or whisky were being put in the bar.

Though supplemented by Service members, the Club was basically kept going by a small and faithful coterie of pre-war members and MacSwiney has listed them: Nigel Sharpe, Dr Billy Lillis, Dr Rex Shirley, Frank Chappelow, an antique dealer, Jack Webb, Horace Morell, Judge Hargreaves, Phillip le Gros, Vera Woods, Mrs A. E. Beamish, John Olliff, Charles Kingsley, H. A. Coldham, Denis Coombe, Claude Lister, Tom Todd, Carla Gerke, Mrs Bengough, Joan Ingram, John and Mrs Hazebroek, Dick and Dawn Sandys, Reggie Bois, Jack and Jill Warboys, Sandy Ashmead Bartlett, Jan Rabl, Colonel Helme, Frank Strawson, Harold 'Tich' Radford, L. K. and Mrs Clark, George and Mrs

Greville, Eric Serin and Mrs Alex McKelvie. A good many have departed this world.

During the first two years of the war there was, understandably, a considerable loss of membership. Financially the Club just kept its head above water with the help of a £10,000 loan from Lloyds Bank and a considerable saving in expenditure through, *inter alia*, a reduction in staff. The LTA refused to help the Club financially. Lord Aberdare, the principal mortgagee, remained chairman of the board and, later on, personally played an active part in running it. The number of secretarial staff was negligible. Greville, a retired banker and player of the same vintage as Major (his Christian name) J. G. Ritchie, began as secretary and was succeeded by Stanley Hellings, who worked for Slazengers in the same role as C. Spychala did so successfully and for so many years after the war. Later Jenkins took over.

THE ANCHOR MEN

The men at the helm were briefly M. J. G. Ritchie who, according to Mrs Fagan, looked 'lost, forlorn and little' towards the end of the war, Nigel Sharpe, Kenneth Hunter, a stockbroker, John Olliff when available from his RAF duties, Judge (later Sir) Gerald Hargreaves, A. C. Bourner, an American who wore a Stetson 'and tipped well' (Mrs Fagan), and Claude Lister who became chairman of the committee in the last year of the war.

One of the early decisions made was that no enemy aliens should be elected members but that those already so should not be asked to resign. Towards the end of the war it was noted that there were many more foreign names among the members, a fact that struck an increasingly strident chord afterwards.

The main aim was to provide all members with the facilities for playing the games available and, as it turned out, that was not too easy. The grass courts, under O'Leary, the head groundsman, remained in good condition and that was much to his credit. He had been called up but the Club had got him exempted and, having done so, officially established his right to use a hole in the wall leading to Greyhound Road – an easy exit to his local pub. The indoor courts soon presented problems. No lights were allowed in the lawn tennis, real tennis, squash or badminton courts and that restricted play to the hours of daylight. Then, in September 1940, Nos. 1 and 2 covered courts were badly damaged by incendiary bombs – it was a good many years before they were fully repaired – and both real tennis courts were requisitioned to store furniture and effects from locally bombed-out homes. Their windows were shattered and boarded up. With so many people wanting to play it came down to just doubles after two o'clock at weekends and members only being allowed to play twice a week on the other five days.

The Club had stocked up with tennis balls at the start of the war. That they had not paid for them was not discovered until Dickie Ritchie resumed his secretaryship after it. Soon no more balls were being made and conservation became vitally important. At first a shilling was charged for every ball lost. Then the grass courts were allowed only three balls a court to be followed by the issue of only four dozen balls a week for the whole Club. Real tennis, of course, was out and there is very little record of any rackets being played other than the 1943 Public Schools Championships in which Winchester (G. H. G. Doggart and J. B. Thursfield) beat Harrow (J. N. Mitchell and J. G. Hogg) 4–2 in the final.

Another picture of wartime Queen's is provided by a Canadian, Bruce Harrison, an Army corporal when he came here in 1943 and, for the last forty-four years, a successful banker with the Toronto Dominion. Strictly only officers were admissable as members and Group-Captain Walter Martin, a former Canadian champion and later Judge-Advocate General to the Forces, was one of them. When Don McDermott, the reigning Canadian champion, and Bruce Harrison arrived, Martin persuaded the Club to make them members – 'Harrison's as good as McDermott,' he added. Two weeks later McDermott was sent to the Middle East but Corporal Harrison stayed on. He remembers the Club as follows:

At the time Stanley Hellings was the secretary and Jack Jenkins the pro. The Club was pretty dilapidated. There was a wonderful man named H. P. Buckingham who would book a grass court for us every Saturday and Sunday. When Hitler bombed the covered courts and the management started watering the whisky he retired. That was more than he could stand.

In those days you had old balls and I am sure they used to blow them up to maintain some pressure. The changing room smelled of liniment. The Club would serve tea, toast and cake. Sometimes members such as Vera Woods, Audrey Richardson, Dawn Sandys and others would bring sandwiches and other foods and we would have a party. One evening John Olliff was in the dog-house at home and when he told his wife that he thought Harrison the funniest man he had met she replied, 'I think him a complete bore.'

At weekends I used to stay in houses in Barons Court to be near the Club. There were many pleasant American officers there, good players too. Ben Lyon and Bebe Daniels were members. Ernest Hemingway and Roly Teakle would sometimes come along. Nigel Sharpe ran charity games and on some Sundays we had exhibition matches with Dick Sandys, Denis Coombe and Claude Lister. Sometimes I used to make up the four. Stanley Hellings had a bad ticker but that did not stop him drinking. I remember one night when the bombing was on, Jack Warboys went to the bar and asked for 'a double tutt, please Mrs Gin' – Mrs Tutt was in the bar that night.

When Harrison returned to Canada in 1945 Dick Sandys, Tom Todd and John Olliff presented him with a silver salver signed by, among others, Mrs Tutt – 'To Bruce Harrison from a group of his friends'. Now Harrison pays fairly frequent visits to this country and stays with Dawn Sandys. I met him at the 1985 Wimbledon.

THE QUEEN'S CLUB STORY
1946–1986

DICKIE Ritchie, appointed Club secretary in 1939, returned home from his years as a Japanese POW in October 1945 and rejoined the Club on 1 December. He felt that work was the best antidote to those lost years and when the Ladies' Committee, with Vera Woods the prime mover, wanted to give him a reception he turned it down as the wrong time to hold an official party.

R. J. R. reflected, 'The Club had got through five years of war without having to close or being taken over by the Services, as it virtually had been during the first war. It was, in fact, the overseas Services, who wanted to play tennis, and a group of faithful members who kept the place alive. But when I got there it was really rather sad. The place was thoroughly run down. The furnishings and fabrics were worn and shoddy. The covered courts leaked and 4 and 5 had been put out of action (in 1943) by incendiary bombs. The real tennis courts were used for storage by the Fulham Council as was one of the covered courts. The squash courts and hard courts were in poor condition. The billiard room had been blitzed and the table had been moved to the dining room to avoid taking on more staff. There was a shortage of fuel, food and drink and so there was little need for a dining room anyway.'

There was little enough staff. Jack Jenkins had migrated from the men's changing room to the role of secretary-manager during the latter and critical years of the war. Bombed out of his own home, he had moved into the Cottage. His reward, in 1946, for thirty years' service to the Club was a piece of silver. Joe Richardson was the barman before retiring in 1954 after forty-three years' service. Mr William Pott was still keeping the accounts and writing the minutes in copper-plate handwriting. He, too,

eventually retired after fifty-five years' service, grossly underpaid throughout that time. Jim O'Leary, unable to do much about the hard courts, somehow managed to keep the grass in good condition and, as a sideline, ran a market garden and kept some chickens in a corner on the east side of the grounds.

Mrs Fagan the cleaner looked after the teas, such as they were. The redoubtable Mrs Tutt ruled over the women's changing room. If she liked you there was nothing she would not do. If she did not it was a different story. Maureen Wilson (later Berryman) was a junior member in 1948 when she first met Mrs Tutt – 'A formidable lady. She had one eye and I was terrified of her.' Only slightly less formidable, it appears, was Mrs Phyllis Satterthwaite, a famous name here and in tournaments in the South of France way back in the twenties – she was also the Duke of Westminster's mistress – with whom Maureen was made to play on the east covered court. All rallies, no scoring.

Ritchie had Lord Aberdare, chairman of the board and controller of the money, and Nigel Sharpe, the Club chairman, behind him but otherwise very little help. Sometimes he even had to serve the teas. In his office he had a table for a desk – the first desk he had came from his father – and next to no secretarial help. Irene Turner and, when she died, Joyce Ward, answered the telephone and booked the courts.

Bridge has always been a strong suit at the Club and it had been one of the main pastimes during the war. Card money, a shilling a player, was introduced to help reimburse the Club for cards, tables and heating, such as it was. It was like a court fee and players were on their honour to put the money in a box. But it was not long before John Archer complained of a shortage of playing cards, scorepads and pencils, probably justifiably as everything was short in those days. And Jack Warboys, well known for calling three no-trumps and his skill on the billiard table, complained about the lack of heat.

There was a shortage of towels in the changing rooms and Ritchie had to point out that sixpence a person did not cover the cost of fuel and laundry for baths and showers. Members were asked to bring their own towels and also to subscribe a coupon or two to help the Club replenish their stock. As before the war, Mrs Bengough, sitting on the terrace or 'in her own chair' in the lounge, continued to observe everything that went on and write frequent letters to the committee on her distinctive purple notepaper.

SOCIAL CHANGES

Re-establishing the traditional competitions, getting life at the Club back to normal and sorting out the membership were among the first priorities. The membership had already changed dramatically in character though not numbers. As mentioned already, the influx of overseas Service members, those from foreign embassies and those who sought refuge in this country after the outbreak of war, altered the social structure of the membership. In the early years the members had been drawn from the leisured and privileged class. In between the wars the spectrum had broadened, though still largely bounded by people from the Public Schools. But many of those who returned from the war and might be expected to join Queen's were fully occupied with re-establishing their former careers and had little time or money for the luxury of such a club.

There were times after the last war when one wondered whether Queen's had become a place of asylum for displaced persons, mainly from Europe, and where they had got the money from. There were jokes about the British needing a passport to get into the Club and about the King's English being a minority language. One of the reasons was that Queen's needed members and those from abroad who joined needed a social centre, somewhere they could meet, play tennis and bridge and become absorbed into the life of London. Money did not appear to be any obstacle and membership seemed easily gained despite various rules designed to vet or stem the flow of foreigners. It was not expensive and the subscription, ten guineas for men, was the same as it had been before the war.

In the first four months of 1946 there were an astonishing 120 applications for membership of the Club. Later came another shoal and the secretary was told 'to note the nationality of the applicants'. There were, from 'home-breds', some very interesting ones – Peter Ustinov, the actor-writer, actor James Mason, an enthusiastic rather than very accomplished real tennis player, Raymond Glendinning, the BBC sports commentator, Hubert Doggart, a fine rackets player at Winchester, later an England cricketer and still later headmaster of a public school in Somerset, Bruce Harris, an *Evening Standard* sportswriter, and Donald MacPhail, a British Davis Cup player.

The Grass Court Championships were the most important event to be re-launched. They were one of the oldest in the calendar, most profitable to the Club and a sound and regular source of income – or so they had been before the war. Coming the week before Wimbledon they would be a 'hosting' event for the world's leading players anxious to get together again after a gap of seven years.

Whatever the difficulties, shortages and frustrations Queen's, like Wimbledon, felt it was of paramount importance to 'put on a good show' or, at least, put on a show. The stands needed reconditioning. The price of the programme was raised from a shilling to one-and-sixpence. But the Club could not afford the thirty-guinea fee for a professional referee – Major Maturin in this case. The Major offered to reduce it to twenty but in the cause of economy the Club asked Ted Avory, a pre-war Cambridge blue and member of the Club – he was elected to the committee shortly afterwards – to referee instead, which he did in his own somewhat eccentric manner.

The weather was perfect. O'Leary's courts were better than hoped for and the women's final in which Pauline Betz, who later won Wimbledon, beat Margaret Osborne 6–8 6–3 6–3 was as fine a match as could be wished for. Jack Kramer, favoured to win Wimbledon, had to retire with a blistered hand. That cost him Wimbledon, too, as Jaroslav Drobny beat him. Pancho Segura, an Ecuadorian living in the US, won the men's title from the Australian Dinny Pails, who with his countryman, Geoff Brown, took the men's doubles. What fun those Aussies were, bringing life to a tired old country. The meeting was a great success, making a profit of £800; without it the Club would have made a loss for the year.

The Club's resident professionals, Joe Pearce, Bill Holmes and Bill Young, had been demobbed early in 1946 and were back in action. Young soon resigned over money but the other two were given increases. However, it was confirmed that the Club could no longer afford to employ ball-boys as it had done in the past. In itself that was a sign of the changing social scene.

GOVERNMENT HELP

With three of the five covered courts completely out of action there was no immediate hope of holding the Covered Court Championships, the oldest event of its kind in the world. Incendiaries had accounted for 4 and 5, the glass roof of No. 3 was damaged and the other two leaked. But No. 2 was patched up sufficiently for it to be used for LTA coaching and No. 1 (the east court) was at least playable. Lord

Templewood, who enjoyed his games on these courts and was president of the LTA, wrote to the Prime Minister, Clement Attlee, a lawn tennis buff, asking for help in restoring No. 3 – Lord Templewood's favourite court – and it was granted. But it was a long time before the Ministry of Works licensed the rebuilding of 4 and 5.

Rackets was the first of the specialist games to get off its mark. Wellington (C. B. Haycraft and J. E. L. Ainslie) won the Schools Championship; John Pawle, a beautiful stylist, won the Amateur singles and paired with Cosmo Crawley, one of the clan, to take the doubles.

When Prince's Club, Knightsbridge, closed, Jim Dear, demobbed from the RAF, joined Queen's. There was little he could do about the real tennis, as one court was still used for storage and the other was not yet derequisitioned, but he made good use of the rackets court. In October 1946 he beat Peter Gray of Rugby 8–0 for the Professional Championship and that set him on course for the World title.

Service with a smile: (left to right) Bill Holmes, Joe Pearce, Jack Jeffrey and Jim Dear

But first he had to beat John Pawle and then Peter Kershaw, the last Amateur Champion before the war. Having cleared those hurdles he met the Canadian professional, Kenneth Chantler, in Montreal and at Queen's for the World title, which he won handsomely.

Dear survived a couple of challenges from Pawle before losing his title to Geoffrey Atkins in 1954. The following year he won the World Real Tennis title beating Albert Johnson of New York by the narrowest of margins, 11 sets to 10. On the last day Dear needed to win the first two sets of the final leg. A pulled leg muscle made this look doubtful but with the help of Dr Stephen Ward and a bottle of Guinness (his normal pre-match tipple), he succeeded.

In these early years after the war when rackets was re-establishing itself, that great enthusiast, Michael Pugh, formed 'a circus' of players to go round the schools to stimulate interest. They used to take Peter Latham, then far too old to play but not to comment and criticise, with them but he often needed encouragement in the form of a bottle of whisky. Once, so it has been said, Latham refused to come down from his bedroom unless he had his bottle. Eventually Pugh capitulated, the Old Man drank half of it and then agreed to make the journey. Latham died in 1953, possibly the greatest of all rackets and real tennis players and certainly the only one so far to hold the two world titles simultaneously.

Michael Pugh was able to reinforce his circus, which already included Anthony Ward with his two sons, Tim and Tom, both Eton rackets players, in the mid-fifties. Tom's record in the game is prodigious and to this day he remains one of the great and most determined competitors, though in recent years one has noticed he equips himself with a concoction when he is playing a match that looks like Coca-Cola but contains something stronger. In my years as *The Times* rackets and real tennis correspondent I found Tom by far the shrewdest and most acute observer of the game. I would take his advice but never a bet, knowing that whatever odds he offered were in his favour. To a lesser degree Stefan Laszlo has the same flair for putting his finger on the hub of the matter at real tennis, as did Christina Wood of the *Daily Telegraph*.

These reflections, though, have taken our story ahead of itself as, for some years after the war, the Club was still struggling to create a personality. In 1947, for instance, the idea of appointing a hostess to arrange anything from a bridge four to games of tennis for members was turned down for lack of funds. The burden of arranging the sporting life of the Club, and most other aspects as well, fell on Ritchie and even many years later I came to the conclusion that but for him many of the events, notably the rackets, would not have got off the ground. Rackets appeared the most disorganized sport, the players neglecting or forgetting to send in their entries or, having done so, failing to turn up for their matches or changing the schedule to suit themselves. Ritchie handled this problem with philosophical calm.

The catering was a constant problem but a licence to serve snacks and self-service lunches was finally granted. In 1949 Premier Caterers were appointed to deal with this side of the Club. They found it unprofitable as no one ever knew how many would turn up for food. Premier retired but the Club tried to steal their chef.

THE CHAIRMAN GAME

For some years after the war there appears to have been a game of musical chairs among the Club committee, most notably in the choice or chairman. Judge Sir Gerald Hargreaves and Nigel Sharpe, a Davis Cup player who had distinguished himself in 1931 by beating Henri Cochet at Wimbledon, were in and out of the Chair. For a term in 1949 Lord Ronaldshay broke up the game, a quiet fellow who was content to let the secretary run the Club. Sir Gerald, when in the Chair, ran the Club as if sitting on the bench. His two loves were playing tennis and music. He played tennis nearly every day at 3.30 or as soon as he could get away from the other sort of court. At home he ran musical parties and enjoyed singing to piano accompaniment. Sharpe, on the other hand, was charming but often authoritarian and obdurate. He did not like change. He had been heavily involved with keeping the Club going during the war. One of his successors, Anthony Ward, found him generous and hospitable but 'accustomed to having his own way and not in favour of radical change'.

There were about 1000 members on the books in 1947 but 1500 was a more desirable figure if the revenue from subscriptions, then about £5500, was to be improved as was obviously necessary. Erroll MacSwiney, the Club's financial director – an honorary post – was constantly pleading for an increase in subscription rates, still the same as pre-

Above: The *dedans* at Queen's, painted by Jean Clark in 1951.
Jim Dear, on court talking to Clarence (Lord) Aberdare and Peter Latham, seated

Top: Peter Latham: arguably the greatest real tennis player of all time

This page

Above: The Queen's Club staff – 1986

Left:
Blitzkrieg – 'Bomber Boris' Becker.
Three weeks after winning the 1985
Stella Artois Championships,
he became the youngest ever
Wimbledon Champion

Opposite:

Ivan Lendl – currently No 1 in the
world, but still not happy on grass

John McEnroe – a brilliantly
talented player

Jimmy Connors – always a fighter and
three times winner of the Grass Court
Championships at the Club

Above: The Championships in progress – the No 1 Court often described by the players
as the finest in the world

Top: The 1985 Championships: HRH the Duchess of Gloucester before the presentation,
with Clive Bernstein, Tournament Director (right)

war. But the committee were terrified that that might prove prohibitive to current and prospective members. The most they would agree to was a ten-shilling locker charge and that raised a query from John Archer: 'Would they be supplied with locks?' The answer was no.

However, some interesting new members did join, among them Barbara Goalen, a famous model, Keith Joseph (now Sir Keith, the much-beleaguered Education Minister), Val Guest and Ralph (later Sir Ralph) Richardson from the world of entertainment and the theatre. Richardson was a keen real tennis player. The playing of real tennis was restricted, though the glass roof of the east court had been repaired. Interest in the game among the members was sluggish. The first two Amateur Championships after the war were played at Lord's and Manchester but Dugald Macpherson and Lord Charles Cullen won the Inter-Club doubles (the Bailey Cup) for the Club for the three years 1947–9. When the Amateur returned to Queen's in 1948, Peter Kershaw won the title having won the Rackets in the last Championship before the war. Kershaw was a stern, aggressive competitor with a fascinating service. He twisted and bent his body like a praying mantis and then delivered a heavily undercut ball. His home court was Manchester.

While real tennis began to root itself at Queen's again so another game, Eton Fives, made its irrevocable break. It had not in fact been played at the Club since the war, the courts having been heavily damaged. But the liaison between the Club and the Eton Fives Association did not end until 1947. The game was active at Queen's before the war, with the Kinnaird Cup (the Amateur Championship), schools events and club matches being regularly played there. In 1937 the second court, near the garages, had been reconditioned and given a glass roof and electric lighting. But there were complaints the following year that the court was dirty and that the reconditioned floor was unsatisfactory. Colonel Bruce, the Club secretary, apologized but the Club and the EFA disagreed over the cost of the refurbishment and who should pay. It ended with the Club nearly suing the EFA and that was the beginning of the end. While the game was played at Queen's some fine players were seen in action, among them George McConnell, a Harrow housemaster with whom I had learnt the game at our prep school in the early twenties, Alan Barber, captain of Oxford at cricket and soccer (and Yorkshire at cricket), Howard Fabian, a Cambridge double 'blue' at those games and a soccer international, C. E. W. Sheepshanks and, of course, the versatile Kenneth Gandar Dower.

The Covered Court Championships returned in 1947, an undistinguished meeting lacking the lure and charisma of Jean Borotra. At the end of the war he had been arrested by the French on suspicion of collaboration with the Germans after being released from a medieval castle in Austria by the Americans. He was cleared by the French High Court and came bounding back to Queen's in 1948 to play in the IC Match and then win the Covered Courts title for the tenth time. The next year he won it for the eleventh and last time but continued to play in the IC Match annually, even when past eighty.

HANDSOME PROFIT

Dickie Ritchie was besieged in his office by an irate public, wanting their money back, during the very wet 1948 Grass Court Championships, but 1949 made up for that when that magnetic character, Ted Schroeder, a beer-drinking, pipe-smoking refrigerator salesman from California, won Queen's and then Wimbledon at his first and only appearance in these two events (years later he returned as a veteran). Attendances at that meeting were the best ever and the £1000 profit was ear-marked for repainting the east and west covered courts.

Once again in the Club's history money was looming large. Lord Aberdare, still chairman of the board, did not interfere with the running of the Club or reduce the facilities but he did not believe in spending too much, pointing out that it was a proprietory, not a members' club. Undoubtedly he saw his considerable investment diminishing since the Club had been designated 'an open space' by the Fulham Council.

Briefly Aberdare entertained a proposal to sell part of the ground, near the front gate, to build a club house for colonial students and he also suggested the 440-yard running track be restored at the cost of numerous hard courts. These ideas fell through and, as Ritchie philosophically put it, 'We may have been short of money [an understatement?] but we are independent and happy, though some members are always dissatisfied.' The usual complaints kept on coming in but Frank Strawson was on target when he pointed out that the condition of the squash courts was 'quite unworthy of the Club'. Despite that, Queen's did hold the Bath Club Cup in 1948.

The New Year's Eve dance taking the forties into the fifties was poorly supported – a bad omen. The rates doubled, membership declined, permission to restore covered courts 4 and 5 were again refused, the billiard room was still blitzed and the Covered Court Championships were again threatened unless the east and west courts' roofs were made waterproof. Boodles, the Bath Club and The Travellers sought weekend facilities but nothing came of it.

It was against this background that new factors entered into the Club's financial saga. MacSwiney, having once again lost his plea for an increase in subscriptions, approached a member, Archie Sandercock, managing director of Glaxo – 'I wanted to borrow £30,000 to pay off Lord Aberdare's mortgage and the bank. Both were pressing. Archie agreed to lend the money and take over the chairmanship of the board. He put up £3000 and was then taken ill. We repaid the £3000 and I then approached Bob Riseley, chairman of the All England Club.' Feelers were also put out to the LTA but they were not keen on making a loan and the idea fell through. Riseley, however, was interested largely because Wimbledon had no covered courts of its own. His interest was in the war-damaged courts 4 and 5 and if Wimbledon could get involved in Queen's he was prepared to include reimbursing Lord Aberdare.

Negotiations had reached the stage of the two sides' lawyers drafting agreements when the whole affair was suddenly called off, turned down by the All England Club committee. Riseley may have been playing his cards close to his chest and taken the committee by surprise, but the general impression was that some of its members did not like the idea of Wimbledon controlling the two largest and most important tenni clubs in the country. That cancellation left Que 's in such straits that they could not even afford to buy a microphone for the Centre Court umpire's chair!

Finally the LTA very probably prodded by Wimbledon, decided to come to the rescue and make a conditional loan. In November 1952 Ritchie wrote to the shareholders asking them whether they would be willing to sell their shares, of which there were 4779, for £1 apiece. He pointed out that the original shares were issued at £10 each, that no dividend had been paid since 1913 and that since the last war they had changed hands for no more than ten shillings. The largest shareholder was MacSwiney with 193. Apart from the Club itself, the freehold land and buildings which had a replacement value of over £90,000, the main asset was the Government compensation for loss of development rights. That was £23,700. About eighty percent of the shareholders were willing to sell. One abstainer was the Oxford University Athletic Club and Bertie Buckler, the LTA chairman, paid them a personal visit without success. Nevertheless sufficient agreed to make the takeover possible; the irony of the whole affair being that the money, £67,500 free of interest, came from Wimbledon, the All England Ground Company, the commercial arm of what is otherwise a private members' Club. £60,000 was immediately advanced to Queen's.

At the Lawn Tennis Association's AGM in December 1953 Lord Templewood, the president, announced the takeover and made three general comments:

1 It was not the LTA's intention to create a rival to Wimbledon but to make Queen's a great tennis centre for London and the training of young players.

2 The LTA aimed to maintain the facilities for rackets, real tennis and squash. (Lord Templewood had played rackets for Harrow and real tennis for Oxford).

3 Lord Aberdare, as chairman of the board of directors and the major mortgage holder, had contributed to the success of the negotiations.

Lord Templewood then rushed to the House of Lords to take charge of a Bill for the protection of birds!

Lord Aberdare handed over the chairmanship of the board to Buckler, who was joined by LTA councillors J. Eaton Griffith (he died in 1984) and V. Penman. MacSwiney remained financial director. Phillip Le Gros replaced Sharpe as the Club chairman. Buckler, a jovial no-nonsense Midlands businessman, summed up the set-up with optimism – 'Prosperity begins to return to the Club'.

Covered courts 4 and 5 were rebuilt. It took seven months and over-enthusiastic architects, deciding that a single glass roof was unsuitable because it let in the sun, built a double one, which in this case meant that play could only take place in artificial light. Later, the heat generated in the glass roof caused the steel-work to flake off and that had to be swept off the courts. The result was that the roofing had to be scrapped and a new one built. The lights were as good as any in Europe and were later installed also in No. 3 court. The Club was equipped with new main gates. The *dedans* of the east real tennis court was redecorated and the roofs of the other three covered courts overhauled. A covered way connecting all the covered courts was built, the car park enlarged and the lounge redesigned and redecorated.

John Olliff, a leading member of the Club and a Davis Cup player – he was also a talented rugby footballer – died during the 1951 Wimbledon, the day after Tony Mottram beat Jaroslav Drobny. In 1953 Peter Latham – perhaps the greatest of all rackets and real tennis players – died in his ninetieth year. He began at the club on 1 January 1888 as one of the professionals. He ended as an honorary member. E. B. Noel once wrote, 'He liked a gallery and liked to give a grand and beautiful exhibition of the games he played but was never spoiled by admiration.' He was World Champion at both games at the age of thirty and during his reign was beaten only once, by 'Punch' Fairs in 1905.

OLD FAITHFULS DEPART

Two more Club stalwarts died in the mid-fifties; M. J. G. Ritchie and F. R. Leighton Crawford. Ritchie was one of the most prolific tournament winners of his era. His career crossed that of the Doherty brothers – he once beat Laurie at Queen's – and in 1907 he reached the Wimbledon challenge round, losing to A. W. Gore. Leighton Crawford, a lesser player but dour and diligent, was known as 'the Mummy' for the way he bound his head and his arm with yards of bandage.

Jim Dear moved to Eton as rackets professional but only stayed a year. While he was away Bill Holmes did his best to fill the gap as real tennis professional. The Club chairmanship was still a game of musical chairs, largely between Nigel Sharpe, Sir Gerald Hargreaves and Phillip Le Gros. The Duke of Edinburgh agreed to become the Club patron in 1953, succeeding the late King George VI.

Around this period a most interesting selection of new members joined the Club. They included Dennis Norden, who later put up his partner Frank Muir; John (later Sir John) Mills, James Mason, A. W. Gamage, Hardy Amies, Vanessa Redgrave (a junior), two MPs in Maurice Edelman (Labour) and Ernest Marples (Conservative), two cricketers, the Nawab of Pataudi, captaining the Indian tourists, and Colin Ingleby-Mackenzie, the Hon. J. J. Astor and

the Aga Khan and some of his progeny. At last, in 1956, MacSwiney achieved a modest rise in subscriptions, to 15 guineas for men, 12 for women. The rules for admitting foreign members were tightened up and, for the first time, the Club bridge team, captained by K. W. 'Konnie' Konstam, won the Devonshire Cup.

The Grass Court Championships that year were hit by poor weather, Lady Crosfield's Garden Party being held on the opening day, inadequate umpiring and a Test Match. The players were given better lunches in lieu of expenses but thought little of it. Neale Fraser and Angela Buxton won the titles, the latter the second British player since the war to do so. (Jean Rinkel was the first in 1953.)

Few men over a long period of time served the Club better than Lord Aberdare who died in 1957. His mortgages kept the place alive when it might have died; his helmsmanship kept it afloat when it might have capsized and sunk. Moreover he decorated the games, rackets and real tennis, that, after the end of football and athletics, maintained Queen's as a unique club in the world of sport. He was a champion at both and a fine cricketer for Middlesex as well – one of those great amateur games-players who no longer exist in this modern world of commercial sport.

This period saw the deaths of many other notable members and officers. The president, the Duke of Athlone, was one and the Duke of Devonshire, president of the LTA, succeeded him. Bertie Buckler was another. Eaton Griffith took over as chairman of the board and straightaway pointed out that the Club was running at a £3000 loss and he would have to do something about it! Another loss was that of George Greville. Greville's death removed a link with the deep past. He was a contemporary of M. J. G. Ritchie and though not in the same class he was an enthusiastic tournament player. When occasionally they met they did not get on well and on one occasion in a handicap final at Eastbourne they had such a row that the ball-girls were reduced to tears and walked off the court. For a time during the last war Greville acted as the Club secretary.

The glimmer of light on what was otherwise a shrouded scene was the appearance of a new member, Frank Taylor. He was to become the father of sponsorship at Queen's. When Taylor arrived at the Club one day and asked to become a member no one was quite sure who he was. He described himself as a builder and said tennis was his hobby.

Noel Berryman arranged a proposer and seconder for him and his wife, Christine. Their enthusiasm for the game was considerable and they played almost daily with Jim Coles, Joe Pearce or Bill Holmes. Frank Taylor was not very good but the professionals soon discovered that he was quite happy provided he was allowed to win his service. It soon sunk in that Frank Taylor was the Taylor of the International Construction company, Taylor Woodrow and, for a fee of £12, the Club staged his firm's finals. In 1958 he paid for new lighting, for covered courts 1, 2 and 3. Later he refurbished and redecorated the women's changing room and that was really only the beginning.

The retirement in 1958 of Jim O'Leary, head groundsman since just after the First World War, removed a landmark from the Club scene. He was not only a great groundsman, a natural son of the earth, but also a character who, when he did not get his way, would resign – only to relent, resign again and so on. He enjoyed his beer. When Dickie Ritchie returned from the war he found, in that corner of the grounds now occupied by the Amateur Fencing Association, O'Leary's already-mentioned market garden, vegetables and chickens which had supplemented his rations and his modest stipend. O'Leary was not pleased when asked to clear the area for the restoration of the hard courts.

ROLLING ON

One day Ritchie was looking out of his office window when he saw O'Leary driving the heavy roller so erratically that it went straight through one of the hedges separating the courts. It was after lunch and O'Leary had just returned from his local. The Monkton Arms, known locally as 'Wrights' after its landlord, was O'Leary's normal haunt. When the hole in the wall O'Leary used as a short cut was bricked up by the Club, he countered by constructing a ladder-bridge over the wall. He occasionally returned to lend a hand after his retirement and the current ground manager, David Kimpton, recalls an occasion when the groundstaff, unrolling the centre court cover, found O'Leary 'sleeping it off' inside.

Very briefly Ernie Peters became head groundsman, retiring when he broke an ankle while helping to build a stand. Ted Blaizey, the maintenance man then and now, took over. Blaizey, now sixty, was formerly a coalman, joining the Club in 1948 having served in the RAF. He was introduced by his brother, a former ball-boy. For a time he worked under O'Leary, whom he regarded as an old-fashioned eccentric who supplemented his income by selling eggs. Blaizey's wages for a seven-day week were £4 17s 0d with an extra three shillings for Sundays. For overtime he ball-boyed for members. In those early days after the war everything at the Club was run on a shoestring and one of Blaizey's implements was a 1930 Shanks mowing machine; most of the equipment was inadequate. Some ten years after the war he discovered some incendiary bombs in the guttering of covered courts 4 and 5.

David Kimpton, who succeeded him, is one of a Fulham family of nine, trained at a Horticultural College and Hurlingham, a worthy successor to such an expert as O'Leary. Officially he became head groundsman in 1970. 'When I arrived at Queen's the grass courts were lawns rather than tennis courts. Too green. Over the years I've changed the seed mixture and renovation programme; spiking, scarification, heavier top dressing and rolling. It was not always easy to get the money for what I wanted to do.' Kimpton was not the only person who had difficulty in wheedling money out of the management but he succeeded and the condition of the courts today bears testimony to his skill and diligence.

When, in 1980, Bob Twynam retired from Wimbledon, the All England Club approached Kimpton. He turned down the offer, preferring the greater activity at Queen's to the more hermit-like life at Wimbledon. It is an interesting fact that when Jim Thorn became Wimbledon's head groundsman his formula for improving the much-criticized courts was very similar to Kimpton's when he began at Queen's.

CHANGE OF OWNERSHIP

The LTA moved into their new headquarters adjacent to the main gate at the Club in July 1959. Whether their proximity improved relations is a moot point. For instance, at the AGM, it was forcefully pointed out that though the Club was no longer owned by shareholders it was still a company owned by the LTA, who had a majority on the board. The board, not the Club members or committee, controlled the pennies. Eaton Griffith, the board chairman, pointed out that the LTA had saved the Club from bankruptcy with money loaned by Wimbledon and that, so far, £80,000 had been advanced free of interest. Moreover a TV contract

Grounds Manager David Kimpton with his team relaying turf

worth £2000 had been lost and no more loans could be expected. This indicated that the LTA had yet to realize the true value of the asset they had acquired.

There was court trouble too. The Covered Court Championships, once one of the 'jewels in the crown' and won that year by Bobby Wilson and Angela Mortimer, were no longer attracting much international entry or public interest. Jack Deloford claimed that the current lack of interest in real tennis could be put down to the Club failing to appoint a professional, as distinct from Hampton Court and Lord's. The board, i.e. the LTA, did not appear willing to appoint one. Indeed one or two LTA members including Derek Hardwick were anti-real tennis, considering it a dying game.

This was confirmed when one of the drastic measures considered for fund-raising turned out to be the conversion of No. 2 court into two badminton courts, letting it out for commercial storage, or even turning it into a bowling alley. In 1959 a basket importer offered £650 a year to store his wares there. Then Brunswicks, manufacturers of bowling alleys, the rights of which were held by Rank, were prepared to pay £30,000 provided they could have both real tennis courts. That would have meant the end of real tennis at Queen's, and a very serious loss indeed, considering this was one of the first games played at the club. Fortunately, negotiations fell through.

In 1961 the Tennis and Rackets Association – through Lord Aberdare and Col. Nigel Renny, whose influence on both games, especially rackets, was considerable – offered the Club an interest-free loan of £1000 if they would put No. 2 court back in play. The Club board agreed but waived the offer of the loan. By the end of the year the court was under repair. Having only one court in action may have impeded the growth of the game but it did not stop the major competitions. Peter Kershaw's Amateur Championship win in 1948, the first held at Queen's after the war, was followed by two years of American domination with Ogden Phipps and Alistair Martin taking the title. The Club's Dugald Macpherson was runner-up on both occasions.

Morys Bruce, Lord Aberdare's son, followed in his father's footsteps and won the title four times from 1953 to 1957, Bob Riseley breaking his run; Geoffrey Atkins, already World Rackets Champion, held sway for a number of years and between 1951 and 1969 David Warburg appeared in the final thirteen times, winning thrice. Then, following a lone intervention from Anthony Tufton, Howard Angus began his remarkable run as champion from 1966 to 1980 inclusive and again in 1982.

J & B RARE

The seed that grew into the revival of real tennis and stalled a possible decline in rackets was sown in 1959 by four men: Dick Bridgeman, a Harrovian and director of Justerini and Brooks, two Etonians, Richard Greenwood and Anthony Ward, and Jack Hurley, whose contribution to real tennis at the Club was massive. It was at that time that the LTA-dominated board of directors at the Club were looking at the game unfavourably.

The Young Professionals Fund was launched with some financial help from the US Ambassador in London, Jock Whitney, whose father had built the Greentree Court in the US in 1915. Until his early death in the eighties it was Bridgeman's consuming hobby. At the same time Bridgeman, Greenwood and Ward conceived the idea of the Queen's Club Weekends at which rackets and real tennis enthusiasts gathered for competition, mostly handicap, and social fun. Between them they mounted over thirty such weekends before Bridgeman died and these get-togethers are now a highly popular part of the Club scene. At the same Hurley organized a much-enlarged match list.

The idea of the Young Professionals Fund was to provide a cadre of professionals at both games for the future; for the schools, where some of the rackets professionals were getting older, and for the real tennis clubs, becoming increasingly popular. Norwood Cripps, trained at Lord's, came to Queen's and was head professional at both games until he went to Eton in 1979. At one time or another Cripps

was joined at Queen's by Peter Ashford, son of an old Queen's Club professional, who later moved to Winchester, by Peter Ellis, who went to Haileybury, and by Terry Whatley, who revived rackets at Clifton. I have a personal feeling for Whatley as he helped me when, at a somewhat advanced age, I took up rackets which I could not afford to play when at Malvern. All three were products of the YPF – as were Kevin King and Gerard Parsons, two more real tennis professionals at Queen's, before moving on.

Cripps made his mark as a gladiatorial real tennis player and he had some splendid battles with Frank Willis and Howard Angus in the various 'open' championships sponsored by *The Field*, Cutty Sark, Unigate and Wimpey. With Alan Lovell he formed the most successful doubles team the game has had. He was a superb volleyer but sometimes over-exuberant off the floor. His successor as head real tennis professional, David Johnson, from Lord's, is generally regarded as a better teacher, especially by the novice with whom he has infinite patience. He makes good play for some of the older and less mobile members like Douglas Evans with whom I enjoyed playing in my more active years. Johnson has never been aggressive enough or possessed of a heavy enough stroke to win in the many competitions that are nowadays played. Like David Cull at Lord's he is of a more gentle nature, though his strokes are excellent.

In the committee room the main topics were again to do with money; MacSwiney's repeated plea for raising the subscriptions and, subsequently, the case of Tommy Anderson, a long-standing member and former Cambridge Rugby 'blue'. MacSwiney pointed out that it was impossible to know how much the Club could afford to spend when they relied for revenue on court fees rather than subscriptions. Eventually he won and the new subscriptions were fixed at 22 guineas for men, 18 for women. That would produce an annual revenue in excess of £15,000, though the membership had slipped from 1100 in 1959 to just over 900 in 1961. Even that sum was not really enough.

Anderson suggested that, among other things, the covered courts be rented out to other clubs after eight o'clock in the evening as at the All England Club, once they had built their own covered courts at Wimbledon. He was supported by many members who voted him onto the committee. But his enthusiasm for reform – Nigel Sharpe was chairman – went too far for their liking. He was asked to resign and, if he refused, he would face expulsion. Fleet Street got wind of this domestic storm and gave it a good airing. It ended when Gerald Gardiner QC headed a deputation of members seeking a withdrawal of the committee's demands and threats. The committee agreed.

FROM COURT TO BAR

Joe Pearce, having been with the Club since the thirties apart from the war, decided he could no longer carry on as a professional. He took over the bar in place of Stanley Suffling, another old retainer and the last of the billiards markers. Joe's early efforts behind the bar caused some amusement but eventually he and his wife, Queenie, formed an excellent team.

Dan Maskell, having begun his career as a ball-boy at Queen's, became the second professional to be made an honorary member, Peter Latham being the first. Ted Dexter, who was in the 1953 Radley rackets pair that reached the Schools Championship final, joined the Club, as did Aiden Crawley, one of the clan of that name and father of Andrew and Randall, and that distinguished *New York Times* columnist – politics not sport – Drew Middleton, while society was represented by Princess Radziwill, Jackie Kennedy's sister.

For some time Ritchie had thought the Club needed someone to organize and arrange games, and until he died Jack Jeffrey did the job. He was succeeded by Jim Coles, one of the lawn tennis professional staff. Coles, like O'Leary, liked his beer and recalled playing Lord Cholmendeley, then eighty-four, one day with a pint too many aboard. 'I couldn't hit the ball straight to him and apologized. He put his arm round my shoulder and suggested we sat down for a bit. He was a real gentleman.' Coles enjoyed playing Charlton Heston, a very useful player, but not Rod Steiger. 'Steiger told me how good he was, so I beat him 6–0 6–0. He gave me a dirty look and we never played again.'

Little-known to the majority of members were the prostitutes who inhabited the flats overlooking the courts. They would parade in the nude when the weather was suitable and Coles said he always put his pupils at the end so that their backs were to the show. The infamous Rachman used to come as a spectator during the Grass Court Championships and bring Mandy Rice-Davies amd Christine Keeler. Coles was asked to go down to Ascot and

give some coaching – for a fat fee. He declined. He also recalled there being a punchup between Roger Taylor and Bob Hewitt in the changing room after an acrimonious match.

There was a brief relief from the financial gloom in 1962 when the Ministry of Housing amd Local Government paid £25,714 to the Club for loss of development rights. The money should have gone to the LTA as the Club's owners but the LTA waived their right and the Club were able to use the money for repairs and maintenance. At the same time and somewhat reluctantly, the Club began negotiations with the Amateur Fencing Association. I use the

Joe Pearce behind the baseline. Later he served for many years behind the bar

word reluctantly because it was the LTA in the person of Eaton Griffith as chairman of the board, who were keen to help the fencers and Griffith's friend, their president, C. L. de Beaumont. The outcome was that the Club sold the AFA that southeast corner of the grounds on which O'Leary had had his market garden, for their new headquarters for a very nominal sum. It deprived the Club of an alternative entrance to the grounds.

Nigel Sharpe, the Club chairman, died in the autumn of 1962. A somewhat aloof person, he had played a leading role in keeping the Club going during the war and in helping his best friend, Dickie Ritchie, get it back on its feet afterwards. He played for Britain in the Davis Cup, once beat Cochet at Wimbledon and, while at Cheltenham College, opened the batting with K. S. Duleepsinghi, that classic – 'beautiful' might be a better word – batsman who later played for England.

Sharpe's successor was Dick Sandys, a doctor from Trinity College, Dublin, practising in Ealing. He and his wife, Dawn, brought a good deal of laughter, fun and Irish charm to the Club. The previous year his daughter, Rosemary, had married Michael Cogswell and their wedding reception was the first ever held at the Club. Though full of fun – eat, drink and be merry – Dick Sandys did not like losing at lawn tennis or golf. Occasionally he was called upon to referee Davis Cup matches and one such match was Britain v Italy at Eastbourne just after the war. Tony Mottram and Geoff Paish faced Gianni Cucelli and the del Bello brothers. It was a close affair and Sandys sat at the side of the court, sometimes reading the *Sporting Life*. On one occasion he was heard to remark to the British captain, 'Kill the wops'. He was equally outspoken in the Club and voiced his dislike of the modern tracksuit, especially when worn in the bar.

A FIRST FOR QUEEN'S

The Federation Cup, an international team knock-out championship for women, was inaugurated in 1963 and the Club was chosen as the first venue. Unfortunately, it coincided with the Grass Court Championships, which attracted an undistinguished entry. The USA won the Federation Cup over Australia, but it was the Sunday after Wimbledon finals day that caused the most fuss when Margaret Smith, the new champion, and Billie-Jean Moffitt, the runner-up, arrived at the Club followed by an unauthorized army of photographers. Jim Coles was on duty that day and had the utmost difficulty in keeping any sort of control. The Club came under some criticism for lack of organization from both the Press and Basil Reay, the LTA secretary.

The Club was still attracting the very occasional titled member and among the latest was the Marquis of Dufferin and Ava. No one took much notice of another new member, Tam Dalyell, an Etonian and a left-wing socialist MP. Nearly twenty years later Dalyell made the headlines as the hell-raiser over the sinking of the *Belgrano* in the Falklands War. Another Labour MP to join was Woodrow Wyatt, owner of various provincial newspapers. Other distinguished new members were the late Editor of *The Times*, Charles Douglas-Home, stage and radio favourites, Bernard Braden and Barbara Kelly, and Jeff Wayne, the musical comedy composer. The Club's association with the world of entertainment stretched back to the First World War and the days of E. B. Noel.

Here in the mid-sixties commercial sponsorship of major events was increasing and becoming more important. Frank Taylor had helped in the past and did so again when Dick Sandys failed to lure Arthur Guinness into sponsoring the Grass Court Championships. Despite a strong entry and two such winners as Roy Emerson and Margaret Smith, it was only Taylor's help that saved the event from losing money.

Largely owing to the drive and energy of Dick Bridgeman, Richard Greenwood, Jack Hurley and Anthony Ward, the current president, rackets and real tennis were thriving. These four men had become established on the Club committee and deservedly so, though they got little encouragement from the Club's owners, the LTA. Among their initiatives were the creation of a Tennis and Rackets membership at 12 guineas, pre-subscribed courts and the Queen's Club Weekends, now well-established and highly popular. There was some pretty brisk gambling at them too. I recall paying over fifty pounds for Michael Bowler in the real tennis handicap auction and spending an apprehensive forty-eight hours until he won and netted me over two hundred pounds.

In 1964 Anthony Tufton won his one-and-only real tennis title, breaking a span of five years during which Geoffrey Atkins and David Warburg hogged the final. Charles Swallow was new to the champions' list too, taking the Amateur Rackets Championship off World Champion, Atkins, 3–2 in the final. Swallow, who had broken a twelve-year domination by John Thompson, James Leonard and Atkins, immediately challenged for the World title but without success. That year, too, Richard Gracey and Martin Smith, Tonbridgians like Thompson, won the first of their five Amateur doubles titles.

Demonstrating the Club's new-found enthusiasm, Stefan Laszlo took a party of real tennis players on the first organized tour of the US and, in 1969, the first to Australia. His wife, by the way, had recently provided the Club with a cup for table tennis, a game with a chequered career there, and it was first won by Clive Bernstein, who must be one of the most prolific winners of Club competitions. Bernstein had recently introduced a 'News Sheet' to keep members informed of what was going on. Among the tit-bits was the fact that Virginia Wade, already embarked on her distinguished lawn tennis career, was posted for not paying her subscription!

GLORIOUS MONEY

When Dick Sandys handed over the chairmanship to Noel Berryman in 1966, the Club was in much better financial shape than when he took over three years earlier. The £25,000 loss-of-development compensation had helped and it was supplemented by two loans, for £25,000 and £45,000, from the LTA – an eightieth birthday present. Some of this went on building a second dining room, modernizing the kitchens, painting the floors of the covered courts, redecorating the *dedans* and laying a new carpet in the card room. Within a year of all this, however, selective employment tax, which could hit the Club for £2500 a year, was introduced and so was the breathalyzer, which soon affected the bar takings.

The strain of increased activity took its toll on some of the staff, among them Joe Pearce, who had a severe attack of bronchitis. His wife, Queenie, took over the bar while he was away. He returned in time to celebrate his fiftieth year with the Club, in 1969. Jim Coles found life as a teaching professional too much and became part-time games manager at weekends. He left the Club the following year, having been replaced on the professional staff by Sidney Upton. The gateman, S. Higgins, also retired.

The end of the sixties was something of a watershed for the staff. The renowned Mrs Tutt, having begun her association with the ladies' changing room back in the thirties, died in 1968. She was succeeded by Mrs Maggie Bird who, now in her late sixties, remains in charge. It is a remarkable fact that these two ladies cover nearly sixty years of The Queen's Club history. Maggie Bird is Irish. She has seventeen children, ten girls and seven boys – 'No pill, no television in my young days' – and came to London from County Cavan near the end of the war. Working in the Shepherds Bush PO she replied to an advertisement for the job at the Club and was taken on by Dickie Ritchie, the secretary.

'It was a lucky day for us when you came through the gate,' remarked Ritchie one day. To which Maggie retorted 'I didn't. I came through a hole in the hedge.' The changing room in those days contained old furniture, including a settee and a large coal fire. Her co-worker – there were only two changing room attendants – was also Irish, Nora Pearce from Cork, who remained for some six years and now helps look after cancer patients at the Hammersmith Hospital while maintaining a long-time friendship with the Boden family.

Maggie's duties included taking the court money and handing out the balls. 'I used to have fights over the money. Some players pretended they had paid when they hadn't and I'd threaten to have them billed. Some people used to come in and say "I want this or I want that". I'd tell them not to talk like that but ask "Can I have?" Virginia Wade and Chris Evert would always support me. They are real ladies, my favourites. During his brief reign as secretary Hassell sacked Maggie and this upset, among others, Clive Bernstein who had her reinstated.

She recalls, among other memories, O'Leary, the former head groundsman, arriving at the Club from hospital wearing only his pyjamas and a Miss Hutchings bitterly complaining that someone had stolen her tennis shoes which, she admitted, she had paid three shillings and sixpence for eleven years previously! Maggie likes the Club as it is now – 'Much cleaner and more pleasant and with a much nicer management. That's my life down there in the changing room; my second home.' She now has three ladies with her – Mrs Mary Butt, Mrs Winnie Maffrey and Mrs Sue Kohn.

The pressure was felt in catering too, especially during tournament time. The volume of catering had fallen off; the cost of food everywhere had risen by twenty-five per cent. Gardnar Merchants took over in time for the Grass Court Championships and introduced a cold buffet instead of a set lunch.

1968 was the year that tennis 'went open', the year that the players could legitimately play for money. Rothmans had already set up a grass court circuit involving Surbiton, Manchester, Beckenham and Queen's with modest prizemoney. With help from Taylor Woodrow some £1400 was available in prizemoney for the Grass Court Championships, a paltry sum compared with what came later. Unfortunately all the finals were rained off. The week, however, left Maureen Wilson with an indelible memory. Then wife of the chairman, Noel Berryman, she hosted an International Club lunch that included Frank Sedgman, Lew Hoad, Roy Emerson, Alex Olmedo and others, all Wimbledon champions returning to the traditional game after years in the professional freezer.

The Covered Court Championships, dormant for the previous two years, were incorporated into the Dewar Cup. They attracted the US Davis Cup team including Arthur Ashe, Stan Smith and Bob Lutz, all of whom were beaten in a week of curious results. The event was not a success because it clashed with a professional promotion at Wembley – the Tournament of Champions. Part of the cause of this was the rivalry between the BBC, who covered Wembley, and ITV, who screened Queen's. The two channels were vying to see which one could capture the game and in a year or two ITV gave up.

Since the retirement of Jim Coles, Mrs Bea Walter had taken over the task of games manager and social secretary. She left to marry but soon returned as Mrs Seal to referee the grass court meeting. (In 1972 she made a name for herself by disqualifying Pancho Gonzales.) Judy Hall, a Worcestershire County player, had taken her place and later married Howard Angus, already well-launched on his astonishing career of winning sixteen Amateur Real Tennis singles titles and the world title at both real tennis and rackets.

The Club Committee had the idea of offering Prince Charles honorary membership but received the prompt reply from the Palace – 'Prince Charles is not at present joining any London Clubs.' The good news was that after a span of thirty-five years the Club membership in 1969 had caught up with what it had been in 1934 – 1681. The bad news was that the Covered Court Championships, already tottering, turned out to be a flop and received some rough treatment from the Press, notably *The Times*. The event was split between Queen's and Wembley and Rex Bellamy, in *The Times*, commented that

'Queen's was bleak, cold and unwelcoming. The few spectators seemed like mourners at a wake,' and that the players thankfully said goodbye to the Club on Wednesday evening. He added that the event's prime need was to get away from the Club. This was a series of comments the Club committee did not enjoy. The fact was that the world's oldest covered courts tournament had at last expired as it had looked like doing for some time.

With the advent of open tennis 'Queen's week' immediately preceding Wimbledon became a much-sought-after date. Edgbaston and Eastbourne had their eyes on it but largely through Vernon Weaver, an LTA councillor, the threats were at least temporarily warded off. When, in 1970, Rod Laver and Margaret Court won, the meeting did have a rival, Eastbourne, but neither that nor the General Election affected its success.

YOBBOS

The Club's image, already tarnished by Press comments on its dreariness (during the Covered Court Championships) and domestic innuendos about English being a minority language among the members, was further dented by the scruffiness of some of the youngsters taking part in the LTA training schemes and junior competitions. Perspiring players would sit in the bar and one youngster walked into it barefoot. The darts board and billiard table were damaged, the latter to such an extent that it had to be dismantled. It was some time before Paul Hutchins and Roger Becker did much about disciplining the youngsters, one of whom they suspended for three weeks. It was not until the late seventies that the Club really smartened up.

The seventies saw a lot of changes. Commander Blowers, successor as book-keeper to William Pott, resigned and Norris Haugh, a schoolmaster and member since 1960, became assistant secretary. In 1975 he succeeded Dickie Ritchie, who retired after thirty years' service to the Club which included the most precarious period in the Club's history. There were times just after the war when, Ritchie confessed, he wondered whether the Club would survive six months. Survive it did and in his retirement, from the committee and as president, Ritchie saw the Club enter a new and prosperous era. In 1985 he handed over the presidency to Anthony Ward. The Ritchie connection with Queen's, father and son, had already extended over ninety years,

Dickie having become a member in 1921, and his father, M. J. G., having joined in the early 1890s.

There are, as a matter of history, very few members left of the same vintage as Dickie Ritchie. Dugald Macpherson preceded Ritchie by a year, having been made a member while still at Harrow. Macpherson was a champion at real tennis and squash, a beautiful player of both games. Charles Kingsley, a former British Davis Cup player and a great friend of the late Esmond Harmsworth (Lord Rothermere), is of the class of '21 and now lives in Malaga, Spain. Then there is 'Pip' Jessel, the fourth of the same vintage, whose enthusiasm for real tennis, squash and bridge was matched by his competitive spirit. He was an infuriating man to play at either court game as he had no backhand. Everyone knew it yet he managed to cover up that deficiency so well that it needed a good player to beat him. There are a few in or approaching their sixty years as members, among them those two great French players, Jean Borotra and René Lacoste,

The Ritchie connection. R. J. and son Richard playing Paradise Tennis in 1961 and (top) R. J. with M. J. G.

Oxford and Cambridge 'blues', Ted Avory and Brian Finnigan – who now lives in Florida – and that very useful player, R. M. Turnbull. Not many.

Joe Pearce, having served twelve years as barman and many more as a lawn tennis professional, retired in 1972 and died a year later. As bartender he was succeeded by Reg Routledge, a former Regular Army senior warrant officer, and his wife, Barbara. They took over the Cottage that, in its time, has housed quite a few staff members. Routledge, having presided over many an officers' mess including the RAOC Headquarters, straightaway attempted to set similar high standards at Queen's and now sees the fruits of his labours. He has served the Club in multifarious ways; as barman (Barbara still works the bar when required), as head waiter, sommelier, archivist and historian, publisher of rare books on real tennis, and, not least by any means, researcher for this history. One of his sons, Michael, plays real tennis and is deputy head groundsman to David Kimpton. The other, Stewart, is a trained butler though not at the Club. Service appears to be in the blood.

Barbara showed her wit one evening not so long ago while tending the bar. A group of rackets players were discussing what the ebullient Tim Hue Williams would be giving his girlfriend for Christmas. As it was claimed he had given her a Rolls-Royce the previous Christmas the choice was limited. 'What about a liveried chauffeur to go with the Rolls?' suggested Barbara.

FATHER AND SON

Peter Ashford, whose father had been a professional at the Club many years previously, joined Norwood Cripps in the real tennis and rackets courts in 1971 and formed an excellent team. Inevitably Ashford, with his flair for organization and dealing with people, moved on – to Winchester as rackets professional in 1975. He has never been a great player at either game but, like Terry Whatley at Clifton, he gets things done and inspires people to play.

The position of the lawn tennis professionals changed considerably in the seventies. Gradually the old-time professionals like Dan Maskell, Jack Jeffrey, Fred Poulson, Bill Holmes and Joe Pearce through to Sidney Upton and Ernie Lowe gave way to their more modern counterpart, the player who retires from competition and takes to coaching. The change was sociological; the days of the ball-boy turned professional had gone. Lowe retired in 1977 leaving Upton as the only survivor of the 'old brigade'.

In the mid-seventies Norman Kitovitz, a former Oxford blue and a barrister, was taken on as a club coach. He resigned in 1979 for no reason other than

The Routledge family: between them nearly fifty years of service to the Club

Erroll MacSwiney – the Club's financial director. A member of the Club
for over fifty years: appointed a director in 1946, Vice Chairman of
the Board 1953–1966 and from 1973, Chairman of the Board 1967–1973

that he felt tired. Michael Davie took over. Roger Becker, former British Davis Cup player, was hired by the LTA to coach their promising young players. For a time he was joined by David Lloyd, another former Davis Cup player. Upton, having joined the staff in 1967, objected to this intrusion by unqualified coaches and was supported by the Professionals' Association. Apart from anything else, men like Becker and Lloyd could command three times as big a fee for their lessons. Neither Becker nor Lloyd appeared willing to take the official coaching course and become registered professionals. An embarrassed LTA tried to work out various solutions but nothing satisfactory enough for Upton, who said he felt unable to work with the two men and retired near the end of the decade, no doubt to spend more time at his hobby – the horses. Understandably he also objected to Becker being referred to as resident professional coach or, as he

was later described, head professional.

For a time MacSwiney became chairman of the board, one of the few non-LTA men to hold the position since the 1953 takeover. He was succeeded by Ted Robbins, an LTA councillor from Surrey who could claim to be the oldest Fleet-Streeter attending Wimbledon by virtue of having spent a brief period of his life on an agency there in the early twenties. The Club chairman, Noel Berryman, recently appointed MBE, died after a tragic fall at his home and Clive Bernstein replaced him. Berryman's widow, Maureen, having taken over the Ladies' committee from Mrs Dorothy Pattison some years previously, handed over the chairmanship to Mrs B. H. Davis.

Judy Hall gradually withdrew from her work in administration and as a part-time coach and, in 1974, Peter Greig, a retired RAF officer, was appointed games manager. The following year a new financial controller, Albert Buck, was called in to disentangle the financial knots. There had been a gap in the organization since the retirement of Mrs Lavendar and the accounts were in a mess. Buck, who had occupied similar posts at the Naval and Military and United Service Clubs put them in order and retired in 1979. Greig became adept at genially persuading people that they were not as good players as they thought. He also turned his office into a cattery and until the committee cried 'halt' the Club became 'a moggies' mecca'. During his ten years with the Club some sixteen cats, many of them abandoned, came under his care. When he left he had six cats at home, four of them from Queen's.

Since the early days, when horses like Tom and Dick were stabled at the Club mainly for the purpose of pulling the heavy rollers, animals have, understandably, not been encouraged in case they soiled the turf. Just before the First World War a dog was hired to assist the night watchman in the days of the suffragette movement. Unfortunately, as already mentioned, it bit the Club secretary. More recently Mr Vilarelle, one of the groundsmen who did some guard duty, was provided with an alsatian. Cats, however, have been the most regular and persistent inhabitants and currently there are two, Tiger and Oscar. Tiger, a fat elderly tabby, is the resident. He used to occupy the most comfortable chair in the lounge but, since the plush redecoration, has been consigned to an old chair in the passage. He is very idle. Oscar, white except for the tip of his tail, is intelligent, proud, independent and active. He lives in one of the nearby flats but regards the Club as his home pitch. Unfortunately he has the disturbing habit of setting off the Club burglar alarm at four in the morning. This annoys both Reg Routledge and the local police.

LOST INCOME

Much of the seventies was taken up with political skirmishing over the Grass Court Championships, the Club's flag carrier in the matter of competitions. The warning signal went up in 1971 – Stan Smith and Margaret Court were the winners – when the meeting made a loss, due almost entirely to the sponsorship money going to the players rather than the Club. Another source of income was lost when ITV declined to discriminate between Queen's and Eastbourne and did not televize either event. With an additional £10,000 income needed, these losses

inevitably led to an increase in subscriptions, which had remained static at 33 guineas (for men) for five years. The suggestion was 45 guineas. (Current subscriptions are the same for men and women, and have been so for some time.)

The situation did not improve the following year when Jimmy Connors and Chris Evert made their first appearances at Queen's and won. The meeting did show a profit of £700 but the committee still viewed events 'with some disquiet'. Jack Kramer and Donald Dell who controlled the Players' Association demanded at least £20,000 prizemoney for the 1973 meeting. Rothmans were prepared to put up that amount but also wanted to mount a £10,000 tournament for women at Eastbourne the same week. A new threat came from John Player, who wanted a *Grand Prix* tournament at Nottingham. The outcome was that Rothmans sponsored the whole of the 1973 meeting, won by Ilie Nastase and Olga Morozova – who beat Evonne Goolagong. It turned out to be a highly successful and profitable meeting. But it was the last one held at the Club for three years.

Soon the 'ante' demanded by the Players' Association went up to £50,000 and only John Player were prepared to spend that money. Queen's had ideas of running an independent tournament or a veterans' championship. Both were deemed impracticable especially when the Club found they could recoup some of the lost revenue by charging Wimbledon a large fee for providing practice courts the week before the Championships. Profitable though this arrangement may have been, it did not go smoothly. There were complaints from the Players' Association that they were not made to feel welcome at the Club. Mr Mynard, in charge of allotting practice courts, may have appeared a trifle gruff, especially with players who turned up in any old clothes.

There was little the Club could do about restoring the Grass Court Championships other than put pressure on the LTA who, as the owners, obviously had a vested interest. Wimbledon were also keen on encouraging a healthy grass court circuit before the Championships began. In the face of rivalry from other centres the need was for a new sponsor and date in the calendar. The chance came in 1977 when Nottingham moved its date back and left the week before Wimbledon free again. Formica came in as possible sponsors but withdrew when they found there would be no TV coverage. Then a new threat appeared when the Berlin *Grand Prix* event was upgraded to a 3-star tournament.

Frank Lowe, an advertising man, and Clive Bernstein, the Club chairman, countered with Rawlings, the soft drinks subsidiary of Whitbread's Brewery who were prepared to put up the £50,000 needed to give the Queen's meeting 3-star status. But it was to be a men-only affair and in the event it was not a great success. Raul Ramirez won, beating Mark Cox in the final. Despite poor weather it did make a £1000 profit and the sponsors were happy enough to cover 1978 with increased prizemoney.

Bernstein, backed by the sponsors, laid £50,000 ($100,000) on the line for the man who won the doubles, Queen's and Wimbledon. This was a fine idea until the Men's International Professional Tennis Council stepped in and turned down the proposal on the grounds they had not been consulted. The result was that the money if won (it was not) would be used for the benefit of British junior tennis. There was some disappointment at the absence in 1978 of top players such as Jimmy Connors and Bjorn Borg – he never played at Queen's – and the sponsors threatened to withdraw unless the entry improved. Tony Roche and John McEnroe were the finalists that year. Little did they know what effect McEnroe would have. He was at the start of his spectacular and controversial career, having qualified and reached the Wimbledon semi-final the previous year.

McENROE ASCENDANT

For the moment the sponsors were wary, despite the advent of TV coverage in 1978. They paid the Club a fee – £2000 that year – and a share of the gate. But the cost of mounting the meeting was well over budget at £115,000 and everyone kept their fingers crossed hoping that TV would return in 1979. It did and the tournament dates were moved back, leaving a gap of a week before Wimbledon. McEnroe returned, won again and ushered in the highly successful years that followed. Undoubtedly the tournament had achieved a special relationship with McEnroe and it was not until 1985 that he broke his link with Queen's and lost his Wimbledon title as well! By that time Whitbread had changed their flag from Rawlings to Stella Artois lager.

The development and sponsorship of the Grass Court Championships may have been a major concern of the seventies but interest in other games, notably real tennis and rackets, was expanding and, at squash, the Club entered its most successful period since the inter-war years. The floors of the two real tennis courts, especially No. 1, needed repair. Anthony Ward saw the job done. The number of members pre-subscribing courts – i.e. buying a bundle of court-bookings at a cut rate at the start of the season – rose from fifty-eight to seventy-four. Peter Ashford joined Norwood Cripps on the professional staff and Dick Bridgeman saw the game flourishing as never before.

Back in 1965 *The Field*, that sporting journal heavily responsible, nearly a hundred years earlier, for the birth of Wimbledon, provided a trophy – *The Field* Trophy – for real tennis at Queen's. That was a major move in the development of open competition and the beginning of sponsorship for both these esoteric games. Ron Hughes, Frank Willis, Howard Angus and Norwood Cripps were the early winners of the Trophy and when *The Field* retired, unable to finance the event, Cutty Sark Whisky took over, followed by Unigate and now George Wimpey.

In the rackets world, Louis Roederer champagne responded in 1971 promoting an open singles championship, won first by Angus and then by William Surtees, John Prenn and William Boone. For some years the event was enhanced by the presence and enthusiasm of Colonel Rutherford, the London agent for Louis Roederer, who at midday would dispense Crystal champagne, the brand leader, in the bar. The fact was not lost on the Press – Christina Wood of the *Telegraph* and McKelvie of *The Times*!

When the Colonel died, the sponsors withdrew and Celestion Loudspeakers, a Prenn family affair, took over and have continued to expand the sponsorship of competitive rackets ever since. The importance the Club now attached to real tennis and rackets, as distinct from the indifference following the LTA takeover in 1953, was seen in 1974 when Anthony Ward was made a member of the board with special responsibility for the two games. Almost immediately the two real tennis courts were equipped with new lights.

In 1973 Angus, having narrowly failed to win Queen's and take the World Rackets title off Surtees in Chicago (where the humidity repeatedly broke his racket strings) succeeded the following year. In 1976 he beat Gene Scott of the US for both the World Real Tennis title in New York and Queen's. Unlike Peter Latham, however, Angus never held the two titles simultaneously.

For a fee of between £750 and £1000 Universal

Pictures shot a scene for the film *Seven Percent Solution* in the real tennis courts. That provided a lot of fun for the Club and Norwood Cripps and Henry Johns were asked to teach the actors the rudiments of the game.

In 1972 the Club won the Bath Club Cup for squash for the first time since 1948 with a team consisting of Robert Dolman, John Ward and Philip Ayton. They won it in two of the next three years. When Ayton and Ward reduced their playing Dolman was joined by Jonathan Leslie and Willie Boone and they won the Cup three years running, 1977–9. Boone was a bonus as he not only shot pheasants but helped cook them for the suppers that followed home matches. The Club had then become so strong at squash that a second team was accepted for the Cup.

The Club's aristocratic roots continued to sprout throughout the seventies and into the eighties. Among new members from great families were the Hon. Michael Astor; the Dowager Marchioness of Cholmondeley, whose husband, I recall, had been a most elegant player in my early days in Norfolk; the Countess of Munster; and the Marquess of Londonderry. In early 1980 Princess Michael of Kent joined and Norman Kitovitz became her coach. The most special member, however, was the Duchess of Gloucester, an enthusiastic player, as Shirley Brasher can vouch. One day in 1979 the Duchess indicated to the Club chairman, Anthony Ward, that she would like to become more involved in the Club and the game. It was the Club's patron, the Duke of Edinburgh, who suggested she should become Vice-Patron, a position she graciously accepted.

DARK CLOUDS

Below the surface, however, there were rumbles of discontent, difficulties in the secretariat, concern over the possibility of the LTA using the Club or part of it as a National Training Centre for young players, and continued dissatisfaction over the catering. The ever-enthusiastic Stefan Laszlo had little difficulty in collecting half the cost of £4000 for new lighting for the No. 2 real tennis court, a problem that was only solved when Howard Angus made some recommendations that cut the cost considerably. Ivar Boden, the vice-chairman to Anthony Ward, described the Club as a place of 'developing dilapidation'. There was a need to upgrade the changing rooms, the catering, the

squash courts and the hard courts. The indoor courts were leaking, there was dry rot in some of the buildings, and areas of the Club were not being used or were shut away.

The LTA recognized that they should improve standards and restore the Club to reasonable repair but not before some senior members, Anthony Ward, Boden and Bernstein among them, had ideas of buying or leasing back the Club from the owners. This body of members was confident it could raise sufficient money to put the Club in order, if not purchase it. That certainly made the LTA realize they had not put anything into the Club for some years. In the late seventies Brian Palmer, not then a member of the committee, was asked to do an in-depth report on the catering. He was well-qualified for the task, his business being wines and spirits, hotels and pubs and a retail chain of shops. He replied that he was unable to cover one section of the Club without examining the whole. This he did.

Just about the time Palmer was finishing his report and making recommendations, the Club suffered its worst physical disaster – a fire – as if some biblical visitation had descended upon it to jolt those who owned and ran the place. An hour before dawn on Tuesday, 26 June 1979 Reg Routledge and his family, asleep in the Cottage, were awakened by the din of fire engines entering the grounds, having axed their way through the main gates. An occupant in one of the homes overlooking the grass courts had noticed smoke coming from the Club and alerted the Brigade.

The fire had begun in the women's dressing room on the ground floor, had spread to the floor above where the administrative records were kept and further into the rackets court gallery. The changing room was gutted, some records destroyed and the gallery was so badly damaged that it was left in a dangerous condition. The ladies moved into part of the men's changing room which was screened off. Virginia Wade called it 'The Stable'.

The cause of the fire was never established. Vandalism was suspected, though never proved, as a door normally kept shut was found to be open. Fortunately the damage was covered by insurance which had recently been re-assessed. In due course the Club's claim for £30,000 was met.

This gave the Ladies' committee under Maureen Wilson the chance of modernizing their changing room and making it attractive with more mirrors, dryers and showers. The old one had been similar to the men's, and the women found it spartan, rather gloomy and utilitarian. It also gave Nicholas Meletiou, having recently completed his finals as an architect with honours, a chance to show his talent. A couple of years earlier this young man had sought and gained permission from Clive Bernstein, the Club chairman at the time, to use Queen's as the topic of his thesis. Having redesigned the ladies' changing room, Meletiou was adopted as the Club architect and later, under the auspices of Brian Palmer and Ivar Boden, became responsible for refurbishing the Club House, the President's Room, the men's changing room and the new Covered Courts complex.

The insurance also allowed the Club to build additional office and board room space on the ground floor and create a much larger rackets gallery of two tiers, not unlike a theatre, with a special 'box' for the Press. The old Press eyrie, jutting out of the wall and perched over the corner of the court, had resembled a ledge on the north face of the Eiger – and was just about as difficult to reach. It was nearly fifty years since I had first clambered onto it with Hubert Winterbotham of the *Daily Telegraph* to watch the Schools rackets. Over the years it had become a favourite nook for many players, in particular the Pugh family. The fire damage repairs did not begin until the summer of 1980, though some work was done on the first floor in time for the Grass Court Championships. Watching rackets was severely restricted.

As London was rebuilt after the Great Fire of 1666, so the Club fire of 1979 seemed to inspire action on the part of those who ran it. Palmer's ideas were adopted, though not all at once. He wanted the Club to be run more like a business, with a proper structure including a management committee, and he wanted the catering to become in-house.

ALL CHANGE IN THE OFFICE

Early in 1980 the Club appointed R. S. Hassell as chief executive, a post similar to that now held by Christopher Gorringe at Wimbledon, with Norris Haugh remaining as secretary. In a clash of personalities Haugh soon resigned. Hassell was allowed to do what he liked. Some of his ideas were sound, some unpopular. He had Portacabins installed through which everyone entering the Club premises had to pass if they wanted to book a court. Peter Greig, the games manager, was in charge – now it

is Mike Hayes – along with Monica Curtiss, the receptionist. This change was suggested many years earlier, long before the days of Portacabins, in order to check who came and went from the Club.

Hassell also wanted tills installed in the dressing rooms so that players could pay straight after their games. This provoked two members of the dressing-room staff to resign. A till on the bar, which was taking £30–40,000 a year, was less contentious. He sacked the caterers, the Kelly sisters, a likeable Irish trio, and brought in a commercial company. He wanted, among other things, to charge non-members for car parking and to review the question of visitors' fees. There was some backing for Hassell's ideas within the Committee but not a majority. They decided he had been given too much latitude, though the concept of a supremo was correct and, in September, he resigned.

With a management committee set up – three club members (later increased to four) to two from the LTA – it was decided to revert to the normal post of secretary and Jonathan Edwardes was appointed. He was a former Army officer who had gained some business experience with Dunhill. He was also a member and had played rackets at Queen's while at Wellington and in the Army Championships. He came at a tough time, a turning point in the Club's history, and his contribution so far has been far beyond the duties of a normal secretary; all credit to him for it.

Edwardes's introduction to working for the Club was dramatic. Within two days of his appointment he was pitchforked into an Extraordinary AGM, the outcome of a Palace revolution. The discontent of the seventies and the awareness of the running down of the Club made members unhappy with almost every aspect of it. There was dissatisfaction over the limitations and restrictions imposed on the use of the Club's facilities by the Stella Artois Championships and the use of the courts and the Club by the Wimbledon competitors. The pot boiled over.

Anthony Ward was still in the chair when the Extraordinary AGM was held on 4 November 1980 in the No. 2 real tennis court. One hundred and eighty three members turned up and it was bitterly cold. There were three resolutions:

1 That the sponsored tournament be abandoned or severely limited in its scope.
2 That the privileges extended to Wimbledon competitors be withdrawn or substantially curtailed.

Pitchforked into a revolution: Secretary Jonathan Edwardes

3   That the interests of Club members should be a major consideration in the allocation of resources.

There was support from the committee for these resolutions though the third had no legal backing. The Club was ninety-five percent owned by the LTA, who through the board of directors controlled both the resources and finances. But the Club did have a friend in the new chairman of the board, Geoff Brown, an LTA councillor who soon became chairman. Brown showed a greater appreciation of the Club's needs and became more involved in its day-to-day working than any of his predecessors. The majority of LTA councillors rarely went near the Club and knew or cared little about it. One was once heard to describe it as 'a can of worms'. In the last few years Brown has done a great deal to satisfy members with regard to the third resolution.

REFRESHING ALE

As to the first, it was pointed out by Cecil Betts that Queen's was the second most important grass court meeting in the country – one of the oldest grass tournaments in the world. It was also financially important to the Club. Clive Bernstein, the tournament director, said that Whitbreads had paid a fee of £15,000 for the privilege of holding it and that

Chairman of the Board of Directors since 1980, Geoff Brown. He
is currently also the President of the Lawn Tennis Association

sum would be increased in future years; £17,500 in 1981 up to £25,000 in 1985. There was also the Club's share of the gate and other bonuses. If, for instance, the meeting were pruned and the number of competitors reduced, it would lose its 3–star *Grand Prix* status.

Regarding the second resolution, Wimbledon was already aware of the burden it was imposing on the Club. Sir Brian Burnett, the All England Club chairman, had agreed to reduce the number of courts and time available to Wimbledon competitors and, as the courts in Aorangi Park (a part of the All England grounds) became available the need for using Queen's would be curtailed even further. It may have been cold at that meeting, with members unprepared to get into long discussions, but two side-issues were not mentioned. The first was the threat to the tournament from the Association of Tennis Professionals who wanted a hefty slice, if not the whole of, the TV rights. The second was the building of the David Lloyd complex at Hayes, near enough to the Club to pose a threat.

The ATP was really an LTA affair but, as Ivar Boden had earlier commented, it was quite unfair to Queen's to have their major showpiece the subject of marketplace bargaining so that neither the Club nor the sponsors were sure whether the grass court meeting would be on or off. Bernstein was confident the meeting would take place and he was right.

The prophets of doom, and there were plenty of them, claimed (though not at this meeting) that the new Lloyd Centre, probably the most up-to-date in the country, would drain off a host of dissatisfied members from Queen's. It may have taken some. Others with money to spare joined both clubs but today in any case the Club has more members than ever before in its history and a very healthy waiting list. The men most responsible for this phenomenon are the three Club chairmen of the period, Anthony Ward, Ivar Boden and Brian Palmer; the LTA's Geoff Brown as chairman of the board, and the tournament director, Clive Bernstein. They saw what was needed and acted.

Through most of the Club's history the catering has posed problems and generally been a loss-maker. In 1983 there was a dramatic drop in the takings and that was put down to the proximity of the David Lloyd centre. It may well have been so. It is a strange fact that until today the only occasion when the catering has made a profit was in the first year of the Great War, when it was run by the Army and Navy.

Providing meals for The Queen's Club and Old Etonian weekends and other functions was well nigh impossible. At one time members such as C. K. Simond and John Ward would entertain in their homes. In the late seventies Gillian Ward and other wives prepared food at home and brought it to the Club. The LTA took their official guests to Hurlingham for meals.

The catering company employed by Hassell left in the autumn of 1980 and was replaced by another under the popular Mr Jaffe, a tennis enthusiast. In the autumn the Club, as Brian Palmer had suggested in his report, took over the catering. The Board voted £55,000 be spent on it. Simon Gelber from the Bath Club was appointed catering manager and extensive rebuilding began of the kitchens – modern and far bigger than anyone thought would be required – the buffet and a new restaurant. Though the restaurant was not opened until after the Stella Artois tournament, all the catering for that event within the Clubhouse was undertaken and grossed a respectable sum of £23,000.

Gelber's hobbies are rugby and cricket and thence, by some strange twist, the life of A. E. Stoddart, the England cricketer and rugby player who was the Club secretary when the First World War broke out and who later shot himself. Gelber brought in as chef Nick Breakes from Trusthouse Forte and they have formed a successful team ever since. They now employ fourteen staff full-time; a far cry from the days of the Kelly sisters.

SLOW START

At first members were reluctant to use the new restaurant but the LTA did so for their more formal lunches and entertaining. Its popularity and its menu have grown in its brief lifetime and the Club now has a respectable wine cellar. There is a luncheon Club with 140 members. Smart dinners and suppers were held for the Queen's and Old Etonian rackets and real tennis weekends, and lunches were served during the Stella Artois in the real tennis courts. Reg Routledge, among his other duties, became the flower arranger. For the 1985 Stella Artois, however, the real tennis courts were pronounced a fire hazard by the GLC and the covered courts were used.

The Functions Room upstairs, part of the earlier men's changing room and overlooking the Club grounds, was completed in September 1984. Since then it has been used extensively by members and

(left to right:) Clive Bernstein, Anthony Ward, Brian Palmer and Ivar Boden – a succession of Chairmen whose unstinting efforts have helped towards a revitalised Club

others for cocktail parties, wedding and other receptions, Masonic dinners and sponsors' lunches. Sir Stanley Rous's ninetieth birthday party was held there in conjunction with the Central Council for Physical Recreation in July 1985. The measure of the success of the Club catering under Gelber is shown in these figures. During the 1985 Stella Artois week the in-house catering, as distinct from the outdoor marquees run by the sponsors, grossed £100,000. For the year 1984–5 the gross was £400,000 including the takings from the smart new bars built into the old lounge and run by Eric Grieve, a Scot from St Andrews who joined the Club in 1983 after serving with the RAF.

The ghosts of E. B. Noel, Freddie Wilson and Peter Latham must look down in wonderment,

Renovations within the Clubhouse:
The dining room (above) and the Members' bar

perhaps envy, at the present luxury of the old Club.

During these last few dynamic years the sport flowed on. William Surtees, having successfully defended his World Rackets title against Willie Boone in 1979 – a few months before the fire destroyed the gallery – lost it to John Prenn in December 1981. Prenn surrendered the title to Boone after matches in Montreal and Queen's three years later. Neil Smith joined the rackets staff from Harrow. Howard Angus, having first won the World Real Tennis title at Queen's in 1976, lost it to Chris Ronaldson, the Hampton Court professional, in April 1981 when, in the second leg, he tore a calf muscle and had to retire. Ronaldson has held the title ever since, surviving his latest challenge from the Australian, Wayne Davies (New York Racquet Club) in 1985 at Queen's.

The professional, Kevin King, moved to Hatfield House and was briefly replaced by Gerard Parsons, who then moved on to Petworth. Henry Johns, the doyen of the real tennis professionals, renewed his association with Queen's after sixty years (many as head pro at Lord's) with two days' coaching a week. The weekly 'open evenings', so popular at rackets, were extended to real tennis.

The death of Dick Bridgeman in September 1982 at an early age was a tragic loss. He was a prime mover in the revival of both games and was responsible for launching the Young Professionals Fund. He was a director of Justerini and Brooks for twenty years. David Norman, a go-getter, took over the chairmanship of the Tennis and Rackets Association. Martin Scott handed over the secretaryship of the T & RA to William Stephens and died shortly after his retirement.

Martin Scott had taken over organizing the Club weekends initiated by Bridgeman, Ward, Greenwood and Hurley. He was succeeded by Dudley MacDonald helped by his wife, Dinah. Unlike his predecessors MacDonald did not come from a rackets playing school but from Shrewsbury noted, among other things, for its rowing and soccer. MacDonald's enthusiasm and that fired by the Monday Club for rackets has increased the number of rackets players competing. More women too. He also obtained sponsorship from Mumm Champagne and the fact that during the weekends a magnum of champagne may be bought for the price of a bottle has been an added lure.

John McEnroe won the first of his hat-trick of Stella Artois titles in 1979 and had a brush or two with authority during the week. He was on his best behaviour the following year but it did not last. He failed to emulate Roy Emerson's four successive titles when Jimmy Connors beat him in the 1982 final, repeating that victory the following year, a complete sell-out. An account of McEnroe's outburst in the 1984 final against the unknown Lief Shiras, which should have led to disqualification, will be found in the section on the Grass Court Championships. In 1985 McEnroe decided that, apart from Wimbledon, he would no longer compete in Britain.

SUDDEN DEATH

McEnroe's association with the Club ended abruptly in 1985 after a brouhaha there during Wimbledon's first week. Having booked time for practice at Queen's he took a court not allocated to him. When the two ladies, one of them Mrs Sheila Boden, the other an American, claimed their court McEnroe berated them with filthy language. They reported him to the Club committee who, in turn, asked him for an explanation. When this was not forthcoming they had no choice but to ask him to resign or face expulsion. He remained silent and broke what, for half a dozen or so years, had been a highly successful partnership between Club and player. There is no doubt that McEnroe was heavily responsible for the success of the Stella Artois meeting. Should one add RIP?

It was during an earlier tournament that David Sellman, better-known at the Club as the bridge organizer and player, found himself umpiring a match between Fred Stolle and the Russian, Alex Metreveli, whom he had never heard of. He noticed a spectator repeatedly shouting at Metreveli in a foreign language. Knowing that sideline coaching was illegal he asked Stolle whether he should take action. 'No,' replied Fred, 'the guy is doing Metreveli more harm than good.' Sellman did his bridge team more good than harm. Two years later, under his leadership, the Club team won the London Trophy and then, in 1984, the Devonshire Cup.

Over the years the Club has maintained its interest in bridge which, during the last war, was heavily responsible for keeping the place together. Early in the 1970s a Pole, Stefan Grzeszczynski, appeared and rekindled interest in the game – at that time he owned a bridge club – and enthusiastically encouraged young people to play tennis. He also owned,

Top The new covered courts were converted into a single championship arena
for the first time for the BASF European Cup in 1986
Above: The winning Swiss team with the 1986 BASF European Cup

at one time, a yellow Rolls-Royce which became something of a landmark in the Club's car park.

The Club was becoming so popular and applications for membership so numerous that it was decided that further applicants must be of a reasonable standard of play. That did not stop the flood and, as the centenary year approaches, the membership stands at 2400, far more than ever before, with a waiting list of over 400. The current subscription is £220 a year for those over twenty-eight, with an entrance fee of £330.

Judged by the Club's successes in competition, that playing standard has always been quite high among young and old. Shirley Brasher's two daughters, Kate and Amanda, Ivar Boden's wife, Sheila, Debbie Parker, Jane Blackett, Judy Rich, Jane Langstaff and Chris Russell-Vick are among the names that appear in competitions. Among older members Bernstein remains the most consistent winner. He and the chairman, Brian Palmer, a former Middlesex County player, won the National Veterans' doubles title three years running, 1981–3. Jimmy Jones, the co-winner of the last Covered Court Championships mixed title before the last war, won the Super-Veterans' title and Tommy Anderson and Kenneth Lo the Over-65 doubles. Lo, by the way, is one of the last mainland Chinese to have played at Wimbledon and is renowned as the proprietor of the *Memories of China* restaurant and as a writer on Chinese cooking. And that faithful old member and revered dealer in fine pictures, André Kalman, is one of those who have won the Club Veterans' singles.

The Club shop, something that Stefan Laszlo began advocating in 1982, was opened in 1984 next door to the reception Portacabin and is managed by Tony Scarlett and Dean Bann. During one week in 1985 it took £3000. Down on the lower ground floor there is a small gymnasium with Mr Sohikish, that learned physio and lawn tennis *aficionado*, as adviser. In an upstairs office Derrick de Moor, an accountant, looks after the money. During the last five years nearly £1,000,000 has been spent on the Club. And that is not counting the cost of the new covered courts. The building of these four new courts began in August 1984. It has meant the loss of the old No. 3 court but will give the Club eight indoor courts when finished. The cost, over £1,000,000 – good old Wimbledon! – has been increased by the fact that the shell housing the courts must be in keeping with the Club, which is a scheduled building. That accounts for the fine brick work.

SENTIMENTAL MEMORIES

One day last summer during the Stella Artois Championships the chairman, Brian Palmer, had a telephone call saying that King Hussein and his American-born wife, Queen Noor, were on the way. They arrived in a large black limousine followed by others containing a host of bodyguards. On the day Jimmy Connors was beaten in his first match Palmer and Geoff Brown hosted a lunch in the upstairs dining room. Like most of the days that week it was dull and damp and Princess Michael, the guest of honour, wore a navy blue trouser suit against the weather. Boris Becker was only a name in the draw sheet. One or two of us older ones, Dickie Ritchie, the president, Geoff Paish, the former Davis Cup player, and I fell to discussing the changes that had taken place at the Club during our time. Understandably we became sentimental about some aspects. The loss of the wood-surfaced indoor courts was one, as all the playing surfaces are now carpet. Some marvellous matches were played on the wood in the old days and Paish had figured in quite a few of them, particularly against Jean Borotra, who must be the greatest wood court player of all time. Bunny Austin, Borotra's chief antagonist, Karl Schroder, the giant Swede, and David Jones, the American whose service thundered into the green baize at the back of the court, were among the memories. Anyone who has played on wood knows how it appears to add thirty to one's game. Today wood has no place in the modern tennis world.

Then there was the earlier men's changing room, out of a large part of which the dining room has been constructed. That old room was one of the Club's landmarks with its great cast-iron Victorian baths. Tall men like Stan Smith and John Newcombe, Lester Stoeffen and Bill Tilden before them, could luxuriate full length in the baths. The cork floor was comfortable on bare feet, the expansive corridors of wide wooden benches provided plenty of room for kit and clothing, sitting and nattering. Now everything is smaller and more 'functional', a horrible word.

The view from the dining room was, on the day of that discussion, of a modern commercial sports promotion; hospitality tents, stands seating thousands, programme sellers, booths for this and that, and crowds of people. Despite the weather David Kimpton's Centre Court had never been better, as good as any in the country. Its colour inspired an

American journalist from Arizona to ask 'Are all grass courts green?' She claimed they had a grass court in Arizona but could not remember the colour. The scene was impressive, with that massive building housing the new covered courts taking shape. The founding fathers would have approved of what they saw inside and outside the Club buildings, though they might mourn the loss of all the other sports and games that made the Club what it was in their day.

In its early years, up to and just after the First World War, Queen's was the greatest sporting complex in the world. Since then it has gone through another war and bombings, and financial crisis after crisis, until it only just survived. Now, like the Phoenix, it has risen again. For the playing of court games there is no other club in the world that can match it.

Top New low-level lighting on the refurbished courts
Above Peter Fleming practising – The new covered courts

THE LONDON GRASS COURT CHAMPIONSHIPS 1946–1986

IT is forty years since the London Grass Court Championships, now the second oldest major grass court meeting in the world, came to life again after the Second World War. You can count the number of Wimbledon champions who have not competed at Queen's during that time on the fingers of two hands. It was the same between the wars. You need both hands, too, to count the number of players who have achieved the double. Queen's and Wimbledon, in the same year – since the last war, eight men. Ted Schroeder, Frank Sedgman, Rod Laver, Roy Emerson, John Newcombe, Jimmy Connors, John McEnroe and Boris Becker, and four women, Pauline Betz, Louise Brough, Ann Jones and Margaret Court. Emerson and Miss Brough did it twice.

During its ninety-five years' existence the meeting has been interrupted twice by war and once in the early seventies when there was a break of three years while sponsors, less reliable or loyal than the major ones are today, were sorting themselves out. Originally, as we have seen, the meeting was played after Wimbledon. Then, as the world took a greater interest in the game and overseas players began to come to this country in the summer in increasing numbers, it moved to a pre-Wimbledon date. Until recently it was held the week before 'The Fortnight'. The drawback to that schedule was that it was so close to Wimbledon that the leading players, fearful of injury, did not always try their hardest. Most of the week's sports stories in the papers centred around pulled muscles and strains.

Under Stella Artois the present week was secured, immediately following the French Championships. For the players the change from clay to grass may be dramatic as Ivan Lendl, having just won his first Grand Slam title in Paris in 1984, found when he lost his opening match at Queen's. But it does give the meeting a character of its own. It is certainly more than a mere preliminary to Wimbledon. Back in 1946, however, the players could not have cared less when Queen's was played so long as they could get back on grass and enjoy free competition again. The world was only just beginning to recover from the war and Britain was a very austere place. Lawn tennis was only just beginning again: form was largely unknown except that the US and Australia seemed to have the best players.

The Australian, Dinny Pails, and the American, Jack Kramer, were favourites for the Wimbledon men's title; Pauline Betz and Margaret Osborne for the women's. All four competed at Queen's in lovely weather and the meeting attracted such massive crowds that the gates had to be closed on finals day with queues of would-be spectators stretching down Palliser Road to Barons Court tube station.

Miss Betz, fundamentally a baseliner who later won Wimbledon, took the women's singles beating Miss Osborne, whose sliced backhand was exposed, 6–8 6–3 6–3 in a final that John Olliff described as one of the finest he had ever seen: 'Such aggressive play has not been seen since Helen Wills played Lili D'Alvarez at Wimbledon in 1927 and 1928'.

Kramer retired with a blistered hand to Pancho Segura and later that same trouble cost him his match against Jaroslav Drobny at Wimbledon. Pails came through to the final after a furious 6–4; 6–4; battle with another Aussie, Geoff Brown who, for a small man, had a dynamic service. Pails served 36 aces and made 25 errors; Brown hit 44 aces and made 40 errors.

Segura, an acrobatic player with a two-handed

backhand, won the final against Pails, 6–4 0–6 6–4. At 4–4 in the final set Segura hit four winning backhand passing shots, a stroke he had not previously played, and that just about knocked out Pails. Eric Filby was the last British survivor, losing to Kramer, in the quarters. Two pre-war notables. Betty Nuthall and *Mme* Simone Matthieu, were among the women competitors.

Bob Falkenburg, a new American star, and Louise Brough were the winners the following year. The famous American coach, Mercer Beasley, said of Falkenburg: 'He is an example of the present American era – all out for points and never mind the defence. He will never be a stylist but he has punch'. At Wimbledon the tall, gangling Falkenburg became known as the 'Praying Mantis' because of his penchant for kneeling down on the court in a praying position.

Falkenburg had to save two match points against

the Kiwi, R. McKenzie, and then put out Lennart Bergelin – Bjorn Borg's guru – before winning the final against Colin Long, an Australian doubles expert. Miss Brough won the women's title, beating Miss Osborne who had survived a match point against her while playing Doris Hart in the semis.

SCHROEDER'S YEAR

The weather during Queen's week has always been fickle and 1948 was one of those years when all the finals were divided. But the sun shone again the next summer, the meeting's 50th anniversary, when Ted Schroeder, described as a Californian refrigerator salesman, attacked the game here like an eighteenth-century buccaneer, never having played in this country before. The pipe-smoking, beer-drinking Schroeder said he would win Wimbledon and did so, but not before a hair-raising series of matches. He won the Queen's final on the Saturday against Gardnar Mulloy, 8–6 6–0, winning the last eight games and met the same man in the first round at

Bird's-eye-view of the grass courts in 1952, with Miss Penrose and Miss Love playing Miss Brough and 'Little Mo' Connolly

Louise Brough (right) partnering Maureen Connolly in the 1952 Ladies' Doubles

Wimbledon on the following Monday. For those who saw it that was a hair-raising contest which Schroeder won by a whisker in the fifth set. He was the twentieth man to have won both Queen's and Wimbledon and was the last American to win the former title until Stan Smith did so in 1971, twenty-two years later.

Miss Brough again beat Mrs Dupont, as Miss Osborne had become, for the women's title and a British pair, Betty Hilton and Joy Gannon (later Mrs Tony Mottram), reached the doubles final. Two British girls, Gem Hoahing and Jean Quertier, also made the last eight of the singles, which had previously been a wholly American preserve.

Slowly the British women improved their record with Jean Walker-Smith beating an American, Barbara Scofield, to reach the quarters in 1950 and Kay Tuckey going one round further in 1951 before losing to Shirley Fry, the ultimate winner. Better still, Betty Wilford reached the final the following year. In 1953 Jean Rinkel, as Miss Quertier had

become, won the title, the first British player to do so for twenty-two years – though it must be said that the Americans were noticeably absent from the singles in that time, confining themselves to doubles.

Meantime a young pigeon-toed but athletic Australian, Frank Sedgman, was fulfilling his promise. He was first noticed in 1948 when, aged twenty, he beat Gardnar Mulloy. Someone forecast he would win Wimbledon in 1953. He beat the prophet by one year as, in 1952, he won Queen's without losing a set and then scored a triple at Wimbledon. In the intervening years Eric Sturgess beat him twice and Art Larsen once. Sedgman was probably the fastest man about the court, the quickest onto the ball and the most determined volleyer – more so even than Schroeder – seen since the war. There were six Australians, Ken McGregor, Don Candy, Mervyn Rose the beaten finalist, Ken Rosewall and Lew Hoad besides himself, in the last eight the year he won.

Hoad and Rosewall were still only eighteen when they met in the 1953 final and their match score was 10–10. Rosewall came to Queen's as the new French Champion but the grass – the first three days were played indoors owing to rain – but Hoad's power game beat him 8–6 10–8. Hoad's tactics, in his own words, were 'Make sure of your service and never play more than one groundstroke when the net is there for the taking.'

Hoad retained his title in 1954, but lost to Jaroslav Drobny, the ultimate winner, at Wimbledon. Rosewall got the better of him 6–2 6–3 in the following year's final, watched by over 3500 spectators. Hoad had some excuse. On the morning of the match he got married to Jennifer Staley, also an Australian player, by special licence at Wimbledon!

The gates were closed several times that bumper week and Australia, disposing of any Americans in sight, provided all four semi-finalists. One who failed to make that stage was Neale Fraser. He lost to John Barrett. As for the women, Louise Brough was still in the driving seat, beating a fifteen-year-old South African, Jean Forbes, in the final.

Fraser, a tall left-hander whose service and reach later carried him to two US titles (1959–1960) and Wimbledon (1960) gained his first win over Rosewall in the 1956 final. The loser was lucky to reach that stage as the Indian, Naresh Kumar, had him down match point and with an empty court which he missed – to lose 9–7 in the final set.

Angela Buxton became the second British girl to take the title since the war and two weeks later reached the Wimbledon final where she lost to Shirley Fry. Her successor at Queen's was little Mimi Arnold who, at eighteen, became the youngest-ever woman to win the title in its sixty-three year history.

PLENTY OF DOUBLES

In the next few years the leading American women and Maria Bueno tended to confine their play to doubles and in 1960 Christine Truman beat Karen Hantze, who served nine double faults, in the final. Two years later Miss Hantze, by then Mrs G. Sussman, won Wimbledon having been beaten at Queen's by Carole Caldwell.

In 1961 two of the game's most distinguished women players, Margaret Smith and Billie-Jean King (Miss Moffitt as she was then), made their first appearances. Miss Smith, who later became Mrs B. M. Court, won the singles and Billie-Jean shared the doubles with Karen Hantze. Mrs Court won the title four times during the next decade, though she came perilously close to defeat in 1970 when Winnie Shaw

led her 6–2 5–0 and 15–0 in the final. That match remains one of the most fascinating seen at Queen's. Miss Shaw (now Mrs Wooldridge) carried into it the memory of their recent clash at Bournemouth. 'There I led her 4–1 in the final set and lost, principally, I think, because she got better. The memory of that may have affected me at Queen's though I don't think I missed very many shots. In plain language I think I choked,' was her explanation.

Ann Jones was the only other Wimbledon champion – she won that title in 1969 – to win Queen's during that time. She reached the final three times, losing to Margaret Smith in 1964, sharing the title with Nancy Richey in 1968 when rain washed out all the finals, and winning in 1969 against Winnie Shaw. The penultimate women's meeting held at Queen's – still sponsored by Rothmans – was 1972 and Chris Evert made her entrance onto the world's stage, beating the Australian, Karen Krantzcke, in the final. Olga Morozova won the last meeting in 1973, beating Evonne Goolagong. The women then went their own way, mounting a highly successful tournament at Eastbourne.

Australia's dominance of the men's singles, begun by John Bromwich in 1950, continued through two decades except for three successive years, 1959, 1960 and 1961. Ashley Cooper repeated his Australian Championships win over Fraser in the 1957 final but withdrew with a torn leg muscle in 1958 when Mal Anderson kept the Australian flag flying. Anderson had come close to defeat in an early round when Jan-Erik Lundquist, a beanpole Swede, served for the match at 6–5 in the final set. He let go an Anderson shot, thinking it would go out, but it landed on the baseline. As if that were not enough, Anderson had to survive two match points before beating Mark, 1–6 11–9 6–3 in the final. Mark had earlier put out a short, bandy-legged, sandy-haired youngster named Rod Laver.

Briefly the Australians lost control. The Indian, Rama Krishnan, thrashed Fraser 6–3 6–0 in 1959 and then the Spaniard, Andres Gimeno, beat Roy Emerson to the title. In 1961 the South African, Bob Hewitt, beat the American, Chuck McKinley, who reached the Wimbledon final that year and won the title the next.

It was as if the Australians had taken a break. Laver did the double in 1962. The losing finalist that year was Roy Emerson, who became the dominant character over the next four years. He beat his compatriot, Owen Davidson, in 1963 and the

The Aussies invade:

Left: Frank Sedgman

Bottom left: Neale Fraser – his serve and reach stopped fellow-Australian Ken Rosewall in 1956

Below: Deadly on the volley. Lew Hoad's one-grip game

Bottom right: Ken Rosewall. Like Hoad, a finalist at 18

Left: Smiles before the 1961 final: Billie-Jean Moffitt, later King, and Margaret Court

All-court tigress Virginia Wade

On her toes. The grace of Maria Bueno partnering Darlene Hard

Right: Wining in 1960: Christine Truman, a people's champion

Judge Sir Carl Aarvold in 1963 presenting the
Cup to Roy Emerson

John Newcombe. He disappointed Britain's Roger Taylor in the
1967 final

Bandy-legged and pigeon-chested, but Rod Laver carved his
name on all the cups

Russian, Toomas Lejus (later convicted of murder
in the USSR and sentenced to life, later commuted)
the following year. Lejus had surprisingly beaten the
reigning US champion, Rafael Osuna, who did not
use the excuse of having twisted an ankle at the start
of the final set but said, 'I fooled around too much.'
In the next two years Emerson was given walk-overs
by Denis Ralston, who withdrew with an injured
thumb, and then Tony Roche who did the same with
an injured ankle.

Though the game had not yet become open the
cost of the meeting was underwritten by Taylor
Woodrow, the building construction company, for
these few years. They certainly prevented a financial
loss in 1964 and some years thereafter. The last
meeting before the advent of 'open tennis' was won
by the next Australian 'giant' John Newcombe, who
beat Roger Taylor, the first Englishman to reach the
final since the war. Newcombe went on to win the
first of his three Wimbledons. So wet was the week
that the doubles events were unfinished.

Above Margaret Court lifted weights in training to beat Billie-Jean King in 1971

Roger Taylor racing against genius – the Nastase backhand volley

It was even wetter in 1968 and not one final was played, though in an earlier round Tom Okker put out Rod Laver. By this time Rothmans had formed a small grass court circuit with prizemoney, consisting of Surbiton, Manchester, Beckenham and Queen's. At the first two the prizemoney was £100 for men and the same for the women. For Beckenham and Queen's it was upped to £500 for the men, £300 for the girls. The total prizemoney on offer at Queen's was £1364, very small beer compared with what came later. At the same time Taylor Woodrow remained the prime sponsors, pumping in £1600 prizemoney and free meals, but no expenses, for the players in 1968.

Rothmans remained with Queen's until the break in 1974 when another sponsor took the meeting and the 'prime time' elsewhere. Up to then there was plenty of excitement with Fred Stolle, Laver and Stan Smith successively beating Newcombe in the men's finals, though that did not deter Newcombe from winning Wimbledon in 1970 and 1971.

GONZALES IN TROUBLE

In 1972 two Americans new to this country dominated the meeting. They were Jimmy Connors, aged nineteen and Chris Evert, aged seventeen. Both were two-handed backhand players and fundamentally baseliners and both won. Another American, Pancho Gonzales, a veteran who had won the US title in 1948 and 1949, made his first appearance and hit the front pages of the newspapers. Connors reached the final after a close call against the Russian, Alex Metreveli, whom he beat 9–7 in the final set in the quarters. He then disposed of Clark Graebner fairly easily. His final opponent was the Englishman, John Paish, son of the former British Davis Cup player. Paish owed his unexpected appearance in the last round to an astonishing win over Stan Smith, Wimbledon champion two weeks later, 2–6 6–3 10–8 and then a hollow victory over Gonzales who was disqualified when leading 7–5 2–3. Paish was no match for Connors in the final.

The disqualification of Gonzales caused a stir. It had happened very rarely at any level of the game and has become even rarer since, much to the detriment of international tennis. At least it showed no

Pancho Gonzales meets his match in referee Mrs Bea Seal
Stan Smith in action in the 1980 Stella Artois Championships

discrimination in favour of a 'top name' and the International Federation was already exhorting referees and umpires to take a tougher line with errant players. Gonzales was serving at 2–3 in the second set when it happened. Three close line calls had gone against him and he stood at love–40. When a fast serve was called 'fault' he exploded: 'That makes four in this goddam game'. He crossed the net, stood towering over the linesman and said he would not continue playing unless this official were changed.

By this time the referee, Mrs Bea Seal, a former British Wightman Cup captain, had appeared and she refused to grant Gonzales' request. There was an altercation between Mrs Seal and Gonzales. She wagged her finger at him. He pushed her, saying 'Don't come too close to me lady or I might lose my temper.' When Gonzales stayed adamant Mrs Seal countered with, 'Then I have to scratch you' – and did.

Rex Bellamy in *The Times* applauded Mrs Seal for the swift and courageous way she asserted her

Baseline baby doll – the young Chris Evert

authority but he questioned the justification of her refusal to change the linesman. Lance Tingay in the *Daily Telegraph* pointed out that firm discipline had recently been lacking in the game. Twelve years later, when John McEnroe created a scene in the Queen's final against Lief Shiras, Bellamy recalled the Gonzales incident and commented that the present-day game could do with an official such as Mrs Seal.

The Gonzales affair was not the first time there had been a scene at Queen's. Some years earlier Gardnar Mulloy had thrown his racket in the direction of a lines-woman. He had also protested over an umpire and when challenged had taken the umpire's chair for a following match – and done the job expertly.

For the next three years the meeting was put on ice as the week and the players departed to Nottingham. That did not mean that the Club, and notably Clive Bernstein, were inactive. Far from it. A sponsor financially strong enough to secure the top players and satisfy Colgate, the overall sponsors of the Grand Prix, had to be found and then the

calendar date had to be recovered before anyone else got it. Bernstein succeeded in his mission. Rawlings, the soft drinks part of Whitbread's Brewery, provided $100,000 prizemoney, sufficient for the tournament to be rated 3-star by Colgate. It coincided with Wimbledon's Centenary (1977) and was confined to men. The women were competing for the Federation Cup at Eastbourne, where in succeeding years they held – and still hold – a very successful tournament of their own.

Bernstein, the showman or ringmaster, put the meeting's revival this way: 'The Rawlings International is designed not only to give you (the public) an opportunity to see great tennis but also give you a sense of involvememt with the players – a sense that comes with the personal atmosphere of the Club itself.' The Queen's set-up was admirably suited to this and the staging of the event, like the facilities, have improved every year. Now that it has moved back a week, separating it from Wimbledon, it has become more of a tournament in its own right – not just a practice meeting. It has also become part of the London summer scene, a festival or carnival, and the public has responded handsomely. The weather was pretty awful that year, 'Queen's has won back its place as part of the pre-Wimbledon scene but it was a horrible week, wet and cold,' wrote Tingay.

COX IN THE FINAL

Jimmy Connors entered but having played one match indoors retired with an injured thumb, giving John Feaver a walk-over. Perhaps the damp got into his bones. Hank Pfister, another of that breed of tall, big-serving Americans, wrought havoc among the more fancied players, beating Marty Riessen, Stan Smith and Roscoe Tanner before Mark Cox put an end to his run in the semi-final. Pfister and his wife Kim could then get on with their honeymoon. Cox was only the second British man to reach the final since the war.

The Mexican, Raul Ramirez, had an exhausting path to the final beginning with an 8–9 9–8 6–4 win over Cliff Drysdale. He followed up with a three-setter against Tom Gullikson, a 9–7 final set victory over Dick Stockton and another three-setter with the American, Jim Delaney. His final win 9–7 7–5 over Cox was tight, too, as the loser had two points for the first set at 5–4 and three for the second, also at 5–4.

The British had one of their better tournaments

as the brothers, David and John Lloyd, reached the doubles final to be beaten by another pair of brothers, Vijay and Anand Amritraj. That was the year young John McEnroe, then eighteen, qualified for Wimbledon and reached the semi-final where Connors beat him. In 1978 he began an association with Queen's that has benefited both the Club and the public richly. The prizemoney that year was increased to $125,000 or £62,500 – the pound was quite high in those days.

McEnroe did not win his first year but made enough noise to be described as 'a self-cursing, line-questioning, fidgeting neurotic'. Still, he pulled in the crowds, despite the weather which caused the meeting to be completed on the Sunday. Tony Roche, a near veteran of thirty-three and a left-hander, beat him, 8–6 9–7 in the final. The young man, it was said, 'never found his grass legs and spent time tumbling around a greasy court'. But he did reach the Wimbledon semi-final again, losing the second year to Connors.

Stella Artois, a lager brewer under licence by Whitbread, replaced Rawlings in 1979 and the meeting was expanded to eight days, ending on a Sunday. It was necessary, too, as the opening day became known as 'Monsoon Day' and by Wednesday all five covered courts were in play. That year McEnroe won the first leg of what later became a hat-trick. But he incurred two penalty points during the week and on one occasion told the umpire, Roy Cope-Lewis, that he would see that he would never again take one of his matches. When Cope-Lewis took the chair for the final, McEnroe showed a spark of humour with his comment, 'I obviously don't carry much influence with my remarks.'

After losing to McEnroe in the quarters, Sandy Mayer suggested that: 'He is so calculating and has worked out a clever routine to upset his opponents.' Peter Fleming came to his doubles partner's defence with: 'Nobody knows the real McEnroe. He's still young, shy and retiring and wants to be liked.' Whatever was said about the young man I had already decided that he was about the most talented player I had seen in a lifetime.

In the semis McEnroe beat Roscoe Tanner while a newcomer from Paraguay, the massive Victor Pecci, fresh from reaching the French final, came through the other half of the draw beating Arthur Ashe. New to grass, Pecci had reached his limit and McEnroe beat him 6–7 6–1 6–1.

Earlier that week a match between Ashe and Bernie Mitton, owing to rain, was spread over six hours and sixteen minutes with a playing time of nearly five hours. Ashe won 7–6 4–6 15–13, the final set tie-break going to 31–29, one of the longest on record at the time.

The weather did not change much in 1980 but McEnroe did. He was on his best behaviour – 'Last year I was awful. This year I feel better because I'm trying to be more relaxed.' The young man showed his change of mood on the Tuesday when, needless to say, it rained. Hundreds of spectators had waited three hours for it to stop in the hope of getting a glimpse of 'Mac'. Though the centre court was scarcely playable, he played Tom Leonard for nearly an hour without a murmur. He won and later beat Paul McNamee who had, a week previously, put him out of the French Championships. In the last three rounds he beat Vijay Amritraj, Pecci and Kim Warwick, dropping only six service points in the final.

Vitas Gerulaitis and Fritz Buehning played a rumbustious match on an outside court. Blowing off steam at some spectators, Gerulaitis was fined £125. One watcher admonished him with: 'Stop swearing, Goldilocks.'

McEnroe did not drop a set when completing his hat-trick in 1981, though he came close to doing so in the final against Brian Gottfried whom he beat 7–6 7–5. A capacity crowd of 4000 were there for the last two days. In the first set tie-break Gottfried was leading 6–3 when McEnroe protested over the positioning of a linesman. Though Gottfried said he had not been distracted by the incident the fact was that McEnroe won the next thirteen points. Later 'Mac' struck a ball near to a lineswoman and then argued that women – Mrs Georgina Clark was the umpire – should not be allowed to umpire matches between top men: 'It's harder to get upset with a woman umpire.' Gottfried told the young man to stop baiting Mrs Clark and questioning so many line-calls.

In the best two matches of the week Kevin Curren put out the No. 2 seed, Roscoe Tanner and, in the doubles final, Pat Dupré and Brian Teacher beat Curren and Denton 3–6 7–6 11–9.

CONNORS STILL WINNING

Ten years after winning the title for the first time Connors returned in 1982 to win again, beating McEnroe in the final 7–5 6–3. *En route* to the final Connors lost only twenty-seven games, nineteen of them to Pfister and Curren, and McEnroe conceded only twenty-five.

It was damp and gloomy at the start of the week when an American newcomer, the coloured Chip Hooper – 'How tall is he? Six-five or six-six?' – and Russell Simpson reached 8–8 in the final set. Simpson wanted to stop. The umpire refused and Hooper ran out without losing another point. Rain interrupted the semis as well, Connors beating Curren and McEnroe ousting Chris Lewis, whom he also beat a year later in the Wimbledon final. The court was still slippery for the final. McEnroe slipped several times and when he came out for the doubles final, with Peter Rennert against Pfister and Amaya, his left ankle was bound up, more as a precaution than anything worse.

Connors beat McEnroe again in the 1983 final, 6–3 6–3. It was his ninety-eighth tournament win and the winner's prizemoney had reached £19,000. At 2–2 in the second set McEnroe aggravated his troublesome left shoulder – 'It was really painful for a while' – and became so tetchy that even a distant dog barking distracted him. Connors' re-jigged service helped him a lot and his return of serve was magnificent.

Ivan Lendl, having avoided grass for some time but with a formidable record on other surfaces, made his first appearance at the meeting. Despite slipping about a damp centre court he opened with a win over Nick Saviano – one service break in each set. McEnroe reckoned that the centre court was unplayable and, while beating Jeff Borowiak, spread himself full length some nine times. Lendl went on to beat Paul McNamee and then Tim Mayotte, 7–6 7–6, before falling to Connors who, in a jocular mood, noticed a lineswoman bending down extremely low to scan her line. 'Are you looking at the line or up my trousers?' queried Connors.

The world's top three men, McEnroe, Lendl and Connors, all competed in 1984 and the sparks flew. There had not been a meeting like this one since Gonzales was disqualified in 1972. The newspapers enjoyed themselves, the public came in abundance.

Lendl arrived having just won the French Championship – his first Grand Slam title – with a 7–5 final set win over McEnroe who had, in his own words, 'blown it'. Still knocking imaginary clay off his shoes – a conditioned reflex? – Lendl lost his first round match to a virtually unknown American, Lief Shiras, ranked 105, 7–5 6–3. Lendl led 4–3 in the first set and then lost five of his next six service

Top: A McEnrow in progress
Above: Jimmy and Mac cross rackets
Right: A tracheotomy for this man. McEnroe admits he choked
Left: Jimmy Connors: 'a magnificent return of serve'

Ivan Lendl. World No. 1 but not on grass

games. 'I'm still very happy after Paris. I'm definitely not going into a corner to cry over this defeat,' was his comment. 'I reckon I must have been 1000 to 1 against going into the match,' said Shiras.

Connors was aced twenty times by Steve Denton and needed six match points before winning 6–4 3–6 9–7. Then he beat Tim Mayotte, 7–6 1–6 9–7 after becoming upset by a line decision early in the final set. In a flash of temper he angrily hit a ball into the net, narrowly missing two ball-girls. That cost him a penalty point and he began pulling faces at the umpire, Jeremy Shales.

McEnroe, though obviously suffering mentally from his finals defeat in Paris, beat Connors, 6–2 6–2 in the semis and held his temper until the final against Shiras who had come through a half denuded of top players. All was well until McEnroe, having won the first set, trailed 1–4 in the second. In the seventh game a lineswoman changed her mind over a passing shot, calling 'Out' and then 'In'. Umpire Roger Smith decided the ball was 'out' and over-ruled the line judge. McEnroe exploded for some three-and-a-half minutes – 'Over a thousand officials and I get a moron like you.'

Thereupon, Jim Moore, the referee, and Kurt Nielsen, the supervisor, arrived on the scene to be greeted with McEnroe's blast: 'You sit there like two bumps on a log doing nothing' – an expression some newspapers misquoted as 'two bums'. The two officials took no action, not even issuing a warning. Later Moore said 'I take a soft line. I was a player once.' Nielsen later resigned from supervising.

Meantime Shiras had made friends with the crowd who were, by then, much on his side. McEnroe attacked him in a way that could be deemed 'insulting' according to the rule book. He beat him too – 6–1 3–6 6–2. 'Send for Mrs Seal,' suggested Bellamy in *The Times*. It did make one wonder what the sponsors, Bernstein and the Queen's committee would have done had McEnroe been disqualified.

The star of 1985 was a tall, carrot-haired youth from West Germany, Boris Becker, aged seventeen. Earlier in the year he had made his mark in this country by winning the Young Masters Championships in Birmingham. It was a dull, damp week weatherwise but that did not deter the crowds, most of whom had obviously booked ahead in anticipation of another John McEnroe-Jimmy Connors episode. But McEnroe, while playing in the French Championships, announced he would no longer compete in England except at Wimbledon. He made harassment by the media his excuse.

Connors, the top seed, went out in his first match to the hard-serving American left-hander, Mike de Palmer, who was then dismissed by Paul McNamee. On the same day McNamee disposed of Tim Mayotte, the winner at Beckenham the previous week. John Lloyd, watched by his wife, fresh from her marvellous win over Martina Navratilova in the French final, briefly flew the flag, beating the American Matt Mitchell but then fell to Wotjek Fibak.

No one took much notice of Becker until he beat the seeded Pat Cash, a semi-finalist at Wimbledon the previous year, 6–4 6–4. 'Bomber Boris' as the Press called him then hammered McNamee 6–4 6–4 and, in the final, demolished Johan Kriek 6–2 6–3 – a very impressive performance. People began to wonder whether here was McEnroe's successor at Wimbledon. The grass courts suited Becker's big game.

THE COVERED COURT CHAMPIONSHIPS
1947–1969

THE Queen's Club returned to normal life slowly after the war. There was no meeting in 1946 and, owing to incendiary bomb damage, there were only two covered courts playable when the Championships were held in 1947.

Understandably the field was undistinguished but there was one remarkable match in which Hedley Baxter, later Britain's Davis Cup captain, beat Henry Billington, already a Davis Cup player, 7–5 5–7 10–8. Both players had match points. At 5–3 in the final set Billington looked to have the easiest volley for the match when the ball hit the tape of the net and jumped over his racket. At 6–5 he had another match point and missed the line by an inch. Then Baxter led 7–6 and 40-love, only to lose the next ten points!

The Dutch hockey international, Ivo Rinkel, won the men's title beating Ernest Wittman 3–6 7–5 7–5 in the final and little Gem Hoahing beat Peggy Dawson-Scott 8–6 6–3 for the women's title. That was Miss Hoahing's fourth tournament win since Wimbledon. Rinkel later married the British Wightman Cup player, Jean Quertier.

Wimbledon had refused to accept Jean Borotra's entry just after the war, there being some uncertainty over his connections with the Germans occupying France. But, at the age of fifty, he was back at Queen's in 1948 to win his tenth title. In 1949 he won his eleventh and last. Both wins were emphatic; he did not lose or ever look like losing a set on either occasion. Geoff Paish, the best of the home players on indoor wood courts, was his final opponent both years. It was 6–3 6–3 6–2 in 1948 – Borotra won the mixed with Mrs Bea Walter two hours later – and 6–4 6–3 6–3 in 1949. A report said Borotra played with 'undiminished zest' and displayed the same bustling game as was first seen at the Dulwich Covered Courts in 1923 – twenty-five years earlier!

Though the home standard of play was low, over seventy men entered for the 1948 singles and thirty were accepted. Three courts were used and the gates were closed for the finals, spectators being forced to squat five deep on the floor of the west court just as they had done many years before, to the irritation of the players.

Gem Hoahing retained her title but lost it the following year when Joan Curry, a pretty mover who could run most players into the ground especially on hard courts, showed her expertise on wood by waltzing through the event, finally beating Jean Quertier 6–1 6–0.

1950 was the beginning of the end for Borotra, then fifty-two, as a champion. Geoff Paish beat him at last, 3–6 5–7 6–1 6–0 6–3, in the semi-final only to lose to Jaroslav Drobny in the final. Paish recalls this win with pride. 'I knew how fit Jean was and how proud he was of his record on the east court. The second set was the vital one – he had rushed the net as much as possible – and losing it so narrowly sapped his stamina enough for me to win the next three.

'But even while losing, his appeal to the gallery was amazing. Every point he won almost raised the roof and I got hardly any applause even for my best shots. And I was the local boy! I recall that David Lurie, a South African, sitting in the gallery at the end of the court, was about the only person clapping me when I won a point. I turned to a linesman and, almost in desperation, asked what sort of shot I had to play to get some applause against the Frenchman. The answer, of course, was that there was nothing I could do. He was too popular. A year later – his last

Right: Borotra and Brugnon (France) playing Olliff and
Coldman (Great Britain) in the Doubles in 1947
Bottom: Borotra, playing with 'undiminished zest'
Covered Court Championships 1947:
the Basque bounding

– when he lost to Tloczynski, I heard one of his many lady admirers turn to her friend and say, 'Well, that's it. I shan't come any more. It won't be the same without Borotra!'

BOROTRA STILL BOUNDING

Borotra, of course, did not bow out in 1951 without a flamboyant flourish, like an old sea-dog going down with flags flying and all guns blazing. In that final fling in 1951 he kept Ignatz Tloczynski on court for three hours before going down 10–9 7–9 6–4 8–6 – Borotra led 4–1 in the third set – and then leapt the net to congratulate his victor after the final point.

Finally he insisted on presenting the Cup to the new champion, Paish, whose fourth final this was. Paish scored a triple that year, the men's doubles with Tony Mottram and the mixed with Jean Quertier.

Borotra's record in these Championships has no parallel. From his first appearance in 1926 to his last in 1951 – he missed only 1927 and 1947 – he won the title eleven times and was only beaten on five occasions, twice by Bunny Austin, once each by Karl Schroder, Geoff Paish and Tloczynski. Henri Cochet was the only other member of the famous 'Musketeers' – René Lacoste was the third – to challenge Queen's: he was fifty when he played in 1950 and, understandably, was beaten by Drobny.

Jaroslav Drobny – still a regular player at the Club

Susan Partridge made her first big impression on the game in 1951. That year she took Maureen Connolly, the seventeen-year-old US champion, to 7–5 in the final set at Wimbledon. She won the singles at Queen's beating Jean Walker-Smith. Miss Partridge came from games-playing stock. Her father Norman, an outstanding cricketer, had been chosen while still at school to play for the Gentlemen against the Players, though the Malvern headmaster would not let him, and her uncle, Geoffrey played soccer (amateur) for England. Her future husband, Philippe Chatrier, later an outstanding President of the International Tennis Federation, was among the Queen's competitors that year.

With the retirement of Borotra from these Championships Drobny became the central figure dominating the singles in 1952, 1953 and 1954. In those three years his final opponents were Tony Mottram, Bobby Wilson and a Pole, Vladimar Skonecki. Only the last named managed to win a set.

To reach his final Mottram had beaten his doubles partner, Paish. As often as possible he went in on Paish's service – something he was unable to do on Drobny's. When Mottram led 5–4 in the third set Drobny served four aces to close the match 6–3 6–4 8–6. He displayed a service power reminiscent of David Jones and Karl Schroder in the thirties.

Bobby Wilson was still a junior when he reached the final and lost to Drobny 6–2 7–5 6–2, but a scribe wrote, 'It was a delight to see a junior of England put up such a fight against a world master.' And 'world master' Drobny became the next year when he won Wimbledon. Yet at Queen's he was taken to five sets by Gerry Oakley, of whom it was once written (Laurie Pignon in the old *Daily Sketch* if I recall correctly) 'He cleans his glasses on court more diligently than any window cleaner of the Crystal Palace.' Drobny had four hard sets with Skonecki in the final.

During those three years a future Wimbledon lady champion appeared on the scene and scored a hat-trick of wins. Angela Mortimer, taught by Arthur Roberts at the Palace Hotel, Torquay, had just returned from her first US tour when she outplayed the holder, Susan Partridge, 6–3 3–6 6–3 to win in 1952. Miss Partridge faltered and lost confidence when she missed a point for 4–3 in the final set. The next year Miss Mortimer beat Georgie Woodgate and Shirley Bloomer, later to marry Chris Brasher, the Olympic steeplechase gold medallist. Miss Mortimer's future husband, John Barrett, a Cambridge man, won the doubles with the Rhodesian, Adrian Black, over Wilson and Mike Davies, both aged seventeen. In one of these years Brian Palmer, the current Club chairman, distinguished himself by beating the eighth seed, Jens Andersen of Denmark, before losing to Laurie Strong, a Middlesex player who went to Canada and later became President of the Canadian LTA.

NEW COURTS

Angela Mortimer's third year, 1954, was also the first that Queen's had come under the LTA flag and there were already signs of a revival. Two more covered courts (4 and 5) were being rebuilt and equipped with the same successful strip lighting that had been installed in court 3 the previous year.

Drobny's reign ended in 1955. Though much briefer than Borotra's it was nevertheless outstanding with four appearances, four wins. But on his fifth appearance he was beaten in four sets by Billy Knight, a fellow left-hander who, in turn, lost to Skonecki, in a long final on the rebuilt court 5 before a packed house. Drobny never liked playing left-handers and was probably just past his peak. With the two rebuilt courts in action both men's events reverted to five sets.

Ann Shilcock, an athletic serve-volleyer, scored a triple, beating Pat Ward in the singles final and winning the women's and mixed doubles with Miss Ward and Billy Knight respectively. During the summer Miss Shilcock had won the Wimbledon doubles title with Angela Mortimer.

The revival hoped for when the LTA took over Queen's a few years earlier did not mature. The aura of Borotra and the huge popularity of Drobny had gone. The Championships were beginning to become just another domestic event with occasional visits from overseas players, few of whom were distinguished or public figures. The organization, and the LTA had a big say in it, was beginning to jigger around with the dates and in 1956, a modest year, the meeting was moved from early October to late November.

Angela Buxton, runner-up to Shirley Fry at Wimbledon that summer, won her first major championship, beating Christine Truman and then the holder, Ann Shilcock. The Austrian, A. Huber, an ice-hockey international and a bit of a clown on court, beat Paish for the men's title. In 1957 there was no tournament.

For the next eight years, to the end of their existence as a meeting independent of a commercial sponsor, the men's singles were dominated by the young Turks of the British game. Mike Davies from South Wales was the first of them. He had hard matches against two others, Bobby Wilson and Alan Mills, before beating Sven Davidson, a Swede then ranked No. 3 in the world, in the final 5–7 6–1 6–2 6–2. Davies was a fighter – perhaps 'scrapper' is a better word.

Bobby Wilson, an artist and stylist taught by his mother, won in 1959 with a notable 6–3 8–6 6–2 victory over the Dane, Kurt Nielsen, Wimbledon runner-up in 1953 and 1955. In an early round match a young man from Essex, Martin Braund, ran out of rackets while engaged in a marathon with Bill Threlfall. Braund managed to save a match point and win 8–6 in the fifth with a borrowed racket. Then he beat Roger Becker.

It was the left-handed Billy Knight's turn the following year. He was a really hard grafter, a difficult man to beat, and he got the better of the more talented Wilson 6–3 6–4 8–6. For the second year running, by the way, Wilson was taken to five sets by Alan Mills, now the Wimbledon referee but then a gentle player who had to work for his points. He did however achieve the distinction of winning a Davis Cup singles 6–0 6–0 6–0 – against Luxembourg.

Tony Mottram (right) with Geoff Paish in 1948

The Queen's Club chairman, Brian Palmer, was beaten in five sets by Laurie Strong, a Middlesex left-hander who went to Canada to work and remained there. Palmer was in good company as Nielsen lost to Mike Sangster, a powerful server from Devon.

Then, along came Tony Pickard from Derbyshire; stylish, flamboyant and brittle. To win in 1961 he beat the up-and-coming Manuel Santana who, it was suspected, was suffering from food poisoning. That may also have been responsible for Santana being taken to five sets by Alan Mills and Mark Otway, a New Zealander. Wilson, the holder, had withdrawn with blistered feet as a result of playing in the Scandinavian Championships. The spectators' support for the first five days of the meeting was minimal.

Wilson won three of the next four years, Sangster breaking the sequence in 1964. Apart from Wilson's final win over Billy Knight in five sets, the match of the week in 1962 was the latter's victory over the blond, beanpole Swede, Jan-Erick Lundquist. Lundquist was a world-class player but also a temperamental one and when, early in the final set against Knight, he was foot-faulted, he blew up. 'It resounded like an explosion' wrote one reporter. The Swede won only four of the next nineteen points and Knight cleared the final set 6–2.

BRITAIN'S BEST

Wilson and Roger Taylor, two of the four best men Britain has produced since the last war, met in the 1963 final, the former winning 16–14 6–2 9–7. Wilson in 1958 had become only the second British man since the war – Tony Mottram was the first – to reach the Wimbledon last eight. Taylor, a burly left-hander from Yorkshire and the son of a Sheffield steel worker, did better than that. Pugnacious at times but always a loyal and resolute fighter, Taylor reached the Wimbledon semi-final three times, in 1967, 1970 and 1973 before turning professional.

For the past seven years the LTA had had to subsidize these Championships to the tune of about £250 a year and however often they changed the dates, from spring to autumn or *vice versa*, the gates except for the finals were poor.

Mike Sangster, another Arthur Roberts product from Torquay – Angela Mortimer being his most successful pupil – and the most powerful server Britain had so far produced since the war, took Wilson's title off him in 1964, 6–3 8–6 6–4. Three years earlier Sangster had reached the Wimbledon semi-final. He was also the most prolific British Davis Cup player, playing sixty-five matches and winning forty-three of them. Without affectation or temperament, he was a solid player.

The end of these Championships as an amateur event came in 1965. Sangster had to retire, with circulation troubles in his racket hand, to Mark Cox at two sets-all. Cox then lost to Wilson in the final. Three years later the left-handed Cox, from Leicestershire and Cambridge University, achieved immortal fame by becoming the first man to beat a professional at the first Open tournament, the British Hard Courts Championships at Bournemouth. His victim was none other than Pancho Gonzales.

If Wilson was the dominant man over the past eight years then two players, Angela Mortimer and Ann Jones, Wimbledon champions in 1961 and 1969 respectively, stood out among the women. Miss Mortimer won in 1959, 1960 – Ann Haydon (later Mrs Jones) retired to her in the final with a back injury. In 1961 she beat her Wimbledon final opponent, Christine Truman, in three sets. Six times the Champion, Miss Mortimer was the most successful of all the ladies to play at Queen's.

Miss Haydon first won in 1962, beating Miss Truman 6–4 4–6 9–7. She lost in the semis to Deirdre Catt the following year but, as Mrs Jones, won in 1964 and 1965 beating the Australian, Fay Toyne, both times. 1966 saw the sad death of Mrs A. Sterry, five times Wimbledon champion who, as Charlotte 'Chattie' Cooper, first won this Covered Courts title in 1895. She was ninety-six.

The Championships, having been dormant for a couple of years, returned to life in 1968 as the fifth leg of the Dewar Cup, an indoor circuit of tournaments. The game had become 'open' to all – amateurs and professionals.

Among the competitors were members of the US Davis Cup team on the way home from playing a match against India. The change of conditions from warm weather and clay courts to London winter and fast wood produced some strange results. Arthur Ashe, the US Open champion and 1975 Wimbledon champion, and Stan Smith, another winner of both titles, were beaten by the Welshman, Gerald Battrick. Charlie Pasarell lost to the New Zealander, Onnie Parun, and Clark Graebner retired to Keith Wooldridge with a back injury. Bob Lutz, the fifth member of the team, got through to the final, to be beaten by the ubiquitous Bob Hewitt in four sets.

The young Mike Sangster being presented with the Boys'
Covered Court trophy by Lord Templewood in 1956

But Smith and Lutz, one of the great doubles teams, did win the men's title, beating Bob Howe and Mike Sangster.

VIRGINIA ON THE MOVE

Margaret Court, already twice Wimbledon champion as Margaret Smith, beat Virginia Wade, winner of the first US Open, 10–8 6–1 in the women's final. And there was the scent of romance in the mixed doubles in which Peter Curtis and Mary-Ann Eisel, who later married, lost to Stan Smith and Margaret Court.

The end to this oldest-of-all covered court meeting came in 1969 when W. D. and H. O. Wills sponsored a £20,000 event that began at Queen's and culminated at Wembley. The prizemoney, £3000 for the men, £1300 for the women, was exceeded

only by Wimbledon. Rod Laver beat Tony Roche in the men's final and in the women's, Ann Jones defeated Billie-Jean King, 9–11 6–2 9–7 – a much closer match than their Wimbledon final.

The meeting was not judged a success, at least from The Queen's Club viewpoint. Joyce Williams, then married to the LTA promotions officer, Gerry, was quoted as saying, 'The players would rather not have a British Covered Court Championships than have it at Queen's'. Then there were the two LTA councillors queuing for lunch. One said, 'I've been watching the tennis'. The other replied, 'Oh, I'd forgotten it was on'. What would great campaigners like M. J. G. Ritchie have said to those comments? Ironically 1969 was the year Fred Perry was made an honorary member of Queen's – and he never played in the Covered Court Championships!

QUEEN'S AND THE INTERNATIONAL CLUB OF GREAT BRITAIN

THE International Lawn Tennis Club of Great Britain was born of a casual conversation between Lord Balfour and A. Wallis Myers, the distinguished *Daily Telegraph* correspondent, during the 1923 Wimbledon. It was formed in 1924 and began an association with The Queen's Club that continued for well over sixty years.

It would be incorrect to say that Queen's is, or ever was, the IC's home base or HQ, for it is a peripatetic organization. Until recently, however, the Club was the scene of the annual match against the IC of France, the oldest annual fixture on either club's list. In 1981 that meeting was moved to the AELTC, Wimbledon, but the centenary match – the hundredth between the two clubs – was celebrated in 1985 at both Queen's and Wimbledon.

The first match the IC played was against Queen's in 1926 as a prelude to the Covered Court Championships. Queen's, whose team included those stalwarts, M. J. G. Ritchie and G. Greville, won handsomely. The following May the two clubs met on grass, the IC, with such players as A. R. F. Kingscote, A. H. Lowe and C. P. Dixon, turning the tables.

In the summer of 1928 Queen's mustered Bill Tilden, Norman Brookes and the brothers I.G. and W. A. R. Collins but only won 5–4 and the following year R. J. Ritchie, son of M. J. G. and a future secretary of the Club, made his first appearance for Queen's. It was in 1929, when the match between the British and the French International Clubs was inaugurated with Queen's as the home base, that the public began to take more than just a casual interest in the affair; largely through one man, Jean Borotra.

Borotra had already won the first of his eleven Covered Court Championships titles at Queen's when he and Christian Boussus led the French IC for their first meeting with their British counterparts. The British Club had Tilden and Nigel Sharpe as their two top strings. The meeting between Borotra and Tilden, on what was probably the fastest court in the world, the east at Queen's, was an affair to savour. They had several times met on grass and clay and Tilden, usually the winner, did not think much of the Frenchman.

Borotra won 10–8 9–7, though Tilden twice served for the first set and once, at 5–4, for the second. Borotra pursued the incongruous, some might say suicidal, tactics of playing Tilden from the back of the court, saving his net rushing for the end of the first set. At 7–8 he won eight successive points and then, helped by a double-fault, took the set. It must be pointed out that the wood surface lessened the effect of Tilden's sliced drives and aided Borotra's net attacks. Borotra's comment made many years later was merely: 'It was a very fast court and that suited my game.'

The French, by the way, won that match and got the better of their early encounters, winning ten of the first fifteen including the one played at Torquay in 1938 when Borotra lost to H. G. N. Lee.

In the 1930s the great battles were between Borotra and Bunny Austin in both the IC match and the Covered Court Championships. Their meeting became part of the London sporting scene, drawing crowds to the Queen's covered courts never equalled after the war. Their first IC meeting was in 1930 when Austin showed so much control and length on the floor that the Frenchman was unable to make a forcing shot with which to get to the net. The ever-popular Borotra was eclipsed as Austin won 6–3 6–3.

The great 1929 International Club match between Britain and France. Tilden played (and lost) for Britain

AUSTIN UNRESTRAINED

It was worse for Borotra the following year. Austin's memory of this encounter may be summed up in his own words: 'I decided to have a go. I lost the first two games and then won the next twelve, much to Borotra's astonishment!' Borotra took revenge in 1933 and 1934 – the latter match drawing larger crowds to Queen's than had witnessed his battle against Tilden in 1929.

These two men set a standard of play on indoor wood courts in that thirties era only once briefly equalled. In 1936 in the Covered Court Championships the big Swede, Karl Schroder, whipped both of them. But Austin outplayed him and Borotra the following year.

The surface, except when it had been repainted – which made it much slower – was much suited to Borotra's ebullient and explosive play. It also seemed to give Austin's game a wider dimension of pace and forcefulness, something he never achieved on grass or clay. All told they met six times in these IC matches, Austin winning four, Borotra twice. But, as Borotra put it, they were the best of three – not five.

Reflecting on his matches against Austin, Borotra confessed: 'For me he was as difficult to play as was Lacoste. He had a very intelligent baseline game and conducted his tactics well. I had only a moderate serve and went to the net even on my second. Austin could pass me, catch me at my feet or lob.'

After the war Borotra's chief rival in these annual get-togethers was Geoff Paish, the best of the British players on wood. In 1948 and 1949 Borotra beat him in both the IC match and the Covered Court Championships. Paish recalled their 1948 meeting – 'As we changed over after the first game of the final set Borotra said: "It hasn't been very good tennis for the crowd so far" and proceeded to win the next six games and the match, 2–6 6–2 6–1.'

In 1950 Paish scored his first win over the great man, then fifty-two, by 6–4 6–3. That, moreover, was the first time Borotra had lost a match on the famous east court since Austin demolished him 6–1 6–1 6–1 in the 1937 Covered Court Championships when, much to Borotra's dismay, the court had been repainted and was consequently much slower.

In succeeding years Borotra twice beat Tony Mottram in these IC matches and in 1955, when aged fifty-seven, defeated Mike Davies in three sets; a splendid achievement as the Welshman was then ranked No. 1 in this country.

In 1981 the autumn meeting between the two clubs was moved to Wimbledon and last year, 1985, they celebrated their one hundredth meeting with a three-day jamboree involving nearly eighty players at both Queen's and the All England Club. The British Club won 35–14 with 25 draws but overall the French lead 53–40 with 7 draws.

Borotra, then eighty-seven, played as he has done in every one of the hundred matches between the Clubs. He lost his single against Gus Holden and, with Henri Pellizza, drew his doubles match against Buzzer Hadingham and Basil Hutchins at set-all.

Jean Borotra and the IC at Queen's Club: 1929–1985

1929	beat W. T. Tilden 10–8, 9–7
	beat N. Sharpe 6–3, 8–6
1930	lost H. W. Austin 3–6, 3–6
	beat Sharpe 6–1, 5–7, 6–2
1931	lost Austin 2–6, 0–6
	beat J. S. Olliff 4–6, 7–5, 6–4
1932	beat H. G. N. Lee 6–0, 6–4
	beat C. E. Malfroy 11–9, 6–4
1933	beat Olliff 4–6, 6–2, 6–4
	beat Austin 1–6, 9–7, 6–3
1934	beat Austin 4–6, 8–6, 6–4
	beat Sharpe 5–7, 8–6, 7–5
1935	beat Sharpe 8–6, 7–5
	beat E. C. Peters 6–8, 6–2, 6–0
1936	lost Austin 0–6, 2–6
	beat C. E. Hare 6–3, 4–6, 6–4
1937	lost Austin 5–7, 11–13
	beat F. H. D. Wilde 6–4, 6–2

1938	beat D. W. Butler 9–7, 7–5
	lost H. G. N. Lee 3–6, 6–2, 6–8 (at Torquay)
1946	beat D. W. Barton 6–0, 6–3
	beat D. W. Butler 6–3, 6–2
1947	beat J. W. Harper 8–6, 6–4
	beat I. Tloczynski 6–1, 6–2
1948	beat G. L. Paish 2–6, 6–2, 6–1
	beat Butler 6–4, 6–2 (Borotra now aged 50)
1949	beat Paish 2–6, 6–3, 6–2
	beat Butler 6–8, 8–6, 6–2
1950*	lost Paish 4–6, 3–6
	beat Butler 5–7, 6–4, 6–4
1951	beat A. J. Mottram 6–3, 6–1
1952	lost E. W. Sturgess 0–6, 1–6
	beat Mottram 3–6, 6–4, 6–1
1953	lost J. Drobny 4–6, 1–6
	lost Paish 4–6, 6–3, 5–7
1954	lost R. K. Wilson 6–8, 8–6, 3–6

The Musketeers: (left to right) Cochet, Brugnon and Borotra

1955	beat M. G. Davies 3–6, 6–3, 6–3	
1956	beat H. Billington 6–1, 9–7	
1957	beat Billington 6–2, 6–3	
1958	beat Billington 6–3, 6–2	
1959	beat E. Wittman 6–1, 7–5	
1960	lost Billington 6–3, 5–7, 5–7	
1961	beat Billington 11–9, 9–7	
1962	beat E. Wittman 3–6, 6–3, 9–7	
	beat Lord Zetland 6–1, 6–4 (now aged 64)	
1963	beat Lord Zetland 6–1, 5–7, 8–6	
1964	beat Lord Zetland 6–1, 6–3	
1965	beat E. J. Filby 6–2, 6–8, 6–2	
1966	beat C. Spychala 6–0, 6–4	
1967	beat J. A. White 6–1, 7–5	
	lost R. E. Carter 6–2, 9–7	
1968	lost Wittman 7–5, 4–6, 4–6	
1969	beat Billington 0–6, 6–3, 6–1	
1970	played no singles	

1971	beat Billington 6–1, 6–2
1972	played no singles
1973	beat Billington 6–2, 6–3
1974	lost E. L. Frith 6–4, 5–7, 2–6
1975	beat R. E. H. Hadingham 6–1, 6–4
1976	beat E. Holden 6–4, 4–6, 6–3
1977	beat Holden 6–2, 6–2
1978	beat Holden 6–4, 4–6, 6–3 (now aged 80)
1979	beat Holden 8–6, 7–9, 6–4
1980	lost B. G. Neal 1–6, 2–6

Played at AELTC

1981	lost Holden 3–6, 7–5, 6–7
1982	lost Frith 3–6, 6–7
1983	lost Holden 6–7, 4–6
1984	beat Holden 6–3, 3–6, 6–4
1985	lost Holden 2–6, 2–6 (now aged 87)

* First defeat on east court since the war

REAL TENNIS
1946–1986

REAL Tennis came but slowly out of its wartime sluber at Queen's. The two courts, having been requisitioned for storing goods and chattels from bombed-out houses and with windows boarded up, were in poor condition. The No. 1 court was released for play almost immediately but early in 1947 the Tennis and Rackets Association pronounced it unfit for championship play and the principal events were held at Lord's or Manchester. Twice in future years (1951 and 1964) the Amateur Championship (The Queen's Club Cup) was held in Manchester and once (1958) at Lord's.

The No. 2 court was not returned to play until 1961 and not before the Club's board of directors, controlled by the LTA since 1953, had considered converting it into badminton courts or a bowling alley or selling off both courts.

The great Peter Latham, in his eighties and living in Stamford Brook, continued to visit the Club and watch what little play there was. After one visit he wrote to Norman Railing whose son, Peter, had begun to follow his father's footsteps though he never reached the same high standard.

The letter showed how sharp were Latham's faculties: 'My Dear Sir, I was awfully pleased to see your son, Peter, playing tennis and playing well. I congratulate him on his stooping which, as you know, is half the battle in playing tennis . . . I manage two or three hours a day out, generally at Queen's. My chilblains, this weather, are not too good.'

Latham's zest for life and games was prodigious. Way back in 1877 he had broken a window of the Manchester Racquet Club while playing tipcat in the street and been made to sweep out the courts as a penalty. Later he became the only man to hold the world titles at real tennis and rackets simultaneously. He drank beer with James Braid when he won the Open gold at Troon and played billiards with Melbourne Inman in a Newmarket pub. In a £1000 a side match in New York he tamed Tom Pettit's railroad service which they said was unplayable and he learned how to tear a pack of cards in two from Eugene Sandow. Latham died in 1953 at the age of 88.

The Times' Obituary to Peter Latham*
A Peerless Player of Rackets and Tennis

The death of Peter Latham yesterday at his home in Chiswick at the age of eighty-eight will be heard of with regret by players of tennis and rackets all over the world. Though it might be said that William Gray before him or Jock Soutar after him were his equals at rackets, or that Mr Jay Gould at his best would have rivalled him at tennis, there can be no question that as a champion of the two games together he was without peer.

*Monday, 28 November 1953

He was born in 1865 and entered the Manchester Rackets Club in his own words as a frail small boy of eleven. He quickly grew in strength, and in 1887, at the age of twenty-two, he defeated Joseph Gray at Rugby and Manchester for the world's championship at rackets. In the following year he went as head professional to Queen's Club, and there and at Charterhouse successfully defended his title against Joseph Gray. In 1891 he beat George Standing at Queen's Club and Prince's Club, and from then for six years was unchallenged at rackets. This

Illustrating Peter Latham's rivalry with Punch Fairs (1. Fairs, 2. Latham, 3 & 4 Fairs, 5. Latham)

enabled him to concentrate his powers on tennis, and so rapidly did he improve that in 1895 at Brighton he won the championship from Charles Saunders, hitherto considered unbeatable, by seven sets to three. Shortly afterwards, on the occasion of one of his matches with the Hon. Alfred Lyttelton, he was presented with a testimonial by his admirers on attaining the double honour. This he held for seven years.

THE GREAT YEARS

Latham's greatest years were 1897 and 1898. In the former year, at the zenith of his career at rackets, came the match with George Standing. Latham won by four games to one at Queen's Club. Crossing to the United States he won two of the first three closely fought games to retain the championship, but it was agreed to continue the New York match as Standing's many supporters contended that their player could not lose in his own court. Amid the greatest excitement, however, Latham, after being within a point of losing, struggled home by four games to three. In the next year Latham probably reached the height of his skill at tennis with the match against

Tom Petitt, of Boston. So confident were Petitt's backers that the match was made for £1000. Latham, playing for the first time against a fast 'railroad' service, made splendid use of his prowess at both games and ran away with the match, winning by seven sets to love.

For the next few years there was no one near him at either game. In 1901 when Sir Charles Rose built his tennis court at Newmarket, Latham went there and to Hardwick. In the following year he easily beat Gilbert Browne at rackets, and though he could probably have held the title for some years after – he was rated scratch in professional handicaps as late as 1909 – having played five matches and won them all he resigned the championship at the age of thirty-seven. His next challenge at tennis came in 1904 when he beat C. Punch Fairs by seven sets to five at Brighton, but in the ensuing year at Queen's Club and Prince's Club he met his one and only defeat in a championship match, Fairs winning by five sets to one. It is fairly certain that for the first time Latham was not at his best, for two years later he regained the title, though much the older man, beating Fairs at Brighton by seven sets to two. After his last triumph at the age of forty-two he retired from championship contests. After that

Latham went again to the United States, where his play at both games was as much appreciated as it was here, and he played exhibition matches at tennis with the then youthful Jay Gould, afterwards the greatest of amateur players.

AT QUEEN'S CLUB

He also played many matches in Paris and visited Bordeaux. In 1916 he returned to Queen's Club and as a player and a teacher was the centre of a post-war revival of tennis. He played two fine matches in 1919 giving half-fifteen to the amateur champion, E. M. Baerlein. Two years later, as an instance of his stamina and of how little his powers had abated, he reached the final of the Professional Handicap at Brighton after a match which went to five sets with E. Johnson, and, though of course receiving odds at this age, actually reached match point in the final only to lose in a fading light to G. F. Covey, then champion of the world. As an exhibition of tennis by both players this match was considered as fine a one as has been seen.

It is clear that to have achieved so much Latham must have possessed exceptional qualities. At rackets a wonderful wrist, balance and footwork gave him a grace

One of the leading amateurs of the day was Richard Hill, runner-up in the 1937 Amateur Championship and a member of the Old Wykehamists Henry Leaf Cup team that had long dominated the competition. Hill was playing at Queen's shortly after the war and not very well. Having missed the tambour umpteen times he stopped, turned to the marker and exclaimed 'The tambour has been moved since I last played here.' Later in the bar he was still muttering about the bombs or something being responsible for his failure to find the tambour.

Hill, later to become *The Times* correspondent for this and other court games, then conducted a correspondence with that newspaper questioning the description of the game as real tennis, royal tennis or, as in the US, court tennis. Tennis was the standard description until the late sixties when John Hennessey, the *Times* sports editor, decided it should be altered to real tennis – a change that infuriated the die-hards – in deference to the world-wide use of 'tennis' to describe lawn tennis. Hill would have preferred 'court tennis' as, like rackets and squash, the game involved the walls of the court. Lawn tennis did not.

The first major post-war event held at Queen's was the 1948 Henry Leaf Cup. Eton with Ronnie

and perfection of style and movement, and there was no weak point in his armour. At tennis it took him years of diligence to master the correct stroke, and to this he added all his natural racket strokes and power of hitting. His backhand stroke will be remembered as the classic model of power and grace, and his backhand boast for the *dedans* which 'made haste' off the main wall as his *tour de force*. Beyond this he was a master of match-play in its various phases. He had, first, the ability of a champion to produce his best on the day, and then a remarkable flair for changing his tactics when things were going against him. It was said of him that some things he might disdain – he never used the 'railroad' service at tennis – but that there was nothing he could not do if the occasion warranted it. And, lastly, he had a real love of the games which lead to the ceaseless application so essential to a champion which was to make him in later days so successful a teacher of players of all standards. For he was equally happy whether tackling a beginner or improving a first-class player. On his eightieth birthday in May, 1945, Peter, as he was known to everyone, was given a luncheon at Lord's which was attended by a large number of distinguished players of various games. Many players and friends will miss a wise counsellor, who up till his last days could entertain them with his rare gift of relating his varied and colourful experiences on and off the court.

Aird, Lord Charles Cullen and R. St. L. Granville, won for the first time, beating Rugby's Michael Pugh, J. G. Pugh and Peter Kershaw. At the age of eighty Edward Leaf, brother of the founder of the competition, turned out for Harrow; the oldest man ever to play in a major competition.

Kershaw's win in the Amateur Championship beating Cullen, the holder, in the semi-final and Lowther Lees in the final, made him the third man, after Edgar Baerlein and Lord Aberdare, to have won this title and the rackets. It also emphasized the lack of an outstanding player since Lees had won the title five years running just before the war. Since then there had been five different champions, Kershaw, Cullen, Lees, Macpherson and Aberdare, and eight different runners-up including Billy Ross-Skinner, Richard Hill and C. M. N. Baker.

INCOMPARABLE BASQUE

That year also Pierre Etchebaster, fifty-three and still the World champion after twenty years, broke his holiday in France to tour some of the courts in this country. He played an exhibition at Queen's against Jim Dear who, receiving half 15, beat him 6–5 6–3 6–1. The Basque master may not have

Pierre Etchebaster (left) and Jim Dear who, receiving half 15, beat him in their exhibition match

been within 30 of his best but Dear, then thirty-eight, gave notice that he was about ready to challenge for the World title.

For the next two years the Americans outclassed the British in the Amateur Championship. Ogden Phipps, the US champion and one of four Americans competing, waltzed through with the loss of no sets and thirty-two games in five matches. His hardest battle was against Bob Riseley in the third round. He won 6–3 6–2 6–4 – world class *v* first class said *The Times* – showing a crushing forehand under the winning gallery and in defence of the *dedans* an equally fierce forehand volley to the foot of the tambour. He went on to beat Cullen and Macpherson in the last two rounds and opinion was that he could have given the field 15 and beaten them.

Alastair Martin, who succeeded Phipps as US champion, won the following year and again Riseley gave him his hardest test. He had a more classic style than Phipps but was equally aggressive and faster about the court. His favourite serve was a railroad from the second gallery; a stroke perfected by Jay Gould and Etchebaster.

Macpherson was the unfortunate finalist again and he has described the experience as 'one of my saddest recollections'. Macpherson claims that he was never a good tennis player but played reasonably good squash in the tennis court, keeping the rally going longer than people liked or expected. His preparation for these two Championships was scanty. 'I spent the whole war sitting in an office or an aeroplane. Coming back to an extremely busy time at my office, I was never able to get back into anything like my 1939 form. But as the Americans were competing in our championships I felt I ought to play – and reached the finals both years. Against Phipps I pulled a leg muscle when leading 2–1 in the first set and that was the end of the match. Against Martin I pulled a back muscle at one set all and that was the

Michael Pugh, who contributed so much to the revival of tennis and rackets
with his elder son Tim

end of that game. They were both much better tennis players than I was.'

Another American player, Bill Lingelbach, came with Martin and they played together in a Bathurst Cup against Britain and France and also in the Bailey Cup which became the Amateur Doubles Championships. Martin beat Riseley again in the former but Lingelbach lost in five sets to Kershaw after having six match points. Riseley and Kershaw beat the American pair to give Britain a 3–1 win in the Bathurst Cup and then, representing Oxford, beat them again in the final of the Bailey Cup, both matches going to five sets. Both Americans returned here some years later, Martin winning the Bailey Cup with Northrup Knox in 1958 and Lingelbach doing so with Knox in 1960.

In the early post-war years the main rivalry in the Henry Leaf Cup was between Eton and Rugby who beat each other in alternate years until in 1953 the Rugby firm of Kershaw, David Warburg and Michael Pugh took over and dominated the competition for eleven years, equalling Winchester's record in the twenties and thirties.

RUGBY ON TOP

Kershaw had already twice won the Amateur title by then, succeeding Martin in 1951, and *The Times* had picked out Warburg as an improving player, developing a good wrist but lacking a cramping service though persisting with the railroad. Pugh, who had done as much if not more than anyone in bringing this game and rackets back to life after the war, was becoming the veteran. He retired from the competition after the 1960 final, three years before his sons, Tom and Tim, helped Anthony Ward take Eton to the final. Rugby, who beat them, were by then reinforced by Geoffrey Atkins, which meant that all three members of their side were past or present champions.

Winchester began their come-back with the arrival on the scene of Howard Angus in 1966 when he, Lord Aberdare, Ben Hay and the Travis brothers, won four years out of the following five. Harrow's Roddy Bloomfield, Dick Bridgeman, Nick Smith and Peter Phillips interrupted them until in 1974 Angus, Lovell, Hay, Peter Seabrook and finally David

Woolley carved up the Cup for eleven straight years before being beaten, at last, by Radley's Julian Snow, Thane Warburg (son of David) and James Male in 1985. The cartel of Eton, Harrow, Winchester and Rugby was at last broken.

The major event of the fifties was Jim Dear's World Championship. He had already won the World rackets title three times (1947, 1948, 1951) and the Open squash title, tantamount to the World title, in 1938. With Etchebaster's retirement the World title was 'up for grabs'. First Dear had to play Ron Hughes of Manchester for the Open title and at Queen's they shared the four sets played; Hughes's elegant play on the floor being matched by Dear's attacking flair and versatility. In Manchester Dear ran away with the three sets needed to give him the right to play Albert Johnson, professional at the New York Racquet Club and son of Ted Johnson of Moreton Morrell. They met in the spring of 1955.

Johnson won the first leg in New York 7–4 and, for Dear, the second at Queen's was touch-and-go, hanging on the second set. In this Dear, having lost the first, lost a 5–3 lead. At 5–5 he reached 40–15 with two grilles and a stroke that died off the tambour. Johnson made it deuce but Dear, having gained advantage played a winning volley from under the grille into Johnson's backhand corner. Eventually Dear won the leg 7–3 and the title.

Johnson had more pace and was quicker about the court but his strokes were less severe. Dear was the stronger volleyer and that counted at Queen's. He was able to force Johnson's railroad service to the backhand corner of the *dedans*, something Ronaldson did thirty years later against Wayne Davies in their challenge match. In an analysis of the winning openings Dear scored sixty-six to Johnson's thirty-eight; thirty-one *dedans* to eleven, twenty-five grilles to seventeen, each man scoring ten winning galleries. Two years later Johnson challenged and they met at Queen's. Dear had left the Club by then and was rackets professional at Wellington. He was forty-seven and that, with lack of regular practice, cost him his title. Johnson beat him 7–3.

While the World and other major championships played at Queen's may represent the peak of the game – and of rackets as well – the significant fact was that neither game was flourishing among ordinary members and that outside competition time the courts were not being fully used. This caused some anxiety within the Tennis and Rackets Association who put it down partially to the fact that the Club had no professionals at either game; they could not afford them, so it was claimed. At the same time it was realized that the existing professionals at both games were getting older and there was a grave shortage of young ones to replace them.

BRIDGEMAN'S BRAINCHILD

In 1958 and 1959 two schemes were launched to try and improve the situation. The Young Professionals' Fund was the brainchild of Dick Bridgeman and Morys, Lord Aberdare, who had recently succeeded to his late father's title. The object was to train a cadre of young men to become professionals and, over the years, this proved highly successful.

The first to come to Queen's were Peter Ellis and Peter Ashford. The former became senior professional at both games before moving to Oxford University; the latter went to Winchester. Ian Church and Norwood Cripps joined the Club staff in 1962, Terry Whatley a year later. Cripps became the best professional player since Jim Dear, before moving to Eton; Terry Whatley made a great success of rackets at Clifton. The line of young men continued to the present day with such professionals as Neil Smith and Gerard Parsons.

Dick Bridgeman was also responsible for the scheme whereby members keen on real tennis and rackets could 'buy' their courts at the start of the season, thereby getting them at reduced rates and providing a fund that would help pay for the professionals. By 1963 there were over one hundred pre-subscribers.

With Anthony Ward and Richard Greenwood, Bridgeman introduced The Queen's Club weekends; competitive get-togethers once or twice a season providing a lot of fun. They have become increasingly successful as social parties and money-raisers. In 1965, for instance, £300 was raised for the Young Professionals' Fund and house parties were given by two members, C. K. Simond and I. P. Roberts and their wives. Nowadays dinner parties are held at the Club. Today the popularity of real tennis and rackets at the Club and these excellent professional staff can be attributed to these events and the men who conceived them over twenty-five years ago.

Unlike the pre-war years when Baerlein and Lees dominated the Amateur Championship, the post-war game did not produce any commanding or outstanding champion until the arrival of Howard Angus in the mid-sixties. The leading American

Dick Bridgeman, who did so much for Young Professionals. Here he
is (left) with his partner choosing wine for the Club

David Johnson, the Queen's Club real tennis head professional

amateurs were ahead of the British, as Northrup Knox showed in 1958 when he beat Lord Aberdare, the holder, 3–0 to win the title, as had Ogden Phipps and Alastair Martin before him. David Warburg, the 1959 and 1961 champion – he won again in 1965 and was runner-up eleven times – had a crack at the Open title in 1962 but Ron Hughes beat him 5–1.

The champions of the era were men of character; some stylish like Charles Cullen, Morys Aberdare (four times a winner), Anthony Tufton and Geoffrey Atkins, three times the champion; others determined and aggressive like Kershaw, Riseley and Warburg. Certainly Kershaw and Riseley were the best doubles team of the period, to be followed by Angus and Warburg.

Aberdare or Bruce as he then was, was more severe than others of his type and this showed when he defended his title against Kershaw in 1954. Kershaw had trained hard for the event but was beaten after three hours' play in five sets, the last two being of a very high standard. When Bruce first won the title in 1953 he was thirty-four. His father, overshadowed by Baerlein and Lees, was forty-seven when first he won in 1932.

Tufton, at Cambridge and full of play, must have been at his peak when he surprisingly beat Warburg for the title in 1964. He was not a natural hitter but possessed a neat floor game and was a useful volleyer, playing through the ball as in lawn tennis rather than cutting it.

Atkins, who beat Warburg in all three of his finals, was a superb mover and had wonderful control of the ball. He was elegant but did not stoop as Latham would have liked and did not cut the ball heavily. Rather he let the ball onto the racket before bringing his wrist through.

BRAINS VERSUS LEGS

Warburg, who figured in so many finals, was canny, determined and strong with a powerful wrist that he used for boasting or forcing low, especially from the hazard end. He lost his title to Angus in 1966. They had first met in the semi-final the previous year and, as Angus has recalled, 'It was a great match up to 4–4 in the first set. He then took the next fourteen games.' It was different in the final the next year. 'He knew more than I did and was stronger in the arm and brain. But I was stronger in the leg,' was how Angus summed up the first of his many finals to come.

Angus, a stocky left-hander built like a sherpa, was in the Winchester rackets pair that reached the Schools Championship final in 1962 and 1963. At Cambridge he took up real tennis under Brian Church, the professional, and with another Old Wykehamist, Ben Hay, beat Oxford 3–0 in the 1964 University match. He was on the winning side for the next two years and lost only one set in all the matches he played against the Dark Blues. In 1966, apart from winning the first of his sixteen 'Amateurs', he with Lord Aberdare and Hay ended Rugby's domination of the Henry Leaf Cup.

After Angus again beat Warburg in the 1967 Amateur final the official report cautiously commented 'Angus gave a brilliant display. It is difficult to see any amateur beating him for several years to come.' A year earlier his brother, Ian, had made a bolder prophecy in a telegram following his first win – 'Well done, you can now win for fifteen years.' He did.

What would E. B. Noel, Freddie Wilson or even Richard Hill have made of Angus? He was not a conventional player in any way, including the fact that he was the first and, so far, the only left-handed champion. He did not stoop. Perhaps he did not need to as he was so near the floor! But he was the nearest thing to perpetual motion yet seen in a court

Geoffrey Atkins (left) and David Warburg, finalists in the
Amateur Singles 1962 (Atkins won)

and that earned him the sobriquet 'The peddlar', coined by Charles Hue Williams.

Early on, Ron Hughes had told Angus 'You'll never be a tennis player. Concentrate on doing what you do well – winning points.' He became very conscious of that. Angus assessed his game this way: 'I hit the ball too hard to do many spins. I set the pace and it was up to my opponents to stop me dominating. I also hit through the ball flat with the wrist turning over late to keep it low over the net, thereby denying good stroke players the chance to make the conventional cut reply. They had to run after the ball. There was a need for the game to be played more athletically, for a new approach.'

Despite this, Angus did cut the ball on the backhand when needed but his forehand remained more of a slice than a traditional cut. He persisted in the railroad service with the occasional variation to the

underarm twist. His boasting was formidable, showing fine control and a strong wrist. Sometimes, when watching Angus, one wondered whether he was playing rackets in a real tennis court.

While Angus was still at Cambridge the game saw the beginnings of sponsorship with 'The Field Trophy', a singles competition open to the sixteen best amateurs and professionals in the country and played at Queen's. It was won in its first year, 1965, by Hughes who beat Jim Dear 3–0 in the final. Frank Willis, the Manchester professional and Open champion, won it the next two years, beating Angus on both occasions though not in the finals.

By 1968 Angus may have established himself as head and shoulders above his amateur contemporaries but he was not yet quite the equal of Willis, a classic player with a very heavy stroke. Willis beat him in the 1968 Open 5–2 at Manchester and Queen's.

An exceptional world champion at work: Howard Angus in 1977
Above: Jim Dear (left) with Malvern professional Ron Hughes, who defeated him for the Field Trophy

ANGUS ON THE MOVE

Angus registered his first win over Willis later that year in the Field Trophy, albeit narrowly by 6–5 in the final set. Willis led 3–1 and 5–3 in that set. When Angus finally took the match with a boasted force that screwed off the floor into the *dedans* Willis clenched his fist and pleaded with the ball not to go in. Willis got his revenge the following season, in five sets. It was in that tournament that Cripps began to make his mark, beating Richard Cooper and Warburg before losing to Willis.

At the end of the sixties and start of the seventies there was a good deal of rivalry between Angus, Willis and Cripps in the Field Trophy. When really fit Willis was too severe for Angus but those occasions became increasingly rare and from 1970 onwards Angus had his measure in the Open, if not the Field.

In 1970 Angus suffered a most unusual defeat at the hands of David Cull in the Field and, the following year, had to withdraw with a damaged shoulder. In 1973 he twisted a suspect ankle in the first set against Cripps in the semi-final. He appeared to recover and was near victory in the fourth set but missed the grille on a vital point. Cripps gained his first win over the amateur but ended with a blistered and bleeding hand. Angus gave him full marks with 'At that time I reckoned Cripps was the best player around.'

A new and exciting player, Chris Ennis, twenty-two and professional at Leamington, appeared on the scene in the early seventies. A mercurial young man, he had a phenomenal instinct for the game and Angus claimed he once saw him anticipate and defend the door from the hazard side.

By 1975 Cutty Sark had become the game's sponsors and taken over the Field Trophy and it was in the semi-final of that event that Ennis scored his bull's-eye and beat Angus. During that match Angus crashed into the main wall and Ennis turned to the *dedans* and smilingly remarked 'I hope he's broken his neck.' He then looked across to Angus with 'You alright?' Ennis went on to beat Cripps in the final. Unfortunately for the game and after partnering Michael Dean, then Oxford's professional, to the doubles final in 1976, he faded out.

The Cutty Sark Doubles, later to become the Unigate and then the George Wimpey, and first won by Charles Swallow and Cripps in 1974, became an increasingly important and exciting event; one in which Cripps made his biggest impression on the game. Cripps and Lovell won the title five years running from 1977 – two competitions that year – to 1980 without losing a set. They missed 1981 but won again in 1982, dropping sets for the first time, to Lachlan Deuchar and Colin Lumley, two Australians, in the semi-final. Chris Ronaldson and Dean, already an established pair, then took over.

In the amateur world there was some disenchantment among the players at the ease with which Angus beat them, especially when he annihilated Roddy Bloomfield 6–0 6–0 6–0 in one Amateur final. Angus confessed 'I was sad it happened. I respected him sufficiently not to lose a point deliberately and he did have sixteen game points being unlucky not to win some of them.' Nevertheless, some people thought he should stand out of the event as did the old-time champions and wait for a challenger. That happened in 1974 as Angus, having already won the World Rackets title, became involved in an eliminator for the World Real Tennis Championship.

LOVELL ARRIVES

The challenger was Alan Lovell, aged twenty, from Oxford where he had been persuaded to take up the game by Chris Ronaldson, the professional who also made his first appearance on the competitive scene. By this time, one should add, these championships and tournaments had become so popular that qualifying competitions were necessary.

Lovell had made his first mark on the senior game when, promoted from the Winchester Henry Leaf second team for the final against Rugby, he beat Warburg. In the Amateur final he beat Anthony Tufton but lost the challenge to Angus. 'Within a month of starting the game at Oxford I was determined to reach the Amateur Championship final within two years.' He succeeded but his reaction after losing to Angus was 'To win a point against Angus is not too difficult but to string four points together for a game is a major problem.'

In his early days as Amateur Champion but before winning the Open Angus had set his sights on one day becoming the World champion. Thinking back he said, 'I remember taking Judy out to dinner and telling her I saw no reason why I should not win it one day. I had been brought up by my father to believe in winners, not losers; to play games to win. It depended on how hard one was prepared to work at the game. I was prepared to work hard; to improve.' Judy, of course, was Judy Hall, a hostess at Queen's for some years. They were married in 1975, the year before Angus did win the World title.

Having beaten Willis 7–5 for the Open title at Manchester, Queen's and Seacourt, Angus in 1974 was faced with playing the American, Gene Scott, a former Davis Cup player, for the right to challenge the World title-holder, Jimmy Bostwick, another American. Angus took the first leg at Queen's 5–4 but only by the narrowest of margins. Scott, whose pre-match practice to pop music caused some interest, led 3–1 on the first day and, at 4–4 on the second, was 4–1 and 5–3 ahead in games with one set point. Angus took the New York leg 5–1.

An indication of the style of play at Queen's was mirrored in the number of winning openings gained by the two players. Angus scored 19, mostly grilles. Scott scored 39, twenty *dedans*, fifteen grilles, four winning galleries. 'My arm was not strong enough to stand that battering,' was Angus's comment. When they met in New York it was different. 'I realized that Gene could cover any shot to the grille or tambour. I had to play tennis, cut the ball into the corners or to chase one and two. I had to avoid getting into a hitting match and prevent him lambasting the ball into the *dedans*,' said Angus. In the title match against Bostwick, Angus, having won the first four sets, fell ill with a respiratory infection, was given a postponement but then lost narrowly.

Norwood Cripps (left) with Alan Lovell. A highly successful partnership

Bostwick retired the following year and that left the field open for Angus and Scott. They met in March 1976 and in the New York leg Angus, after losing the first three sets, won the next seven. At Queen's he won the first day's play 3–1, scoring 16 winning openings to 12, a very different affair to their previous encounter at the Club. That left Angus with one set to win and this he did the following day to become the first British amateur to win the World Championship. The full score of this contest was, in favour of Angus, 2–6 5–6 4–6 6–3 6–2 6–5 6–2 6–1 6–2 6–0 6–2 6–2 5–6 6–3 6–4 – 11 sets to 4. A year later he resisted a challenge from Scott at Hampton Court.

Meantime, Lovell was maturing as a player and the 1977 Amateur final in which he took Angus to five sets was about the best played for fifteen years. Lovell led two sets to one and 3–1. At the end he said he was more tired mentally than physically.

GREAT DOUBLES TEAM

Lovell's first title of any consequence was the Cutty Sark Open doubles which he won with Norwood Cripps. Thus began the most successful doubles partnership the game had yet seen. In that 1977 final they beat the holders, Willis and David Cull. The match was delayed as Willis, driving down from Manchester as was his habit, was held up by two punctures and a traffic jam. Quite often he would arrive in some disarray which he shrugged off in his jovial way.

At Queen's as elsewhere the game's popularity increased immeasurably. Though competitions were beginning to increase – they proliferated in the eighties – the Club remained the centre. In singles Willis and Cripps began to fade and Ennis had unfortunately left the game. It was now the turn of players like Lovell, Chris Ronaldson, who had gone from Oxford to Australia, and Barry Toates, also from Australia, to chase the Master. Toates was originally a product of the Young Professionals Fund and trained at Cambridge; a pleasing stroke player and character who would converse with the *dedans* in the middle of a rally. Graham Hyland was another newcomer, an Australian virtuoso but a suspect match player.

Ronaldson scored his first win over Angus in the 1978 Cutty Sark final 6–5 6–2 4–6 0–6 6–4. He still considers that one of his best matches – 'I remember being down 3–4 and love-40 in the final set. Angus tried and failed to beat chase better than a yard. That was my break-through,' said the victorious Ronaldson after the match. Angus was less equivocal – 'I had not prepared properly for the event and did not deserve to win.' Earlier Ronaldson had had a tussle with Lovell and when he lost four set points in the third set exclaimed 'I must try something.' He did and served a high ball that fell dead in the corner.

There was, by the way, one extraordinary match that season in the Henry Leaf Cup final between Winchester and Eton. Willie Boone, a tyro at the game, led Peter Seabrook, the Winchester third string, 5-love and 40-love in the final set and lost because he did not know how to finish it off. Providing Seabrook did not make a silly mistake or suffer an unexpected *coup de théâtre* he had only to keep the ball in play.

Unigate took over from Cutty Sark as the game's sponsors in 1979. Chris Ronaldson made an abortive challenge for the World title – Angus thrashed him at Hampton Court – and returned to Troon where he was then professional 'with my tail between my legs'.

Angus, having won the Amateur title for the fifteenth time, beating Lovell again, had to withdraw from further competition that season (1980), having been hit in the eye by a rackets ball. That left the

Wayne Davies in play in the 1983 George Wimpey Open. He lost to Ronaldson
Ronaldson: practice paid off again in 1985
Wayne Davies, 'needing any breaks that were going'

1981 World Champion Chris Ronaldson, following the presentation. He defeated
Howard Angus

field clear for Ronaldson though Lovell and Cripps continued to win the doubles – the Unigate Doubles by then. Lovell also had a successful Unigate singles, beating Cripps and Willis for the first time before going down to Ronaldson. That year also, Oxford and Cambridge, represented by Simon Kverndal, William Hollington and Amam Kanwar, beat a team of young Americans for the Van Allen Trophy at Queen's.

The Angus era, stretching back sixteen years, ended in 1981 when he lost both his major titles. Lovell beat him in the Amateur Championship final 6–2 6–3 6–5 and summed up his success with 'For years I played pretty tennis against Howard. This time I decided to bash the ball.'

NEW CHAMPION

Then Ronaldson, having warded off Willis and Toates in eliminators at Queen's, captured the World title when Angus, down five sets to one, 5–4

and 30–15, pulled a calf muscle and had to retire. The score in Ronaldson's favour was 6–5 6–5 6–5 6–2 2–6 6–2 5–4.

It was not a highly satisfactory end to the former champion's career. Undoubtedly he had lost some of his will to win. His work and his family had taken priority over the game. To get to work in the Midlands he was getting up at 5.45 a.m., returning home late, grabbing something to eat and trying to practise. But it was bound to happen sooner or later and Ronaldson, not a great mover but consistent, without any weakness to attack and a clever user of the court and his own resources, deserved his triumph.

Almost immediately, Ronaldson came under siege from the Australians. Hyland was close to beating him in the George Wimpey Open – Wimpey had taken over from Unigate with considerable enthusiasm – and Wayne Davies, Lachlan Deuchar and Colin Lumley were on the scene. In May 1984 Queen's staged a match between England and the

Club members enjoying a game

Rest of the World which the former won narrowly. Ronaldson, Toates, Lovell, Cripps, David Johnson and Kevin Sheldon played for England; the Rest were all Australians, Wayne Davies, Deuchar, Lumley, Paul Tabley and the man who once batted twelve hours and seven minutes while amassing 307 for his country, Bob Cowper.

Late that year Davies, not physically strong but possessing a strong forcing forehand and volley, won the first two sets against Ronaldson in the Open Championship but then lost his grip on the match. He had already lodged his challenge for the World title. Ronaldson went into that contest, played in March 1985, full of confidence. He had practised returning the railroad into the backhand corner, a difficult shot, and it paid off. Davies led 4–1 in the first set and needed to win it to have any chance. 'He needed any breaks that were going. Everything had to go right for him. But it didn't,' said

Ronaldson, who won 6–5 6–3 5–6 6–3 6–1 6–2 6–4 6–1.

At the T. & R. A. Dinner held in the court in 1984 David Norman, the chairman, was at pains to point out that they regard Queen's as the HQ of real tennis and rackets in this country and, indeed, the world. And with the host of championships from juniors to the peak of those games held there, it has become so. A glance at the record section will confirm that.

At that same dinner the Speaker of the House of Commons, Bernard Weatherill, recalled the story of the two real tennis players who wore glasses. They fell off one of the players and broke. The other took his off as he did not want to put his opponent at a disadvantage. He had been told that by Billy Ross Skinner, one of the monuments of the game at Queen's and elsewhere; a man who never said a bad word about anyone. A lot of people have played on the Club's two courts in nearly a century and the great majority have done so in the spirit of Billy Ross Skinner.

RACKETS
1946–1986
J. R. Thompson

SECRETARY of the Club from 1939 to 1975 was R. J. Ritchie. Predominantly interested in lawn tennis as he was, he did a great deal to encourage rackets and to help in re-establishing the game in the Queen's court after the Second World War. J. A. S. Edwardes, the present secretary, is still a keen player. He had two years in the Wellington pair in 1957 and 1958 and he was Army Champion in 1966, 1970 and 1971. The future of rackets at Queen's is assured with the secretaryship in his capable hands.

From The Queen's Club's financial viewpoint, rackets has been one of the least profitable games. Since the Second World War, rackets players must be grateful to those members of the Club Committee who have given their support to the continuation of rackets at the Club. Dick Bridgeman was one. A member of The Queen's Club Committee for eighteen years and Chairman of the Tennis and Rackets Association from 1979 until his untimely death in 1982, he was 1st string for Harrow in 1949 and 1950, reaching the final of the Public Schools Championship with R. J. McAlpine in 1950. After leaving school he played regularly in amateur rackets and tennis championships. He captained and managed two rackets tours to the USA in 1960 and 1962. But his greatest contribution to the two games undoubtedly was the untiring work he did for the Young Professionals Fund, which has enabled so many young professionals to be trained. He had the foresight to see that without money to pay for the training of new professionals after the war, rackets and real tennis would not survive. Those interested in these games should realize how great a benefactor he has been in furthering the cause of rackets and real tennis at Queen's and elsewhere.

Anthony Ward was another long-serving Queen's committee member and a past Chairman of the Club and now President in the centenary year. He was two years in the Eton rackets pair, reaching the final with J. R. Greenwood in 1944. His encouragement for rackets and real tennis and his running of the 200 Club to raise money for the Young Professionals Fund have contributed greatly.

Mention has already been made of the mysterious fire in 1979 in the Ladies' Dressing Room, beside the entrance to the court, which caused extensive damage to the rackets gallery above. Maybe this was a blessing in disguise as the old gallery was becoming very dilapidated. The new gallery, smaller than its predecessor, can accommodate sufficient spectators for the major championships in more comfort. In 1983, extensive repairs to the front and right-hand wall of the court were carried out most successfully by Cornwall Bros of Maidstone, although as a result the court is a little slower than before.

PLENTEOUS PRENNS

Rackets players at Queen's have recently been helped by generous sponsors. Louis Roederer in the 1970's and more recently Celestion Loudspeakers Ltd have done so much for both amateurs and professionals in financing much of the expense of championships and providing prizemoney for the professionals. The Prenn family in particular have provided lavish receptions after the major championship finals, which has helped to make the game more widely known. They have also subsidized the Queen's subscriptions for young players which has enabled them to continue playing rackets after leaving school.

There is good reason to hope that the south court may soon be converted back into use for rackets and this would relieve the present congestion in the north court during the major championships.

The World Championship

After the Second World War and David Milford's retirement, another Anglo-American Challenge Match was arranged to decide the World title. The British representative became Jim Dear. He had started as a ball-boy at Queen's in 1927 and had moved to Prince's as the only rackets and squash professional. When Prince's closed during the war he returned to Queen's in 1946. He had fully earned his right to challenge, having defeated Peter Gray, the professional at Rugby and also John Pawle and Peter Kershaw, the best amateurs. In North America, Ken Chantler, the popular Montreal professional, had beaten Bobby Grant, the much fancied hard-hitting amateur, to win the American Open Championship.

Top: left to right, Anthony Ward, President in the Club's centenary year, and John Clench with Roddy Bloomfield and Michael Coulman, the 1955 Oxford University pair
Two scribes – Christina Wood (*Daily Telegraph*) and Roy McKelvie (*The Times*)

In 1947, the first leg, played at Montreal, resulted in a convincing win for Dear by 15–9 16–17 15–10 15–11 15–11. In the second leg at Queen's, Dear again won convincingly by 4 games to 0 to become the first post-war World Champion by 8 games to 1. Chantler won many friends as the first Canadian to contest a World Championship match and he is still officiating at the Montreal Club today, forty years later. Jim Dear held the World title for the next seven years, resisting two challenges from John Pawle, the Amateur Champion of 1946 and 1947 in the process. The first of these in 1948 produced a high-quality match, Dear just winning the very close first leg at Queen's by 4 games to 3, 15–5 6–15 12–15 9–15 15–9 15–5 15–12. After leading by 3 games to 1, Pawle began to be troubled with a back injury so that Dear won the last 3 games. In the second leg, Pawle again started well, but his injury had not fully recovered and Dear ran out the winner by 15–18 15–10 15–1 16–13 to retain his title by 8 games to 4.

John Pawle challenged again in 1951 and in the two legs, both played at Queen's, Dear was again

Top: Marlborough's A. J. Crosby with his sons Jim, Fred and Arthur, lined up at Queen's
Right: The 1947 World Championship final: Jim Dear beat Ken Chantler 8–1.

victorious by 15–6 7–15 12–15 15–2 15–7 15–6 and by 15–9 15–9 15–6 15–8, to retain the title by 8 matches to 2. By 1954, a new star was on the horizon in Geoffrey Atkins, the Amateur Champion of 1952 and 1953. He had learnt his rackets at Rugby under that expert teacher Peter Gray. In 1954, Dear and Atkins played two superb matches at Queen's, in which Atkins, playing brilliantly, won the first leg, 15–9 15–1 15–8 5–15 17–16. Dear, after a slow start, fought back with all his experience to win the fourth game, but was unfortunate to lose the very close crucial fifth. Dear started the 2nd leg in superb form to win the first 3 games, but Atkins then brought out his great fighting qualities to take the next two games for the title, the score being 15–10 18–17 15–6 10–15 10–15 18–16 4 games to 2 in Dear's favour, but Atkins had won overall by 6 games to 5.

Jim Dear, then forty-four, was the last professional to hold the World title. He was a wonderful all-round court game player. He had been British Open Squash Champion on 1938, World Rackets Champion, 1947–1954 and was to become the World Real Tennis Champion in 1955 – a unique triple achievement.

UNRUFFLED ATKINS

After his victory, Atkins was mainly domiciled in the USA for the next twenty years and was the dominant player on both sides of the Atlantic during that time. His classical effortless style and graceful footwork enabled him to cover the court with deceptive ease. With never a hair out of place, he always appeared calm in a crisis and his court manners were an example to all. Atkins held off four challenges for the title. In 1963, James Leonard, a shrewd, intelligent Etonian, earned the right to challenge by defeating Atkins in the final of the 1962 Amateur Champion-

Charles Swallow defeating Atkins in the 1964 final

ship by 3 games to 2. However, in the World Challenge matches at Queen's, Atkins won comfortably
by 17–15 15–12 8–15 15–11 15–16 and by 15–8
15–6 in the second leg to retain the title by 6 games
to 1. In 1964, Charles Swallow, a tall, fluent stroke
player, also defeated Atkins in the final of the 1964
Championship by 3 games to 2. The World title
match between Atkins and Swallow at Queen's produced high-quality rackets, with Swallow leading by
2 games to 1 in the first leg and by 2 games to love
in the second. However Atkins, as ever cool in the
crisis, was able to fight back in both matches and to
retain his title by 8 games to 5.

James Leonard challenged again in 1967 but lost
by 7 games to 2 in Chicago and at Queen's. Swallow
tried again in 1970, also at Chicago and Queen's,
but Atkins retained the title yet again by 6 games to
3. In 1971, at the age of forty-four, Geoffrey Atkins
resigned the World title after seventeen years during
which he had resisted the challenge of many fine
young players.

With the World title again vacant, another Anglo-
American match was arranged. After various elimin-
ating matches between Charles Hue Williams, Tom
Pugh, Richard Gracey, James Leonard, Howard
Angus and Martin Smith, the Amateur Champion
Howard Angus was eventually selected as the British
contender. Willie Surtees, an Englishman living in
the USA and another of Peter Gray's ex-pupils from
Rugby, was the North American representative. In
the first leg at Queen's Angus won with ease by 4
games to 1. In the second leg in Chicago, Angus had
trouble with the gut of his racquets in the central
heating. Surtees won the first 3 games and with
everything depending on the next game, Surtees just
got home by, 18–13 to claim the title by 5 games to
4.

However, in the following year, 1973, Angus
turned the tables in no uncertain fashion. He won
the first leg in Chicago by 4 games to 0 after narrowly
taking the first game by 17–15. In the second leg at
Queen's, Angus lost the first game by 8–15 but made
no mistake in the second, winning it by 15–3 to
become the first left-handed World Champion.
Howard Angus, a product of Winchester, was an
excellent mover and retriever and a very good match
player. In 1974, Surtees came back to challenge
again, regaining the title by 5 games to 1, winning
by 4 games to 0 in Chicago and taking the one game

Willie Surtees – a handsome champion

Willie Boone, the second southpaw World Champion, collecting his trophy
from Sebastian Coe. David Norman, Chairman of the Tennis and Rackets
Association, is in the centre

necessary at Queen's by 15–11. Howard Angus went on to win the World Real Tennis Championship in 1976 and 1977, but, no doubt to his own disappointment, he never quite managed to be World Champion at both rackets and tennis simultaneously. Willie Surtees was a fine champion. He had a superb backhand stroke, hitting the ball hard and low and he possessed many of the match-winning qualities, which had set Atkins above his rivals.

THE PRENN-BOONE AGE

Since 1977, British rackets, particularly amongst the amateurs, has achieved new high standards of excellence. With more championships and competitions, the players are fitter than in the past and the competition is keener. Generous sponsorship by Celestion Loudspeakers Ltd since 1980 has helped financially and with publicity for the major championships.

Since 1977, two outstanding players have emerged from this increased activity, namely John Prenn from Harrow and Willie Boone, from Eton. These two great players have contested the finals of the Amateur Championship and the Open Championship for the past eight years and their keen rivalry has done much to raise the general standard of play and to increase spectator interest in the game. They are both members of Queen's.

John Prenn, although he had lost to Willie Boone in the final of the Amateur Championship in 1981, gained his revenge in the Open Championship, winning by 4 games to 0. This victory enabled him to challenge Willie Surtees for the World Championship. Sponsored by Celestion Loudspeakers the matches took place in December 1981. Surtees won the first leg in Chicago by 4 games to 2. However, Prenn played magnificently in the second leg at Queen's to take the match and the World title by 4

Above: John Prenn and William Boone in the 1985 Amateur
Singles Final – style versus brawn
Right John Prenn

games to 0 and to win by 6 games to 4 on aggregate. John Prenn is very quick about the court and a great retriever with a classical backhand stroke. He varies his service cleverly, sometimes using an overhead lawn tennis service effectively.

For the next three years Prenn and Boone continued their close-fought battles in the British Championships. In 1982 and 1983 Prenn narrowly beat Boone in the Open Championship finals (best of 7 games) and also the Amateur Championship (best of 5 games). However, towards the end of 1983, Prenn developed a persistent back injury. This undoubtedly affected his performances in 1984 as he did not reach the final of the Amateur Championship in 1984 and later he had to withdraw from the Open Championship. Boone won both the Amateur and Open Championships which earned him the right to challenge Prenn for his World title.

After two postponements, due to Prenn's injury, they finally met in Montreal on 24 November, 1984 and at Queen's for the second leg on 1 December. In the event the left-handed Boone with his vicious service and hard-hitting showed clear superiority in both matches. At Montreal, on a muggy day, the game was postponed for an hour at 3 games to 2 because the court began to sweat. On resumption Boone took the last game to win by 15–10 15–2 15–11 11–15 11–15 15–17. A week later at Queen's, Boone was again in devastating form to win the second leg by 15–6 15–10 15–6 2–15 15–5 to take the title by 8 games to 3. Boone is the second left-hander to be World Champion. He is a strong man, who hits the ball very hard. He also possesses tremendous service power and is very sound in the rallies; he is indeed a worthy World Champion.

It is worth mentioning that six of the last eleven World Rackets Champions have been from Queen's, namely: Peter Latham and Jim Dear, both professionals, and the amateurs Geoffrey Atkins, Howard Angus, John Prenn and Willie Boone.

The British Open Championships

Until 1971, occasional challenge matches for the British Open Rackets Championships, usually played at Queen's, took place. Often these matches were arranged to find a British challenger for the World Championship. In 1959, Geoffrey Atkins, the holder, was living abroad and had to relinquish the title and an invitation competition was arranged, which was won by John Thompson. The following year he was challenged and defeated by Jim Dear, the last time that a professional has held the title. In 1971 an annual invitation competition for the Open Championship was inaugurated, originally sponsored by Louis Roederer and later by Celestion Loudspeakers. So far there have only been four winners in fifteen years, namely: Howard Angus (six times), Willie Surtees (once), John Prenn (six times) and Willie Boone (twice). Since 1979, the great rivalry between John Prenn and Willie Boone has added great interest to the finals of this event. Since 1978 the Open Championship has accepted anyone who wished to enter.

In 1981, the British Open Doubles Championship was instituted and sponsored by Celestion Loudspeakers. It has been won on all five occasions by Willie Boone and Randall Crawley, an outstanding partnership.

The Amateur Singles Championship

In the Amateur Singles, J. H. Pawle, a fine stylish Harrovian won the first four championships after the War (1946–49) with the evergreen Milford winning twice more at the age of forty-five (1950–51). In 1952 the great G. W. T. Atkins won for the next two years (1952–53). In the next fifteen years he usually won the championship when he was available during his years in the USA or Japan. However, in 1962 J. W. Leonard defeated him 3–2 and in 1964, C. J. Swallow repeated the feat. During Atkins's absence in the 1950s, J. R. Thompson, Milford's doubles partner and colleague at Marlborough, won on five occasions (1945–55 and 1957–59), the last time in an extraordinary final against J. M. G. Tildesley. Tildesley, a most talented Rugbeian, in his last year at Oxford, led Thompson by 15–11 15–0 14–8 at match point. However, Thompson, the holder, somehow managed to save this game and eventually won the match by 11–15 0–15 17–16 15–13 15–8 showing remarkable stamina at the age of forty. J. W. Leonard, the last undergraduate to win the Amateur Championships, won on four occasions (1961, '62, '68 and '69) and the stylish C. J. Swallow also on four occasions (1964, '66, '68, and '69). They were both fine players who unsuccessfully challenged Atkins for the World Championship.

M. G. M. Smith won twice (1970 and 1971) to be followed by H. R. Angus who won for the next four years (1972–75). Angus, a Wykehamist, became World Champion during this period. C. J.

James Male: victory over Prenn and Boone to win the Amateur title in 1985

The Amateur Doubles Championship

C. S. Crawley and J. H. Pawle, who had won the last Amateur Doubles Championship before the Second World War, won the first championship after the War (1946) before the younger generation came on the scene with R. A. A. Holt and A. R. Taylor, who won in 1947 and 1949. However after the War, D. S. Milford found a new partner in J. R. Thompson, his colleague at Marlborough and after some close finals with Holt and Taylor, the schoolmasters went on to win the championship, Thompson at the front of the court while Milford operated from the back with all his subtle genius. Each won on one other occasion, Milford with P. M. Whitehouse in 1938 and Thompson with C. T. M. Pugh in 1966.

Their sequence was interrupted by G. W. T. Atkins and P. Kershaw, who won in 1953 and again in 1961 and 1962.

In more recent years, the Tonbridgians, R. M. K. Gracey and M. G. M. Smith had five victories (1964, '65, '69, '70, and '71) and C. J. Hue Williams, a fine doubles player, won with C. J. Leonard (1967–68) and with H. R. Angus (1972–73) and with G. W. T. Atkins (1974). For five successive years

The 1952 Amateur Doubles final. (Left to right:) D. S. Milford, J. R. Thompson, P. Kershaw and G. W. T. Atkins

Hue Williams had a single win in 1977 before W. R. Boone and J. A. N. Prenn monopolized the final up to the present day. Boone the present Amateur, Open and World Champion has won five times (1976, '78, '81, '84 and '85), while Prenn has four times (1979, '80, '82 and '83.) Boone, with his power of service and exhilarating hitting and Prenn, with his retrieving ability and agility, have given us some of the best rackets ever seen at Queen's in their finals in recent years.

Winners in the eighty-seven Amateur Championships have been:

E. M. Baerlein	9 wins
H. K. Foster	8 wins
D. S. Milford	7 wins
J. R. Thompson	5 wins
G. W. T. Atkins	5 wins
W. R. Boone	5 wins
J. H. Pawle	4 wins
J. W. Leonard	4 wins
C. J. Swallow	4 wins
H. R. Angus	4 wins
J. A. N. Prenn	4 wins

(1980–84), W. R. Boone and R. S. Crawley have been outstanding winners. Boone's power and Crawley's stylish support have carried all before them. In 1985 they were surprisingly beaten by C. J. Hue Williams and J. A. N. Prenn in the final by 4 games to love.

Most frequent winners from the eighty-five Amateur Doubles Championships have been:

D. S. Milford and J. R. Thompson	10
Hon. C. N. Bruce and H. W. Leatham	6
R. M. K. Gracey and M. G. M. Smith	5
W. R. Boone and R. S. Crawley	5
H. K. Foster and P. Ashworth	4

Most winning shares have been:

D. S. Milford	11	
J. R. Thompson	11	
Hon. C. N. Bruce	10	(4 different partners)
H. K. Foster	8	(5 different partners)
W. R. Boone	8	
P. Ashworth	7	
H. W. Leatham	7	
E. M. Baerlein	6	
C. J. Hue Williams	6	(4 different partners)

The Public Schools Championship

During the 1939–45 war period, the championship continued, except for 1942 when it was not played. In 1941 it was held at Wellington College. The outstanding pairs were Haileybury (J. K. Drinkall and A. Fairbairn) who won in 1940 and 1941 and Winchester (H. E. Webb and G. H. J. Myrtle) who won in 1944 and 1945. As Winchester (G. H. G. Doggart and J. B. Thursfield) had also won in 1943, Winchester became the first school to win the championship three years in succession at Queen's.

After the war, Malvern, whose courts had been requisitioned and damaged during the war, were unable to re-enter the championship until 1955 and Haileybury did not re-start until 1954. Winchester were again predominant, winning the cup again for three successive years, 1949–51. M. R. Coulman created a record by being four years in the Winchester pair and winning the cup for the last three, in 1949 as second string to P. M. Welsh and in 1950 and 1951 as first string to A. D. Myrtle. In 1967–70, Eton surpassed Winchester's record by winning the championship four years in succession, M. J. J. Faber

appearing in three of these victories in 1967 as second string to Lord Wellesley and in 1968 and 1969 as first string with W. R. Boone followed by A. G. Milne. The winning Eton pair in 1970 were R. W. Drysdale and N. H. P. Bacon.

Malvern again produced two brothers, M. W. Nicholls and P. C. Nicholls who won in 1974. In 1975 Malvern won again with P. C. Nicholls and M. A. Tang, beating Harrow (A. C. S. Piggott and P. Greig) by 4 games to 0 in the final. The 1976 final was memorable in that Malvern again with the winning pair of 1975, Nicholls and Tang, led Marlborough by 3 games to 0 in the final. So well did Marlborough (D. K. Watson and M. N. P. Mockridge) fight back that they took the next four games against the holders to win a remarkable match. Radley (J. S. Male and J. P. Snow) were the 1982 winning pair and Tonbridge (G. R. Cowdrey and R. H. Reiss), winning in 1983 and again with A. M. Spurling and R. Owen-Browne in 1984.

Westminster were represented in the championship on eight occasions, the last in 1926. Rossall played once in 1904 and Cheltenham, who were regular participants until the Second World War, have not used their court since, but there are hopes that they will soon be re-starting. R. N. C. Dartmouth entered seven times, the last in 1939, but discontinued when their age of entry was changed.

In 1948, the under-16 singles event for the Incledon-Webber Cup was instituted and in 1966 a further level singles competition for the Renny Cup was added for those not selected for the Foster Cup. In 1963, the under-16 doubles competition started and in 1973 second pairs were able to enter for the Public Schools Doubles Championship and nowadays can also compete for the Professional Association Cup, a competition for second pairs only. Finally in 1981/82, a doubles and singles competition were instituted for under-15 players, the singles for the Jim Dear Cup.

Each of the twelve competing schools with rackets courts has a resident professional, whose job is to coach the boys and to provide racquets and balls and to look after the court. In recent years the Rackets Professional Association, under the direction of Peter Ashford (Winchester), has been responsible for organizing and running the various schools competitions. The popularity and success of school rackets owes much to the dedicated work of the professionals and also to Queen's, who stage these events for a week at Christmas and Easter.

The Radley pair (J. S. Male and J. P. Snow) collect the Cup from
Dick Bridgeman in 1983

It is worth recording some points of interest in connection with public schools rackets. It has been rare for brothers to win the Public Schools Doubles Championship as a pair and on three occasions they have come from Malvern namely:

1892 H. K. Foster and W. L. Foster (Malvern)
1908 M. K. Foster and N. J. A. Foster (Malvern)
1974 M. W. Nicholls and P. C. Nicholls (Malvern)
1980 J. H. C. Mallinson and R. A. C. Mallinson (Wellington)

Pairs that have won the Championship in two successive years have occurred on five occasions, namely:

1871–72 G. A. Webbe and A. A. Hadow (Harrow) at Prince's.
1936–37 P. D. Manners and N. W. Beeson (Malvern) at Queen's.
1940–41 J. K. Drinkall and A. Fairbairn (Haileybury) at Queen's and Wellington.
1944–45 H. E. Webb and G. H. J. Myrtle (Winchester) at Queen's.
1950–51 M. R. Coulman and A. D. Myrtle (Winchester) at Queen's.

There have been only two occasions when a winning pair has been defeated in the final the following year, namely:

1932 R. Pullbrook and J. H. Pawle (Harrow) defeated R. A. Gray and R. F. Lumb by 4 games to 2. The following year Gray and Lumb reversed the result beating Pullbrook and Pawle by 4 games to 2.
1975 P. C. Nicholls and M. A. Tang (Malvern) defeated A. C. S. Piggott and P. Greig (Harrow) by 4 games to 0. The following year they led D. K. Watson and M. N. P. Mockridge (Marlborough) by 3 games to 0 in the final only to lose eventually by 4 games to 3, so well did the Marlburians fight back.

It is not surprising that the Public Schools have produced all the amateur winners of the World Championship, namely:

1862–63 Sir William Hart Dyke (Harrow, before P. S. Championship)
1937–47 D. S. Milford (Rugby pair, 1921–24)
1954–70 G. W. T. Atkins (Rugby pair, 1945)
1972 and 1974–81 W. L. C. Surtees (Rugby pair, 1964–65)
1973 H. R. Angus (Winchester pair, 1962–63)
1981–84 J. A. N. Prenn (Harrow pair, 1971)
1984–   W. R. Boone (Eton pair, 1968)

All these World Champions will have had their first experience of championship competition at The

Queen's Club in the Public Schools Championship.

The following former Amateur Singles Champions also started their championship experience at Queen's:

In 1972 C. J. Swallow presented the Swallow Trophy, a handsome bronze figure of a rackets player standing on a marble plinth for an open under-24 singles championship. This excellent competition to encourage the younger players has taken place at Queen's ever since, with the number of entries increasing each year. An open under-24 doubles competition began at Queen's in 1983 for the Sutton Trophy.

J. R. Thompson and R. M. K. Gracey presented a cup for the over-40s and this doubles competition has taken place at Queen's since 1980. In 1984

the Masters over-40 singles championship first took place for a salver presented by D. M. Norman.

The Noel-Bruce Cup

In the competition for the Noel-Bruce Cup, Rugby's dominance continued after the War when David Milford and P. Kershaw won for seven years in succession. In 1953, John Thompson and Colin Cowdrey at last managed to beat them to give Tonbridge their first success. Rugby won again in 1954 with Cowdrey away playing cricket overseas. However Tonbridge came back to win for the next five years in succession with Thompson partnered by Cowdrey when available, or Richard Gracey.

From 1962–1965, Eton had a four-year run of success with James Leonard, Tom Pugh or David

AMATEUR SINGLES CHAMPIONS

Amateur Champion	Name	School Pair
1888	C. D. Buxton	Harrow 1882–84
1889	E. M. Butler	Harrow 1884–85
1890	P. Ashworth	Harrow 1887
1891	H. Philipson	Eton 1884–85
1892, 1893, 1901	F. Dames-Longworth	Charterhouse 1880–81
1894–1900, 1904	H. K. Foster	Malvern 1889–92
1902	E. H. Miles	Marlborough (not in pair)
1903, 1905, 1908–11, 1920–21, 1923	E. M. Baerlein	Eton 1897–98
1906	Maj. S. H. Sheppard	–
1907	E. B. Noel	Winchester 1897–98
1912–1913	B. S. Foster	Malvern 1898–1900
1914, 1924	H. W. Leatham	Charterhouse 1908
1922, 1931	Hon. C. N. Bruce	Winchester 1903–04
1925	C. C. Pell	U.S.A.
1926–28	J. C. F. Simpson	Rugby 1915–16
1929	C. S. Crawley	Harrow 1920–22
1930, 1935–38, 1950–51	D. S. Milford	Rugby 1921–24
1932–34	I. Akers-Douglas	Eton 1927–28
1939	P. Kershaw	Rugby 1934
1946–49	J. H. Pawle	Harrow 1932–34
1952–53, 1956, 1960, 1963	G. W. T. Atkins	Rugby 1945
1954–55, 1957–59	J. R. Thompson	Tonbridge 1934–37
1961–62, 1965, 1967	J. W. Leonard	Eton 1957–58
1964, 1966, 1968–69	C. J. Swallow	Charterhouse 1954–56
1970–71	M. G. M. Smith	Tonbridge 1959–60
1972–75	H. R. Angus	Winchester 1962–63
1976, 1978, 1981, 1984, 1985	W. R. Boone	Eton 1968
1977	C. J. Hue-Williams	Harrow 1961
1979–80, 1982–83	J. A. N. Prenn	Harrow 1971

Immaculate footwork required – for this and cricket – Colin Cowdrey

Norman. Harrow (Charles Hue Williams and J. Q. Greenstock) had their first success in 1967, followed by Charterhouse's only win in 1968 with Charles Swallow and Mike Hooper. Tonbridge then had a run of six successive years with Richard Gracey and Martin Smith. It was Harrow's turn to win from 1975–78 with a four-year run for Hue Williams and John Prenn. Since 1979 the winners have either been Eton with Willie Boone partnered by either Andrew Milne, David Norman or Tom Pugh, or Harrow with Hue Williams and Prenn.

(See appendix for results and winners table.)

The University Match

Sadly, the prestige of the University Rackets match has declined over the years. This is partly due to the smaller number of public school rackets players going up to Oxford and Cambridge as these universities have steadily decreased the proportion of their entries from independent schools. In addition,

neither Oxford nor Cambridge can nowadays provide facilities for rackets. At Oxford before the First World War there were two courts in Museum Road, two in Pembroke Street and two at the end of Manor Road and Cross Road. These were requisitioned by the army during the First World War and were never restored thereafter. Since then Oxford rackets players have had to rely on the hospitality of Radley College, the nearest available court.

The court at Portugal Place, Cambridge is still in a reasonable state of repair, but since the First World War it has been almost exclusively used for badminton. Occasionally an enthusiastic undergraduate has re-established the game temporarily, but there are no permanent facilities available.

It is not without interest that all the amateur World Champions up to 1981 were former Oxford and Cambridge players, namely: Sir William Hart Dyke (O., 1858–60), D. S. Milford (O., 1926–28), G. W. T. Atkins (C., 1950–51), H. R. Angus (C., 1965–66) and W. J. C. Surtees (O., 1967–69). Of the thirty Amateur Champions, twenty-three were former representatives of Oxford or Cambridge, although in the last ten years the three winners of the Amateur Championship, W. R. Boone, C. J. Hue Williams and J. A. N. Prenn were not former university players. In the early days it was not unusual for a resident undergraduate to win the Amateur Championship. J. W. Leonard, the Amateur Champion in 1961 while still at Oxford, was the last undergraduate to appear in the final. Not only is this indicative of the lower standard of University rackets, but it also points to the general rise in standard of amateur rackets in the last twenty years.

The Services at Queen's

Queen's has always opened its doors to the Services for their rackets championships. The Royal Navy Singles Championship started after the 1914–18 War and was played at The Prince's Club, Knightsbridge until 1939. It was revived after the Second World War at Queen's, but due to lack of entries it was discontinued after 1948. The Royal Naval College, Dartmouth had ended the fourteen-year old entry by then and the two rackets courts have only been used occasionally since. Commander H. F. H. Layman, who did so much to encourage rackets in the Navy, won the Championship six times and probably would have done so more often if his duties at sea had not prevented him.

The Army has played its Rackets Championships at Queen's each year except in 1980, when it was held at the Royal Military Academy, Sandhurst. It was held at Sandhurst that year to celebrate some refurbishment of the one court in use and to promote rackets at the Academy. The Championships returned to The Queen's Club the next year and two real tennis events were introduced to make use of the facilities there. The Army Championships include three rackets events, Singles, Regimental Doubles and Combined Services (past and present). These events have attracted a good entry which in recent years has been consistently higher than that of many amateur competitions. This has been mainly due to the efforts and enthusiasm of firstly Tim Toyne-Sewell and then Barry Aitken when they acted as Secretary in the late 1970s and early 1980s. Both learnt rackets in the Army, Tim Toyne-Sewell with the KOSB and Barry Aitken while instructing at Sandhurst, and they have been encouraging others to follow their example and play in the Championships irrespective of standard ever since. Indeed the Army has always been mindful that it needs to train up rackets players as well as recruit them.

The Army Singles Championship in the 1970s and early 1980s was dominated by two players, Christopher Braithwaite and Mark Nicholls. Between them they won 12 out of the 14 singles competitions between 1972 and 1985. Christopher Braithwaite won seven times ('72, '73, '74, '79, '84, '85) and Mark Nicholls five times ('78, '80, '81, '82 and '83). In that time they played each other in four finals before Mark Nicholls left the Army in 1983. Both players were evenly matched and all but one of their encounters went the full distance. Of the two competitions unaccounted for, Andrew Myrtle won his seventh title in 1976 as a forty-four-year-old Colonel, having won his first in 1955 as a Second Lieutenant. In 1977 David Reed-Felstead beat Andrew Myrtle two months before the latter was promoted to Brigadier. Although David Reed-Felstead has only won the title once he has come close several times and was runner-up in three recent years '82, '84 and '85.

The Regimental Doubles has been one of the principal vehicles for promoting the game within the Army. This is because there is an onus on recognized players to encourage another person in their regiment to learn the game and so form a pair. A recent example of this was Alex Finlayson who gave enough instruction to a newly joined subaltern, Nick Oulton,

to enable the 16th/5th The Queens Royal Lancers to reach the 1985 Semi-Final. Of course some regiments have been fortunate in having a couple of experienced players and there have been some useful pairs. These have included the Blues and Royals (David Reed-Felstead with first David Hardy and then Charles Fraser) 4th/7th Royal Dragoon Guards (Mark Nicholls and Charles Wright), 15th/19th The Kings Royal Hussars (Christopher Brathwaite and Mark Evans), Scots Guards (Ian Mackay-Dick and Campbell Gordon), Kings Own Scottish Borderers (Andrew Myrtle and Tim Toyne-Sewell) and the Royal Green Jackets (Alistair Drew and Peter Chamberlin). In the past the Royal Artillery have had some good pairs but they have had a lean spell in the '70s and '80s without an experienced player. The Royal Engineers have had a good record in this event with pairs headed by Malcolm Maclagan, Richard Beasley and lastly Ian Dobbie and John Woollen. The standard of this competition is usually lower than the Combined Services event but the 15th/19th had the achievement of winning both cups in 1980.

THE FAITHFUL, OLD AND YOUNG

The main feature of the Combined Services event is that it has attracted a wide, interesting and high-quality entry over the years. Faithful support for the competition has come from Roger Crosby, who completed National Service in the Royal Army Service Corps before becoming rackets professional at Harrow School, Jonathan Edwardes, the present secretary of The Queen's Club, ex-Gurkha and ex-Army Rackets Champion and Lord Simon Reading. Dick Bridgeman also played each year while President of the Army Tennis and Rackets Association. The Royal Navy and the Royal Air Force have both entered pairs in the event, the former more frequently than the latter. Royal Navy players have included Bruce Trentham, James Luard and Charles Banner. The RAF pair Nick Meredith and Jerry Greville-Heygate reached the 1985 Quarter-Final. However, the event has recently been dominated by Geoffrey Atkins and Tom Pugh who won in '82, '83 and '84 until losing to Paul and Mark Nicholls in '85.

The Army has enjoyed a long acquaintance with Queen's and looks forward to holding future Army Rackets and Real Tennis Championship there. The Club has provided their facilities for an enjoyable week, many Army players have actually learnt their rackets there, and it has consequently helped to widen the interest in the game. Playing the Rackets Championship at Queen's has promoted the game of rackets not least because of the press coverage provided by *The Times* and *Telegraph* correspondents who can travel there easily.

The Professionals Today

The contribution to the game of the Club's rackets professionals has been inestimable. Norwood Cripps, now at Eton, was Senior Rackets Professional at Queen's from 1962–79 and he was Professional Rackets Champion from 1977–79 and in 1981 and 1983. Terry Whatley, trained at Marlborough and Professional Champion in 1980 and now at Clifton was also apprenticed at Queen's. The present Professional Champion, Neil Smith, is now the Queen's Rackets Professional and he is fully upholding the distinguished record of his predecessors together with Peter Ellis at Haileybury and Peter Ashford at Winchester, who also served their apprenticeships at Queen's. Amateur players over the years are forever indebted to these men whose loyal service to the Club in and around the rackets court, supplying rackets and balls, has too often gone unsung.

At Random with Tom Pugh

Whether playing rackets or real tennis Peter Kershaw, a champion at both games, wore the same outfit; long, baggy khaki trousers, shoes laced with black real tennis gut – 'It doesn't slip loose' – and with a red handkerchief with white spots hanging out of his pocket.

In the rackets court he had a distinct ritual when about to serve from the backhand court. First, he would prowl away from the service box usually towards the front wall. He would then turn round, tap his racket on the floor and scowl at his opponent. Finally he would return to the service box, tap his racket again and look over his shoulder at the man about to receive service. The day of reckoning came when Kershaw and Milford met John Thompson and a young Richard Gracey in the final of the Noel-Bruce Cup. Thompson took the backhand court and quietly said to Gracey, 'When Kershaw serves you the first serve of the match I want you to go up to the service line and stand there.'

Kershaw then begins his ritual and on his return from his meandering finds himself scowling not at an opponent at the back of the court but one standing practically in the opposite service box. This throws him. He looks again and can't believe his eyes. He skips a couple of paces, taps his racket and looks again. At last he serves plumb into Gracey's racket. Gracey volleys it straight past him. For years Kershaw's serve from the backhand court had been regarded as a lethal stroke and here was some young idiot volleying it. Needless to say, Thompson and Gracey won.

Thompson, eleven times Amateur Doubles Champion, revolutionized the doubles game. He was the first person to work out that you actually won doubles by not losing points rather than by positively winning them except, of course, from the service box. He realized that you do not win with brilliant shots but by getting everything back, by covering your partner and, when one or other is beaten, by scooping the ball off the back wall. That was something none of us, I am sure, was taught at school. If Thompson made more than half a dozen unforced errors in a match it was something exceptional.

Dick Bridgeman, never more than a good club player, once bet Kenneth Wagg, a pre-war Amateur doubles champion, £250 that with Geoffrey Atkins he could beat any pair Wagg liked to nominate. Wagg chose the current doubles champions, James Leonard and Charles Swallow, but farmed out his bet whereas Bridgeman kept the whole of his stake. The match, by the way, was staged for charity. Dick and Geoffrey won 4–1. It was Dick's brilliance that knocked Leonard and Swallow off court. It was astounding stuff. No one had ever seen him play like it before or since. Geoffrey played the perfect second string role.

Over the past twenty or so years Charles Hue Williams has been Mr Doubles. First he got Leonard out of retirement to win the Amateur twice in 1967 and 1968. Then he won with Howard Angus twice in the early seventies, once serving over thirty aces in the final. He won with Atkins in 1974 and since then has been successful with Johnny Prenn. Charles's weakness is lack of mobility though he has always been superbly fit. If you could, or can, make him run then he is at a disadvantage. But he has a very cool temperament.

There is, of course, another way of playing doubles, as Jim Dear once showed – others have done the same – in a pro-am. He was playing with an American, Dave Pearson from Chicago; a tremendous enthusiast but possessed of a very bad temperament on court. He got so wild that he threw his racket into the gallery and he and Jim soon found themselves down three games. At the end of the third game Jim took him aside and said 'Mr Pearson, do you want to win this match?' 'Hell, sure I'm very keen to win – very keen,' came the answer. To which Jim replied 'Well, Mr Pearson, if you stand by the door I think we'll have a much better chance.' They won 4–3.

Jim came into rackets a strange way. Back in the pre-war days when he was a ball-boy there was a competition for junior professionals. The senior pros

'Mr Doubles' – Charles Hue Williams

used to get £25 for entering a junior and Charles Read, then senior pro at Queen's, did not have a junior to enter. He noticed Dear and said 'Jim, I've entered you for the Junior Rackets Championship.' Jim replied 'I've never played rackets, Mr Read'. 'Never mind, here's a racket and some balls, get onto court and start practising.' This Jim did for a few days by himself until someone asked him for a game. That was the only time he was on court with anyone else until the competition began.

Jim beat all the other young professionals and later on that inspired him to claim that the most important part of one's training is actually done in the court on one's own. That was his policy when he first taught me squash when I was nine and for a couple of years when he was at Eton and I was a boy there. He would come into court and spend about ten minutes showing you how to serve or kill the ball off the back wall. He would then retire and let you get on with it for about twenty minutes. Essentially you had to do the work yourself.

The one snag to this method was that you cannot learn to take service and Jim found this when first he played the American Ken Chantler. The whole match was a series of service runs. Eventually, in 1947, he beat Chantler for the World Championship and then came up against John Pawle, the amateur champion. Pawle was a beautiful stylist, a wonderful stroke producer, but his great failing was a lack of stamina. He used to slow down the play by walking about, almost bringing the game to a grinding halt. My father used to criticize him for this. But in one of their matches he did give Jim Dear some trouble until he ran out of steam.

I only saw David Milford play singles near the end of his career but did play against him and Thompson in the final of the Amateur Doubles. That was the last time they played together while I was playing with Richard Gracey. The gamesmanship that was going on was way above our league. It seemed that Milford not only had the referee on his side but knew how to play all the tricks. To youngsters like Richard and I it was frustrating. Milford may have been a hitter in his earlier days but he became a spoiler while Thompson never made a mistake. They had worked out that you win a doubles rally by being the last person to make a mistake; not the first person to make a winner.

The match, in our opinion, turned when we were one game-all and 12-all. I was serving to Milford in the backhand court. I served an ace. Milford,

Veteran antagonists – Boone and Randall Crawley versus Prenn and Charles Hue Williams

knowing he couldn't return it, called 'Fault'. The referee gave it as a fault and they put us out. They won the game and the match. I consider that brilliant gamesmanship though at the time we felt we'd been cheated. But a final of the championship is not just a matter of beautiful play. Gamesmanship and cunning come into big events.

The two champion gamesmen were, in my opinion, Milford and James Leonard. James was so good at it that, in the end, people read things into his play that never existed. It all began with his first major *coup* in the final of the Public Schools singles. The court was damp and he was losing to Peter Rylands when he suddenly stopped and asked for the court to be swept, which it was. This was good thinking for a sixteen-year-old and it took all the steam out of Rylands' game. That story had become folklore by the time James began his career in the senior game.

Some years later Leonard met Miles Connell in the final of the Amateur Singles. In an earlier match I noticed that Connell footfaulted when serving from the forehand box. I mentioned this to James, who timed his trap perfectly. They had just finished their

knock-up and were about to begin the match when James went across to Connell and said, 'Oh, Miles, incidentally when I was watching you yesterday I noticed you footfaulted all the time from the forehand court.' The result was that Connell spent much of the first game, which he lost, looking at his foot instead of concentrating on his serve. Not surprisingly he lost the match.

James and I used to sit at home, drinking my father's claret, and discuss tactics. For instance, everyone prefers to knock up second before a match. We found the thing to do if you lost the toss was to get lost in the clubhouse; to stand by the fire or in the bar talking to some respected people. When the opponents had finished their knock-up and were ready to start, you were not there. They had to come looking for us and, seeing us talking to senior people, could hardly complain.

Then there was the taking of lets. We would always look for a let when serving as it gave us another chance of an ace. If we couldn't get the quick serve and kill, or we were pushed onto the defensive, or it was an even rally, we would look for a let.

Partners. Willie Boone and Tom Pugh, winners of the 1984 Noel-Bruce Cup

Comparing the leading post-war players, the world champions, is not easy and I'm inclined to go for Jim Dear as the best of them. He had such wonderful control of the ball. He could play a stop volley, a drop shot, a reverse angle – shots you expect to see in a squash court – from anywhere. Geoffrey Atkins had a wonderful forehand and could kill your best shot stone dead but he had a definite weakness deep in the backhand court, though it was terribly difficult to exploit it.

I recall when he was playing Charles Swallow for the World title he asked me to give him some practice before the second leg – the first had been in Chicago – at Queen's. We had about three sessions and all he wanted was for me to serve to his backhand court. In a week he taught himself to take serve up court on the volley. That was the measure of his great ability to adapt. He never appeared to move in a hurry and had marvellous anticipation. My father always said we never saw Geoffrey within four or five points of his peak because there was nobody to stretch him that far.

Willie Surtees had a backhand almost in the same class as Atkins's forehand but he never bothered to develop a killing service. The fact that New York was his home court did not help. It is difficult to serve in that court because the ball comes off the back wall; it is impossible to bring the ball down. So Surtees just concentrated on improving his stroke production in the rallies.

I'm sure Geoffrey Atkins would have beaten Surtees. I think John Prenn and Willie Boone would have done so too. They are so fit and have an almost professional approach to the game. They must play more than any of their predecessors. Howard Angus, a terrific player seeing he didn't play very much, did take the World title off Surtees one year. Howard got to anything and could turn on a sixpence.

There are far more people today playing rackets to a higher standard then there were twenty-five to thirty years ago. The polythene ball has helped enormously; a faster, truer game. When I came out of the Navy in the 1950s there was hardly anyone to play with, apart from brother Tim and our cousins,

Peter and Roger Eckersley. Then Dick Bridgeman joined us and with the help of people like David Scholey and Jack Hurley the Queen's weekend was born. Now they have Monday night sessions when any duffer can come along and learn the game. That is a huge step forward.

It must all be very different from the old days; the days of Peter Latham, for instance. He was never beaten and they say he could give H. K. Foster, often regarded as the greatest amateur in the old days, five points a game and beat him. Shortly before he died Tim and I visited Peter Latham, then in his eighties. He was perched up in bed with a bundle of pillows. A light hung from the ceiling and he wore a shade to keep it out of his eyes. His talk was rambling and he said 'An extraordinary thing happened this morning. I was going down to Brighton to play an exhibition with Punch Fairs. I got myself to the station and was standing on the platform when I realized I was in my pyjamas.'

SQUASH
1946–1986

APART from Queen's winning the Bath Club Cup in the 1947–8 season, the post-war game there did not flourish until the 1970s. The condition of the courts became worse during the war, as Frank Strawson continued to point out, and with all the post-war restrictions there was little that could be done about it. Strawson never lived to see the courts as they now are – strip lighting, false ceilings. He died while playing a match in Court 3.

The 1947–8 season did at least mark the card when the ageless Macpherson led a winning team that included Alan Seymour-Haydon, John Peake and Maurice Baring. In beating the Army and Navy Club, the United Service Club, the RAC and the Bath Club, Queen's dropped only two rubbers. In the deciding rubber of the last match, against the Bath Club, Macpherson beat Roger Pulbrook 9–3 5–9 3–9 9–2 9–3. Some claimed that this was his hundredth rubber for the Club in this competition.

It was not until the 1960s and the arrival of Robert Dolman from Oxford University that the Club began to prosper competitively. His first and lasting impression of the game at Queen's is of the courts – 'Certainly not to everyone's taste and almost universally disliked by our opponents. Despite some renovations they managed to retain their character and a certain eccentricity which those who played on them regularly came to appreciate and enjoy.' Dolman had experienced cold courts while at Magdalen College, Oxford, but they were nothing like Queen's – 'a unique combination of the Arctic, white dust and the pitch black void provided by the old rackets court setting'. The lob and the dropshot were effective shots, both of them being devalued on hot courts. Understandably the Club enjoyed playing at home whereas the visitors hated it.

Queen's, claims Dolman, had another advantage in having Sidney Upton as marker. Though a very useful squash professional in his time – he beat John Stokes in the 1947 Amateur *v* Professionals match – Upton was at the Club primarily as a lawn tennis professional. He was certainly not a professional marker. He took on the job as there was no one else to do it and never really mastered it. Though fair and courteous he would let out a shout in the middle of a rally and then deny having made a sound. Generally that seemed to work in the Club's favour. Afterwards he would join the teams for supper.

WILLIE'S BIRDS

The Bath Club Cup involved a higher standard of hospitality and entertainment than was normal and Queen's was in no position to match that of other clubs. The catering was poor. The staff left before suppertime and on one occasion the teams found waiting for them enough chicken soup for forty people and nothing else. On another occasion the Club managed to poison the opposition. The catering improved when Willie Boone joined the team, and shot and cooked his own pheasants for the team suppers. It was claimed that Dolman played Boone at second string rather than himself in order 'to keep him sweet'.

When he joined the team Dolman replaced Humphrey Truman in a side captained by Dennis Hughes. The latter was a virtuoso, especially on cold courts, until he suffered a stroke and had to retire. Dolman can only recall Hughes losing one home match – to Jeremy Lyon, then England's No. 1. John Ward known as 'Ward the Tennis' as distinct from the other John Ward, was the third member and the side were regular runners-up to the Lansdowne. When Hughes retired Dolman and Ward were joined by Philip Ayton, who later became England's No. 1 and winner of a record seventy-six caps. Like Hughes he became a master on the Club courts. Occasionally supplemented by Truman and Howard Angus, this team won the Bath Club Cup in the 1971–2 season and in two of the next three seasons.

In the mid-seventies Ayton began to reduce his playing and the Club were lucky enough to recruit Johnny Leslie who took over as England's leading amateur, becoming No. 1. in 1976 and holding that position until the game went open in 1980. 'Ward the Tennis' played less too and Willie Boone, currently the World Rackets Champion, replaced him. The left-handed Boone was a different type of player from the others, exploding the idea that only touch players thrived at Queen's. He hit harder than anyone else and went on winning. Boone, Leslie and Dolman won the Cup in 1976–7 and 1977–8.

During these successful years others were occasionally drafted into the side, players such as Roger Taylor, who had a surprisingly delicate touch, Buster Mottram, very fit and competitive and Jim Moore, not very fit but entertaining.

When Leslie first joined the Club in 1973 he found the courts not only cold but 'quirky'. Recently the approach to No. 2 court has been over rubble and debris and one opposing team had to run the gauntlet of missiles thrown over the wall by dwellers in nearby council houses. Nevertheless during his years the Club has been so successful and so strong that a second team has been competing in the Bath Club Cup and, one season, reached the top division. The current side, Leslie, Boone and Tom Candy, are the Cup-holders and one reason for that may be that each member agreed to pay the others five pounds for every rubber he lost. Since then none has recorded a single defeat! Queen's have now won the Bath Club Cup sixteen times, more than any other Club including the RAC, who have recorded fifteen wins.

Jonathan Leslie – leading amateur from 1976 to 1980

APPENDIX A
QUEEN'S CLUB PRESIDENTS
1887–1986

1887–1888	The Rt. Hon. the Earl of Wharncliffe
1888–1889	The Rt. Hon. the Earl of Jersey
1889–1890	The Rt. Hon. the Earl of Clarendon
1890–1891	The Rt. Hon. the Lord Windsor
1891–1892	W. H. Grenfell Esq
1892–1893	The Rt. Hon. the Earl of Londesborough
1893–1894	The Rt. Hon. the Earl of Londesborough
1894–1895	The Rt. Hon the Earl of Dalkeith
1895–1896	The Rt. Hon. the Viscount Curzon, M.P.
1896–1897	The Rt. Hon. the Viscount Curzon, M.P.
1897–1898	The Rt. Hon. the Lord Wenlock, G.C.I.E.
1898–1899	The Most Hon. the Marquess of Granby
1899–1900	The Most Hon. the Marquess of Granby
1900–1901	The Rt. Hon. the Earl of Chesterfield
1901–1902	The Rt. Hon. the Earl of Chesterfield
1902–1912	The Rt. Hon. the Lord Alverstone, G.C.M.G.
1912–1915	The Rt. Hon. the Lord Alverstone, G.C.M.G.
1915–1930	The Rt. Hon. the Earl of Balfour, K.G.
1930–1938	H. R. H. Prince Arthur of Connaught, K.G.
1939–1957	Major General the Earl of Athlone, K.G.
1957–1962	His Grace the Duke of Devonshire, M.C.
1963–1981	His Honour Judge Carl D. Aarvold, O.B.E., T.D.
1981–1984	R. J. Ritchie Esq
1984–	A. J. H. Ward Esq

The Rt. Hon. the Earl of
Wharncliffe

The Rt. Hon. the Earl of
Jersey

The Rt. Hon. the Earl of
Clarendon

The Rt. Hon. the Lord
Windsor

W. H. Grenfell Esq

The Rt. Hon. the Earl of
Londesborough

The Rt. Hon. the Earl of
Dalkeith

The Rt. Hon. the Viscount
Curzon, M.P.

The Rt. Hon. the Lord
Wenlock, G.C.I.E.

The Rt. Hon. the Marquess
of Granby

The Rt. Hon. the Earl of
Chesterfield

The Rt. Hon. the Lord
Alverstone, G.C.M.G.

The Rt. Hon. the Earl of
Balfour, K.G.

H. R. H. Prince Arthur of
Connaught, K.G.

Major General the Earl of
Athlone, K.G.

His Grace the Duke of
Devonshire, M.C.

His Honour Judge Carl D.
Aarvold, O.B.E., T.D.

R. J. Ritchie, Secretary
1939–74, President 1981–85

A. J. H. Ward, Chairman
1978–80, President 1985–

APPENDIX B

GENERAL COMMITTEE
CHAIRMEN
1949–1986

1	year to Annual General Meeting 1949:	Nigel Sharpe
1	year to Annual General Meeting 1950:	Sir Gerald Hargreaves
1	year to Annual General Meeting 1951:	Nigel Sharpe
1	year to Annual General Meeting 1952:	Sir Gerald Hargreaves
2	years to Annual General Meeting 1954:	Nigel Sharpe
1	year to Annual General Meeting 1955:	Lt. Col. P. W. Le Gros
7	years to Annual General Meeting 1962:	Nigel Sharpe
3	years to Annual General Meeting 1965:	Dr. R. J. Sandys
3	years to Annual General Meeting 1968:	N. Berryman M.B.E.
3	years to Annual General Meeting 1971:	Dr. R. J. Sandys
2½	years to decease	N. Berryman O.B.E.
3	years to Annual General Meeting 1977:	H. C. Bernstein
3	years to Annual General Meeting 1980:	A. J. H. Ward
3	years to Annual General Meeting 1983:	I. McG. Boden
	To date	B. C. Palmer

CHAMPIONSHIP AND TOURNAMENT RECORDS

CONTENTS

Davis Cup: 1905–1974

1905 USA beat France 5–0
H. Ward (USA) beat M. Germot 6–2, 6–2, 6–1;
beat M. Decugis 6–2, 6–2, 6–1.
W. J. Clothier (USA) beat Germot 6–3, 5–7, 6–1,
6–3; beat Decugis 6–3, 6–4, 6–4.
Ward and B. C. Wright (USA) beat Decugis and
Germot 6–2, 6–2, 6–2.

1905 Australasia beat Austria 5–0
N. E. Brookes (Australasia) beat R. Kinzl 6–0,
6–1, 6–2; beat C. von Wessely 6–0, 6–2, 6–2.
A. F. Wilding (Australasia) beat Kinzl 6–3, 4–6,
6–2, 6–4; beat von Wessely 4–6, 6–3, 7–5,
6–1.
Brookes and A. W. Dunlop (Australasia) beat
Kinzl and von Wessely 9–7, 6–3, 7–5.

1905 USA beat Australasia 5–0 in Final Round
B. C. Wright (USA) beat N. E. Brookes 12–10,
5–7, 12–10, 6–4; beat A. F. Wilding 6–3, 6–3
(best of three).
W. A. Larned (USA) beat Brookes 14–12, 6–0,
6–3; beat Wilding 6–3, 6–2, 6–4.
H. Ward and Wright (USA) beat Brookes and
A. W. Dunlop 6–4, 7–5, 5–7, 6–2.

1913 Canada beat South Africa 4–1
R. B. Powell (Canada) beat R. F. Le Sueur 6–3,
6–4, 3–6, 7–5; beat V. R. Gauntlett ret.
B. O. Schwengers (Canada) beat Le Sueur 6–3,
6–3, 6–3; lost to Gauntlett 9–11, 3–6, 0–6.
Powell and Schwengers (Canada) beat
Gauntlett and Le Sueur 7–5, 6–3, 3–6, 6–3.

1930 Great Britain beat Germany 3–2
H. W. Austin (GB) beat D. D. Prenn 6–3, 6–4,
7–5; lost to H. Landmann 3–6, 6–8, 7–5, 6–4,
4–6.
H. G. N. Lee (GB) beat Landmann 5–7, 6–3,
6–2, 6–3; lost to Prenn 4–6, 9–7, 3–6, 2–6.
J. C. Gregory and I. G. Collins (GB) beat
H. Kleinschroth and W. Dessart 6–2, 6–4,
6–3.

1933 Great Britain beat Finland 5–0
F. J. Perry (GB) beat B. Grotenfelt 6–0, 6–3, 6–1;
beat A. Grahn 6–1, 6–2, 6–4.
H. W. Austin (GB) beat Grahn 6–0, 6–2, 6–2;
beat Grotenfelt 6–0, 6–1, 6–4.
Perry and G. P. Hughes (GB) beat Grahn and
Grotenfelt 6–1, 6–1, 6–3

1933 Australia beat South Africa 3–2
J. H. Crawford (Australia) beat V. G. Kirby 8–6,
6–1, 6–3; beat C. J. J. Robbins 6–4, 6–1, 6–0.
V. B. McGrath (Australia) beat Robbins 7–5, 6–4,
4–6, 10–8; lost to Kirby 8–6, 0–6, 4–6, 2–6.
Crawford and McGrath (Australia) lost to Kirby
and N. G. Farquharson 4–6, 4–6, 4–6.

1968 Great Britain beat Finland 5–0
M. J. Sangster (GB) beat P. Saila 6–4, 8–6, 6–4;
beat P. Peterson-Dyggve 7–5, 6–2, 6–2.
M. Cox (GB) beat Peterson-Dyggve 6–2, 6–4,
6–0; beat Saila 6–4, 4–6, 6–1, 6–4.
R. K. Wilson and P. R. Hutchins (GB) beat Saila
and H. Hedman 6–1, 6–2, 6–1.

1974 Great Britain beat Iran 5–0 (*played on covered
courts*)
R. Taylor (GB) beat M. Bahrani 6–0, 6–0, 6–2;
beat A. Madani 6–1, 6–3, 6–1.
J. M. Lloyd (GB) beat Madani 6–1, 7–5, 6–2;
beat Bahrani 7–5, 7–5, 6–4.
Lloyd and M. J. Farrell (GB) beat Madani and
K. Javan 6–1, 6–1, 6–1.

King's Cup: 1962

1962 Jugoslavia beat Great Britain 3–2
N. Pilic (Jugoslavia) lost to J. A. Pickard 4–6,
8–10; lost to M. J. Sangster 5–7, 4–6.
B. Jovanovic (Jugoslavia) beat Pickard 6–2, 6–0;
beat Sangster 8–6, 6–1.
Jovanovic and Pilic beat Pickard and
Sangster 6–2, 6–2, 7–5.

Federation Cup: 1963

1st Round

Australia beat Belgium 3–0; Miss M. Smith bt. Miss
C. Mercelis 6–3, 6–1; Miss J. Lehane bt. Miss
E. Bellens 6–0, 6–3; Miss Smith and Miss L. Turner
bt. Miss Mercelis and Miss M. Marechal 6–1, 6–0.

Hungary beat Denmark 3–0: Mrs S. Kormoczy bt. Miss
P. Balling 6–4, 6–0; Mrs I. Brosmann bt. Mrs
V. Johansen 7–5, 6–4; Mrs Brosmann and Mrs
K. Bardoczy bt. Miss Balling and Mrs Johansen 6–2,
3–6, 6–3.

South Africa beat Czechoslovakia 2–1; Miss
R. Schuurman lost to Mrs V. Sukova 3–6, 6–2, 6–8;
Miss M. Hunt bt. Miss M. Prochova 6–2, 6–2; Miss
Schurrman and Miss Hunt bt. Mrs Sukova and
Miss Prochova 6–3, 6–2.

France beat Germany 2–1; Miss F. Durr lost to Miss E. Buding 3–6, 4–6; Miss J. Lieffrig bt. Miss M. Dittmeyer 6–3, 4–6, 6–2; Miss Durr and Miss Lieffrig bt. Miss Buding and Miss R. Ostermann 6–3, 6–3.

Austria beat Norway 2–1: Miss S. Pachta bt. Miss L. Paldan 6–3, 6–2; Miss A. Winkler lost to Miss R. Hankeres 4–6, 3–6; Miss Pachta and Miss E. Hardy bt. Miss Paldan and Miss T. Schirmer 6–3, 6–3.

Great Britain beat Canada 3–0: Mrs P. F. Jones bt. Miss A. Barclay 6–0, 6–1; Miss C. C. Truman bt. Mrs L. Browne 8–6, 6–3; Mrs Jones and Miss Truman bt. Miss Barclay and Mrs Browne 6–1, 6–3.

Netherlands beat Switzerland 3–0: Mrs E. de Jong-Duldig bt. Mrs A. Wavre 6–1, 6–4; Mrs J. Ridderhof-Seven bt. Miss J. Bourgnon 8–6, 6–4; Mrs de Jong-Duldig and Mrs Ridderhof-Seven bt. Miss Bourgnon and Miss A. M. Studer 6–1, 6–3.

United States beat Italy 3–0: Miss D. R. Hard bt. Miss L. Pericoli 6–4, 3–6, 6–2; Miss B. J. Moffitt bt. Miss S. Lazzarino 6–8, 6–1, 6–2; Miss Hard and Miss C. Caldwell bt. Miss Pericoli and Miss Lazzarino 6–4, 6–1.

2nd Round

Australia beat Hungary 3–0: Miss Smith bt. Mrs Kormoczy 6–0, 6–1; Miss Lehane bt. Mrs Brosmann 6–1, 6–2; Miss Smith and Miss Turner bt. Mrs Brosmann and Mrs Bardoczy 6–1, 6–1.

South Africa beat France 3–0: Miss Schuurman bt. Miss Durr 6–3, 3–6, 6–3; Miss Hunt bt. Miss Lieffrig 6–4, 5–7, 6–2; Miss Schuurman and Miss Hunt bt. Miss Durr and Miss Lieffrig 7–5, 6–1.

Great Britain beat Austria 3–0: Miss Truman bt. Miss Pachta 6–2, 6–1; Miss D. M. Catt bt. Miss Winkler 6–2, 6–3; Mrs Jones and Miss Truman bt. Miss Pachta and Miss Herdy 6–1, 6–0.

United States beat Netherlands 3–0: Miss Hard bt. Mrs. de Jong-Duldig 6–2, 6–2; Miss Moffitt bt. Mrs Ridderhof-Seven 6–2, 6–2; Miss Moffitt and Miss Caldwell bt. Mrs de Jong-Duldig and Mrs Ridderhof-Seven 6–0, 6–3.

Semi-Final

Australia beat South Africa 3–0: Miss Smith bt. Miss Schuurman 6–3, 6–2; Miss Lehane bt. Miss Hunt 4–6, 9–7, 6–1; Miss Smith and Miss Turner bt. Miss Schuurman and Miss Hunt 5–7, 6–3, 6–3.

United States beat Great Britain 3–0: Miss Hard bt. Mrs Jones 6–2, 6–4; Miss Moffitt bt. Miss Truman 6–3, 3–6, 6–4; Miss Hard and Miss Caldwell bt. Mrs Jones and Miss Truman 2–6, 9–7, 6–3.

Final

United States beat Australia 2–1: Miss Hard lost to Miss Smith 3–6, 0–6; Miss Moffitt bt. Miss Turner 5–7, 6–0, 6–3; Miss Hard and Miss Moffitt bt. Miss Smith and Miss Turner 3–6, 13–11, 6–3.

Maureen Connolly Cup (21 and Under International): 1985

USA beat GB 6–5   (GB Names first)

Miss S. Gomer bt Miss J. Holden 6–0, 6–1; lost Miss T. Phelps 4–6, 7–5, 3–6

Miss A. Brown lost Miss Phelps 2–6, 3–6; bt Miss Holdern 6–3, 4–6, 6–3

Miss S. Reeves lost Miss A. Hulbert 7–5, 5–7, 4–6; bt Miss R. Reis 6–3, 4–6, 6–2

Miss J. Louis lost Miss Reis 6–4, 5–7, 0–6; bt Miss Hulbert 6–2, 6–2

Miss J. Wood lost Miss W. Wood 6–7, 3–6

Miss J. Wood and Miss Louis lost Miss Hulbert and Miss Reis 6–4, 5–7, 2–6

Miss Brown and Miss Gomer bt Miss Phelps and Miss W. Wood 6–4, 7–6.

London Grass Court Championships

MEN'S SINGLES: 1890–1985

	WINNER	RUNNER–UP
1890	H. S. Barlow	W. Baddeley
1891	H. S. Barlow	J. Pim
1892	E. W. Lewis	J. Pim
1893	J. Pim	H. S. Mahony
1894	H. S. Mahony	H. S. Barlow
1895	H. S. Barlow	H. S. Mahony
1896	H. S. Mahony	R. F. Doherty
1897	H. L. Doherty	M. J. G. Ritchie
1898	H. L. Doherty	H. S. Mahony
1899	H. S. Mahony	A. W. Gore
1900	A. W. Gore	A. W. Lavy
1901	C. P. Dixon	G. Greville
1902	M. J. G. Ritchie	G. M. Simond
1903	G. Greville	G. M. Simond
1904	M. J. G. Ritchie	H. S. Mahony
1905	H. Ward	B. C. Wright
1906	M. J. G. Ritchie	J. M. Flavelle
1907	A. F. Wilding	M. J.G. Ritchie

1908	K. Powell	M. J. G. Richie
1909	M. J. G. Ritchie	H. K. Parker
1910	A. F. Wilding	M. J. G. Ritchie
1911	A. F. Wilding	A. E. Beamish
1912	A. F. Wilding	O. Froitzheim
1913	F. G. Lowe	W. F. Johnson
1914	F. G. Lowe	P. M. Davson
1919	P. O'Hara Wood	L. Raymond
1920	W. M. Johnston	W. T. Tilden
1921	Z. Shimidzu	M. Sleem
1922	H. G. Mayes	D. M. Greig
1923	V. Richards	S. M. Jacob
1924	A. R. F. Kingscote	F. G. Lowe
1925	F. G. Lowe	H. G. Mayes
1926	H. G. Mayes	F. G. Lowe
1927	H. G. Mayes	D. M. Evans
1928	W. T. Tilden	F. T. Hunter
1929	W. T. Tilden and F. T. Hunter divided	
1930	W. L. Allison	G. S. Mangin
1931	J. S. Olliff	E. R. Avory
1932	J. H. Crawford	H. Timmer
1933	E. Vines and L. R. Stoefen divided	
1934	S. B. Wood	F. X. Shields
1935	D. N. Jones and W. L. Allison divided	
1936	J. D. Budge	D. N. Jones
1937	J. D. Budge	H. W. Austin
1938	H. W. Austin	Kho Sin Kie
1939	G. von Cramm	G. Mahommed
1946	P. Segura	D. Pails
1947	R. Falkenburg	C. F. Long
1948	R. Falkenburg and E. W. Sturgess divided	
1949	F. R. Schroeder	G. Mulloy
1950	J. E. Bromwich	A. Larsen
1951	E. W. Sturgess	F. A. Sedgman
1952	F. A. Sedgman	M. G. Rose
1953	L. A. Hoad	K. R. Rosewall
1954	L. A. Hoad	M. G. Rose
1955	K. R. Rosewall	L. A. Hoad
1956	N. A. Fraser	K. R. Rosewall
1957	A. J. Cooper	N. A. Fraser
1958	M. J. Anderson	R. Mark
1959	R. Krishnan	N. A. Fraser
1960	A. Gimeno	R. S. Emerson
1961	R. A. J. Hewitt	C. R. McKinley
1962	R. G. Laver	R. S. Emerson
1963	R. S. Emerson	O. K. Davidson
1964	R. S. Emerson	T. Lejus
1965	R. S. Emerson w.o.	R. D. Ralston scr.
1966	R. S. Emerson w.o.	A. D. Roche scr.
1967	J. D. Newcombe	R. Taylor
1968	T. S. Okker and C. E. Graebner divided	
1969	F. S. Stolle	J. D. Newcombe
1970	R. G. Laver	J. D. Newcombe
1971	S. R. Smith	J. D. Newcombe
1972	J. S. Connors	J. G. Paish
1973	I. Nastase	R. Taylor
1974	no meeting	
1975	no meeting	
1976	no meeting	
1977	R. Ramirez	M. Cox
1978	A. D. Roche	J. P. McEnroe
1979	J. P. McEnroe	V. Pecci
1980	J. P. McEnroe	K. G. Warwick
1981	J. P. McEnroe	B. E. Gottfried
1982	J. S. Connors	J. P. McEnroe
1983	J. S. Connors	J. P. McEnroe
1984	J. P. McEnroe	L. Shiras
1985	B. Becker	J. Kriek

MEN'S DOUBLES: 1903–1985

	WINNERS	RUNNERS-UP
1903	G. Greville and M. J. G. Ritchie	J. M. Flavelle and G. L. Orme
1904	R. F. Doherty and W. V. Eaves	G. Greville and 'D. A. Mann'
1905	W. A. Larned and W. J. Clothier	H. Ward and B. C. Wright
1906	T. M. Mavrogordato and E. Gwynne Evans	F. G. Lowe and A. H. Lowe
1907	A. F. Wilding and N. E. Brookes	R. F. Doherty and W. V. Eaves
1908	M. J. G. Ritchie and A. D. Prebble	G. A. Thomas and R. J. McNair
1909	A. W. Gore and H. Roper Barrett	T. R. Quill and H. A. Parker
1910	M. J. G. Ritchie and A. F. Wilding	T. M. Mavrogordato and C. P. Dixon
1911	M. J. G. Ritchie and C. P. Dixon	H. Kleinschroth and F. W. Rahe
1912	J. C. Parke and A. E. Beamish	C. P. Dixon and H. Roper Barrett
1913	F. W. Rahe and H. Kleinschroth	C. Tindell Green and J. E. H. Zimmerman
1914	A. F. Wilding and N. E. Brookes	P. M. Davson and W. C. Crawley
1919	N. E. Brookes and G. L. Patterson–	C. E. Lyle and W. A. Ingram divided
1920	W. M. Johnson and W. T. Tilden	R. N. Williams and C. S. Garland
1921	'Dixie' and A. M. Lovibond	Z. Shimidzu and C. P. Dixon
1922	The Hon. F. M. B. Fisher and H. Hunt	J. J. Lezard and D. R. Rutnam
1923	H. A. Carless and C. P. Luck	E. F. Busby and E. G. Serin
1924	A. C. Chappelow and S. H. Young	D. J. Wardley and J. E. Dunning

1925	G. C. Golding and D. J. Wardley	H. W. Backhouse and R. de Quetteville	
1926	A. H. Cattaruzza and W. Robson	Col. A. Berger and Major R. Bernard	
1927	T. Harada and Y. Ohta	B. Hillyard and A. Wallis Myers	
1928	W. T. Tilden and F. T. Hunter	J. H. Crawford and H. C. Hopman	
1929	W. T. Tilden and F. T. Hunter	W. L. Allison and J. van Ryn	
1930	G. W. Lott and J. H. Doeg	W. L. Allison and J. van Ryn	
1931	G. von Cramm and J. Brugnon	R. Boyd and E. Zappa	
1932	J. H. Crawford and H. C. Hopman	R. Miki and J. H. Satch	
1933	H. E. Vines and H. Gledhill	V. G. Kirby and N. G. Farquharson	
1934	I. G. Collins and F. H. D. Wilde	C. E. Malfroy and K. C. Gandar Dower	
1935	G. P. Hughes and C. R. D. Tuckey	J. D. Budge and G. C. Mako	
1936	J. D. Budge and C. G. Mako	W. L. Allison and J. van Ryn	
1937	J. D. Budge and C. G. Mako	C. Boussus and Y. Petra	
1938	G. P. Hughes and F. H. D. Wilde	G. C. Mako and F. Kukuljevic	
1939	J. S. Olliff and G. von Cramm	I. G. Collins and R. K. Tinkler	
1946	D. Pails and G. E. Brown	A. Buser and A. Huonder	
1947	J. E. Bromwich and D. Pails	J. A. Kramer and R. Falkenburg	
1948	S. C. Misra and R. L. Sawhney E. Morea and A. D. Russell divided		
1949	G. E. Brown and O. W. Sidwell	G. Mulloy and F. R. Schroeder	
1950	W. F. Talbert and G. Mulloy	J. E. Bromwich and A. K. Quist	
1951	F. A. Sedgman and K. McGregor	J. Drobny and E. W. Sturgess	
1952	J. Drobny and J. E. Patty	D. W. Candy and M. G. Rose	
1953	P. Washer and J. Brichant	M. G. Rose and R. N. Hartwig	
1954	E. V. Seixas and M. A. Trabert	M. G. Rose and R. N. Hartwig	
1955	R. N. Hartwig and L. A. Hoad	M. G. Rose and G. A. Worthington	
1956	H. Richardson and E. V. Seixas	L. A. Hoad and K. R. Rosewall	
1957	N. A. Fraser and L. A. Hoad – H. Richardson and E. V. Seixas divided		
1958	L. Ayala and D. W. Candy – M. G. Rose and B. Mackay divided		
1959	T. W. Gorman and R. A. J. Hewitt	K. Nielsen and T. Ulrich	
1960	R. G. Laver and R. Mark	R. N. Howe and A. A. Segal	
1961	R. A. J. Hewitt and F. S. Stolle	L. Ayala and R. Krishnan	
1962	R. A. J. Hewitt and F. S. Stolle	R. N. Howe and R. Krishnan	
1963	R. A. J. Hewitt and F. S. Stolle – R. S. Emerson and M. Santana divided		
1964	R. A. J. Hewitt and F. S. Stolle	R. S. Emerson and K. N. Fletcher	
1965	R. S. Emerson and F. S. Stole w.o.	R. D. Ralston and H. Richardson scr.	
1966	R. S. Emerson and F. S. Stolle w.o.	J. D. Newcombe and A. D. Roche	
1967	unfinished		
1968	E. Buchholz and R. D. Ralston – J. D. Newcombe and A. D. Roche divided		
1969	O. K. Davidson and R. D. Ralston	O. Bengtson and T. Koch	
1970	T. S. Okker and M. C. Riessen	A. R. Ashe and C. M. Pasarell	
1971	T. S. Okker and M. C. Riessen	S. R. Smith and E. J. van Dillen	
1972	J. H. McManus and J. H. Osborne	J. Fassbender and K. Meiler	
1973	T. S. Okker and M. C. Riessen	R. F. Keldie and R. J. Moore	
1974	no tournament		
1975	no tournament		
1976	no tournament		
1977	A. and V. Amritraj	D. A. and J. M. Lloyd	
1978	R. A. J. Hewitt and F. D. McMillan	F. V. McNair and R. Ramirez	
1979	T. R. and T. E. Gullikson	S. E. Stewart and M. C. Riessen	
1980	R. J. Frawley and G. Masters	P. McNamee and S. E. Stewart	
1981	P. Dupre and B. Teacher	K. Curren and S. B. Denton	
1982	J. P. McEnroe and P. Rennert	V. C. Amaya and H. Pfister	
1983	B. E. Gottfried and P. McNamee	K. Curren and S. Denton	
1984	P. Cash and P. McNamee	B. M. Mitton and B. Walts	
1985	K. Flach and R. Seguso	P. Cash and J. B. Fitzgerald	

WOMEN'S SINGLES: 1890–1973

	WINNER	RUNNER-UP
1890	Miss M. Jacks	Miss M. Shackle
1891	Miss M. Shackle	Miss P. Legh
1892	Miss M. Shackle	Miss E. L. Austin
1893	Miss M. Shackle	Miss E. Lane
1894	Miss E. L. Austin	Miss C. Cooper
1895	Miss M. Shackle	Miss E. L. Austin
1896	Miss C. Cooper	Miss A. Templeman
1897	Miss C. Cooper	Miss E. L. Austin
1898	Miss C. Cooper	Miss E. L. Austin
1899	Miss E. L. Austin	Miss C. Cooper
1900	Miss C. Cooper	Mrs G. Greville
1901	Mrs G. Greville	Miss E. W. Thomson
1902	Mrs G. W. Sterry	Mrs N. Durlacher
1903	Miss A. M. Morton	Mrs G. Greville
1904	Miss A. M. Morton	Miss E. M. Stawell-Brown
1905	Miss E. W. Thomson	Mrs G. Greville
1906	Miss E. W. Thomson	Miss M. Coles
1907	Miss V. M. Pinckney	Mrs D. Lambert Chambers
1908	Miss V. M. Pinckney	Mrs D. Lambert Chambers
1909	Mrs H. Edgington	Mrs M. O'Neill
1910	Mrs G. Lamplough	Miss E. G. Johnson
1911	Miss M. Coles	Miss A. M. Morton
1912	Mrs D. R. Larcombe	Miss E. D. Holman
1913	Mrs D. R. Larcombe	Mrs H. Edgington
1914	Mrs D. R. Larcombe	Miss B. Tulloch
1919	Mrs D. R. Larcombe	Miss E. D. Holman
1920	Miss E. D. Holman w.o.	Mrs D. Larcombe scr.
1921	Mrs R. C. Clayton	Miss E. D. Holman
1922	Mrs R. C. Clayton	Mrs Keays
1923	Miss E. M. Ryan	Mrs A. E. Beamish
1924	Miss E. M. Ryan	Mrs D. K. Craddock
1925	Miss E. M. Ryan	Miss E. H. Harvey
1926	Mrs John Hill	Miss E. Bennett
1927	Mrs John Hill	Mrs Broadbridge
1928	Miss J. C. Ridley	Mme H. Nicolopoulo
1929	Miss E. M. Ryan	Miss E. A. Goldsack
1930	Mrs W. D. List	Mrs D. Stocks
1931	Mrs J. B. Pittman	Mrs L. A. Godfree
1932	Mrs D. B. Andrus	Mlle J. Jedrzejowska
1933	Mrs J. B. Pittman and Mrs H. Wills-Moody divided	
1934	Mlle J. Goldschmidt	Mrs D. B. Andrus
1935	Sta A. Lizana and Mme S. Henrotin divided	
1936	Miss J. Jedrzejowska	Miss S. D. B. Noel
1937	Miss J. Jedrzejowska	Miss K. E. Stammers
1938	Miss J. Jedrzejowska	Fru H. Sperling
1939	Miss J. Jedrzejowska	Fru H. Sperling
1946	Miss P. M. Betz	Miss M. E. Osborne
1947	Miss A. L. Brough	Miss M. E. Osborne
1948	Miss D. J. Hart and Mrs M. Dupont divided	
1949	Miss A. L. Brough	Mrs M. Dupont
1950	Miss D. J. Hart	Mrs M. Dupont
1951	Miss S. J. Fry	Miss N. Chaffee
1952	Mrs H. Redick-Smith	Miss E. M. Wilford
1953	Mrs I. F. Rinkel	Mrs W. Brewer
1954	Miss A. L. Brough	Miss S. J. Fry
1955	Miss A. L. Brough	Miss J. Forbes
1956	Miss A. Buxton	Miss P. E. Ward
1957	Miss M. Arnold	Mrs Z. Körmöczy
1958	Miss B. Carr	Miss M. Varner
1959	Miss Y. Ramirez	Miss C. Mercelis
1960	Miss C. C. Truman	Miss K. Hantze
1961	Miss M. Smith	Miss N. Richey
1962	Miss R. H. Bentley	Mrs J. W. Cawthorn
1963	Miss R. A. Ebbern	Miss R. H. Bentley
1964	Miss M. Smith	Mrs P. F. Jones
1965	Miss A. M. van Zyl	Miss C. C. Truman
1966	Miss F. Durr	Miss J. A. M. Tegart
1967	Miss N. Richey	Miss K. A. Melville
1968	Mrs P. F. Jones and Miss N. Richey divided	
1969	Mrs P. F. Jones	Miss W. M. Shaw
1970	Mrs B. M. Court	Miss W. M. Shaw
1971	Mrs B. M. Court	Mrs L. W. King
1972	Miss C. M. Evert	Miss K. M. Krantzcke
1973	Mrs O. Morozova	Miss E. F. Goolagong

WOMEN'S DOUBLES: 1919–1973

	WINNERS	RUNNERS-UP
1919	Miss E. M. Ryan and Mrs D. Lambert Chambers	Mrs D. R. Larcombe and Mrs P. Satterthwaite
1920	Mrs D. R. Larcombe and Mrs P. Satterthwaite	Mrs D. K. Craddock and Mrs C. M. B. Marriott
1921	Mrs R. J. McNair and Mrs A. C. Geen	Mrs Atkey and Mrs Foulger
1922	Mrs Bruce May and Mrs Van Praagh	Mrs Johnson Brown and Mrs Ellis
1923	Mrs R. Horsley and Mrs G. N. Hume	Mrs M. Bersey and Miss B. Beauchamp
1924	Mrs R. Watson and Mrs R. J. McNair	Mrs H. S. Cobb and Miss Seager
1925	Mrs D. Lambert Chambers and Miss E. H. Harvey	Mrs H. W. Backhouse and Mrs. Carritt
1926	Mrs D. Lambert Chambers and Miss E. H. Harvey	Mrs John Hill and Miss E. R. Clarke
1927	Miss E. L. Heine and Mrs G. Peacock	Mrs B. C. Covell and Mrs G. Sterry
1928	Miss E. Bennett and Miss E. H. Harvey	Miss E. R. Clarke and Miss M. A. Thomas
1929	Miss E. A. Goldsack and Mrs Jameson	Mrs D. Bundy and Miss M. Morrill

1930	Frl. C. Aussem and Miss E. M. Ryan	Mrs E. Fearnley Whittingstall and Miss B. M. Nuthall	
1931	Mrs J. van Ryn and Mrs L. A. Harper	Mrs L. A. Godfree and Mrs A. D. Stocks	
1932	Miss D. E. Round and Mrs L. R. C. Michell	Mrs L. A. Harper and Miss S. Palfrey	
1933	Mme R. Mathieu and Miss E. M. Ryan	Miss E. H. Harvey and Mrs P. Holcroft Watson	
1934	Mrs P. D. Howard and Mlle C. Rosambert	Mme S. Henrotin and Mrs D. B. Andrus	
1935	Mlle J. Jedrzejowska and Miss S. D. B. Noel	Mrs H. C. Hopman and Miss J. Hartigan	
1936	Mrs D. B. Andrus and Mme S. Henrotin	Mlle N. Adamson and Mlle J. De Meulemeester	
1937	Mrs D. B. Andrus and Mme S. Henrotin	Miss E. H. Harvey and Miss R. M. Hardwick	
1938	Mrs E. L. Heine Miller and Miss M. Morphew	Miss J. Jedrzejowska and Miss M. A. Thomas	
1939	Mrs D. B. Andrus and Mme S. Henrotin	Miss A. M. Yorke and Miss J. Jedrzejowska	
1946	Miss A. L. Brough and Miss M. E. Osborne	Miss P. Betz and Miss D. J. Hart	
1947	Miss A. L. Brough and Miss M. E. Osborne	Mrs H. C. Hopman and Miss N. Bolton	
1948	abandoned		
1949	Mrs P. C. Todd and Miss G. Moran	Mrs B. E. Hilton and Miss J. Gannon	
1950	Mrs M. Dupont and Miss A. L. Brough	Miss D. J. Hart and Miss S. J. Fry	
1951	Miss D. J. Hart and Miss S. J. Fry	Mrs M. Dupont and Miss N. Bolton	
1952	Miss A. L. Brough and Miss M. Connolly	Miss B. Penrose and Miss G. Love	
1953	Miss M. Connolly and Miss J. Sampson	Mrs I. F. Rinkel and Miss H. Fletcher	
1954	Miss A. L. Brough and Mrs M. Dupont	Miss B. M. Kimbrell and Mrs B. M. Lewis	
1955	Miss D. R. Hard and Mrs J. Fleitz	Miss A. Mortimer and Miss J. A. Shilcock	
1956	Miss A. L. Brough and Miss S. J. Fry	Miss A. Buxton and Miss A. Gibson	
1957	Miss A. Gibson and Miss D. R. Hard	Mrs K. Hawton and Mrs T. D. Long	
1958	Miss M. E. Bueno and Miss A. Gibson – Mrs K. Hawton and Mrs T. D. Long divided		
1959	Mrs J. Fleitz and Miss C. C. Truman	Miss J. Arth and Miss D. R. Hard	
1960	Miss M. E. Bueno and Miss D. R. Hard	Miss K. Hantze and Miss J. S. Hopps	
1961	Miss K. Hantze and Miss B. J. Moffitt	Miss M. L. Hunt and Miss L. M. Hutchings	
1962	Miss J. Bricka and Miss M. Smith	Miss M. E. Bueno and Miss D. R. Hard	
1963	Miss A. Dmitrieva and Miss J. A. M. Tegart	Miss A. Mortimer and Mrs A. Ochoa	
1964	Mrs P. Haygarth and Mrs P. F. Jones	Miss D. M. Catt and Miss D. E. Starkie	
1965	Miss M. Smith and Miss L. R. Turner	Miss M. E. Bueno and Miss B. J. Moffitt	
1966	Miss N. Baylon and Miss A. M. van Zyl	Miss R. Casals and Mrs L. W. King	
1967	abandoned		
1968	Mrs B. M. Court and Miss V. Eade – Miss P. Bartkowicz and Miss S. R. de Fina divided		
1969	Miss R. Casals and Mrs L. W. King	Miss F. Durr and Mrs P. F. Jones	
1970	Miss R. Casals and Mrs L. W. King	Miss K. A. Melville and Miss K. M. Krantzcke	
1971	Miss R. Casals and Mrs L. W. King	Mrs P. W. Curtis and Miss V. J. Zeigenfuss	
1972	Miss R. Casals and Mrs L. W. King	Miss B. I. Kirk and Mrs Q. C. Pretorius	
1973	Miss R. Casals and Mrs L. W. King	Miss F. Durr and Miss B. F. Stove	

MIXED DOUBLES: 1905–1972

	WINNERS	RUNNERS-UP
1905	A. W. Dunlop and Miss E. W. Thomson	N. E. Brookes and Miss A. M. Morton
1906	H. Pollard and Miss M. Coles	G. Greville and Mrs Greville
1907	N. E. Brookes and Mrs D. Lambert Chambers	R. F. Doherty and Miss G. S. Eastlake-Smith
1908	G. A. Thomas and Mrs D. Lambert Chambers	W. C. Crawley and Miss V. M. Pinckney
1909	F. W. Rahe and Mrs E. G. Parton	D. P. Rhodes and Mrs G. Greville
1910	J. B. Ward and Miss B. Tulloch	O. Froitzheim and Mrs G. Greville
1911	R. J. McNair and Mrs McNair	S. N. Doust and Mrs B. Armstrong
1912	J. C. Parke and Mrs D. R. Larcombe	M. J. G. Ritchie and Miss E. D. Holman
1913	C. P. Dixon and Mrs D. R. Larcombe	'Alfred' and Mrs M. O'Neill
1914	A. W. Dunlop and Mrs D. R. Larcombe	G. T. C. Watt and Miss B. Tulloch
1919	Sir G. A. Thomas and Mrs D. R. Larcombe	S. N. Doust and Mrs 'James'
1920	B. I. C. Norton and Mrs D. R. Larcombe	F. H. Jarvis and Miss D. C. Shepherd
1921	A. D. Prebble and Mrs A. C. Geen	R. S. Barnes and Mrs J. L. Leisk
1922	G. T. C. Watt and Mrs R. C. Clayton	R. G. de Quetteville and Miss B. Tulloch

1923	P. M. Davson and Miss E. M. Ryan	D. M. Greig and Mrs D. Lambert Chambers
1924	Col. A. Berger and Mrs R. J. McNair	B. L. Cameron and Miss R. Watson
1925	G. R. Crole-Rees and Miss E. H. Harvey	D. Stralem and Miss R. L. French
1926	Major Bernard and Mrs Furness	Mr and Mrs H. W. Backhouse
1927	C. H. Kingsley and Mrs John Hill	Col. A. Berger and Mrs D. Lambert Chambers
1928	W. F. Coen and Frl. C. Aussem	N. E. Brookes and Frl. von Reznicek
1929	W. L. Allison and Miss E. Cross	G. Lyttleton-Rogers and Miss M. Morrill
1930	Dr. J. C. Gregory and Miss E. M. Ryan	G. M. Lott and Miss M. Greef
1931	J. D. P. Wheatley and Miss N. M. Lyle	Dr. J. C. Gregory and Mrs J. B. Pittman
1932	R. Miki and Miss D. E. Round	Mr and Mrs J. H. Crawford
1933	E. Maier and Miss E. M. Ryan	R. Nunoi and Miss S. D. B. Noel
1934	A. Martin-Legeay and Mme S. Henrotin	J. Lesueur and Mme S. Mathieu
1935	A. Martin-Legeay and Mme S. Henrotin– W. L. Allison and Miss H. H. Jacobs divided	
1936	J. D. Budge and Mrs S. Fabyan	C. E. Hare and Mlle J. Jedrzejowska
1937	L. de Borman and Miss S. D. B. Noel	H. Billington and Mlle J. Jedrzejowska
1938	J. S. Olliff and Mrs E. L. Heine Miller	C. G. Mako and Mlle J. Jedrzejowska
1939	E. T. Cooke and Mrs S. Fabyan	R. L. Riggs and Mlle J. Jedrzejowska
1947	C. Tanacescu and Mrs M. Rurac	I. F. Rinkel and Miss J. Quertier
1948	abandoned	
1949	G. E. Brown and Miss J. Fitch	G. A. Worthington and Mrs T. D. Long
1950	G. L. Paish and Miss J. Quertier	E. Morea and Miss B. Scofield
1951	N. Cockburn and Mrs H. Bartlett	D. W. Candy and Mrs W. H. L. Gordon
1952	B. M. Woodroffe and Miss G. Love w.o.	M. G. Rose and Miss M. Connolly scr.
1953	K. R. Rosewall and Miss M. Connolly – R. N. Hartwig and Mrs D. P. Knode divided	
1954	L. A. Hoad and Miss M. Connolly	H. Burrows and Miss P. E. Ward
1955	N. A. Fraser and Miss B. Penrose	G. L. Forbes and Miss D. R. Hard
1956	G. Mulloy and Miss A. Gibson	R. N. Howe and Miss D. R. Hard

1957	N. A. Fraser and Miss A. Gibson – L. Ayala and Mrs T. D. Long divided	
1958	abandoned	
1959	R. G. Laver and Miss D. R. Hard	N. Pietrangeli and Miss M. E. Bueno
1960	R. G. Laver and Miss D. R. Hard	R. Mark and Miss J. S. Hopps
1961	J. Javorsky and Mrs V. Sukova	R. N. Howe and Miss I. Buding
1962	R. N. Howe and Miss M. E. Bueno	M. P. Hann and Miss C. Yates-Bell
1963	abandoned	
1964	abandoned	
1965	abandoned	
1966	T. S. Okker and Miss T. Groenman	J. Leschly and Miss E. Lundquist
1967	abandoned	
1968	S. Likhachev and Miss G. Baksheeva – A. Metreveli and Miss O. Morozova divided	
1969	abandoned	
1970	O. K. Davidson and Miss W. M. Shaw	W. Giltinan and Miss E. F. Goolagong
1971	abandoned	
1972	C. S. Dibley and Miss K. M. Krantzcke	A. Metreveli and Mrs O. Morozova

VETERANS DOUBLES: 1964–1973

1964	J. Mehta and M. V. Deo
1965	G. R. MacCall and G. Mulloy
1966	W. T. Anderson and A. V. Martini
1967	J. Drobny and A. V. Martini
1968	S. Match and G. Mulloy
1969	J. Faunce and G. Mulloy
1970	W. T. Anderson and A. Kalman
1971	F. R. Schroeder and L. S. Straus
1972	G. Mulloy and T. Vincent
1973	J. J. Borough and J. W. Gunn

Members' (Grass Court) Tournaments
MEN'S SINGLES: 1974–1982

1974	A. H. Coles
1975	J. A. N. Prenn
1976	P. H. Frick
1977	P. H. Frick
1978	M. M. Parfitt
1979	rain stopped play
1980	M. P. Bryant
1981	no competition
1982	P. W. Blincow

LADIES' SINGLES: 1974–1982

1974   Mrs G. M. Foster
1975   Miss S. Rodgers
1976   Miss K. J. Brasher
1977   Miss K. J. Brasher
1978   Miss J. Tacon
1979   rain stopped play
1980   Miss J. Hamilton
1981   no competition
1982   Miss C. Bann

MEN'S DOUBLES: 1974–1982

1974   not played – rain
1975   O. S. Prenn and J. A. N. Prenn
1976   H. C. Bernstein and S. D. Ludlum
1977   H. C. Bernstein and S. D. Ludlum
1978   M. M. Parfitt and M. P. Bryant
1979   rained off
1980   M. P. Byrant and P. R. Thomas
1981   cancelled
1982   S. Arisawa and A. Pisker

LADIES' DOUBLES: 1974–1981

1974   Mrs G. Appleby and Miss M. L. Douglas
1975   Mrs G. Appleby and Miss M. L. Douglas
1976   Mrs S. J. Brasher and Miss K. J. Brasher
1977   Mrs A. Harris and Miss M. Douglas
1978   Miss M. Douglas and Mrs G. Appleby
1979   no competition
1980   Mrs S. Cornish and Mrs B. Stevenson
1981   rain stopped play

MIXED DOUBLES: 1974–1981

1974   no play – rain
1975   A. H. Coles and Miss S. Rodgers
1976   I. McG. Boden and Mrs S. Boden
1977   H. C. Bernstein and Mrs S. Cornish
1978   D. C. Sellman and Mrs B. Stevenson
1979   H. C. Bernstein and Mrs S. Cornish
1980   H. C. Bernstein and Mrs S. Cornish
1981   rain stopped play

VETERANS MEN'S SINGLES: 1974–1984

	OVER 45	OVER 55	OVER 65
1974	J. H. H. Fisher		
1975	J. H. H. Fisher		
1976	J. H. H. Fisher	G. Hesz	
1977	G. M. Foster	V. A. D. Turner	
1978	G. M. Foster	D. J. Mabey	C. M. Jones
1979	no competitions		
1980	—	I. McG. Boden	C. M. Jones
1981	no competitions		
1982	—	J. H. H. Fisher	C. M. Jones
1983	no competitions		
1984	—	A. Kalman	

VETERANS MEN'S DOUBLES: 1974–1980
The Stefan Challenge Cup

1974   H. C. Bernstein and S. Stefan
1975   I. McG. Boden and N. K. Haugh
1976   H. C. Bernstein and S. Stefan
1977   J. D. Nixon and N. K. Haugh
1978   L. Lane and G. M. Foster
1979   no competitions due to rain
1980   R. Saunders and P. G. Knightley

Oxford v. Cambridge: 1887–1904

1887   Oxford won singles 6–3,
         Cambridge won doubles 6–3
1888   abandoned owing to rain
1889   Oxford won singles 5–3,
         Cambridge won doubles 9–0
1890   Singles drawn 4–4, Cambridge won doubles 8–1
1891   Oxford won singles 5–4,
         Cambridge won doubles 7–2
1892   Cambridge won singles 9–0, won doubles 8–1
1893   Cambridge won singles 5–4, won doubles 7–2
1894   Cambridge won singles 5–4, doubles 7–2
1895   Cambridge won singles 9–0, doubles 8–1
1896   Cambridge won singles 9–0, doubles 9–0
1897   Cambridge won singles 4–3, doubles 7–2
1898   Cambridge won singles 5–4, doubles 5–4
1899   Oxford won singles 6–3,
         Cambridge won doubles 5–4
1900   Oxford won singles 5–4,
         Cambridge won doubles 5–4
1901   Oxford won singles 5–4, doubles 6–3
1902   Cambridge won singles 5–4, doubles 5–4
1903   Oxford won singles 7–2, doubles 7–2
1904   Cambridge won singles 5–4, doubles 5–4

Young Professionals Lawn Tennis Match

1937   F. Hollingshead

Lawn Tennis: Hard Courts

Members' Tournaments

GENTLEMEN'S SINGLES: 1946–1985

1946	E. Wittmann	1966	N. Kitovitz
1947	E. Wittmann	1967	G. Villaneuva
1948	G. E. Godsell	1968	O. S. Prenn
1949	G. E. Godsell	1969	C. J. Mottram
1950	G. E. Godsell	1970	R. G. Clarke
1951	I. Tloczynski	1971	R. G. Clarke
1952	I. Tloczynski	1972	R. G. Clarke
1953	I. Tloczynski	1973	C. S. Wells
1954	I. Tloczynski	1974	P. W. Blincow
1955	G. E. Mudge	1975	P. W. Blincow
1956	O. S. Prenn	1976	P. W. Blincow
1957	R. S. Condy	1977	N. F. Herrero
1958	R. S. Condy	1978	P. W. Blincow
1959	M. Kizlink	1979	D. B. S. Young
1960	L. P. Coni	1980	S. Arisawa
1961	R. S. Condy	1981	R. Taylor
1962	F. S. Field	1982	T. A. Morgan
1963	F. S. Field	1983	S. King
1964	H. C. Bernstein	1984	P. W. Blincow
1965	N. Kitovitz	1985	S. King

LADIES' SINGLES: 1946–1985

1946	Mrs B. Carris
1947	Miss C. G. Hoahing
1948	Miss G. E. Woodgate
1949	Miss R. F. Woodgate
1950	Mrs T. M. Dubuisson
1951	Miss I. Hutchings
1952	Miss I. Hutchings
1953	Miss D. Herbst
1954	Miss A. Buxton
1955	Miss I. Hutchings
1956	Miss I. Hutchings
1957	Mrs R. Deloford
1958	Miss C. Levy
1959	Mrs H. Sladek
1960	Mrs A. Silk
1961	Mrs N. K. Haugh
1962	Mrs A. Silk
1963	Miss M. L. Douglas
1964	Mrs N. K. Haugh
1965	Miss S. Okin
1966	Miss C. A. Camp
1967	Miss C. A. Camp
1968	Miss C. S. Colman
1969	Miss L. D. Blachford
1970	Miss J. A. Congdon
1971	Mrs G. Appleby
1972	Miss A. M. Coe
1973	Mrs H. Barat
1974	Miss S. N. Imhof
1975	Miss J. A. Eyre
1976	Miss K. J. Brasher
1977	Miss K. J. Brasher
1978	Mrs S. Thomas
1979	Mrs S. J. Brasher
1980	Mrs P. Barratt
1981	Miss C. Bann
1982	Miss J. Reeves
1983	Miss J. Rich
1984	Miss C. Bann
1985	(not held)

MEN'S DOUBLES: 1969–1985

1969	P. Willetts and R. P. Boyd
1970	D. K. Martin and C. E. McHugo
1971	R. P. Boyd and R. S. Burns
1972	S. D. Ludlum and A. I. Mitha
1973	H. C. Bernstein and J. L. Moore
1974	H. C. Bernstein and J. L. Moore
1975	B. Joannides and K. J. Havelock
1976	F. S. Field and P. H. Frick
1977	divided
1978	P. R. Thomas and J. Markson
1979	M. P. Bryant and M. M. Parfitt
1980	M. P. Byrant and P. R. Thomas
1981	divided
1982	J. Markson and D. B. S. Young
1983	T. A. Morgan and S. King
1984	A. Pisker and B. Crystal
1985	J. Markson and D. B. S. Young

LADIES' DOUBLES: 1978–1985

1978	Mrs J. Soley and Miss C. Russell-Vick
1979	Miss A. Buxton and Mrs S. J. Brasher
1980	Miss A. Buxton and Mrs P. Barratt
1981	(not held)
1982	Mrs S. J. and Miss A. Brasher
1983	Mrs J. Segal and Mrs D. Donovan
1984	(not held)
1985	(not held)

MIXED DOUBLES: 1963–1985

1963	H. C. Bernstein and Mrs S. Nicol
1964	J. Abel and Miss M. B. H. McAnally
1965	H. C. Bernstein and Mrs S. Nicol
1966	J. M. Cope and Miss S. Edgecombe

1967 J. Wayne and Miss C. Webb
1968 J. Wayne and Miss C. Webb
1969 H. C. Bernstein and Mrs S. Cornish
1970 R. S. Burns and Mrs S. Cornish
1971 H. C. Bernstein and Mrs S. Cornish
1972 divided
1973 J. J. Marnoch and Mrs A. P. Bradford
1974 H. C. Bernstein and Mrs S. Cornish
1975 C. S. Wells and Miss R. Lewis
1976 R. G. Harris and Mrs A. Harris
1977 divided
1978 H. C. Bernstein and Mrs S. Cornish
1979 H. C. Bernstein and Mrs S. Cornish
1980 H. C. Bernstein and Mrs S. Cornish
1981 rain prevented play
1982 H. C. Bernstein and Mrs S. Cornish
1983 (not held)
1984 J. Wayne and Miss C. Bann
1985 (not held)

MEN'S VETERANS SINGLES: 1976–1985

	OVER 45	OVER 55	OVER 65
1976	—	V. A. D. Turner	—
1977	—	V. A. D. Turner	—
1978	G. M. Foster	D. J. Mabey	C. M. Jones
1979	—	J. H. H. Fisher	C. M. Jones
1980	—	J. H. H. Fisher	P. Forda
1981	—	J. H. H. Fisher	—
1982		R. F. Stephens	
1983		J. H. H. Fisher	
1984		A. Kalman	
1985	G. M. Foster	G. M. Foster	

Schools' Competitions

SCHOOLBOYS' SINGLES: 1919–1966
Challenge Cup presented by D. Macleod, Esq.

1919 C. H. Weinberg (Westminster)
1920 E. A. Dearman (Marlborough)
1921 C. E. St. J. Evers (Haileybury)
1922 H. K. Lester (The Leys)
1923 H. W. Austin (Repton)
1924 H. W. Austin (Repton)
1925 H. W. Austin (Repton)
1926 J. S. Olliff (St. Paul's)
1927 E. R. Avory (Stowe)
1928 R. J. Ritchie (Eastbourne College)
1929 J. W. Nuthall (Repton)
1930 A. S. C. Hulton (Charterhouse)
1931 W. F. Moss (Charterhouse)
1932 C. R. Fawcus (Rugby)
1933 R. Pulbrook (Harrow)
1934 G. M. Zarifi (Lycée de Marseilles)

1935 C. J. Hovell (St. Paul's)
1936 H. T. Baxter (Christ's College)
1937 J. Michelmore (Charterhouse)
1938 G. L. Paish (Whitgift)
1939 J. W. Bacon (Downside)
1940–1946 no competition
1947 D. R. Male (Aldenham)
1948 J. A. T. Horn (Forest)
1949 J. E. Barrett (U. C. S.)
1950 A. A. W. Kimpton (Eton)
1951 P. Wooldridge (Guildford)
1952 G. D. Owen (Rugby)
1953 B. R. Hatton (U.C.S.)
1954 B. R. Hatton (U.C.S.)
1955 J. I. Tattersall (Herbert Strutt)
1956 J. A. H. Curry (K.C.S. Wimbledon)
1957 D. K. Simons (Felsted)
1958 L. F. Strong (Tottenham)
1959 M. W. Francis (Mill End)
1960 R. G. Davies (Eltham)
1961 R. G. Davies (Eltham)
1962 C. W. T. Atkins (Highgate)
1963 C. W. T. Atkins (Highgate)
1964 P. Kingham (Wimbledon County)
1965 M. Barnett (Pinner County)
1966 G. K. Fuggle (Kent College)

SCHOOLBOYS' DOUBLES: 1919–1966
Challenge Cup presented by D. Macleod, Esq.

1919 J. Riba and N. Mahony (Beaumont)
1920 J. Riba and N. Mahony (Beaumont)
1921 C. E. W. Mackintosh and R. E. Freason (Eastbourne)
1922 G. S. Fletcher and C. G. Fletcher (Charterhouse)
1923 H. W. Austin and B. H. Valentine (Repton)
1924 G. S. Fletcher and C. G. Fletcher (Charterhouse)
1925 H. W. Austin and R. K. Tinkler (Repton)
1926 B. H. Valentine and C. J. Dunn (Repton)
1927 J. L. H. Fletcher and E. M. Buzzard (Charterhouse)
1928 R. K. Tinkler and J. W. Nuthall (Repton)
1929 A. S. C. Hulton and W. F. Moss (Charterhouse)
1930 A. S. C. Hulton and W. F. Moss (Charterhouse)
1931 W. F. Moss and J. C. Moss (Charterhouse)
1932 J. W. Waring and D. H. Mackenzie (Malvern)
1933 J. D. Anderson and R. H. Williamson (Uppingham)
1934 F. J. C. Mennell and A. E. Vickery (Ottersham)
1935 C. J. Hovell and R. G. W. Smith (St. Paul's)
1936 J. P. R. Whelan and J. H. Page (Canford)
1937 L. A. B. Pilkington and A. H. Cambell (Sherborne)
1938 K. Shute and W. Shute (King's College, Rochester)

1939   J. D. P. Tanner and J. Michelmore
       (Charterhouse)
1940–1946   no competition
1947   G. R. B. Brown and J. G. H. Hirsch (K. C. S.)
1948   J. E. Barrett and S. W. Greenbury (U.C.S.)
1949   J. E. Barrett and D. T. Seymour (U.C.S.)
1950   J. W. Neill and G. D. Owen (Rugby)
1951   J. W. Neill and G. D. Owen (Rugby)
1952   J. W. Neill and G. D. Owen (Rugby)
1953   B. R. Hatton and R. B. Stuart (U.C.S.)
1954   B. R. Hatton and R. B. Stuart (U.C.S.)
1955   L. P. Coni and R. M. T. Earlam (Stowe)
1956   G. S. Clarke and D. P. Gordon
       (Westminster)
1957   G. R. T. Bateman and P. G. Howard
       (Marlborough)
1958   P. W. Malkin and D. K. Martin (St. Paul's)
1959   A. R. Davies and R. G. Davies (Eltham)
1960   A. R. Davies and R. G. Davies (Eltham)
1961   R. G. Davies and J. Hopkins (Eltham)
1962   C. W. T. Atkins and A. J. Parfitt (Highgate)
1963   R. Gibbons and J. M. M. Hooper (St. George's
       and Charterhouse)
1964   I. Gibbs and T. Woodcock (Stoneleigh County
       and Holy Family)
1965   M. Barnett and R. J. S. Fraser (Pinner County
       and Emanuel)
1966   R. J. S. Fraser and M. A. Mitha (Emanuel and
       Seaford College)

SCHOOLGIRLS' SINGLES: 1927–1985

Yatman Challenge Cup

1927   Miss S. D. B. Noel (Glendower)
1928   Miss S. D. B. Noel (Glendower)
1929   Miss A. McOstrich (Queen's College)
1930   Miss P. Brazier (County High School, Worthing)
1931   Miss O. Garrish (Malvern Girls' College)
1932   Miss M. Whitmarsh (The Grove)
1933   Miss M. G. Figgis (St. Felix)
1934   Miss D. Rowe (Eversley)
1935   Miss C. G. Hoahing (Twickenham County
       School)
1936   Miss M. Lincoln (Putney High School)
1937   Miss R. Thomas (Wallington County School)
1938   Miss N. Zinovieff (Redmoor School)
1939   Miss M. Greaunt (Jersey College)
1940–1946   no competition
1947   Miss J. Knight (Northampton School for Girls)
1948   Miss J. Knight (Northampton School for Girls)
1949   Miss L. M. Cornell (Sutton High School)
1950   Miss L. M. Cornell (Sutton High School)
1951   Miss S. J. Bloomer (Sherborne School for Girls)
1952   Miss J. M. Boundy (Enfield)
1953   Miss P. Della Porta (Roedean)

1954   Miss J. Chittenden (Godolphin and Latymer)
1955   Miss J. Chittenden (Godolphin and Latymer)
1956   Miss J. Chittenden (Godolphin and Latymer)
1957   Miss J. Hall (Edgbaston High School)
1958   Miss C. A. Silver (Queen's College)
1959   Miss C. A. Rosser (St. Margaret's)
1960   Miss D. F. Franklin (Woodford County High
       School)
1961   Miss S. V. Wade (Wimbledon County School)
1962   Miss P. Mundy (Wimbledon High School)
1963   Miss C. M. Myers (Ursuline Convent,
       Wimbledon)
1964   Miss C. J. Sivers (Finchley County School)
1965   Miss B. E. Orchard (Queen Anne's, Caversham)
1966   Miss E. J. Allen (Felixstowe College)
1967   Miss M. E. Forbes (Watford G.S.)
1968   Miss C. E. Rendel (Benenden)
1969   Miss C. M. Panton (Cobham Hall)
1970   Miss V. E. M. Veale (Clifton High School)
1971   Miss A. C. Derby (Heathfield, Harrow)
1972   Miss S. O. Elliott (Vyners Grammar School,
       Ickenham)
1973   Miss T. M. Eaton (Southampton College)
1974   Miss J. P. Willson (Guildford County School)
1975   Miss M. Ballheimer (Orange Hill Sen. H.)
1976   Miss A. M. Walters (Millfield)
1977   Miss D. Parnell (Withington School, Manchester)
1978   Miss A. B. Hill (Red Maids' School, Bristol)
1979   Miss J. L. Wrigley (Dr. Challoner's High School)
1980   Miss S. J. Ryder (Millfield School)
1981   Miss C. Bann (Coloma Convent School, Croydon)
1982   Miss C. Bhaguandas (Highgate Wood School)
1983   Miss C. Gaskin (Sutton High School)
1984   Miss A. Brasher (Repton School)
1985   Miss E. Bishop

SCHOOLGIRLS' SENIOR DOUBLES: 1927–1980

Challenge Cup presented by Mrs S. Courtauld

1927   Miss M. Buick and Miss M. Goldson
       (Malvern Girls' College)
1928   Miss D. B. Gibson and Miss S. Spedding
       (St. Leonards, St. Andrews)
1929   Miss O. Garrish and Miss M. Roberts (Malvern
       Girls' College)
1930   Miss L. Watson and Miss B. Watson (Princess
       Helena College, Ealing)
1931   Miss K. E. Stammers and Miss M. Whitmarsh
       (The Grove, Watford)
1932   Miss N. Dickin and Miss M. Whitmarsh
       (The Grove, Watford)
1933   Miss M. Gardiner and Miss A. Joseph (St. Paul's)
1934   Miss M. Caudwell and Miss A. Callins (Malvern
       Girls' College)

1935 Miss M. Lincoln and Miss V. Steenbrugge (Putney High School)
1936 Miss V. Heaton and Miss P. Lane (Sherborne School for Girls)
1937 Miss E. M. Teayes and Miss S. Elton (Dorchester)
1938 Miss E. Curtis and Miss J. MacKenzie (Benenden)
1939 Miss E. Curtis and Miss J. MacKenzie (Benenden)
1940–1946 no competition
1947 Miss J. P. Mead and Miss P. Cunane (Sherborne School for Girls)
1948 Miss J. Knight and Miss B. J. Loakes (Northampton School for Girls)
1949 Miss E. Watson and Miss I. Williams (Queen Elizabeth, Barnet)
1950 Miss D. Spiers and Miss H. Mousley (North London Collegiate)
1951 Miss J. M. Boundy and Miss S. Brasted (Enfield School for Girls)
1952 Miss H. J. Bell and Miss S. Fisher (Sherborne School for Girls)
1953 Miss H. J. Bell and Miss S. Fisher (Sherborne School for Girls)
1954 Miss S. Fisher and Miss J. M. Young (Sherborne School for Girls)
1955 Miss P. H. Banks and Miss J. M. Chamberlain (Queen Anne's, Caversham)
1956 Miss P. H. Banks and Miss J. M. Chamberlain (Queen Anne's, Caversham)
1957 Miss S. M. E. Porter and Miss D. Rawsthorne (Oldershaw)
1958 Miss R. F. Wolstenholme and Miss S. E. Wolstenholme (Berkhamsted)
1959 Miss B. M. Nicholson and Miss C. A. Rosser (St. Margaret's)
1960 Miss R. Bate and Miss J. M. Hope (Queen's, Chester)
1961 Miss A. M. Dawes and Miss J. Scott (Hove County School)
1962 Miss E. A. Moeller and Miss F. E. Truman (Queen Anne's, Caversham)
1963 Miss H. Mellotte and Miss E. J. Worsfold (St. Maurs)
1964 Miss A. Grey and Miss S. E. Kitchin (St. Helens, Northwood)
1965 Miss M. Forbes and Miss H. M. Reid (Watford Grammar School)
1966 Miss E. J. Allen and Miss S. C. Hale (Felixstowe College)
1967 Miss C. L. Ricketts and Miss S. Milne (Roedean)
1968 Miss C. A. Morgan and Miss A. Thornley (Millfield School)
1969 Miss S. A. Darwell and Miss G. M. Fletcher (North London Collegiate)

1970 Miss J. R. Harrison and Miss V. E. M. Veale (Clifton High School)
1971 Miss S. M. Jones and Miss S. Preece (King Edward VI, Birmingham, and Sutton Coldfield Tech. College)
1972 Miss A. Williams and Miss R. Paine (Harrow County Grammar School)
1973 Miss E. A. Cooke and Miss V. M. Cooke (Newbury Girls' School)
1974 Miss D. A. Jevans and Miss E. Locke (Loughton County High School and Chingford Junior High School).
1975 Miss P. A. Roberts and Miss J. Matthews (Croft Lodge Convent and Torquay Girls')
1976 Miss S. Bakewell and Miss E. Locke (Croft Lodge Convent, Torquay, and Chingford Senior High)
1977 Miss S. Bakewell and Miss D. Taylor (Croft Lodge Convent, Torquay, and Pilgrim School, Bedford)
1978 Miss A. Loughrey and Miss C. Power (Quarry Bank and Holly Lodge)
1979 Miss K. L. Cass and Miss J. Blyth-Lewis (The Perse School for Girls and Tonbridge Girl's School)
1980 Miss A. Forbes and Miss S. Grace (Talbot Heath School, Bournemouth, and Cams Hill School, Fareham)

BRITISH SCHOOLS' LTA CHAMPIONSHIP

Barclays Supersavers Challenge Cup

1983 North London Collegiate School (Miss J. Redstone and Miss E. Wilson)
1984 Broxbourne School (Miss J. Pearson and Miss A. Skipp)
1985 Marist Convent, Ascot (Miss S. Eve and Miss L. Eve)

INTER-SCHOOL GIRLS' DOUBLES: 1976–1985

The People to People Bowl

1976 Millfield School (Miss R. M. D'Sa and Miss A. M. Walters)
1977 Dr Challoner's High School (Miss J. L. Wrigley and Miss K. Thompson)
1978 The Perse School for Girls (Miss K. L. Cass and Miss J. Lilley)
1979 The Perse School for Girls (The Misses K. L. and M. Cass)
1980 Dr Challoner's High School (Miss N. McNab and Miss D. Cantrell)
1981 St Albans High School (Miss L. Day and Miss J. V. Wood)
1982 St Albans High School (Miss J. V. Wood and Miss L. Day)

BRITISH SCHOOLS LTA GIRLS' INTERMEDIATE
SCHOOL TEAM
DOUBLES CHAMPIONSHIP (15 and Under)

1983   Bancroft's School, Woodford Green
        (Miss C. Bateman and Miss S. Timms)
1984   Thorpe House School, Norwich (Miss N. Hughes
        and Miss S. Elvin)
1985   Newcastle-upon-Tyne Church High School (Miss
        C. Storey and Miss G. Jenkins)

SCHOOLBOYS' UNDER–16 SINGLES: 1920–1966

For The Queen's Club Cup

1920   J. A. L. Hill (Marlborough)
1921   H. W. Austin (Repton)
1922   C. G. Fletcher (Charterhouse)
1923   J. S. Olliff (St. Paul's)
1924   D. B. F. Burt (Wellington)
1925   G. de St. Croix (Clifton)
1926   J. W. Nuthall (Repton)
1927   K. H. Bicker-Caarten (Chillon)
1928   J. Monahan (Stonyhurst)
1929   R. Pulbrook (Harrow)
1930   H. D. B. Faber (Epsom)
1931   J. S. Nuthall (Repton)
1932   C. O'Connor (Douai)
1933   A. W. Allen (Bootham)
1934   H. T. Baxter (Christ's College)
1935   R. S. Abdesselam (Lycée D'Alger)
1936   H. A. Clark (Taunton)
1937   G. L. Paish (Whitgift)
1938   G. F. Anson (Harrow)
1939   D. O. Warwick (Repton)
1940–1946   no competition
1947   S. W. Greenbury (U.C.S.)
1948   G. D. Owen (Rugby)
1949   D. H. Wheeler (K.C.S., Wimbledon)
1950   D. C. Rhodes (K.C.S., Wimbledon)
1951   C. J. Day (Chislehurst)
1952   D. E. W. Archdale (St. Paul's)
1953   M. L. Booth (King's School, Macclesfield)
1954   J. I. Tattersall (Herbert Strutt)
1955   C. M. Hirchfield (Whitgift)
1956   R. B. B. Avory (Stowe)
1957   D. J. Moys (Mercers)
1958   T. L. Sandor (St. Paul's)
1959   V. T. M. Smith (Sir Roger Manwood)
1960   G. R. Stilwell (Parmiters)
1961   K. O. Ajegbo (Eltham)
1962   M. Barnett (Pinner County)
1963   J. G. Paish (Purley G.S.)
1964   G. K. Fuggle (Kent College)
1965   A. F. C. Whitaker (Cheltenham)
1966   P. J. Vickers-Willis (Wimbledon College)

SCHOOLGIRLS' UNDER–16 SINGLES: 1927–1985

Challenge Bowl presented by Mrs G. T. C. Watt

1927   Miss M. Burgess Smith (London Collegiate)
1928   Miss P. Brazier (County High School, Worthing)
1929   Miss P. Brazier (County High School, Worthing)
1930   Miss S. Hewitt (Byculla)
1931   Miss M. Whitmarsh (The Grove, Watford)
1932   Miss E. Kiddle (St. George's)
1933   Miss D. Rowe (Eversley)
1934   Miss C. G. Hoahing (Twickenham County
        School)
1935   Miss R. Thomas (Wallington County School)
1936   Miss R. Thomas (Wallington County School)
1937   Miss P. Gannon (North Middlesex School)
1938   Miss J. B. Rudd (Wimbledon County School)
1939   Miss J. Bridger (Roedean)
1940–1946   no competition
1947   Miss J. P. Mead (Sherborne School for Girls)
1948   Miss L. M. Cornell (Mitcham County)
1949   Miss E. Barnett (Q. E. Barnet)
1950   Miss A. Buxton (Queens House)
1951   Miss J. M. Boundy (Enfield)
1952   Miss M. Archard (St. Martin's)
1953   Miss G. Pears (Northwood)
1954   Miss B. Lygon (Francis Holland)
1955   Miss J. E. Lintern (Channing)
1956   Miss S. M. E. Porter (Oldershaw)
1957   Miss A. L. Owen (Cheltenham)
1958   Miss F. E. Walton (North London Collegiate)
1959   Miss R. A. Blakelock (Springfield Park)
1960   Miss J. C. French (Loughton)
1961   Miss S. Percivall (North London Collegiate)
1962   Miss L. Cullen-Smith (Cheadle Hulme)
1963   Miss B. E. Orchard (Queen Anne's, Caversham)
1964   Miss V. Grisogono (St. Paul's Girls' School)
1965   Miss C. R. Walker (Priorsfield)
1966   Miss F. M. Gardner (Lady Eleanor Holles)
1967   Miss A. Lloyd (Francis Holland)
1968   Miss L. Geeves (Cecil Rhodes)
1969   Miss G. L. Coles (Harvington)
1970   Miss G. Parsons (St Austell G.S.)
1971   Miss C. Russell-Vick (Ancaster House School,
        Bexhill)
1972   Miss K. A. Harrison (Dame Alice Owen's)
1973   Miss C. A. Vigar (Kendrick School, Reading)
1974   Miss A. P. Cooper (St. Hilary's Sevenoaks)
1975   Miss E. Locke (Chingford Senior High School)
1976   Miss D. L. Morgan (Prendergast Grammar
        School)
1977   Miss D. Taylor (Pilgrim School, Bedford)
1978   Miss K. L. Cass (The Perse School for Girls,
        Cambridge)
1979   Miss C. Gaskin (Sutton High School)
1980   Miss C. Bann (Coloma Convent School, Croydon)

1981 Miss D. Walker (Southgate)
1982 Miss J. Wood (St. Albans High School)
1983 Miss F. A. Couldridge (Talbot Heath School,
      Bournemouth)
1984 Miss H. Walker (Crispin School, Somerset)
1985 Miss C. Tee

SCHOOLGIRLS' UNDER–16 DOUBLES: 1970–1982

Sponsored by Commercial Union

1970 Miss A. C. Derby and Miss H. R. Herson
      (Heathfield, Harrow, and St. Mary's, Eastcote)
1971 Miss L. Clare and Miss E. Pooler
      (Croydon High School)
1972 Miss L. Dawes and Miss K. A. Harrison
      (St. Helen's, Northwood, and Dame Alice
      Owen's)
1973 Miss D. Locke and Miss E. Locke
      (Chingford Senior and Chingford Junior)
1974 Miss A. Bramwell and Miss S. Davies
      (North London Collegiate and St. Helen's,
      Northwood)
1975 Miss P. J. Eyre and Miss K. J. Brasher
      (Hinchley Wood Secondary and St. Paul's)
1976 Miss R. Burges and Miss F. Young
      (Talbot Heath School, Bournemouth)
1977 Miss J. L. Wrigley and Miss K. Thompson
      (Dr Challoner's High School)
1978 Miss E. J. Walters and Miss R. E. Eakins
      (Bishop Fox's Girls' School, Taunton, and King's
      Lynn High School)
1979 Miss N. Lusty and Miss J. Carroll
      (Notting Hill and Ealing High School)
1980 Miss C. Gaskin and Miss C. Bann
      (Sutton High School and Coloma Convent
      School, Croydon)
1981 Miss D. Newbery and Miss K. Brown
      (Radcliffe Comprehensive and Holy Cross
      Convent)
1982 Miss J. V. Wood and Miss F. A. Couldridge
      (St. Albans High School and Talbot Heath
      School, Bournemouth)

NESTLÉ WINNERS: 1963–1983

1963 *English Finals*
      Boys: J. Baker
      Girls: P. Spencer

1964 *English Finals*
      Boys: K. Weatherley
      Girls: J. Buckhorn

1965 *English Finals*
      Boys: J. Stillman beat S. Creed 6–2, 6–1.
      Girls: D. Oakley beat B. Orchard 6–2, 2–6, 6–2.

1966 Not held at Queen's

1967 *English Finals*
      Boys: K. Foulner beat A. Mitha
      Girls: L. Charles beat P. Grist

1968 Not held at Queen's

1969 Not held at Queen's

1970 *English Finals*
      Boys: C. Mabbutt beat P. Woodhouse 6–1, 4–6,
          6–1.
      Girls: S. Barker beat D. Southey, 6–0, 6–2.
      International Finals
      Boys: K. Menton (Ireland) beat C. Mabbutt
      Girls: S. Minford (Ireland) beat S. Barker

1971 *English Finals*
      Boys: M. Smith beat J. Scott 6–2, 6–4.
      Girls: M. Tyler beat D. Eyre 6–4, 6–2.
      International Finals
      Boys: K. Revie (Scotland) beat M. Smith 6–1,
          6–2.
      Girls: M. Tyler beat E. Robb (Scotland) 6–1, 6–4.

1972 *English Finals*
      Boys: P. Blincow beat R. Vigar 8–10, 7–5, 7–5.
      Girls: D. Eyre beat P. Jennings 6–2, 6–1.
      International Finals
      Boys: P. Blincow beat R. Tweedlie (Scotland) 7–5,
          6–4.
      Girls: D. Eyre beat M. Andrew (Scotland) 6–1,
          6–0.

1973 *English Finals*
      Boys: P. Thomas
      Girls: J. Eyre
      International Finals
      Boys: S. Sorenson (Ireland)
      Girls: J. Eyre

1974 *English Finals*
      Boys: W. Gowans beat M. Grive 6–0, 6–3.
      Girls: J. Strain beat M. Page-Jones 6–3, 7–6.
      International Finals
      Boys: W. Gowans beat K. Fitzgibbon (Ireland)
          6–1, 6–3.
      Girls: J. Strain beat A. Brotherston (Scotland) 6–1,
          6–7, 6–2.

1975 *English Finals*
      Boys: I. Currie beat J. Dier 6–4, 4–6, 6–4.
      Girls: E. Locke beat J. Matthews 7–6, 6–1.
      International Finals
      Boys: I. Currie beat A. Chisholm (Scotland) 6–1,
          6–2.
      Girls: J. Erskine (Scotland) beat E. Locke 6–4,
          6–0.

1976 *English Finals*
    Boys: N. Blincow beat S. Collar 7–6, 6–3.
    Girls: R. Hutton beat K. Brasher 2–6, 7–5, 6–1.
    International Finals
    Boys: H. Tinney (Ireland) beat N. Blincow 6–4,
      2–6, 6–4.
    Girls: E. Lightbody (Wales) beat R. Hutton 6–3,
      6–4.

1977 *English Finals*
    Boys: J. Bates beat P. Hughesman 6–1, 6–0.
    Girls: J. Blyth-Lewis beat L. Machin 6–2, 6–3.
    International Finals
    Boys: J. Bates beat A. McNab (Scotland) 6–3,
      6–3.
    Girls: J. Blyth-Lewis beat L. Tuff (Ireland) 7–5,
      6–4.

1978 *English Finals*
    Boys: R. Smith beat R. Coull
    Girls: J. Gasser beat T. Sawyer
    International Finals
    Boys: P. Hannon (Ireland) beat R. Smith 6–3,
      6–2.
    Girls: J. Gasser beat D. Boothman (Scotland) 6–2,
      6–0.

1979 *English Finals*
    Boys: R. Coull beat N. Fulwood 6–4, 6–3.
    Girls: S. Reeves beat C. Berry 6–3, 6–3.
    International Finals
    Boys: A. McNeill (Scotland) beat R. Coull 4–6,
      6–4, 6–3.
    Girls: S. Reeves beat C. Ruane (Ireland) 6–0, 6–1.

1980 *English Finals*
    Boys: N. Beedham beat P. Treen 6–1, 6–3.
    Girls: S. Longbottom beat V. Adams 6–4, 7–5.

    International Finals
    Boys: N. Beedham beat T. Hartland (Wales) 6–3,
      6–1.
    Girls: S. Longbottom beat L. Browne (Scotland)
      7–6, 6–3.

1981 *English Finals*
    Boys: H. Slater beat G. Thomas 7–5, 6–2.
    Girls: S. Nicholson beat A. Grant 6–3, 6–1.
    International Finals
    Boys: H. Slater beat M. Walker (Wales) 6–1, 6–2.
    Girls: S. Nicholson beat M. Buckley (Ireland) 6–1,
      6–0.

1982 *English Finals*
    Boys: C. Peat beat A. Brice 7–5, 6–3.
    Girls: A. Grant beat A. Brasher 6–0, 6–1.
    International Finals
    Boys: C. Peet beat N. Jones (Wales) 7–6, 6–2.
    Girls: A. Grant beat S. Richards (Wales) 6–1, 6–1.

1983 *English Finals*
    Boys: J. Goodall beat L. Matthews 6–1, 6–1
    Girls: F. Couldridge beat S. McCarthy 6–2, 6–4.
    International Finals
    Boys: J. Goodall beat I. McKinlay (Scotland) 6–2,
      6–0.
    Girls: F. Couldridge beat A. Wood (Scotland)
      6–4, 6–0.

1984 Not held at Queen's

1985 *English Finals*
    Boys: D. Ahl beat S. Wilkins 6–2, 6–4
    Girls: A. Fleming beat S. Timms 6–2, 6–2
    International Finals
    Boys: D. Ahl beat A. Fisher (Wales) 6–4, 6–4
    Girls: A. Fleming beat S. Loosemore (Wales) 6–0,
      6–4

Lawn Tennis: Covered Courts

Olympic Games: 1908

Men's Singles: A. W. Gore; Silver Medal –
C. A. Caridia; Bronze – M. J. G. Ritchie.
Ladies' Singles: Miss G. Eastlake-Smith; Silver Medal –
Miss A. N. G. Greene; Bronze – Mrs Adlerstrale.
Men's Doubles: A. W. Gore and H. Roper Barrett; Silver
Medal – C. M. Simond and G. A. Caridia; Bronze –
G. Setterwell and W. Bostrom.

World Covered Court Championships: 1920

Men's Singles: F. G. Lowe beat W. C. Crawley 6–1,
6–3, 6–1.
Ladies' Singles: Mrs A. E. Beamish beat Miss
K. McKane 6–1, 1–6, 6–3.
Men's Doubles: P. M. Davson and T. M. Mavrogordato
beat F. M. B. Fisher and A. E. Beamish 4–6, 10–8,
13–11, 3–6, 6–3.
Mixed Doubles: F. M. B. Fisher and Mrs G. E. Peacock
w.o. S. N. Doust and Miss McKane scr.

The Covered Court Championships

MEN'S SINGLES: 1895–1969

	WINNER	RUNNER-UP
1895	E. W. Lewis	W. V. Eaves
1896	E. W. Lewis	W. V. Eaves
1897	W. V. Eaves	E. W. Lewis
1898	W. V. Eaves	H. L. Doherty
1899	W. V. Eaves	H. S. Mahony
1900	A. W. Gore	M. J. G. Ritchie
1901	H. L. Doherty	A. W. Gore
1902	H. L. Doherty	M. J. G. Ritchie
1903	H. L. Doherty	G. W. Hillyard
1904	H. L. Doherty	M. J. G. Ritchie
1905	H. L. Doherty	M. J. G. Ritchie
1906	H. L. Doherty	A. W. Gore
1907	A. F. Wilding	G. A. Caridia
1908	A. W. Gore	A. F. Wilding
1909	M. J. G. Ritchie	A. W. Gore
1910	F. G. Lowe	A. H. Lowe
1911	A. H. Gobert	F. G. Lowe
1912	A. H. Gobert	A. F. Wilding
1913	P. M. Davson	E. Larsen
1914	M. J. G. Ritchie	P. M. Davson
1919	P. M. Davson	M. J. G. Ritchie
1920	A. H. Gobert	P. M. Davson
1921	A. H. Gobert	W. C. Crawley
1922	A. H. Gobert	B. I. C. Norton
1923	J. D. P. Wheatley	Dr. A. H. Fyzee
1924	P. D. B. Spence	J. D. P. Wheatley
1925	S. M. Jacob	P. D. B. Spence
1926	J. Borotra	D. M. Greig
1927	E. Higgs	G. R. O. Crole-Rees
1928	J. Borotra	G. R. O. Crole-Rees
1929	J. Borotra	N. Sharpe
1930	J. Borotra	H. W. Austin
1931	J. Borotra	J. Satoh
1932	J. Borotra	H. G. N. Lee
1933	J. Borotra	H. W. Austin
1934	H. W. Austin	J. Borotra
1935	J. Borotra	N. Sharpe
1936	K. Schroder	J. Borotra
1937	H. W. Austin	K. Schroder
1938	J. Borotra	D. W. Butler
1947	I. F. Rinkel	E. Wittman
1948	J. Borotra	G. L. Paish
1949	J. Borotra	G. L. Paish
1950	J. Drobny	G. L. Paish
1951	G. L. Paish	I. Tloczynski
1952	J. Drobny	A. J. Mottram
1953	J. Drobny	R. K. Wilson
1954	J. Drobny	W. Skonecki
1955	V. Skonecki	W. A. Knight
1956	A. Huber	G. L. Paish
1957	no competition	
1958	M. G. Davies	S. Davidson
1959	R. K. Wilson	K. Nielsen
1960	W. A. Knight	R. K. Wilson
1961	J. A. Pickard	M. Santana
1962	R. K. Wilson	W. A. Knight
1963	R. K. Wilson	R. Taylor
1964	M. J. Sangster	R. K. Wilson
1965	R. K. Wilson	M. Cox
1966	no competition	
1967	no competition	
1968	R. A. J. Hewitt	R. C. Lutz
1969	R. G. Laver	A. D. Roche

MEN'S DOUBLES: 1890–1969

	WINNERS	RUNNERS-UP
1890	G. W. Hillyard and H. S. Scrivener	E. Renshaw and H. S. Barlow
1891	G. W. Hillyard and H. S. Scrivener	J. H. Crispe and H. S. Mahoney
1892	E. G. Meers and H. S. Mahoney	G. W. Hillyard and H. S. Scrivener
1893	W. Renshaw and H. S. Barlow	W. Baddeley and H. Baddeley
1894	E. G. Meers and H. S. Mahony	'Pilkington' and G. C. Ball-Greene
1895	W. V. Eaves and C. H. Martin	W. Renshaw and H. S. Barlow
1896	W. V. Eaves and C. H. Martin	F. L. Riseley and A. H. Riseley
1897	H. A. Nisbet and G. Greville	W. V. Eaves and C. H. Martin
1898	R. F. Doherty and H. L. Doherty	H. A. Nisbet and G. Greville
1899	R. F. Doherty and H. L. Doherty	E. W. Lewis and G. Greville
1900	R. F. Doherty and H. L. Doherty	M. J. G. Ritchie and 'A. Porter'
1901	R. F. Doherty and H. L. Doherty	W. V. Eaves and G. W. Hillyard
1902	R. F. Doherty and H. L. Doherty	M. J. G. Ritchie and H. M. Sweetman
1903	R. F. Doherty and H. L. Doherty	C. H. L. Cazalet and G. W. Hillyard
1904	H. L. Doherty and G. W. Hillyard	M. J. G. Ritchie and G. Greville
1905	H. L. Doherty and G. W. Hillyard	M. J. G. Ritchie and G. M. Simond
1906	R. F. Doherty and H. L. Doherty	A. W. Gore and G. A. Garidia
1907	M. J. G. Ritchie and A. F. Wilding	A. W. Gore and G. A. Caridia

Year	Winner	Runner-up
1908	M. J. G. Ritchie and A. F. Wilding	A. W. Gore and 'L. A. O. Seer'
1909	A. W. Gore and H. Roper Barrett	A. H. Lowe and F. G. Lowe
1910	S. N. Doust and L. O. S. Poidevin	A. W. Gore and H. Roper Barrett
1911	A. H. Gobert and M. J. G. Ritchie	A. H. Lowe and F. G. Lowe
1912	S. N. Doust and A. F. Wilding	A. H. Gobert and M. J. G. Ritchie
1913	S. N. Doust and A. F. Wilding	A. W. Gore and 'Lamb'
1914	P. M. Davson and T. M. Mavrogordato	P. Hicks and W. A. Ingram
1919	R. Lycett and R. W. Heath	T. M. Mavrogordato and P. M. Davson
1920	A. H. Gobert and R. Lycett	T. M. Mavrogordato and P. M. Davson
1921	T. M. Mavrogordato and P. M. Davson	A. H. Gobert and R. Lycett
1922	R. Lycett and S. N. Doust	T. M. Mavrogordato and P. M. Davson
1923	S. N. Doust and A. W. Asthalter	E. Hamilton Price and J. D. P. Wheatley
1924	C. H. Kingsley and P. D. B. Spence	A. Berger and 'Flaneur'
1925	C. H. Kingsley and P. D. B. Spence	J. D. P. Wheatley and S. N. Doust
1926	G. R. O. Crole-Rees and C. G. Eames	M. Sleem and A. H. Fyzee
1927	G. R. O. Crole-Rees and C. G. Eames	E. Higgs and D. M. Greig
1928	J. D. P. Wheatley and C. H. Kingsley	G. R. O. Crole-Rees and C. G. Eames
1929	G. R. O. Crole-Rees and C. G. Eames	J. D. P. Wheatley and E. C. Peters
1930	H. W. Austin and J. S. Olliff	W. A. Ingram and F. H. D. Wilde
1931	H. W. Austin and J. S. Olliff	J. Satoh and R. Miki
1932	H. G. N. Lee and G. L. Tuckett	R. Miki and J. Yamagishi
1933	G. L. Rogers and V. G. Kirby	R. K. Tinkler and C. R. D. Tuckey
1934	J. S. Olliff and D. D. Prenn	R. Miki and G. L. Rogers
1935	D. D. Prenn and D. N. Jones	F. H. D. Wilde and J. S. Olliff
1936	C. E. Hare and F. H. D. Wilde	H. G. N. Lee and K. Schroder
1937	D. W. Butler and F. H. D. Wilde	G. L. Rogers and K. Schroder
1938	J. S. Olliff and H. Billington	C. E. Malfroy and F. H. D. Wilde
1947	R. E. Carter and I. F. Rinkel	H. Billington and I. Tloczynski
1948	C. J. Hovell and C. M. Jones	D. H. Slack and H. F. Walton
1949	H. Billington and G. L. Paish	H. A. Clark and A. Hamburger
1950	H. Cochet and J. Drobny	G. D. Oakley and R. L. Sawney
1951	A. J. Mottram and G. L. Paish	H. T. Baxter and A. G. Roberts
1952	A. J. Mottram and G. L. Paish	J. Drobny and O. G. Williams
1953	J. E. Barrett and D. L. M. Black	M. G. Davies and R. K. Wilson
1954	J. Drobny and R. K. Wilson	G. D. Oakley and V. Skonecki
1955	R. N. Howe and V. Skonecki	M. G. Davies and R. K. Wilson
1956	G. L. Paish and J. A. Pickard	D. B. Hughes and G. D. Oakley
1957	no competition	
1958	M. G. Davies and R. K. Wilson	W. A. Knight and J. A. Pickard
1959	A. R. Mills and G. L. Paish	R. Becker and R. K. Wilson
1960	M. J. Sangster and R. K. Wilson	A. R. Mills and G. L. Paish
1961	L. P. Coni and M. A. Otway	J. R. McDonald and A. R. Mills
1962	A. R. Mills and R. K. Wilson	W. A. Knight and J. A. Pickard
1963	B. Jovanovic and N. Pilic	M. J. Sangster and R. Taylor
1964	R. Taylor and R. K. Wilson	K. Brebnor and F. D. McMillan
1965	A. R. Mills and R. K. Wilson	J. E. Barrett and R. D. Bennett
1966	no competition	
1967	no competition	
1968	R. C. Lutz and S. R. Smith	R. N. Howe and M. J. Sangster
1969	R. S. Emerson and R. G. Laver	R. A. Gonzales and R. A. J. Hewitt

LADIES' SINGLES: 1890–1969

Year	WINNER	RUNNER-UP
1890	Miss M. Jacks	Miss M. Pick
1891	Miss M. Shackle	Miss M. Jacks
1892	Miss M. Shackle	Miss M. Arbuthnot
1893	Miss M. Shackle	Miss M. Arbuthnot
1894	Miss E. L. Austin	Miss M. Arbuthnot
1895	Miss C. Cooper	Miss E. L. Austin
1896	Miss E. L. Austin	Miss C. Cooper

1897	Miss E. L. Austin	Miss R. Dyas
1898	Miss E. L. Austin	Miss P. Legh
1899	Miss E. L. Austin	Miss C. Cooper
1900	Miss T. Lowther	Miss P. Tulloch
1901	Mrs G. M. Hillyard	Miss T. Lowther
1902	Miss T. Lowther	Mrs G. W. Hillyard ret'd.
1903	Miss T. Lowther	Mlle Masson
1904	Miss D. K. Douglass	Mrs G. Greville
1905	Miss H. Lane	Miss G. S. Eastlake-Smith
1906	Miss D. K. Douglass	Miss T. Lowther
1907	Miss G. S. Eastlake-Smith	Miss M. Coles
1908	Mrs D. Lambert Chambers	Miss G. S. Eastlake-Smith
1909	Miss D. Boothby	Mrs M. O'Neill
1910	Mrs D. Lambert Chambers	Mrs M. O'Neill
1911	Mrs D. Lambert Chambers	Miss H. Aitchison
1912	Miss E. D. Holman	Mrs H. Edgington
1913	Mrs D. Lambert Chambers	Miss E. D. Holman
1914	Miss E. D. Holman	Mrs M. O'Neill
1919	Mrs D. Lambert Chambers	Miss E. D. Holman
1920	Miss E. M. Ryan	Miss E. D. Holman
1921	Miss E. D. Holman	Mrs G. Peacock
1922	Miss E. D. Holman	Mrs D. K. Craddock
1923	Mrs R. C. Clayton	Mrs H. Edginton
1924	Mrs A. E. Beamish	Mrs D. K. Craddock
1925	Miss J. Reid-Thomas	The Hon. Mrs Colston
1926	Miss P. Saunders	Miss M. E. Dix
1927	Miss E. Bennett	Miss C. Hardie
1928	Mrs L. A. Godfree	Miss E. Bennett
1929	Mrs L. R. C. Michell	Miss J. C. Ridley
1930	Miss J. C. Ridley	Miss J. Fry
1931	Miss M. Heeley	Miss J. Morfey
1932	Miss M. C. Scriven	Miss K. E. Stammers
1933	Mrs M. R. King	Miss K. E. Stammers
1934	Mrs M. R. King	Miss R. M. Hardwick
1935	Miss M. C. Scriven	Miss E. H. Harvey
1936	Sta. A. Lizana	Miss R. M. Hardwick
1937	Miss M. C. Scriven	Mrs M. R. King
1938	Miss M. C. Scriven	Mrs R. D. McKelvie
1947	Miss C. G. Hoahing	Mrs E. W. Dawson-Scott
1948	Miss C. G. Hoahing	Miss P. J. Curry
1949	Miss P. J. Curry	Miss J. Quertier
1950	Miss J. Quertier	Miss P. J. Curry
1951	Miss J. S. V. Partridge	Mrs J. J. Walker-Smith
1952	Miss A. Mortimer	Miss J. S. V. Partridge
1953	Miss A. Mortimer	Miss R. F. Woodgate

1954	Miss A. Mortimer	Miss S. J. Bloomer
1955	Miss J. A. Shilcock	Miss P. E. Ward
1956	Miss A. Buxton	Miss J. A. Shilcock
1957	no competition	
1958	Miss J. A. Shilcock	Miss C. C. Truman
1959	Miss A. Mortimer	Miss P. E. Ward
1960	Miss A. Mortimer	Miss A. S. Haydon
1961	Miss A. Mortimer	Miss C. C. Truman
1962	Miss A. S. Haydon	Miss C. C. Truman
1963	Miss D. M. Catt	Miss R. Schuurman
1964	Mrs P. F. Jones	Miss F. M. E. Toyne
1965	Mrs P. F. Jones	Miss F. M. E. Toyne
1966	no competition	
1967	no competition	
1968	Mrs B. M. Court	Miss S. V. Wade
1969	Mrs P. F. Jones	Mrs L. W. King

LADIES' DOUBLES: 1929–1969

	WINNERS	RUNNERS-UP
1929	(Invitation event) Mrs L. R. C. Michell and Miss M. E. Dix	Miss J. C. Ridley and Miss E. Goldsack
1931	Mrs L. R. C. Michell and Miss E. H. Harvey	Miss M. Heeley and Miss A. M. Yorke
1932	Mrs L. R. C. Michell and Miss D. E. Round	Miss A. M. Yorke and Miss J. M. Ingram
1933	Mrs L. R. C. Michell and Miss M. C. Scriven	Miss R. M. Hardwick and Miss K. E. Stammers
1934	Mrs J. B. Pittman and Miss A. M. Yorke	Mrs L. A. Godfree and Miss S. D. B. Noel
1935	Mrs J. B. Pittman and Miss A. M. Yorke	Miss R. M. Hardwick and Miss E. H. Harvey
1936	Miss M. Whitmarsh and Miss A. M. Yorke	Miss E. H. Harvey and Miss J. M. Ingram
1937	Miss J. Saunders and Miss V. E. Scott	Miss E. H. Harvey and Miss M. C. Scriven
1938	Miss E. A. Dearman and Miss J. M. Ingram	Miss J. Saunders and Miss V. E. Scott
1939–47	no competition	
1948	Miss P. J. Curry and Miss J. Quertier	Mrs B. M. Walter and Mrs P. J. Halford
1949	Mrs P. J. Halford and Miss P. O'Connell	Mrs B. M. Walter and Miss G. E. Woodgate
1950	Miss R. Anderson and Miss P. J. Curry	Miss J. Quertier and Mrs R. F. Chandler
1951	Mrs E. W. Dawson-Scott and Miss E. M. Wilford	Miss J. Quertier and Mrs J. J. Walker-Smith
1952	Miss J. Quertier and Miss H. Fletcher	Miss R. J. R. Bullied and Miss A. Mortimer
1953	Mrs P. Chatrier and Miss J. A. Shilcock	Miss H. Fletcher and Miss A. Mortimer

	Winners	Runners-up
1954	Miss R. J. R. Bullied and Miss A. Mortimer	Miss R. Walsh and Miss R. F. Woodgate
1955	Miss J. A. Shilcock and Miss P. E. Ward	Mrs L. M. Cawthorn and Miss R. F. Woodgate
1956	Miss J. A. Shilcock and Miss P. E. Ward	Miss S. J. Bloomer and Miss A. Buxton
1957	no competition	
1958	Miss J. A. Shilcock and Miss P. E. Ward	Miss S. M. Armstrong and Miss C. C. Truman
1959	Miss A. Mortimer and Miss P. E. Ward	Miss P. Wheeler and Miss C. Webb
1960	Mrs S. J. Brasher and Miss S. M. Armstrong	Miss A. S. Haydon and Miss A. Mortimer
1961	Miss D. M. Catt and Miss A. Mortimer	Mrs S. J. Brasher and Mrs V. A. Roberts
1962	Miss A. S. Haydon and Miss C. C. Truman	Mrs D. Roberts and Mrs V. A. Roberts
1963	Mrs P. F. Jones and Miss R. Schuurman	Miss D. M. Catt and Miss D. E. Starkie
1964	Miss P. R. McClenaughan and Miss F. M. E. Toyne	Mrs P. F. Jones and Miss S. V. Wade
1965	Mrs P. F. Jones and Miss S. V. Wade	Miss A. Mortimer and Mrs V. A. Roberts
1966	no competition	
1967	no competition	
1968	Miss M. A. Eisel and Miss W. M. Shaw	Mrs G. T. Janes and Miss F. E. Truman
1969	Mrs P. F. Jones and Miss S. V. Wade	Miss R. Casals and Mrs B. J. King

MIXED DOUBLES: 1898–1969

	WINNERS	RUNNERS-UP
1898	R. F. Doherty and Miss C. Cooper	G. Greville and Miss E. L. Austin
1899	R. F. Doherty and Miss C. Cooper	G. Greville and Miss E. L. Austin
1900	R. F. Doherty and Miss C. Cooper	E. D. Black and Miss B. Tulloch
1901	G. W. and Mrs Hillyard	H. L. Doherty and Miss T. Lowther
1902	H. L. Doherty and Miss T. Lowther	G. W. and Mrs Hillyard scr.
1903	H. L. Doherty and Miss T. Lowther	R. F. Doherty and Mlle Masson
1904	G. and Mrs Greville	A. D. Prebble and Miss D. Boothby
1905	R. F. Doherty and Miss G. S. Eastlake-Smith	M. J. G. Ritchie and Miss M. B. Squire
1906	A. F. Wilding and Miss D. K. Douglass	R. F. Doherty and Miss G. S. Eastlake-Smith
1907	A. F. Wilding and Miss G. S. Eastlake-Smith	J. B. Ward and Miss M. Coles
1908	A. F. Wilding and Miss G. S. Eastlake-Smith	M. J. G. Ritchie and Miss A. N. G. Green
1909	F. Rahe and Miss E. L. Boswoth	D. P. Rhodes and Miss B. Tulloch
1910	H. Roper Barrett and Mrs M. O'Neill	S. N. Doust and Miss Adams
1911	A. F. Wilding and Mrs D. Lambert Chambers	H. Roper Barrett and Mrs M. O'Neill
1912	A. H. Gobert and Mrs M. O'Neill	N. S. B. Kidson and Miss T. Hore
1913	S. N. Doust and Mrs D. Lambert Chambers	'Lamb' and Mrs M. O'Neill
1914	E. Gwynne Evans and Miss E. D. Holman	S. N. Doust and Mrs D. Lambert Chambers
1919	R. Lycett and Miss E. M. Ryan	E. Gwynne-Evans and Miss E. D. Holman
1920	R. Lycett and Miss E. M. Ryan	G. T. C. Watt and Mrs Craddock
1921	F. M. B. Fisher and Mrs G. Peacock	R. Lycett and Miss E. M. Ryan
1922	R. Lycett and Miss K. McKane	F. M. B. Fisher and Mrs G. Peacock
1923	A. W. Asthalter and Mrs H. Edgington	J. D. P. Wheatley and Miss E. L. Colyer
1924	C. G. Eames and Mrs A. E. Beamish	C. H. Kingsley and Miss J. C. Ridley
1925	P. B. D. Spence and Miss E. L. Colyer	C. R. Crole-Rees and Mrs A. D. Stocks
1926	S. N. Doust and Miss J. Ridley	D. M. Greig and Miss E. Bennett
1927	G. R. O. Crole-Rees and Mrs John Hill	C. G. Eames and Mrs E. A. Beamish
1928	G. R. O. Crole-Rees and Mrs L. R. C. Michell	J. D. P. Wheatley and Miss E. Bennett
1929	G. R. O. Crole-Rees and Mrs L. R. C. Michell	J. D. P. Wheatley and Mrs R. Lycett
1930	C. H. Kingsley and Miss J. C. Ridley	J. S. Olliff and Mrs L. A. Godfree
1931	J. S. Olliff and Miss P. G. Brazier	R. Miki and Miss M. Heeley
1932	J. Borotra and Miss B. Nuthall	R. Miki and Miss D. E. Round
1933	J. Borotra and Miss B. Nuthall	D. N. Jones and Mrs H. Dyson
1934	J. Borotra and Miss M. C. Scriven	R. Miki and Mrs M. R. King

1935	J. Borotra and Miss M. C. Scriven	F. H. D. Wilde and Mrs M. R. King
1936	J. S. Olliff and Miss F. James	C. E. Hare and Miss R. M. Hardwick
1937	K. Schroder and Miss J. Saunders	D. W. Butler and Miss P. O'Connell
1938	C. M. Jones and Miss E. H. Harvey	D. W. Butler and Miss V. E. Scott
1947	I. F. Rinkel and Mrs P. J. Halford	J. S. Olliff and Mrs E. W. Dawson-Scott
1948	J. Borotra and Mrs B. M. Walter	C. M. Jones and Miss P. O'Connell
1949	G. L. Paish and Miss J. Quertier	H. T. Baxter and Mrs E. W. Dawson-Scott
1950	G. L. Paish and Miss J. Quertier	J. Drobny and Miss R. Anderson
1951	G. L. Paish and Miss J. Quertier	C. J. Hovell and Mrs P. J. Halford
1952	G. L. Paish and Mrs I. F. Rinkel	H. Billington and Miss J. S. V. Partridge
1953	G. D. Oakley and Mrs P. Chatrier	C. W. Hannam and Miss S. J. Bloomer
1954	M. G. Davies and Miss D. Spiers	P. V. V. Sherwood and Miss P. A. Hird
1955	W. A. Knight and Miss J. A. Shilcock	M. G. Davies and Miss D. Spiers
1956	G. L. Paish and Miss J. A. Shilcock	G. D. Oakley and Miss P. A. Hird
1957	no competition	
1958	M. G. Davies and Miss P. E. Ward	J. E. Barrett and Miss S. M. Armstrong
1959	no competition	
1960	W. A. Knight and Mrs S. J. Brasher	J. A. Pickard and Miss A. S. Haydon
1961	J. R. McDonald and Miss D. M. Catt	J. E. Barrett and Miss P. E. Hird
1962	P. Darmon and Mme P. Darmon	M. J. Sangster and Miss D. M. Catt
1963	G. D. Oakley and Miss C. C. Truman	R. McKenzie and Mrs P. F. Jones
1964	R. N. Howe and Miss P. R. McClenaughan	J. E. Barrett and Miss A. Mortimer
1965	R. J. Carmichael and Mrs P. F. Jones	R. N. Howe and Miss S. V. Wade
1966	no competition	
1967	no competition	
1968	S. R. Smith and Mrs B. M. Court	P. W. Curtis and Miss M. A. Eisel
1969	no competition	

London Covered Court Championships

GENTLEMEN'S SINGLES: 1903–1939

1903	A. W. Gore	1924	P. D. B. Spence
1904	M. Decugis	1925	P. D. B. Spence
1905	A. W. Gore	1926	O. G. N. Turnbull
1906	A. F. Wilding	1927	S. M. Jacob
1907	M. Decugis	1928	N. Sharpe
1908	K. Powell	1929	J. S. Olliff
1909	M. J. G. Ritchie	1930	Y. Ohta
1910	A. F. Wilding	1931	I. Aoki
1911	M. J. G. Ritchie	1932	no competition
1912	T. M. Mavrogordato	1933*	H. W. Austin
1913	A. F. Wilding	1934	N. Sharpe
1914–1918	no competition	1935	D. D. Prenn
1919	T. M. Mavrogordato	1936	N. Sharpe
1920	F. G. Lowe	1937	R. A. Shayes
1921	M. Sleem	1938	N. Sharpe
1922	M. J. G. Ritchie	1939	L. Shaffi
1923	J. B. Gilbert		

LADIES' SINGLES: 1905–1939

1905	Miss D. K. Douglass
1906	Miss G. S. Eastlake-Smith
1907	Miss A. N. G. Greene
1908	Miss E. L. Bosworth
1909	Mrs H. Edgington
1910	Miss H. Lane
1911	Miss H. Aitcheson
1912	Miss B. Tulloch
1913	Mrs H. Edgington
1914–1918	no competition
1919	Mrs A. E. Beamish
1920	Mrs A. E. Beamish
1921	Miss K. McKane
1922	Miss K. McKane
1923	Mrs B. C. Covell
1924	Mrs A. E. Beamish
1925	Mrs A. E. Beamish
1926	Mrs A. E. Beamish
1927	Mrs John Hill
1928	Miss P. Saunders
1929	Mrs L. R. C. Michell
1930	Miss P. E. Mudford
1931	Mrs F. M. Strawson
1932	no competition
1933*	Miss J. Jedrzejowska
1934	Miss E. H. Harvey
1935	Miss R. M. Hardwick
1936	Miss A. E. L. McOstrich
1937	Miss K. E. Stammers
1938	Miss J. Saunders
1939	Mrs M. L. King

*From 1933 played as the Spring Open Covered Court Tournament

MEN'S DOUBLES: 1902–1939

1902	H. L. Doherty and R. F. Doherty
1903	H. S. Mahony and M. J. G. Ritchie
1904	R. F. Doherty and H. L. Doherty
1905	A. W. Gore and G. A. Caridia
1906	R. F. Doherty and G. M. Simond
1907	R. F. Doherty and G. M. Simond
1908	F. G. Lowe and A. H. Lowe
1909	M. J. G. Ritchie and R. B. Powell
1910	A. F. Wilding and M. J. G. Ritchie
1911	A. H. Lowe and F. G. Lowe
1912	M. J. G. Ritchie and T. M. Mavrogordato
1913	C. P. Dixon and P. M. Davson
1914–1918	no competition
1919	P. M. Davson and T. M. Mavrogordato
1920	P. M. Davson and T. M. Mavrogordato
1921	P. M. Davson and T. M. Mavrogordato
1922	S. N. Doust and J. B. Gilbert
1923	C. H. Kingsley and C. Ramaswami
1924	P. D. B. Spence and C. H. Kingsley
1925	C. H. Kingsley and J. D. P. Wheatley
1926	G. R. O. Crole-Rees and C. G. Eames
1927	G. R. O. Crole-Rees and C. G. Eames
1928	E. Higgs and D. M. Greig
1929	G. R. O. Crole-Rees and C. G. Eames
1930	J. S. Olliff and N. Sharpe
1931	I. Aoki and R. Miki
1932	no competition
1933	H. W. Austin and F. J. Perry
1934	V. G. Kirby and R. Miki
1935	C. E. Hare and D. D. Prenn
1936	C. E. Hare and F. H. D. Wilde
1937	L. Shaffi and M. D. Deloford
1938	C. E. Malfroy and F. H. D. Wilde
1939	C. M. Jones and M. D. Deloford

MIXED DOUBLES: 1904–1939

1904	R. F. Doherty and Miss G. S. Eastlake-Smith
1905	H. L. Doherty and Miss E. W. Thomson
1906	no competition
1907	R. F. Doherty and Miss G. S. Eastlake-Smith
1908	R. B. Powell and Mrs R. J. McNair
1909	R. B. Powell and Mrs R. J. McNair
1910	T. M. Mavrogordato and Mrs E. G. Parton
1911	S. N. Doust and Mrs R. J. McNair
1912	E. O. Pockley and Mrs D. Lambert Chambers
1913	A. F. Wilding and Mrs Colston
1914–1918	no competition
1919	F. M. B. Fisher and Mrs D. Lambert Chambers
1920	F. M. B. Fisher and Mrs G. Peacock
1921	S. N. Doust and Miss K. McKane
1922	D. M. Greig and Mlle M. Cousin

1923	D. M. Greig and Mrs D. Lambert Chambers
1924	C. G. Eames and Mrs A. E. Beamish
1925	P. D. B. Spence and Miss E. L. Colyer
1926	A. Berger and Mrs F. M. Strawson
1927	W. A. Ingram and Mrs Pleydell Bouverie
1928	G. R. O. Crole-Rees and Miss P. Saunders
1929	S. W. Harris and Miss J. C. Ridley
1930	P. D. B. Spence and Miss B. Nuthall
1931	I. Aoki and Miss A. M. Yorke
1932	no competition
1933	F. J. Perry and Miss B. Nuthall
1934	V. G. Kirby and Miss E. H. Harvey
1935	I. Aoki and Miss R. M. Hardwick
1936	J. S. Olliff and Miss B. Nuthall
1937	J. S. Olliff and Miss K. E. Stammers
1938	C. E. Malfroy and Miss E. H. Harvey
1939	C. M. Jones and Miss E. H. Harvey

British Junior Covered Court Championships

BOY'S SINGLES: 1956–1986

1956	M. J. Sangster
1957	M. J. Sangster
1958	J. I. Tattersall
1959	J. Baker
1960	T. J. Reynolds
1961	M. Cox
1962	S. J. Matthews
1963	P. W. Curtis
1964	M. E. Ratcliff
1965	G. Battrick
1966	D. A. Lloyd
1967	J. de Mendoza
1968	S. A. Warboys
1969	M. W. Collins beat G. M. Newton 6–3, 6–3
1970	R. A. V. Walker beat C. J. Mottram 6–2, 1–6, 6–3
1971	C. J. Mottram beat M. J. Farrell 9–7, 3–6, 6–2
1972	J. M. Lloyd beat R. A. Lewis 6–8, 6–2, 6–4
1973	J. R. Smith beat C. M. Robinson 10–8, 8–6
1974	P. Bradnam beat A. H. Lloyd 6–4, 6–4
1975	W. J. Gowans beat R. C. Beven 4–6, 6–3, 8–6
1976	A. N. Paton beat C. Bradnam 6–3, 1–6, 6–4
1977	N. A. Rayner beat J. M. Dier 4–6, 7–6, 10–8
1978	D. C. M. Atkinson beat K. Harris 7–6, 6–7, 14–12
1979	M. J. Bates beat P. S. J. Farrell 6–4, 7–6
1980	P. S. J. Farrell beat J. Bates 7–6, 6–4
1981	N. Fulwood beat D. Felgate 6–3, 6–3
1982	P. Heath beat J. Poxon 6–3, 6–2
1983	J. M. J. Clunie beat P. A. Moore 3–6, 6–4, 6–2
1984	R. A. W. Whichello beat S.C.S. Cole 6–4, 6–3
1985	R. A. W. Whichello beat J. M. Goodall 3–6, 6–2, 10–8
1986	D. Sapsford

GIRLS' SINGLES: 1956–1986

1956   C. C. Truman
1957   S. M. Armstrong
1958   C. C. Truman
1959   C. Webb
1960   R. A. Blakelock
1961   F. E. Walton
1962   S. J. Holdsworth
1963   M. B. H. McAnally
1964   M. Veale
1965   W. M. Shaw
1966   J. A. Congdon
1967   C. Molesworth
1968   V. A. Burton
1969   V. A. Burton beat D. P. Oakley 6–2, 6–0
1970   L. D. Blachford beat A. Coe 8–6, 6–1
1971   G. L. Coles beat L. D. Blachford 6–2, 6–1
1972   S. Barker beat G. L. Coles 6–2, 4–6, 6–2
1973   L. J. Mottram beat S. Barker 8–6, 6–3
1974   L. J. Mottram beat B. R. Thompson 6–2, 6–1
1975   M. Tyler beat J. Cottrell 6–1, 6–1
1976   J. M. Durie beat C. J. Drury 7–6, 6–4
1977   C. J. Drury beat K. M. Glancy 6–4, 6–4
1978   K. J. Brasher beat K. M. Glancy 7–6, 6–1
1979   K. J. Brasher beat D. K. A. Taylor 6–2, 6–4
1980   E. Jones beat L. Pennington 6–4, 6–3
1981   A. Brown beat S. Reeves 7–5, 6–1
1982   A. Brown beat S. L. Gomer 6–4, 7–6
1983   B. Borneo beat J. Louis 6–2, 2–6, 6–3
1984   A. L. Grunfeld beat L. C. Gould 7–6, 6–1
1985   J. V. Wood beat R. E. Charlton 6–2, 6–1
1986   S. McCarthy

BOYS' DOUBLES: 1955–1986

1955–56   R. W. Dixon and M. J. Sangster
1956–57   M. J. Sangster and M. J. Woolven
1957–58   H. M. Harvey and M. J. Sangster
1958–59   R. B. B. Avory and J. Baker
1959–60   D. K. Martin and T. D. Phillips
1960–61   S. J. Matthews and G. R. Stilwell
1961–62   S. J. Matthews and G. R. Stilwell
1962–63   P. R. Hutchins and M. E. Ratcliff
1963–64   D. A. Lloyd and K. F. Weatherley
1964–65   G. Battrick and J. M. M. Hooper
1965–66   J. G. Paish and J. P. R. Williams
1966–67   J de Mendoza and J. P. R. Williams
1967–68   S. J. Creed and P. W. Etheridge
1968–69   G. M. Newton and I. A. Thomson
1970   M. J. Farrell and J. M. Lloyd
1971   C. J. Mottram and P. Siviter
1972   R. A. Leslie and R. A. Lewis
1973   P. Bradnam and J. Trafford
1974   C. Bradman and P. Bradnam

1975   P. A. Bourdon and R. G. Haak
1976   M. D. Grive and N. A. Rayner
1977   M. R. E. Appleton and J. M. Dier
1978   H. B. Becker and A. A. Simcox
1979   R. P. Boulton and N. Gerrard
1980   J. Bates and P. Farrell
1981   S. Bale and D. Shaw
1982   P. A. Heath and J. D. Poxon
1983   B. Knapp and R. A. W. Whichello
1984   B. Knapp and R. A. W. Whichello
1985   R. A. W. Whichello and J. M. Goodall
1986   D. Sapsford and S. Booth

GIRLS' DOUBLES: 1955–1986

1955–56   Miss D. M. Catt and Miss C. C. Truman
1956–57   Miss S. M. Armstrong and
           Miss M. R. O'Donnell
1957–58   Miss D. M. Catt and Miss J. M. Trewby
1958–59   Miss J. E. Kemp and Miss J. M. Tee
1959–60   Miss M. M. Lee and Miss A. L. Owen
1960–61   Miss F. T. A. Anstey and F. E. Walton
1961–62   Miss M. B. H. McAnally and
           Miss S. V. Wade
1962–63   Miss M. B. H. McAnally and
           Miss S. V. Wade
1963–64   Miss A. F. Morris and Miss S. M. Veale
1964–65   Miss A. F. Morris and Miss W. M. Shaw
1965–66   Miss J. A. Congdon and Miss B. L. Davies
1966–67   Miss J. P. Cooper and Miss C. Molesworth
1967–68   Miss S. M. Langdale and
           Miss W. G. Slaughter
1968–69   Miss L. J. Charles and Miss W. G. Slaughter
1970   Miss L. D. Blachford and Miss A. Lloyd
1971   Miss A. M. Coe and Miss N. A. Dwyer
1972   Miss S. Barker and Miss N. Salter
1973   Miss S. Barker and Miss N. A. Dwyer
1974   Miss L. J. Mottram and
        Miss B. R. Thompson
1975   Miss C. A. Leatham and Miss M. Tyler
1976   Miss A. P. Cooper and Miss D. A. Jevans
1977   Miss A. P. Cooper and Miss D. A. Jevans
1978   Miss K. M. Glancy and Miss D. L. Morgan
1979   Miss K. J. Brasher and Miss D. K. A. Taylor
1980   Miss C. Gaskin and Miss E. Jones
1981   Miss A. Brown and Miss E. Jones
1982   Miss C. Gaskin and Miss S. L. Gomer
1983   Miss C. Gillies and Miss A. M. Grant
1984   Miss S. Longbottom and Miss J. Smith
1985   Miss A. M. Grant and Miss J. Louis
1986   Miss K. Hand and Miss V. Lake.

Covered Court Tournament: 1985

*A new competition, first held 1985 following
the opening of the new covered courts*

Men's Singles: I. Currie
Ladies' Singles: Miss J. Rich
Men's Doubles: S. King and T. A. Morgan
Ladies' Doubles: Mrs. S. J. Brasher and Mrs F. Morgan
Mixed Doubles: J. Markson and Miss J. Rich
Men's Veterans Over 45 Singles: B. C. Palmer
Men's Veterans Over 55 Singles: S. Howard
Men's Veterans Over 65 Singles: T. R. H. Frank
Men's Veterans Over 45 Doubles: T. Davies and R. Acker
Men's Veterans Over 55 Doubles: G. Sacerdote and S. Howell

Members' American Lawn Tennis Tournaments

1978	February	P. A. Clayton and Miss D. S. Parker
	April	L. Lane and N. K. Haugh
	December	T. F. Candy and R. M. Khatau
	May	abandoned owing to weather
1979	February	K. Farmanfarmai and Mrs S. Thomas
	December	R. Reichman and R. Loughton
	May	abandoned owing to weather
1980	March	R. F. Stephens and G. M. Foster
	May	D. C. Sellman and Miss A. Buxton
	December	G. Bamford and J. A. S. Edwardes
1981	April	G. Bamford and Miss C. Russell-Vick
	November	A. Fuss and C. McDonagh
1982	February	M. Schmeitzner and Mrs E. Sinclair
	April	M. P. Gill and Mrs B. Thompson
	May	C. Haswell and Miss L. Forrester
	November	S. Lyster and Miss P. Grade
1983	January	R. F. Stephens and Miss U. Rohrs
	February	D. de la Plain and Miss K. J. Brasher
	November	D. Bann and Miss C. Bann
1984	January	C. Haswell and Miss A. Brasher
	March	R. Tsiboe and Mrs J. Segal
	November	J. Markson and Miss J. Rich
	December	C. Boden and Mrs S. Boden
1985	January	J. Markson and Miss J. Rich
	February	R. Acker and Miss N. Quine
	March	P. Eberle and Miss W. Wassen
	Octover	C. Hiswell and S. Hiswell
	November	M. Schmeitzner and N. Quine

British Women's Tennis Association Winter Tournament: 1975–1985

1975	*Sponsored by Commercial Union*
	Under 23: L. Mottram
	Under 18: J. Durie
1976	*Sponsored by Colgate Palmolive* (1976–1981)
	Under 21: A. Cooper
	Under 16: K. Brasher
1977	Under 21: K. Brasher
	Under 16: J. Reardon
1978	Under 21: K. Brasher
	Under 16: D. Taylor
1979	Under 21: D. Parker
	Under 15: H. Narborough
1980	Under 21: K. Brasher
	Under 15: S. Longbottom
1981	Ladies' Singles: S. Reeves
	Under 15: S. Mair
1982	*Sponsored by Sunsilk*
	Ladies' Singles: A. Hobbs
	Under 15: R. Charlton
1983	*Sponsored by Sunsilk*
	Ladies' Singles Championship: K. Brasher
	Ladies' Singles: K. Hand
1984	*Sponsored by Sunsilk*
	Ladies' Singles: S. Reeves
	Under 14: V. Heath
1985	*Sponsored by Abbey Life*
	Ladies' Singles: B. Borneo
	Under 14: K. Fisher

IC v. IC of France

LONDON (QUEEN'S)

1929	French IC	10–5
1930	IC	9–6
1931	French IC	8–7
1932	IC	9–6
1933	French IC	8–7
1934	French IC	8–7
1935	French IC	11–4
1936	IC	12–7
1937	Drawn	8–8
1938	French IC	10–5
1939	—	
1946	French IC	8–4
1947	French IC	8–4
1948	Drawn	6–6
1949	French IC	7–6
1950	French IC	7–6
1951	IC	7–5
1952	IC	8–5
1953	IC	8–5

1954	IC	11–2
1955	IC	11–2
1956	French IC	8–7
1957	IC	8–4
1958	IC	13–3
1959	IC	12–4
1960	French IC	15–11
1961	IC	10–4
1962	French IC	11–8
1963	IC	11–8
1964	French IC	10–6
1965	IC	–
1966	IC	10–8
1967	IC	18–4
1968	French IC	13–12
1969	IC	15–7

1970	IC	14–12
1971	IC	16–9
1972	French IC	12–7
1973	IC	14–6
1974	IC	13–8
1975	Drawn	10–10
1976	IC	10–8
1977	IC	10–7
1978	IC	15–11
1979	French IC	8–7
1980	IC	16–6
1981	IC	8–7
1982	French IC	13–12
1983	IC	16–7
1984	French IC	12–9
1985	IC	48–27

Real Tennis

World Championship: 1905–1985

1905   C. Fairs beat P. Latham 5–1,
       Queen's and Prince's
1955   J. P. Dear beat A. B. Johnson 11–10,
       New York and Queen's
1957   A. B. Johnson beat J. P. Dear 7–3,
       Queen's
1976   H. R. Angus beat E. L. Scott 11–4,
       New York and Queen's
1981   C. J. Ronaldson beat H. R. Angus 5–1,
       (Angus retired injured), Queen's
1985   C. J. Ronaldson beat W. F. Davies 7–1,
       Queen's

Olympic Games: 1908

Gold Medal: J. Gould beat E. H. Miles
Bronze Medal: Hon. N. S. Lytton

Bathurst Cup: 1922–1960

1922   Great Britain beat France 5–0
1924   USA beat Great Britain 3–1
1928   USA beat France 3–0
       Great Britain beat USA 3–0
1930   Great Britain beat USA 5–0
1932   Great Britain beat USA 3–0
1934   France beat USA 3–2
       Great Britain beat France 3–0
1938   Great Britain beat France 3–0
1948   Great Britain beat France 5–0
1950   Great Britain beat France 5–0
       Great Britain beat USA 3–1
1955   Great Britain beat USA 4–1
       Great Britain beat Australia 3–0
1958   USA beat Great Britain 3–0
1960   USA beat Great Britain 3–2

Queen's Club Spring Handicap: 1898–1927

Instituted 1898. Open to members only.
No competition since 1927

1898 H. A. Nisbet (Winchester)
1899 A. D. Whatman (Eton)
1900 H. S. Mahony
1901 E. A. Biedermann (Eton and Oxford)
1902 B. J. Wolfe Barry (Winchester and Oxford)
1903 A. A. Surtees (Rugby and Cambridge)
1904 H. S. Mahony
1905 E. B. Noel (Winchester and Cambridge)
1906 Maj. A. Cooper-Key (Wellington)
1907 C. E. Tatham (Marlborough and Cambridge)
1908 Hon. E. A. Pomeroy
1909 H. M. Leaf (Marlborough and Cambridge)
1910 Hon. N. S. Lytton (Eton)
1911 R. Walker (Charterhouse and Oxford)
1912 E. A. C. Druce (Marlborough and Cambridge)
1913 E. A. C. Druce (Marlborough and Cambridge)
1914 E. A. C. Druce (Marlborough and Cambridge)
1915–1920 no competition
1921 G. R. Westmacott (Eton and Oxford)
1922 Hon. C. N. Bruce (Winchester and Oxford)
1923 V. H. Pennell (Charterhouse and Cambridge)
1927 R. W. Gandar Dower

Amateur Tennis Championship: 1888–1985

Queen's Club Cup:
Championship of Queen's Club 1888
Amateur Championship since 1889

	WINNER	RUNNER-UP	
1888	J. M. Heathcote	Sir E. Grey	3–1
1889	Sir E. Grey	E. B. C. Curtis	3–1
1890	E. B. C. Curtis	Sir E. Grey	3–1
1891	Sir E. Grey	Lord Windsor	Scr.
1892	H. E. Crawley	Sir E. Grey	3–2
1893	H. E. Crawley	Sir E. Grey	3–2
1894	H. E. Crawley	Sir E. Grey	3–2
1895	Sir E. Grey	H. E. Crawley	3–2
1895	Sir E. Grey	H. E. Crawley	3–0
1896	Sir E. Grey	H. E. Crawley	3–2
1897	J. B. Gribble	H. E. Crawley	3–1
1898	Sir E. Grey	H. E. Crawley	3–0
1899	E. H. Miles	J. B. Gribble	3–1
1900	E. H. Miles	J. B. Gribble	3–0
1901	E. H. Miles	J. B. Gribble	3–0
1902	E. H. Miles	J. B. Gribble	3–0
1903	E. H. Miles	V. H. Pennell (*ret.*)	2–0
1904	V. H. Pennell	E. H. Miles	3–2
1905	E. H. Miles	V. H. Pennell	3–0
1906	E. H. Miles	Jay Gould (USA)	3–1
1907	Jay Gould (USA)	V. H. Pennell	3–0
1908	Jay Gould (USA)	E. H. Miles	3–1
1909	E. H. Miles	Hon. N. S. Lytton	3–1
1910	E. H. Miles	Hon. N. S. Lytton	3–2
1911	Hon. N. S. Lytton	E. H. Miles	3–1
1912	E. M. Baerlein	Hon. N. S. Lytton	3–0
1913	Hon. N. S. Lytton	E. M. Baerlein	3–2
1914	E. M. Baerlein	Joshua Crane (USA)	3–0
1919	E. M. Baerlein	V. H. Pennell	3–2
1920	E. M. Baerlein	E. A. C. Druce	3–0
1921	E. M. Baerlein	C. S. Cutting (USA)	3–0
*1922	E. M. Baerlein	W. Renshaw	3–1
1923	E. M. Baerlein	V. H. Pennell	3–2
1924	E. M. Baerlein	Hon. C. N. Bruce	3–1
1925	E. M. Baerlein	Hon. C. N. Bruce	3–0
*1926	E. M. Baerlein	Hon. C. N. Bruce	3–0
1927	E. M. Baerlein	Hon. C. N. Bruce	3–1
1928	L. Lees	R. H. Hill	3–2
1929	E. M. Baerlein	L. Lees	3–1
1930	E. M. Baerlein	W. C. Wright (USA)	3–0
*1931	L. Lees	E. M. Baerlein	3–0
1932	Lord Aberdare	L. Lees	3–2
1933	L. Lees	Lord Aberdare	3–1
1934	L. Lees	Lord Aberdare	3–0
1935	L. Lees	Lord Aberdare	3–0
1936	L. Lees	C. M. N. Baker	3–0
1937	L. Lees	R. H. Hill	3–0
1938	Lord Aberdare	W. M. Ross-Skinner	3–0
1939	W. D. Macpherson	L. Lees	3–1
†1946	L. Lees	W. D. Macpherson	3–1
*1947	Lord Cullen	P. Kershaw	3–0
1948	P. Kershaw	L. Lees	3–0
1949	Ogden Phipps (USA)	W. D. Macpherson	3–0
1950	A. B. Martin (USA)	W. D. Macpherson	3–1
*1951	P. Kershaw	D. J. Warburg	3–0
1952	Lord Cullen	R. C. Riseley	3–2
1953	Hon. M. G. L. Bruce	P. Kershaw	3–0
1954	Hon. M. G. L. Bruce	P. Kershaw	3–2
1955	R. C. Riseley	P. Kershaw	3–1
1956	Hon. M. G. L. Bruce	D. J. Warburg	3–0
1957	Hon. M. G. L. Bruce	D. J. Warburg	3–2
†1958	N. R. Knox (USA)	Lord Aberdare	3–0
1959	D. J. Warburg	J. D. Whatman	3–2
1960	G. W. T. Atkins	D. J. Warburg	3–1
1961	D. J. Warburg	G. W. T. Atkins	3–0
1962	G. W. T. Atkins	D. J. Warburg	3–0
1963	G. W. T. Atkins	D. J. Warburg	3–1
‡1964	A. C. S. Tufton	D. J. Warburg	3–2
1965	D. J. Warburg	A. C. S. Tufton	3–2
1966	H. R. Angus	D. J. Warburg	3–1
1967	H. R. Angus	D. J. Warburg	3–1
1968	H. R. Angus	D. J. Warburg	3–0
1969	H. R. Angus	D. J. Warburg	3–1
1970	H. R. Angus	A. C. S. Tufton	3–0

1971	H. R. Angus	R. B. Bloomfield	3–0
1972	H. R. Angus	R. B. Bloomfield	3–0
1973	H. R. Angus	A. C. S. Tufton	3–0
1974	H. R. Angus	A. C. Lovell	3–0
1975	H. R. Angus	A. C. Lovell	3–0
1976	H. R. Angus	J. D. Ward	3–0
1977	H. R. Angus	A. C. Lovell	3–2
1978	H. R. Angus	J. D. Ward	3–0
1979	H. R. Angus	A. C. Lovell	3–0
1980	H. R. Angus	A. C. Lovell	3–1
1981	A. C. Lovell	H. R. Angus	3–0
1982	H. R. Angus	A. C. Lovell	3–0
1983	A. C. Lovell	H. R. Angus	3–0
‡1984	A. C. Lovell	M. F. Dean	3–0
1985	A. C. Lovell	H. R. Angus	3–2

* Played at Manchester 1922, 1926, 1931, 1947, 1951, 1957, 1964.
† Played at Lord's 1946, 1958.
‡ Played at Cambridge 1964, 1984.

Inter-Club Four-Handed Championship: 1920–1984

The 'Bailey Cup', instituted 1920 at The Queen's Club.
From 1954 The Amateur Doubles Championship

1920 E. M. Baerlein and W. Renshaw (M)*
1921 E. M. Baerlein and W. Renshaw (M)
1922 E. M. Baerlein and W. Renshaw (M)
1923 Hon. C. N. Bruce and R. H. Hill
1924 Jay Gould and C. S. Cutting (Paris)
1925 E. M. Baerlein and L. Lees (M)
1926 L. Lees and M. Woosnam (M)
1927 Jay Gould and W. C. Wright (Philadelphia)
1928 L. Lees and M. Woosnam (M)
1929 E. M. Baerlein and L. Lees (M)
1930 E. M. Baerlein and L. Lees (M)
1931 E. M. Baerlein and L. Lees (M)
1932 Lord Aberdare and W. D. Macpherson
1933 Lord Aberdare and W. D. Macpherson
1934 E. M. Baerlein and L. Lees (M)
1935 E. M. Baerlein and L. Lees (M)
1936 E. M. Baerlein and L. Lees (M)
1937 E. M. Baerlein and L. Lees (M)
1938 Lord Aberdare and W. D. Macpherson
1939 Lord Aberdare and R. C. Riseley
1940–1945 no competition
1946 L. Lees and P. Kershaw (M)
1947 W. D. Macpherson and Lord Cullen
1948 W. D. Macpherson and Lord Cullen
1949 W. D. Macpherson and Lord Cullen
1950 R. C. Riseley and P. Kershaw (Oxford)
1951 P. Kershaw and M. A. Pugh (M)
1952 R. C. Riseley and P. Kershaw (Oxford)

1953 R. C. Riseley and P. Kershaw (Oxford)
1954 Lord Cullen and Hon. M. G. L. Bruce
1955 P. Kershaw and R. C. Riseley
1956 P. Kershaw and R. C. Riseley
1957 Hon. M. G. L. Bruce and J. D. Whatman (M)
1958 N. R. Knox and A. B. Martin (Lord's)
1959 Lord Aberdare and J. D. Whatman
1960 N. R. Knox and W. E. Lingelbach
1961 Lord Aberdare and J. D. Whatman
1962 A. C. S. Tufton and J. W. Leonard
1963 A. C. S. Tufton and J. W. Leonard
1964 A. C. S. Tufton and J. W. Leonard
1965 W. T. Vogt and E. Newbold Black
1966 D. J. Warburg and R. L. O. Bridgeman
1967 H. R. Angus and D. J. Warburg
1968 H. R. Angus and D. J. Warburg
1969 H. R. Angus and D. J. Warburg
1970 H. R. Angus and D. J. Warburg
1971 no competition
1972 H. R. Angus and D. J. Warburg
1973 H. R. Angus and D. J. Warburg
1974 H. R. Angus and D. J. Warburg
1975 J. A. R. Clench and A. C. Lovell
1976 H. R. Angus and D. J. Warburg
1977 A. C. Lovell and A. G. Windham (Petworth)
1978 A. C. Lovell and A. G. Windham
1979 A. C. Lovell and A. G. Windham
1980 H. R. Angus and R. D. B. Cooper
1981 A. C. Lovell and M. F. Dean
1982 P. G. Seabrook and J. D. Ward
1983 A. C. Lovell and M. F. Dean
1984 A. C. Lovell and M. F. Dean (Cambridge)
1985 A. C. Lovell and M. F. Dean (Hatfield)

* Played at Queen's, except as shown in brackets.
  (M) indicates Manchester.

Ladies Real Tennis Singles

*The Mrs N. Berryman Cup**

1966 Mrs J. L. Deloford
1967 Mrs J. L. Deloford
1968 Mrs J. L. Deloford
1969 no competition
1970 Miss J. F. Haye
1971 Mrs J. C. Danby
1972 no competition

* It was agreed that the cup would continue to be owned by The
  Queen's Club until it was clear that the competition would be
  recognised by the T & RA as the national championship, when it
  would be donated, with Mrs Berryman's (now Mrs Bill Wilson)
  agreement. Accordingly, it was given to Nigel Bruce, the T & RA
  Secretary, in 1978, and is now known as 'The British Ladies Open
  Tennis Singles Cup' for which the competition is now held at
  Seacourt, Hayling Island.

Old Boys' Public Schools Tennis Championship: 1922–1985

Henry Leaf Cup

1922   *Old Wykehamists*
Hon. C. N. Bruce, R. H. Hill,
G. D. Huband

1923   *Old Rugbeians*
J. F. Marshall, J. C. F. Simpson,
H. S. Kershaw

1924   *Old Wykehamists*
Hon. C. N. Bruce, R. H. Hill,
D. R. Jardine

1925   *Old Wykehamists*
Hon. C. N. Bruce, R. H. Hill,
W. M. Ross-Skinner

1926–1927   *Old Wykehamists*
Hon. C. N. Bruce, R. H. Hill,
N. F. H. Freudenthal

1928   *Old Wykehamists*
Hon. C. N. Bruce, N. F. H. Freudenthal

1929   *Old Wykehamists*
Lord Aberdare, N. F. H. Freudenthal

1930–1932   *Old Wykehamists*
Lord Aberdare, N. F. H. Freudenthal,
W. M. Ross-Skinner

1933   *Old Wykehamists*
Lord Aberdare, N. F. H. Freudenthal

1934   *Old Wykehamists*
R. H. Hill, W. M. Ross-Skinner

1935   no competition

1936   *Old Wykehamists*
Lord Aberdare, R. H. Hill, N. F. H. Railing

1937   *Old Wykehamists*
R. H. Hill, N. F. H. Railing, A. L. Grant

1938   *Old Wykehamists*
Lord Aberdare, N. F. H. Railing,
W. M. Ross-Skinner

1939   *Old Harrovians*
W. D. Macpherson,
K. C. Gandar Dower, C. S. Crawley

1946   *Old Wykehamists*
W. M. Ross-Skinner, Lord Aberdare,
A. R. V. Barker

1947   no competition

1948   *Old Etonians*
Lord Cullen, R. Aird, R. St. L. Granville

1949   *Old Rugbeians*
P. Kershaw, D. J. Warburg, M. A. Pugh

1950   *Old Etonians*
Lord Cullen, R. Aird, R. St. L. Granville

1951   *Old Rugbeians*
P. Kershaw, D. J. Warburg, M. A. Pugh

1952   *Old Etonians*
R. Aird, Lord Cullen, R. St. L. Granville

1953   *Old Rugbeians*
P. Kershaw, D. J. Warburg, M. A. Pugh

1954   *Old Rugbeians*
P. Kershaw, D. J. Warburg, M. A. Pugh

1955   *Old Rugbeians*
P. Kershaw, D. J. Warburg, M. A. Pugh

1956   *Old Rugbeians*
P. Kershaw, D. J. Warburg, M. A. Pugh

1957   *Old Rugbeians*
D. J. Warburg, P. Kershaw, M. A. Pugh

1958   *Old Rugbeians*
D. J. Warburg, P. Kershaw, M. M. Morton

1959   *Old Rugbeians*
D. J. Warburg, P. Kershaw, M. A. Pugh

1960   *Old Rugbeians*
D. J. Warburg, P. Kershaw, M. A. Pugh

1961   *Old Rugbeians*
G. W. T. Atkins, D. J. Warburg,
P. Kershaw

1962   *Old Rugbeians*
D. J. Warburg, G. W. T. Atkins,
P. Kershaw

1963   *Old Rugbeians*
G. W. T. Atkins, D. J. Warburg,
P. Kershaw

1964   *Old Etonians*
A. C. S. Tufton, J. A. R. Clench,
J. W. Leonard

1965   *Old Rugbeians*
D. J. Warburg, P. Kershaw,
J. G. H. Hogben

1966   *Old Wykehamists*
H. R. Angus, Lord Aberdare, P. B. Hay

1967   *Old Wykehamists*
H. R. Angus, P. B. Hay, J. R. N. Travis

1968   *Old Harrovians*
R. B. Bloomfield, N. W. Smith,
R. L. O. Bridgeman

1969   *Old Wykehamists*
H. R. Angus, P. B. Hay, M. S. Travis

1970   *Old Wykehamists*
H. R. Angus, P. B. Hay, J. R. N. Travis

1971   *Old Harrovians*
R. B. Bloomfield, R. L. O. Bridgeman,
P. T. G. Philipps

1972   *Old Harrovians*
R. B. Bloomfield, R. L. O. Bridgeman,
N. W. Smith

1973   *Old Harrovians*
R. B. Bloomfield, R. L. O. Bridgeman,
N. W. Smith

1974   *Old Wykehamists*
H. R. Angus, A. C. Lovell, P. B. Hay

1975   *Old Wykehamists*
H. R. Angus, A. C. Lovell, P. B. Hay

1976	*Old Wykehamists*
	H. R. Angus, A. C. Lovell, P. G. Seabrook
1977	*Old Wykehamists*
	H. R. Angus, A. C. Lovell, P. G. Seabrook
1978	*Old Wykehamists*
	H. R. Angus, A. C. Lovell, P. G. Seabrook
1979	*Old Wykehamists*
	H. R. Angus, A. C. Lovell, P. G. Seabrook
1980	*Old Wykehamists*
	H. R. Angus, A. C. Lovell, P. G. Seabrook
1981	*Old Wykehamists*
	H. R. Angus, A. C. Lovell, P. G. Seabrook
1982	*Old Wykehamists*
	A. C. Lovell, H. R. Angus, P. G. Seabrook
1983	*Old Wykehamists*
	H. R. Angus, A. C. Lovell, P. G. Seabrook
1984	*Old Wykehamists*
	A. C. Lovell, H. R. Angus, D. Woolley
1985	*Old Radleians*
	J. Snow, T. Warburg, J. S. Male

The Open Tennis Handicap for the Druce Cup: 1936–1984

1936	M. A. Pugh	1965	R. J. Potter
1937	P. Kershaw	1966	P. M. Johns
1938	F. W. H. Loudon	1967	S. I. de Laszlo
1939–1946	no competition	1968	P. R. Wilson
1947	R. C. Riseley	1969	J. A. R. Clench
1948	Major J. K. Forte	1970	C. H. W. Robson
1949	R. C. Riseley	1971	J. A. R. Clench
1950	D. J. Warburg	1972	M. H. L. Bowler
1951	D. J. Warburg	1973	R. J. Potter
1952	W. M. Ross Skinner	1974	W. R. Boone
1953	W. S. S. Maclay	1975	J. G. M. Walsh
1954	no competition	1976	J. A. R. Clench
1955	D. J. Warburg	1977	K. Farmanfarmai
1956	D. J. Warburg	1978	T. F. Candy
1957	R. A. Colville	1979	no competition
1958	C. A. A. Black	1980	E. J. Cannon
1959	J. A. R. Clench	1981	R. C. MacKenzie
1960	N. W. Smith	1982	no competition
1961	J. L. Deloford	1983	no competition
1962	P. M. Johns	1984	J. W. R. Larken
1963	A. C. S. Tufton	1985	D. M. Norman
1964	A. C. S. Tufton		

British Open Doubles Championship: 1971–1985

Sponsored by Cutty Sark 1974–1978; Unigate 1979–1981; George Wimpey 1982 et seq.

| | WINNERS | RUNNERS-UP | |
| 1971 | N. A. R. Cripps and R. Hughes | H. R. Angus and N. W. Smith | 3–1 |

1972	C. Ennis and F. Willis	C. J. Swallow and N. A. R. Cripps	3–1
1973	C. J. Swallow and N. A. R. Cripps	C. Ennis and F. Willis	3–0
1974	C. J. Swallow and N. A. R. Cripps	C. Ennis and F. Willis	3–0
1975	C. J. Swallow and N. A. R. Cripps	H. R. Angus and D. J. Warburg	3–2
1976	F. Willis and D. W. Cull	C. Ennis and M. F. Dean	3–1
1977 (May)	A. C. Lovell and N. A. R. Cripps	F. Willis and D. W. Cull	3–1
1977 (Dec)	A. C. Lovell and N. A. R. Cripps	F. Willis and D. W. Cull	3–0
1978	A. C. Lovell and N. A. R. Cripps	C. J. Ronaldson and M. F. Dean	3–0
1979	A. C. Lovell and N. A. R. Cripps	C. J. Ronaldson and M. F. Dean	3–0
1980	A. C. Lovell and N. A. R. Cripps	B. Toates and F. Willis	3–0
1981	C. J. Ronaldson and M. F. Dean	W. F. Davies and L. Deuchar	3–2
1982	A. C. Lovell and N. A. R. Cripps	C. J. Ronaldson and M. F. Dean	3–0
1983	C. J. Ronaldson and M. F. Dean	C. Lumley and L. Deuchar	3–1
1984	W. F. Davies and L. Deuchar	C. J. Ronaldson and M. F. Dean	3–1
1985	W. F. Davies and L. Deuchar	C. J. Ronaldson and M. F. Dean	3–0

British Open Singles Championship: 1965–1984

The Field Trophy 1965–1973. Sponsored by Cutty Sark 1974–1978; by Unigate 1979–1981 and by George Wimpey 1982 et seq.

	WINNER	RUNNER-UP	
1965	R. Hughes	J. P. Dear	3–0
1966	F. Willis	N. A. R. Cripps	3–0
1967	F. Willis	G. W. T. Atkins	3–1
1968	H. R. Angus	F. Willis	3–2
1969	F. Willis	H. R. Angus	3–2
1970	H. R. Angus	F. Willis	3–1
1971	N. A. R. Cripps	F. Willis	3–1
1972	F. Willis	N. A. R. Cripps	3–0
1973	N. A. R. Cripps	F. Willis	3–1
1974	H. R. Angus	N. A. R. Cripps	3–2
1975	C. Ennis	N. A. R. Cripps	3–2
1976	H. R. Angus	N. A. R. Cripps	3–2*
1977	H. R. Angus	N. A. R. Cripps	3–0

* Played at Hampton Court.

1978	C. J. Ronaldson	H. R. Angus	3–2
1979	H. R. Angus	C. J. Ronaldson	3–0
1980(1)	C. J. Ronaldson	H. R. Angus	3–2
1980(2)	C. J. Ronaldson	A. C. Lovell	3–1
1981	C. J. Ronaldson	W. F. Davies	3–2
1982	C. J. Ronaldson	G. J. Hyland	3–2
1983	C. J. Ronaldson	L. Deuchar	3–0
1984	C. J. Ronaldson	W. F. Davies	3–2

Broadwood Cup: 1967–1984

Presented by R. L. O. Bridgeman, A. J. H. Ward and J. R. Greenwood

1967	J. L. Deloford	1977	no competition
1968	J. L. Deloford	1978	P. R. Wilson
1969	W. M. Ross Skinner	1979	P. R. Wilson
1970	S. I. de Laszlo	1980	B. C. Rich
1971	no competition	1981	R. L. Brown
1972	W. Eller	1982	B. C. Rich
1973	A. F. Lee	1983	B. C. Rich
1974	A. D. G. Sharp	1984	Y. Adam
1975	C. K. Simond		
1976	P. R. Wilson		

Oxford v. Cambridge

SINGLES: 1968–1976

1968	A. M. A. Hankey (Cambridge)
1969	W. J. C. Surtees (Oxford)
1970	A. G. Windham (Cambridge)
1971	C. M. Wilmot (Oxford)
1972	C. J. Moore (Oxford)
1973	J. P. Willcocks (Oxford)
1974	A. C. Lovell (Oxford)
1975	A. C. Lovell (Oxford)
1976	A. C. Lovell (Oxford)

DOUBLES: 1968–1976

1968	A. M. A. Hankey and J. O. Newton (Cambridge)
1969	W. J. C. Surtees and M. S. Travis (Oxford)
1970	P. T. Calvert and A. G. Windham (Cambridge)
1971	A. G. Windham and G. W. H. Dunnett (Cambridge)
1972	C. J. Moore and D. P. Jessell (Oxford)
1973	A. C. Lovell and J. C. A. Leslie (Oxford)
1974	A. C. Lovell and P. G. Seabrook (Oxford)
1975	A. C. Lovell and P. G. Seabrook (Oxford)
1976	A. C. Lovell and R. F. Hollington (Oxford)

England v. Rest of the World: 1984

In this special event, R. O. W. were all Australia. England beat Rest of the World 4–3

K. Sheldon (England) beat R. M. Cowper 6–2, 6–2, 6–5
A. C. Lovell (England) beat P. Tabley 6–2, 6–5, 6–3
C. J. Ronaldson (England) beat W. F. Davies 6–4, 6–4, 6–1
D. Johnson (England) lost to C. J. Lumley 4–6, 5–6, 2–6
B. Toates (England) lost to L. Deuchar 5–6, 5–6, 3–6
N. A. R. Cripps and Lovell beat Tabley and Lumley 6–3, 6–3, 2–6, 6–1
Ronaldson and Toates lost to Davies and Deuchar 5–6, 4–6, 3–6

The Eric Angus Cup: 1978–1985

Under-24 Championship sponsored by George Wimpey 1983 et seq.

1978	A. C. Lovell
1979	W. A. Hollington
1980	W. A. Hollington
1981	W. A. Hollington
1982	J. Howell
1983	L. Deuchar
1984	G. Parsons

The Stephens Tayleur Trophy: 1983–1985

The British under-24 Doubles Championship

1983	N. Pendrigh and L. Deuchar
1984	N. Pendrigh and G. Parsons
1985	M. Gooding and J. Snow

The British Junior Championship: 1983–1984

| 1983 | E. Popplewell |
| 1984 | R. Elmitt |

The Army Singles: 1983–1985

1983	M. W. Nicholls
1984	D. M. Reed-Felstead
1985	J. Maxwell

Rackets

Olympic Games: 1908

Singles, Gold Medal: E. B. Noel w.o. H. M. Leaf scr.
Doubles, Gold Medal: V. H. Pennell and J. J. Astor

Amateur Singles Championship: 1888–1986

Sponsored by Celestion 1981 et seq.

	WINNER	RUNNER-UP	
1888	C. D. Buxton	E. M. Hadow	3–0
1889	E. M. Butler	C. D. Buxton	3–2
1890	P. Ashworth	W. C. Hedley	3–0
1891	H. Philipson	P. Ashworth	3–2
1892	F. Dames Longworth	H. Philipson	3–0
1893	F. Dames Longworth	H. K. Foster	3–1
1894	H. K. Foster	F. Dames Longworth	3–1
1895	H. K. Foster	G. F. Vernon	3–1
1896	H. K. Foster	E. H. Miles	3–0
1897	H. K. Foster	P. Ashworth	3–2
1898	H. K. Foster	W. L. Foster	3–0
1899	H. L. Foster	E. H. Miles	3–0
1900	H. K. Foster	P. Ashworth	3–0
1901	F. Dames Longworth	J. Howard	3–1
1902	E. H. Miles	F. Dames Longworth	3–1
1903	E. M. Baerlein	E. H. Miles	3–2
1904	H. K. Foster	E. M. Baerlein	3–0
1905	E. M. Baerlein	E. H. Miles	3–0
1906	S. H. Sheppard	P. Ashworth	3–1
1907	E. B. Noel	B. S. Foster	3–2
1908	E. M. Baerlein	E. B. Noel	3–1
1909	E. M. Baerlein	H. Brougham	3–1
1910	E. M. Baerlein	P. Ashworth	3–0
1911	E. M. Baerlein	H. A. Denison	3–0
1912	B. S. Foster	G. G. Kershaw	3–1
1913	B. S. Foster	H. W. Leatham	3–0
1914	H. W. Leatham	E. M. Baerlein	3–2
1920	E. M. Baerlein	Hon. C. N. Bruce	3–1
1921	E. M. Baerlein	Hon. C. N. Bruce	3–0
1922	Hon. C. N. Bruce	E. M. Baerlein	3–0
1923	E. M. Baerlein	Hon. C. N. Bruce	3–1
1924	H. W. Leatham	T. O. Jameson	3–2
1925	C. C. Pell (USA)	H. W. Leatham	3–0
1926	J. C. F. Simpson	H. W. Leatham	3–2
1927	J. C. F. Simpson	Hon. C. N. Bruce	3–2
1928	J. C. F. Simpson	Hon. C. N. Bruce	3–0
1929	C. S. Crawley	H. D. Hake	3–0
1930	D. S. Milford	I. Akers-Douglas	3–0
1931	Lord Aberdare	I. Akers-Douglas	3–0
1932	I. Akers-Douglas	J. C. F. Simpson	3–1
1933	I. Akers-Douglas	C. S. Crawley	3–1
1934	I. Akers-Douglas	A. M. Hedley	3–0
1935	D. S. Milford	I. Akers-Douglas	3–1
1936	D. S. Milford	J. H. Pawle	3–1
1937	D. S. Milford	R. C. Riseley	3–0
1938	D. S. Milford	I. Akers-Douglas	3–0
1939	P. Kershaw	R. A. A. Holt	3–0
1946	J. H. Pawle	I. Akers-Douglas	3–1
1947	J. H. Pawle	D. S. Milford	3–2
1948	J. H. Pawle	D. S. Milford	3–2
1949	J. H. Pawle	D. S. Milford	3–2
1950	D. S. Milford	G. H. G. Doggart	3–0
1951	D. S. Milford	G. W. T. Atkins	3–2
1952	G. W. T. Atkins	M. C. Cowdrey	3–0
1953	G. W. T. Atkins	D. S. Milford	3–2
1954	J. R. Thompson	D. S. Milford	3–1
1955	J. R. Thompson	D. S. Milford	3–2
1956	G. W. T. Atkins	J. R. Thompson	3–1
1957	J. R. Thompson	M. R. Coulman	3–2
1958	J. R. Thompson	R. M. K. Gracey	3–0
1959	J. R. Thompson	J. M. G. Tildesley	3–2
1960	G. W. T. Atkins	J. R. Thompson	3–0
1961	J. W. Leonard	R. M. K. Gracey	3–0
1962	J. W. Leonard	G. W. T. Atkins	3–2
1963	G. W. T. Atkins	J. W. Leonard	3–2
1964	C. J. Swallow	G. W. T. Atkins	3–2
1965	J. W. Leonard	M. S. Connell	3–1
1966	C. J. Swallow	J. W. Leonard	3–1
1967	J. W. Leonard	C. T. M. Pugh	3–2
1968	C. J. Swallow	R. M. K. Gracey	3–0
1969	C. J. Swallow	J. W. Leonard	3–0
1970	M. G. M. Smith	C. T. M. Pugh	3–1
1971	M. G. M. Smith	H. R. Angus	3–2
1972	H. R. Angus	M. G. M. Smith	3–1
1973	H. R. Angus	M. G. M. Smith	3–1
1974	H. R. Angus	C. J. Hue Williams	3–1
1975	H. R. Angus	D. M. Norman	3–1
1976	W. R. Boone	J. A. N. Prenn	3–2
1977	C. J. Hue Williams	W. R. Boone	3–0
1978	W. R. Boone	J. A. N. Prenn	3–2
1979	J. A. N. Prenn	W. R. Boone	3–0
1980	J. A. N. Prenn	W. R. Boone	3–0
1981	W. R. Boone	J. A. N. Prenn	3–2
1982	J. A. N. Prenn	W. R. Boone	3–2
1983	J. A. N. Prenn	W. R. Boone	3–2
1984	W. R. Boone	M. W. Nicholls	3–0
1985	W. R. Boone	J. A. N. Prenn	3–2
1986	J. S. Male	W. R. Boone	3–2

Amateur Doubles Championship: 1890–1985

Sponsored by Celestion 1981 et seq.

1890	P. Ashworth and Capt. W. C. Hedley
1891	P. Ashworth and E. L. Metcalfe
1892	E. M. Butler and M. C. Kemp
1893	F. H. Browning and H. K. Foster
1894	H. K. Foster and C. S. C. F. Ridgeway
1895	F. Dames Longworth and F. H. Browning
1896–1897	H. K. Foster and P. Ashworth
1898	H. K. Foster and W. L. Foster
1899–1900	H. K. Foster and P. Ashworth
1901	F. Dames Longworth and V. H. Pennell
1902	E. M. Baerlein and E. H. Miles
1903	H. K. Foster and B. S. Foster
1904–1905	E. M. Baerlein and E. H. Miles
1906	E. H. Miles and F. Dames Longworth
1907	W. L. Foster and B. S. Foster
1908	F. Dames Longworth and V. H. Pennell
1909	E. M. Baerlein and P. Ashworth
1910–1911	B. S. Foster and Hon. C. N. Bruce
1912	H. W. Leatham and H. A. Denison
1913	B. S. Foster and H. Brougham
1914 & 1920	E. M. Baerlein and G. G. Kershaw
1921	Hon. C. N. Bruce and H. W. Leatham
1922–1923	J. C. F. Simpson and R. C. O. Williams
1924–1927	Hon. C. N. Bruce and H. W. Leatham
1928	Hon. C. N. Bruce and A. C. Raphael
1929	J. C. F. Simpson and R. C. O. Williams
1930	Lord Aberdare and H. W. Leatham
1931	J. C. F. Simpson and C. S. Crawley
1932–1933	K. A. Wagg and I. Akers-Douglas
1934	Lord Aberdare and P. W. Kemp-Welch
1935	K. A. Wagg and L. Akers-Douglas
1936–1937	C. S. Crawley and J. C. F. Simpson
1938	D. S. Milford and P. M. Whitehouse
1939 & 1946	C. S. Crawley and J. H. Pawle
1947	R. A. A. Holt and Maj. A. R. Taylor
1948	D. S. Milford and J. R. Thompson
1949	R. A. A. Holt and Maj. A. R. Taylor
1950–1952	D. S. Milford and J. R. Thompson
1953	P. Kershaw and G. W. T. Atkins
1954–1959	D. S. Milford and J. R. Thompson
1960	C. J. Swallow and J. M. G. Tildesley
1961–1962	G. W. T. Atkins and P. Kershaw
1963	J. W. Leonard and C. J. Swallow
1964–1965	R. M. K. Gracey and M. G. M. Smith
1966	J. R. Thompson and C. T. M. Pugh
1967–1968	J. W. Leonard and C. J. Hue Williams
1969–1971	R. M. K. Gracey and M. G. M. Smith
1972–1973	H. R. Angus and C. J. Hue Williams
1974	G. W. T. Atkins and C. J. Hue Williams
1975–1977	W. R. Boone and C. T. M. Pugh
1978–1979	H. R. Angus and A. G. Milne
1980–1984	W. R. Boone and R. S. Crawley
1985	C. J. Hue Williams and J. A. N. Prenn

Public Schools Singles Championship:

(Handicap from 1946 to 1953)

1946	W. J. Collins (Eton)
1947	J. D. Thornton (Winchester)
1948	I. C. de Sales la Terriere (Eton)
1949	M. C. Cowdrey (Tonbridge)
1950	A. D. Myrtle (Winchester)
1951	M. D. Scott (Winchester)
1952	T. Mesquita (Wellington)
1953	R. B. Bloomfield (Harrow)

The H. K. Foster Cup 1954–1985

1954	J. M. G. Tildesley (Rugby)
1955	C. J. Swallow (Charterhouse)
1956	P. D. Rylands (Tonbridge)
1957	J. W. Leonard (Eton)
1958	J. L. Cuthbertson (Rugby)
1959	G. P. Milne (Eton)
1960	G. P. Milne (Eton)
1961	M. G. Griffith (Marlborough)
1962	H. R. Angus (Winchester)
1963	G. B. Trentham (Wellington)
1964	A. H. V. Monteuuis (Tonbridge)
1965	W. J. C. Surtees (Rugby)
1966	R. S. Crawley (Harrow)
1967	M. J. J. Faber (Eton)
1968	M. J. J. Faber (Eton)
1969	C. N. Hurst-Brown (Wellington)
1970	R. W. Drysdale (Eton)
1971	M. Thatcher (Harrow)
1972	D. G. Parsons (Clifton)
1973	M. W. Nicholls (Malvern)
1974	M. W. Nicholls (Malvern)
1975	A. S. C. Pigott (Harrow)
1976	M. N. P. Mockridge (Marlborough)
1977	R. G. P. Ellis (Haileybury)
1978	R. G. P. Ellis (Haileybury)
1979	R. G. P. Ellis (Haileybury)
1980	J. S. Male (Radley)
1981	J. S. Male (Radley)
1982	J. P. Snow (Radley)
1983	A. Spurling (Tonbridge)
1984	R. Owen-Browne (Tonbridge)
1985	J. I. Longley (Tonbridge)

School Winners:

Eton	6
Tonbridge	5
Haileybury	3
Harrow	3
Radley	3
Rugby	3
Marlborough	2
Malvern	2
Wellington	2
Charterhouse	1
Clifton	1
Winchester	1
	31

Public Schools Championship: 1868–1985

Played at Prince's 1868–1886, Lord's 1887, Queen's since 1888 (except 1941, when final was at Wellington)

	WINNERS	RUNNERS-UP	
1868	*Eton* C. J. Ottaway and W. F. Tritton	*Cheltenham* J. J. Read and A. T. Myers	4–3
1869	*Eton* C. J. Ottaway and J. P. Rodger	*Rugby* S. K. Gwyer and H. W. Gardner	4–0
1870	*Rugby* H. W. Gardner and T. S. Pearson	*Eton* J. P. Rodger and F. C. Ricardo	4–2
1871	*Harrow* G. A. Webbe and A. A. Hadow	*Eton* F. C. Ricardo and A. W. Ridley	4–3
1872	*Harrow* G. A. Webbe and A. A. Hadow	*Eton* E. O. Wilkinson and W. W. Whitmore	4–1
1873	*Harrow* P. F. Hadow and F. D. Leyland	*Rugby* J. J. Barrow and J. Harding	4–0
1874	*Harrow* F. D. Leyland and C. W. M. Kemp	*Winchester* H. J. B. Hollings and H. R. Webbe	4–0
1875	*Eton* J. Oswald and D. Lane	*Winchester* H. R. Webbe and A. L. Ellis	4–1
1876	*Harrow* H. E. Meek and L. K. Jarvis	*Eton* Hon. I. F. W. Bligh and V. A. Butler	4–1
1877	*Eton* C. A. C. Ponsonby and Hon. I. F. W. Bligh	*Marlborough* G. M. Butterworth and F. M. Lucas	4–1
1878	*Eton* C. A. C. Ponsonby and J. D. Cobbold	*Harrow* H. F. de Paravicini and M. C. Kemp	4–0
1879	*Harrow* M. C. Kemp and Hon. F. R. de Moleyns	*Rugby* C. F. H. Leslie and W. G. Stutfield	4–0
1880	*Harrow* M. C. Kemp and E. M. Hadow	*Eton* P. St. L. Grenfell and J. C. B. Eastwood	4–2
1881	*Harrow* E. M. Hadow and A. F. Kemp	*Marlborough* A. W. Martyn and H. M. Leaf	4–1
1882	*Eton* R. H. Pemberton and A. C. Richards	*Harrow* H. E. Crawley and C. D. Buxton	4–2
1883	*Harrow* H. E. Crawley and C. D. Buxton	*Eton* R. H. Pemberton and H. Phillipson	4–2
1884	*Harrow* E. M. Butler and C. D. Buxton	*Eton* H. Phillipson and J. H. B. Noble	4–3
1885	*Harrow* E. M. Butler and E. Crawley	*Eton* H. Phillipson and H. W. Forster	4–3
1886	*Harrow* E. Crawley and N. T. Holmes	*Haileybury* J. D. Campbell and H. M. Walters	4–2
1887	*Harrow* P. Ashworth and R. D. Cheales	*Charterhouse* H. L. Meyer and R. Nicholson	4–1
1888	*Charterhouse* E. C. Streatfield and W. Shelmerdine	*Harrow* R. D. Cheales and E. W. F. Castleman	4–2
1889	*Winchester* E. J. Neve and T. B. Case	*Charterhouse* W. Shelmerdine and F. S. Cokayne	4–2
1890	*Harrow* A. H. M. Butler and W. F. G. Wyndham	*Wellington* G. J. Mordaunt and R. H. Raphael	4–3
1891	*Wellington* C. J. Mordaunt and R. H. Raphael	*Malvern* H. K. Foster and W. L. Foster	4–2
1892	*Malvern* H. K. Foster and W. L. Foster	*Harrow* B. N. Bosworth-Smith and F. G. H. Clayton	4–2
1893	*Charterhouse* E. Garnett and V. H. Pennell	*Eton* P. W. Cobbold and H. Harben	4–3
1894	*Charterhouse* V. H. Pennell and E. Garnett,	*Malvern* C. J. Burnup and H. H. Marriott	4–2

1895	*Harrow*	*Clifton*	4–0
	J. H. Stogdon and	R. O. de Gex and	
	A. S. Crawley	A. H. C. Kearsey	
1896	*Rugby*	*Eton*	4–3
	W. E. Wilson-Johnston and	H. C. B. Underdown and E. A. Biedermann	
	G. T. Hawes		
1897	*Harrow*	*Winchester*	4–3
	L. F. Andrewes and	E. B. Noel and	
	W. F. A. Rattigan	R. A. Williams	
1898	*Harrow*	*Eton*	4–2
	W. F. A. Rattigan and	E. M. Baerlein and	
	L. F. Andrewes	J. E. Tomkinson	
1899	*Eton*	*Harrow*	4–1
	S. MacNaghten and	F. B. Wilson and	
	I. A. de la Rue	S. J. G. Hoare	
1900	*Malvern*	*Rugby*	4–0
	B. S. Foster and	S. C. Blackwood and	
	W. H. B. Evans	O. Fleischmann	
1901	*Marlborough*	*Haileybury*	4–0
	A. J. Graham and	S. M. Toyne and	
	L. E. Gillett	P. F. Reid	
1902	*Harrow*	*Rugby*	4–2
	G. A. Phelips and	K. M. Agnew and	
	C. Browning	J. V. Nesbitt	
1903	*Harrow*	*Rugby*	4–2
	G. A. Phelips and	K. M. Agnew and	
	L. M. MacLean	J. Powell	
1904	*Winchester*	*Malvern*	4–0
	Hon. C. N. Bruce and E. L. Wright	G. N. Foster and A. P. Day	
1905	*Eton*	*Wellington*	4–1
	J. J. Astor and	H. Brougham and	
	M. W. Bovill	T. Hone	
1906	*Charterhouse*	*Wellington*	4–1
	C. V. L. Hooman and	H. Brougham and	
	R. M. Garnett	E. C. Harrison	
1907	*Wellington*	*Malvern*	4–1
	H. Brougham and	M. K. Foster and	
	E. C. Harrison	F. T. Mann	
1908	*Malvern*	*Rugby*	4–1
	M. K. Foster and	C. F. B. Simpson and	
	N. J. A. Foster	C. C. Watson	
1909	*Charterhouse*	*Eton*	4–1
	H. A. Denison and	J. C. Craigie and	
	H. W. Leatham	V. Bulkeley-Johnson	
1910	*Charterhouse*	*Eton*	4–0
	H. W. Leatham and	E. L. Bury & Hon.	
	H. A. Denison	J. N. Manners	
1911	*Rugby*	*Winchester*	4–3
	C. F. B. Simpson and W. H. Clarke	L. de O. Tollemache and D. F. McConnel	
1912	*Charterhouse*	*Wellington*	4–0
	G. A. Wright and	E. G. Bartlett and	
	C. B. Leatham	W. G. Grenville Grey	
1913	*Wellington*	*Haileybury*	4–0
	E. G. Bartlett and	D. H. Hake and	
	F. A. Carnegy	L. F. Marson	
1914	*Charterhouse*	*Wellington*	4–3
	L. D. B. Monier-Williams and	E. A. Simson and C. P. Hancock	
	J. H. Strachen		
1919	*Marlborough*	*Malvern*	4–1
	G. S. Butler and	C. G. W. Robson and	
	G. W. F. Haslehurst	N. E. Partridge	
1920	*Malvern*	*Eton*	4–1
	C. G. W. Robson and J. A. Deed	H. P. Guinness and R. Aird	
1921	*Wellington*	*Eton*	4–1
	P. N. Durlacher and	R. Aird and	
	L. Lees	H. D. Sheldon	
1922	*Eton*	*Radley*	4–2
	G. S. Incledon-Webber and O. C. Smith-Bingham	F. C. Dawnay and A. E. Blair	
1923	*Rugby*	*Radley*	4–2
	D. S. Milford and	F. C. Dawnay and	
	G. M. Goodbody	A. E. Blair	
1924	*Rugby*	*Eton*	4–2
	D. S. Milford and	C. J. Child and	
	E. F. Longrigg	T. A. Pilkington	
1925	*Harrow*	*Eton*	4–3
	A. C. Raphael and	C. J. Child and	
	N. M. Ford	T. A. Pilkington	
1926	Wellington	Harrow	4–3
	R. C. Dobson and	N. M. Ford and	
	J. Powell	A. M. Crawley	
1927	*Eton*	*Harrow*	4–0
	K. A. Wagg and	R. H. A.	
	I. Akers-Douglas	G-Calthorpe and G. L. Raphael	
1928	*Eton*	*Winchester*	4–3
	I. Akers-Douglas and I. A. de Lyle	P. J. Brett and W. D. Evans	
1929	*Winchester*	*Haileybury*	4–0
	N. McCaskie and	E. N. Evans and	
	R. H. Priestley	R. W. Bulmore	
1930	*Radley*	*Eton*	4–1
	P. I. Van der Gucht and W. H. Vestey	R. Grant and J. de P. Whitaker	
1931	*Harrow*	*Eton*	4–2
	R. Pullbrook and	A. M. Hedley and	
	J. M. F. Lightly	J. C. Atkinson-Clark	
1932	*Harrow*	*Rugby*	4–2
	R. Pullbrook and	R. A. Gray and	
	J. H. Pawle	R. F. Lumb	

1933	*Rugby*	*Harrow*	4–2
	R. A. Gray and	R. Pullbrook and	
	R. F. Lumb	J. H. Pawle	
1934	*Rugby*	*Haileybury*	4–2
	R. F. Lumb and	W. M. Robertson and	
	P. Kershaw	F. R. E. Malden	
1935	*Winchester*	*Marlborough*	4–2
	J. T. Faber and	P. M. Whitehouse	
	A. B. Kingsley	and J. D. L. Dickson	
1936	*Malvern*	*Clifton*	4–0
	P. D. Manners and	W. E. Brassington	
	N. W. Beeson	and S. G. Greenbury	
1937	*Malvern*	*Tonbridge*	4–3
	P. D. Manners and	J. R. Thompson and	
	N. W. Beeson	P. Pettman	
1938	*Rugby*	*Malvern*	4–2
	A. Kershaw and	P. D. Manners and	
	J. D. L. Repard	D. Chalk	
1939	*Rugby*	*Winchester*	4–0
	J. D. L. Repard and	A. R. Taylor and	
	W. H. D. Dunnett	H. E. W. Bowyer	
1940	*Haileybury*	*Rugby*	4–1
	J. K. Drinkall and	L. G. H. Hingley and	
	A. Fairbairn	P. M. Dagnall	
1941	*Haileybury*	*Clifton*	4–0
	J. K. Drinkall and	R. J. Potter and	
	A. Fairbairn	L. J. Waugh	
1943	*Winchester*	*Harrow*	4–2
	G. H. G. Doggart	I. N. Mitchell and	
	and J. B. Thursfield	J. G. Hogg.	
1944	*Winchester*	*Eton*	4–2
	H. E. Webb and	A. J. H. Ward and	
	G. H. J. Myrtle	J. R. Greenwood	
1945	*Winchester*	*Eton*	4–1
	H. E. Webb and	J. A. R. Clench and	
	G. H. J. Myrtle	W. H. R. Brooks	
1946	*Wellington*	*Harrow*	4–1
	C. B. Haycraft and	G. R. Simmonds and	
	J. E. L. Ainslie	J. A. Glynne-Percy	
1947	*Harrow*	*Eton*	4–2
	G. R. Simmonds and	R. F. H. Ward and	
	R. K. F. C.	W. J. Collins	
	Treherne-Thomas		
1948	*Harrow*	*Wellington*	4–3
	D. W. Taylor and	A. H. Swift and	
	T. A. M. Pigott	R. L. Lees	
1949	*Winchester*	*Eton*	4–3
	P. M. Welsh and	I. C. de Sales la	
	M. R. Coulman	Terrière and	
		A. C. D. Ingleby-	
		Mackenzie	
1950	*Winchester*	*Harrow*	4–2
	M. R. Coulman and	R. L. O. Bridgeman	
	A. D. Myrtle	and R. J. McAlpine ·	
1951	*Winchester*	*Tonbridge*	4–2
	M. R. Coulman and	M. C. Cowdrey and	
	A. D. Myrtle	J. F. Campbell	
1952	*Rugby*	*Wellington*	4–2
	D. R. W. Harrison	P. de Mesquita and	
	and J. G. H. Hogben	M. W. Bolton	
1953	*Winchester*	*Radley*	4–3
	R. T. C. Whatmore	E. R. Dexter and	
	and D. B. D. Lowe	I. A. K. Dipple	
1954	*Harrow*	*Marlborough*	4–2
	C. A. Strang and	N. R. C. Marr and	
	R. B. Bloomfield	P. R. H. Anderson	
1955	*Eton*	*Winchester*	4–1
	C. T. M. Pugh and	C. N. Copeman and	
	Lord Chelsea	M. M. Mitchell	
		Thompson	
1956	*Charterhouse*	*Marlborough*	4–1
	C. J. Swallow and	P. Pyemont and	
	J. Carless	N. C. Harris	
1957	*Tonbridge*	*Marlborough*	4–1
	M. S. Connell and	P. Pyemont and	
	P. D. Rylands	N. C. Harris	
1958	*Eton*	*Winchester*	4–1
	J. W. Leonard and	P. J. L. Wright and	
	D. M. Norman	Nawab of Pataudi	
1959	*Winchester*	*Eton*	4–3
	Nawab of Pataudi and	D. M. Norman and	
	C. E. M. Snell	R. M. Bailey	
1960	*Marlborough*	*Winchester*	4–2
	A. J. Price and	C. E. M. Snell and	
	M. G. Griffith	P. B. Hay	
1961	*Eton*	*Marlborough*	4–2
	G. P. Milne and	M. G. Griffith and	
	B. A. Fitzgerald	J. Hopper	
1962	*Marlborough*	*Winchester*	4–3
	M. G. Griffith and	H. R. Angus and	
	J. Hopper	C. J. H. Green	
1963	*Eton*	*Winchester*	4–1
	R. A. Pilkington and	H. R. Angus and	
	M. D. T. Faber	C. L. Sunter	
1964	*Eton*	*Tonbridge*	4–3
	M. D. T. Faber and	T. F. Tyler and	
	G. W. Pilkington	A. H. V. Monteuuis	
1965	*Rugby*	*Eton*	4–3
	W. J. C. Surtees and	G. W. Pilkington and	
	A. M. A. Hankey	A. R. Bonsor	
1966	*Malvern*	*Radley*	4–0
	P. F. C. Begg and	J. K. Rogers and	
	P. D'A. Mander	B. M. Osborne	
1967	*Eton*	*Harrow*	4–3
	Lord Wellesley and	R. N. Readman and	
	M. J. J. Faber	R. S. Crawley	

1968 *Eton*   *Rugby*   4–0
      M. J. J. Faber and   S. R. Miller and
      W. R. Boone   J. C. A. Leslie
1969 *Eton*   *Harrow*   4–0
      M. J. J. Faber and   C. H. Braithwaite and
      A. G. Milne   G. R. J. McDonald
1970 *Eton*   *Rugby*   4–0
      R. W. Drysdale and   T. H. Wetherill and
      N. H. P. Bacon   J. H. M. Griffiths
1971 *Harrow*   *Clifton*   4–2
      M. Thatcher and   J. P. Willcocks and
      J. A. N. Prenn   D. G. Parsons
1972 *Winchester*   *Haileybury*   4–0
      A. C. Lovell and   J. E. Dawes and
      P. G. Seabrook   R. F. Hollington
1973 *Tonbridge*   *Malvern*   4–1
      N. B. S. Hawkins   J. G. Hughes and
      and C. S. Cowdrey   M. W. Nicholls
1974 *Malvern*   *Eton*   4–2
      M. W. Nicholls and   T. M. Brudenell and
      P. C. Nicholls   D. M. Lindsay
1975 *Malvern*   *Harrow*   4–0
      P. C. Nicholls and   A. C. S. Pigott and
      M. A. Tang   P. Greig
1976 *Marlborough*   *Malvern*   4–3
      D. K. Watson and   P. C. Nicholls and
      M. N. P. Mockridge   M. A. Tang
1977 *Malvern*   *Marlborough*   4–3
      P. J. Rosser and   D. K. Watson and
      A. J. B. MacDonald   C. F. Worlidge
1978 *Haileybury*   *Harrow*   4–1
      R. G. P. Ellis and   D. J.G. Thomas and
      P. Wallis   M. L. J. Paul
1979 *Harrow*   *Eton*   4–1
      D. J. G. Thomas and   D. J. C. Faber and
      M. L. J. Paul   A. D. Pease
1980 *Wellington*   *Marlborough*   4–0
      J. H. C. Mallinson   A. J. Naylor and
      and R. A. C.   M. R. C. Swallow
      Mallinson
1981 *Tonbridge*   *Clifton*   4–2
      G. R. Cowdrey and   P. B. Morris and
      P. Reiss   T. R. V. Robins
1982 *Radley*   *Tonbridge*   4–0
      J. S. Male and   G. R. Cowdrey and
      J. P. Snow   A. M. Spurling
1983 *Tonbridge*   *Eton*   4–1
      A. M. Spurling and   A. C. B. Giddins and
      R. Owen-Browne   M. H. Brooks
1984 *Harrow*   *Wellington*   4–1
      D. G. Dick and   D. S. C. Mallinson
      S. O'N. Segrave   and A. H. Gordon
1985 *Tonbridge*   *Eton*   4–0
      R. Owen-Browne and   P. Baily and
      S. M. S. Davies   M.C. Smail

TABLE SHOWING FIRST YEAR OF ENTRY

At Prince's Club, Hans Place (1868–1886):

1868 Eton, Harrow, Charterhouse, Cheltenham
1869 Rugby, Haileybury
1871 Wellington
1873 Winchester, Marlborough
1883 Malvern
1886 Clifton
1887 Radley (Played at Lord's)

At Queen's Club (from 1888):

1898 Tonbridge
1904 Rossall
1908 Westminster
1920 R. N. C. Dartmouth
1984 The following schools no longer enter for the P. S. Championships and their last appearance is shown in brackets.

Cheltenham (1939), R. N. C. Dartmouth (1939), Rossall (1904), Westminster (1926). Rossall and Westminster no longer have courts. Cheltenham are hoping to get their court back into play in the near future. R.N.C. Dartmouth have for many years had no 14-year-old entry.

TABLE OF WINNERS AND FINALISTS UP TO 1985

School	Year of entry	Winners	Finalist runners-up	Pts	Place
Charterhouse	1868	9	2	20	7
Cheltenham	1868	0	1	1	13
Clifton	1886	0	5	5	12
Eton	1868	20	29	69	2
Haileybury	1869	3	6	12	10
Harrow	1868	28	15	71	1
Malvern	1883	10	8	28	5
Marlborough	1873	5	9	19	8
Radley	1887	2	4	8	11
Rugby	1869	11	11	33	4
Tonbridge	1898	5	4	14	9
Wellington	1871	7	8	22	6
Winchester	1873	13	11	37	3

(R.N.C. Dartmouth, Rossall and Westminster have never reached the final.) (Points allocated are: 2 for a win, 1 for runner-up.)

Public Schools Old Boys' Championship: 1929–1985

Noel-Bruce Cup

1929 *Old Etonians*
      R. C. O. Williams and
      I. Akers-Douglas

1930 *Old Rugbeians* D. S. Milford and J. C. F. Simpson	1964 *Old Etonians* D. M. Norman and C. T. M. Pugh
1931 *Old Rugbeians* D. S. Milford and J. C. F. Simpson	1965 *Old Etonians* J. W. Leonard and C. T. M. Pugh
1932 *Old Etonians* K. A. Wagg and I. Akers-Douglas	1966 *Old Rugbeians* G. W. T. Atkins and J. G. H. Hogben
1933 *Old Rugbeians* D. S. Milford and J. C. F. Simpson	1967 *Old Harrovians* C. J. Hue Williams and J. Q. Greenstock
1934 *Old Rugbeians* D. S. Milford and J. C. F. Simpson	1968 *Old Carthusians* C. J. Swallow and J. M. M. Hooper
1935 *Old Wykehamists* N. McCaskie and J. T. Faber	1969 *Old Tonbridgians* R. M. K. Gracey and M. G. M. Smith
1936 *Old Rugbeians* R. F. Lumb and P. Kershaw	1970 *Old Tonbridgians* R. M. K. Gracey and M. G. M. Smith
1937 *Old Rugbeians* R. F. Lumb and P. Kershaw	1971 *Old Tonbridgians* R. M. K. Gracey and M. G. M. Smith
1938 *Old Rugbeians* R. F. Lumb and P. Kershaw	1972 *Old Tonbridgians* R. M. K. Gracey and M. G. M. Smith
1939–1945 no competition	1973 *Old Tonbridgians* R. M. K. Gracey and M. G. M. Smith
1946 *Old Rugbeians* D. S. Milford and P. Kershaw	1974 *Old Tonbridgians* R. M. K. Gracey and M. G. M. Smith
1947 *Old Rugbeians* D. S. Milford and P. Kershaw	1975 *Old Harrovians* C. J. Hue Williams and J. A. N. Prenn
1948 *Old Rugbeians* D. S. Milford and P. Kershaw	1976 *Old Harrovians* C. J. Hue Williams and J. A. N. Prenn
1949 *Old Rugbeians* D. S. Milford and P. Kershaw	1977 *Old Harrovians* C. J. Hue Williams and J. A. N. Prenn
1950 *Old Rugbeians* D. S. Milford and P. Kershaw	1978 *Old Etonians* W. R. Boone and A. G. Milne
1951 *Old Rugbeians* D. S. Milford and P. Kershaw	1979 *Old Etonians* W. R. Boone and A. G. Milne
1952 *Old Rugbeians* D. S. Milford and P. Kershaw	1980 *Old Harrovians* C. J. Hue Williams and J. A. N. Prenn
1953 *Old Tonbridgians* J. R. Thompson and M. C. Cowdrey	1981 *Old Etonians* W. R. Boone and A. G. Milne
1954 *Old Rugbeians* D. S. Milford and P. Kershaw	1982 *Old Harrovians* C. J. Hue Williams and J. A. N. Prenn
1955 *Old Tonbridgians* J. R. Thompson and M. C. Cowdrey	1983 *Old Etonians* W. R. Boone and D. M. Norman
1956 *Old Tonbridgians* J. R. Thompson and R. M. K. Gracey	1984 *Old Etonians* W. R. Boone and C. T. M. Pugh
1957 *Old Tonbridgians* J. R. Thompson and M. C. Cowdrey	1985 *Old Harrovians* C. J. Hue Williams and J. A. N. Prenn
1958 *Old Tonbridgians* J. R. Thompson and R. M. K. Gracey	
1959 *Old Tonbridgians* J. R. Thompson and R. M. K. Gracey	
1960 *Old Rugbeians* G. W. T. Atkins and P. Kershaw	
1961 *Old Tonbridgians* J. R. Thompson and R. M. K. Gracey	
1962 *Old Etonians* J. W. Leonard and C. T. M. Pugh	
1963 *Old Etonians* J. W. Leonard and C. T. M. Pugh	

Summary of results:

Old Rugbeians	17 wins
Old Tonbridgians	13 wins
Old Etonians	10 wins
Old Harrovians	8 wins
Old Carthusians	1 win
Old Wykehamists	1 win
	50

Oxford v. Cambridge

Played at Oxford 1855, unknown 1858, Prince's 1859–1886, Manchester 1887, Queen's since 1888. Second string match first counted towards result in 1937

SINGLES: 1858–1985

	WINNER	RUNNER-UP	
1855	no match		
1858	*Oxford*		
	W. H. Dyke	J. M. Moorsom	3–1
1859	*Oxford*		
	W. H. Dyke	J. M. Moorsom	3–1
1860	*Oxford*		
	W. H. Dyke	J. M. Moorsom	3–0
1861	*Oxford*		
	R. D. Walker	A. Ainslie	3–1
1862	*Cambridge*		
	A. Ainslie	R. D. Walker	3–1
1863	*Cambridge*		
	A. Ainslie	R. D. Walker	3–1
1864	*Cambridge*		
	A. W. T. Daniell	R. D. Walker	3–0
1865	*Cambridge*		
	C. D. Rudd	R. T. Reid	3–0
1866	*Cambridge*		
	J. W. Knight-Bruce	W. E. Maitland	3–1
1867	*Cambridge*		
	C. E. Parker	R. T. Reid	3–2
1868	*Cambridge*		
	W. S. O. Warner	C. J. P. Clay	3–0
1869	*Oxford*		
	C. J. P. Clay	W. B. Money	3–0
1870	*Oxford*		
	C. J. P. Clay	M. H. Stow	3–0
1871	*Oxford*		
	C. J. Ottoway	W. Yardley	3–0
1872	*Oxford*		
	C. J. Ottoway	E. J. Sanders	3–0
1873	*Oxford*		
	C. J. Ottoway	E. J. Sanders	3–0
1874	*Oxford*		
	R. O. Milne	E. J. Sanders	3–1
1875	*Oxford*		
	R. O. Milne	J. M. Batten	3–1
1876	*Oxford*		
	T. S. Drury	E. O. Pleydell-Bouverie	3–2
1877	*Oxford*		
	A. J. Webbe	Hon. A. Lyttelton	3–2
1878	*Oxford*		
	A. J. Webbe	E. O. Pleydell-Bouverie	3–1
1879	*Cambridge*		
	Hon. I. F. W. Bligh	S. C. Snow	3–0
1880	*Cambridge*		
	Hon. I. F. W. Bligh	F. A. Jones	3–1
1881	*Oxford*		
	C. F. H. Leslie	C. T. Studd	3–0
1882	*Cambridge*		
	C. T. Studd	C. F. H. Leslie	3–1
1883	*Cambridge*		
	J. D. Cobbold	W. W. Paine	3–0
1884	*Cambridge*		
	H. M. Leaf	E. H. Buckland	3–2
1885	*Cambridge*		
	H. E. Crawley	E. H. Buckland	3–0
1886	*Cambridge*		
	H. E. Crawley	E. H. Buckland	3–2
1887	*Oxford*		
	J. H. B. Noble	H. E. Crawley	3–2
1888	*Oxford*		
	H. Philipson	C. D. Buxton	3–0
1889	*Cambridge*		
	E. M. Butler	E. L. Metcalfe	3–1
1890	*Cambridge*		
	P. Ashworth	E. L. Metcalfe	3–2
1891	*Cambridge*		
	P. Ashworth	E. L. Metcalfe	3–0
1892	*Cambridge*		
	C. P. Dixon	F. S. Cokayne	3–1
1893	*Oxford*		
	H. K. Foster	S. D. Corbett	3–0
1894	*Oxford*		
	H. K. Foster	P. W. Cobbold	3–2
1895	*Oxford*		
	H. K. Foster	P. W. Cobbold	3–0
1896	*Oxford*		
	H. K. Foster	P. W. Cobbold	3–0
1897	*Cambridge*		
	E. Garnett	R. E. Foster	3–0
1898	*Oxford*		
	R. E. Foster	E. Garnett	3–1
1899	*Cambridge*		
	E. B. Noel	R. A. Williams	3–0
1900	*Oxford*		
	L. F. Andrewes	E. B. Noel	3–2
1901	*Cambridge*		
	E. M. Baerlein	L. F. Andrewes	3–0
1902	*Cambridge*		
	E. M. Baerlein	I. A. de la Rue	3–0
1903	*Cambridge*		
	F. B. Wilson	A. J. Graham	3–0
1904	*Cambridge*		
	E. W. Bury	A. J. Graham	3–0
1905	*Cambridge*		
	E. W. Bury	Hon C. N. Bruce	3–0
1906	*Oxford*		
	G. N. Foster	St. J. F. Wolton	3–1

1907	*Oxford*		
	G. N. Foster	W. G. W. Pound	3–0
1908	*Oxford*		
	Hon C. N. Bruce	G. T. C. Watt	3–0
1909	*Oxford*		
	H. Brougham	C. C. Watson	3–0
1910	*Oxford*		
	A. Tyler	F. A. Sampson	3–1
1911	*Cambridge*		
	F. A. Sampson	Hon J. N. Manners	3–1
1912	*Cambridge*		
	H. W. Leatham	Hon J. N. Manners	3–0
1913	*Cambridge*		
	H. W. Leatham	C. F. B. Simpson	3–1
1914	*Cambridge*		
	H. W. Leatham	R. A. Boddington	3–0
1920	*Oxford*		
	J. C. F. Simpson	R. H. Hill	3–0
1921	*Oxford*		
	J. C. F. Simpson	R. H. Hill	3–0
	Oxford 2		
	R. C. O. Williams	H. D. Hake	
1922	*Oxford*		
	J. C. F. Simpson	R. H. Hill	3–1
	Oxford 2		
	J. F. Park	R Aird	
1923	*Cambridge*		
	R. Aird	C. S. Crawley	3–1
	Oxford 2		
	J. F. Park	O. M. Robson	3–0
1924	*Oxford*		
	C. S. Crawley	R. J. O. Meyer	3–2
	Oxford 2		
	J. F. Park	O. M. Robson	3–2
1925	*Oxford*		
	C. S. Crawley	L. G. Crawley	3–1
1926	*Oxford*		
	D. S. Milford	K. S. Duleepsinhji	3–1
	Oxford 2		
	T. A. Pilkington	P. W. Kemp-Welch	3–1
1927	*Cambridge*		
	P. W. Kemp-Welch	D. S. Milford	3–0
	Cambridge 2		
	L. D. Cambridge	F. C. Dawnay	3–1
1928	*Oxford*		
	D. S. Milford	P. W. Kemp-Welch	3–1
	Oxford 2		
	F. C. Dawnay	C. M. N. Baker	3–0
1929	*Oxford*		
	I. Akers-Douglas	R. H. A. Greville-Calthorpe	3–0
	Oxford 2		
	P. V. F. Catalet	M. D. MacLagan	
1930	*Oxford*		
	I. Akers-Douglas	R. H. A. G.-Calthorpe	3–0
1930	*Cambridge 2*		
	C. M. N. Baker	N. McCaskie	3–0
1931	*Oxford*		
	N. McCaskie	J. M. Stow	3–2
	Oxford 2		
	E. N. Evans	R. H. Priestley	3–1
1932	*Oxford*		
	N. McCaskie	R. H. Priestley	3–1
	Oxford 2		
	I. A. de H. Lyle	J. M. Stow	3–0
1933	*Cambridge*		
	J. M. Stow	C. J. Malim	3–1
	Oxford 2		
	W. H. Vestey	A. H. S. Reid	3–2
1934	*Cambridge*		
	E. F. A. Royds	R. C. Riseley	3–1
	Oxford 2		
	R. Pulbrook	A. H. S. Reid	3–2
1935	*Oxford*		
	R. C. Riseley	J. H. Pawle	3–0
	2nd Strings—No match		
1936	*Oxford*		
	R. C. Riseley	J. H. Pawle	3–1
	Oxford 2		
	R. Pulbrook	E. F. A. Royds	
1937	*Oxford*		
	R. C. Riseley	J. H. Pawle	3–0
	Oxford 2		
	P. Kershaw	J. T. Faber	3–0
1938	*Oxford*		
	P. Kershaw	J. R. Thompson	3–0
	Oxford 2		
	P. M. Whitehouse	M. B. Baring	3–0
1939	*Cambridge*		
	P. D. Manners	Hon. M. G. L. Bruce	3–0
	Cambridge 2		
	R. A. A. Holt	T. H. Read	3–0
1947	*Oxford*		
	H. E. Webb	P. M. Dagnall	3–1
	Oxford 2		
	J. K. Drinkall	D. B. S. Weston	3–0
1948	*Oxford*		
	H. E. Webb	G. H. G. Doggart	3–0
	Cambridge 2		
	I. N. Mitchell	D. C. St. C. Miller	3–0
1949	*Cambridge*		
	G. H. G. Doggart	D. C. St. C. Miller	3–0
	Cambridge 2		
	I. N. Mitchell	J. G. A. Campbell	3–1
1950	*Cambridge*		
	G. W. T. Atkins	W. J. Collins	3–1
	Cambridge 2		
	G. H. G. Doggart	C. B. Haycraft	3–0

Year	Winner			
1951	*Cambridge*			
	G. W. T. Atkins	W. J. Collins	3–0	
	Oxford 2			
	E. N. C. Oliver	A. H. Swift	3–0	
1952	*Oxford*			
	M. C. Cowdrey	A. H. Swift	3–0	
	Oxford 2			
	E. N. C. Oliver	W. S. S. Maclay	3–1	
1953	*Oxford*			
	M. C. Cowdrey	C. H. W. Robson	3–1	
	Oxford 2			
	E. N. C. Oliver	J. J. M. Barron	3–2	
1954	*Oxford*			
	M. C. Cowdrey	C. H. W. Robson	3–0	
	Oxford 2			
	M. R. Coulman	J. A. Kidd	3–0	
1955	*Oxford*			
	M. R. Coulman	C. H. W. Robson	3–2	
	Oxford 2			
	D. R. W. Harrison	C. A. Strang	3–2	
1956	*Oxford*			
	M. R. Coulman	P. B. Steele	3–0	
	Oxford 2			
	R. B. Bloomfield	R. G. Newman	3–0	
1957	*Cambridge*			
	J. G. H. Hogben	R. B. Bloomfield	3–2	
	Oxford 2			
	M. D. Scott	P. R. C. Steele	3–2	
1958	*Oxford*			
	J. M. G. Tildesley	J. G. H. Hogben	3–2	
	Oxford 2			
	P. G. Palumbo	D. B. D. Lowe	3–2	
1959	*Oxford*			
	J. M. G. Tildesley	T. B. L. Coghlan	3–0	
	Oxford 2			
	C. J. Swallow	P. R. Chamberlin	3–0	
1960	*Oxford*			
	C. J. Swallow	P. R. Chamberlin	3–0	
	Oxford 2			
	J. M. G. Tildesely	M. H. L. Bowler	3–1	
1961	*Oxford*			
	J. W. Leonard	J. W. T. Wilcox	3–0	
	Oxford 2			
	C. J. Swallow	M. G. M. Smith	3–1	
1962	*Cambridge*			
	M. G. M. Smith	J. L. Cuthbertson	3–0	
	Cambridge 2			
	P. L. J. Wright	C. D. Palmer-Tomkinson	3–1	
1963	*Cambridge*			
	M. G. M. Smith	J. R. A. Townsend	3–1	
	Cambridge 2			
	M. G. Griffith	J. Q. Greenstock	3–1	
1964	*Oxford*			
	J. R. A. Townsend	M. G. Griffith	3–1	
1964	*Oxford 2*			
	J. Q. Greenstock	P. B. Hay	3–1	
1965	*Cambridge*			
	H. R. Angus	J. Q. Greenstock	3–0	
	Oxford 2			
	M. R. J. Guest	M. G. Griffith	3–1	
1966	*Cambridge*			
	H. R. Angus	M. R. J. Guest	3–0	
	Cambridge 2			
	M. D. T. Faber	G. B. Trentham	3–0	
1967	*Cambridge*			
	M. D. T. Faber	G. B. Trentham	3–2	
	Oxford 2			
	W. J. C. Surtees	A. M. A. Hankey	3–1	
1968	*Oxford*			
	W. J. C. Surtees	A. M. A. Hankey	3–0	
	Oxford 2			
	A. R. Bonsor	M. Pettman	3–0	
1969	*Oxford*			
	W. J. C. Surtees	M. Pettman	3–0	
	Cambridge 2			
	J. Bailey	P. F. C. Begg	3–1	
1970	*Oxford*			
	M. J. J. Faber	A. G. Windham	3–0	
	Oxford 2			
	C. M. Wilmot	P. W. Gore	3–0	
1971	*Oxford*			
	M. J. J. Faber	N. G. H. Draffen	3–0	
	Oxford 2			
	J. C. A. Leslie	S. S. Cobb	3–1	
1972	*Oxford*			
	M. J. J. Faber	J. P. Willcocks	3–1	
	Oxford 2			
	V. A. Cazalet	E. de C. Bryant	3–0	
1973	*Cambridge*			
	J. P. Willcocks	V. A. Cazalet	3–0	
	Cambridge 2			
	J. H. M. Griffiths	C. J. Sutton-Mattocks	3–0	
1974	*Cambridge*			
	J. P. Willcocks	A. C. Lovell	3–1	
	Cambridge 2			
	J. H. M. Griffiths	P. C. Seabrook	3–0	
1975	*Oxford*			
	A. C. Lovell	J. H. M. Griffiths	3–1	
	Oxford 2			
	P. C. Seabrook	C. J. Hopton	3–0	
1976	*Oxford*			
	A. C. Lovell	M. W. Nicholls	3–0	
	Oxford 2			
	R. F. Hollington	C. J. Hopton	3–0	
1977	*Oxford*			
	W. A. Hollington	P. C. Nicholls	3–0	
	Cambridge 2			
	M. W. Nicholls	R. F. Hollington	3–1	

1978	*Oxford*		
	J. Orders	P. C. Nicholls	3–1
	Cambridge 2		
	M. W. Nicholls	F. C. Satow	3–0
1979	*Oxford*		
	W. A. Hollington	A. J. B. McDonald	3–0
	Oxford 2		
	F. C. Satow	P. C. Nicholls	3–2
1980	*Oxford*		
	F. C. Satow	A. J. B. McDonald	3–0
	Oxford 2		
	W. A. Hollington	W. J. Maltby	3–0
1981	*Oxford*		
	R. G. P. Ellis	W. J. Maltby	3–0
	Cambridge 2		
	A. J. B. McDonald	W. A. Hollington	3–1
1982	*Oxford*		
	R. G. P. Ellis	N. Pendrigh	3–1
	Oxford 2		
	J. H. C. Mallinson	S. C. Bourge	3–1
1983	*Cambridge*		
	P. Titchener	J. H. C. Mallinson	3–0
	Cambridge 2		
	T. R. V. Robins	D. J. C. Faber	3–0
1984	*Oxford*		
	W. R. Bristowe	P. Titchener	3–1
	Cambridge 2		
	T. R. V. Robins	M. R. C. Swallow	3–2
1985	*Cambridge*		
	P. Titchener	C. E. R. M. Hall	3–1
	Oxford 2		
	W. R. Bristowe	T. R. V. Robins	3–2

DOUBLES: 1855–1985

	WINNERS	RUNNERS-UP	
1855	*Cambridge*		
	T. W. Bury and	J. G. Codey and	4–3
	W. F. Moorsom	W. H. Davey	
1858	*Oxford*		
	W. H. Dyke and	J. M. Moorsom and	4–1
	J. P. G. Gundry	W. H. Benthall	
1859	*Oxford*		
	W. H. Dyke and	J. M. Moorsom and	4–1
	J. P. F. Gundry	J. H. Marshall	
1860	*Oxford*		
	W. H. Dyke and	J. M. Moorsom and	4–2
	R. W. Munro	A. Ainslie	
1861	*Cambridge*		
	A. Ainslie and	R. D. Walker and	4–0
	R. Sainsbury	C. H. Kennard	

1862	*Cambridge*		
	A. Ainslie and	R. D. Walker and	4–1
	R. Sainsbury	C. H. Kennard	
1863	*Oxford*		
	R. D. Walker and	A. Ainslie and	4–2
	C. H. Kennard	H. M. Plowden	
1864	*Oxford*		
	R. D. Walker and	A. W. T. Daniell	4–1
	R. A. H. Mitchell	and G. T. Warner	
1865	*Cambridge*		
	C. D. Rudd and	R. T. Reid and	4–1
	C. E. Parker	E. Worsley	
1866	*Cambridge*		
	J. W. Knight-Bruce	W. F. Maitland and	4–2
	and W. S. O. Warner	W. T. Phipps	
1867	*Oxford*		
	R. J. Reid and	C. E. Parker and	4–3
	C. J. P. Clay	W. S. O. Warner	
1868	*Cambridge*		
	W. S. O. Warner	C. J. P. Clay and	4–1
	and M. H. Stow	C. L. Kennaway	
1869	*Oxford*		
	C. J. P. Clay and	W. B. Money and	4–0
	C. L. Kennaway	W. Lee-Warner	
1870	*Oxford*		
	C. J. P. Clay and	M. H. Stow and	4–2
	C. J. Ottaway	C. Brudenell-Bruce	
1871	*Oxford*		
	C. J. Ottaway and	W. Yardley and	4–0
	W. H. Hadow	W. E. Pretyman	
1872	*Oxford*		
	C. J. Ottaway and	E. J. Sanders and	4–2
	W. H. Hadow	G. E. B. Wrey	
1873	*Oxford*		
	C. J. Ottaway and	E. J. Sanders and	4–0
	R. O. Milne	J. H. Gurney	
1874	*Oxford*		
	R. O. Milne and	E. J. Sanders and	4–2
	T. S. Pearson	J. M. Barten	
1875	*Oxford*		
	R. O. Milne and	J. M. Batten and	4–0
	T. S. Drury	H. A. Bull	
1876	*Cambridge*		
	E. O. Pleydell-Bouverie and Hon. A. Lyttelton	T. S. Drury and A. J. Webbe	4–3
1877	*Cambridge*		
	Hon. A. Lyttelton and E. O. Pleydell-Bouverie	A. J. Webbe and H. J. B. Hollins	4–1
1878	*Cambridge*		
	E. O. Pleydell-Bouverie and Hon. I. F. W. Bligh	A. J. Webbe and H. C. Jenkins	4–0

1879	*Cambridge*		
	Hon. I. F. W. Bligh and E. O. Pleydell-Bouverie	S. C. Snow and A. L. Ellis	4–1
1880	*Cambridge*		
	Hon. I. F. W. Bligh and A. G. Steel	F. A. Jones and F. L. Evelyn	4–0
1881	*Cambridge*		
	C. T. Studd and A. G. Steel	C. F. H. Leslie and M. C. Kemp	4–1
1882	*Cambridge*		
	J. D. Cobbold and F. M. Lucas	C. F. H. Leslie and M. C. Kemp	4–2
1883	*Cambridge*		
	J. D. Cobbold and H. M. Leaf	W. W. Paine and H. Steward	4–0
1884	*Cambridge*		
	H. M. Leaf and F. Dames-Longworth	E. H. Buckland and C. F. H. Leslie	4–3
1885	*Cambridge*		
	H. E. Crawley and L. Sanderson	E. H. Buckland and J. H. B. Noble	4–2
1886	*Cambridge*		
	H. E. Crawley and C. D. Buxton	E. H. Buckland and G. B. Bovill	4–0
1887	*Cambridge*		
	H. E. Crawley and C. D. Buxton	J. H. B. Noble and H. A. B. Chapman	4–0
1888	*Cambridge*		
	E. M. Butler and C. D. Buxton	H. Philipson and J. H. B. Noble	4–0
1889	*Cambridge*		
	E. M. Butler and P. Ashworth	E. L. Metcalfe and T. R. Spyers	4–1
1890	*Cambridge*		
	P. Ashworth and H. L. Meyer	E. L. Metcalfe and F. H. Browning	4–2
1891	*Oxford*		
	E. L. Metcalfe and F. S. Cokayne	P. Ashworth and E. H. Miles	4–3
1892	*Oxford*		
	F. S. Cokayne and A. D. Erskine	S. W. M. Burns and G. J. V. Weigall	4–0
1893	*Oxford*		
	H. K. Foster and C. S. C. F. Ridgeway	P. W. Cobbold and W. G. Hilton-Price	4–0
1894	*Oxford*		
	H. K. Foster and C. S. C. F. Ridgeway	P. W. Cobbold and S. D. Corbett	4–1
1895	*Oxford*		
	H. K. Foster and F. G. H. Clayton	P. W. Cobbold and W. G. Hilton-Price	4–3
1896	*Oxford*		
	H. K. Foster and I. L. Johnson	P. W. Cobbold and E. Garnett	4–2
1897	*Cambridge*		
	E. Garnett and J. H. Stogdon	R. E. Foster and R. H. de Montmorency	4–2
1898	*Oxford*		
	R. E. Foster and A. S. Crawley	E. Garnett and T. A. Cock	4–1
1899	*Cambridge*		
	E. B. Noel and E. M. Baerlein	R. A. Williams and R. H. de Montmorency	4–3
1900	*Oxford*		
	L. F. Andrewes and S. J. G. Hoare	E. B. Noel and W. K. P. ffrench	4–1
1901	*Cambridge*		
	E. M. Baerlein and E. B. Noel	L. F. Andrewes and I. A. de la Rue	4–2
1902	*Cambridge*		
	E. M. Baerlein and F. B. Wilson	I. A. de la Rue and A. J. Graham	4–1
1903	*Oxford*		
	A. J. Graham and G. T. Bartholomew	F. B. Wilson and A. P. Boone	4–3
1904	*Oxford*		
	A. J. Graham and G. T. Branston	E. W. Bury and R. P. Keigwin	4–2
1905	*Cambridge*		
	E. W. Bury and R. P. Keigwin	Hon. C. N. Bruce and H. M. Butterworth	4–2
1906	*Cambridge*		
	St. J. F. Wolton and W. G. W. Pound	G. N. Foster and H. M. Butterworth	4–3
1907	*Oxford*		
	G. N. Foster and C. V. L. Hooman	W. G. W. Pound and St. J. F. Wolton	4–1
1908	*Oxford*		
	Hon. C. N. Bruce and H. Brougham	G. T. C. Watt and L. C. Crockford	4–0
1909	*Oxford*		
	H. Brougham and R. O. Lagden	C. C. Watson and L. C. Crockford	4–1
1910	*Oxford*		
	A. Tyler and A. J. Evans	F. A. Sampson and W. E. Wallace	4–0
1911	*Cambridge*		
	F. A. Sampson and A. H. Lang	Hon. J. N. Manners and V. Bulkeley-Johnson	4–0

1912	*Cambridge*		
	H. W. Leatham and F. A. Sampson	Hon. J. N. Manners and V. Bulkeley-Johnson	4–1
1913	*Cambridge*		
	H. W. Leatham and A. H. Lang	C. F. B. Simpson and R. A. Boddington	4–2
1914	*Cambridge*		
	H. W. Leatham and C. B. Leatham	R. A. Boddington and L. de O. Tollemache	4–0
1920	*Oxford*		
	J. C. F. Simpson and V. A. Cazalet	R. H. Hill and H. D. Hake	4–1
1921	*Oxford*		
	J. C. F. Simpson and R. C. O. Williams	R. H. Hill and H. D. Hake	4–1
1922	*Cambridge*		
	R. H. Hill and R. Aird	J. C. F. Simpson and J. F. Park	4–3
1923	*Cambridge*		
	R. Aird and O. M. Robson	C. S. Crawley and J. F. Park	4–0
1924	*Oxford*		
	C. S. Crawley and J. F. Park	R. J. O. Meyer and O. M. Robson	4–3
1925	*Oxford*		
	C. S. Crawley and D. S. Milford	L. G. Crawley and A. S. Howard	4–1
1926	*Oxford*		
	D. S. Milford and T. A. Pilkington	K. S. Duleepsinhji and P. W. Kemp-Welch	4–3
1927	*Oxford*		
	D. S. Milford and F. C. Dawnay	P. W. Kemp-Welch and L. D. Cambridge	4–1
1928	*Oxford*		
	D. S. Milford and F. C. Dawnay	P. W. Kemp-Welch and L. D. Cambridge	4–2
1929	*Oxford*		
	I. Akers-Douglas and P. V. F. Cazalet	R. H. A. Greville-Calthorpe and M. D. Maclagan	4–3
1930	*Oxford*		
	I. Akers-Douglas and K. A. Wagg	R. H. A. Greville-Calthorpe and C. M. N. Baker	4–2
1931	*Oxford*		
	N. McCaskie and E. N. Evans	J. M. Stow and R. H. Priestley	4–3
1932	*Oxford*		
	N. McCaskie and I. A. de H. Lyle	R. H. Priestley and J. M. Stow	4–2
1933	*Cambridge*		
	J. M. Stow and A. H. S. Reid	W. H. Vestey and J. de P. Whitaker	4–2
1934	*Oxford*		
	R. C. Riseley and R. Pulbrook	E. F. A. Royds and A. H. S. Reid	4–0
1935	*Oxford*		
	R. C. Riseley and P. Kershaw	J. H. Pawle and E. F. A. Royds	4–3
1936	*Cambridge*		
	J. H. Pawle and E. F. A. Royds	R. C. Riseley and R. Pulbrook	4–1
1937	*Oxford*		
	R. C. Riseley and P. Kershaw	J. H. Pawle and J. T. Faber	4–1
1938	*Oxford*		
	P. Kershaw and P. M. Whitehouse	J. R. Thompson and M. B. Baring	4–0
1939	*Cambridge*		
	P. D. Manners and R. A. A. Holt	Hon. M. G. L. Bruce and T. H. Read	4–0
1947	*Oxford*		
	H. E. Webb and J. K. Drinkall	P. M. Dagnall and D. B. S. Weston	4–1
1948	*Oxford*		
	H. E. Webb and D. C. St. C. Miller	G. H. G. Doggart and I. N. Mitchell	4–2
1949	*Oxford*		
	D. C. St. C. Miller and J. G. A. Campbell	G. H. G. Doggart and I. N. Mitchell	4–3
1950	*Cambridge*		
	G. W. T. Atkins and G. H. G. Doggart	W. J. Collins and C. B. Haycraft	4–2
1951	*Cambridge*		
	G. W. T. Atkins and A. H. Swift	W. J. Collins and E. N. C. Oliver	4–2
1952	*Oxford*		
	M. C. Cowdrey and E. N. C. Oliver	A. H. Swift and W. S. S. Maclay	4–0
1953	*Oxford*		
	M. C. Cowdrey and E. N. C. Oliver	C. H. W. Robson and J. J. M. Barron	4–0
1954	*Oxford*		
	M. C. Cowdrey and M. R. Coulman	C. H. W. Robson and J. J. M. Barron	4–0
1955	*Oxford*		
	M. R. Coulman and D. R. W. Harrison	C. H. W. Robson and C. A. Strang	4–0
1956	*Oxford*		
	M. R. Coulman and R. B. Bloomfield	R. G. Newman and P. B. Steele	4–0

1957 *Cambridge*
J. G. H. Hogben and　R. B. Bloomfield and　4–2
R. R. C. Steele　　　M. D. Scott

1958 *Oxford*
J. M. G. Tildesley　J. G. H. Hogben and　4–1
and P. G. Palumbo　D. B. D. Lowe

1959 *Oxford*
J. M. G. Tildesley　T. B. L. Coghlan and　4–0
and C. J. Swallow　P. R. Chamberlain

1960 *Oxford*
C. J. Swallow and　P. R. Chamberlain　　4–0
J. M. G. Tildesley　and M. H. L. Bowler

1961 *Oxford*
J. W. Leonard and　M. G. M. Smith and　4–0
C. J. Swallow　　J. W. T. Wilcox

1962 *Cambridge*
M. G. M. Smith and　C. D. Palmer-　　　4–2
P. J. L. Wright　　Tomkinson and
　　　　　　　　J. L. Cuthbertson

1963 *Cambridge*
M. G. M. Smith and　J. R. A. Townsend　4–1
M. G. Griffith　　and J. Q. Greenstock

1964 *Oxford*
J. R. A. Townsend　M. G. Griffith and　4–3
and J. Q. Greenstock　P. B. Hay

1965 *Oxford*
J. Q. Greenstock　M. G. Griffith and　4–1
and M. R. J. Guest　H. R. Angus

1966 *Cambridge*
H. R. Angus and　M. R. J. Guest and　4–3
M. D. T. Faber　　G. B. Trentham

1967 *Oxford*
G. B. Trentham and　M. D. T. Faber and　4–3
W. J. C. Surtees　A. M. A. Hankey

1968 *Oxford*
W. J. C. Surtees　A. M. A. Hankey　4–2
and A. R. Bonsor　and M. E. Pettman

1969 *Oxford*
W. J. C. Surtees　M. E. Pettman and　4–1
and P. F. C. Begg　J. Bailey

1970 *Oxford*
M. J. J. Faber and　A. G. Windham and　4–1
C. M. Wilmot　　P. W. Gore

1971 *Oxford*
M. J. J. Faber and　N. G. H. Draffer　4–0
J. C. A. Leslie　　and S. S. Cobb

1972 *Oxford*
M. J. J. Faber and　J. P. Willcocks and　4–0
V. A. Cazalet　　E. de C. Bryant

1973 *Cambridge*
J. P. Willcocks and　V. A. Cazalet and　4–0
J. H. M. Griffiths　C. J. Sutton-
　　　　　　　　Mattocks

1974 *Cambridge*
J. P. Willcocks　　A. C. Lovell and　4–3
and J. H. M. Griffiths　P. G. Seabrook

1975 *Oxford*
A. C. Lovell and　J. H. M. Griffiths　4–1
P. G. Seabrook　　and C. J. Hopton

1976 *Oxford*
A. C. Lovell and　M. W. Nicholls and　4–0
R. F. Hollington　C. J. Hopton

1977 *Cambridge*
P. C. Nicholls and　R. F. Hollington and　4–1
M. W. Nicholls　W. A. Hollington

1978 *Oxford*
F. C. Satow and　M. W. Nicholls and　4–1
J. Orders　　　P. C. Nicholls

1979 *Cambridge*
A. J. B. McDonald　W. A. Hollington　4–3
and P. C. Nicholls　and F. C. Satow

1980 *Oxford*
F. C. Satow and　A. J. B. McDonald　4–1
W. A. Hollington　and W. J. Maltby

1981 *Oxford*
W. A. Hollington　A. J. B. McDonald　4–1
and R. G. P. Ellis　and W. J. Maltby

1982 *Oxford*　　　　　　　　　　4–0
R. G. P. Ellis and　S. C. Bourge and
J. H. C. Mallinson　N. Pendrigh

1983 *Oxford*
J. H. C. Mallinson　P. Titchener and　4–2
and D. J. C. Faber　T. R. V. Robins

1984 *Cambridge*
P. Titchener and　W. R. Bristowe and　4–0
T. R. V. Robins　M. R. C. Swallow

1985 *Oxford*
W. R. Bristowe and　P. Titchener and　4–1
C. E. R. M. Hall　T. R. V. Robins

Services Championships

ROYAL NAVY SINGLES: 1919–1948
Prince's Club Challenge Cup

1919–1920　Lieut. J. C. Leach
1921　　　Capt. J. M. Pipon
1922　　　Cdr. H. H. de Burgh
1923　　　Cdr. B. F. Adams
1924　　　Lieut. Cdr. S. W. Beadle
1925　　　Lieut. T. E. Halsey
1926　　　Lieut. J. W. Hale
1927　　　Sub. Lieut. D. E. Holland-Martin
1928　　　Lieut. H. F. H. Layman
1929　　　Lieut. Cdr. T. H. Troubridge

1930	Lieut. Cdr. I. C. McD. Sanderson
1931–1932	Lieut. Cdr. H. F. H. Layman
1933	Lieut. D. E. Holland-Martin
1934	Lieut. Cdr. H. F. H. Layman
1935	Lieut. A. P. Pellew
1937–1938	Cdr. H. F. H. Layman
1939	Lieut. A. P. Pellew
1947	Lieut. Cdr. A. P. Pellew
1948	Lieut. Cdr. J. P. Harvey

No further contests

ARMY SINGLES: 1903–1985

1903	Capt. S. H. Sheppard, RE
1904–1905	Lieut. H. Balfour-Bryant, 2nd Bn. HLI
1906	Maj. S. H. Sheppard, RE
1907	Lieut. H. Balfour-Bryant, 2nd Bn. HLI
1908	Lieut. J. J. Astor, 1st Life Guards
1909	Capt. A. Berger, Army Service Corps
1910	Capt. W. E. Wilson-Johnston, 36th Sikhs
1911	Capt. A. C. G. Luther, 2nd Bn. KOYLI
1912	Lieut. A. H. Muir, 15th Sikhs
1913	Capt. A. C. G. Luther, 2nd Bn. KOYLI
1914	Lieut. Hon. J. N. Manners, 2nd Bn. Grenadier Guards
1920	Maj. A. J. H. Sloggett, 2nd Bn. The Rifle Brigade
1921	Maj.-Gen. S. H. Sheppard, RE
1922–1924	Capt. T. O. Jameson, 3rd Bn. The Rifle Brigade
1925	Col. W. E. Wilson-Johnston, IA
1926–1927	Lieut. G. N. Scott-Chad, 1st Bn. Coldstream Guards
1928	Lieut. A. C. Gore, 2nd Bn. The Rifle Brigade
1929–1930	Lieut. G. N. Scott-Chad, 1st. Bn. Coldstream Guards
1931	Capt. A. C. Gore, 2nd Bn. The Rifle Brigade
1932	Lieut. R. H. Anstruther-Gough-Calthorpe, Royal Scots Greys
1933	2nd Lieut. J. R. Cairnes, 8th King's Royal Irish Hussars
1934–1938	Lieut. R. H. Anstruther-Gough-Calthorpe, Royal Scots Greys
1939	2nd Lieut. J. B. De Pree, Seaforth Highlanders
1946	Capt. A. R. Taylor, Grenadier Guards
1947–1949	Maj. A. R. Taylor, Grenadier Guards
1950	Capt. A. R. Taylor, Grenadier Guards
1951	Capt. W. R. H. Brooks, Grenadier Guards
1952	Offr./Cdt. M. R. Coulman, RMA, Sandhurst
1953	2nd Lieut. M. R. Coulman, 60th Rifles
1954	2nd Lieut. R. H. B. Neame, 17/21 Lancers

1955	2nd Lieut. A. D. Myrtle, KOSB
1957	2nd Lieut. M. W. Bolton, RE
1958–1959	Lieut. M. W. Bolton, RE
1960–1962	Capt. A. D. Myrtle, KOSB
1963	Lieut. H. N. J. Peto, 9/12 L
1964–1965	Major A. D. Myrtle, KOSB
1966	Capt. J. A. S. Edwardes, 10 GR
1967	Major C. M. Wilmot, Queen's
1968	Offr/Cdt. D. M. Reed-Felstead RMA
1969	Major C. M. Wilmot, Queen's
1970	Capt. J. A. S. Edwardes, 10 GR
1971	Capt. J. A. S. Edwardes, 10 GR
1972–1973	Offr./Cdt. C. H. Braithwaite
1974	2nd Lieut. C. H. Braithwaite, 15/19 H
1975	Lieut. C. H. Braithwaite, 15/19 H
1976	Col. A. D. Myrtle, late KSOB
1977	Capt. D. Reed-Felstead, RHGD
1978	2nd Lieut. M. W. Nicholls, 4/7 DG
1979	Lieut. C. H. Braithwaite, 15/19 H
1980	Lieut. M. W. Nicholls, 4/7 DG
1981	Lieut. M. W. Nicholls, 4/7 DG
1982	Capt. M. W. Nicholls, 4/7 DG
1983	Capt. M. W. Nicholls, 4/7 DG
1984	Capt. C. H. Braithwaite, 15/19 H
1985	Major C. H. Braithwaite, 15/19 H

ARMY INTER-REGIMENTAL DOUBLES: 1892–1985

1892–1894	*12th Royal Lancers* Capt. J. C. B. Eastwood and Lieut. E. Crawley
1895	*RE, Chatham* Lieut. J. E. Hamilton and Lieut. E. M. Blair
1896–1898	*12th Royal Lancers* Capt. J. C. B. Eastwood and Lieut. E. Crawley
1899	*85th KSLI* Lieut. Col. J. Spens and Lieut. E. M. Sprot
1900	no competition
1901	*2nd Bn. HLI* Lieut. P. Balfour and Lieut. H. Balfour-Bryant
1902–1907	*2nd Bn. HLI* Lieut. H. Balfour-Bryant and Lieut. P. Bramwell-Davis
1908	*1st Life Guards* Lieut. J. J. Astor and Lieut. Lord Somers
1909	*50th Brigade, RFA* Col. C. D. King and Capt. H. H. Bond
1910–1911	*Army Service Corps* Maj. Puckle and Capt. A. Berger

1912	*2nd Bn. KOYLI* Capt. A. C. G. Luther and Lieut. C. E. D. King	1947–1949	*Grenadier Guards* Maj. A. R. Taylor and Lieut. G. W. T. Atkins
1913	*15th Sikhs* Lieut. A. H. Muir and Lieut. H. E. Growse	1950	*Grenadier Guards* Capt. A. R. Taylor and Capt. W. R. H. Brooks
1914	*2nd Bn. KOYLI* Capt. A. C. G. Luther and Lieut. C. E. D. King	1951	*Royal Artillery* Maj. P. A. C. Don and Capt. J. L. H. Gordon
1920–1922	*3rd Bn. The Rifle Brigade* Capt. H. G. Moore-Gwyn and Capt. T. O. Jameson	1952	*Green Jackets* Lieut. P. M. Welsh and Offr./Cdt. M. R. Coulman
1923	*The Rifle Brigade* Maj. A. J. H. Sloggett and Capt. H. G. Moore-Gwyn	1953	*Green Jackets* 2nd Lieut. M. R. Coulman and 2nd Lieut. P. M. Welsh
1924	*The Rifle Brigade* Capt. H. G. Moore-Gwyn and Lieut. A. C. Gore	1954	*RMA Sandhurst* Offr./Cdt. P. de Mesquita and Offr./Cdt. M. W. Bolton
1925–1927	*Coldstream Guards* Lieut. G. N. Scott-Chad and Lieut. J. R. Duckworth-King	1955	*RMA Sandhurst* Offr./Cdt. M. W. Bolton and Offr./Cdt. J. W. Knowles
1928	*The Rifle Brigade* Maj. H. G. Moore-Gwyn and Lieut. A. C. Gore	1957	*Royal Engineers* Lieut. Col. M. D. Maclagan and 2nd Lieut. M. W. Bolton
1929	*The Rifle Brigade* Capt. E. S. B. Williams and Lieut. A. C. Gore	1958	*Grenadier Guards* Capt. W. R. H. Brooks and 2nd Lieut. A. D. Mayhew
1930	*Coldstream Guards* Capt. G. N. Scott-Chad and 2nd Lieut. Sir John Child	1959	*Royal Engineers* Lieut. Col. M. D. Maclagan and Lieut. M. W. Bolton
1931	*The Rifle Brigade* Maj. H. G. Moore-Gwyn and Lieut. A. C. Gore	1960	*RMA Sandhurst* Offr./Cdt. J. A. S. Edwardes and Offr./Cdt. M. L. Dunning
1932	*King's Royal Rifle Corps* Capt. J. N. Cheney and Capt. C. J. Wilson	1961	*Royal Fusiliers* Lieut. C. G. R. Nevill and 2nd Lieut. Ross-Collins
1933	*The Rifle Brigade* Maj. H. G. Moore-Gwyn and Lieut. A. C. Gore	1962	*KOSB* Brig. D. W. McConnell and Capt. A. D. Myrtle
1934	*Royal Artillery* 2nd Lieut. P. T. O'Brien Butler and 2nd Lieut. P. A. C. Don	1963	*Royal Armoured Corps* Capt. A. D. Williams and Lieut. N. J. Peto
1935	*King's Royal Rifle Corps* Capt. J. N. Cheney and Maj. T. N. F. Wilson	1964	*2nd Green Jackets* Capt. J. R. E. Nelson and Lieut. M. L. Dunning
1936	*Royal Artillery* Lieut. P. T. O'Brien Butler and Lieut. C. P. Hamilton	1965	*KOSB* Major A. D. Myrtle and Lieut. T. P. Toyne-Sewell
1937	*3rd Bde., RHA* Lieut. P. T. O'Brien Butler and Lieut. C. P. Hamilton	1966	*Royal Armoured Corps* Capt. N. J. Peto and Lieut. F. M. Strang-Steel
1938–1939	*The Rifle Brigade* Maj. A. C. Gore and Lieut. F. A. V. Parker	1967	*RMA Sandhurst* Offr./Cdts. R. M. Beazley and D. M. Reed-Felstead
1946	*King's Royal Rifle Corps* Maj-Gen. T. N. F. Wilson and Capt. A. J. B. Marsham	1968	*17/21st Lancers* Capt. F. M. Strang-Steel and 2nd Lieut. C. Pyemont

1969	*17/21st Lancers* 2nd Lieut. C. Pyemont and 2nd Lieut. S. S. Cobb
1970	*17/21st Lancers* Capt. F. M. Strang-Steel and Lieut. C. Pyemont
1971	*Black Watch* Major C. I. A. Grant and 2nd Lieut. B. M. Osborne
1972	*RMA Sandhurst* Offr./Cdt. C. H. Braithwaite and Offr. Cdt. A. I. Finlayson
1973	*RMA Sandhurst* Offr./Cdt. C. H. Braithwaite and Offr. Cdt. A. I. Finlayson
1974	*Royal Armoured Corps* 2nd Lieut. C. H. Braithwaite and 2nd Lieut. A. I. Finlayson
1975	*Royal Armoured Corps* Lieut. C. H. Braithwaite and Lieut. A. I. Finlayson
1976	*Scottish Division* Col. A. D. Myrtle and Capt. B. M. Osborne
1977	*KOSB* Col. A. D. Myrtle and Major T. P. Toyne-Sewell
1978	*Royal Armoured Corps* Capt. C. M. Craggs and Lieut. M. B. H. Evans
1979	*Royal Armoured Corps* Capt. A. J. Finlayson and Lieut M. W. Nicholls
1980	*15/19th The King's Royal Hussars* Capt. C. H. Braithwaite and Lieut. M. B. H. Evans
1981	*15/19th The King's Royal Hussars* Capt. C. H. Braithwaite and Lieut. M. B. H. Evans
1982	*4/7th Dragoon Guards* Capt. M. W. Nicholls and Lt. Col. C. T. J. Hardy
1983	*4/7th Dragoon Guards* Capt. M. W. Nicholls and Lt. Col. C. T. J. Wright
1984	*5th Innis. Dragoon Guards* Lieut. J. Hanson Smith and 2nd Lieut M. Hough
1985	*Household Cavalry* Major D. M. Reed-Felstead and Lieut C. T. de Fraser.

ARMY OPEN (VICTORY) COMPETITION:
1946–1948

1946	C. S. Crawley and P. V. F. Cazalet
1947	C. S. Crawley and K. A. Wagg
1948	R. A. A. Holt and K. A. Wagg

COMBINED SERVICES (PAST AND PRESENT):
1949–1985

SINGLES

1949	G. W. T. Atkins
1950	Lt.-Col. M. D. Maclagan
1951	G. W. T. Atkins
1952	G. W. T. Atkins
1953	G. W. T. Atkins
1954	M. R. Coulman
1955	W. H. D. Dunnett
1957	T. M. E. Pugh
1958	C. J. Swallow
1959	C. T. M. Pugh
1960	T. M. E. Pugh
1961	C. T. M. Pugh
1962	C. J. Swallow
1963	C. J. Swallow
1964	C. J. Swallow
1965	C. T. M. Pugh
1966	C. J. Swallow
1967	M. S. Connell

DOUBLES

1949	Maj. A. R. Taylor and Lieut. G. W. T. Atkins
1950	Capt. A. R. Taylor and Lieut. G. W. T. Atkins
1951	W. J. Collins and E. N. C. Oliver
1952	R. A. A. Holt and A. R. Taylor
1953	2nd Lieut. M. R. Coulman and 2nd Lieut. P. M. Welsh
1954	R. A. A. Holt and A. R. Taylor
1955	Lieut.-Col. M. D. Maclagan and W. M. Robertson
1957	T. M. E. Pugh and W. M. Robertson
1958	P. Kershaw and C. T. M. Pugh
1959	P. Kershaw and C. T. M. Pugh
1960	Major W. R. H. Brooks and Capt. A. D. Myrtle
1961	T. M. E. Pugh and W. H. D. Dunnett
1962	C. J. Swallow and J. G. H. Hogben
1963	C. T. M. and T. M. E. Pugh
1964	Major A. D. Myrtle and M. R. Coulman
1965	C. J. Swallow and R. L. O. Bridgeman
1966	C. J. Swallow and M. S. Connell
1967	C. T. M. and T. M. E. Pugh
1968	R. L. O. Bridgeman and Major A. D. Myrtle
1969	Major A. D. Myrtle and 2nd Lieut. R. M. Beazley
1970	R. L. O. Bridgeman and T. M. E. Pugh

1971   S. S. Cobb and R. M. Beazley
1972   C. T. M. and T. M. E. Pugh
1973   R. L. O. Bridgeman and
       Lieut.-Col. A. D. Myrtle
1974   2nd Lieut. C. H. Braithwaite and
       2nd Lieut. A. I. Finlayson
1975   Lieut. C. H. Braithwaite and
       Lieut. A. I. Finlayson
1976   G. W. T. Atkins and C. T. M. Pugh
1977   R. L. O. Bridgeman and A. J. H. Ward
1978   Major T. P. Toyne-Sewell and
       2nd Lieut. M. W. Nicholls
1979   Capt. A. I. Finlayson and Lieut. M. B. H. Evans
1980   Capt. C. H. Braithwaite and
       Lieut. M. B. H. Evans
1981   The Marquis of Reading and J. A. S. Edwardes
1982   G. W. T. Atkins and C. T. M. Pugh
1983   G. W. T. Atkins and C. T. M. Pugh
1984   G. W. T. Atkins and C. T. M. Pugh
1985   M. W. Nicholls and P. C. Nicholls

British Open Championship: 1929–1971

The Sheppard Cup

	WINNER	RUNNER-UP	
1929	J. C. F. Simpson	*C. R. Read	5–1
1930	J. C. F. Simpson	*C. R. Read	5–0
1932	Lord Aberdare	J. C. F. Simpson	6–2
1933	I. Akers-Douglas	Lord Aberdare (retired)	4–0
1934	*A. G. Cooper	I. Akers-Douglas	7–4
1936	D. S. Milford	*A. G. Cooper	8–3
1946	*J. P. Dear	P. Kershaw	8–1
1951	*J. P. Dear	J. H. Pawle	8–2
1954	G. W. T. Atkins	*J. P. Dear	6–4
(a)(c)1959	J. R. Thompson	R. M. K. Gracey	3–1
1960	*J. P. Dear	J. R. Thompson	7–4
1961	G. W. T. Atkins – claimed	*J. P. Dear – resigned	
(a)1967	J. W. Leonard	C. J. Swallow	7–4
1970	C. J. Swallow	J. W. Leonard	7–4
1971	(Jan) M.G.M.Smith	C. J. Swallow	7–4
1971	(Nov) H. R. Angus	M. G. M. Smith	6–2

* = Professional
(c) Invitation competition
(a) = G. W. T. Atkins living abroad and so relinquished the title

Louis Roederer British Open Championship: 1971–1980

	WINNER	RUNNER-UP	
1971	H. R. Angus	R. M. K. Gracey	3–1
1972	H. R. Angus	M. G. M. Smith	3–1
1973	H. R. Angus	M. G. M. Smith	3–2
1974	W. J. C. Surtees	H. R. Angus	3–1
1975	H. R. Angus	W. J. C. Surtees	4–1
1976	H. R. Angus	J. A. N. Prenn	4–1
1977	J. A. N. Prenn	W. R. Boone	4–1
1978	H. R. Angus	W. R. Boone	4–1
1979	W. R. Boone	J. A. N. Prenn	4–1
1980	J. A. N. Prenn	W. R. Boone	4–2

1971–1974 best of 5 games. From 1975 best of 7 games for semi-final and final.

Celestion British Open Championship: 1981–1985

	WINNER	RUNNER-UP	
1981	J. A. N. Prenn	W. R. Boone	4–0
1982	J. A. N. Prenn	W. R. Boone	4–2
1983	J. A. N. Prenn	W. R. Boone	4–1
1984	W. R. Boone	R. S. Crawley	4–0
1985	J. A. N. Prenn	W. R. Boone	4–1

Best of 7 games for semi-final and final.

British Open Doubles Championship: 1981–1985

Sponsored by Celestion Loudspeakers Limited

	WINNERS	RUNNERS-UP	
1981	W. R. Boone and R. S. Crawley	C. J. Hue Williams and J. A. N. Prenn	4–0
1982	W. R. Boone and R. S. Crawley	C. J. Hue Williams and J. A. N. Prenn	4–0
1983	W. R. Boone and R. S. Crawley	M. W. Nicholls and P. C. Nicholls	4–1
1984	W. R. Boone and R. S. Crawley	J. A. N. Prenn and J. S. Male	4–0
1985	W. R. Boone and R. S. Crawley	J. A. N. Prenn and J. S. Male	4–3

Age Limit Championships

OPEN UNDER-24 SINGLES: 1973–1985

Swallow Trophy

	WINNER	RUNNER-UP	
1973	A. G. Milne		
1974	A. G. Milne	W. R. Boone	3–1
1975	J. A. N. Prenn	B. R. Weatherill	3–1

1976	J. A. N. Prenn	P. G. Seabrook	3–2
1977	J. A. N. Prenn	D. G. Parsons	3–0
1978	A. C. Lovell	D. G. Parsons	3–0
1979	P. C. Nicholls	A. J. B. McDonald	3–0
1980	P. C. Nicholls	R. G. P. Ellis	3–0
1981	P. C. Nicholls	S. Hazell	3–1
1982	P. C. Nicholls	S. Hazell	3–1
1983	S. Hazell	J. Spurling	3–0
1984	S. Hazell	R. G. P. Ellis	3–2
1985	J. S. Male	N. P. A. Smith	3–0

MASTERS OVER-40 OPEN SINGLES: 1984–1985

Norman Salver

	WINNER	RUNNER-UP	
1984	R. M. K. Gracey	C. J. Hue Williams	3–0
1985	C. J. Hue Williams	R. M. K. Gracey	3–1

UNDER-24 OPEN DOUBLES: 1983–1985

Sutton Trophy

1983	N. P. A. Smith and S. Hazell
1984	P. A. Brake and G. R. Cowdrey
1985	J. S. Male and N. P. A. Smith

OVER-40 OPEN DOUBLES: 1980–1984

Thompson-Gracey Cup

1980	G. W. T. Atkins and M. S. Connell
1981	R. M. K. Gracey and D. M. Norman
1982	R. M. K. Gracey and C. T. M. Pugh
1983	C. T. M. Pugh and D. M. Norman
1984	R. M. K. Gracey and M. G. M. Smith

Squash Rackets

THE BATH CLUB CUP: 1926–1985

Won by Queen's Club:

1926, 1930, 1931, 1932, 1936, 1939, 1948, 1972, 1973, 1975, 1977, 1978, 1979, 1980, 1981, 1985

Public Schools Squash Rackets Handicap: 1927–1967

Cup presented by Edward W. Evans Esq.

1927	D. C. Clarke (Haileybury)
1928	C. J. Grace (Marlborough)
1929	T. C. S. Haywood (Winchester)
1930	R. W. Beadle (Marlborough)
1931	J. A. Gillies (Winchester)
1932	K. A. H. Read (Lancing)
1933	P. C. Samuelson (Charterhouse)
1934	V. A. Barry (Oratory)
1935	D. Rowlandson (Marlborough)
1936	N. F. Borrett (Framlingham)
1937	R. S. Woodward (Lancing)
1938	D. G. Yeats Brown (Tonbridge)
1939	C. L. Welford (Tonbridge)
1940–1947	no competition
1948	M. G. Case (Marlborough)
1949	M. G. Case (Marlborough)
1950	J. R. Partridge (Malvern)
1951	W. J. Downey (Sedbergh)

1952	N. H. R. A. Broomfield (Haileybury)
1953	N. H. R. A. Broomfield (Haileybury)
1954	N. H. R. A. Broomfield (Haileybury)
1955	N. H. R. A. Broomfield (Haileybury)
1956	G. J. Sharman (Lancing)
1957	D. Jude (Lancing)
1958	K. A. White (Brighton)
1959	T. D. Phillips (Mill Hill)
1960	T. D. Phillips (Mill Hill)
1961	M. S. Khan (Millfield)
1962	C. N. Stiff (Hurstpierpoint)
1963	Philip Goodwin (Lancing)
1964	Paul Goodwin (Lancing)
1965	C. Orriss (Hymers)
1966	S. H. Courtney (City of London)
1967	M. T. Greenwood (Cheltenham)

British Women's Championship: 1922–1939

Played at Queen's Club 1922–1939 inclusive

The first six championships were contested in groups on an all-play-all basis, the most successful players qualifying for concluding knock-out rounds. In the second championship there were no semi-finals, because only the top player in each of two groups went forward – meeting in the final. The 1928 championship was the first played entirely on a knock-out basis. Until 1974, the championship was restricted to amateurs.

	WINNER	RUNNER-UP
1922 (Feb.)	Miss J. I. Cave	Miss N. F. Cave
1922 (Nov.)	Miss S. Huntsman	Miss N. F. Cave
1923 (Dec.)	Miss N. F. Cave	Miss J. I. Cave

1924 (Dec.)	Miss J. I. Cave	Miss N. F. Cave
1925 (Dec.)	Miss C. M. Fenwick	Miss N. F. Cave
1926 (Dec.)	Miss C. M. Fenwick	Miss N. F. Cave
1928 (Jan.)	Miss J. I. Cave	Miss C. M. Fenwick
1929 (Jan.)	Miss N. F. Cave	Miss J. I. Cave
1930 (Jan.)	Miss N. F. Cave	Miss C. M. Fenwick
1931 (Jan.)	Miss C. M. Fenwick	Miss N. F. Cave
1932 (Feb.)	Miss S. D. B. Noel	Miss J. I. Cave
1933 (Apr.)	Miss S. D. B. Noel	Miss S. Keith Jones
1934 (Feb.)	Miss S. D. B. Noel	Miss M. E. Lumb
1934 (Dec.)	Miss M. E. Lumb	Miss A. Lytton-Milbanke
1936 (Mar.)	Miss M. E. Lumb	Miss A. Lytton-Milbanke
1937 (Jan.)	Miss M. E. Lumb	Mrs I. H. McKechnie
1938 (Feb.)	Miss M. E. Lumb	Mrs I. H. McKechnie
1939 (Mar.)	Miss M. E. Lumb	Miss S. D. B. Noel

Soccer

Oxford v. Cambridge: 1888–1921

Played exclusively at Queen's

1888	Oxford	3–2		1903	Oxford	1–0
1889	Draw	1–1		1904	Cambridge	5–0
1890	Cambridge	3–1		1905	Oxford	2–1
1891	Oxford	2–1		1906	Cambridge	3–1
1892	Cambridge	5–1		1907	Oxford	2–1
1893	Oxford	3–2		1908	Oxford	4–1
1894	Cambridge	3–1		1909	Draw	1–1
1895	Oxford	3–0		1910	Cambridge	2–1
1896	Oxford	1–0		1911	Oxford	3–2
1897	Oxford	1–0		1912	Cambridge	3–1
1898	Cambridge	1–0		1913	Draw	2–2
1899	Cambridge	3–1		1914	Cambridge	2–1
1900	Oxford	2–0		1920	Draw	2–2
1901	Oxford	3–2		1921	Oxford	2–1
1902	Oxford	2–0				

Arthur Dunn Cup: 1904–1921

Finals played at Queen's

	WINNERS	RUNNERS-UP	
1904	O. Carthusians	O. Rossalians	2–0
1905	O. Carthusians	O. Reptonians	2–0
1906	O. Carthusians	O. Reptonians	2–0
1907	O. Reptonians	O. Brightonians	4–1
1908	O. Carthusians	O. Wykehamists	2–1
1909	O. Malvernians	O. Salopians	3–0
1910	O. Carthusians	O. Rossalians	2–1
1911	O. Reptonians	O. Carthusians	1–0
1912	O. Reptonians	O. Cholmelians	3–0
1913	O. Brightonians	O. Aldenhamians	2–1
1920	O. Wykehamists	O. Malvernians	3–0
1921	O. Carthusians	O. Aldenhamians	2–0

Rugby

Oxford v. Cambridge: 1887–1921

Played exclusively at Queen's

1887–1888	Cambridge 1DG, 2T to 0
1888–1889	Cambridge 1G, 2T to 0
1889–1890	Oxford 1G, 1T to 0
1890–1891	Drawn 1G to 1G
1891–1892	Cambridge 2T to 0
1892–1893	Drawn no score
1893–1894	Oxford 1T to 0
1894–1895	Drawn 1G to 1G
1895–1896	Cambridge 1G to 0
1896–1897	Oxford 1G, 1DG to 1G, 1T
1897–1898	Oxford 2T to 0
1898–1899	Cambridge 1G, 2T to 0
1899–1900	Cambridge 2G, 4T to 0
1900–1901	Oxford 2G to 1G, 1T

1901–1902	Oxford 1G, 1T to 0
1902–1903	Drawn 1G, 1T to 1G, 1T
1903–1904	Oxford 3G, 1T to 2G, 1T
1904–1905	Cambridge 3G to 2G

(modern scoring values adopted)

1905–1906	Cambridge 3G (15) to 2G, 1T (13)
1906–1907	Oxford 4T (12) to 1G, 1T (8)
1907–1908	Oxford 1G, 4T (17) to 0
1908–1909	Drawn 1G (5) to 1G (5)
1909–1910	Oxford 4G, 5T (35) to 1T (3)
1910–1911	Oxford 4G, 1T (23) to 3G 1T (18)
1911–1912	Oxford 2G, 3T (19) to 0
1912–1913	Cambridge 2G (10) to 1T (3)
1913–1914	Cambridge 1DG, 3T (13) to 1T (3)
1919–1920	Cambridge 1DG, 1PG (7) to 1G (5)
1920–1921	Oxford 1G, 4T (17) to 1G, 3T (14)

Athletics

Oxford v. Cambridge: 1888–1928

Held exclusively at Queen's

1888	Cambridge	5 to 4
1889	Cambridge	5½ to 3½
1890	Cambridge	6 to 3
1891	Cambridge	6½ to 2½
1892	Cambridge	5 to 4
1893	Oxford	7 to 2
1894	Oxford	6 to 3
1895	Cambridge	5 to 4
1896	Cambridge	5 to 4
1897	Oxford	5 to 4
1898	Oxford	7 to 2
1899	Tie	5 to 5
1900	Oxford	6 to 4
1901	Oxford	6 to 4
1902	Oxford	5 to 4
1903	Cambridge	8 to 2
1904	Cambridge	8 to 2
1905	Oxford	6⅓ to 3⅔
1906	Oxford	7 to 3
1907	Oxford	8½ to 1½
1908	Cambridge	6 to 4
1909	Oxford	6 to 4
1910	Cambridge	7 to 3
1911	Cambridge	6 to 4
1912	Tie	5 to 5
1913	Tie	5 to 5
1914	Cambridge	6 to 4
1915–1919	no contests	
1920	Oxford	5½ to 4½
1921	Tie	5 to 5
1922	Cambridge	9 to 1
1923	Oxford	7 to 4
1924	Tie	5½ to 5½
1925	Oxford	6 to 5
1926	Cambridge	8 to 3
1927	Cambridge	9 to 2
1928	Cambridge	8 to 3

100 YARDS

Oxford 39 wins; Cambridge 46 wins; 4 dead heats.

Record number of wins: 4 by *C. R. Thomas* (1897–1900 inc. 2 ties); H. M. Abrahams (1920–23).

YEAR	WINNER	COLLEGE	SEC.
1888	H. M. Fletcher	Trinity	10.8
1889	R. W. Turner	Trinity Hall	10.6
1890	E. E. B. Prest	Trinity Hall	10.8
1891	A. Ramsbotham C. J. B. Monypenny	Exeter Jesus	10.4
1892	A. Ramsbotham C. J. B. Monypenny	Exeter Jesus	10.4
1893	A. Ramsbotham C. B. Fry	Exeter Wadham	10.5
1894	G. Jordan	University	10.4
1895	G. Jordon	University	10.75
1896	G. Jordan	University	10.25
1897	F. L. Carter C. R. Thomas	Caius Jesus	10.2
1898	C. R. Thomas	Jesus	10.4
1899	C. R. Thomas	Jesus	10.4
1900	C. R. Thomas A. M. Hollins	Jesus Hertford	10.25
1901	A. E. Hind	Trinity Hall	10.6
1902	R. W. Barclay	Trinity	10.4
1903	R. W. Barclay	Trinity	10.25
1904	R. W. Barclay	Trinity	10.2
1905	J. H. Morrell	Magdalen	10.4
1906	K. G. Macleod	Pembroke	10.6
1907	N. G. Chavasse K. G. Macleod	Trinity Pembroke	10.5
1908	K. G. Macleod	Pembroke	10.4
1909	L. C. Hull	B.N.C.	10.4
1910	H. R. Ragg	St. John's	10.4
1911	D. Macmillan	Trinity	10.0†
1912	D. Macmillan	Trinity	10.0†
1913	H. M. Macintosh	Corpus Christi	10.4
1914	H. M. Macintosh	Corpus Christi	10.2
1920	H. M. Abrahams	Caius	10.0†
1921	H. M. Abrahams	Caius	10.2
1922	H. M. Abrahams	Caius	10.2
1923	H. M. Abrahams	Caius	10.0†
1924	C. F. N. Harrison	Trinity	10.2
1925	A. E. Porritt	Magdalen	10.0†
1926	A. E. Porritt	Magdalen	9.9*
1927	J. W. J. Rinkel	Clare	10.0
1928	J. W. J. Rinkel	Clare	10.1

No contests were held 1915 to 1919, and no official contests from 1940 to 1945.

The names of winners from *Oxford* are printed in italics.

* Indicates that the performance was either the best of the first three contests or was at that date a series record.

† Indicates that the performance at that date equalled the then existing series record.

Times in the early days were taken only to the nearest quarter and then to the nearest fifth of a second. For the sake of convenience, all times have been decimalized.

Oxford athletes have won 477 events compared with 460 won by Cambridge athletes. There have been 14 tied events.

440 YARDS

Oxford 39 wins; Cambridge 49 wins; 2 dead heats.

Record number of wins: 4 by A. G. K. Brown (1935–38).

YEAR	WINNER	COLLEGE	SEC.
1888	*A. G. le Maitre*	St. John's	51.4
1889	R. W. Turner	Trinity Hall	51.4
1890	*W. B. Thomas*	Christ Church	50.2†
1891	*P. R. Lloyd*	Pembroke	50.6
1892	C. J. B. Monypenny	Jesus	49.8*
1893	*A. Ramsbotham*	Exeter	50.4
1894	*G. Jordan*	University	50.8
1895	W. Fitzherbert	Trinity Hall	50.0
1896	W. Fitzherbert	Trinity Hall	49.6*
1897	*G. Jordan*	University	49.8
1898	F. L. Carter	Caius	50.4
	C. G. Davison	Sidney Sussex	
1899	*A. M. Hollins*	Hertford	51.4
1900	*A. M. Hollins*	Hertford	50.6
1901	*L. J. Cornish*	Lincoln	52.8
1902	R. W. Barclay	Trinity	50.6
1903	R. W. Barclay	Trinity	50.5
1904	R. W. Barclay	Trinity	50.6
1905	*J. H. Morrell*	Magdalen	51.2
1906	*K. Cornwallis*	University	51.0
1907	*C. M. Chavasse*	Trinity	50.6
1908	E. H. Ryle	Trinity	51.0
1909	*L. C. Hull*	B.N.C.	50.6
1910	W. T. Wetenhall	Caius	51.2
1911	F. G. Black	Pembroke	51.6
1912	D. Macmillan	Trinity	49.4*
1913	D. Gordon Davies	Downing	51.0
1914	D. Gordon Davies	Downing	50.0
1920	*B. G. D'U. Rudd*	Trinity	49.6
	G. M. Butler	Trinity	
1921	G. M. Butler	Trinity	49.8
1922	G. M. Butler	Trinity	51.2
1923	H. M. Abrahams	Caius	50.8
1924	*D. M. Johnson*	Balliol	51.0
1925	*W. E. Stevenson*	Balliol	51.0
1926	J. W. J. Rinkel	Clare	50.8
1927	J. W. J. Rinkel	Clare	51.0
1928	J. W. J. Rinkel	Clare	50.4

880 YARDS

Oxford 25 wins; Cambridge 27 wins; 1 dead heat.

Record number of wins: 3 by *K. Cornwallis* (1904–06);
P. J. Baker (now Noel-Baker) (1910–12);
D. G. A. Lowe (1923–25); *D. J. N. Johnson* (1954–56).

YEAR	WINNER	COLLEGE	MIN.	SEC.
1899	H. E. Graham	Jesus	1	59.6
1900	H. E. Graham	Jesus	1	58.6*
1901	*J. R. Cleave*	B.N.C.	1	59.4

YEAR	WINNER	COLLEGE	MIN.	SEC.
1902	not contested			
1903	T. B. Wilson	Pembroke	2	02.0
1904	*K. Cornwallis*	University	1	54.8*
1905	*K. Cornwallis*	University	1	56.6
1906	*K. Cornwallis*	University	1	56.4
1907	*P. Stormonth-Darling*	New College	2	00.0
1908	T. H. Just	Trinity	1	55.8
1909	*P. Stormonth-Darling*	New College	1	59.0
1910	P. J. Baker	King's	1	57.6
1911	P. J. Baker	King's	1	58.2
1912	P. J. Baker	King's	1	56.6
1913	H. S. O. Ashington	King's	2	00.2
1914	R. E. Atkinson	Emmanuel	1	56.4
1920	*B. G. D'U. Rudd*	Trinity	1	57.4
1921	E. D. Mountain	Corpus Christi	1	57.8
1922	E. D. Mountain	Corpus Christi	2	00.4
1923	D. G. A. Lowe	Pembroke	2	00.8
1924	D. G. A. Lowe	Pembroke	1	57.2
1925	D. G. A. Lowe	Pembroke	1	57.2
1926	R. S. Starr	Christ's	1	59.8
1927	H. L. Elvin	Trinity Hall	2	00.2
1928	C. E. G. Green	Christ's	2	01.8

ONE MILE

Oxford 52 wins; Cambridge 37 wins.

Record number of wins: 4 *F. J. K. Cross* (1886–89),
W. E. Lutyens (1892–95), *R. G. Bannister* (1947–50).

YEAR	WINNER	COLLEGE	MIN.	SEC.
1888	*F. J. K. Cross*	New College	4	29.4
1889	*F. J. K. Cross*	New College	4	23.6*
1890	*W. Pollock-Hill*	Keble	4	21.6*
1891	*B. C. Allen*	Corpus Christi	4	26.6
1892	W. E. Lutyens	Sidney Sussex	4	24.6
1893	W. E. Lutyens	Sidney Sussex	4	22.0
1894	W. E. Lutyens	Sidney Sussex	4	19.8*
1895	W. E. Lutyens	Sidney Sussex	4	23.4
1896	H. F. Howard	Trinity Hall	4	29.4
1897	H. F. Howard	Trinity Hall	4	27.6
1898	*A. Danson*	Balliol	4	25.8
1899	A. Hunter	Trinity	4	35.0
1900	F. G. Cockshott	Trinity	4	28.6
1901	F. G. Cockshott	Trinity	4	26.8
1902	*E. L. Gay-Roberts*	Queen's	4	25.8
1903	H. W. Gregson	Christ's	4	27.4
1904	H. W. Gregson	Christ's	4	20.0
1905	*C. C. Henderson-Hamilton*	Trinity	4	17.8*
1906	A. R. Welsh	Trinity	4	21.2
1907	*S. P. L..Lloyd*	Magdalen	4	28.0
1908	*S. P. L. Lloyd*	Magdalen	4	29.8
1909	P. J. Baker	King's	4	27.6
1910	W. Gavin	Trinity	4	26.8

1911	P. J. Baker	King's	4	29.4
1912	*A. N. S. Jackson*	B.N.C.	4	21.4
1913	*A. N. S. Jackson*	B.N.C.	4	24.2
1914	*A. N. S. Jackson*	B.N.C.	4	23.2
1920	H. B. Stallard	Caius	4	27.6
1921	H. B. Stallard	Caius	4	22.0
1922	H. B. Stallard	Caius	4	22.4
1923	*W. R. Milligan*	University	4	25.0
1924	D. G. A. Lowe	Pembroke	4	33.2
1925	R. S. Starr	Christ's	4	30.8
1926	R. S. Starr	Christ's	4	27.6
1927	F. L. Hamer	Christ's	4	35.6
1928	C. E. G. Green	Christ's	4	25.4

THREE MILES

Oxford 53 wins; Cambridge 31 wins; 1 dead-heat.
Record number of wins: 3 by 8 athletes the last being
N. F. Hallows (1906–08)

YEAR	WINNER	COLLEGE	MIN.	SEC.
1888	*W. Pollock-Hill*	Keble	15	28.2
1889	*W. Pollock-Hill*	Keble	15	20.4
1890	*W. Pollock-Hill*	Keble	15	20.6
1891	C. Ekin	Clare	15	12.2
1892	B. C. Allen	Corpus Christi	15	13.8
1893	F. S. Horan	Trinity Hall	14	44.6*
1894	F. S. Horan	Trinity Hall	15	07.0
1895	F. S. Horan	Trinity Hall	14	50.4
1896	*J. M. Fremantle*	Hertford	15	12.0
1897	*J. M. Fremantle*	Hertford	15	07.0
1898	*J. M. Fremantle*	Hertford	15	34.0
1899	H. W. Workman	Pembroke	15	32.6
1900	H. W. Workman	Pembroke	15	01.4
1901	H. W. Workman	Pembroke	14	58.0
1902	H. W. Gregson	Christ's	15	07.4
1903	H. P. W. Macnaghten	King's	15	13.4
1904	A. R. Churchill	Caius	14	57.6
1905	A. S. D. Smith	Jesus	15	08.0
1906	*N. F. Hallows*	Keble	15	14.0
1907	*N. F. Hallows*	Keble	15	06.6
1908	*N. F. Hallows*	Keble	14	53.4
1909	*A. M. Brown*	Oriel	15	00.0
1910	*A. E. Cator*	Keble	14	45.8
1911	C. H. A. Porter	B. N. C.	15	06.0
1912	E. Gawan-Taylor	Pembroke	14	47.0
1913	D. N. Goussen	St. John's	14	47.0
1914	G. M. Sproule	Balliol	14	34.8*
1920	E. A. Montague	Magdalen	14	45.0
1921	E. A. Montague	Magdalen	14	54.0
1922	W. R. Seagrove	Clare	15	02.6
1923	N. A. McInnes	New College	15	22.0
1924	P. H. M. Bryant	Queen's	15	11.2
1925	V. E. Morgan	Christ Church	15	00.0
1926	T. C. Fooks	Christ's	15	07.4

1927	*I. Thomas*	St. John's	15	05.0
1928	*W. A. M. Edwards*	Oriel	15	00.4

120 YARDS HIGH HURDLES

Oxford 44 wins; Cambridge 44 wins; 1 dead-heat.
Record number of wins: 3 by *E. T. Garnier* (1896–98);
G. R. Garnier (1901–03); Lord Burghley (1925–27)

YEAR	WINNER	COLLEGE	SEC.
1888	J. Le Fleming	Clare	17.2
1889	J. L. Greig	Clare	16.6
1890	J. L. Greig	Clare	16.8
1891	H. Le Fleming	Clare	16.4
1892	H. Le Fleming	Clare	16.4
1893	*H. T. S. Gedge* / *E. L. Collis*	Keble / Keble	16.4
1894	*W. J. Oakley*	Christ Church	16.6
1895	*W. J. Oakley*	Christ Church	16.4
1896	*E. T. Garnier*	Oriel	16.6
1897	*E. T. Garnier*	Oriel	16.6
1898	*E. T. Garnier*	Oriel	16.4
1899	W. G. Paget-Tomlinson	Trinity Hall	16.0†
1900	W. G. Paget-Tomlinson	Trinity Hall	16.2
1901	*G. R. Garnier*	Oriel	17.0
1902	*G. R. Garnier*	Oriel	16.2
1903	*G. R. Garnier*	Oriel	16.0†
1904	F. H. Teall	Sidney Sussex	16.4
1905	F. H. Teall	Sidney Sussex	16.4
1906	*E. R. J. Hussey*	Hertford	16.5
1907	K. Powell	King's	15.6*
1908	K. Powell	King's	16.0
1909	*G. R. L. Anderson*	Trinity	16.0
1910	*M. V. Macdonald*	Lincoln	16.0
1911	P. R. O'R. Phillips	Pembroke	16.2
1912	H. S. O. Ashington	King's	17.0
1913	H. S. O. Ashington	King's	16.2
1914	*V. B. Havens*	Christ Church	17.2
1920	*H. P. Jeppe*	Trinity	16.6
1921	*G. A. Trowbridge*	Trinity	15.8
1922	L. F. Partridge	St. Catharine's	16.0
1923	*R. Stapleton*	Queen's	16.2
1924	*S. H. Thomson*	St. Catharine's	15.8
1925	Lord Burghley	Magdalene	15.8
1926	Lord Burghley	Magdalene	15.5*
1927	Lord Burghley	Magdalene	15.5†
1928	G. C. Weightman Smith	Selwyn	15.4*

200 YARDS HURDLES

YEAR	WINNER	COLLEGE	SEC.
1864	E. H. Wynne-Finch	Trinity	26.75

220 YARDS LOW HURDLES

Oxford 17 wins; Cambridge 19 wins.
Record number of wins: 3 Lord Burghley (1925–27)

YEAR	WINNER	COLLEGE	SEC.
1922	W. S. Bristowe	Caius	26.2
1923	*T. Huhn*	University	25.8*
1924	W. S. Bristowe	Caius	26.2
1925	Lord Burghley	Magdalene	24.8*
1926	Lord Burghley	Magdalene	25.4
1927	Lord Burghley	Magdalene	26.0
1928	G. C. Weightman-Smith	Selwyn	24.8†

HIGH JUMP

Oxford 41 wins; Cambridge 43 wins; 5 two-way ties.
Record number of wins: 4 by J. H. Gurney (1870–73) and by *W. P. Montgomery* (1885–88) (each had one tie)

YEAR	WINNER	COLLEGE	FT.	IN.
1888	*W. P. Montgomery*	Merton	5	10½
1889	*H. J. Scott* E. B. Badcock	Merton Trinity	5	8
1890	T. Jennings	Gonville & Caius	5	8¾
1891	H. Le Fleming	Clare	5	9½
1892	H. Le Fleming	Clare	5	9½
1893	*E. D. Swanwick*	Trinity	5	11
1894	*E. D. Swanwick*	Trinity	5	10¼
1895	*G. A. Gardiner*	New College	5	9
1896	*E. O. Kirlew*	Christ Church	5	8½
1897	E. O. Kirlew E. H. Cholmeley	Christ Church Jesus	5	7⅝
1898	H. S. Adair	Oriel	5	9
1899	*H. S. Adair*	Oriel	5	8¼
1900	*W. E. B. Henderson*	Trinity	5	9¼
1901	G. Howard-Smith	Trinity	5	10¼
1902	G. Howard-Smith	Trinity	5	9¾
1903	G. Howard-Smith	Trinity	5	10½
1904	E. E. Leader	Trinity	5	11
1905	*P. M. Young* E. E. Paget-Tomlinson E. E. Leader	Oriel Trinity Hall	5	7
1906	*P. M. Young*	Oriel	5	7¼
1907	*P. M. Young*	Oriel	5	8½
1908	A. C. B. Bellerby	Emmanuel	5	8
1909	A. C. B. Bellerby	Emmanuel	5	11¾
1910	A. C. B. Bellerby L. Z. Ludinszky	Emmanuel Downing	5	8
1911	H. A. Dubois	Fitzwilliam Hall	5	8¾
1912	*J. C. Masterman*	Worcester	5	8
1913	*J. de B. Crossley*	Balliol	5	8⅛
1914	H. S. O. Ashington	King's	5	8
1920	*H. S. White*	B.N.C.	5	9
1921	E. S. Burns	St. Catharine's	5	10
1922	E. S. Burns	St. Catharine's	5	10½
1923	*R. J. Dickinson*	Oriel	5	11
1924	*R. J. Dickinson* C. T. Van Geyzel	Oriel Trinity Hall	5	11
1925	C. J. Van Geyzel	Trinity Hall	5	11½
1926	A. G. De L. Willis J. D. S. Pendlebury	Emmanuel Pembroke	5	9½
1927	J. D. S. Pendlebury	Pembroke	6	0
1928	*E. Bradbrooke* *C. E. S. Gordon*	Queen's Christ Church	5	10

POLE VAULT

Oxford 16 wins; Cambridge 18 wins.
Record number of wins: 3 by *R. L. Hyatt* (1925–27); F. R. Webster (1935–37); *A. J. Burger* (1950–52)

YEAR	WINNER	COLLEGE	FT.	IN.
1923	*D. R. Michener*	Hertford	10	6
1924	G. S. Baird	King's	11	0
1925	*R. L. Hyatt*	Balliol	11	6*
1926	*R. L. Hyatt*	Balliol	11	10*
1927	*R. L. Hyatt*	Balliol	11	3
1928	*G. P. Faust*	St. Catharine's	12	0*

LONG JUMP

Oxford 47 wins; Cambridge 42 wins.
Record number of wins: 3 by 5 athletes with H. M. Abrahams (1920–22–23) most recently

YEAR	WINNER	COLLEGE	FT.	IN.
1888	W. C. Kendall	St. John's	20	10¾
1889	J. L. Greig	Clare	21	0½
1890	J. L. Grieg	Clare	22	7¾
1891	R. J. Leakey T. Jennings	Corpus Christi Gonville and Caius	20	7½
1892	*C. B. Fry*	Wadham	23	5*
1893	*C. B. Fry*	Wadham	23	0½
1894	*C. B. Fry*	Wadham	22	4
1895	W. Mendelson	Jesus	22	5½
1896	E. Batchelor	Gonville & Caius	22	7
1897	*G. C. Vassall*	Oriel	22	7
1898	*G. C. Vassall*	Oriel	22	5½
1899	*G. C. Vassall*	Oriel	23	3
1900	*G. W. F. Kelly*	Lincoln	21	8
1901	*L. J. Cornish*	Lincoln	21	6¼
1902	*L. J. Cornish*	Lincoln	21	4¼
1903	*T. A. Leach*	B.N.C.	22	3
1904	*T. A. Leach*	B.N.C.	21	2¼
1905	*G. Le Blanc-Smith*	University	21	1
1906	*P. M. Young*	Oriel	22	3
1907	*P. M. Young*	Oriel	22	4

Year	Winner	College	FT.	IN.
1908	*W. H. Bleaden*	B.N.C.	22	3
1909	M. G. D. Murray	Trinity	22	0½
1910	M. G. D. Murray	Trinity	21	5½
1911	*D. A. J. J. Hartley*	Merton	21	5
1912	H. S. O. Ashington	King's	23	1
1913	H. S. O. Ashington	King's	23	5¾*
1914	H. S. O. Ashington	King's	23	6¼*
1920	H. M. Abrahams	Caius	22	7
1921	*L. S. C. Ingrams*	Pembroke	22	0½
1922	H. M. Abrahams	Caius	22	0
1923	H. M. Abrahams	Caius	23	7¼*
1924	*C. E. W. Macintosh*	University	23	4
1925	*C. E. W. Macintosh*	University	23	2½
1926	*R. L. Hyatt*	Balliol	21	9½
1927	V. B. V. Powell	Caius	22	3½
1928	G. W. Pomeroy	St. Catharine's	22	4

SHOT PUTT

Oxford 39 wins; Cambridge 49 wins.
Record number of wins: 4 by *J. H. Ware* (1883–86);
A. Irfan (1934–37); D. R. Harrison (1958–61)

YEAR	WINNER	COLLEGE	FT.	IN.
1888	E. O'F. Kelly	Gonville & Caius	37	0
1889	C. Rolfe	Clare	35	6½
1890	M. B. Elder	Jesus	37	5
1891	S. H. Barber	King's	35	7
1892	*C. A. White*	New College	36	2½
1893	*E. Hind*	Keble	34	11½
1894	C. H. Rivers	St. John's	37	8½
1895	E. J. M. Watson	Trinity	37	9
1896	J. H. Bulloch	Trinity	38	2
1897	J. H. Bulloch	Trinity	37	6½
1898	*F. G. Snowball*	Queen's	37	4
1899	G. W. Clark	Gonville & Caius	34	0
1900	*E. E. B. May*	Oriel	36	8
1901	*E. E. B. May*	Oriel	34	9
1902	*W. W. Coe*	Hertford	43	10*
1903	H. A. Leeke	Corpus Christi	37	8
1904	Hon. G. W. Lyttleton	Trinity	37	7
1905	Hon. G. W. Lyttleton	Trinity	37	11
1906	Hon. G. W. Lyttleton	Trinity	38	3¾
1907	*R. L. Robinson*	Magdalen	37	7
1908	J. L. Michie	Trinity	37	2½
1909	*W. H. Bleaden*	B.N.C.	36	2
1910	M. J. Susskind	Pembroke	37	0
1911	*W. A. Zeigler*	Wadham	39	6½
1912	*W. A. Zeigler*	Wadham	40	10

Year	Winner	College	FT.	IN.
1913	*W. A. Zeigler*	Wadham	43	3
1914	R. S. Woods	Downing	41	1
1920	R. S. Woods	Downing	40	9
1921	*A. I. Reese*	Lincoln	39	2
1922	*A. I. Reese*	Lincoln	38	9½
1923	*F. K. Brown*	Exeter	42	8
1924	*S. H. Thomson*	St. Catharine's	42	2
1925	*R. L. Hyatt*	Balliol	41	6
1926	R. L. Howland	St. John's	40	4
1927	R. L. Howland	St. John's	42	2
1928	R. L. Howland	St. John's	42	10

HAMMER THROW

Oxford 26 wins; Cambridge 25 wins.
Record number of wins: 4 by G. H. Hales (1874–77)

YEAR	WINNER	COLLEGE	FT.	IN.
1888	H. Woolner	Trinity	93	10
1889	*K. L. Macdonald*	St. John's	91	5
1890	N. M. Cohen	Jesus	94	2
1891	T. Jennings	Gonville & Caius	102	10
1892	H. A. Cooper	Trinity Hall	96	4
1893	*G. S. Robertson*	Exeter	105	1½
1894	*G. S. Robertson*	Exeter	101	4½
1895	*G. S. Robertson*	Exeter	116	7
1896	A. B. Johnston	Pembroke	107	7
1897	J. A. Halliday	Trinity	97	6
1898	L. O. T. Baines	Trinity Hall	102	7
1899	*J. D. Greenshields*	Oriel	110	1
1900	*J. D. Greenshields*	Oriel	115	2
1901	*E. E. B. May*	Oriel	113	3
1902	*W. W. Coe*	Hertford	111	10
1903	H. A. Leeke	Corpus Christi	126	8
1904	M. Spicer	Trinity Hall	114	10
1905	*A. H. Fyffe*	University	128	6
1906	*A. H. Fyffe*	University	136	3
1907	*A. M. Stevens*	Balliol	146	9*
1908	*A. M. Stevens*	Balliol	139	8
1909	R. H. Lindsay-Watson	Trinity	148	10*
1910	G. E. Putnam	Christ Church	146	8
1911	G. E. Putnam	Christ Church	153	3*
1912	*W. A. Ziegler*	Wadham	139	4
1913	*W. A. Ziegler*	Wadham	114	7
1914	*E. T. Adams*	Worcester	123	7
1920	*G. A. Feather*	Wadham	100	11
1921	*M. C. Nokes*	Magdalen	148	0

Eton Fives

Kinnaird Cup: 1930–1939

Played exclusively at Queen's

	WINNERS	RUNNERS-UP			
1930	A. H. Fabian and J. Aguirre (Cholmelians)	R. G. de Quetteville and R. A. Redhead (Etonians)	1935	J. M. Peterson and C. E. W. Sheepshanks (Salopians/Etonians)	A. H. Fabian and R. A. Blair (Cholmeleians)
1931	W. M. Welch and H. G. de Grey-Warter (Harrovians)	K. C. Gandar Dower and G. R. McConnell (Harrovians)	1936	D. M. Backhouse and A. T. Barber (Salopians)	A. J. Conyers and T. G. Lund (Aldenhamians/ Westminsters)
1932	K. C. Gandar Dower and G. R. McConnell (Harrovians)	Hon P. F. Remnant and Hon R. J. F. Remnant (Etonians)	1937	A. H. Fabian and J. K. G. Webb (Cholmeleians)	R. H. V. Cavendish and S. R. Allsopp (Etonians)
1933	W. M. Welch and H. G. de Grey-Warter (Harrovians)	D. M. Backhouse and A. T. Barber (Salopians)	1938	J. M. Peterson and C. E. W. Sheepshanks (Salopians/Etonians)	R. A. Blair and A. G. A. Turnbull (Cholmeleians)
1934	D. M. Backhouse and A. T. Barber (Salopians)	A. J. Conyers and A. W. S. Sim (Aldenhamians)	1939	A. H. Fabian and J. K. G. Webb (Cholmeleians)	G. R. McConnell and W. M. Welch (Harrovians)

Billiards and Snooker

Billiard Handicap Cup: 1894–1971

Presented by W. M. Cranston Esq.

1894	M. F. Goodbody		1922	G. M. Thomas
1895	A. N. MacNicoll		1923	H. Peterson
1896	R. Bayley Smith		1924	C. W. Tabbush
1897	L. Tamworth		1925	C. Goodall
1898	P. R. Tremewen		1926	R. J. McNair
1899	S. D. Winkworth		1927	D. I. Galsworthy
1900	M. Roberts		1928	J. S. Olliff
1901	R. Bailey Smith		1929	J. S. Olliff
1902	E. L. Phillips		1930	D. I. Galsworthy
1903	H. S. Mahony		1931	C. W. Tabbush
1904	H. Cholmondeley Pennell		1932	Maj. Gen. C. A. Foulkes
1905	G. M. Simond		1933	K. C. Gandar Dower
1906	M. Roberts		1934	Maj. Gen. C. A. Foulkes
1907	C. L. Beddington		1935	Dr. V. Clifford
1908	G. Stoddart		1936	J. C. Warboys
1909	A. C. Stern		1937	G. E. Bean
1910	D. E. Seligman		1938–1960	no competition
1911	J. N. Wilson		1961	H. W. Morrall
1912	R. Sambourne		1962	N. Berryman
1913	E. L. Phillips		1963	Air Commodore W. F. Langdon
1914–1918	no competition		1964	H. W. Morrall
1919	R. Sambourne		1965	N. Berryman
1920	G. F. De Teissier		1966	Air Commodore W. F. Langdon
1921	R. Sambourne		1967–1968	no competition
			1969	N. Berryman
			1970	N. Berryman
			1971	J. R. N. Lisle

Billiard Spring Handicap: 1907–1938

1907	F. J. Plaskitt
1908	C. Smith
1909	C. Smith
1910	E. L. Phillips
1911	R. Sambourne
1912	M. Roberts
1913	C. Smith
1914	E. L. Phillips
1915–1919	no competition
1920	J. N. Wilson
1921	S. Walter
1922	no competition
1923	S. Walter
1924	no competition
1925	H. Peterson
1926	no competition
1927	H. L. R. Dent
1928–1934	no competition
1935	M. W. Bovill
1936	Capt. J. L. Holt
1937	J. S. Olliff
1938	C. Mollison

Members' Straight Snooker Handicap: 1937–1971

From 1938, Cup presented by G. A. Harding

1937	J. C. Warboys
1938	E. A. Vivian
1955	
1961	A. W. Davson
1962	Air Commodore W. F. Langdon
1963	R. S. Condy
1964	H. W. Morrall
1965	Air Commodore W. F. Langdon
1966	Air Commodore W. F. Langdon
1967–1968	no competition
1969	
1970	N. Berryman
1971	N. Berryman

Table Tennis

Table Tennis Championship: 1961–1978

The Laszlo Cup, presented by Mrs S. Laszlo, 1961

1961	H. C. Bernstein	1970	J. D. Nixon
1962	S. I. de Laszlo	1971	J. D. Nixon
1963	H. C. Bernstein	1972	C. J. Mottram
1964	no competition	1973	J. D. Nixon
1965	no competition	1974	P. W. Blincow
1966	K. Glass	1975	
1967	J. R. N. Lisle	1976	
1968	R. Leslie	1977	J. D. Nixon
1969	R. Leslie	1978	H. C. Bernstein

INDEX

PHOTOGRAPHIC ACKNOWLEDGEMENTS

The author and publishers wish to thank the following for permission to reproduce photographs:
Sir Carl Aarvold, page 235 *FOURTH ROW left*; Lord Aberdare, page 129; BBC Hulton Picture Library, pages 23, 28, 29 *left and right*, 80 *above and below*, 84 *above, below left and below right*, 85 *above left,. above right and below*, 115, 116, 118, 177 *above left*, 190, 234 *left, centre and right* and 235 *TOP ROW left, right and far right, SECOND ROW far left*; Camera Press, page 204; Mrs. Joyce Church, pages 145 and 153; Neal Clayton, page 218; Peter Dazeley, pages 151, 158, 159, 164, 165, 167, 168 *above and below*, 172 *below* and 235 *FOURTH ROW right and far right*; David Frith Collection, page 34; Richard Greenwood, pages 51 *right*, 64 *above and below*, and 65; David Griew, page 37; Tommy Hindley, pages 170 *above and below*, 172 *above*, 184, 185 *above and below right*, 186 and 212; Illustrated London News, pages 18/19, 33, 41, 45 *below*, 49, 52, 62/63, 72, 73 *above and below*, 74, 83 *above, centre and below*, 106, 130, 131, 195, 199 and 235 *SECOND ROW left, right and far right, THIRD ROW right*; Robin Eley Jones, page 233; London Regional Transport, page 16; Alan Lovell, page 209; Eamonn McCabe, page 217; Mansell Collection, page 235 *TOP ROW far left*; National Portrait Gallery, London, page 235 *THIRD ROW far right*; John O'Grady, page 230; Geoffrey Paish, page 191; Photo Source, pages 180 *above* and 181 *above and below*; Press Association, page 235 *THIRD ROW far left and left, FOURTH ROW far left*; Derek Rowe, page 219 *above left*; Sport and General, pages 125 *above and below*, 135, 157 *above and below*, 174, 175, 177 *above right, below left and below right*; 178 *above left, above right, below left and below right*; 179 *above left, above right and below*; 180 *below*, 182, 188 *above and below*, 189, 193, 197, 201, 206, 207 *above*, 214 *above*, 215 *below*, 216 and 225; Sporting Pictures, page 207 *below*; Syndication International, pages 58 and 108; Tennis and Rackets Association, pages 45 *above*, 46, 87, 123 and 211; Reginald Thompson, pages 214 *below*, 219 *left and above right*, 221 *above*, 223, 228 and 229; Whitbread and Company, page 185 *below left*; Wimpey Group Services, page 210 *above, centre and below*; The Zachary family, pages 92/93 and 95.

COLOUR SECTION
All-Sport, pages 2 *below*, 3 *below* and 4 *below*; Colorsport, page 3 *above right*; Peter Dazeley, page 2 *above*; Tommy Hindley, page 3 *above left*, Le Roye Productions, page 4 *above*.